The Las

The Broker

John Grisham

arrow books.

This edition published by Arrow Books in 2007

This novel is a work of fiction. Names and characters are the product
of the author's imagination and any resemblance to actual
person's living or dead is entirely coincidental

Arrow Books
The Random House Group Limited
20 Vauxhall Bridge Road, London SW1V 2SA

www.randomhouse.co.uk

Addresses for companies within The Random House Group Limited
can be found at:
www.randomhouse.co.uk/offices.htm

The Random House Group Limited Reg. No. 954009

A CIP catalogue record for this book
is available from the British Library

ISBN 9780099521860

The Random House Group Limited makes every effort to ensure
that the papers used in its books are made from trees that
have been legally sourced from well-managed and credibly
certified forests. Our paper procurement policy can be found at:
www.randomhouse.co.uk/paper.htm

Printed and bound in Great Britain by
Cox & Wyman Ltd, Reading, Berkshire

John Grisham lives with his family in Virginia and Mississippi. His novels are *A Time to Kill*, *The Firm*, *The Pelican Brief*, *The Client*, *The Chamber*, *The Rainmaker*, *The Runaway Jury*, *The Partner*, *The Street Lawyer*, *The Testament*, *The Brethren*, *A Painted House*, *Skipping Christmas*, *The Summons*, *The King of Torts*, *Bleachers*, *The Last Juror* and *The Broker*. He has also written his first work of non-fiction *The Innocent Man*.

Also available by John Grisham

Fiction

A Time to Kill
The Firm
The Pelican Brief
The Client
The Chamber
The Rainmaker
The Runaway Jury
The Partner
The Street Lawyer
The Testament
The Brethren
A Painted House
Skipping Christmas
The Summons
The King of Torts
Bleachers
The Last Juror
The Broker

Non-fiction

The Innocent Man

The Last Juror

Part One

Part One

Chapter 1

After decades of patient mismanagement and loving neglect, *The Ford County Times* went bankrupt in 1970. The owner and publisher, Miss Emma Caudle, was ninety-three years old and strapped to a bed in a nursing home in Tupelo. The editor, her son Wilson Caudle, was in his seventies and had a plate in his head from the First War. A perfect circle of dark grafted skin covered the plate at the top of his long, sloping forehead, and throughout his adult life he had endured the nickname of Spot. Spot did this. Spot did that. Here, Spot. There, Spot.

In his younger years, he covered town meetings, football games, elections, trials, church socials, all sorts of activities in Ford County. He was a good reporter, thorough and intuitive. Evidently, the head wound did not affect his ability to write. But sometime after the Second War the plate apparently shifted, and Mr. Caudle stopped writing everything but the obituaries. He loved obituaries. He spent hours on them. He filled paragraphs of eloquent prose detailing the lives of even the humblest of Ford Countians. And the death of a wealthy or prominent citizen was front page news, with Mr. Caudle seizing the moment. He never missed a wake or a funeral, never wrote anything bad about anyone. All received glory in the end. Ford County was a wonderful place to die. And Spot was a very popular man, even though he was crazy.

The only real crisis of his journalistic career happened in 1967, about the time the civil rights movement finally made it to Ford County. The paper had never shown the slightest hint of racial tolerance. No black faces appeared in its pages, except those belonging to known or suspected criminals. No black wedding announcements. No black honor students or baseball teams. But in 1967, Mr. Caudle made a startling discovery. He awoke one morning to the realization that black people were dying in Ford County, and their deaths were not being properly reported. There was a whole, new, fertile world of obituaries waiting out there, and Mr. Caudle set sail in dangerous and uncharted waters. On Wednesday, March 8, 1967, the *Times* became the first white-owned weekly in Mississippi to run the obituary of a Negro. For the most part, it went unnoticed.

The following week, he ran three black obituaries, and people were beginning to talk. By the fourth week, a regular boycott was under way, with subscriptions being canceled and advertisers holding their money. Mr. Caudle knew what was happening, but he was too impressed with his new status as an integrationist to worry about such trivial matters as sales and profits. Six weeks after the historic obituary, he announced, on the front page and in bold print, his new policy. He explained to the public that he would publish whatever he damned well pleased, and if the white folks didn't like it, then he would simply cut back on their obituaries.

Now, dying properly is an important part of living in Mississippi, for whites and blacks, and the thought of being laid to rest without the benefit of one of Spot's glorious send-offs was more than most whites could stand. And they knew he was crazy enough to carry out his threat.

The next edition was filled with all sorts of obituaries, blacks and whites, all neatly alphabetized and desegregated. It sold out, and a brief period of prosperity followed.

The bankruptcy was called involuntary, as if others had eager volunteers. The pack was led by a print supplier from Memphis that was owed $60,000. Several creditors had not been paid in six months. The old Security Bank was calling in a loan.

I was new, but I'd heard the rumors. I was sitting on a desk in the front room of the *Times*'s offices reading a magazine, when a midget in a pair of pointed toes strutted in the front door and asked for Wilson Caudle.

5

'He's at the funeral home,' I said.

He was a cocky midget. I could see a gun on his hip under a wrinkled navy blazer, a gun worn in such a manner so that folks would see it. He probably had a permit, but in Ford County one was not really needed, not in 1970. In fact, permits were frowned upon. 'I need to serve these papers on him,' he said, waving an envelope.

I was not about to be helpful, but it's difficult being rude to a midget. Even one with a gun. 'He's at the funeral home,' I repeated.

'Then I'll just leave them with you,' he declared.

Although I'd been around for less than two months, and though I'd gone to college up North, I had learned a few things. I knew that good papers were not served on people. They were mailed or shipped or hand-delivered, but never served. The papers were trouble, and I wanted no part of them.

'I'm not taking the papers,' I said, looking down.

The laws of nature require midgets to be docile, noncombative people, and this little fella was no exception. The gun was a ruse. He glanced around the front office with a smirk, but he knew the situation was hopeless. With a flair for the dramatic, he stuffed the envelope back into his pocket and demanded, 'Where's the funeral home?'

I pointed this way and that, and he left. An

hour later, Spot stumbled through the door, waving the papers and bawling hysterically. 'It's over! It's over!' he kept wailing as I held the Petition for Involuntary Bankruptcy. Margaret Wright, the secretary, and Hardy, the pressman, came from the back and tried to console him. He sat in a chair, face in hands, elbows on knees, sobbing pitifully. I read the petition aloud for the benefit of the others.

It said Mr. Caudle had to appear in court in a week over in Oxford to meet with the creditors and the Judge, and that a decision would be made as to whether the paper would continue to operate while a trustee sorted things out. I could tell Margaret and Hardy were more concerned about their jobs than about Mr. Caudle and his breakdown, but they gamely stood next to him and patted his shoulders.

When the crying stopped, he suddenly stood, bit his lip, and announced, 'I've got to tell Mother.'

The three of us looked at each other. Miss Emma Caudle had departed this life years earlier, but her feeble heart continued to work just barely enough to postpone a funeral. She neither knew nor cared what color Jell-O they were feeding her, and she certainly cared nothing about Ford County and its newspaper. She was blind and deaf and weighed less than eighty pounds, and now Spot was about to discuss involuntary bankruptcy with her. At that point, I realized that he, too, was no longer with us.

He started crying again and left. Six months later I would write his obituary.

Because I had attended college, and because I was holding the papers, Hardy and Margaret looked hopefully at me for advice. I was a journalist, not a lawyer, but I said that I would take the papers to the Caudle family lawyer. We would follow his advice. They smiled weakly and returned to work.

At noon, I bought a six-pack at Quincy's One Stop in Lowtown, the black section of Clanton, and went for a long drive in my Spitfire. It was late in February, unseasonably warm, so I put the top down and headed for the lake, wondering, not for the first time, just exactly what I was doing in Ford County, Mississippi.

I grew up in Memphis and studied journalism at Syracuse for five years before my grandmother got tired of paying for what was becoming an extended education. My grades were unremarkable, and I was a year away from a degree. Maybe a year and a half. She, BeeBee, had plenty of money, hated to spend it, and after five years she figured my opportunity had been sufficiently funded. When she cut me off I was very disappointed, but I did not complain, to her anyway. I was her only grandchild and her estate would be a delight.

I studied journalism with a hangover. In the early days at Syracuse, I aspired to be an investigative reporter with the *New York Times* or the *Washington Post*. I wanted to save the world by uncovering corruption and environmental abuse and government waste and the injustice suffered by the weak and oppressed. Pulitzers were waiting for me. After a year or so of such lofty dreams, I saw a movie about a foreign correspondent who dashed around the world looking for wars, seducing beautiful women, and somehow finding the time to write award-winning stories. He spoke eight languages, wore a beard, combat boots, starched khakis that never wrinkled. So I decided I would become such a journalist. I grew a beard, bought some boots and khakis, tried to learn German, tried to score with prettier girls. During my junior year, when my grades began their steady decline to the bottom of the class, I became captivated by the idea of working for a small-town newspaper. I cannot explain this attraction, except that it was at about this time that I met and befriended Nick Diener. He was from rural Indiana, and for decades his family had owned a rather prosperous county newspaper. He drove a fancy little Alfa Romeo and always had plenty of cash. We became close friends.

Nick was a bright student who could have handled medicine, law, or engineering. His only goal, however, was to return to Indiana and run the family business. This baffled me until we got drunk one night and he told me how much his father cleared each year off their small weekly – circulation six thousand. It was a gold mine, he said. Just local news, wedding announcements, church socials, honor rolls, sports coverage, pictures of basketball teams, a few recipes, a few obituaries, and pages of advertising. Maybe a little politics, but stay away from controversy. And count your money. His father was a millionaire. It was laid-back, low-pressure journalism with money growing on trees, according to Nick.

This appealed to me. After my fourth year, which should've been my last but wasn't close, I spent the summer interning at a small weekly in the Ozark Mountains of Arkansas. The pay was peanuts but BeeBee was impressed because I was employed. Each week I mailed her the paper, at least half of which was written by me. The owner/editor/publisher was a wonderful old gentleman who was delighted to have a reporter who wanted to write. He was quite wealthy.

After five years at Syracuse my grades were irreparable, and the well ran dry. I returned to Memphis, visited BeeBee, thanked her for her efforts, and told her I loved her. She told me to find a job.

At the time Wilson Caudle's sister lived in Memphis, and through the course of things this lady met BeeBee at one of those hot tea drinkers' parties. After a few phone calls back and forth, I was packed and headed to Clanton, Mississippi, where Spot was eagerly waiting. After an hour of orientation, he turned me loose on Ford County.

In the next edition he ran a sweet little story

with a photo of me announcing my 'internship' at the *Times*. It made the front page. News was slow in those days.

The announcement contained two horrendous errors that would haunt me for years. The first and less serious was the fact that Syracuse had now joined the Ivy League, at least according to Spot. He informed his dwindling readership that I had received my Ivy League education at Syracuse. It was a month before anyone mentioned this to me. I was beginning to believe that no one read the paper, or, worse, those who did were complete idiots.

The second misstatement changed my life. I was born Joyner William Traynor. Until I was twelve I hammered my parents with inquiries about why two supposedly intelligent people would stick Joyner on a newborn. The story finally leaked that one of my parents, both of whom denied responsibility, had insisted on Joyner as an olive branch to some feuding relative who allegedly had money. I never met the man, my namesake. He died broke as far as I was concerned, but I nonetheless had Joyner for a lifetime. When I enrolled at Syracuse I was J. William, a rather imposing name for an eighteen-year-old. But Vietnam and the riots and all the rebellion and social upheaval convinced me that J. William sounded too corporate, too establishment. I became Will.

Spot at various times called me Will, William, Bill, or even Billy, and since I would answer to all of them I never knew what was next. In the announcement, under my smiling face, was my new name. Willie Traynor. I was horrified. I had never dreamed of anyone calling me Willie. I went to a prep school in Memphis and then to college in New York, and I had never met a person named Willie. I wasn't a good ole boy. I drove a Triumph Spitfire and had long hair.

What would I tell my fraternity brothers at Syracuse? What would I tell BeeBee?

After hiding in my apartment for two days, I mustered the courage to confront Spot and demand he do something. I wasn't sure what, but he'd made the mistake and he could damned well fix it. I marched into the *Times* office and bumped into Davey Bigmouth Bass, the sports editor of the paper. 'Hey, cool name,' he said. I followed him into his office, seeking advice.

'My name's not Willie,' I said.

'It is now.'

'My name's Will.'

'They'll love you around here. A smart-ass from up North with long hair and a little imported sports car. Hell, folks'll think you're pretty cool with a name like Willie. Think of Joe Willie.'

'Who's Joe Willie?'

'Joe Willie Namath.'

'Oh him.'

'Yeah, he's a Yankee like you, from Pennsylvania or some place, but when he got to Alabama he went from Joseph William to Joe

12

Willie. The girls chased him all over the place.'

I began to feel better. In 1970, Joe Namath was probably the most famous athlete in the country. I went for a drive and kept repeating 'Willie.' Within a couple of weeks the name was beginning to stick. Everybody called me Willie and seemed to feel more comfortable because I had such a down-to-earth name.

I told BeeBee it was just a temporary pseudonym.

The *Times* was a very thin paper, and I knew immediately that it was in trouble. Heavy on the obits, light on news and advertising. The employees were disgruntled, but quiet and loyal. Jobs were scarce in Ford County in 1970. After a week it was obvious even to my novice eyes that the paper was operating at a loss. Obits are free – ads are not. Spot spent most of his time in his cluttered office, napping periodically and calling the funeral home. Sometimes they called him. Sometimes the families would stop just hours after Uncle Wilber's last breath and hand over a long, flowery, handwritten narrative that Spot would seize and carry delicately to his desk. Behind a locked door, he would write, edit, research, and rewrite until it was perfect.

He told me the entire county was mine to cover. The paper had one other general reporter, Baggy Suggs, a pickled old goat who spent his hours hanging around the courthouse across the street sniffing for gossip and drinking bourbon with a small club of washed-up lawyers too old and too drunk to practice anymore. As I would soon learn, Baggy was too lazy to check sources and dig for anything interesting, and it was not unusual for his front page story to be some dull account of a boundary dispute or a wife beating.

Margaret, the secretary, was a fine Christian lady who ran the place, though she was smart enough to allow Spot to think he was the boss. She was in her early fifties and had worked there for twenty years. She was the rock, the anchor, and everything at the *Times* revolved around her. Margaret was soft-spoken, almost shy, and from day one was completely intimidated by me because I was from Memphis and had gone to school up North for five years. I was careful not to wear my Ivy Leagueness on my shoulder, but at the same time I wanted these rural Mississippians to know that I had been superbly educated.

She and I became gossiping pals, and after a week she confirmed what I already suspected – that Mr. Caudle was indeed crazy, and that the newspaper was indeed in dire financial straits. But, she said, the Caudles have family money!

It would be years before I understood this mystery.

In Mississippi, family money was not to be confused with wealth. It had nothing to do with cash or other assets. Family money was a status, obtained by someone who was white, somewhat educated beyond high school, born in a large home with a front porch – preferably one surrounded by cotton or soybean fields, although this was not mandatory – and partially reared by a beloved black maid named Bessie or Pearl, partially reared by doting grandparents who once owned the ancestors of Bessie or Pearl, and lectured from birth on the stringent social graces of a privileged people. Acreage and trust funds helped somewhat, but Mississippi was full of insolvent blue bloods who inherited the status of family money. It could not be earned. It had to be handed down at birth.

When I talked to the Caudle family lawyer, he explained, rather succinctly, the real value of their family money. 'They're as poor as Job's turkey,' he said as I sat deep in a worn leather chair and looked up at him across his wide and ancient mahogany desk. His name was Walter Sullivan, of the prestigious Sullivan & O'Hara firm. Prestigious for Ford County – seven lawyers. He studied the bankruptcy petition and rambled on about the Caudles and the money they used to have and how foolish they'd been in running a once profitable paper into the ground. He'd represented them for thirty years, and back when Miss Emma ran things the *Times* had five thousand subscribers and pages filled with advertisements. She kept a $500,000 certificate of deposit at Security Bank, just for a rainy day.

Then her husband died, and she remarried a local alcoholic twenty years her junior. When sober, he was semiliterate and fancied himself as a tortured poet and essayist. Miss Emma loved him dearly and installed him as coeditor, a position he used to write long editorials blasting everything that moved in Ford County. It was the beginning of the end. Spot hated his new stepfather, the feelings were mutual, and their relationship finally climaxed with one of the more colorful fistfights in the history of downtown Clanton. It took place on the sidewalk in front of the *Times* office, on the downtown square, in front of a large and stunned crowd. The locals believed that Spot's brain, already fragile, took additional damage that day. Shortly thereafter, he began writing nothing but those damned obituaries.

The stepfather ran off with her money, and Miss Emma, heartbroken, became a recluse.

'It was once a fine paper,' Mr. Sullivan said. 'But look at it now. Less than twelve hundred subscriptions, heavily in debt. Bankrupt.'

'What will the court do?' I asked.

'Try and find a buyer.'

'A buyer?'

'Yes, someone will buy. The county has to have a newspaper.'

I immediately thought of two people – Nick Diener and BeeBee. Nick's family had become rich off their county weekly. BeeBee was already loaded and she had only one beloved grandchild. My heart began pounding as I smelled opportunity.

Mr. Sullivan watched me intently, and it was

obvious he knew what I was thinking. 'It could be bought for a song,' he said.

'How much?' I asked with all the confidence of a twenty-three-year-old cub reporter whose grandmother was as stout as lye soap.

'Probably fifty thousand. Twenty-five for the paper, twenty-five to operate. Most of the debts can be bankrupted, then renegotiated with the creditors you need.' He paused and leaned forward, elbows on his desk, thick grayish eyebrows twitching as if his brain was working overtime. 'It could be a real gold mine, you know.'

BeeBee had never invested in a gold mine, but after three days of priming the pump I left Memphis with a check for $50,000. I gave it to Mr. Sullivan, who put it in a trust account and petitioned the court for the sale of the paper. The Judge, a relic who belonged in the bed next to Miss Emma, nodded benignly and scrawled his name on an order that made me the new owner of *The Ford County Times*.

It takes at least three generations to be accepted in Ford County. Regardless of money or breeding, one cannot simply move there and be trusted. A dark cloud of suspicion hangs over any newcomer, and I was no exception. The people there are exceedingly warm and gracious and polite, almost to the point of being nosy with their friendliness. They nod and speak to everyone on the downtown streets. They ask about

17

your health, the weather, and they invite you to church. They rush to help strangers.

But they don't really trust you unless they trusted your grandfather.

Once word spread that I, a young green alien from Memphis, had bought the paper for fifty, or maybe a hundred, or perhaps even two hundred thousand dollars, a great wave of gossip shook the community. Margaret gave me the updates. Because I was single, there was a chance I was a homosexual. Because I went to Syracuse, wherever that was, then I was probably a Communist. Or worse, a liberal. Because I was from Memphis, I was a subversive intent on embarrassing Ford County.

Just the same, as they all conceded quietly among themselves, I now controlled the obituaries! I was somebody!

The new *Times* debuted on March 18, 1970, only three weeks after the midget arrived with his papers. It was almost an inch thick and loaded with more photos than had ever been published in a county weekly. Cub Scout troops, Brownies, junior high basketball teams, garden clubs, book clubs, tea clubs, Bible study groups, adult softball teams, civic clubs. Dozens of photos. I tried to include every living soul in the county. And the dead ones were exhalted like never before. The obits were embarrassingly long. I'm sure Spot was proud, but I never heard from him.

The news was light and breezy. Absolutely no

editorials. People love to read about crime, so on the bottom left-hand corner of the front page I launched the Crime Notes Section. Thankfully, two pickups had been stolen the week before, and I covered these heists as if Fort Knox had been looted.

In the center of the front page there was a rather large group shot of the new regime – Margaret, Hardy, Baggy Suggs, me, our photographer, Wiley Meek, Davey Bigmouth Bass, and Melanie Dogan, a high school student and part-time employee. I was proud of my staff. We had worked around the clock for ten days, and our first edition was a great success. We printed five thousand copies and sold them all. I sent a box of them to BeeBee, and she was most impressed.

For the next month, the new *Times* slowly took shape as I struggled to determine what I wanted it to become. Change is painful in rural Mississippi, so I decided to do it gradually. The old paper was bankrupt, but it had changed little in fifty years. I wrote more news, sold more ads, included more and more pictures of groups of endless varieties. And I worked hard on the obituaries.

I had never been attracted to long hours, but since I was the owner I forgot about the clock. I was too young and too busy to be scared. I was twenty-three, and through luck and timing and a rich grandmother, I was suddenly the owner of a weekly newspaper. If I had hesitated and studied the situation, and sought advice from bankers and accountants, I'm sure someone would have talked some sense into me. But when you're twenty-three, you're fearless. You have nothing, so there's nothing to lose.

I figured it would take a year to become profitable. And, at first, revenue increased slowly. Then Rhoda Kassellaw was murdered. I guess it's the nature of the business to sell more papers after a brutal crime when people want details. We sold twenty-four hundred papers the week before her death, and almost four thousand the week after.

It was no ordinary murder.

Ford County was a peaceful place, filled with people who were either Christians or claimed to be. Fistfights were common, but they were usually the work of the lower classes who hung around beer joints and such. Once a month a redneck would take a shot at a neighbor or perhaps his own wife, and each weekend had at least one stabbing in the black tonks. Death rarely followed these episodes.

I owned the paper for ten years, from 1970 to 1980, and we reported very few murders in Ford County. None was as brutal as Rhoda Kassellaw's; none was as premeditated. Thirty years later, I still think about it every day.

Chapter 2

Rhoda Kassellaw lived in the Beech Hill community, twelve miles north of Clanton, in a modest gray brick house on a narrow, paved country road. The flower beds along the front of the house were weedless and received daily care, and between them and the road the long wide lawn was thick and well cut. The driveway was crushed white rock. Scattered down both sides of it was a collection of scooters and balls and bikes. Her two small children were always outdoors, playing hard, sometimes stopping to watch a passing car.

It was a pleasant little country house, a stone's throw from Mr. and Mrs. Deece next door. The young man who bought it was killed in a trucking accident somewhere in Texas, and, at the age of twenty-eight, Rhoda became a widow. The insurance on his life paid off the house and the car. The balance was invested to provide a modest monthly income that allowed her to remain home and dote on the children. She spent hours outside, tending her vegetable garden, potting flowers, pulling weeds, mulching the beds along the front of the house.

She kept to herself. The old ladies in Beech Hill considered her a model widow, staying home, looking sad, limiting her social appearances to an occasional visit to church. She should attend more regularly, they whispered.

Shortly after the death of her husband, Rhoda planned to return to her family in Missouri. She was not from Ford County, nor was her husband. A job took them there. But the house was paid for, the kids were happy, the neighbors were nice, and her family was much too concerned about how much life insurance she'd collected. So she stayed, always thinking of leaving but never doing so.

Rhoda Kassellaw was a beautiful woman when she wanted to be, which was not very often. Her shapely, thin figure was usually camouflaged under a loose cotton drip-dry dress, or a bulky chambray workshirt, which she preferred when gardening. She wore little makeup and kept her long flaxen-colored hair pulled back and stuck together on top of her head. Most of what she ate came from her organic garden, and her skin had a soft healthy glow to it. Such an attractive young widow would normally have been a hot property in the county, but she kept to herself.

After three years of mourning, however, Rhoda became restless. She was not getting younger; the years were slipping by. She was too young and too pretty to sit at home every Saturday and read bedtime stories. There had to be some action out there, though there was certainly none in Beech Hill.

She hired a young black girl from down the road to baby-sit, and Rhoda drove north for an hour to the Tennessee line, where she'd heard there were some respectable lounges and dance clubs. Maybe no one would know her there. She enjoyed the dancing and the flirting, but she never drank and always came home early. It became a routine, two or three times a month.

Then the jeans got tighter, the dancing faster, the hours longer and longer. She was getting noticed and talked about in the bars and clubs along the state line.

He followed her home twice before he killed her. It was March, and a warm front had brought a premature hope of spring. It was a dark night, with no moon. Bear, the family mutt, sniffed him first as he crept behind a tree in the backyard. Bear was primed to growl and bark when he was forever silenced.

Rhoda's son Michael was five and her daughter Teresa was three. They wore matching Disney cartoon pajamas, neatly pressed, and watched their mother's glowing eyes as she read them the story of Jonah and the whale. She tucked them in and kissed them good night, and when Rhoda turned off the light to their bedroom, he was already in the house.

An hour later she turned off the television, locked the doors, and waited for Bear, who did not appear. That was no surprise because he often chased rabbits and squirrels into the woods and came home late. Bear would sleep on the back porch and wake her howling at dawn. In her bedroom, she slipped out of her light cotton dress and opened the closet door. He was waiting in there, in the dark.

He snatched her from behind, covered her mouth with a thick and sweaty hand, and said, 'I have a knife. I'll cut you and your kids.' With the other hand he held up a shiny blade and waved it before her eyes.

'Understand?' he hissed into her ear.

She trembled and managed to shake her head. She couldn't see what he looked like. He threw her to the floor of the cluttered closet, face down, and yanked her hands behind her. He took a brown wool scarf an old aunt had given her and wrapped it roughly around her face. 'Not one sound,' he kept growling at her. 'Or I'll cut your kids.' When the blindfold was finished he grabbed her hair, snatched her to her feet, and dragged her to her bed. He poked the tip of the blade into her chin and said, 'Don't fight me. The knife's right here.' He cut off her panties and the rape began.

He wanted to see her eyes, those beautiful eyes he'd seen in the clubs. And the long hair. He'd bought her drinks and danced with her twice, and when he'd finally made a move she had stiff-armed him. Try these moves, baby, he mumbled just loud enough for her to hear.

He and the Jack Daniel's had been building courage for three hours, and now the whiskey numbed him. He moved slowly above her, not rushing things, enjoying every second of it. He mumbled in the self-satisfying grunts of a real man taking and getting what he wanted.

The smell of the whiskey and his sweat nauseated her, but she was too frightened to throw up. It might anger him, cause him to use the knife. As she started to accept the horror of the moment, she began to think. Keep it quiet. Don't wake up the kids. And what will he do with the knife when he's finished?

His movements were faster, he was mumbling louder. 'Quiet, baby,' he hissed again and again. 'I'll use the knife.' The wrought-iron bed was squeaking; didn't get used enough, he told himself. Too much noise, but he didn't care.

The rattling of the bed woke Michael, who then got Teresa up. They eased from their room and crept down the dark hall to see what was happening. Michael opened the door to his mother's bedroom, saw the strange man on top of her, and said, 'Mommy!' For a second the man stopped and jerked his head toward the children.

The sound of the boy's voice horrified Rhoda, who bolted upward and thrust both hands at her assailant, grabbing whatever she could. One small fist caught him in the left eye, a solid shot that stunned him. Then she yanked off her blind-fold while kicking with both legs. He slapped her and tried to pin her down again. 'Danny Padgitt!' she shouted, still clawing. He hit her once more.

'Mommy!' Michael cried.

'Run, kids!' Rhoda tried to scream, but she was struck dumb by her assailant's blows.

'Shut up!' Padgitt yelled.

'Run!' Rhoda shouted again, and the children backed away, then darted down the hallway, into the kitchen, and outside to safety.

In the split second after she shouted his name, Padgitt realized he had no choice but to silence her. He took the knife and hacked twice, then scrambled from the bed and grabbed his clothing.

Mr. and Mrs. Aaron Deece were watching late television from Memphis when they heard Michael's voice calling and getting closer. Mr. Deece met the boy at the front door. His pajamas were soaked with sweat and dew and his teeth were chattering so violently he had trouble speaking. 'He hurt my mommy!' he kept saying. 'He hurt my mommy!'

Through the darkness between the two houses, Mr. Deece saw Teresa running after her brother. She was almost running in place, as if she wanted to get to one place without leaving the other. When Mrs. Deece finally got to her by the Deece garage, she was sucking her thumb and unable to speak.

Mr. Deece raced into his den and grabbed two shotguns, one for him, one for his wife. The children were in the kitchen, shocked to the point of being paralyzed. 'He hurt Mommy,' Michael kept saying. Mrs. Deece cuddled them, told them everything would be fine. She looked at her shotgun when her husband laid it on the table. 'Stay here,' he said as he rushed out of the house.

He did not go far. Rhoda almost made it to the Deece home before she collapsed in the wet grass. She was completely naked, and from the neck down covered in blood. He picked her up and carried her to the front porch, then shouted at his wife to move the children toward the back of the house and lock them in a bedroom. He could not allow them to see their mother in her last moments.

As he placed her in the swing, Rhoda whispered, 'Danny Padgitt. It was Danny Padgitt.'

He covered her with a quilt, then called an ambulance.

Danny Padgitt kept his pickup in the center of the road and drove ninety miles an hour. He was half-drunk and scared as hell but unwilling to admit it. He'd be home in ten minutes, secure in the family's little kingdom known as Padgitt Island.

Those little faces had ruined everything. He'd think about it tomorrow. He took a long pull on the fifth of Jack Daniel's and felt better.

It was a rabbit or a small dog or some varmint, and when it darted from the shoulder he caught a glimpse of it and reacted badly. He instinctively hit the brake pedal, just for a split second because he really didn't care what he hit and rather enjoyed the sport of roadkilling, but he'd punched too hard. The rear tires locked and the pickup fishtailed. Before he realized it Danny was in serious trouble. He jerked the wheel one way, the wrong way, and the truck hit the gravel shoulder where it began to spin like a stock car on the backstretch. It slid into the ditch, flipped twice, then crashed into a row of pine trees. If he'd been sober he would've been killed, but drunks walk away.

He crawled out through a shattered window, and for a long while leaned on the truck, counting his cuts and scratches and considering his options. A leg was suddenly stiff, and as he climbed up the bank to the road he realized he could not walk far. Not that he would need to.

The blue lights were on him before he realized it. The deputy was out of the car, surveying the scene with a long black flashlight. More flashing lights appeared down the road.

The deputy saw the blood, smelled the whiskey, and reached for the handcuffs.

Chapter 3

The Big Brown River drops nonchalantly south from Tennessee and runs as straight as a hand-dug channel for thirty miles through the center of Tyler County, Mississippi. Two miles above the Ford County line it begins twisting and looping, and by the time it leaves Tyler County it looks like a scared snake, curling desperately and going nowhere. Its water is thick and heavy, muddy and slow, shallow in most places. The Big Brown is not known for its beauty. Sand, silt, and gravel bars line its innumerable bends and curves. A hundred sloughs and creeks feed it with an inexhaustible supply of slow-moving water.

Its journey through Ford County is brief. It dips and forms a wide circle around two thousand acres in the northeasternmost corner of the county, then leaves and heads back toward Tennessee. The circle is almost perfect and an island is almost formed, but at the last moment the Big Brown turns away from itself and leaves a narrow strip of land between its banks.

The circle is known as Padgitt Island, a deep, dense woodland covered in pine, gum, elm, oak, and a myriad of swamps and bayous and sloughs, some connected but most isolated. Little of the rich soil had ever been cleared. Nothing was harvested on the island except timber and lots of corn – for illegal whiskey. And marijuana, but that was a later story.

On the thin strip of land between the banks of the Big Brown a paved road entered and left, came and went, always with someone watching. The road was built long ago by the county, but very few taxpayers ever dared to use it.

The entire island had been in the Padgitt family since Reconstruction, when Rudolph Padgitt, a carpetbagger from the North, arrived a bit late after the War and found all the prime land taken. He searched in vain, found nothing attractive, then somehow stumbled upon the snake-infested island. On the map, it looked promising. He put together a band of newly freed slaves and, with guns and machetes, fought his way onto the island. No one else wanted it.

Rudolph married a local whore and began cutting timber. Since timber was in great demand after the War, he became prosperous. The local proved to be quite fertile and soon there was a horde of little Padgitts on the island. One of his ex-slaves had learned the art of distillery. Rudolph became a corn farmer who neither ate nor sold his crop, but instead used it to produce what was soon known as one of the finest whiskeys in the Deep South.

For thirty years Rudolph made moonshine until he died of cirrhosis in 1902. By then an entire clan of Padgitts inhabited the island, and were quite proficient at milling timber and producing illegal whiskey. Scattered about the island were half a dozen distilleries, all well protected and concealed, all operating with state-of-the-art machinery.

The Padgitts were famous for their whiskey, though fame was not something they sought. They were secretive and clannish, fiercely private and deathly afraid that someone might infiltrate their little kingdom and disrupt their considerable profits. They said they were loggers, and it was well known that they produced timber and were prosperous at it. The Padgitt Lumber Company was very visible on the main highway near the river. They claimed to be legitimate people, taxpayers and such, with their children in the public schools.

During the 1920s and 1930s, when alcohol was illegal and the nation was thirsty, Padgitt whiskey could not be distilled fast enough. It was shipped in oak barrels across the Big Brown and hauled by trucks up North, as far away as Chicago. The patriarch, president, and director of production and marketing was a tight-fisted old warrior named Clovis Padgitt, eldest son of

Rudolph and the local. Clovis had been taught at an early age that the best profits were those from which no taxes were extracted. That was lesson number one. Number two preached the marvelous message of dealing strictly in cash. Clovis was a hard-nosed cash and no-taxes man, and the Padgitts were rumored to have more money than the Mississippi state treasury.

In 1938, three revenue agents sneaked across the Big Brown in a rented flatboat in search of the source of Old Padgitt. Their covert invasion of the island was flawed in many ways, the obvious being the original idea itself. But for some reason they chose midnight as their hour to cross the river. They were dismembered and buried in deep graves.

In 1943, a strange event occurred in Ford County – an honest man was elected Sheriff. Or High Sheriff, as he is commonly known. His name was Koonce Lantrip, and he wasn't really that honest but certainly sounded good on the stump. He vowed to end corruption, to clean up county government, to put the bootleggers and moonshiners, even the Padgitts, out of business. It made for a nice speech and Lantrip won by eight votes.

His supporters waited and waited, and, finally, six months after taking office he organized his deputies and crossed the Big Brown on the only bridge, an ancient wooden structure that had been built by the county in 1915 at the insistence of Clovis. The Padgitts sometimes used it in the springtime when the river was high. No one else was allowed to cross it.

Two of the deputies were shot in the head, and Lantrip's body was never found. It was carefully laid to rest on the banks of a swamp by three Padgitt Negroes. Buford, the eldest son of Clovis, supervised the burial.

The massacre was hot news in Mississippi for weeks, and the Governor threatened to send in the National Guard. But the Second War was raging, and D-Day soon captured the attention of the country. There wasn't much left of the National Guard anyway, and those who were able to fight had little interest in attacking Padgitt Island. The beaches of Normandy would be more inviting.

With the noble experiment of an honest Sheriff behind them, the good people of Ford County elected one from the old school. His name was Mackey Don Coley and his father had been the High Sheriff back in the twenties when Clovis was in charge of Padgitt Island. Clovis and the senior Coley had been rather close, and it was widely known that the Sheriff was a rich man because Old Padgitt was allowed to move so freely out of the county. When Mackey Don announced his candidacy, Buford sent him $50,000 in cash. Mackey Don won in a landslide. His opponent claimed to be honest.

There was a widely held but unprofessed belief in Mississippi that a good Sheriff must be a little crooked to ensure law and order.

Whiskey, whoring, and gambling were simply facts of life, and a good Sheriff must be knowledgeable in these affairs to properly regulate them and protect the Christians. Those vices could not be eliminated, so the High Sheriff must be able to coordinate them and synchronize the orderly flow of sin. For his coordinating efforts, he was to be paid a little extra from the purveyors of such wickedness. He expected it. Most of the voters expected it. No honest man could live on such a humble salary. No honest man could move quietly through the shadows of the underworld.

For the better part of a hundred years following the Civil War, the Padgitts owned the Sheriffs of Ford County. They bought them outright with sacks of cash. Mackey Don Coley received a hundred thousand a year (it was rumored), and during election years he got whatever he needed. And they were generous with other politicians. They quietly bought and kept influence. They asked little; they just wanted to be left alone on their island.

After the Second War, the demand for moonshine began a steady decline. Since generations of Padgitts had been schooled to operate outside the law, Buford and the family began to diversify into other forms of illicit commerce. Selling only timber was dull, and subject to too many market factors, and, most important, did not generate the piles of cash the family expected. They ran guns, stole cars, counterfeited, bought and burned buildings to collect insurance. For twenty years they operated a highly successful brothel on the county line, until it mysteriously burned in 1966.

They were creative and energetic people, always scheming and searching for opportunity, always waiting for someone to rob. There were rumors, quite significant at times, that the Padgitts were members of the Dixie Mafia, a loose-knit gang of redneck thieves who ran rampant through the Deep South in the sixties. These rumors were never verified and were in fact discounted by many because the Padgitts were simply too secretive to share their business with anyone. Nonetheless, the rumors persisted for years, and the Padgitts were the source of endless gossip in the cafés and coffee shops around the square in Clanton. They were never considered local heroes, but certainly legends.

In 1967, a younger Padgitt fled to Canada to avoid the draft. He drifted to California where he tried marijuana and realized he had a taste for it. After a few months as a peacenik, he got homesick and sneaked back to Padgitt Island. He brought with him four pounds of pot, which he shared with all his cousins, and they, too, were quite taken with it. He explained that the rest of the country, and primarily California, was toking like crazy. As usual, Mississippi was at least five years behind the trend.

The stuff could be grown cheaply, then hauled to the cities where there was demand. His father,

Gill Padgitt, grandson of Clovis, saw the opportunity, and soon many of the old cornfields were converted to cannabis. A two-thousand-foot strip of land was cleared for a runway and the Padgitts bought themselves an airplane. Within a year there were daily flights to the outskirts of Memphis and Atlanta, where the Padgitts had established their network. To their delight and with their help, marijuana finally became popular in the Deep South.

The moonshining slowed considerably. The brothel was gone. The Padgitts had contacts in Miami and Mexico and the cash was coming in by the truckloads. For years, no one in Ford County had a hint that the Padgitts were trafficking in drugs. And they never got caught. No Padgitt was ever indicted for a drug-related offense.

In fact, not a single Padgitt had ever been arrested. A hundred years of moonshining, stealing, gunrunning, gambling, counterfeiting, whoring, bribing, even killing, and eventually drug manufacturing, and not a single arrest. They were smart people, careful, deliberate, patient with their schemes.

Then Danny Padgitt, Gill's youngest son, was arrested for the rape and murder of Rhoda Kassellaw.

Chapter 4

Mr. Deece told me the next day that when he was certain Rhoda was dead he finally left her in the swing on the front porch. He went to his bathroom, where he stripped and showered and saw her blood spin down the drain. He changed into work clothes and waited for the police and the ambulance. He watched her house while holding a loaded shotgun, anxious to blast anything that moved. But there was no movement, no sound. In the distance he could barely hear a siren.

His wife kept the children locked in the back bedroom, where she huddled with them in the bed, under a blanket. Michael kept asking about his mother, and who was that man? But Teresa was too traumatized to speak. She managed only a low groaning sound as she sucked her fingers and shook as if she were freezing.

Before long Benning Road was alive with red and blue flashing lights. Rhoda's body was photographed at length before it was taken away. Her home was cordoned off by a squad of deputies, led by Sheriff Coley himself. Mr. Deece, still holding his shotgun, gave his statement to an investigator, then to the Sheriff.

Shortly after 2 A.M., a deputy arrived with the news that a doctor in town had been notified and had suggested that the children be brought in for a look. They rode in the backseat of a patrol car, Michael clutching Mr. Deece, and Teresa in the lap of his wife. At the hospital, they were given a mild sedative and placed together in a semiprivate room where the nurses brought them cookies and milk until they finally went to sleep. Later in the day an aunt arrived from Missouri and took them away.

My phone rang seconds before midnight. It was Wiley Meek, the paper's photographer. He'd picked up the story on the police scanner and was already hanging around the jail waiting to ambush the suspect. Cops were everywhere, he said, his excitement barely under control. Hurry, he urged me. This could be the big one.

At the time I lived above an old garage next to a decaying but still grand Victorian mansion known as the Hocutt House. It was filled with elderly Hocutts, three sisters and a brother, and they took turns being my landlord. Their five-acre estate was a few blocks from the Clanton square and had been built a century earlier with family money. It was covered with trees, overgrown flower beds, thick patches of mature weeds, and enough animals to stock a game preserve. Rabbits, squirrels, skunks, possums, raccoons, a million birds, a frightening assortment of green and black snakes – all non-poisonous I was reassured – and dozens of cats. But no dogs. The Hocutts hated dogs. Each cat had a name, and a major clause in my verbal lease was that I would respect the cats.

Respect them I did. The four-room loft apartment was spacious and clean and cost me the ridiculous sum of $50 a month. If they wanted their cats respected at that price, fine with me.

Their father, Miles Hocutt, had been an eccentric doctor in Clanton for decades. Their mother died during childbirth, and, according to local legend, Dr. Hocutt became very possessive of the children after her death. To protect them from the world, he concocted one of the biggest lies ever told in Ford County. He explained to his children that insanity ran deeply in the family, and thus they should never marry lest they produce some hideous strain of idiot offspring. His children worshiped him, believed him, and were probably already exposed to some measure of unbalance. They never married. The son, Max Hocutt, was eighty-one when he leased me the apartment. The twins, Wilma and Gilma, were seventy-seven, and Melberta, the baby, was seventy-three and completely out of her mind.

It was Gilma, I think, who was peeking from

the kitchen window as I descended the wooden stairway at midnight. A cat was asleep on the bottom step, directly in my path, but I respectfully stepped over it. I wanted to kick it into the street.

Two cars were parked in the garage. One was my Spitfire, top up to keep the cats out, and the other was a long, shiny black Mercedes with red-and-white butcher knives painted on the doors. Under the knives were phone numbers in green paint. Someone had once told Mr. Max Hocutt that he could completely write off the cost of a new car, any car, if he used it for business and some sort of logo was painted on the doors. He bought a new Mercedes and became a knife sharpener. He said his tools were in the trunk.

The car was ten years old and had been driven less than eight thousand miles. Their father had also preached to them the sinfulness of women driving, so Mr. Max was the chauffeur.

I eased the Spitfire down the gravel drive and waved at Gilma peeking from behind the curtain. She jerked her head away and disappeared. The jail was six blocks away. I had slept for about thirty minutes.

Danny Padgitt was being fingerprinted when I arrived. The Sheriff's office was in the front section of the jail, and it was packed with deputies and reserves and volunteer firemen and everybody with access to a uniform and a police scanner. Wiley Meek met me on the front sidewalk.

'It's Danny Padgitt!' he said with great excitement.

I stopped for a second and tried to think. 'Who?'

'Danny Padgitt, from the island.'

I'd been in Ford County less than three months and had yet to meet a single Padgitt. They, as always, kept to themselves. But I'd heard various installments of their legend, with much more to follow. Telling Padgitt stories was a common form of entertainment in Ford County.

Wiley gushed on, 'I got some great shots just as they got him out of the car. Had blood all over him. Great pictures! The girl's dead!'

'What girl?'

'The one he killed. Raped her too, at least that's the rumor.'

Danny Padgitt, I mumbled to myself as the sensational story began to sink in. I had my first glimpse of the headline, no doubt the boldest one the *Times* had run in many years. Poor old Spot had shied away from the jolting stories. Poor old Spot had gone bankrupt. I had other plans.

We pushed our way inside and looked around for Sheriff Coley. I'd met him twice during my brief stint with the *Times* and I had been impressed with his polite and warm nature. He called me mister and said sir and ma'am to everyone, always with a smile. He'd been the Sheriff since the massacre in 1943, so he was pushing seventy years of age. He was tall and gaunt without the obligatory thick stomach required of most Southern sheriffs. On the surface he was a gentleman, and both times I'd met him I'd later wondered how such a nice man could be so corrupt. He emerged from a back room with a deputy, and I, practicing my assertiveness, rushed to him.

'Sheriff, just a couple of questions,' I said sternly. There were no other reporters present. His boys – the real deputies, the part-timers, the wannabes, the jackleg constables with home-made uniforms – they all got quiet and gave me their sneers. I was still very much the brash new rich boy who'd somehow wrangled control of their newspaper. I was a foreigner, with no right to barge in at a time like this and start asking questions.

Sheriff Coley smiled as usual, as if these encounters happened all the time around midnight. 'Yes sir, Mr. Traynor.' He had a slow rich drawl that was very soothing. This man couldn't tell a lie, could he?

'What can you tell us about the murder?'

With his arms folded across his chest, he gave a few of the basics in copspeak. 'White female, age thirty-one, was attacked in her home on Benning Road. Raped, stabbed, murdered. Can't give you her name until we talk to her kinfolks.'

'And you've made an arrest?'

'Yes sir, but no details now. Just give us a

couple of hours. We're investigatin'. That's all, Mr. Traynor.'

'Rumor has it that you have Danny Padgitt in custody.'

'I don't deal in rumors, Mr. Traynor. Not in my profession. Yours neither.'

Wiley and I drove to the hospital, sniffed around for an hour, heard nothing we could print, then drove to the scene on Benning Road. The cops had cordoned off the house and a few of the neighbors were huddled quietly behind a strand of yellow police ribbon near the mailbox. We eased next to them, listening intently, hearing almost nothing. They seemed too stunned to talk. After a few minutes of gawking at the house, we crept away.

Wiley had a nephew who was a part-time deputy, and we found him guarding the Deece home where they were still inspecting the front porch and the swing where Rhoda took her last breath. We pulled him off to the side, behind a row of Mr. Deece's crepe myrtles, and he told us everything. All off the record, of course, as if the gory details would somehow be kept quiet in Ford County.

There were three small cafés around the square in Clanton, two for the whites, one for the blacks. Wiley suggested we get an early table and just listen.

I do not eat breakfast, and I'm usually not awake during the hours in which it is served. I don't mind working until midnight, but I prefer to sleep until the sun is overhead and in full view. As I quickly realized, one of the advantages of owning a small weekly was that I could work late and sleep late. The stories could be written anytime, as long as the deadlines were met. Spot himself was known to drift in not long before noon, after, of course, dropping by the funeral home. I liked his hours.

The second day I lived in my apartment above the Hocutt garage, Gilma banged on my door at nine-thirty in the morning. And banged and banged. I finally staggered through my small kitchen in my underwear and saw her squinting through the blinds. She announced that she was just about to call the police. The other Hocutts were down below, wandering around the garage, looking at my car, certain that a crime had been committed.

She asked what I was doing. I said that I had been sleeping until I heard somebody banging on the damned door. She asked me why I was still asleep at nine-thirty on a Wednesday morning. I rubbed my eyes and tried to think of an appropriate response. I was suddenly aware that I was almost nude and standing in the presence of a seventy-seven-year-old virgin. She kept looking at my thighs.

They'd been up since five, she explained. Nobody sleeps till nine-thirty in Clanton. Was I drunk? They were just concerned, that's all. As I closed the door I told her I was sober, still sleepy, thanks for being concerned but I would often be in bed past 9 A.M.

I'd been to the Tea Shoppe a couple of times for late morning coffee and once for lunch. As the owner of the paper, I felt it necessary to circulate and be seen, at a reasonable hour. I was keenly aware that I would be writing about Ford County, its people and places and happenings, for years to come.

Wiley said the cafés would be crowded early. 'Always after football games and car wrecks,' he said.

'What about murders?' I asked.

'It's been a long time,' he said.

He was right, the place was packed when we walked in, just after 6 A.M. He offered some hellos, shook some hands, exchanged a couple of insults. He was from Ford County and knew everyone. I nodded and smiled and caught the odd looks. It would take years. The people were friendly, but also wary of outsiders.

We found two seats at the counter and I asked for coffee. Nothing else. The waitress did not approve of this. She warmed to Wiley, though, when he reconsidered and ordered scrambled eggs, country ham, biscuits, grits, and a side of hash browns, enough cholesterol to choke a mule.

The talk was of the rape and murder and nothing else. If the weather could cause arguments, imagine what such a heinous crime could stir up. The Padgitts had had the run of the

45

county for a hundred years; it was time to send 'em all to jail. Surround the island with the National Guard if necessary. Mackey Don had to go; he'd been in their pockets for too long. Let a bunch of crooks run free and they think they're above the law. Now this.

Not much was said about Rhoda because little was known. Someone knew she'd been hanging around the lounges on the state line. Someone said she'd been sleeping with a local lawyer. Didn't know his name. Just a rumor.

The rumors roared around the Tea Shoppe. A couple of the loudmouths took turns holding court, and I was surprised at how reckless they were with their versions of the truth. Too bad I couldn't print all the wonderful gossip we heard.

Chapter 5

We did, however, print a lot. The headline proclaimed that Rhoda Kassellaw had been raped and murdered, and that Danny Padgitt had been arrested for it. The headline could've been read from twenty yards down any sidewalk around the courthouse square.

Under it were two photos; one of Rhoda as a senior in high school, and one of Padgitt as he was led into the jail in handcuffs. Wiley had ambushed him all right. It was a perfect shot, with Padgitt sneering at the camera. There was blood on his forehead from the wreck, and blood on his shirt from the attack. He looked nasty, mean, insolent, drunk, and guilty as hell, and I knew the photo would cause a sensation. Wiley thought we'd better avoid it, but I was twenty-three years old and too young to be restrained. I wanted my readers to see and know the ugly truth. I wanted to sell newspapers.

The photo of Rhoda had been obtained from

a sister in Missouri. The first time I talked to her, by phone, she had had almost nothing to say and quickly hung up. The second time she thawed just a little, said the children were being seen by a doctor, that the funeral would take place Tuesday afternoon in a small town near Springfield, and, as far as the family was concerned, the entire state of Mississippi could burn in hell.

I told her that I understood completely, that I was from Syracuse, that I was one of the good guys. She finally agreed to send me a photo.

Using a host of unnamed sources, I described in detail what happened the previous Saturday night on Benning Road. When I was sure of a fact, I drove it home. When I wasn't so sure, I nibbled around the edges with enough innuendo to convey what I thought happened. Baggy Suggs sobered up long enough to reread and edit the stories. He probably kept us from getting sued or shot.

On page two there was a map of the crime scene and a large photo of Rhoda's home, one taken the morning after the crime, complete with cop cars and yellow police ribbon everywhere. The photo also included the bikes and toys of Michael and Teresa scattered around the front yard. In many ways, the photo was more ominous than one of the corpse itself, which I didn't have but tried to get. The photo stated plainly that children lived there, and that children were involved in a crime so brutal that most Ford Countians were still trying to believe it really happened.

How much did the children see? That was the burning question.

I didn't answer it in the *Times*, but I got as close as possible. I described the house and its interior layout. Using an unnamed source, I estimated that the children's beds were about thirty feet from their mother's. The children fled the house before Rhoda, they were in shock by the time they got next door, they were seen by a doctor in Clanton and were undergoing therapy of some nature back home in Missouri. They saw a lot.

Would they testify at a trial? Baggy said there was no way; they were simply too young. But I pulled the question out of the air and posed it anyway, to give the readers something else to argue and fret over. After exploring the possibility of parading the children into a court-room, I concluded that 'experts' agreed that such a scenario was unlikely. Baggy enjoyed being considered an expert.

Rhoda's obituary was as long as I could possibly make it, which, given the tradition of the *Times*, was not unusual.

We went to press about 10 P.M. on Tuesday night; the paper was in the racks around the Clanton square by 7 A.M. on Wednesday. The circulation had dropped to fewer than twelve hundred at the time of the bankruptcy, but after a month of my fearless leadership we had close to

49

twenty-five hundred subscribers – five thousand was a realistic goal.

For the Rhoda Kassellaw murder we printed eight thousand copies and put them everywhere – by the doors of the cafés around the square, in the halls of the courthouse, on the desks of every county employee, in the lobbies of the banks. We mailed three thousand free copies to potential subscribers, as part of a sudden, one-time special promotion effort.

According to Wiley, it was the first murder in eight years. It was a Padgitt! It was a wonderfully sensational story and I saw it as my golden moment. Sure I went for the shock, for the sensational, for the bloodstains. Sure it was yellow journalism, but what did I care?

I had no idea the response would be so quick and unpleasant.

At 9 A.M., Thursday morning, the main courtroom on the second floor of the Ford County Courthouse was full. It was the domain of the Honorable Reed Loopus, an aging Circuit Court Judge from Tyler County, who passed through Clanton eight times a year to dispense justice. He was a legendary old warrior who ruled with an iron fist and, according to Baggy – who spent most of his working life hanging around the courthouse either picking up gossip or creating it – was a thoroughly honest Judge who had somehow managed to avoid the tentacles of the Padgitt money. Perhaps because he was from another county, Judge Loopus believed criminals should serve long sentences, preferably at hard labor, though he could no longer order such.

The Monday after the murder, the Padgitt lawyers had scrambled around trying to get Danny out of jail. Judge Loopus was preoccupied with a trial in another county – his district covered six of them – and he refused to be pushed into a quick bail hearing. Instead, he set the matter for 9 A.M. Thursday, thus allowing the town several days to ponder and speculate.

Because I was a member of the press, indeed the owner of the local paper, I felt it was my duty to arrive early and get a good seat. Yes, I was a bit smug. The other spectators were there out of curiosity. I, however, had very important work to do. Baggy and I were sitting in the second row when the crowd began to assemble.

Danny Padgitt's principal lawyer was a character named Lucien Wilbanks, a man I would quickly learn to hate. He was what was left of a once prominent clan of lawyers and bankers and such. The Wilbanks family had worked long and hard to build Clanton, then Lucien came along and had pretty much ruined a fine family name. He fancied himself as a radical lawyer, which, for that part of the world in 1970, was quite rare. He wore a beard, swore like a sailor, drank heavily, and preferred clients who were rapists and murderers and child molesters. He was the only white member of the NAACP in Ford County, which alone was enough to get you shot there. He didn't care.

Lucien Wilbanks was abrasive and fearless and downright mean, and he waited until everyone was settled in the courtroom – just before Judge Loopus entered – to walk slowly over to me. He was holding a copy of the latest *Times*, which he began waving as he started swearing. 'You little son of a bitch!' he said, quite loudly, and the courtroom became perfectly still. 'Who in hell do you think you are?'

I was too mortified to attempt an answer. I felt Baggy inch away. Every single person in the courtroom was staring at me, and I knew I had to say something. 'Just telling the truth,' I managed to say with as much conviction as I could muster.

'It's yellow journalism!' he roared. 'Sensational tabloid garbage!' The paper was just a few inches from my nose.

'Thank you,' I said, like a real wise guy. There were at least five deputies in the courtroom, none of whom were showing any interest in breaking this up.

'We'll file suit tomorrow!' he said, his eyes glowing. 'A million dollars in damages!'

'I got lawyers,' I said, suddenly terrified that I was about to be as bankrupt as the Caudle family. Lucien tossed the paper into my lap, then turned and went back to his table. I was finally able to exhale; my heart was pounding. I could feel my cheeks burning from embarrassment and fear.

But I managed to keep a stupid grin on my face. I couldn't show the locals that I, the editor/publisher of their paper, was afraid of anything. But a million dollars in damages! I immediately thought of my grandmother in Memphis. That would be a difficult conversation.

There was a commotion up behind the bench and a bailiff opened a door. 'Everyone rise,' he announced. Judge Loopus crept through it and shuffled to his seat, his faded black robe trailing behind him. Once situated, he surveyed the crowd, and said, 'Good morning. A rather nice turnout for a bail hearing.' Such routine matters generally attracted no one, except for the accused, his lawyer, and perhaps his mother. There were three hundred people watching this one.

It wasn't just a bail hearing. It was round one of a rape/murder trial, and few people in Clanton wanted to miss it. As I was keenly aware, most folks would not be able to attend the proceedings. They would rely on the *Times*, and I was determined to give them the details.

Every time I looked at Lucien Wilbanks, I thought about the lawsuit for a million dollars. Surely he wasn't going to sue my paper, was he? For what? There had been no libel, no defamation.

Judge Loopus nodded at another bailiff and a side door opened. Danny Padgitt was escorted in, his hands cuffed at his waist. He was wearing a neatly pressed white shirt, khaki pants, and loafers. His face was clean shaven and free of any apparent injuries. He was twenty-four, a year older than me, but he looked much younger. He was clean cut, handsome, and I couldn't help but think he ought to be in college somewhere. He managed a slow strut, then the sneer as the bailiff removed the handcuffs. He looked around at the crowd, and for a moment seemed to enjoy the attention. He showed all the confidence of someone whose family had unlimited cash, which it would use to get him out of his little jam.

Seated directly in back of him, behind the bar in the first row, were his parents and various other Padgitts. His father Gill, grandson of the infamous Clovis Padgitt, had a college degree and was rumored to be the chief money launderer in the gang. His mother was well dressed and somewhat attractive, which I found unusual for someone dimwitted enough to marry into the Padgitt clan and spend the rest of her life secluded on the island.

'I've never seen her before,' Baggy whispered to me.

'How often have you seen Gill?' I asked.

'Maybe twice, in the last twenty years.'

The State was represented by the county prosecutor, a part-timer named Rocky Childers. Judge Loopus addressed him: 'Mr. Childers, I assume the State is opposed to bail.'

Childers stood and said, 'Yes sir.'

'On what grounds?'

'The horrific nature of the crimes, Your

Honor. A vicious rape, in the victim's own bed, in front of her small children. A simultaneous murder caused by at least two knife wounds. The attempted flight of the accused, Mr. Padgitt.' Childers's words cut through the hushed courtroom. 'The great likelihood that if Mr. Padgitt leaves jail we will never see him again.'

Lucien Wilbanks couldn't wait to stand up and start bickering. He was on his feet immediately. 'We object to that, Your Honor. My client has no criminal record whatsoever, never been arrested before.'

Judge Loopus looked calmly over his reading glasses and said, 'Mr. Wilbanks, I do hope that is the first and last time you interrupt anyone in this proceeding. I suggest you sit down, and when the Court is ready to hear from you, then you will be so advised.' His words were icy, almost bitter, and I wondered how many times these two had tangled in this very courtroom.

Nothing bothered Lucien Wilbanks; his skin was as thick as rawhide.

Childers then gave us a bit of history. Eleven years earlier, in 1959, a certain Gerald Padgitt had been indicted for stealing cars over in Tupelo. It took a year to find a couple of deputies willing to enter Padgitt Island to serve a warrant, and though they survived, they were unsuccessful. Gerald Padgitt either fled the country or secluded himself somewhere on the island. 'Wherever he is,' Childers said, 'he's never been arrested, never been found.'

'You ever hear of Gerald Padgitt?' I whispered to Baggy.

'Nope.'

'If this defendant is released on bail, Your Honor, we'll never see him again. It's that simple.' Childers sat down.

'Mr. Wilbanks,' His Honor said.

Lucien stood slowly and waved a hand at Childers. 'As usual, the prosecutor is confused,' he began pleasantly. 'Gerald Padgitt is not charged with these crimes. I don't represent him and really don't give a damn what happened to him.'

'Watch your language,' Loopus said.

'He's not on trial here. This is about Danny Padgitt, a young man with no criminal record whatsoever.'

'Does your client own real estate in this county?' Loopus asked.

'No, he does not. He's only twenty-four.'

'Let's get to the bottom line, Mr. Wilbanks. I know his family owns considerable acreage. The only way I'll grant bail is if it's all pledged to secure his appearance for trial.'

'That's outrageous,' Lucien growled.

'So are his alleged crimes.'

Lucien flung his legal pad onto the table. 'Give me a minute to consult with the family.'

This caused quite a stir among the Padgitts. They huddled behind the defense table with Wilbanks and there was disagreement from the very start. It was almost funny watching these

56

very wealthy crooks shake their heads and get mad at each other. Family fights are quick and bitter, especially when money is at stake, and every Padgitt present seemed to have a different opinion about which course to take. One could only imagine what it was like when they were dividing their loot.

Lucien sensed that an agreement was unlikely, and to avoid embarrassment he turned and addressed the Court. 'That's impossible, Your Honor,' he announced. 'The Padgitt land is owned by at least forty people, most of them absent from this courtroom. What the Court is requiring is arbitrary and overly burdensome.'

'I'll give you a few days to put it together,' Loopus said, obviously enjoying the discomfort he was causing.

'No sir. It's just not fair. My client is entitled to a reasonable bail, same as any other defendant.'

'Then bail is denied until the preliminary hearing.'

'We waive the preliminary.'

'As you wish,' Loopus said, taking notes.

'And we request that the case be presented to the grand jury as soon as possible.'

'In due course, Mr. Wilbanks, same as all other cases.'

'Because we will move for a change of venue as soon as possible.' Lucien said this boldly, as if an important proclamation was needed.

'It's a bit early for that, don't you think?' Loopus said.

'It will be impossible for my client to get a fair trial in this county.' Wilbanks was gazing around the courtroom as he continued, almost ignoring the Judge, who, for the moment, seemed curious.

'An effort is already under way to indict, try, and convict my client before he has the chance to defend himself, and I think the Court should intervene immediately with a gag order.'

Lucien Wilbanks was the only one who needed gagging.

'Where are you going with this, Mr. Wilbanks?' Loopus asked.

'Have you seen the local paper, Your Honor?'

'Not lately.'

All eyes seemed to settle upon me, and once again my heart stopped dead still.

Wilbanks glared at me as he continued. 'Front page stories, bloody photographs, unnamed sources, enough half-truths and innuendos to convict any innocent man!'

Baggy was inching away again, and I was very much alone.

Lucien stomped across the courtroom and tossed a copy up to the bench. 'Take a look at this,' he growled. Loopus adjusted his reading glasses, pulled the *Times* up high, and sank back into his fine leather chair. He began reading, apparently in no particular hurry.

He was a slow reader. At some point my heart

began functioning again, returning with the fury of a jackhammer. And I noticed my collar was wet where it rested on the back of my neck. Loopus finished the front page and slowly opened it up. The courtroom was silent. Would he toss me into jail right there? Nod to a bailiff to slap handcuffs on me and drag me away? I wasn't a lawyer. I'd just been threatened with a million-dollar lawsuit, by a man who'd certainly filed many, and now the Judge was reading my rather lurid accounts while the entire town waited for his verdict.

A lot of hard glances were coming my way, so I found it easier to scribble on my reporter's pad, though I couldn't read anything I was writing. I worked hard at keeping a straight face. What I really wanted to do was bolt from the courtroom and race back to Memphis.

Pages rattled, and His Honor was finally finished. He leaned slightly forward to the microphone and uttered words that would instantly make my career. He said, 'It's very well written. Engaging, perhaps a bit macabre, but certainly nothing out of line.'

I kept scribbling, as if I hadn't heard this. In a sudden, unforeseen, and rather harrowing skirmish, I had just prevailed over the Padgitts and Lucien Wilbanks. 'Congratulations,' Baggy whispered.

Loopus refolded the newspaper and laid it down. He allowed Wilbanks to rant and rave for a few minutes about leaks from the cops, leaks

59

from the prosecutor's office, potential leaks from the grand jury room, all of them somehow coordinated by a conspiracy of unnamed people determined to treat his client unfairly. What he was really doing was performing for the Padgitts. He had lost his attempt to get bail, so he had to impress them with his zealousness.

Loopus bought none of it.

As we would soon learn, Lucien's act had been nothing but a smokescreen. He had no intention of moving the case from Ford County.

Chapter 6

When I bought the *Times*, its prehistoric building came with the deal. It had very little value. It was on the south side of the Clanton square, one of four decaying structures built wall to wall by someone in a hurry; long and narrow, three levels, with a basement that all employees feared and shied away from. There were several offices in the front, all with stained and threadbare carpet, peeling walls, the smell of last century's pipe smoke forever fused to the ceilings.

In the rear, as far away as possible, was the printing press. Every Tuesday night, Hardy, our pressman, somehow coaxed the old letterpress to life and managed to produce yet another edition of our paper. His space was rank with the sharp odor of printer's ink.

The room on the first floor was lined with bookshelves sagging under the weight of dusty tomes that had not been opened in decades; collections of history and Shakespeare and Irish

61

poetry and rows of badly outdated British encyclopedias. Spot thought such books would impress anyone who ventured in.

Standing in the front window, and looking through dingy panes of glass, across which someone had long ago painted the word 'TIMES,' one could see the Ford County Courthouse and the bronze Confederate sentry guarding it. A plaque below his feet listed the names of the sixty-one county boys who died in the Great War, most at Shiloh.

The sentry could also be seen from my office, which was on the second floor. It, too, was lined with bookshelves holding Spot's personal library, an eclectic collection that appeared to have been as neglected as the one downstairs. It would be years before I moved any of his books.

The office was spacious, cluttered, filled with useless artifacts and worthless files and adorned with fake portraits of Confederate generals. I loved the place. When Spot left he took nothing, and after a few months no one seemed to want any of his junk. So it remained where it was, neglected as always, virtually untouched by me, and slowly becoming my property. I boxed up his personal things – letters, bank statements, notes, postcards – and stored them in one of the many unused rooms down the hall where they continued to gather dust and slowly rot.

My office had two sets of French doors that opened to a small porch with a wrought-iron railing, and there was enough room out there for four people to sit in wicker chairs and watch the square. Not that there was much to see, but it was a pleasant way to pass the time, especially with a drink.

Baggy was always ready for a drink. He brought a bottle of bourbon after dinner, and we assumed our positions in the rockers. The town was still buzzing over the bail hearing. It had been widely assumed that Danny Padgitt would be sprung as soon as Lucien Wilbanks and Mackey Don Coley could get matters arranged. Promises would be made, money would change hands, Sheriff Coley would somehow personally guarantee the boy's appearance at trial. But Judge Loopus had other plans.

Baggy's wife was a nurse. She worked the night shift in the emergency room at the hospital. He worked days, if his rather languid observations of the town could be considered labor. They rarely saw each other, which was evidently a good thing because they fought constantly. Their adult children had fled, leaving the two of them to wage their own little war. After a couple of drinks, Baggy always began the cutting remarks about his wife. He was fifty-two, looked at least seventy, and I suspected that the booze was the principal reason he was aging badly and fighting at home.

'We kicked their butts,' he said proudly. 'Never before has a newspaper story been so clearly exonerated. Right there in open court.'

'What's a gag order?' I asked. I was an ill-informed rookie, and everybody knew it. No sense in pretending I knew something when I didn't.

'I've never seen one. I've heard of them, and I think they're used by judges to shut up the lawyers and the litigants.'

'So they don't apply to newspapers?'

'Never. Wilbanks was grandstanding, that's all. The guy is a member of the ACLU, only one in Ford County. He understands the First Amendment. There's no way a court can tell a newspaper not to print something. He was having a bad day, it was apparent his client was staying in jail, so he had to showboat. Typical maneuver by lawyers. They teach it in law school.'

'So you don't think we'll get sued?'

'Hell no. Look, first of all, there's no lawsuit. We didn't libel or defame anyone. Sure we got kinda loose with some of the facts, but it was all small stuff, and it was probably true anyway. Second, if Wilbanks had a lawsuit he would have to file it here, in Ford County. Same courthouse, same courtroom, same Judge. The Honorable Reed Loopus, who, this morning, read our stories and declared them to be just fine. The lawsuit was shot down before Wilbanks typed the first word. Brilliant.'

I certainly didn't feel brilliant. I'd been worrying about the million dollars in damages and wondering where I might find such a sum. The bourbon was finally settling in and I relaxed.

It was Thursday night in Clanton and few people were out. Every shop and store and office around the square was locked tight.

Baggy, as usual, had been relaxed for a long time. Margaret had whispered to me that he often had bourbon for breakfast. He and a one-legged lawyer called Major liked to have a nip with their coffee. They would meet on the balcony outside Major's office across the square and smoke and drink and argue law and politics while the courthouse came to life. Major lost a leg at Guadalcanal, according to his version of the Second War. His law practice was specialized to the point that he did nothing but type wills for the elderly. He typed them himself – had no need for a secretary. He worked about as hard as Baggy, and the two were often seen in the court-room, half-soused, watching yet another trial.

'I guess Mackey Don's got the boy in the suite,' Baggy said, his words starting to slur.

'The suite?' I asked.

'Yeah – have you seen the jail?'

'No.'

'It's not fit for animals. No heat, no air, plumbing works about half the time. Filthy conditions. Rotten food. And that's for the whites. The blacks are at the other end, all in one long cell. Their only toilet is a hole in the floor.'

'I think I'll pass.'

'It's an embarrassment to the county, but, sadly, it's the same in most places around here. Anyway, there's one little cell with air

65

conditioning and carpet on the floor, one clean bed, color television, good food. It's called the suite and Mackey Don puts his favorites there.'

I was mentally taking notes. To Baggy, it was business as usual. To me, a recent college attendee and sometime journalism student, a real muckraking story was in the works. 'You think Padgitt's in the suite?'

'Probably. He came to court in his own clothes.'

'As opposed to?'

'Those orange jail coveralls everybody else wears. You haven't seen them?'

Yes, I had seen them. I had been in court one time, a month or so earlier, and I suddenly recalled seeing two or three defendants sitting in the courtroom, waiting for a judge, all wearing different shades of faded orange coveralls. 'Ford County Jail' was printed across the front and back of the shirts.

Baggy took a sip and expounded. 'You see, for the preliminary hearings and such, the defendants, if they're still in jail, always come to court dressed like prisoners. In the old days, Mackey Don would make them wear the coveralls even during their trials. Lucien Wilbanks got a guilty verdict reversed on the grounds that the jury was predisposed to convict since his client certainly looked guilty as hell in his orange jail suit. And he was right. Kinda hard to convince a jury you're not guilty when you're dressed like an inmate and wearing rubber shower shoes.'

I marveled once again at the backwardness of Mississippi. I could see a criminal defendant, especially a black one, facing a jury and expecting a fair trial, wearing jail garb designed to be spotted from half a mile away. 'Still fightin' the War,' was a slogan I'd heard several times in Ford County. There was a frustrating resistance to change, especially where crime and punishment were concerned.

Around noon the following day I walked to the jail looking for Sheriff Coley. Under the pretext of asking him questions about the Kassellaw investigation, I planned to see as many of the inmates as possible. His secretary informed me, rather rudely, that he was in a meeting, and that was fine with me.

Two prisoners were cleaning the front offices. Outside, two more were pulling weeds from a flower bed. I walked around the block and behind the jail I saw a small open area with a basketball goal. Six prisoners were loitering under the shade of a small oak tree. On the east side of the jail I saw three prisoners standing in a window, behind bars, gazing down at me.

Thirteen inmates in all. Thirteen orange suits.

Wiley's nephew was consulted about things around the jail. At first he was reluctant to talk, but he had a deep hatred of Sheriff Coley, and he thought he could trust me. He confirmed what Baggy had suspected – Danny Padgitt was living the good life in an air-conditioned cell and eating whatever he wanted. He dressed as he wished, played checkers with the Sheriff himself, and made phone calls all day long.

The next edition of the *Times* did much to solidify my reputation as a hard-charging, fearless, twenty-three-year-old fool. On the front page was a huge photo of Danny Padgitt being led into the courthouse for his bail hearing. He was handcuffed and wore street clothes. He was also giving the camera one of his patented go-to-hell looks. Just above it was the massive headline: BAIL DENIED FOR DANNY PADGITT. The story was lengthy and detailed.

Alongside was another story, almost as long and much more scandalous. Quoting unnamed sources, I described at length the conditions of Mr. Padgitt's incarceration. I mentioned every possible perk he was getting, including personal time with Sheriff Coley over the checkerboard. I talked about his food and diet, color television, unlimited phone use. Everything I could possibly verify. Then I compared this with how the other twenty-one inmates were living.

On page two, I ran an old black-and-white file photo of four defendants being led into the courthouse. Each, of course, was wearing the coveralls. Each had handcuffs and unruly hair. I blacked out their faces so, whoever they were, they would not suffer any more embarrassment. Their cases had long since been closed.

I'd placed another picture of Danny Padgitt as

he was led into the courthouse next to the file photo. Except for the handcuffs, he could've been on his way to a party. The contrast was startling. The boy was being pampered by Sheriff Coley, who, so far, had refused to discuss the matter with me. Big mistake.

In the story, I detailed my efforts to chat with the Sheriff. My phone calls had not been returned. I'd gone to the jail twice and he wouldn't meet with me. I'd left a list of questions for him, which he chose to ignore. I painted the picture of an aggressive young reporter desperately searching for the truth and being stiff-armed by an elected official.

Since Lucien Wilbanks was one of the least popular men in Clanton, I included him in the fray. Using the phone, which I was quickly learning was a great equalizer, I called his office four times before he called me back. At first he had no comment about his client or the charges, but when I persisted with questions about his treatment at the jail he erupted. 'I don't run the damned jail, son!' he growled, and I could almost see his red eyes glowing at me. I quoted him on that.

'Have you interviewed your client at the jail?' I asked.

'Of course.'

'What was he wearing?'

'Don't you have better things to report?'

'No sir. What was he wearing?'

'Well he wasn't naked.'

That was too good a quote to pass up, so I put it in bold print in a sidebar.

With a rapist/murderer, a corrupt Sheriff, and a radical lawyer on one side, and me standing alone on the other, I knew I couldn't lose the fight. The response to the story was astounding. Baggy and Wiley reported that the cafés were buzzing with admiration for the fearless young editor of the paper. The Padgitts and Lucien had been despised for a long time. Now it was time to get rid of Coley.

Margaret said we were swamped with phone calls from readers incensed with the soft treatment Danny was receiving. Wiley's nephew reported that the jail was in chaos and Mackey Don was at war with his deputies. He was coddling a murderer – 1971 was an election year. Folks were angry out there and they might all lose their jobs.

Those two weeks at the *Times* were crucial to its survival. The readers were hungry for details, and, through timing, dumb luck, and some guts, I gave them just what they wanted. The paper was suddenly alive; it was a force. It was trusted. The people wanted it to report with detail and without fear.

Baggy and Margaret told me that Spot would have never used the bloody pictures and challenged the Sheriff. But they were still quite timid. I can't say that my brashness had in any way emboldened my staff. The *Times* was, and would be, a one-man show with a rather weak supporting staff.

Little did I care. I was telling the truth and damning the consequences. I was a local hero. Subscriptions jumped to almost three thousand. Ad revenue doubled. Not only was I shining a new light into the county, I was making money at the same time.

Chapter 7

The bomb was a rather basic incendiary device that, if detonated, would have quickly engulfed our printing room. There the fire would have been energized by various chemicals and no less than 110 gallons of printer's ink, and would have raced quickly through the front offices. After a few minutes, with no sprinkler system and no alarms, who knows how much of the upper two floors could have been saved. Probably not much. It was very likely that the fire, if properly detonated in the early hours of Thursday morning, would've burned most of the four buildings in our row.

It was discovered sitting ominously, still intact, next to a pile of old papers in the printing room, by the village idiot. Or, I should say, one of the village idiots. Clanton had more than its share.

His name was Piston, and he, like the building and the ancient press and the untouched libraries upstairs and down, came with the deal. Piston was not an official employee of the *Times*, but he nonetheless showed up every Friday to collect his $50 in cash. No checks. For this fee he sometimes swept the floors and occasionally rearranged the dirt on the front windows, and he hauled out the trash when someone complained. He kept no hours, came and went as he pleased, didn't believe in knocking on doors when meetings were in progress, liked to use our phones and drink our coffee, and though he at first looked rather sinister – eyes wide apart and covered with thick glasses, oversized trucker's cap pulled down low, scraggly beard, hideous buck teeth – he was harmless. He provided his janitorial services for several businesses around the square, and somehow survived. No one knew where he lived, or with whom, or how he got about town. The less we knew about Piston, the better.

Piston was in early Thursday morning – he'd had a key for decades – and said that he first heard something ticking. Upon closer examination he noticed three, five-gallon plastic cans laced together with a wooden box sitting on the floor next to them. The ticking sound came from the box. Piston had been around the printing room for many years and occasionally helped Hardy on Tuesday nights when he ran the paper.

For most folks, panic would quickly follow curiosity, but for Piston it took a while. After poking around the cans to make sure that they

were in fact filled with gasoline, and after deter-
mining that a series of dangerous-looking wires
tied everything together, he walked to Margaret's
office and called Hardy. He said the ticking was
getting louder.

Hardy called the police, and around 9 A.M. I
was awakened with the news.

Most of downtown was evacuated by the time
I arrived. Piston was sitting on the hood of a car,
by then thoroughly distraught at having survived
such a close call. He was being attended by some
acquaintances and an ambulance driver, and he
seemed to be enjoying the attention.

Wiley Meek had photographed the bomb
before the police removed the gasoline cans and
placed them safely in the alley behind our
building. 'Woulda blown up half of downtown,'
was Wiley's uneducated evaluation of the bomb.
He nervously darted around the scene, recording
the excitement for future use.

The chief of police explained to me that the
area was off limits because the wooden box had
not been opened and whatever was in there was
still ticking. 'It might explode,' he said gravely, as
if he was the first one smart enough to realize the
danger. I doubted if he had much experience
with bombs, but I went along. An official from
the state crime lab was being rushed in. It was
decided that the four buildings in our row would
remain unoccupied until this expert finished his
business.

A bomb in downtown Clanton! The news

spread faster than the fire would have, and all work stopped. The county offices emptied, as well as the banks and stores and cafés, and before long large groups of spectators were crowded across the street, under the huge oaks on the south side of the courthouse, a safe distance away. They gawked at our little building, obviously concerned and frightened but also waiting for some excitement. They'd never seen a bomb blast before.

The Clanton city police had been joined by the Sheriff's deputies, and every uniform in the county was soon present, milling about on the sidewalks, doing absolutely nothing. Sheriff Coley and the police chief huddled and conferred and watched the throng across the street, then barked some orders here and there, but if any of their orders were followed it wasn't noticeable. It was obvious to all that the city and county had no bomb drills.

Baggy needed a drink. It was too early for me. I followed him into the rear of the courthouse, up a narrow flight of stairs I'd not seen before, through a cramped hallway, then up another twenty steps to a small dirty room with a low ceiling. 'Used to be the old jury room,' he said. 'Then it was the law library.'

'What is it now?' I asked, almost afraid of the answer.

'The Bar Room. Get it? Bar? Lawyers? Booze?'

'Got it.' There was a card table with folding

legs and a beaten look that indicated years of use. Around it were half a dozen mismatched chairs, all county hand-me-downs that had been passed from one county office to another and finally ditched in this dingy little room.

In one corner there was a small refrigerator with a padlock. Baggy, of course, had a key, and inside he found a bottle of bourbon. He poured a generous shot into a paper cup and said, 'Grab a chair.' We pulled two of them up to the window, and below was the scene we had just left. 'Not a bad view, huh?' he said proudly.

'How often you come here?'

'Twice a week, maybe, sometimes more. We play poker every Tuesday and Thursday at noon.'

'Who's in the club?'

'It's a secret society.' He took a sip and smacked his lips as if he'd been in the desert for a month. A spider made its way down a thick web along the window. Dust was half an inch thick on the sills.

'I guess they're losin' their touch,' he said, gazing down at the excitement.

'They?' I was almost afraid to ask.

'The Padgitts.' He said this with a certain smugness, then allowed it to hang in the air for my benefit.

'You're sure it's the Padgitts?' I asked.

Baggy thought he knew everything, and he was right about half the time. He smirked and grunted, took another sip, then said, 'They've been burnin' buildings forever. It's one of their scams – insurance fraud. They've made a bloody fortune off insurance companies.' A quick sip. 'Odd, though, that they would use gasoline. Your more talented arsonists stay away from gasoline because it's easily detected. You know that?'

'No.'

'True. A good fire marshal can smell gasoline within minutes after the blaze is out. Gasoline means arson. Arson means no insurance payoffs.' A sip. 'Of course, in this case, they probably wanted you to know it's arson. Makes sense, doesn't it?'

Nothing made sense at that moment. I was too confused to say much.

Baggy was content to do the talking. 'Come to think of it, that's probably the reason it wasn't detonated. They wanted you to see it. If it went off, then the county wouldn't have the *Times*, which might upset some folks. Might make some other folks happy.'

'Thanks.'

'Anyway, that explains it better. It was a subtle act of intimidation.'

'Subtle?'

'Yes, compared to what could've been. Believe me, those guys know how to burn buildings. You were lucky.'

I noticed how he had quickly disassociated himself from the paper. It was 'I' who was lucky, not 'we.'

The bourbon had found its way to the brain and was loosening the tongue. 'About three years ago, maybe four, there was a large fire at one of their lumber mills, the one on Highway 401, just off the island. They never burn anything on the island because they don't want the authorities snoopin' around. Anyway, the insurance company smelled a rat, refused to pay, so Lucien Wilbanks filed this big lawsuit. It came to trial, in front of the Honorable Reed Loopus. I heard ever' word of it.' A long, satisfying drink.

'Who won?'

He ignored me completely because the story was not yet properly laid out. 'It was a big fire. The boys from Clanton took off with all their trucks. The volunteers from Karaway took off, ever' yokel with a siren went screamin' off toward Padgitt Island. Nothin' like a good fire around here to get the boys worked up. That and a bomb, I guess, but I can't remember the last bomb.'

'And so . . .'

'Highway 401 runs through some lowland near Padgitt Island, real swampy. There's a bridge over Massey's Creek, and when the fire trucks came flyin' up to the bridge they found a pickup layin' on its side, like it had rolled over. The road was completely blocked; couldn't go around because there was nothin' but swamps and ditches.' He smacked his lips and poured more from the bottle. It was time for me to say something, but whatever I said would be completely ignored anyway. This was the way Baggy preferred to be prompted.

'Whose pickup was it?' I asked, the words barely out of my mouth before he was shaking his head as if the question was completely off the mark.

'The fire was ragin' like hell. Fire trucks backed up all along 401 because some clown had flipped his pickup. Never found him. No sign of a driver. No sign of an owner because there was no registration. No tags. The vehicle ID had been sanded off. The truck was never claimed. Wasn't damaged much either. All this came out at trial. Ever'body knew the Padgitts set the fire, flipped one of their stolen trucks to block the road, but the insurance company couldn't prove it.'

Down below Sheriff Coley had found his bullhorn. He was asking the people to please stay off the street in front of our office. His shrieking voice added urgency to the situation.

'So the insurance company won?' I said, anxious to get to the end.

'Helluva trial. Went on for three days. Wilbanks can usually cut a deal with one or two people on the jury. Been doin' it for years and never gets caught. Plus he knows ever'body in the county. The insurance boys were up from Jackson, and they didn't have a clue. The jury stayed out for two hours, came back with a verdict for the claim, a hundred grand, and for good measure, tacked on a million in punitive damages.'

'One point one million!' I said.

'You got it. The first million-dollar verdict in Ford County. Lasted about a year until the Supreme Court took an ax to it and cut out the punitive.'

The notion of Lucien Wilbanks having such sway over jurors was not comforting. Baggy neglected his bourbon for a moment and gazed at something below. 'This is a bad sign, son,' he finally said. 'Really bad.'

I was his boss and didn't like to be referred to as 'son,' but I let it slide. I had more pressing matters at hand. 'The intimidation?' I said.

'Yep. The Padgitts rarely leave the island. The fact that they've brought their little show on the road means they're ready for war. If they can intimidate the newspaper, then they'll try it with the jury. They already own the Sheriff.'

'But Wilbanks said he wants a change of venue.'

He snorted and rediscovered his drink. 'Don't bet on it, son.'

'Please call me Willie.' Odd how I was now clinging to that name.

'Don't bet on it, Willie. The boy's guilty; his only chance is to have a jury that can be bought or scared. Ten to one odds the trial takes place right here, in this building.'

After two hours of waiting in vain for the ground to shake, the town was ready for lunch. The crowd broke up and drifted away. The expert from the state crime lab finally arrived and went to work in the printing room. I wasn't allowed in the building, which was fine with me.

Margaret, Wiley, and I had a sandwich in the gazebo on the courthouse lawn. We ate quietly, chatted briefly, the three of us keeping an eye on our office across the street. Occasionally someone would see us and stop for an awkward word or two. What do you say to bombing victims when the bomb doesn't go off? Fortunately, the townsfolk had had little practice in that area. We collected some sympathy and a few offers of help.

Sheriff Coley ambled over and gave a preliminary report on our bomb. The clock was of the wind-up alarm variety, available in stores everywhere. At first glance the expert thought there was a problem with the wiring. Very amateurish, he said.

'How will you investigate this?' I asked with an edge.

'We'll check for prints, see if we can find any witnesses. The usual.'

'Will you talk to the Padgitts?' I asked, even edgier. I was, after all, in the presence of my employees. And though I was scared to death, I wanted to impress them with how utterly fearless I was.

'You know somethin' I don't?' he shot back.

'They're suspects, aren't they?'

'Are you the Sheriff now?'

'They're the most experienced arsonists in the

county, been burning buildings for years with impunity. Their lawyer threatened me in court last week. We've had Danny Padgitt on the front page twice. If they're not suspects, then who is?'

'Just go ahead and write the story, son. Call 'em by name. You seem determined to get sued anyway.'

'I'll take care of the paper,' I said. 'You catch the criminals.'

He tipped his hat to Margaret and walked away.

'Next year's reelection year,' Wiley said as we watched Coley stop and chat with two ladies near a drinking fountain. 'I hope he has an opponent.'

The intimidation continued, at Wiley's expense. He lived a mile from town on a five-acre hobby farm, where his wife raised ducks and watermelons. That night as he parked in his drive and was getting out of his car, two goons jumped from the shrubs and assaulted him. The larger man knocked him down and kicked him in the face, while the other one rummaged through his backseat and pulled out two cameras. Wiley was fifty-eight years old and an ex-Marine, and at some point in the melee he managed to land a kick that sent the larger assailant to the ground. There they exchanged blows and as Wiley was gaining the upper hand the other thug banged him over the head with one of his cameras. Wiley said he didn't remember much after that.

His wife eventually heard the ruckus. She found Wiley on the ground, semiconscious, with both cameras shattered. In the house, she put ice packs on his face and determined that there were no broken bones. The ex-Marine did not want to go to the hospital.

A deputy arrived and made a report. Wiley had caught only a glimpse of his attackers and he'd certainly never seen them before. 'They're back on the island by now,' he said. 'You won't find them.'

His wife prevailed, and an hour later they called me from the hospital. I saw him between X rays. His face was a mess, but he managed to smile. He grabbed my hand and pulled me close. 'Next week, front page,' he said through cut lips and swollen jaws.

A few hours later I left the hospital and went for a long drive through the countryside. I kept glancing at my mirror, half-expecting another load of Padgitts to come roaring up, guns blazing.

It was not a lawless county, where organized criminals ran roughshod over the law-abiding people. It was just the opposite – crime was rare. Corruption was generally frowned upon. I was right and they were wrong, and I decided I'd be damned before I knuckled under. I'd buy myself a gun; hell, everybody else in the county carried two or three. And if necessary I'd hire a guard of some sort. My paper would grow even bolder as the murder trial approached.

Chapter 8

Prior to the bankruptcy, and my unlikely rise in prominence in Ford County, I had heard a fascinating story about a local family. Spot never pursued it because it would've required some light research and a trip across the railroad tracks.

Now that the paper was mine, I decided it was too good to pass up.

Over in Lowtown, the colored section, there lived an extraordinary couple – Calia and Esau Ruffin. They had been married for over forty years and had raised eight children, seven of whom had earned PhD's and were now college professors. Details on the remaining one were sketchy, though, according to Margaret, his name was Sam and he was hiding from the law.

I called the house and Mrs. Ruffin answered the phone. I explained who I was and what I wanted, and she seemed to know everything about me. She said she'd been reading the *Times* for fifty years, front to back, everything including the obits and the want ads, and after a moment or two offered the opinion that the paper was in much better hands now. Longer stories. Fewer mistakes. More news. She spoke slowly, clearly, with precise diction I had not heard since I left Syracuse.

When I finally had an opening, I thanked her and said I'd like to meet and talk about her remarkable family. She was flattered and insisted that I come over for lunch.

Thus began an unusual friendship that opened my eyes to many things, not the least of which was Southern cuisine.

My mother died when I was thirteen. She was anorexic, there were only four pallbearers. She weighed less than a hundred pounds and looked like a ghost. Anorexia was only one of her many problems.

Because she did not eat, she did not cook. I cannot remember a single hot meal she prepared for me. Breakfast was a bowl of Cheerios, lunch a cold sandwich, dinner some frozen mess I usually ate in front of the television, alone. I was an only child and my father was never at home, which was a relief because his presence caused friction between them. He preferred to eat, she did not. They feuded over everything.

I never went hungry; the pantry was always full of peanut butter and cereal and such. I occasionally ate with a friend and I always marveled at how real families cooked and spent so much time at the table. Food was simply not important around our house.

As a teenager I existed on frozen dinners. At Syracuse it was beer and pizza. For the first twenty-three years of my life, I ate only when I was hungry. This was wrong, I soon learned in Clanton. In the South, eating has little to do with hunger.

The Ruffin home was in a nicer section of Lowtown, in a row of neatly preserved and painted shotgun houses. The street addresses were on the mailboxes, and when I rolled to a stop I was smiling at the white picket fence and flowers – peonies and irises – that lined the sidewalk. It was early April, I had the top down on my Spitfire, and as I turned off the ignition I smelled something delicious. Pork chops!

Calia Ruffin met me at the low swing-gate that opened into her immaculate front lawn. She was a stout woman, thick in the shoulders and trunk, with a handshake that was firm and felt like a man's. She had gray hair and was showing the effects of raising so many children, but when she smiled, which was constantly, she lit up the world with two rows of brilliant, perfect teeth. I had never seen such teeth.

'I'm so glad you came,' she said, halfway up the brick walkway. I was so glad too. It was about noon. Typically, I had yet to eat a bite, and the aromas wafting from the porch were making me dizzy.

'A lovely house,' I said, gazing at the front of it. It was clapboard, painted a sparkling white, and gave the impression that someone was usually hanging around with a brush and bucket. A green tin-roofed porch ran across the entire front.

'Why thank you. We've owned it for thirty years.'

I knew that most of the dwellings in Lowtown were owned by white slumlords across the tracks. To own a home was an unusual accomplishment for blacks in 1970.

'Who's your gardener?' I asked as I stopped to smell a yellow rose. There were flowers everywhere – edging the walkway, along the porch, down both sides of their property line. 'That would be me,' she said with a laugh, teeth gleaming in the sunlight.

Up three steps and onto the porch, and there it was – the spread! A small table next to the railing was prepared for two people – white cotton cloth, white napkins, flowers in a small vase, a large pitcher of iced tea, and at least four covered dishes.

'Who's coming?' I asked.

'Oh, just the two of us. Esau might drop by later.'

'There's enough food for an army.' I inhaled as deeply as possible and my stomach ached in anticipation.

'Let's eat now,' she said, 'before it gets cold.'

I restrained myself, walked casually to the table and pulled back a chair for her. She was delighted that I was such a gentleman. I sat across from her and was ready to yank off the lids and dive headfirst into whatever I found when she took both my hands and lowered her head. She began to pray.

It would be a lengthy prayer. She thanked the Lord for everything good, including me, 'her new friend.' She prayed for those who were sick and those who might become so. She prayed for rain and sun and health and humility and patience, and though I began to worry about the food getting cold I was mesmerized by her voice. Her cadence was slow, with thought given to each word. Her diction was perfect, every consonant treated equally, every comma and period honored. I had to peek to make sure I wasn't dreaming. I had never heard such speech from a Southern black, or a Southern white for that matter.

I peeked again. She was talking to her Lord, and her face was perfectly content. For a few seconds, I actually forgot about the food. She squeezed my hands as she petitioned the Almighty with eloquence that came only from years of practice. She quoted Scripture, the King James Version for sure, and it was a bit odd to hear her use words like 'thou' and 'thine' and 'whither' and 'goest.' But she knew precisely what she was doing. In the clutches of this very holy woman, I had never felt closer to God.

I couldn't imagine such a lengthy devotional over a table crowded with eight children. Something told me, though, that when Calia Ruffin prayed everybody got still.

Finally, she ended with a flourish, a long burst in which she managed to appeal for the forgiveness of her sins, which I presumed were few and far between, and for my own, which, well, if she only knew.

She released me and began removing lids from bowls. The first contained a pile of pork chops smothered in a sauce that included, among many ingredients, onions and peppers. More steam hit my face and I wanted to eat with my fingers. In the second there was a mound of yellow corn, sprinkled with green peppers, still hot from the stove. There was boiled okra, which, she explained as she prepared to serve, she preferred over the fried variety because she worried about too much grease in her diet. She was taught to batter and fry everything, from tomatoes to pickles, and she had come to realize that this was not altogether healthy. There were butter beans, likewise unbattered and unfried, but rather cooked with ham hocks and bacon. There was a platter of small red tomatoes covered with pepper and olive oil. She was one of the very few cooks in town who used olive oil, she said as she continued her narrative. I was hanging on every word as my large plate was being tended to.

A son in Milwaukee shipped her good olive oil because such was unheard of in Clanton.

She apologized because the tomatoes were store bought; hers were still on the vine and wouldn't be ready until summertime. The corn, okra, and butter beans had been canned from her garden last August. In fact, the only real 'fresh' vegetables were the collard greens, or 'spring greens' as she called them.

A large black skillet was hidden in the center of the table, and when she pulled the napkin off it there were at least four pounds of hot corn bread. She removed a huge wedge, placed it in the center of my plate, and said, 'There. That will get you started.' I had never had so much food placed in front of me. The feast began.

I tried to eat slowly, but it was impossible. I had arrived with an empty stomach, and somewhere in the midst of the competing aromas and the beauty of the table and the rather long-winded blessing and the careful description of each dish, I had become thoroughly famished. I packed it in, and she seemed content to do the talking.

Her garden had produced most of the meal. She and Esau grew four types of tomatoes, butter beans, string beans, black-eyed peas, crowder peas, cucumbers, eggplant, squash, collards, mustard greens, turnips, vidalia onions, yellow onions, green onions, cabbage, okra, new red potatoes, russet potatoes, carrots, beets, corn, green peppers, cantaloupes, two varieties of watermelon, and a few other things she couldn't recall at the moment. The pork chops were provided by her brother, who still lived on the old family place out in the country. He killed two hogs for them every winter and they stuffed their freezer. In return, they kept him in fresh vegetables.

'We don't use chemicals,' she said, watching me gorge myself. 'Everything is natural.'

It certainly tasted like it.

'But it's all put-up, you know, from the winter. It'll taste better in the summertime when we pick and eat it just a few hours later. Will you come back then, Mr. Traynor?'

I grunted and nodded and somehow managed to convey the message that I would return any time she wanted.

'Would you like to see my garden?' she asked.

I nodded again, both jaws filled to capacity.

'Good. It's out back. I'll pick you some lettuce and greens. They're coming in nicely.'

'Wonderful,' I managed to utter.

'I figure a single man like you needs all the help he can get.'

'How'd you know I was single?' I took a gulp of tea. It could have served as dessert – there was so much sugar in it.

'Folks are talking about you. Word gets around. There are not too many secrets in Clanton, on both sides of the tracks.'

'What else have you heard?'

'Let's see. You rent from the Hocutts. You come from up North.'

'Memphis.'

'That far?'

'It's an hour away.'

'Just joking. One of my daughters went to college there.'

I had many questions about her children, but I was not ready to take notes. Both hands were busy eating. At some point I called her Miss Calia, instead of Miss Ruffin.

'It's Callie,' she said. 'Miss Callie will do just fine.' One of the first habits I picked up in Clanton was referring to the ladies, regardless of age, by sticking the word 'Miss' in front of their names. Miss Brown, Miss Webster, for new acquaintances who had a few years on them. Miss Martha, Miss Sara, for the younger ones. It was a sign of chivalry and good breeding, and since I had neither it was important to seize as many local customs as possible.

'Where did Calia come from?' I asked.

'It's Italian,' she said, as if that would explain everything. She ate some butter beans. I carved up a pork chop. Then I said, 'Italian?'

'Yes, that was my first language. It's a long story, one of many. Did they really try to burn down the paper?'

'Yes, they did,' I said, wondering if I'd heard this black lady in rural Mississippi just say that her first language was Italian.

'And they assaulted Mr. Meek?'

'They did.'

'Who is they?'

'We don't know yet. Sheriff Coley is investigating.' I was anxious to get her impression of our Sheriff. While I waited, I went after another wedge of corn bread. Soon there was butter dripping from my chin.

'He's been the Sheriff for a long time, hasn't he?' she said.

I'm sure she knew the exact year in which Mackey Don Coley had first bought himself into office. 'What do you think of him?' I asked.

She drank some tea and contemplated. Miss Callic did not rush her answers, especially when talking about others. 'On this side of the tracks, a good Sheriff is one who keeps the gamblers and the bootleggers and the whoremongers away from the rest of us. In that regard, Mr. Coley has done a proper job.'

'Can I ask you something?'

'Certainly. You're a reporter.'

'Your speech is unusually articulate and precise. How much education did you receive?' It was a sensitive question in a society where, for many decades, education had not been stressed. It was 1970, and Mississippi still had no public kindergartens and no mandatory school attendance laws.

She laughed, giving me the full benefit of those teeth. 'I finished the ninth grade, Mr. Traynor.'

'The ninth grade?'

'Yes, but my situation was unusual. I had a wonderful tutor. It's another long story.'

I began to realize that these wonderful stories Miss Callie was promising would take months, maybe years to develop. Perhaps they would evolve on the porch, over a weekly banquet.

'Let's save it for later,' she said. 'How is Mr. Caudle?'

'Not well. He will not come out of his house.'

'A fine man. He will always be close to the heart of the black community. He had such courage.'

I thought Spot's 'courage' had more to do with widening the range of his obituaries than with a commitment to the fair treatment of all. But I had learned how important dying was to black folks – the ritual of the wake, often lasting a week; the marathon memorial services, with open caskets and much wailing; the mile-long funeral processions; and, lastly, the final grave-side farewells fraught with emotion. When Spot had so radically opened his obituary page to blacks he had become a hero in Lowtown.

'A fine man,' I said, reaching for my third pork chop. I was beginning to ache a bit, but there was so much food left on the table!

'You're doing him proud with your obituaries,' she said with a warm smile.

'Thank you. I'm still learning.'

'You have courage too, Mr. Traynor.'

'Could you call me Willie? I'm only twenty-three.'

'I prefer Mr. Traynor.' And that issue was settled. It would take four years before she could break down and use my first name. 'You have no fear of the Padgitt family,' she announced.

That was news to me. 'It's just part of my job,' I said.

'Do you expect the intimidation to continue?'

'Probably so. They are accustomed to getting whatever they want. They are violent, ruthless people, but a free press must endure.' Who was I kidding? One more bomb or assault and I'd be back in Memphis before sunrise.

She stopped eating and her eyes turned toward the street, where she looked at nothing in particular. She was deep in thought. I, of course, kept stuffing my face.

Finally, she said, 'Those poor little children. Seeing their mother like that.'

That image finally caused my fork to stop. I wiped my mouth, took a long breath, and let the food settle for a moment. The horror of the crime was left to everyone's imagination, and for days Clanton had whispered about little else. As always happens, the whispers and rumors got amplified, different versions were spun off and repeated, and enlarged yet again. I was curious as to how the stories were playing in Lowtown.

'You told me on the phone you've been reading the *Times* for fifty years,' I said, almost belching.

'Indeed I have.'

'Can you remember a more brutal crime?'

She paused for a second as she reviewed five decades, then slowly shook her head. 'No, I cannot.'

'Have you ever met a Padgitt?'

'No. They stay on the island, and always have. Even their Negroes stay out there, making whiskey, doing their voodoo, all sorts of foolishness.'

'Voodoo?'

'Yes, it's common knowledge on this side of the tracks. Nobody here messes with the Padgitt Negroes, never have.'

'Do people on this side of the tracks believe Danny Padgitt raped and killed her?'

'The ones who read your newspaper certainly do.'

That stung more than she would ever know. 'We just report the facts,' I said smugly. 'The boy was arrested. He's been charged. He's in jail awaiting trial.'

'Isn't there a presumption of innocence?'

Another squirm on my side of the table. 'Of course.'

'Do you think it was fair to use a photograph of him handcuffed, with blood on his shirt?' I was struck by her sense of fairness. Why would she, or any other black in Ford County, care if Danny Padgitt was treated fairly? Few people had ever worried about black defendants getting decent treatment by the police or the press.

'He had blood on his shirt when he arrived at the jail. We didn't put it there.' Neither one of us was enjoying this little debate. I took a sip of tea and found it difficult to swallow. I was stuffed all the way down.

She looked at me with one of those smiles and had the nerve to say, 'What about some dessert? I baked a banana pudding.'

I could not say no. Nor could I hold another bite. A compromise was called for. 'Let's wait a while, give things a chance to settle.'

'Then have some more tea,' she said, already refilling my glass. Breathing was difficult, so I reclined as much as possible in my chair and decided to act like a journalist. Miss Callie, who'd eaten far less than I, was finishing a serving of okra.

According to Baggy, Sam Ruffin had been the first black student to enroll in the white schools in Clanton. It happened in 1964 when Sam was a seventh grader, age twelve, and the experience had been difficult for everyone. Especially Sam. Baggy warned me that Miss Callie might not talk about her youngest child. There was a warrant for his arrest and he had fled the area.

She was reluctant at first. In 1963, the courts ruled that a white school district could not deny admission to a black student. Forced integration was still years in the future. Sam was her youngest, and when she and Esau made the decision to take him to the white school they hoped they would be joined by other black families. They were not, and for two years Sam was the only black student at Clanton Junior

97

High School. He was tormented and beaten, but he quickly learned to handle his fists and with time was left alone. He begged his parents to take him back to the Negro school, but they held their ground, even after he moved to the senior high. Relief was coming, they kept telling themselves. The desegregation fight was raging across the South and blacks were continually promised that the mandate of *Brown versus Board of Education* would be carried out.

'It is hard to believe that it is now 1970, and the schools here are still segregated,' she said. Federal lawsuits and appellate decisions were pummeling white resistance throughout the South, but, typically, Mississippi was fighting to the bitter end. Most white folks I knew in Clanton were convinced that their schools would never be integrated. I, a Northerner from Memphis, could see the obvious.

'Do you regret sending Sam to the white school?'

'Yes and no. Someone had to be courageous. It was painful knowing he was very unhappy, but we had taken a stand. We were not going to retreat.'

'How is he today?'

'Sam is another story, Mr. Traynor, one I might talk about later, or not. Would you like to see my garden?'

It was more of a command than an invitation. I followed her through the house, down a narrow hallway lined with dozens of framed photographs of children and grandchildren. The inside was as meticulous as the outside. The kitchen opened to the back porch and from there the Garden of Eden stretched to the rear fence. Not a single square foot was wasted.

It was a postcard of beautiful colors, neat rows of plants and vines, narrow dirt footpaths so that Callie and Esau could tend to their spectacular bounty.

'What do you do with all this food?' I asked in amazement.

'We eat some, sell a little, give most away. No one goes hungry around here.' At that moment my stomach was aching like never before. Hunger was a notion I couldn't comprehend. I followed her into the garden, moving slowly along the footpaths as she pointed out the herb patch and melons and all the other delicious fruits and vegetables she and Esau tended to with great care. She commented on every plant, including an occasional weed, which she snatched almost with anger and flung back into some vines. It was impossible for her to walk through the garden and ignore the details. She looked for insects, killed a nasty green worm on a tomato vine, searched for weeds, made mental notes about future chores for Esau. The leisurely stroll was doing wonders for my digestive system.

So this is where food comes from, I thought to my ignorant self. What did I expect? I was a city kid. I'd never been in a vegetable garden before.

I had many questions, all banal, so I held my tongue.

She examined a stalk of corn and was not pleased with whatever she saw. She tore off a snap bean, broke it in two, analyzed it like a scientist, and offered the guarded opinion that they needed much more sun. She saw a patch of weeds and informed me Esau would be sent to pull them as soon as he got home. I did not envy Esau.

After three hours, I left the Ruffin home stuffed yet again with banana pudding. I also left with a sack of 'spring greens,' which I had no idea what to do with, and precious few notes on which to write a story. I also had an invitation to return the following Thursday for another lunch. Lastly, I had Miss Callie's handwritten list of all the errors she'd found in that week's edition of the *Times*. Almost all were typographical errors and misspelled words – twelve in all. Under Spot, the average had been about twenty. Now it was down to around ten. It was a lifelong habit of hers. 'Some folks like crossword puzzles,' she said. 'I like to look for mistakes.'

It was hard not to take this personally. She certainly didn't intend to criticize anyone. I vowed to proofread the copy with much more enthusiasm.

I also left with the feeling that I had entered a new and rewarding friendship.

Chapter 9

We ran another large photo on the front page. It was Wiley's shot of the bomb before the police dismantled it. The headline above it screamed: BOMB PLANTED IN TIMES OFFICE.

My story began with Piston and his unlikely discovery. It included every detail I could substantiate, and a few I could not. No comment from the chief of police, a few meaningless sentences from Sheriff Coley. It ended with a summary of the findings by the state crime lab, and a prediction that, if detonated, the bomb would have caused 'massive' damage to the buildings on the south side of the square.

Wiley would not allow me to use a photo of his badly bruised face, though I pleaded desperately with him to do so. On the bottom half of the front page I ran the headline TIMES PHOTOGRAPHER ASSAULTED AT HOME. Again, my story spared no detail, though Wiley insisted he be allowed to edit it.

In both stories, and with no effort at being subtle, I linked the crimes and implied rather strongly that little was being done by the authorities, especially Sheriff Coley, to prevent further intimidation. I never named the Padgitts. I didn't have to. Everyone in the county knew they were bullying me and my newspaper.

Spot had been too lazy for editorials. He'd written only one during my stint as an employee. A congressman from Oregon had filed some nutty bill that would somehow affect the cutting of redwood trees – more cutting or maybe less, it really wasn't clear. This had upset Spot. For two weeks he labored over an editorial and finally ran a two-thousand-word tirade. It was obvious to anyone with a high school education that he wrote with a pen in one hand and a dictionary in the other. The first paragraph was filled with more six-syllable words than anyone had ever seen and was virtually unreadable. Spot was shocked when there was no response from the community. He expected a flood of sympathetic letters. Few of his readers could have survived the flood from Webster's.

Finally, three weeks later, a hand-scrawled note was slid under the front door of the office. It read:

Dear Editor: I'm sorry you're so worked up over the redwoods, which we don't have in Mississippi. If Congress starts messing with pulpwood, would you please let us know?

It was unsigned, but Spot ran it anyway. He was relieved that someone out there was paying attention. Baggy told me later that the note was written by one of his drinking buddies in the courthouse.

My editorial began, 'A free and uninhibited press is crucial to sound democratic government.' Without being windy or preachy, I went on for four paragraphs extolling the importance of an energetic and inquisitive newspaper, not only for the country but for every small community as well. I vowed that the *Times* would not be frightened away from reporting local crimes, whether they were rapes and murders or corrupt acts by public officials.

It was bold, gutsy, and downright brilliant. The townsfolk were on my side. It was, after all, the *Times* versus the Padgitts and their Sheriff. We were taking a mighty stand against bad people, and though they were dangerous they were evidently not intimidating me. I kept telling myself to act brave, and I really had no choice. What was my paper supposed to do – ignore the Kassellaw murder? Take it easy on Danny Padgitt?

My staff was elated with the editorial. Margaret said it made her proud to work for the *Times*. Wiley, still nursing his wounds, was now carrying a gun and looking for a fight. 'Give 'em hell, rookie,' he said.

Only Baggy was skeptical. 'You're gonna get yourself hurt,' he said.

And Miss Callie once again described me as courageous. Lunch the following Thursday lasted for only two hours and included Esau. I actually began taking notes about her family. More important, she'd found only three errors in that week's edition.

I was alone in my office early Friday afternoon when someone made a noisy entrance downstairs, then came clamoring up. He shoved my door open without so much as a 'Hello' and stuck both hands in his pants pockets. He looked vaguely familiar; we'd met somewhere around the square.

'You got one of these, boy?' he growled, yanking his right hand out and momentarily freezing my heart and lungs. He slid a shiny pistol across my desk as if it were a set of keys. It spun wildly for a few seconds before resting directly before me, the barrel mercifully pointing toward the windows.

He lunged across the desk, thrust out a massive hand, and said, 'Harry Rex Vonner, a pleasure.' I was too stunned to speak or move, but eventually honored him with an embarrassingly weak handshake. I was still watching the gun.

'It's a Smith and Wesson thirty-eight, six-shooter, damned fine firearm. You carry one?'

I shook my head no. The name alone sent chills to my feet.

Harry Rex kept a nasty black cigar tucked into

the left side of his mouth. It gave the impression of having spent most of the day there, slowly disintegrating like a plug of chewing tobacco. No smoke because it wasn't lit. He dropped his massive body into a leather chair as if he might stay for a couple of hours.

'You a crazy sumbitch, you know that?' He didn't speak as much as he growled. Then I caught the name. He was a local lawyer, once described by Baggy as the meanest divorce attorney in the county. He had a large fleshy face with short hair that shot in all directions like windblown straw. His ancient khaki suit was wrinkled and stained and said to the world that Harry Rex didn't give a damn about anything.

'What am I supposed to do with this?' I asked, pointing at the gun.

'First you load it, I'll give you some bullets, then you stick it in your pocket and carry it with you everywhere you go, and when one of them Padgitt thugs jumps out from behind the bushes you blast him right between the eyes.' To help convey his message, he moved his index finger through the air like a bullet and poked himself between the eyes.

'It's not loaded?'

'Hell no. Don't you know anything about guns?'

'Afraid not.'

'Well, you'd better learn, boy, at the rate you're goin'.'

'That bad, huh?'

'I did a divorce one time, ten years ago I guess, for a man whose young wife liked to sneak over to the brothel and make a few bucks. The guy worked offshore, stayed gone all the time, had no idea what she was up to. He finally found out. The Padgitts owned the whorehouse and one of them had taken a shine to the young lady.' Somehow the cigar stayed in place, bobbing up and down with the narrative. 'My client was heartbroken and he wanted blood. He got it. They caught him out one night and beat him senseless.'

'They?'

'The Padgitts I'm sure, or some of their operatives.'

'Operatives?'

'Yeah, they got all sorts of thugs who work for them. Leg breakers, bomb throwers, car stealers, hit men.'

He allowed the 'hit men' to hang in the air while he watched me flinch. He gave the impression of one who could tell stories forever without being unduly burdened by veracity. Harry Rex had a nasty grin and a twinkle in his eyes, and I strongly suspected some embellishment was under way.

'And of course they were never caught,' I said.

'Padgitts never get caught.'

'What happened to your client?'

'He spent a few months in the hospital. The brain damage was pretty severe. In and out of institutions, really sad. Broke his family. He drifted to the Gulf Coast where they elected him to the state senate.'

I smiled and nodded at what I hoped was a lie, but I didn't pursue it. Without touching the cigar with his hands, he flicked his tongue somehow and cocked his head, and it slid to the right side of his mouth.

'You ever eat goat?' he asked.

'Say what?'

'Goat?'

'No. I didn't know it was edible.'

'We're roastin' one this afternoon. The first Friday of each month I throw a goat party at my cabin in the woods. Some music, cold beer, fun and games, about fifty folks, all carefully selected by me, the cream of society. No doctors, no bankers, no country club assholes. A classy bunch. Why don't you stop by? I got a firin' range out behind the pond. I'll take the pistol and we'll figure out how to use the damned thing.'

Harry Rex's ten-minute drive into the country took almost half an hour, and that was on the paved county road. When I crossed the 'third creek past Heck's old Union 76 station,' I left the asphalt and turned onto gravel. For a while it was a nice gravel road with mailboxes indicating some hope of civilization, but after three miles the mail route stopped and so did the gravel. When I saw a 'rusted-out Massey Ferguson tractor with no tires,' I turned left onto a dirt

107

road. His crude map referred to it as a pig trail, though I had never seen one of those. After the pig trail disappeared into a dense forest, I gave serious thought to turning back. My Spitfire wasn't designed for the terrain. By the time I saw the roof of his cabin, I'd been driving for forty-five minutes.

There was a barbed-wire fence with an open metal gate, and I stopped there because the young man with the shotgun wanted me to. He kept it on his shoulder as he looked scornfully at my car. 'What kind is it?' he grunted.

'Triumph Spitfire. It's British.' I was smiling, trying not to offend him. Why did a goat party need armed security? He had the rustic look of someone who'd never seen a car made in another country.

'What's your name?' he asked.

'Willie Traynor.'

I think the 'Willie' made him feel better, so he nodded at the gate. 'Nice car,' he said as I drove through.

The pickup trucks outnumbered the cars. Parking was haphazard in a field in front of the cabin. Merle Haggard was wailing from two speakers placed in the windows. One group of guests huddled over a pit where smoke was rising and the goat was roasting. Another group was tossing horseshoes beside the cabin. Three well-dressed ladies were on the porch, sipping something that was certainly not beer. Harry Rex appeared and greeted me warmly.

'Who's the boy with the shotgun?' I asked.

'Oh him. That's Duffy, my first wife's nephew.'

'Why is he out there?' If the goat party included something illegal, I at least wanted some notice.

'Don't worry. Duffy ain't all there, and the gun ain't loaded. He's been guardin' nothin' for years.'

I smiled as if this made perfect sense. He guided me to the pit where I saw my first goat, dead or alive. With the exception of head and hide, it appeared to be intact. I was introduced to the many chefs. With each name I got an occupation – a lawyer, a bail bondsman, a car dealer, a farmer. As I watched the goat spin slowly on a spit, I soon learned that there were many competing theories on how to properly barbecue one. Harry Rex handed me a beer and we moved on to the cabin, speaking to anyone we bumped into. A secretary, a 'crooked real estate agent,' the current wife of Harry Rex. Each seemed pleased to meet the new owner of the *Times*.

The cabin sat on the edge of a muddy pond, the kind snakes find attractive. A deck protruded over the water, and there we worked the crowd. Harry Rex took great delight in introducing me to his friends. 'He's a good boy, not your typical Ivy League asshole,' he said more than once. I didn't like to be referred to as a 'boy,' but then I was getting used to it.

I settled into a small group that included two ladies who looked as though they'd spent years in the local honky-tonks. Heavy eye makeup, teased hair, tight clothing, and they immediately took an interest in me. The conversation began with the bomb and the assault on Wiley Meek and the prevailing cloud of fear the Padgitts had spread over the county. I acted as if it was just another routine episode in my long and colorful career in journalism. They drilled me with questions and I did more talking than I wanted to.

Harry Rex rejoined us and handed me a suspicious-looking jar of clear liquid. 'Sip it slowly,' he said, much like a father.

'What is it?' I asked. I noticed that others were watching.

'Peach brandy.'

'Why is it in a fruit jar?' I asked.

'That's the way they make it,' he said.

'It's moonshine,' one of the painted ladies said. The voice of experience.

Not often would these rural folks see an 'Ivy Leaguer' take his first drink of moonshine, so the crowd drew closer. I was certain I had consumed more alcohol in the prior five years at Syracuse than anyone else present, so I threw caution to the wind. I lifted the jar, said, 'Cheers,' and took a very small sip. I smacked my lips, said, 'Not bad.' And tried to smile like a freshman at a fraternity party.

The burning began at the lips, the point of initial contact, and spread rapidly across the tongue and gums and by the time it hit the back of my throat I thought I was on fire. Everyone was watching. Harry Rex took a sip from his jar.

'Where does it come from?' I asked, as nonchalantly as possible, flames escaping through my teeth.

'Not far from here,' someone said.

Scorched and numb, I took another sip, quite anxious for the crowd to ignore me for a while. Oddly enough, the third sip revealed a hint of peach flavoring, as if the taste buds had to be shocked before they could work. When it was apparent that I was not going to breathe fire, vomit, or scream, the conversation resumed. Harry Rex, ever anxious to speed along my education, thrust forward a plate of fried something. 'Have one of these,' he said.

'What is it?' I asked, suspicious.

Both of my painted ladies curled up their noses and turned away, as if the smell might make them ill. 'Chitlins,' one of them said.

'What's that?'

Harry Rex popped one in his mouth to prove they weren't poison, then shoved the plate closer to me. 'Go ahead,' he said, chomping away at this delicacy.

Folks were watching again, so I picked out the smallest piece and put it in my mouth. The texture was rubbery, the taste was acrid and foul. The smell had a barnyard essence. I chewed as hard as possible, choked it down, then followed with a gulp of moonshine. And for a few seconds I thought I might faint.

'Hog guts, boy,' Harry Rex said, slapping me on the back. He threw another one in his large mouth and offered me the plate. 'Where's the goat?' I managed to ask. Anything would be an improvement.

Whatever happened to beer and pizza? Why would these people eat and drink such disagreeable things?

Harry Rex walked away, the putrid smell of the chitlins following him like smoke. I placed the fruit jar on the railing, hoping it would tumble and disappear. I watched others pass around their moonshine, one jar usually good for an entire group. There was absolutely no concern over germs and such. No bacteria could've survived within three feet of the vile brew.

I excused myself from the deck, said I needed to find a restroom. Harry Rex emerged from the back door of the cabin holding two pistols and a box of ammo. 'We'd better take a few shots before it gets dark,' he said. 'Follow me.'

We stopped at the goat spit where a cowboy named Rafe joined us. 'Rafe's my runner,' Harry Rex said as the three of us headed for the woods.

'What's a runner?' I asked.

'Runs cases.'

'I'm the ambulance chaser,' Rafe said helpfully. 'Although usually the ambulance is behind me.'

I had so much to learn, though I was making

some real progress. Chitlins and moonshine in one day were no small feat. We walked a hundred yards or so down an old field road, through some woods, then came to a clearing. Between two magnificent oaks Harry Rex had constructed a semicircle wall of hay bales twenty feet high. In the center was a white bedsheet, and in the middle of it was the crude outline of a man. An attacker. The enemy. The target.

Not surprisingly, Rafe whipped out his own handgun. Harry Rex was handling mine. 'Here's the deal,' he said, beginning the lesson. 'This is a double action revolver with six cartridges. Press here and the cylinder pops out.' Rafe reached over and deftly loaded six bullets, something he had obviously done many, many times. 'Snap it back like this, and you're ready to fire.'

We were about fifty feet from the target. I could still hear the music from the cabin. What would the other guests think when they heard gunfire? Nothing. It happened all the time.

Rafe took my handgun and faced the target. 'For starters, spread your legs to shoulders' width, bend the knees slightly, use both hands like this, and squeeze the trigger with your right index finger.' He demonstrated as he spoke, and, of course, everything looked easy. I was standing less than five feet away when the gun fired, and the sharp crack jolted my nerves. Why did it have to be so loud?

I had never heard live gunfire.

The second shot hit the target square in the

chest, and the next four landed around the mid-section. He turned to me, opened the cylinder, spun out the empty cartridges, and said, 'Now you do it.'

My hands were shaking as I took the gun. It was warm and the smell of gunpowder hung heavy around us. I managed to shove in the six cartridges and snap the cylinder shut without hurting anyone. I faced the target, lifted the gun with both hands, crouched like someone in a bad movie, closed my eyes and pulled the trigger. It felt and sounded like a small bomb of some sort.

'You gotta keep your eyes open, dammit,' Harry Rex growled.

'What did I hit?'

'That hill beyond the oak trees.'

'Try it again,' Rafe said.

I tried to look down the gunsight but it was shaking too badly to be of any use. I squeezed the trigger again, this time with my eyes open, waiting to see where my bullet hit. I noticed no entry wound anywhere near the target.

'He missed the sheet,' Rafe mumbled behind me.

'Fire again,' Harry Rex said.

I did, and again couldn't see where the bullet landed. Rafe gently took my left arm and eased me forward another ten feet. 'You're doin' fine,' he said. 'We got plenty of ammo.'

I missed the hay on the fourth shot, and Harry Rex said, 'I guess the Padgitts are safe after all.'

'It's the moonshine,' I said.

'It just takes practice,' Rafe said, moving me forward yet again. My hands were sweating, my heart was galloping away, my ears were ringing.

On number five I hit the sheet, barely, in the top right-hand corner, at least six feet from the target. On number six I missed everything again and heard the bullet hit a branch up in one of the oaks.

'Nice shot,' Harry Rex said. 'You almost hit a squirrel.'

'Shut up,' I said.

'Relax,' Rafe said. 'You're too tense.' He helped me reload, and this time he squeezed my hands around the gun. 'Breathe deeply,' he said over my shoulder. 'Exhale right before you pull the trigger.' He steadied the gun as I looked down the sight, and when it fired the target took a hit in the groin.

'Now we're in business,' Harry Rex said.

Rafe released me, and, like a gunslinger at high noon, I unloaded the next five shots. All hit the sheet, one would've taken off the target's ear. Rafe approved and we loaded up again.

Harry Rex had a 9-millimeter Glock automatic from his vast collection, and as the sun slowly disappeared we took turns blasting away. He was good and had no trouble drilling ten straight shots into the upper torso from fifty feet. After four rounds, I began to relax and enjoy the sport of it. Rafe was an excellent teacher, and as I progressed he passed on tips here and there. 'It just takes practice,' he kept saying.

When we finished, Harry Rex said, 'The gun's a gift. You can come out here anytime for target practice.'

'Thanks,' I said. I stuck the gun in my pocket like a real redneck. I was delighted that the ritual was over, that I had accomplished something that every other male in the county had experienced by his twelfth birthday. I didn't feel any safer. Any Padgitt who jumped from the bushes would have the advantage of surprise, and the benefit of years of target practice. I could almost envision myself grappling with my own gun in the darkness and finally unloading a bullet that would more likely hit me than any assailant.

As we were walking back through the woods, Harry Rex said from behind me, 'That bleached blonde you met, Carleen.'

'Yeah,' I said, suddenly nervous.

'She likes you.'

Carleen had lived at least forty very hard years. I could think of nothing to say.

'She's always good for a hop in the sack.'

I doubted if Carleen had missed too many sacks in Ford County. 'No thanks,' I said. 'I got a girl in Memphis.'

'So?'

'Good call,' Rafe said under his breath.

'A girl here, a girl there. What's the big difference?'

'I gotta deal for you, Harry Rex,' I said. 'If I need your help picking up women, I'll let you know.'

'Just a roll in the hay,' he mumbled.

I did not have a girl in Memphis, but I knew several. I'd rather make the drive than stoop to the likes of Carleen.

The goat had a distinctive taste; not good, but, after the chitlins, not nearly as bad as I had feared. It was tough and smothered in sticky barbeque sauce, which, I suspected, was applied in generous layers to counter the taste of the meat. I toyed with a slice of it and washed it down with beer. We were on the deck again with Loretta Lynn in the background. The moonshine had made the rounds for a while and some of the guests were dancing above the pond. Carleen had disappeared earlier with someone else, so I felt safe. Harry Rex sat nearby, telling everyone how effective I'd been shooting squirrels and rabbits. His talent for storytelling was remarkable.

I was an oddity but every effort was made to include me. Driving the dark roads home, I asked myself the same question I posed every day. What was I doing in Ford County, Mississippi?

Chapter 10

The gun was too big for my pocket. For a few hours I tried walking around with it, but I was terrified the thing would discharge down there very near my privates. So I decided to carry it in a ragged leather briefcase my father had given me. For three days the briefcase went everywhere, even to lunch, then I grew weary of that too. After a week I left the pistol under the seat of my car, and after three weeks I had pretty much forgotten about it. I did not go to the cabin for more target practice, though I did attend a few other goat parties in which I avoided chitlins, moonshine, and an increasingly aggressive Carleen.

The county was quiet, a lull before the frenzy of the trial. The *Times* said nothing about the case because nothing was happening. The Padgitts were still refusing to pledge their land for Danny's bail, so he remained a guest in Sheriff Coley's special cell, watching television, playing cards or checkers, getting plenty of rest, and eating better food than the common inmates.

The first week in May, Judge Loopus was back in town, and my thoughts returned to my trusty Smith & Wesson.

Lucien Wilbanks had filed a motion requesting a change of venue, and the Judge set it for a hearing at 9 A.M. on a Monday morning. Half the county was there, it seemed. Certainly most of the regulars from around the square. Baggy and I got to the courtroom early and secured good seats.

The defendant's presence was not required, but evidently Sheriff Coley wanted to show him off. They brought him in, handcuffed and wearing new orange coveralls. Everyone looked at me. The power of the press had brought about change.

'It's a setup,' Baggy whispered.

'What?'

'They're baitin' us into runnin' a picture of Danny in his cute little jail outfit. Then Wilbanks can run back to the Judge and claim the jury pool has been poisoned yet again. Don't fall for it.'

My naïveté shocked me again. Wiley had been positioned outside the jail in another effort to ambush Padgitt when they loaded him up for court. I could see a large front page photo of him in his orange coveralls.

Lucien Wilbanks entered the courtroom from behind the bench. As usual, he seemed angry and perturbed, as if he'd just lost an argument with the Judge. He walked to the defense table, tossed down his legal pad, and scanned the crowd. His eyes locked onto me. They narrowed and his jaws clenched, and I thought he might hop over the bar and attack. His client turned around and began looking too. Someone pointed, and Mr. Danny Padgitt himself commenced glaring at me as if I might be his next victim. I was having trouble breathing, but I tried to keep calm. Baggy inched away.

In the front row behind the defense crowd were several Padgitts, all older than Danny. They, too, joined the staring, and I had never felt so vulnerable. These were violent men who knew nothing but crime, intimidation, leg breaking, killing, and there I was in the same room with them while they dreamed of ways to cut my throat.

A bailiff called us to order and everybody stood to acknowledge the entrance of His Honor. 'Please be seated,' he said.

Loopus scanned the papers while we waited, then he adjusted his reading glasses and said, 'This is a motion to change venue, filed by the defense. Mr. Wilbanks, how many witnesses do you have?'

'Half a dozen, give or take. We'll see how things go.'

'And the State?'

A short round man with no hair and a black suit bounced to his feet and said, 'About the same.' His name was Ernie Gaddis, the longtime, part-time District Attorney from up in Tyler County.

'I don't want to be here all day,' Loopus mumbled, as if he had an afternoon golf game. 'Call your first witness, Mr. Wilbanks.'

'Mr. Walter Pickard.'

The name was unknown to me, which was expected, but Baggy had never heard of him either. During the preliminary questions it was established that he had lived in Karaway for over twenty years, went to church every Sunday and the Rotary Club every Thursday. For a living he owned a small furniture factory.

'Must buy lumber from the Padgitts,' Baggy whispered.

His wife was a schoolteacher. He had coached Little League baseball and worked with the Boy Scouts. Lucien pressed on and did a masterful job of laying the groundwork that Mr. Pickard knew his community well.

Karaway was a smaller town eighteen miles west of Clanton. Spot had always neglected the place and we sold very few papers there. And even fewer ads. In my youthful eagerness, I was already contemplating the expansion of my empire. A small weekly in Karaway would sell a thousand copies, I thought.

'When did you first hear that Miss Kassellaw had been murdered?' Wilbanks asked.

'Couple of days after it happened,' Mr. Pickard said. 'News is sometimes slow getting to Karaway.'

'Who told you?'

'One of my employees came in with the story. She has a brother who lives around Beech Hill, where it happened.'

'Did you hear that someone had been arrested for the murder?' Lucien asked. He prowled around the courtroom like a bored cat. Just going through the motions, yet missing nothing.

'Yes, the rumor was that one of the young Padgitts had been arrested.'

'Did you later confirm this?'

'Yes.'

'How?'

'I saw the story in *The Ford County Times*. There was a large photo of Danny Padgitt on the front page, right next to a large photo of Rhoda Kassellaw.'

'Did you read the reports in the *Times?*'

'I did.'

'And did you form an opinion about Mr. Padgitt's guilt or innocence?'

'He looked guilty to me. In the photo he had blood all over his shirt. His face was placed right next to that of the victim's, you know, side by side. The headline was huge and said something like, DANNY PADGITT ARRESTED FOR MURDER.'

'So you assumed he was guilty?'

'It was impossible not to.'

'What's been the reaction to the murder in Karaway?'

'Shock and outrage. This is a peaceful county. Serious crimes are rare.'

'In your opinion, do folks over there generally believe Danny Padgitt raped and murdered Rhoda Kassellaw?'

'Yes, especially after the way the newspaper has treated the story.'

I could feel stares from all directions, but I kept telling myself that we had done nothing wrong. People suspected Danny Padgitt because the rotten sonofabitch had committed the crimes.

'In your opinion, can Mr. Padgitt receive a fair trial in Ford County?'

'No.'

'Upon what do you base this opinion?'

'He's already been tried and convicted by the newspaper.'

'Do you think your opinion is shared by most of your friends and neighbors over in Karaway?'

'I do.'

'Thank you.'

Mr. Ernie Gaddis was on his feet, holding a legal pad as if it were a weapon. 'Say you're in the furniture business, Mr. Pickard?'

'Yes, that's correct.'

'You buy lumber locally?'

'We do.'

'From whom?'

Pickard readjusted his weight and pondered the question. 'Gates Brothers, Henderson, Tiffee, Voyles and Sons, maybe one or two others.'

Baggy whispered, 'Padgitt owns Voyles.'

'You buy any lumber from the Padgitts?' Gaddis asked.

'No sir.'

'Now or at any time in the past?'

'No sir.'

'Any of these lumberyards owned by the Padgitts?'

'Not to my knowledge.'

The truth was that no one really knew what the Padgitts owned. For decades they'd had their tentacles in so many businesses, legitimate or otherwise. Mr. Pickard may not have been well known in Clanton, but, at that moment, he was suspected of having some relationship with the Padgitts. Why would he voluntarily testify on Danny's behalf?

Gaddis shifted gears. 'Now, you said that the bloody photograph had much to do with your assumption that the boy is guilty, that right?'

'It made him look very suspicious.'

'Did you read the entire story?'

'I believe so.'

'Did you read where it says that Mr. Danny Padgitt was involved in an auto accident, that he was injured, and that he was also charged with drunk driving?'

'I believe I read that, yes.'

'Would you like for me to show it to you?'

'No, I remember it.'

'Good, then why were you so quick to assume the blood came from the victim and not from Mr. Padgitt himself?'

Pickard shifted again and looked frustrated.

'I simply said that the photos and the stories, when taken together, make him look guilty.'

'You ever serve on a jury, Mr. Pickard?'

'No sir.'

'Do you understand what's meant by the presumption of innocence?'

'Yes.'

'Do you understand that the State of Mississippi must prove Mr. Padgitt guilty beyond a reasonable doubt?'

'Yes.'

'Do you believe everyone accused of a crime is entitled to a fair trial?'

'Yes, of course.'

'Good. Let's say you got a summons for jury service in this case. You've read the newspaper reports, listened to all the gossip, all the rumors, all that mess, and you arrive in this very courtroom for the trial. You've already testified that you believe Mr. Padgitt to be guilty. Let's say you're selected for the jury. Let's say that Mr. Wilbanks, a very skilled and experienced lawyer, attacks the State's case and raises serious doubts about our proof. Let's say there's doubt in your mind, Mr. Pickard. Could you at that point vote not guilty?'

He nodded as he followed along, then said, 'Yes, under those circumstances.'

'So, regardless of how you now feel about guilt or innocence, you would be willing to listen to the evidence and weigh it fairly before you decide the case?'

The answer was so obvious that Mr. Pickard had no choice but to say, 'Yes.'

'Of course,' Gaddis agreed. 'And what about your wife? You mentioned her. She's a school-teacher, right? She would be as openminded as you, wouldn't she?'

'I think so. Yes.'

'And what about those Rotarians over there in Karaway. Are they as fair as you?'

'I suppose so.'

'And your employees, Mr. Pickard. Surely you hire honest, fair-minded people. They'd be able to ignore what they've read and heard and try this boy justly, wouldn't they?'

'I suppose.'

'No further questions, Your Honor.'

Mr. Pickard hustled off the witness stand and hurried from the courtroom. Lucien Wilbanks stood and said, rather loudly, 'Your Honor, the defense calls Mr. Willie Traynor.'

A brick to the nose could not have hit Mr. Willie Traynor with more force. I gasped for air and heard Baggy say, too loudly, 'Oh shit.'

Harry Rex was sitting in the jury box with some other lawyers, taking in the festivities. As I wobbled to my feet, I looked at him desperately for help. He was rising too.

'Your Honor,' he said. 'I represent Mr. Traynor, and this young man has not been notified that he would be a witness.' Go Harry Rex! Do something!

The Judge shrugged and said, 'So? He's here.

What's the difference?' There was not a trace of concern in his voice, and I knew I was nailed.

'Preparation for one thing. A witness has a right to be prepped.'

'I believe he's the newspaper editor, is he not?'

'He is.'

Lucien Wilbanks was walking toward the jury box as if he might take a swing at Harry Rex. He said, 'Your Honor, he's not a litigant, and he will not be a witness at trial. He wrote the stories. Let's hear from him.'

'It's an ambush, Judge,' Harry Rex said.

'Sit down, Mr. Vonner,' His Honor said, and I took a seat in the witness chair. I fired a look at Harry Rex as if to say, 'Nice work, lawyer.'

A bailiff stood in front of me and said, 'Are you armed?'

'What?' I was beyond nervous and nothing made sense.

'A gun. Do you have a gun?'

'Yes.'

'Can I have it, please?'

'Uh, it's in the car.' Most of the spectators thought this was funny. Evidently, in Mississippi, one cannot properly testify if one is armed. Another silly rule. Moments later the rule made perfect sense. If I'd had a gun, I would've begun firing in the direction of Lucien Wilbanks.

The bailiff then swore me to tell the truth, and I watched as Wilbanks began pacing. The crowd behind him looked even larger. He began pleasantly enough with some preliminary inquiries about me and my purchase of the paper. I managed the correct answers, though I was extremely suspicious of every question. He was going somewhere; I had no idea where.

The crowd seemed to enjoy this. My sudden takeover of the *Times* was still the source of interest and speculation, and, suddenly, there I was, in plain view of everyone, chatting about it under oath and on the record.

After a few minutes of niceties, Mr. Gaddis, who I assumed was on my side since Lucien certainly was not, stood and said, 'Your Honor, this is all very informative. Where, exactly, is it going?'

'Good question. Mr. Wilbanks?'

'Hang on, Judge.'

Lucien then produced copies of the *Times* and passed them to me, Gaddis, and Loopus. He looked at me and said, 'Just for the record, Mr. Traynor, how many subscribers does the *Times* have now?'

'About forty-two hundred,' I answered with a little pride. When the bankruptcy hit Spot had squandered all but twelve hundred or so.

'And how many copies are sold at the newsstand?'

'Roughly a thousand.'

Roughly twelve months earlier I had been living on the third floor of a fraternity house in Syracuse, New York, attending class occasionally, working hard to be a good soldier in the sexual revolution, drinking prodigious amounts of alcohol, smoking pot, sleeping until noon anytime I felt like it, and for exercise I'd hustle over to the next antiwar rally and scream at the police. I thought I had problems. How I'd gone from there to a witness chair in the Ford County courtroom was suddenly very unclear to me.

However, at that crucial moment in my new career, I had several hundred of my fellow citizens, and subscribers, staring at me. It was not the time to appear vulnerable.

'What percentage of your newspapers are sold in Ford County, Mr. Traynor?' he asked, as casually as if we were talking business over coffee.

'Virtually all. I don't have the exact numbers.'

'Well, do you have any newsstands outside of Ford County?'

'No.'

Mr. Gaddis attempted another lame rescue. He stood and said, 'Your Honor, please, where is this going?'

Wilbanks suddenly raised his voice and lifted a finger toward the ceiling. 'I will argue, Your Honor, that potential jurors in this county have been poisoned by the sensational coverage thrust upon us by *The Ford County Times*. Mercifully, and justifiably, this newspaper has not been seen or read in other parts of the state. A change of venue is not only fair, but mandatory.'

The word 'poisoned' changed the tone of the proceedings dramatically. It stung me and frightened me, and once again I asked myself if I had done something wrong. I looked at Baggy for consolation, but he was ducking behind the lady in front of him.

'I'll decide what's fair and mandatory, Mr. Wilbanks. Proceed,' Judge Loopus said sharply.

Mr. Wilbanks held up the paper and pointed to the front page. 'I refer to the photograph of my client,' he said. 'Who took this photograph?'

'Mr. Wiley Meek, our photographer.'

'And who made the decision to put it on the front page?'

'I did.'

'And the size? Who determined that?'

'I did.'

'Did it occur to you that this might be considered sensational?'

Damned right. Sensational was what I was after. 'No,' I replied coolly. 'It happened to be the only photo we had of Danny Padgitt at the moment. He happened to be the only person arrested for the crime. We ran it. I'd run it again.'

My haughtiness surprised me. I glanced at Harry Rex and saw one of his nasty grins. He was nodding. Go get 'em, boy.

'So in your opinion it was fair to run this photo?'

'I don't think it was unfair.'

'Answer my question. In your opinion, was it fair?'

'Yes, it was fair, and it was accurate.'

Wilbanks seemed to record this, then filed it

away for future use. 'Your report has a rather detailed description of the interior of the home of Rhoda Kassellaw. When did you inspect the home?'

'I have not.'

'When did you enter the home?'

'I have not.'

'You've never seen the interior of the house?'

'That's correct.'

He flipped open the newspaper, scanned it for a moment, then said, 'You report that the bedroom of Miss Kassellaw's two small children was down a short hallway, approximately fifteen feet from her bedroom door, and you estimate that their beds were about thirty feet from hers. How do you know this?'

'I have a source.'

'A source. Has your source been in the house?'

'Yes.'

'Is your source a police officer or a deputy?'

'He will remain confidential.'

'How many confidential sources did you use for these stories?'

'Several.'

From my journalism studies I vaguely remembered the case of a reporter who, in a similar situation, relied on sources and then refused to reveal their identity. This had somehow upset the Judge, who ordered the reporter to divulge his sources. When he refused again, the Judge held him in contempt and the cops hauled him away to jail where he spent many weeks hiding the identity of his informants. I couldn't remember the ending, but the reporter was eventually let go and the free press endured.

In a flash, I saw myself being handcuffed by Sheriff Coley and dragged away, screaming for Harry Rex, then thrown into the jail where I'd be stripped and handed a pair of those orange coveralls.

It would certainly be a bonanza for the *Times*. Boy, the stories I could write from in there.

Wilbanks continued, 'You report that the children were in shock. How do you know this?'

'I spoke with Mr. Deece, the next-door neighbor.'

'Did he use the word "shock"?'

'He did.'

'You report that the children were examined by a doctor here in Clanton on the night of the crime. How did you know this?'

'I had a source, and later I confirmed this with the doctor.'

'And you report that the children are now undergoing some type of therapy back home in Missouri. Who told you that?'

'I talked to their aunt.'

He tossed the newspaper on the table and took a few steps in my direction. His bloodshot eyes narrowed and glared at me. Here, the pistol would've been useful.

'The truth is, Mr. Traynor, you tried to paint the unmistakable picture that these two little innocent children saw their mother get raped and murdered in her own bed, isn't that right?'

I took a deep breath and weighed my response. The courtroom was silent, waiting. 'I have reported the facts as accurately as possible,' I said, staring straight at Baggy, who, though he was peeking around the lady in front of him, at least was nodding at me.

'In an effort to sell newspapers, you relied on unnamed sources and half-truths and gossip and wild speculation, all in an effort to sensationalize this story.'

'I have reported the facts as accurately as possible,' I said again, trying to remain calm.

He snorted and said, 'Is that so?' He grabbed the newspaper again and said, 'I quote: "Will the children testify at trial?" Did you write that, Mr. Traynor?'

I couldn't deny it. I kicked myself for writing it. It was the last section of the reports that Baggy and I had haggled over. We'd both been a little squeamish, and, with hindsight, we should have followed our instincts.

Denial was not possible. 'Yes,' I said.

'Upon what accurate facts did you base that question?'

'It was a question I heard asked many times after the crime,' I said.

He flung the newspaper back on his table as if it were pure filth. He shook his head in mock bewilderment. 'There are two children, right, Mr. Traynor?'

'Yes. A boy and a girl.'

'How old is the little boy?'

'Five.'

'And how old is the little girl?'

'Three.'

'And how old are you, Mr. Traynor?'

'Twenty-three.'

'And in your twenty-three years, how many trials have you covered as a reporter?'

'None.'

'How many trials have you seen, period?'

'None.'

'Since you are so ignorant about trials, what type of legal research did you do in order to accurately prepare yourself for these stories?'

At this point I would have probably turned the gun on myself.

'Legal research?' I repeated, as if he were speaking another language.

'Yes, Mr. Traynor. How many cases did you find where children age five or younger were allowed to testify in a criminal trial?'

I glanced in the direction of Baggy, who, evidently was now under the wooden bench. 'None,' I said.

'Perfect answer, Mr. Traynor. None. In the history of this state, no child under the age of eleven has ever testified in a criminal trial. Please write that down somewhere, and remember it the next time you attempt to inflame your readers with yellow journalism.'

'Enough, Mr. Wilbanks,' Judge Loopus said, a little too gently for my liking. I think he and the other lawyers, probably including Harry Rex, were enjoying this quick butchering of someone who'd meddled in legal affairs and gotten it all wrong. Even Mr. Gaddis seemed content to let me bleed.

Lucien was wise enough to stop when the blood was flowing. He growled something like, 'I'm through with him.' Mr. Gaddis had no questions. The bailiff motioned for me to step down, off the witness chair, and I tried desperately to walk upright back to the bench where Baggy was still hunkering down, like a stray dog in a hailstorm.

I scribbled notes through the rest of the hearing, but it was a failing effort to look busy and important. I could feel the stares. I was humiliated and wanted to lock myself in my office for a few days.

Wilbanks ended things with an impassioned plea to move the case somewhere far away, maybe even the Gulf Coast, where perhaps a few folks had heard of the crime but no one had been 'poisoned' by the *Times*'s coverage of it. He railed against me and my newspaper, and he went overboard. Mr. Gaddis, in his closing remarks, reminded the Judge of the old saying, 'Strong and bitter words indicate a weak cause.'

I wrote that down. Then I hustled out of the courtroom as if I had an important deadline.

Chapter 11

Baggy rushed into my office late the following morning with the hot news that Lucien Wilbanks had just withdrawn his motion to change venue. As usual, he was full of analysis.

His first windy opinion was that the Padgitts didn't want the trial moved to another county. They knew Danny was dead guilty and that he would almost certainly be convicted by a properly selected jury anywhere. Their sole chance was to get a jury they could either buy or intimidate. Since all guilty verdicts must be unanimous, they needed only a single vote in Danny's favor. Just one vote and the jury would hang itself; the Judge would be required by law to declare a mistrial. It would certainly be retried, but with the same result. After three or four attempts, the State would give up.

I was sure Baggy had been at the courthouse all morning, replaying with his little club the venue hearing and borrowing the conclusions of

136

the lawyers. He explained gravely that the hearing the day before had been staged by Lucien Wilbanks, for two reasons. First, Lucien was baiting the *Times* into running another large photo of Danny, this one in jailhouse garb. Second, Wilbanks wanted to get me on the witness stand to peel off some skin. 'He damned sure did that,' Baggy said.

'Thanks, Baggy,' I said.

Wilbanks was setting the stage for the trial, one that he knew all along would take place in Clanton, and he wanted the *Times* to tone down its coverage.

The third, or fourth, reason was that Lucien Wilbanks never missed an opportunity to grandstand in front of a crowd. Baggy had seen it many times and he shared a few stories.

I'm not sure I followed all of his expansive thinking, but at that moment nothing else made sense. It seemed such a waste of time and effort to put on a two-hour hearing, knowing full well it was all a show. I figured worse things have happened in courtrooms.

The third feast was a pot roast, and we ate on the porch as it rained steadily.

As usual, I confessed that I'd never had a pot roast, so Miss Callie described the recipe and the preparation in detail. She lifted the lid off a large iron pot in the center of the table and closed her eyes as the thick aroma wafted upward. I had only been awake for an hour, and at that moment I could've eaten the tablecloth.

It was her simplest dish, she said. Take a beef rump roast, leave the fat on it, place it in the bottom of the pot, then cover it with new potatoes, onions, turnips, carrots, and beets; add some salt, pepper, and water, put it in the oven on slow bake, and wait five hours. She filled my plate with beef and vegetables, then covered it all with a thick sauce. 'The beets give it all a purple tint,' she explained.

She asked me if I wanted to say the blessing, and I declined. Praying was not something I had done in a long time. She was far more gifted. She took my hands and we closed our eyes. As she spoke to heaven the rain tapped the tin roof above our heads.

'Where's Esau?' I asked after my first three large bites.

'At work. Sometimes he can get free for lunch, often he cannot.' She was preoccupied with something and finally said, 'Can I ask you a question that's somewhat personal?'

'Sure, I guess.'

'Are you a Christian child?'

'I'm sure I am. My mother used to take me to church on Easter.'

That was not satisfactory. Whatever she was looking for, that wasn't it. 'What kind of church?'

'Episcopalian. St. Luke's in Memphis.'

'I'm not sure we have one of those in Clanton.'

'I haven't seen one.' Not that I'd been

searching diligently for a house of worship. 'What kind of church do you attend?' I asked.

'Church of God in Christ,' she answered quickly and her entire face had a serene glow. 'My pastor is the Reverend Thurston Small, a fine man of God. A powerful preacher too. You should come hear him.'

I'd heard stories about how blacks worship, how the entire Sabbath was spent at church, how services ran late into the night and broke up only when the spirit was finally exhausted. I had vivid memories of suffering through Episcopal Easter services that, by law, could run no longer than sixty minutes.

'Do white people worship with you?' I asked.

'Only during the election years. Some of the politicians come sniffing around like dogs. They make a bunch of promises.'

'Do they stay for the entire service?'

'Oh no. They're always too busy for that.'

'So it's possible to come and go?'

'For you, Mr. Traynor, yes. We'll make an exception.' She launched into a long story about her church, which was within walking distance of her home, and a fire that destroyed it not too many years earlier. The fire department, which of course was on the white side of town, was never in a hurry when responding to calls in Lowtown. They lost their church, but it was a blessing! Reverend Small rallied the congregation. For nearly three years they met in a warehouse loaned to them by Mr. Virgil Mabry, a fine Christian man. The building was one block off Main Street and many white folks didn't like the idea of Negroes worshiping on their side of town. But Mr. Mabry held firm. Reverend Small raised the money, and three years after the fire they cut the ribbon on a new sanctuary, one twice as big as the old. Now it was full every Sunday.

I loved it when she talked. It allowed me to eat nonstop, which was a priority. But I was still captivated by her precise diction, her cadence, and her vocabulary, which had to be college level.

When she finished with the new sanctuary, she asked, 'Do you read the Bible often?'

'No,' I said, shaking my head and chewing on a hot turnip.

'Never?'

Lying never crossed my mind. 'Never.'

That disappointed her again. 'How often do you pray?'

I paused for a second and said, 'Once a week, right here.'

She slowly placed her knife and fork beside her plate and frowned at me as if something profound was about to be said. 'Mr. Traynor, if you don't go to church, don't read your Bible, and don't pray, I'm not so sure you're really a Christian child.'

I wasn't so sure either. I kept chewing so I wouldn't have to speak and defend myself. She continued, 'Jesus said, "Judge not, that ye be not judged." It's not my place to pass judgment on anyone's soul, but I must confess that I'm worried about yours.'

I was worried too, but not to the point of disrupting lunch.

'Do you know what happens to those who live outside the will of God?' she asked.

Nothing good, I knew that much. But I was too hungry and too frightened to answer. She was preaching now, not eating, and I was not enjoying myself.

'Paul wrote in Romans, "The wages of sin is death, but the gift of God is eternal life through Jesus Christ our Lord." Do you know what that means, Mr. Traynor?'

I had a hunch. I nodded and took a mouthful of beef. Had she memorized the entire Bible? Was I about to hear it all?

'Death is always physical, but a spiritual death means eternity away from our Lord Jesus. Death means an eternity in hell, Mr. Traynor. Do you understand this?'

She was making things very clear. 'Can we change the subject?' I said.

Miss Callie suddenly smiled and said, 'Of course. You're my guest and it's my job to make sure you feel welcome.' She took up her fork again and for a long time we ate and listened to the rain.

'It's been a very wet spring,' she said. 'Good for beans but my tomatoes and melons need some sunshine.'

I was comforted to know she was planning

future meals. My story about Miss Callie and Esau and their remarkable children was almost complete. I was dragging out the research in hopes of spending a few more Thursday lunches on her porch. At first I had felt guilty for having so much food prepared just for me; we ate only a fraction of it. But she assured me that nothing was thrown out. She and Esau and perhaps some friends would make sure the leftovers were properly put away. 'Nowadays, I only cook three times a week,' she admitted with a hint of shame.

Dessert was peach cobbler and vanilla ice cream. We agreed to wait an hour so we could pace ourselves. She brought two cups of strong black coffee and we moved to the rocking chairs where we did our work. I pulled out my reporter's pad and pen and began making up questions. Miss Callie loved it when I wrote down things she said.

Her first seven children had Italian names – Alberto (Al), Leonardo (Leon), Massimo (Max), Roberto (Bobby), Gloria, Carlota, and Mario. Only Sam, the youngest and the one rumored to be on the lam, had an American name. During my second visit she had explained that she had been raised in an Italian home, right there in Ford County, but it was a very long story and she was saving it for later.

The first seven had all been valedictorians of their classes at Burley Street High, the colored school. Each had earned a PhD and now taught in college. The biographical details filled pages, and Miss Callie, rightly so, could talk about her children for hours.

And so she talked. I scribbled notes, rocked gently in my chair, listened to the rain, and finally fell asleep.

Chapter 12

Baggy had some reservations about the Ruffin story. 'It's really not news,' he said as he read it. I'm sure Hardy had alerted him that I was considering a large, front page story about a family of Negroes. 'This stuff is usually on page five,' he said.

Absent a murder, Baggy's notion of front page news was a hot property line dispute being waged in the courtroom with no jurors, a handful of half-asleep lawyers, and a ninety-year-old Judge brought back from the grave to referee such matters.

In 1967, Mr. Caudle had shown guts in running black obituaries, but in the three years since then the *Times* had taken little interest in anything on the other side of the railroad tracks. Wiley Meek was reluctant to go over with me and photograph Callie and Esau in front of their home. I managed to schedule the picture taking on a Thursday, at midday. Fried catfish, hush puppies, and coleslaw. Wiley ate until he had trouble breathing.

Margaret was also skittish about the story, but, as always, she deferred to the boss. In fact, the entire office was cool to the idea. I didn't care. I was doing what I thought was right; plus there was a big trial around the corner.

And so, on Wednesday, May 20, 1970, during a week in which there was absolutely nothing to print about the Kassellaw murder, the *Times* devoted more than half of its front page to the Ruffin family. It began with a large headline – RUFFIN FAMILY BOASTS SEVEN COLLEGE PROFESSORS. Under it was a large photo of Callie and Esau sitting on their front steps, smiling proudly at the camera. Below them were the senior portraits of all eight children – Al through Sam. My story began:

> When Calia Harris was forced to drop out of school in the tenth grade, she promised herself her children would be able to finish not only high school but college as well. The year was 1926, and Calia, or Callie as she prefers to be called, was, at the age of fifteen, the oldest of four children. Education became a luxury when her father died of tuberculosis. Callie worked for the DeJarnette family until 1929, when she married Esau Ruffin, a carpenter and part-time preacher. They rented a small duplex in Lowtown for $15 a month and began saving every

penny. They would need all they could
save.
   In 1931, Alberto was born.

In 1970, Dr. Alberto Ruffin was a professor of sociology at the University of Iowa. Dr. Leonardo Ruffin was a professor of biology at Purdue. Dr. Massimo Ruffin was a professor of economics at the University of Toledo. Dr. Roberto Ruffin was a professor of history at Marquette. Dr. Gloria Ruffin Sanderford taught Italian at Duke. Dr. Carlota Ruffin was a professor of urban studies at UCLA. Dr. Mario Ruffin had just completed his PhD in medieval literature and was a professor teaching at Grinnell College in Iowa. I mentioned Sam but didn't dwell on him.

By phone I had talked to all seven of the professors, and I quoted liberally from them in my story. The themes were common – love, sacrifice, discipline, hard work, encouragement, faith in God, faith in family, ambition, perseverance; no tolerance for laziness or failure. Each of the seven had a success story that could have filled an entire edition of the *Times*. Each had worked at least one full-time job while struggling through college and grad school. Most had worked two jobs. The older ones helped the younger ones. Mario told me he received five or six small checks each month from his siblings and parents.

The five older ones had been so tenacious in

their studies that they had postponed marriage until in their late twenties and early thirties. Carlota and Mario were still single. Likewise, the next generation was being carefully planned. Leon had the oldest grandchild, age five. There were a total of five. Max and his wife were expecting their second.

There was so much material on the Ruffins that I ran only Part One that week. When I went to Lowtown for lunch the next day, Miss Callie met me with tears in her eyes. Esau met me too, with a firm handshake and a stiff, awkward, manly hug. We devoured a lamb stew and compared notes on how the story was being received. Needless to say, it was the talk of Lowtown, with neighbors stopping by all Wednesday afternoon and Thursday morning with extra copies. I had mailed a half dozen or so to each of the professors.

Over coffee and fried apple pies, their preacher, Reverend Thurston Small, parked in the street and made his way to the porch. I was introduced, and he seemed pleased to meet me. He quickly accepted a dessert and began a lengthy summary of how important the Ruffin story was to the black community of Clanton. Obituaries were fine, and in most Southern towns dead black folks were still ignored. Thanks to Mr. Caudle, progress was being made on one front. But to run such a grand and dignified profile of an outstanding black family on the front page was a giant step for racial tolerance in the town. I didn't see it that way. It was just a good human interest story about Miss Callie Ruffin and her extraordinary family.

The reverend enjoyed food and he also had a knack for embellishment. On his second pie, he became monotonous in his praise for the story. He gave no indication of leaving anytime that afternoon, so I finally excused myself.

Other than being the unofficial and somewhat unreliable janitor for several businesses around the square, Piston had another job. He had an unlicensed courier service. Every hour or so he would appear inside the front doors of his clients – primarily law offices, but also the three banks, some Realtors, insurance agents, and the *Times* – and he would stand there for a few moments waiting for something to deliver. A simple shake of the head by a secretary would send him on his way to his next stop. If a letter or small package needed to be delivered, the secretaries would wait for Piston to pop in. He would grab whatever it was and jog it over to its destination. If it weighed over ten pounds, forget it. Since he was on foot, his service was limited to the square and maybe one or two blocks around it. At almost any hour of the working day Piston could be seen downtown – walking, if he had no package, and jogging if he did.

The bulk of his traffic was letters between law offices. Piston was much faster than the mail, and much cheaper. He charged nothing.

He said it was his service to his community, though at Christmas he fully expected a ham or a cake.

He darted in late Friday morning with a hand-addressed letter from Lucien Wilbanks. I was almost afraid to open it. Could it be the million-dollar lawsuit he'd promised? It read:

> Dear Mr. Traynor:
>
> I enjoyed your profile on the Ruffin family, a most remarkable clan. I had heard of their achievements, but your story provided great insight. I admire your courage.
>
> I hope you continue in this more positive vein.
>
> Sincerely,
> Lucien Wilbanks

I detested the man, but who wouldn't have appreciated the note? He enjoyed his reputation as a wild-eyed radical liberal who embraced unpopular causes. As such, his support at that moment gave limited comfort. And I knew it was only temporary.

There were no other letters. No anonymous phone calls. No threats. School was out and the weather was hot. The ominous and much-dreaded winds of desegregation were gathering strength. The good folks of Ford County had more important matters to worry about.

After a decade of strife and tension over civil rights, many white Mississippians were fearful that the end was near. If the federal courts could integrate the schools, could churches and housing be next?

The following day, Baggy went to a public meeting in the basement of a church. The organizers were trying to measure the support for a private, all-white school in Clanton. The crowd was large, frightened, angry, and determined to protect the children. A lawyer summarized the status of various federal appeals and delivered the distressing opinion that the final mandate would come that summer. He predicted that black kids in grades ten through twelve would be sent to Clanton High School and that white kids in grades seven through nine would be sent to Burley Street in Lowtown. This caused men to shake their heads and women to cry. The thought of white kids being shipped across the tracks was simply unacceptable.

A new school was organized. We were asked not to report the story, at least not then. The organizers wanted to gain some financial commitments before going public. We complied with their requests. I was anxious to avoid controversy.

A federal judge in Memphis ordered a massive busing plan that ripped the city apart. Inner-city black kids would be hauled to the white suburbs, and along the way they would pass the white kids going in the other direction. Tension was even greater there, and I found myself trying to avoid the city for a while.

It would be a long, hot summer. It seemed as if we were waiting for things to explode.

I skipped a week, then ran the second part of Miss Callie's story. On the bottom of the front page I lined up current photos of the seven Ruffin professors. My story dealt with where they were now and what they were doing. Without exception they professed great love for Clanton and Mississippi, though none planned to ever return permanently. They refused to judge a place that had kept them in inferior schools, kept them on one side of the tracks, kept them from voting and eating in most restaurants and drinking water from the fountain on the courthouse lawn. They refused to dwell on anything negative. Instead, they thanked God for his goodness, for health, for family, for their parents, and for their opportunities.

I marveled at their humility and kindness. Each of the seven promised to meet me during the Christmas vacation when we would sit on Miss Callie's porch and eat pecan pie and tell stories.

I finished my lengthy profile with an intriguing detail about the family. From the day each Ruffin child left home, he or she was instructed by Esau to write at least one letter a week to their mother. This they did, and the letters never stopped. At some point, Esau decided that Callie should receive a letter a day. Seven professors. Seven days in a week. So Alberto wrote his letter on Sunday, and mailed it. Leonardo wrote his on Monday, and mailed it. And so on. Some days Callie received two or three letters, some days none. But the short walk to the mailbox was always exciting.

And she kept every letter. In a closet in the front bedroom, she showed me a stack of cardboard boxes, all filled with hundreds of letters from her children.

'I'll let you read them sometime,' she said, but for some reason I didn't believe her. Nor did I want to read them. They would be far too personal.

Chapter 13

Ernie Gaddis, the District Attorney, filed a motion to enlarge the jury pool. According to Baggy, who was becoming more of an expert each day, in the typical criminal trial the Circuit Court clerk summoned about forty people for jury duty. About thirty-five would show up and at least five of those would be too old or too sick to be qualified. Gaddis argued in his motion that the increased notoriety of the Kassellaw murder would make it more difficult to find impartial jurors. He asked the Court to summon at least a hundred prospective jurors.

What he didn't say in writing, but what everybody knew, was that the Padgitts would have a harder time intimidating one hundred than forty. Lucien Wilbanks objected strenuously and demanded a hearing. Judge Loopus said one was not necessary and ordered a larger jury pool. He also took the unusual step of sealing the list of prospective jurors. Baggy and his drinking buddies, and everyone else around the courthouse, were shocked by this. It had never been done. The lawyers and litigants always got a complete list of the jury pool two weeks before trial.

The order was generally viewed as a major setback to the Padgitts. If they didn't know who was in the pool, then how could they bribe or frighten them?

Gaddis then asked the Court to have the jury summons mailed, not personally served by the Sheriff's office. Loopus liked this idea too. Evidently he was well aware of the cozy relationship between the Padgitts and our Sheriff. Not surprisingly, Lucien Wilbanks screamed over this plan. In his rather frantic responses he made the point that Judge Loopus was treating his client differently and unfairly. Reading his filings, I was amazed at how he could rant so clearly for so many pages.

It was becoming obvious that Judge Loopus was determined to preside over a secure and unbiased trial. He had been the District Attorney back in the 1950s before ascending to the bench, and he was known for his pro-prosecution leanings. He certainly appeared to have little concern for the Padgitts and their legacy of corruption. Plus, on paper (and certainly in my paper), the case against Danny Padgitt appeared to be airtight.

On Monday, June 15, amid great secrecy, the Circuit Court clerk mailed a hundred summonses for jury duty to registered voters all over Ford County. One arrived in the rather busy mailbox of Miss Callie Ruffin, and when I arrived for lunch on Thursday she showed it to me.

In 1970, Ford County was 26 percent black, 74 percent white, with no fractions for Others or those who weren't certain. Six years after the tumultuous summer of 1964 and its massive push to register blacks, and five years after the Voting Rights Act of 1965, few bothered to sign up in Ford County. In the statewide elections of 1967, almost 70 percent of the eligible whites in the county had voted, while only 12 percent of the blacks did so. Registration drives in Lowtown were met with general indifference. One reason was that the county was so white that no black could ever be elected to a local office. So why bother?

Another reason was the historical abuse at the point of enrolling. For a hundred years whites had used a variety of tricks to deny blacks proper registration. Poll taxes, literacy exams, the list was long and miserable.

Yet another reason was the hesitancy by most blacks to be registered in any manner by white authorities. Registration could mean more taxes, more supervision, more surveillance, more intrusions. Registration could mean serving on juries.

According to Harry Rex, who was a slightly more reliable courthouse source than Baggy, there had never been a black juror in Ford County. Since potential jurors were selected from the voter registration rolls and nowhere else, few showed up in a jury pool. Those who survived the early rounds of questioning were routinely excused before the final twelve were empaneled. In criminal cases, the prosecution routinely challenged blacks under the belief that they would be too sympathetic to the accused. In civil cases, the defense challenged them because they were feared as too liberal with the money of others.

However, these theories had never been tested in Ford County.

Callie and Esau Ruffin registered to vote in 1951. Together, they marched into the office of the Circuit Court clerk and asked to be added to the voter rolls. The deputy clerk, as she was trained to do, handed them a laminated card with the words 'Declaration of Independence' across the top. The text was written in German.

The clerk, assuming that Mr. and Mrs. Ruffin were as illiterate as most blacks in Ford County, said, 'Can you read this?'

'This is not English,' Callie said. 'It's German.'

'Can you read it?' the clerk asked, realizing that she might have her hands full with this couple.

'I can read as much of it as you can,' Callie said politely.

The clerk withdrew the card and handed over another. 'Can you read this?' she asked.

'I can,' Callie said. 'It's the Bill of Rights.'

'What does number eight say?'

Callie read it slowly, then said, 'The Eighth Amendment prohibits excessive fines and cruel punishments.'

At about this time, depending on whose version was being described, Esau leaned in and said, 'We are property owners.' He placed the deed to their home on the counter and the deputy clerk examined it. Property ownership was not a prerequisite to voting, but it was a huge asset if you were black. Not knowing what else to do, she said, 'Fair enough. The poll tax will be two dollars each.' Esau handed over the money, and with that they joined the voter rolls with thirty-one other blacks, none of whom were women.

They never missed an election. Miss Callie had always worried because so few of her friends bothered to register and vote, but she was too busy raising eight children to do much about it. Ford County was spared the racial unrest that was common throughout most of the state, so there was never an organized drive to register blacks.

At first I couldn't tell if she was anxious or excited. I'm not sure she knew either. The first black female voter might now become the first black juror. She had never backed away from a challenge, but she had grave moral concerns about judging another person. "Judge not, that ye be not judged,"' she said more than once, quoting Jesus.

'But if everyone followed that verse of Scripture, our entire judicial system would fail, wouldn't it?' I asked.

'I don't know,' she said, gazing away. I had never seen Miss Callie so preoccupied.

We were eating fried chicken with mashed potatos and gravy. Esau had not made it home for lunch.

'How can I judge a man I know to be guilty?' she asked.

'First, you listen to the evidence,' I said. 'You have an open mind. It won't be difficult.'

'But you know he killed her. You all but said so in your paper.' Her brutal honesty hit hard every time.

'We just reported the facts, Miss Callie. If the facts make him look guilty, then so be it.'

The gaps of silence were long and many that day. She was deep in thought and ate little.

'What about the death penalty?' she asked. 'Will they want to put that boy in the gas chamber?'

'Yes ma'am. It's a capital murder case.'

'Who decides whether he is put to death?'

'The jury.'

'Oh my.'

She was unable to eat after that. She said her blood pressure had been up since she received

158

the jury summons. She had already been to the doctor. I helped her to the sofa in the den and took her a glass of ice water. She insisted that I finish my lunch, which I happily did in silence. Later, she rallied a bit and we sat on the porch in the rockers, talking about anything but Danny Padgitt and his trial.

I finally hit paydirt when I asked her about the Italian influence in her life. Over our first lunch she had told me that she learned Italian before she learned English. Seven of her eight children had Italian names.

She needed to tell me a long story. I had absolutely nothing else to do.

In the 1890s, the price of cotton rose dramatically as demand increased around the world. The fertile regions of the South were under pressure to produce more. The large plantation owners in the Mississippi Delta desperately needed to increase their crops, but they faced a severe labor shortage. Many of the blacks who were physically able had fled the land their ancestors toiled as slaves for better jobs and certainly better lives up North. Those left behind were, understandably, less than enthusiastic about chopping and picking cotton for brutally low wages.

The landowners hit upon a scheme to import industrious and hardworking European immigrants to raise cotton. Through contacts with Italian labor agents in New York and New

Orleans, connections were made, promises swapped, lies told, contracts forged, and in 1895 the first boatload of families arrived in the Delta. They were from northern Italy, from the region of Emilia-Romagna, near Verona. For the most part they were poorly educated and spoke little English, though in any language they quickly realized they were on the bad end of a huge scam. They were given miserable living accommodations, in a subtropical climate, and while battling malaria and mosquitoes and snakes and rotten drinking water they were told to raise cotton for wages no one could live on. They were forced to borrow money at scandalous rates from the landowners. Their food and supplies came from the company store, at steep prices.

Because the Italians worked hard the landowners wanted more of them. They dressed up their operations, made more promises to more Italian labor agents, and the immigrants kept coming. A system of peonage was fine tuned, and the Italians were treated worse than most black farmworkers.

Over time some efforts were made to divide profits and transfer ownership of land, but the cotton markets fluctuated so wildly that the arrangements could never be stabilized. After twenty years of abuse, the Italians finally scattered and the experiment became history.

Those who remained in the Delta were considered second-class citizens for decades. They were excluded from schools, and because they were Catholic they were not welcome in churches. The country clubs were off limits. They were 'dagos' and shoved to the bottom of the social ladder. But because they worked hard and saved their money, they slowly accumulated land.

The Rossetti family landed near Leland, Mississippi, in 1902. They were from a village near Bologna, and had the misfortune of listening to the wrong labor agent in that city. Mr. and Mrs. Rossetti brought with them four daughters, the oldest of which was Nicola, age twelve. Though they often went hungry the first year, they managed to avoid outright starvation. Penniless when they arrived, after three years of peonage the family had racked up $6,000 in debts to the plantation with no possible way of paying them off. They fled the Delta in the middle of the night and rode a boxcar to Memphis, where a distant relative took them in.

At the age of fifteen, Nicola was stunningly beautiful. Long dark hair, brown eyes – a classic Italian beauty. She looked older than her years and managed to get a job in a clothing store by telling the owner she was eighteen. After three days, the owner offered her a marriage proposal. He was willing to divorce his wife of twenty years and say good-bye to his children if Nicola would run away with him. She said no. He offered Mr. Rossetti $5,000 as an incentive. Mr. Rossetti said no.

In those days, the wealthy farming families in

northern Mississippi did their shopping and socializing in Memphis, usually within walking distance of the Peabody Hotel. It was there that Mr. Zachary DeJarnette of Clanton had the blind luck of bumping into Nicola Rossetti. Two weeks later they were married.

He was thirty-one, a widower with no children and in the midst of a serious search for a wife. He was also the largest landowner in Ford County, where the soil was not as rich as in the Delta, but still quite profitable if you owned enough of it. Mr. DeJarnette had inherited over four thousand acres from his family. His grandfather had once owned the grandfather of Calia Harris Ruffin.

The marriage was a package deal. Nicola was wise beyond her years, and she was also desperate to protect her family. They had suffered so much. She saw an opportunity and took full advantage of it. Before she agreed to marriage, Mr. DeJarnette promised to not only employ her father as a farm supervisor but to provide his family with very comfortable housing. He agreed to educate her three younger sisters. He agreed to pay off the peonage debts from the Delta. So smitten was Mr. DeJarnette that he would've agreed to anything.

The first Italians in Ford County arrived not in a broken ox cart, but rather by first-class passage on the Illinois Central Rail Line. A welcoming party unloaded their brand-new luggage and helped them into two 1904 Ford Model T's. The Rossettis were treated like royalty as they followed Mr. DeJarnette from party to party in Clanton. The town was instantly abuzz with descriptions of how beautiful the bride was. There was talk of a formal wedding ceremony, to sort of buttress the quickie service in Memphis, but since there was no Catholic church in Clanton the idea was scrapped. The bride and groom had yet to address the sticky issue of religious preference. At that time, if Nicola had asked Mr. DeJarnette to convert to Hinduism he would have quickly done so.

They finally made it to the main house at the edge of town. When the Rossettis turned into the long front drive and glimpsed the stately antebellum mansion built by the first Mr. DeJarnette, they all broke into tears.

It was decided that they would live there until an overseer's house could be renovated and made suitable. Nicola assumed her duties as the lady of the manor and tried her best to get pregnant. Her younger sisters were provided with private tutors, and within weeks were speaking good English. Mr. Rossetti spent each day with his son-in-law, who was only three years his junior, and learned how to run the plantation.

And Mrs. Rossetti went to the kitchen where she met Callie's mother, India.

'My grandmother cooked for the DeJarnettes, so did my mother,' Miss Callie was saying. 'I thought I would too, but it didn't work out that way.'

'Did Zack and Nicola have children?' I asked.

I was on my third or fourth glass of tea. It was hot and the ice had melted. Miss Callie had been talking for two hours, and she had forgotten about the jury summons and the murder trial.

'No. It was very sad because they wanted children so badly. When I was born in 1911, Nicola practically took me away from my mother. She insisted I have an Italian name. She kept me in the big house with her. My mother didn't mind – she had plenty of other children, plus she was in the house all day long.'

'What did your father do?' I asked.

'Worked on the farm. It was a good place to work, and to live. We were very lucky because the DeJarnettes took care of us. They were good, fair people. Always. It wasn't that way for a lot of Negro folk. Back then your life was controlled by the white man who owned your house. If he was mean and abusive, then your life was miserable. The DeJarnettes were wonderful people. My father, grandfather, and great-grandfather worked their land, and they were never mistreated.'

'And Nicola?'

She smiled for the first time in an hour. 'God blessed me. I had two mothers. She dressed me in clothes she bought in Memphis. When I was a toddler she taught me to speak Italian while I was learning English. She taught me to read when I was three years old.'

'You still speak Italian?'

'No. It was a long time ago. She loved to tell me stories of being a little girl in Italy, and she promised me that one day she would take me there, to see the canals in Venice and the Vatican in Rome and the tower in Pisa. She loved to sing and she taught me about the opera.'

'Was she educated?'

'Her mother had some education, Mr. Rossetti did not, and she had made sure Nicola and her sisters could read and write. She promised me I would go to college somewhere up North, or maybe even in Europe where folks were more tolerant. The notion of a black woman going to college in the 1920s was downright crazy.'

The story was running in many directions. I wanted to record some of it but I had not brought a notepad. The image of a young black girl living in an antebellum home speaking Italian and listening to the opera in Mississippi fifty years earlier had to be unique.

'Did you work in the house?' I asked.

'Oh yes, when I got older. I was a housekeeper, but I never had to work as hard as the others. Nicola wanted me close by. At least an hour every day we would sit in her parlor and practice speaking. She was determined to lose her Italian accent, and she was just as determined that I would have perfect diction. There was a retired schoolteacher from town, a Miss Tucker, an old maid, I'll never forget her, and Nicola would send a car for her every morning. Over hot tea we would read a lesson and Miss Tucker would correct even the slightest mispronunciation. We studied grammar. We memorized vocabulary. Nicola drilled herself until she spoke perfect English.'

'What happened to college?'

She was suddenly exhausted and story time was over. 'Ah, Mr. Traynor, it was very sad. Mr. DeJarnette lost everything back in the 1920s. He'd invested heavily in railroads and ships and stocks and such stuff, and went broke almost overnight. He shot himself, but that's another story.'

'What happened to Nicola?'

'She managed to hold on to the big house until the Second War, then she moved back to Memphis with Mr. and Mrs. Rossetti. We swapped letters every week for years, I still have them. She died four years ago, at the age of seventy-six. I cried for a month. I still cry when I think of her. How I loved that woman.' Her words trailed off and I knew from experience that she was ready for a nap.

Late that night I buried myself in the *Times* archives. On September 12, 1930, there was a front page story about the suicide of Zachary DeJarnette. Despondent over the collapse of his businesses, he had left a new will and a farewell note for his wife Nicola, then, to make things easier for everyone, he had driven to the funeral home in Clanton. He walked in the rear door with a double-barreled shotgun, found the embalming room, took a seat, took off a shoe, put the gun in his mouth, and pulled the trigger with a big toe.

Chapter 14

On Monday, June 22, all but eight of the hundred jurors arrived for the trial of Danny Padgitt. As we soon found out, four were dead and four had simply vanished. For the most part, the rest looked very anxious. Baggy said that usually jurors have no idea what kind of case they might be selected to decide when they arrive. Not so with the Padgitt trial. Every breathing soul in Ford County knew that the big day had finally come.

Few things draw a crowd in a small town like a good murder trial, and the courtroom was full long before 9 A.M. The prospective jurors filled one side, spectators the other. The old balcony practically sagged above us. The walls were lined with people. As a show of strength, Sheriff Coley had every available uniformed body milling around, looking important, doing nothing productive. What a perfect time to pull a bank heist, I thought.

Baggy and I were in the front row. He had convinced the Circuit Court clerk that we were entitled to press credentials, thus special seating. Next to me was a reporter from the newspaper in Tupelo, a pleasant gentleman who reeked of cheap pipe tobacco. I filled him in on the details of the murder, off the record. He seemed impressed with my knowledge.

The Padgitts were there in full force. They sat in chairs pulled close to the defense table and huddled around Danny and Lucien Wilbanks like the den of thieves they really were. They were arrogant and sinister and I couldn't help but hate every one of them. I didn't know them by name; few people did. But as I watched them I wondered which one had been the incompetent arsonist who'd sneaked into our printing room with gallons of gasoline. I had my pistol in my briefcase. I'm sure they had theirs close by. A false move here or there and an old-fashioned gunfight would erupt. Throw in Sheriff Coley and his poorly trained but trigger-happy boys, and half the town would get wiped out.

I caught a few stares from the Padgitts, but they were much more worried about the jurors than me. They watched them closely as they filed into the courtroom and took their instructions from the clerk. The Padgitts and their lawyers looked at lists that they had found somewhere. They compared notes.

Danny was nicely but casually dressed in a white long-sleeved shirt and a pair of starched khakis. As instructed by Wilbanks, he was smiling a lot, as if he were really a nice kid whose innocence was about to be revealed.

Across the aisle, Ernie Gaddis and his smaller crew were likewise observing the prospective jurors. Gaddis had two assistants, one a paralegal and one a part-time prosecutor named Hank Hooten. The paralegal carried the files and brief-cases. Hooten seemed to do little but just be there so Ernie would have someone to confer with.

Baggy leaned over as if it was time to whisper. 'That guy there, brown suit,' he said, nodding at Hooten. 'He was screwin' Rhoda Kassellaw.'

I was shocked and my face showed it. I jerked to the right and looked at Baggy. He nodded smugly and said what he always said when he had the scoop on something really nasty. 'That's what I'm tellin' you,' he whispered. This meant that he had no doubts. Baggy was often wrong but never in doubt.

Hooten appeared to be about forty with prematurely gray hair, nicely dressed, somewhat handsome. 'Where's he from?' I whispered. The courtroom was noisy as we waited for Judge Loopus.

'Here. He does some real estate law, low-pressure stuff. A real jerk. Been divorced a couple of times, always on the prowl.'

'Does Gaddis know his assistant was seeing the victim?'

'Hell no. Ernie would pull him from the case.'

169

'You think Wilbanks knows?'

'Nobody knows,' Baggy said with even greater smugness. It was as if he had personally caught them in bed, then kept it to himself until that very moment in the courtroom. I wasn't sure I believed him.

Miss Callie arrived a few minutes before nine. Esau escorted her into the courtroom, then had to leave when he couldn't find a seat. She checked in with the clerk and was placed in the third row; she was given a questionnaire to fill out. She looked around for me but there were too many people between us. I counted four other blacks in the pool.

A bailiff bellowed for us to rise, and it sounded like a stampede. Judge Loopus told us to sit, and the floor shook. He went straight to work and appeared to be in good spirits. He had a courtroom full of voters and he was up for reelection in two years, though he had never had an opponent. Six jurors were excused because they were over the age of sixty-five. Five were excused for medical reasons. The morning began to drag. I couldn't take my eyes off Hank Hooten. He certainly had the look of a ladies' man.

When the preliminary questions were over, the panel was down to seventy-nine duly qualified jurors. Miss Callie was now in the second row, not a good sign if she wanted to avoid jury service. Judge Loopus yielded the floor to Ernie Gaddis, who introduced himself to the panel again and explained in great length that he was there on behalf of the State of Mississippi, the taxpayers, the citizens who had elected him to prosecute those who commit crimes. He was the people's lawyer.

He was there to prosecute Mr. Danny Padgitt, who had been indicted by a grand jury, made up of their fellow citizens, for the rape and murder of Rhoda Kassellaw. He asked if it was possible that anyone had not heard something about the murder. Not a single hand went up.

Ernie had been talking to juries for thirty years. He was friendly and smooth and gave the impression that you could discuss almost anything with him, even in open court. He moved slowly into the area of intimidation. Has anyone outside your family contacted you about this case? A stranger? Has a friend tried to influence your opinion? Your summons was mailed to you; the jury list is locked under seal. No one is supposed to know that you're a potential juror. Has anyone mentioned it to you? Anyone threatened you? Anyone offered you anything? The courtroom was very quiet as Ernie led them through these questions.

No one raised a hand; none was expected. But Ernie was successful in conveying the message that these people, the Padgitts, had been moving through the shadows of Ford County. He hung an even darker cloud above them, and he left the impression that he, as the District Attorney and the people's lawyer, knew the truth.

He began his finish with a question that cut through the air like a rifle shot. 'Do all of you folks understand that jury tampering is a crime?'

They seemed to understand.

'And that I, as the prosecutor, will pursue, indict, bring to trial, and do my utmost to convict any person involved with jury tampering. Do you understand this?'

When Ernie finished we all felt as though we'd been tampered with. Anyone who'd talked about the case, which of course was every person in the county, seemed in danger of being indicted by Ernie and hounded to the grave.

'He's effective,' whispered the reporter from Tupelo.

Lucien Wilbanks began with a lengthy and quite dull lecture about the presumption of innocence and how it is the foundation of American jurisprudence. Regardless of what they'd read in the local newspaper, and here he managed a scornful glance in my general direction, his client, sitting right there at the moment, was an innocent man. And if anyone felt otherwise, then he or she was duty bound to raise a hand and say so.

No hands. 'Good. Then by your silence you're telling the Court that you, all of you, can look at Danny Padgitt right now and say he is innocent. Can you do that?' He hammered them on this for far too long, then shifted to the burden of proof with another lecture on the State's monumental challenge to prove his client guilty

172

beyond a reasonable doubt.

These two sacred protections – the presumption of innocence and proof beyond a reasonable doubt – were granted to all of us, including the jurors, by the very wise men who wrote our Constitution and Bill of Rights.

We were approaching noon and everybody was anxious for a break. Wilbanks seemed to miss this and he kept rattling on. When he sat down at twelve-fifteen, Judge Loopus announced that he was starving. We would recess until two o'clock.

Baggy and I had a sandwich upstairs in the Bar Room with several of his cronies, three aging washed-up lawyers who hadn't missed a trial in years. Baggy really wanted a glass of whiskey, but for some odd reason felt the call of duty. His pals did not. The clerk had given us a list of jurors as they were currently seated. Miss Callie was number twenty-two, the first black and the third female.

It was the general feeling that the defense would not challenge her because she was black, and blacks, according to the prevailing theory, were sympathetic to those accused of crimes. I wasn't sure how a black person could be sympathetic to a white thug like Danny Padgitt, but the lawyers were unshakable in their belief that Lucien Wilbanks would gladly take her.

Under the same theory, the prosecution would exercise one of its arbitrary, peremptory challenges and strike her from the panel. Not so, said Chick Elliot, the oldest and drunkest of the gang.

'I'd take her if I were prosecuting,' he argued, then knocked back a potent shot of bourbon.

'Why?' Baggy asked.

'Because we know her so well, now, thanks to the *Times*. She came across as a sensible, God-fearing, Bible-quoting patriot, who raised all those kids with a heavy hand and a swift kick in the ass if they screwed up.'

'I agree,' said Tackett, the youngest of the three. Tackett, though, had a tendency to agree with whatever the prevailing theory happened to be. 'She'd make an ideal juror for the prosecution. Plus, she's a woman. It's a rape case. I'd take all the women I could get.'

They argued for an hour. It was my first session with them, and I suddenly understood how Baggy collected so many differing opinions about so many issues. Though I tried not to show it, I was deeply concerned that my long and generous stories about Miss Callie would somehow come back to haunt her.

After lunch, Judge Loopus moved into the most serious phase of questioning – the death penalty. He explained the nature of a capital offense and the procedures that would be followed, then he yielded again to Ernie Gaddis.

Juror number eleven was a member of some obscure church and he made it very clear that he could never vote to send a person to the gas chamber. Juror number thirty-four was a veteran of two wars and he felt rather strongly that the death penalty wasn't used often enough. This, of course, delighted Ernie, who singled out individual jurors and politely asked them questions about judging others and imposing the death sentence. He eventually made it to Miss Callie. 'Now, Mrs. Ruffin, I've read about you, and you seem to be a very religious woman. Is this correct?'

'I do love the Lord, yes sir,' she answered, as clear as always.

'Are you hesitant to sit in judgment of another human?'

'I am, yes sir.'

'Do you want to be excused?'

'No sir. It's my duty as a citizen to be here, same as all these other folks.'

'And if you're on the jury, and the jury finds Mr. Padgitt guilty of these crimes, can you vote to put him to death?'

'I certainly wouldn't want to.'

'My question was, "Can you?"'

'I can follow the law, same as these other folks. If the law says that we should consider the death penalty, then I can follow the law.'

Four hours later, Calia H. Ruffin became the last juror chosen – the first black to serve on a trial jury in Ford County. The drunks up in the Bar Room had been right. The defense wanted her because she was black. The State wanted her because they knew her so well. Plus, Ernie Gaddis had to save his jury strikes for less-appealing characters.

Late that night I sat alone in my office working on a story about the opening day and jury selection. I heard a familiar noise downstairs. Harry Rex had a way of shoving open the front door and stomping on the wooden floors so that everybody at the *Times*, regardless of the time of day, knew he had arrived. 'Willie boy!' he yelled from below.

'Up here,' I yelled back.

He rumbled up the stairs and fell into his favorite chair. 'Whatta you think of the jury?' he said. He appeared to be completely sober.

'I only know one of them,' I said. 'How many do you know?'

'Seven.'

'You think they picked Miss Callie because of my stories?'

'Yep,' he said, brutally honest as always. 'Everybody's been talkin' about her. Both sides felt like they knew her. It's 1970 and we've never had a black juror. She looked as good as any. Does that worry you?'

'I guess it does.'

'Why? What's wrong with servin' on a jury? It's about time we had blacks doin' it. She and her husband have always been anxious to break down barriers. Ain't like it's dangerous. Well, normally it ain't dangerous.'

I hadn't talked to Miss Callie and I would not be able to do so until after the trial. Judge Loopus had ordered the jurors sequestered for the week. By then they were hiding in a motel in another town.

'Any suspicious characters on the jury?' I asked.

'Maybe. Everybody's worried about that crippled boy from out near Dumas. Fargarson. Hurt his back in a sawmill owned by his uncle. The uncle sold timber to the Padgitts many years ago. The boy has some attitude. Gaddis wanted to bump him but he ran out of challenges.'

The crippled boy walked with a cane and was at least twenty-five years old. Harry Rex referred to anyone younger than himself, and especially me, as 'boy.'

'But with the Padgitts you never know,' he continued. 'Hell, they could own half the jury by now.'

'You don't really believe that, do you?'

'Naw, but a hung jury wouldn't surprise me either. It might take two or three shots at this boy before Ernie gets him.'

'But he will go to prison, won't he?' The thought of Danny Padgitt escaping punishment frightened me. I had invested myself in the town of Clanton, and if its justice was so corruptible then I didn't want to stay.

'They'll hang his ass.'

'Good. The death penalty?'

'I'd bet on it, eventually. This is the buckle of the Bible Belt, Willie. An eye for an eye, all that crap. Loopus'll do everything he can to help Ernie get a death verdict.'

I then made the mistake of asking him why he was working so late. A divorce client had left

177

town on business, then sneaked back to catch his wife with her boyfriend. The client and Harry Rex had spent the last two hours in a borrowed pickup behind a hot-sheets motel north of town. As it turned out, the wife had two boyfriends. The story took half an hour to tell.

Chapter 15

Tuesday morning, almost two hours were wasted as the lawyers wrangled over some hotly contested motions back in the Judge's chambers. 'Probably the photographs,' Baggy kept saying. 'They always fight over the photographs.' Since we were not privy to their little war, we waited impatiently in the courtroom, holding our seats. I wrote pages of useless notes in a chicken-scratch handwriting that any veteran reporter would admire. The scribbling kept me busy and it kept my eyes away from the ever-present stares of the Padgitts. With the jury out of the room they turned their attention to the spectators, especially me.

The jurors were locked away in the deliberation room, with deputies at the door as if someone might gain something by attacking them. The room was on the second floor, with large windows that looked upon the east side of the courthouse lawn. At the bottom of one window was a noisy air-conditioning unit that could be heard from any point on the square when it was at full throttle. I thought of Miss Callie and her blood pressure. I knew she was reading the Bible and maybe this was calming her. I had called Esau early that morning. He was very upset that she had been sequestered and hauled away.

Esau was in the back row, waiting with the rest of us.

When Judge Loopus and the lawyers finally appeared they looked as though they had all been fistfighting. The Judge nodded at the bailiff and the jurors were led in. He welcomed them, thanked them, asked about their accommodations, apologized for the inconvenience, apologized for the delay that morning, then promised that things would move forward.

Ernie Gaddis assumed a position behind the podium and began his opening statement to the jury. He had a yellow legal pad, but he didn't look at it. With great efficiency, he rattled off the necessary elements the State would prove against Danny Padgitt. When all the exhibits were in, and all the witnesses were finished, and the lawyers were quiet, and the Judge had spoken, it would be left to the jury to serve justice. There was no doubt in his mind that they would find Danny Padgitt guilty of rape and murder. He didn't waste a word, and every word found its mark. He was mercifully brief. His confident tone and concise remarks conveyed the clear message that he had the facts, the case, and he would get his verdict. He did not need long, emotional arguments to convince the jury.

Baggy loved to say, 'When lawyers have a weak case they do a lot more talking.'

Oddly, Lucien Wilbanks deferred his opening remarks until the defense put on its case, an option rarely exercised. 'He's up to something,' Baggy mumbled as if he and Lucien were thinking together. 'No surprise there.'

The first witness for the State was Sheriff Coley himself. Part of his job was testifying in criminal cases, but it was doubtful he'd ever dreamed of doing so against a Padgitt. In a few months he would be up for re-election. It was important for him to look good before the voters.

With Ernie's meticulous planning and prodding, they walked through the crime. There were large diagrams of the Kassellaw home, the Deece home, the roads around Beech Hill, the exact spot where Danny Padgitt was arrested. There were photographs of the area. Then, there were photographs of Rhoda's corpse, a series of eight by ten's that were handed to the jurors and passed around. Their reactions were amazing. Every face was shocked. Some winced. A few mouths flew open. Miss Callie closed her eyes and appeared to pray. Another lady on the jury, Mrs. Barbara Baldwin, gasped at first sight and turned away. Then she looked at Danny Padgitt as if she could shoot him at point-blank range. 'Oh my God,' one of the men mumbled.

Another covered his mouth as if he might throw up.

The jurors sat in padded swivel chairs that rocked slightly. As the gruesome photos were passed around, not a single chair was still. The pictures were inflammatory, highly prejudicial, yet always admissible, and as they caused a commotion in the jury box I thought Danny Padgitt was as good as dead. Judge Loopus allowed only six as exhibits. One would have sufficed.

It was just after 1 P.M., and everyone needed a break. I doubted that the jurors had much of an appetite.

The State's second witness was one of Rhoda's sisters from Missouri. Her name was Ginger McClure, and I had talked to her several times after the murder. When she realized I had gone to school at Syracuse and was not a native of Ford County, she had thawed somewhat. She had reluctantly sent me a photo for the obituary. Later, she had called and asked if I could send her copies of the *Times* when it mentioned Rhoda's case. She expressed frustration in getting details from the District Attorney's office.

Ginger was a slim redhead, very attractive and well dressed, and when she settled into the witness chair she had everyone's attention.

According to Baggy, someone from the victim's family always testified. Death became real when the loved ones took the stand and looked at the jurors.

Ernie wanted Ginger to be viewed by the jury and arouse their sympathy. He also wanted to remind the jury that the mother of two small children had been taken from them in a premeditated murder. Her testimony was brief. Wisely, Lucien Wilbanks had no questions on cross-examination. When she was excused, she walked to a reserved chair behind the bar, near the seat of Ernie Gaddis, and assumed the position as representative of the family. Her every move was watched until the next witness was called.

Then it was back to the gore. A forensic pathologist from the state crime lab was called to discuss the autopsy. Though he had plenty of photos, none were used. None were needed. In layman's terms, her cause of death was obvious – a loss of blood. There was a four-inch gash beginning just below her left ear and running almost straight down. It was almost two inches deep, and, in his opinion, and he'd seen many knife wounds, it was caused by a rapid and powerful thrust from a blade that was approximately six inches long and an inch wide. The person using the knife was, more than likely, right-handed. The gash cut completely through the left jugular vein, and at that point the victim had only a few minutes to live. A second gash was six-and-a-half inches long, one inch deep, and ran from the tip of the chin and to the right ear, which it almost sliced in two. This wound by itself probably would not have resulted in death.

The pathologist described these wounds as if he were talking about a tick bite. No big deal. Nothing unusual. In his business he saw this carnage every day and talked about it with juries. But for everyone else in the courtroom, the details were unsettling. At some point during his testimony, every single juror looked at Danny Padgitt and silently voted 'Guilty.'

Lucien Wilbanks began his cross pleasantly enough. The two had hooked up before in trials. He made the pathologist admit that some of his opinions might possibly be wrong, such as the size of the murder weapon and whether the assailant was right-handed. 'I stated that these were probabilities,' the doctor said patiently. I got the impression that he'd been grilled so many times nothing rattled him. Wilbanks poked and probed a bit, but he was careful not to revisit the damning evidence. The jury had heard enough of the cuts and gashes; it would be foolish to cover this ground again.

A second pathologist followed. Concurrent with the autopsy, he had made a thorough examination of the body and found several clues as to the identity of the killer. In the vaginal area, he found semen that matched perfectly with Danny Padgitt's blood. Under the nail of Rhoda's right index finger he had found a tiny piece of human skin. It too matched the defendant's blood type.

On cross-examination, Lucien Wilbanks asked him if he had personally examined Mr. Padgitt.

No, he had not. Where on his body was Mr. Padgitt scraped or scratched or clawed in such a way?

'I did not examine him,' the pathologist said.

'Did you examine photographs of him?'

'I did not.'

'So if he lost some skin, you can't tell the jury where it came from can you?'

'I'm afraid not.'

After four hours of graphic testimony, everybody in the courtroom was exhausted. Judge Loopus sent the jury away with stern warnings about avoiding outside contact. It seemed overkill in light of the fact that they were being hidden in another town and guarded by police.

Baggy and I raced back to the office and typed frantically until almost ten. It was Tuesday, and Hardy liked to have the presses running no later than 11 P.M. On those rare weeks when there were no mechanical problems, he could run five thousand copies in less than three hours.

Hardy set the type as quickly as possible. There was no time for editing and proofreading, but I wasn't too concerned about that edition because Miss Callie was on the jury and wouldn't be able to catch our mistakes. Baggy was hitting the sauce as we finished up and couldn't wait to leave. I was about to head for my apartment when Ginger McClure strolled in the front door and said hello as if we were old friends. She was wearing tight jeans and a red blouse. She asked if I had anything to drink. Not at the office, but that wouldn't stop us.

We left the square in my Spitfire and drove to Quincy's, where I bought a six-pack of Schlitz. She wanted to see Rhoda's house one last time, from the road, not too close. As we headed that way I cautiously inquired about the two children. The report was mixed. Both were living with another sister – Ginger was quick to tell me she was recently divorced – and both were undergoing intense counseling. The little boy appeared to be almost normal, though he sometimes drifted off into prolonged periods of silence. The little girl was much worse. She had constant nightmares about her mother and had lost the ability to control her bladder. She was often found curled in a fetal position, sucking her fingers and groaning pitifully. The doctors were experimenting with various drugs.

Neither child would tell the family or the doctors how much they saw that night. 'They saw their mother get raped and stabbed,' she said, killing off the first beer. Mine was still half full.

The Deece home looked as if Mr. and Mrs. Deece had been asleep for days. We turned into the gravel driveway of what was once the happy little Kassellaw home. It was empty, dark, and had an abandoned look to it. There was a FOR SALE sign in the yard. The house was the only significant asset in Rhoda's small estate. The proceeds would all go to the children.

At Ginger's request, I cut the lights and turned off the engine. It was not a good idea because the neighbors were understandably jumpy. Plus, my Triumph Spitfire was the only one of its kind in Ford County and as such was naturally a suspicious vehicle.

She gently placed her hand on mine and said, 'How did he get in the house?'

'They found some footprints at the patio door. It was probably unlocked.' And during a long silence both of us replayed the attack, the rape, the knife, the children fleeing through the darkness, yelling for Mr. Deece to come save their mother.

'Were you close to her?' I asked, then I heard the distant approach of a vehicle.

'When we were kids, but not recently. She left home ten years ago.'

'How often did you visit here?'

'Twice. I moved away too, to California. We sort of lost touch. After her husband died, we begged her to come back to Springfield, but she said she liked it here. Truth was, she and my mother never got along.'

A pickup truck slowed on the road just behind us. I tried to act unconcerned, but I knew how dangerous things could be in such a dark part of the county. Ginger was staring at the house, lost in some horrible image, and seemed not to hear. Thankfully, the truck did not stop.

'Let's go,' she said, squeezing my hand. 'I'm scared.'

When we drove away, I saw Mr. Deece crouching in the shadows of his garage, holding a shotgun. He was scheduled to be the last witness called by the State.

Ginger was staying at a local motel, but she did not want to go there. It was after midnight, our options were thin, so we drove to the Hocutt place, where I led her up the stairs, over the cats, and into my apartment.

'Don't get any ideas,' she said as she kicked off her shoes and sat on the sofa. 'I'm not in the mood.'

'Neither am I,' I lied.

Her tone was almost flippant, as though her mood might change real soon and when it did then we could have a go at it. I was perfectly happy to wait.

I found colder beer in the kitchen and we settled into our places as if we might talk until sunrise. 'Tell me about your family,' she said.

It was not my best subject, but, for this lady, I could talk. 'I'm an only child. My mother died when I was thirteen. My father lives in Memphis, in an old family house that he never leaves because both he and the house have a few loose boards. He has an office in the attic, and he stays there all day and night trading stocks and bonds. I don't know how well he trades, but I have a hunch he loses more than he gains. We speak by phone once a month.'

'Are you wealthy?'

'No, my grandmother is wealthy. My mother's

mother, BeeBee. She loaned me the money to buy the paper.'

She thought about this as she sipped her beer. 'There were three of us girls, two now. We were pretty wild growing up. My father went out for milk and eggs one night and never came home. My mother has tried twice more since then, can't seem to get it right. I'm divorced. My older sister is divorced. Rhoda is dead.' She reached across with the bottle and tapped mine. 'Here's to a couple of screwed-up families.'

We drank to that.

Divorced, childless, wild, and very cute. I could spend time with Ginger.

She wanted to know about Ford County and its characters – Lucien Wilbanks, the Padgitts, Sheriff Coley, and so on. I talked and talked and kept waiting for her mood to change.

It did not. Sometime after 2 A.M. she stretched out on the sofa, and I went to bed alone.

Chapter 16

Three of the Hocutts – Max, Wilma, and Gilma – were loitering around the garage under my apartment when Ginger and I made our exit a few hours later. I guess they wanted to meet her. They looked at her scornfully as I made cheerful introductions. I half-expected Max to say something ridiculous like, 'We did not contemplate illicit sex when we leased this place to you.' But nothing offensive was said, and we quickly drove to the office. She jumped in her car and disappeared.

The latest edition was stacked floor to ceiling in the front room. I grabbed a copy for a quick perusal. The headline was fairly restrained – DANNY PADGITT TRIAL BEGINS: JURY SEQUESTERED. There were no photos of the defendant. We had used enough of those already, and I wanted to save a big one for the following week when, hopefully, we could nail the little thug leaving the courthouse after receiving his death sentence. Baggy and I had filled the columns with the things we'd seen and heard during the first two days, and I was quite proud of our reporting. It was straightforward, factual, detailed, well written, and not the least bit lurid. The trial itself was big enough to carry the moment. And, truthfully, I had already learned my lesson about trying to sensationalize things. By 8 A.M. the courthouse and the square were blanketed with complimentary copies of the *Times*.

There were no preliminary skirmishes on Wednesday morning. At precisely 9 A.M. the jurors were led in and Ernie Gaddis called his next witness. His name was Chub Brooner, the longtime investigator for the Sheriff's department. According to both Baggy and Harry Rex, Brooner was famous for his incompetence.

To wake up the jury and captivate the rest of us, Gaddis produced the bloody white shirt Danny Padgitt was wearing the night he was arrested. It had not been washed; the splotches of blood were dark brown. Ernie gently waved it around the courtroom for all to see as he chatted with Brooner. It had been removed from the body of Danny Padgitt by a deputy named Grice, in the presence of Brooner and Sheriff Coley. Tests had revealed two types of blood – O Positive and B Positive. Further tests by the state crime lab matched the B Positive with the blood of Rhoda Kassellaw.

I watched Ginger as she looked at the shirt. After a few minutes she looked away and began writing something. Not surprisingly, she looked even better her second day in the courtroom. I was very concerned about her moods.

The shirt was ripped across the front. Danny had cut himself when he crawled out of his wrecked truck and had received twelve stitches. Brooner did a passable job of explaining this to the jury. Ernie then pulled out an easel and placed on it two enlarged photographs of the footprints found on the patio of Rhoda's home. On the exhibit table he picked up the shoes Padgitt was wearing when he arrived at the jail. Brooner stumbled through testimony that should have been much easier, but the point was made that everything matched.

Brooner was terrified of Lucien Wilbanks and began stuttering at the first question. Lucien wisely ignored the fact that Rhoda's blood was found on Danny's shirt, and chose instead to hammer Brooner on the art and science of matching up footprints. The investigator's training had not been comprehensive, he finally admitted. Lucien zeroed in on a series of ridges on the heel of the right shoe, and Brooner couldn't locate them in the print. Because of weight and motion, a heel usually leaves a better print than the rest of the sole, according to Brooner's testimony on direct. Lucien harangued him to the point of confusing everyone, and I had to admit that I was skeptical of the footprints. Not that it mattered. There was plenty of other evidence.

'Was Mr. Padgitt wearing gloves when he was arrested?' Lucien asked.

'I don't know. I didn't arrest him.'

'Well, you boys took his shirt and his shoes. Did you take any gloves?'

'Not to my knowledge.'

'You've reviewed the entire evidence file, right, Mr. Brooner?'

'I have.'

'In fact, as chief investigator, you're very familiar with every aspect of this case, aren't you?'

'Yes sir.'

'Have you seen any reference to any gloves worn by or taken from Mr. Padgitt?'

'No.'

'Good. Did you dust the crime scene for fingerprints?'

'Yes.'

'Routine, isn't it?'

'Yes, always.'

'And of course you fingerprinted Mr. Padgitt when he was arrested, right?'

'Yes.'

'Good. How many of Mr. Padgitt's fingerprints did you find at the crime scene?'

'None.'

'Not a single one, did you?'

'None.'

With that, Lucien picked a good moment to

sit down. It was difficult to believe that the murderer could enter the house, hide there for a while, rape and murder his victim, then escape without leaving behind fingerprints. But Chub Brooner did not inspire a lot of confidence. With him in charge of the investigation, there seemed an excellent chance that dozens of fingerprints could have been missed.

Judge Loopus called for the morning recess, and as the jurors stood to leave I made eye contact with Miss Callie. Her face exploded into one huge grin. She nodded, as if to say, 'Don't worry about me.'

We stretched our legs and whispered about what we had just heard. I was delighted to see so many people in the courtroom reading the *Times*. I walked to the bar and leaned down to speak to Ginger. 'You doin' okay?' I asked.

'I just want to go home,' she said softly.

'How about lunch?'

'You got it.'

The State's last witness was Mr. Aaron Deece. He walked to the stand shortly before 11 A.M., and we braced for his recollection of that night. Ernie Gaddis led him through a series of questions designed to personalize Rhoda and her two children. They had lived next door for seven years, perfect neighbors, wonderful people. He missed them greatly, couldn't believe they were gone. At one point Mr. Deece wiped a tear from his eye.

This was completely irrelevant to the issues at hand, and Lucien gamely allowed it for a few minutes. Then he stood and politely said, 'Your Honor, this is very touching, but it's really not admissible.'

'Move along, Mr. Gaddis,' Judge Loopus said.

Mr. Deece described the night, the time, the temperature, the weather. He heard the panicked voice of little Michael, age five, calling his name, crying for help. He found the children outside, in their pajamas, wet with dew, in shock from fear. He took them inside where his wife put blankets on them. He got his shoes and his guns and was flying out of the house when he saw Rhoda, stumbling toward him. She was naked and, except for her face, she was completely covered in blood. He picked her up, carried her to the porch, placed her on a swing.

Lucien was on his feet, waiting.

'Did she say anything?' Ernie asked.

'Your Honor, I object to this witness testifying to anything the victim said. It's clearly heresay.'

'Your motion is on file, Mr. Wilbanks. We've had our debate in chambers, and it is on the record. You may answer the question, Mr. Deece.'

Mr. Deece swallowed hard, inhaled and exhaled, and looked at the jurors. 'Two or three times, she said, "It was Danny Padgitt. It was Danny Padgitt."'

For dramatic effect, Ernie let those bullets crack through the air, then ricochet around the courtroom while he pretended to look at some notes. 'You ever met Danny Padgitt, Mr. Deece?'

'No sir.'

'Had you ever heard his name before that night?'

'No sir.'

'Did she say anything else?'

'The last thing she said was, "Take care of my babies." '

Ginger was touching her eyes with a tissue. Miss Callie was praying. Several of the jurors were looking at their feet.

He finished his story – he called the Sheriff's department; his wife had the children in a bedroom behind a locked door; he took a shower because he was covered with blood; the deputies showed up, did their investigating; the ambulance came and took away the body; he and his wife stayed with the children until around two in the morning, then rode with them to the hospital in Clanton. They stayed with them there until a relative arrived from Missouri.

There was nothing in his testimony that could be challenged or impeached, so Lucien Wilbanks declined a cross-examination. The State rested, and we broke for lunch. I drove Ginger to Karaway, to the only Mexican place I knew, and we ate enchiladas under an oak tree and talked about everything but the trial. She was subdued and wanted to leave Ford County forever.

I really wanted her to stay.

Lucien Wilbanks began his defense with a little pep talk about what a nice young man Danny Padgitt really was. He had finished high school with good grades, he worked long hours in the family's timber business, he dreamed of one day running his own company. He had no police record whatsoever. His only brush with the law had been one, just one, speeding ticket when he was sixteen years old.

Lucien's persuasive skills were reasonably well honed, but he was collapsing under the weight of the effort. It was impossible to make a Padgitt appear warm and cuddly. There was quite a bit of squirming in the courtroom, some smirks here and there. But we weren't the ones deciding the case. Lucien was talking to the jurors, looking them in the eyes, and no one knew if he and his client had already locked up a vote or two.

However, Danny was not a saint. Like most handsome young men he had discovered he enjoyed the company of ladies. He had met the wrong one, though, a woman who happened to be married to someone else. Danny was with her the night Rhoda Kassellaw was murdered.

'Listen to me!' he bellowed at the jurors. 'My client did not kill Miss Kassellaw! At the time of this horrible murder, he was with another woman, in her home not far from the Kassellaw place. He has an airtight alibi.'

This announcement sucked the air out of the courtroom, and for a long minute we waited for the next surprise. Lucien played the drama perfectly. 'This woman, his lover, will be our first witness,' he said.

They brought her in moments after Lucien finished his opening remarks. Her name was Lydia Vince. I whispered to Baggy and he said he'd never heard of her; didn't know any Vinces from out in Beech Hill. There were a lot of whispers in the courtroom as folks tried to place her, and gauging from the frowns and puzzled looks and head shakes it appeared as though the woman was a complete unknown. Lucien's preliminary questions revealed that she was living in a rented house on Hurt Road back in March but was now living in Tupelo, that she and her husband were going through a divorce, that she had one child, that she grew up in Tyler County, and that she was currently unemployed. She was about thirty years old, somewhat attractive in a cheap way – short skirt, tight blouse over a big chest, bottle-blond hair – and she was utterly terrified of the proceedings.

She and Danny had been having an adulterous affair for about a year. I glanced at Miss Callie and was not surprised to see this was not sitting well.

On the night Rhoda was murdered, Danny was at her house. Malcolm Vince, her husband, was supposedly in Memphis, doing something with the boys, she really didn't know what. He was gone a lot in those days. She and Danny had sex twice and sometime around midnight he was preparing to leave when her husband's truck turned into the driveway. Danny sneaked out the rear door and disappeared.

The shock of a married woman admitting in open court that she had committed adultery was designed to convince the jury that she had to be telling the truth. No one, respectable or otherwise, would admit this. It would damage her reputation, if she cared about such things. It would certainly impact her divorce, perhaps jeopardize custody of her child. It might even allow her husband to sue Danny Padgitt for alienation of affection, though it was doubtful the jurors were thinking that far ahead.

Her answers to Lucien's questions were brief and very well rehearsed. She refused to look at the jurors or at her alleged former lover. Instead, she kept her eyes down and appeared to be looking at Lucien's shoes. Both the lawyer and the witness were careful not to venture outside the script. 'She's lyin',' Baggy whispered loudly, and I agreed.

When the direct examination was over, Ernie Gaddis stood and walked deliberately to the podium, staring with great suspicion at this self-confessed adulteress. He kept his reading glasses on the tip of his nose, and looked above them with wrinkled brow and narrow eyes. Very much the professor who'd just caught a bad student cheating.

'Miss Vince, this house on Hurt Road. Who owned it?'

'Jack Hagel.'

'How long did you live there?'

'About a year.'

'Did you sign a lease?'

She hesitated for a split second too long, then said, 'Maybe my husband did. I really don't remember.'

'How much was the rent each month?'

'Three hundred dollars.'

Ernie wrote down each answer with great effort, as though each detail was about to be diligently investigated and lies would be revealed.

'When did you leave this house?'

'I don't know, about two months ago.'

'So how long did you live in Ford County?'

'I don't know, a couple of years.'

'Did you ever register to vote in Ford County?'

'No.'

'Did your husband?'

'No.'

'What's his name again?'

'Malcolm Vince.'

'Where does he live now?'

'I'm not sure. He moves around a lot. Last I heard he was somewhere around Tupelo.'

'And y'all are getting a divorce now, right?'

'Yes.'

'When did you file for divorce?'

Her eyes lifted quickly and she glanced at Lucien, who was listening hard but refusing to watch her. 'We haven't actually filed papers yet,' she said.

'I'm sorry, I thought you said you were going through a divorce.'

'We've split, and we've both hired lawyers.'

'And who is your attorney?'

'Mr. Wilbanks.'

Lucien flinched, as if this was news to him. Ernie let it settle in, then continued, 'Who is your husband's lawyer?'

'I can't remember his name.'

'Is he suing you for divorce, or is it the other way around?'

'It's a mutual thing.'

'How many other men were you sleeping with?'

'Just Danny.'

'I see. And you live in Tupelo, right?'

'Right.'

'You say you're unemployed, right?'

'For now.'

'And you've separated from your husband?'

'I just said we've split.'

'Where do you live over in Tupelo?'

'An apartment.'

'How much is the rent?'

'Two hundred a month.'

'And you live there with your child?'

'Yes.'

'Does the child work?'

'The child is five years old.'

'So how do you pay the rent and utilities?'

'I get by.' No one could have possibly believed her answer.

'What kind of car do you drive?'

She hesitated again. It was the kind of question that required an answer that could be verified with a few phone calls. 'A '68 Mustang.'

'That's a nice car. When did you get it?'

Again, there was a paper trail here, and even Lydia, who wasn't bright, could see the trap. 'Coupla months ago,' she said, defiantly.

'Is the car titled in your name?'

'It is.'

'Is the apartment lease in your name?'

'It is.'

Paperwork, paperwork. She couldn't lie about it, and she certainly couldn't afford it. Ernie took some notes from Hank Hooten and studied them suspiciously.

'How long did you sleep with Danny Padgitt?'

'Fifteen minutes, usually.'

In a tense courtroom, the answer provided scattered laughter. Ernie removed his glasses, rubbed them with the end of his tie, gave her a nasty grin, and rephrased the question. 'Your affair with Danny Padgitt, how long did it last?'

'Almost a year.'

'Where did you first meet him?'

'At the clubs, up at the state line.'

'Did someone introduce the two of you?'

'I really don't remember. He was there, I was there, we had a dance. One thing led to another.'

There was no doubt that Lydia Vince had

spent many nights in many honky-tonks, and she'd never run from a new dance partner. Ernie needed just a few more lies that he could nail down.

He asked a series of questions about her background and her husband's – birth, education, marriage, employment, family. Names and dates and events that could be verified as true or false. She was for sale. The Padgitts had found a witness they could buy.

As we left the courtroom late that afternoon, I was confused and uneasy. I had been convinced for many months that Danny Padgitt killed Rhoda Kassellaw, and I still had no doubts. But the jury suddenly had something to hang itself with. A sworn witness had committed a dreadful act of perjury, but it was possible that a juror could have a reasonable doubt.

Ginger was more depressed than me, so we decided to get drunk. We bought burgers and fries and a case of beer and went to her small motel room where we ate and then drowned our fears and hatred of a corrupt judicial system. She said more than once that her family, fractured as it was, could not hold up if Danny Padgitt were let go. Her mother was not stable anyway, and a not-guilty verdict would push her over the cliff. What would they tell Rhoda's children one day?

We tried watching television, but nothing held our interest. We grew weary of worrying about the trial. As I was about to fall asleep, Ginger walked out of the bathroom naked, and the night took a turn for the better. We made love off and on until the alcohol prevailed and we fell asleep.

Chapter 17

Unknown to me – and there was no reason it should have been known to me because I was such a newcomer to the community and certainly not involved in judicial affairs, and besides I literally had my hands full of Ginger and for a few wonderful hours we lost interest in the trial – a secret meeting took place shortly after adjournment on Wednesday. Ernie Gaddis went to Harry Rex's office for a post-trial drink and both admitted they were sick over Lydia's testimony. They began making phone calls, and within an hour they had rounded up a group of lawyers they could trust, and a couple of politicians as well.

The opinion was unanimous that the Padgitts were in the process of wiggling out of what appeared to be a solid case against them. They had managed to find a witness they could bribe. Lydia had obviously been paid to concoct her story, and she was either too broke or too stupid to understand the risks of perjury. Regardless, she had given the jury a reason, albeit a weak one, to second-guess the prosecution.

An acquittal in such an open-and-shut case would infuriate the town and mock the court system. A hung jury would send a similar message – justice could be bought in Ford County. Ernie, Harry Rex, and the other lawyers worked hard every day manipulating the system on behalf of their clients, but the rules were applied fairly. The system worked because the judges and jurors were impartial and unbiased. To allow Lucien Wilbanks and the Padgitts to corrupt the process would cause irreparable damage.

There was a consensus that a hung jury was entirely possible. As a believable witness, Lydia Vince left much to be desired, but the jurors were not as savvy about fabricated testimony and crooked clients. The lawyers agreed that Fargarson, 'the crippled boy,' appeared hostile to the prosecution. After two full days and almost fifteen hours of watching the jurors, the lawyers felt they could read them.

Mr. John Deere also had them worried. His real name was Mo Teale and he'd been a mechanic down at the tractor place for over twenty years. He was a simple man with a limited wardrobe. Late Monday afternoon when the jury was finally selected and Judge Loopus sent them home to hurriedly pack for the bus, Mo had simply loaded up his week's supply of work uniforms. Each morning he marched into the jury box wearing a bright yellow shirt with green trim and green pants with yellow trim, as if he was ready for another vigorous day of pulling wrenches.

Mo sat with his arms crossed and frowned whenever Ernie Gaddis was on his feet. His body language terrified the prosecution.

Harry Rex thought it was important to find Lydia's estranged husband. If they were in fact going through a divorce, it was more than likely not an amicable one. It was difficult to believe she was having an affair with Danny Padgitt, but at the same time it seemed likely that the woman was no stranger to extramarital activity. The husband might have testimony that could severely discredit Lydia's.

Ernie wanted to dig into her private life. He wanted to create doubt about her finances so he could yell at the jury, 'How can she live so comfortably when she's unemployed and going through a divorce?'

'Because she got twenty-five thousand dollars from the Padgitts,' one of the lawyers said. Speculation about the amount of the bribe became a running debate as the night wore on.

The search for Malcolm Vince began with Harry Rex and two others calling every lawyer within five counties. Around 10 P.M. they found a lawyer in Corinth, two hours away, who said he had met with a Malcolm Vince once about a divorce, but had not been retained. Mr. Vince was living in a trailer somewhere out in the boondocks near the Tishomingo County line. He could not remember where he worked, but he was sure he had written it down in his file at the office. The District Attorney himself got on the phone and coaxed the lawyer back to the office.

At eight o'clock the next morning, about the time I was leaving Ginger at the motel, Judge Loopus readily agreed to order a subpoena for Malcolm Vince. Twenty minutes later, a Corinth city policeman stopped a forklift in a warehouse and informed its operator that a subpoena had just been issued for his appearance in a murder trial over in Ford County.

'What the hell for?' Mr. Vince demanded.

'I'm just following orders,' the policeman said.

'What am I supposed to do?'

'You got two choices, pal,' explained the cop. 'Stay here with me till they come get you, or we can leave now and get it over with.' Malcolm's boss told him to leave and hurry back.

After a ninety-minute delay, the jury was brought in. Mr. John Deere was as spiffy as ever, but the rest were beginning to look tired. It seemed like the trial had been going on for a month.

Miss Callie searched me out and gave me a restrained grin, not one of her spectacular day-brighteners. She was still clutching a small New Testament.

Ernie rose and informed the court that he had

no further questions for Lydia Vince. Lucien said he was through with her too. Ernie said he had a rebuttal witness he would like to call out of order. Lucien Wilbanks objected and they haggled over it at the bench. When Lucien learned who the witness was, he became visibly upset. A good sign.

Evidently Judge Loopus was concerned about a bad verdict as well. He ruled against the defense, and a thoroughly bewildered Malcolm Vince was called into the packed courtroom to testify. Ernie had spent less than ten minutes with him in a back room, so he was as unprepared as he was confused.

Ernie started slow, with the basics – name, address, employment, recent family history. Malcolm somewhat reluctantly admitted being married to Lydia and shared her desire to escape from the union. He said he had seen neither his wife nor his child in about a month. His recent employment history was spotty at best, but he tried to send her $50 a week to support the child.

He knew she was unemployed but living in a nice apartment. 'You're not paying for her apartment?' Ernie asked with great suspicion, glancing warily at the jury.

'No sir, I am not.'

'Is her family paying for her apartment?'

'Her family couldn't pay for one night in a motel,' Malcolm said with no small amount of satisfaction.

Once excused, Lydia had left the courtroom

and was probably in the process of fleeing the country. Her act was complete, her performance over, her fee collected. She would never again set foot in Ford County. It's doubtful her presence would have inhibited Malcolm's testimony, but her absence gave him free rein to take all the cheap shots he wanted.

'You're not close to her family?' Ernie asked, a throwaway question.

'Most of them are in jail.'

'I see. She testified yesterday that a couple of months ago she bought a 1968 Ford Mustang. Did you help her with this purchase?'

'I did not.'

'Any idea how this unemployed woman could make this purchase?' Ernie asked, glancing at Danny Padgitt.

'No.'

'Do you know if she's made any other unusual purchases lately?'

Malcolm looked at the jury, saw some friendly faces, and said, 'Yeah, she bought a new color television for herself and a new motorcycle for her brother.'

It appeared as if everyone at the defense table had stopped breathing. The strategy over there had been to sneak Lydia in quietly, let her tell her lies, verify the alibi, get her off the stand, then push the case to a verdict before she could be discredited. She had known very few people in the county and now lived an hour away.

The strategy was unraveling with disastrous

results, and the entire courtroom could see and feel the tension between Lucien and his client.

'Do you know a man by the name of Danny Padgitt?' Ernie asked.

'Never heard of him,' Malcolm said.

'Your wife testified yesterday that she had been having an affair with him for almost a year.'

It's rare to see an unsuspecting husband confronted with such news in such a public manner, but Malcolm seemed to handle it well. 'That so?' he said.

'Yes sir. She testified the affair ended about two months ago.'

'Well, sir, I'll tell you – that's kinda hard to believe.'

'And why is that?'

Malcolm was squirming, suddenly interested in his feet. 'Well, it's really kinda personal, you know,' he said.

'Yes, Mr. Vince, I'm sure it is. But sometimes personal matters have to be discussed in open court. A man is on trial here, charged with murder. This is serious business, and we need to know the truth.'

Malcolm swung his left leg over his right knee and scratched his chin for a few seconds. 'Well, sir, it's like this. We stopped havin' sex about two years ago. That's why we're gettin' a divorce, you know.'

'Any particular reason you stopped having sex?' Ernie asked as he held his breath.

'Yes sir. She told me she hated sex with me,

said it made her sick to her stomach. Said she preferred sex with, you know, other ladies.'

Though he knew what answer was coming, Ernie managed to appear sufficiently shocked. Along with everyone else. He backed away from the podium and huddled with Hank Hooten, just a brief break to allow the jurors to fully absorb the blow. Finally, he said, 'No further questions, Your Honor.'

Lucien approached Malcolm Vince as if he were staring at a loaded gun. He picked around the edges for a few minutes. According to Baggy, a good trial lawyer never asks a question unless he knows the answer, especially with a witness as dangerous as Malcolm Vince. Lucien was a good lawyer, and he had no idea what Malcolm might blurt out.

He admitted he had no affection for Lydia, that he couldn't wait to get through with the divorce, that the last few years with her had not been pleasant, and so on. Typical divorce chatter. He remembered hearing of the Kassellaw murder the next morning. He'd been out the night before and returned home very late. Lucien scored a very weak point by proving that Lydia was indeed alone that night, as she had testified.

But it mattered little. The jurors and the rest of us were still struggling with the enormity of Lydia's sins.

*

After a long recess, Lucien rose slowly and addressed the Court. 'Your Honor, the defense has no other witnesses. However, my client wishes to testify. I want it stated clearly in the record that he will testify against my advice.'

'Duly noted,' Loopus said.

'A very stupid mistake. Unbelievable,' Baggy whispered loud enough for half the courtroom to hear.

Danny Padgitt jumped up and strutted to the witness stand. His attempt at smiling came across as nothing but a smirk. His attempt at confidence came across as cockiness. He was sworn to tell the truth, but no one expected to hear it.

'Why do you insist on testifying?' was Lucien's first question, and the courtroom was still and silent.

'Because I want these good people to hear what really happened,' he answered, looking at the jurors.

'Then tell them,' Lucien said, waving his hand at the jury.

His version of events was wonderfully creative because there was no one to rebut him. Lydia was gone, Rhoda was dead. He began by saying that he had spent a few hours with his girlfriend, Lydia Vince, who lived less than half a mile from Rhoda Kassellaw. He knew exactly where Rhoda lived because he had visited her on several occasions. She wanted a serious romance but he'd been too occupied with Lydia. Yes, he and

Rhoda had had intimate relations on two occasions. They'd met at the clubs at the state line and spent many hours drinking and dancing. She was hot and loose and known to sleep around.

As insult was added to injury, Ginger lowered her head and covered her ears. It was not missed by the jury.

He didn't believe Lydia's husband's garbage about her homosexual tendencies; the woman enjoyed the intimacy of men. Malcolm was lying so he could win custody of their child.

Padgitt was not a bad witness, but then he was testifying for his life. Every answer was quick, there were too many fake smiles toward the jury box, his narrative was clean and neat and fit too nicely together. I listened to him and watched the jurors and I didn't see much sympathy. Fargarson, the crippled boy, appeared just as skeptical as he had with every other witness. Mr. John Deere still sat with his arms wrapped across his chest, frowning. Miss Callie had no use for Padgitt, but then she would probably send him to prison for the adultery as quickly as for the murder.

Lucien kept it brief. His client had plenty of rope with which to hang himself, no sense making it easier for the State. When Lucien sat down he glared at the elder Padgitts as if he truly hated them. Then he braced himself for what was about to come.

Cross-examining such a guilty criminal is a

prosecutor's dream. Ernie deliberately walked to the exhibit table and lifted Danny's bloody shirt. 'Exhibit number eight,' he said to the court reporter, holding it up for the jury to see again.

'Where'd you buy this shirt, Mr. Padgitt?'

Danny froze, uncertain as to whether he should deny it was his, or admit ownership, or try and recall where he bought the damned thing.

'You didn't steal it, did you?' Ernie roared at him.

'I did not.'

'Then answer my question, and please try to remember you're under oath. Where did you buy this shirt?' As Ernie talked he held the shirt in front of him with his fingertips, as if the blood was still wet and might spot his suit.

'Over in Tupelo, I think. I really don't remember. It's just a shirt.'

'How long have you owned it?'

Another pause. How many men can remember when they bought a particular shirt?

'A year or so, maybe. I don't keep notes on clothes.'

'Neither do I,' Ernie said. 'When you were in bed with Lydia that night, had you removed this shirt?'

A very cautious, 'Yes.'

'Where was it while the two of you were, uh, having relations?'

'On the floor, I guess.'

Now that it was firmly established that the

shirt was his, Ernie was free to slaughter the witness. He pulled out the report from the state crime lab, read it to Danny, and asked him how his own blood came to be stained on the shirt. This led to a discussion about his driving abilities, his tendency to speed, the type of vehicle, and the fact that he was legally drunk when he flipped his truck. With Ernie pounding away, I doubt if a case of driving under the influence had ever sounded so deadly. Not surprisingly, Danny had a thin skin and began to bristle at Ernie's pointed and sardonic questioning.

On to Rhoda's bloodstains. If he was in bed with Lydia, with the shirt on the floor, how in the world did Rhoda's blood find its way from her bedroom to Lydia's, a half mile away?

It was a conspiracy, Danny said, advancing a new theory and digging a hole he would never get out of. Too much time alone in a jail cell can be dangerous for a guilty criminal. Well, he tried to explain, someone either stained his shirt with Rhoda's blood, a theory that lightened up the crowd considerably, or, it was more likely that some mysterious person who examined the shirt was simply lying, all in an effort to convict him. Ernie had a field day with both scenarios, but he landed his heaviest blows with a series of brutal questions about why Danny, who certainly had the money to hire the best lawyers around, didn't hire his own expert to come to court and explain the tainted blood exams to the jury.

Perhaps no expert was found because no expert could reach the ridiculous conclusions Padgitt wanted.

Same for the semen. If Danny had been producing it over at Lydia's, how could it arrive at Rhoda's? No problem – it was part of a broad conspiracy to nail him for the crime. The lab reports were fabricated; the police work was faulty. Ernie hammered him until we were all exhausted.

At twelve-thirty, Lucien stood and suggested a break for lunch. 'I'm not done!' Ernie yelled across the courtroom. He wanted to finish the annihilation before Lucien could get his hands on his client and try to rehabilitate him, a task that seemed impossible. Padgitt was on the ropes, battered and gasping for air, and Ernie was not going to a neutral corner.

'Continue,' Judge Loopus said, and Ernie suddenly shouted at Padgitt, 'What did you do with the knife?'

The question startled everyone, especially the witness, who jerked backward and quickly said, 'I, uh, – ' then went silent.

'You what! Come on, Mr. Padgitt, tell us what you did with the knife, the murder weapon.'

Danny shook his head fiercely and looked too scared to speak. 'What knife?' he managed to say. He could not have looked guiltier if the knife had dropped out of his pocket onto the floor.

'The knife you used on Rhoda Kassellaw.'

'It wasn't me.'

Like a slow and cruel executioner, Ernie took a long pause and huddled with Hank Hooten again. He then picked up the autopsy report and asked Danny if he remembered the testimony of the first pathologist. Was his report also a part of this conspiracy? Danny wasn't sure how to answer. All of the evidence was being used against him, so, yes, he figured it must be bogus as well.

And the piece of his skin found under her fingernail, that was part of the conspiracy? And his own semen? And on and on; Ernie hammered away. Occasionally, Lucien would glance over his shoulder at Danny's father with a look that said, 'I told you so.'

Danny's presence on the stand allowed Ernie to once more trot out all the evidence, and the impact was devastating. His weak protests that everything was tainted by a conspiracy sounded ridiculous, even laughable. Watching him get thoroughly decimated before the jury was quite gratifying. The good guys were winning. The jury seemed primed to pull out rifles and form a firing squad.

Ernie tossed his legal pad on his table and appeared ready for lunch, finally. He jammed both hands into his front pockets, glared at the witness, and said, 'Under oath, you're telling this jury you didn't rape and murder Rhoda Kassellaw?'

'I didn't do it.'

'You didn't follow her home from the state line that Saturday night?'

'No.'

'You didn't sneak in her patio door?'

'No.'

'And hide in her closet until she put her children to bed?'

'No.'

'And you didn't attack her when she came in to put on her night clothes?'

'No.'

Lucien stood and said angrily, 'Objection, Your Honor, Mr. Gaddis is testifying here.'

'Overruled!' Loopus snapped at the defense table. The Judge wanted a fair trial. To counteract all the lying done by the defense, the prosecution was being allowed considerable freedom in describing the murder scene.

'You didn't blindfold her with a scarf?'

Padgitt was continually shaking his head as the narrative approached its climax.

'And cut off her panties with your knife?'

'No.'

'And you didn't rape her in her own bed, with her two little children asleep not far away?'

'I did not.'

'And you didn't wake them with your noise?'

'No.'

Ernie walked as close to the witness chair as the Judge would allow, and he looked sadly at his jury. Then he turned to Danny and said, 'Michael and Teresa ran to check on their mother, didn't they, Mr. Padgitt?'

'I don't know.'

'And they found you on top of her, didn't they?'

'I wasn't there.'

'Rhoda heard their voices, didn't she? Did they yell at you, beg you to get off?'

'I wasn't there.'

'And Rhoda did what any mother would do – she yelled for them to run, didn't she, Mr. Padgitt?'

'I wasn't there.'

'You weren't there!' Ernie bellowed, and the walls seemed to shake. 'Your shirt was there, your footprints were there, you left your semen there! You think this jury is stupid, Mr. Padgitt?'

The witness kept shaking his head. Ernie walked slowly to his chair and pulled it from under the table. As he was about to sit, he said, 'You're a rapist. You're a murderer. And you're a liar, aren't you, Mr. Padgitt?'

Lucien was up and yelling. 'Objection, Your Honor. This is enough.'

'Sustained. Any further questions, Mr. Gaddis?'

'No, Your Honor, the State is finished with this witness.'

'Any redirect, Mr. Wilbanks?'

'No, Your Honor.'

'The witness may step down.' Danny slowly got to his feet. Long gone was the smirk, the swagger. His face was red with anger and wet with sweat.

As he was about to step out of the witness box

and return to the defense table, he suddenly turned to the jury and said something that stunned the courtroom. His face wrinkled into pure hatred, and he jabbed his right index finger into the air. 'You convict me,' he said, 'and I'll get every damned one of you.'

'Bailiff!' Judge Loopus said as he grabbed for his gavel. 'That's enough, Mr. Padgitt.'

'Every damned one of you!' Danny repeated, louder. Ernie jumped to his feet, but could think of nothing to say. And why should he? The defendant was strangling himself. Lucien was on his feet, equally uncertain about what to do. Two deputies raced forward and shoved Padgitt toward the defense table. As he walked away he glared at the jurors as if he might just throw a grenade right then.

When things settled, I realized my heart was pounding with excitement. Even Baggy was too stunned to speak.

'Let's break for lunch,' His Honor said, and we fled the courtroom. I was no longer hungry. I felt like racing to my apartment and taking a shower.

Chapter 18

The trial resumed at 3 P.M. All the jurors were present; the Padgitts hadn't knocked one off during lunch. Miss Callie gave me a grin, but her heart was not in it.

Judge Loopus explained to the jury that it was now time for the closing arguments, after which he would read to them his formal instructions, and they should have the case to decide in a couple of hours or so. They listened carefully, but I'm sure they were still reeling from the shock of being so flagrantly intimidated. The entire town was reeling. The jurors were a sampling of us, the rest of the community, and to threaten them was to do the same to everyone.

Ernie went first, and within minutes the bloody shirt was back in play. He was careful, though, not to overdo it. The jurors understood. They knew the evidence well.

The District Attorney was thorough but surprisingly brief. As he made his last appeal for a verdict of guilty, we watched the faces of the jurors. I saw no sympathy for the defendant. Fargarson, the crippled boy, was actually nodding as he followed along with Ernie. Mr. John Deere had uncrossed his arms and was listening to every word.

Lucien was even briefer, but then he had far less to work with. He began by addressing his client's final words to the jury. He apologized for his behavior. He blamed it on the pressure of the moment. Imagine, he asked the jurors, being twenty-four years old and facing either life in prison or, worse, the gas chamber. The stress on his young client – he always referred to him as 'Danny' as if he was an innocent little boy – was so enormous that he was concerned about his mental stability.

Since he could not pursue the goofy conspiracy theory advanced by his client, and since he knew better than to dwell on the evidence, he spent half an hour or so praising the heroes who'd written our Constitution and the Bill of Rights. The way Lucien interpreted the presumption of innocence and the requirement that the State prove its case beyond a reasonable doubt made me wonder how any criminal ever got convicted.

The State had the chance for a rebuttal; the defense did not. So Ernie got the last word. He ignored the evidence and did not mention the defendant, but chose instead to talk about Rhoda. Her youth and beauty, her simple life out in Beech Hill, the death of her husband, and the challenge of raising two small children alone.

This was very effective, and the jurors were absorbing every word. 'Let's not forget about her,' was Ernie's refrain. A polished orator, he saved the best for last.

'And let's not forget about her children,' he said as he looked into the eyes of the jurors. 'They were there when she died. What they saw was so horrible that they will be forever scarred. They have a voice here in this courtroom, and their voice belongs to you.'

Judge Loopus read his instructions to the jury, then sent them back to begin their deliberations. It was after 5 P.M., a time when the shops around the square were closed and the merchants and their customers were long gone. Traffic was normally light, parking was easy.

But not when a jury is out!

Much of the crowd lingered on the courthouse lawn, smoking, gossiping, predicting how long a verdict would take. Others crowded into the cafés for a late coffee or an early dinner. Ginger followed me to my office where we sat on the balcony and watched the activity around the courthouse. She was emotionally wasted and wanted to do nothing but get out of Ford County.

'How well do you know Hank Hooten?' she asked at one point.

'Never met him. Why?'

'He caught me during lunch, said he knew

Rhoda well, said he knew for a fact that she was not sleeping around, especially not with Danny Padgitt. I told him I did not believe for an instant that she was seeing that scumbag.'

'Did he say he dated her?' I asked.

'He wouldn't say, but I got the impression he did. When we were going through her things, a week or so after the funeral, I found his name and phone number in her address book.'

'You've met Baggy,' I said.

'Yes.'

'Well, Baggy's been around forever, thinks he knows it all. He told me Monday when the trial started that Rhoda and Hank were seeing each other. He said Hank's been through a couple of wives, likes to be known as a ladies' man.'

'So he's not married?'

'I don't think so. I'll ask Baggy.'

'I guess I should feel better knowing my sister was sleeping with a lawyer.'

'Why would that make you feel better?'

'I don't know.'

She'd kicked off her heels and her short skirt was even higher up her thighs. I began to rub them, and my thoughts drifted away from the trial.

But only for a moment. There was a commotion around the front door of the courthouse, and I heard someone yell something about a 'verdict.'

After deliberating for less than one hour, the jury

was ready. When the lawyers and spectators were in place, Judge Loopus told a bailiff, 'Bring 'em in.'

'Guilty as hell,' Baggy whispered to me as the door opened and Fargarson came limping out first. 'Quick verdicts are always guilty.'

For the record, Baggy had predicted a hung jury, but I didn't remind him of that, not then anyway.

The foreman handed a folded sheet of paper to the bailiff, who then gave it to the Judge. Loopus examined it for a long time, then leaned down close to his microphone. 'Would the defendant please rise,' he said. Both Padgitt and Lucien stood, slowly and awkwardly, as if the firing squad was taking aim.

Judge Loopus read, 'As to count one, the charge of rape, we the jury find the defendant, Danny Padgitt, guilty. As to count two, the charge of capital murder, we the jury find the defendant, Danny Padgitt, guilty.'

Lucien didn't flinch and Padgitt tried not to. He looked at the jurors with as much venom as he could convey, but he was getting more of it in return.

'You may be seated,' His Honor said, then turned to the jury. 'Ladies and gentlemen, thank you for your service so far. This completes the guilt-or-innocence phase of the trial. Now we move to the capital phase in which you will be asked to decide whether this defendant gets a death sentence or life in prison. You will now return to your hotel, and we will recess until nine in the morning. Thank you and good night.'

It was over so quickly that most of the spectators didn't move for a moment. They led Padgitt out, in handcuffs this time, and his family seemed completely bewildered. Lucien had no time to chat with them.

Baggy and I went to the office where he began typing with a fury. The deadline was days away, but we wanted to capture the moment. Typically, though, he faded after half an hour when the sour mash called. It was almost dark when Ginger returned, in tight jeans, tight shirt, hair down, a look that said 'Take me somewhere.'

We stopped at Quincy's again, where I bought another six-pack for the road, and with the top down and the warm muggy air blowing by us, we headed for Memphis, ninety minutes away.

She said little, and I didn't poke around. She had been forced by her family to attend the trial. She hadn't asked for this nightmare. Luckily, she'd found me for a little fun.

I'll never forget that night. Racing the dark empty backroads, drinking a cold beer, holding hands with a beautiful lady who'd come looking for me, one I'd already slept with and was sure to do so again.

Our sweet little romance had but a few hours left. I could almost count them. Baggy thought the penalty phase would take less than a day, so the trial would end tomorrow, Friday. Ginger

227

couldn't wait to leave Clanton and shake the dust off her shoes, and of course there was no way I could leave with her. I'd checked an atlas – Springfield, Missouri, was far away, at least a six-hour drive. Commuting would be difficult, though I'd certainly try if she wanted me to.

But something told me Ginger would vanish from my life as quickly as she had appeared. I was sure she had a boyfriend or two back home, so I wouldn't be welcome. And if she saw me in Springfield she would be reminded of Ford County and its horrible memories.

I squeezed her hand and vowed to make the most of those last few hours.

In Memphis, we headed for the tall buildings by the river. The most famous restaurant in town was a rib place called the Rendezvous, a landmark owned by a family of Greeks. Almost all of the good food in Memphis was cooked by either Greeks or Italians.

Downtown Memphis in 1970 was not a safe place. I parked in a garage and we hustled across an alley to the door of the Rendezvous. Smoke from its pits boiled from vents and hung like thick fog among the buildings. It was the most delicious smell I had ever encountered, and I, like most other patrons, was famished by the time we walked down a flight of stairs and entered the restaurant.

Thursdays were slow. We waited five minutes, and when they called my name we followed a waiter as he zigzagged around tables, through smaller rooms, deeper into the caverns. He winked at me and gave us a table for two in a dark corner. We ordered ribs and beer and groped each other while we waited.

The guilty verdict was a huge relief. Anything else would've been a civic disaster, and Ginger would've fled town and never looked back. She would flee tomorrow, but I had her for the moment. We drank to the verdict. For Ginger it meant justice had indeed prevailed. For me, it meant that too, but it also gave us another night together.

She ate little, which allowed me to finish my slab of ribs and go to work on hers. I told her about Miss Callie and the lunches on her porch, about her remarkable children, and her background. Ginger said she adored Miss Callie, same as she adored the other eleven.

Such admiration would not last long.

As I had expected, my father was holed up in the attic, which is what he had always called his office. It was really the top floor of a Victorian tower at the front corner of our shabby and ill-maintained home in midtown Memphis. Ginger wanted to see it, and in the darkness it looked much more imposing than in daylight. It was in a wonderful, shady old neighborhood filled with declining homes owned by declining families surviving gamely in genteel poverty.

'What does he do up there?' she asked. We were sitting in my car, with the engine off, at the curb. Mrs. Duckworth's ancient schnauzer was barking at us four doors down.

'I told you already. He trades stocks and bonds.'

'At night?'

'He's doing market research. He never comes out.'

'And he loses money?'

'He certainly doesn't make any.'

'Are we going to say hello?'

'No. It'll just piss him off.'

'When was the last time you saw him?'

'Three, four months ago.' Visiting with my father was the last thing I wanted to do at that moment. I was consumed with lust and anxious to get started. We drove out of the city, into the suburbs, and found a Holiday Inn next to the interstate.

Chapter 19

Friday morning, in the hallway outside the courtroom, Esau Ruffin found me and had a pleasant surprise. Three of his sons, Al, Max, and Bobby (Alberto, Massimo, and Roberto), were with him, anxious to say hello to me. I had spoken to all three a month earlier when I was doing the feature on Miss Callie and her children. We shook hands and exchanged pleasantries. They politely thanked me for my friendship with their mother, and for the kind words I'd written about their family. They were as soft-spoken, pleasant, and as articulate as Miss Callie.

They had arrived late the night before to give her moral support. Esau had talked to her once all week – each juror had been given one phone call – and she was holding up well but worried about her blood pressure.

We chatted for a moment as the crowd pushed toward the courtroom and walked in together.

They sat directly behind me. A few moments later when Miss Callie took her seat, she looked at me and saw her three sons. The smile was like a bolt of lightning. The fatigue around her eyes vanished immediately.

During the trial, I had seen in her face a certain amount of pride. She was sitting where no black person had ever sat, shoulder to shoulder with fellow citizens, judging a white person for the first time in Ford County. I'd also had hints of the anxiety that comes with venturing into untested waters.

Now that her sons were there to watch, pride filled her face, and there was no evidence of fear. She sat a bit straighter, and though she'd missed nothing in the courtroom so far, her eyes darted everywhere, anxious to capture what was coming and finish her task.

Judge Loopus explained to the jurors that in the penalty phase the State would offer evidence of aggravating circumstances in support of its request for the death penalty. The defense would offer mitigating proof. He did not expect it to take long. It was Friday; the trial had already lasted forever; the jurors and everybody else in Clanton wanted Padgitt shipped off so life could return to normal.

Ernie Gaddis correctly gauged the mood in the courtroom. He thanked the jurors for their proper verdict of guilty and confessed that he felt no further testimony was necessary. The crime was so heinous that nothing more aggravating could be added to it. He asked the jurors to remember the graphic photos of Rhoda in the swing on Mr. Deece's front porch, and the pathologist's testimony about her vicious wounds and how she died. And her children, please don't forget her children.

As if anybody could.

He delivered an impassioned plea for the death penalty. He gave a brief history of why we, as good solid Americans, believed so strongly in it. He explained why it was a deterrent and a punishment. He quoted Scripture.

In almost thirty years of prosecuting crimes in six counties, he had never seen a case that so mightily begged for the death penalty. Watching the faces of the jurors, I was convinced he was about to get what he asked for.

He wrapped it up by reminding the jurors that each had been selected on Monday after promising that they could follow the law. He read them the law enacting the death penalty. 'The State of Mississippi has proven its case,' he said, closing the thick green law book. 'You have found Danny Padgitt guilty of rape and murder. The law now calls for the death penalty. You are duty bound to deliver it.'

Ernie's spellbinding performance lasted for fifty-one minutes – I was trying to record everything – and when he finished I knew the jury would hang Padgitt not once but twice.

According to Baggy, in a capital case the defendant, after protesting his innocence throughout the trial and being nailed by the jury, usually took the stand and said he was very sorry for whatever crime he'd been denying all week. 'They beg and cry,' Baggy had said. 'It's quite a show.'

But Padgitt's disaster the day before precluded him from getting near the jury. Lucien called to the witness stand his mother, Lettie Padgitt. She was a fiftyish woman with pleasant features and short graying hair, and she wore a black dress as if she was already mourning the death of her son. Led by Lucien, she unsteadily began testimony that seemed scripted down to every pause in her cadence. There was Danny the little boy, fishing every day after school, breaking his leg falling from a tree house, and winning the spelling bee in the fourth grade. He was never any trouble in those days, none at all. In fact, Danny had caused no trouble at all growing up, a real joy. His two older brothers were always into something, but not Danny.

The testimony was so silly and self serving that it bordered on ridiculous. But there were three mothers on the jury – Miss Callie, Mrs. Barbara Baldwin, and Maxine Root – and Lucien was aiming for one of them. He needed just one.

Not surprisingly, Mrs. Padgitt was soon in tears. She would never believe that her son had committed such a terrible crime, but if the jury felt so, then she would try and accept it. But why take him away? Why kill her little boy? What would the world gain if he were put to death?

Her pain was real. Her emotions were raw and difficult to watch, to sit through. Any human being would feel sympathy for a mother about to lose a child. She finally collapsed and Lucien left her sobbing on the witness stand. What began as a stilted performance ended in a gut-wrenching plea that forced most of the jurors to lower their eyes and study the floor.

Lucien said he had no other witnesses. He and Ernie made brief final summations, and by 11 A.M. the jury once again had the case.

Ginger disappeared into the crowd. I went to the office and waited, and when she didn't show I walked across the square to Harry Rex's office. He sent his secretary out for sandwiches and we ate in his cluttered conference room. Like most lawyers in Clanton, he'd spent the entire week in the courtroom watching a case that meant nothing to him financially.

'Is your gal gonna stick?' he asked with a mouth full of turkey and Swiss.

'Miss Callie?' I asked.

'Yeah. She okay with the gas chamber?'

'I have no idea. We haven't discussed it.'

'She's got us worried, along with that damned crippled boy.'

Harry Rex had quietly involved himself in the case in such a way that one would think he was working for Ernie Gaddis and the State. But he wasn't the only lawyer in town secretly abetting the prosecution.

'It took them less than sixty minutes to find him guilty,' I said. 'Isn't that a good sign?'

'Maybe, but jurors do strange things when it's time to sign a death warrant.'

'So? Then he'll get life. From what I hear about Parchman, life there would be worse than the gas chamber.'

'Life ain't life, Willie,' he said, wiping his face with a paper towel.

I put my sandwich down while he took another bite.

'What is life?' I asked.

'Ten years, maybe less.'

I tried to understand this. 'You mean a life sentence in Mississippi is ten years?'

'You got it. After ten years, less with good time, a murderer sent to prison for life is eligible for parole. Insane, don't you think?'

'But why – '

'Don't try and understand it, Willie, it's just the law. Been on the books for fifty years. And what's worse is the jury doesn't know it. Can't tell 'em. Want some coleslaw?'

I shook my head.

'Our distinguished Supreme Court has said that the jury, if it knows how light a life sentence really is, might be more inclined to give the death penalty. Thus, it's unfair to the defendant.'

'Life is ten years,' I mumbled to myself. In Mississippi, the liquor stores are locked up on Election Day, as if the voters would otherwise get drunk and elect the wrong people. Another unbelievable law.

'You got it,' Harry Rex said, then finished his sandwich with one huge bite. He pulled an envelope off a shelf, opened it, then slid a large black-and-white photo across to me. 'Busted, buddy,' he said with a laugh.

It was a photo of me, making my quick exit from Ginger's room at the motel on Thursday morning. I looked tired, hungover, guilty of something, but also oddly satisfied.

'Who took this?' I asked.

'One of my boys. He was working on a divorce case, saw your little Communist car pull in that night, decided to have some fun.'

'He wasn't the only one.'

'She's a hot one. He tried to shoot through the curtains, but couldn't get an angle.'

'Shall I autograph it for you?'

'Just keep it.'

After three hours of deliberation, the jury slipped a note to Judge Loopus. They were deadlocked and making little progress. He called things to order, and we raced across the street.

If the jury could not reach a unanimous verdict for the death penalty, then, by law, the judge imposed a life sentence.

Fear pervaded the crowd as we waited for the jurors. Something was going wrong back there. Had the Padgitts finally found their mark?

Miss Callie was stonefaced, a look I'd never

seen. Mrs. Barbara Baldwin had obviously been crying. Several of the men gave the impression that their fistfight had just been broken up, and that they were anxious to resume the brawl.

The foreman stood and very nervously explained to His Honor that the jury was divided and had made absolutely no progress in the last hour. He was not optimistic about a unanimous verdict, and all were ready to go home.

Judge Loopus then asked each juror if he or she thought a unanimous verdict could be reached. They unanimously said no.

I could feel the anger rise among the crowd. People were fidgeting and whispering, and this certainly didn't help the jurors.

Judge Loopus then delivered what Baggy later described as the 'dynamite charge,' an off-the-cuff lecture about following the law and keeping promises made during jury selection. It was a stern and lengthy admonishment, loaded with no small measure of desperation.

It didn't work. Two hours later, a stunned courtroom listened as Judge Loopus quizzed the jurors again, with the same result. He grudgingly thanked them and sent them home.

When they were gone, he called Danny Padgitt forward, and on the record, gave him a tongue lashing that made my skin crawl. He called him a rapist, murderer, coward, liar, and worst of all a thief for having taken from two small children the only parent they had. It was a scalding, withering assault. I tried to write it word for word, but it was so compelling I had to stop and listen. A rabid street preacher could not have heaped such abuse upon sin.

If he had the power, he would sentence him to death, and a rapid and painful one at that.

But the law was the law, and he had to follow it. He sentenced him to life and ordered Sheriff Coley to immediately transport him to the state penitentiary at Parchman. Coley slapped handcuffs on him and he was gone.

Loopus banged his gavel and bolted from the courtroom. A fight erupted in the back of the courtroom when one of Danny's uncles bumped into Doc Crull, a local barber and noted hot-head. It quickly drew a crowd and several others cursed the Padgitts and told them to get back to their island. 'Go back to your swamp!' someone kept yelling. Deputies broke it up, and the Padgitts left the courtroom.

The crowd lingered for a while, as if the trial weren't finished, as if justice had not been completely served. There was anger and cursing, and I got a whiff of how lynch mobs got organized.

Ginger didn't show. She said she would stop by the office after she checked out and say good-bye, but she obviously changed her mind. I could see her speeding through the night, crying and cursing and counting the miles until she was out of Mississippi. Who could blame her?

Our three-day fling came to an abrupt end the way both of us expected but neither had

239

admitted. I could not imagine our paths ever crossing again, and if they did it would be another round or two in the sack before we got distracted with life and moved on. She would go through many men before she found one who would last. I sat on the porch outside my office and waited for her to park below, knowing she was probably in Arkansas by then. We'd started the day in bed together, anxious to return to court to watch her sister's murderer get his death sentence.

In the heat of the moment, I began writing an editorial about the verdict. It would be a scathing attack on the criminal laws of the State. It would be honest and heartfelt, and it would also play well with the audience.

Esau called and interrupted me. He was at the hospital with Miss Callie and asked me to hurry down.

She had fainted as she was getting into the car outside the courthouse. Esau and the three sons had rushed her in, and wisely so. Her blood pressure was dangerously high, and the doctor was worried about a stroke. After a couple of hours, though, she had stabilized and her outlook was better. I held her hand briefly, told her I was very proud of her, and so on. What I really wanted was the inside story on what happened back in the jury room.

It was a story I would never get.

I drank coffee with Al, Max, Bobby, and Esau until midnight in the hospital canteen. She had not said a word about the jury's deliberations.

We talked about them and their brothers and sisters, and their children and careers and life growing up in Clanton. The stories poured forth, and I almost pulled out a pen and notepad.

Chapter 20

For the first six months I lived in Clanton, I usually fled the place on weekends. There was so little to do. Other than an occasional goat roasting at Harry Rex's, and one dreadful cocktail party, which I left twenty minutes after I arrived, there had been no socializing. Virtually all the young people my age were married, and their idea of a blowout was an ice cream 'supper' on Saturday night at one of the innumerable churches in town. Most of those who went away to college never came back.

Out of boredom, I occasionally spent the weekends in Memphis, usually at the apartment of a friend, almost never at home. I made several trips to New Orleans where an old girlfriend from high school was living and enjoying the party life. But the *Times* was mine for the near future anyway. I was a resident of Clanton. I had to come to grips with life in a small town, dull weekends and all. The office became my refuge.

I went there on Saturday after the verdict, around noon. I had several stories about the trial I wanted to write, plus my editorial was far from finished. There were seven letters lying on the floor, just inside the front door. This had been a tradition at the *Times* for many years. On those rare occasions when Spot wrote something that prompted a reaction from a reader, more often than not the letter to the editor was hand-delivered and slid under the front door.

Four were signed, three were anonymous. Two were typed, the rest handwritten, one I could hardly read. All seven expressed outrage that Danny Padgitt had escaped with his life. I was not surprised by the town's thirst for blood. I was also dismayed that six of the seven made some reference to Miss Callie. The first one was typed and unsigned. It read:

Dear Editor: Our community has sunk to a new low when an outlaw like Danny Padgitt can rape and murder and get by with it. The presence of a Negro on the jury should wake us up to the fact that these people do not think the way law-abiding white people think.

Mrs. Edith Caravelle from Beech Hill, in a beautiful hand, wrote:

Dear Editor: I live one mile from where the murder took place. I am the mother of two teenagers. How do I explain the verdict to

243

them? The Bible says: 'An eye for an eye.' I guess that doesn't apply to Ford County.

Another anonymous author wrote, on perfumed pink stationery with flowers around the border:

Dear Editor: See what happens when blacks are placed in positions of responsibility. An all-white jury would have strung up Padgitt in the courtroom. Now the Supreme Court is telling us that blacks should teach our children, police our streets, and run for public office. God help us.

As the editor (and owner and publisher) I had complete control over what was printed in the *Times*. I could edit the letters, ignore them, pick and choose the ones I wanted to print. On controversial issues and events, letters to the editor stoked the fires and got folks upset. And they sold newspapers, because that's the only place they could be printed. They were absolutely free and allowed anyone the forum to sound off.

As I read the first wave, I decided that I would print nothing that would harm Miss Callie. And I became angry that people were assuming she had somehow hung the jury and prevented a death sentence.

Why was the town so anxious to blame an unpopular verdict on the only black on the jury? And with no proof whatsover? I vowed to find out what really happened in the jury room, and I immediately thought of Harry Rex. Baggy, of course, would stumble in Monday morning with his customary hangover and pretend to know exactly how the jury split. Odds were he'd be wrong. If anyone could get to the truth, it would be Harry Rex.

Wiley Meek stopped by with the town gossip. Folks were hot in the coffee shops. Padgitt was a dirty word. Lucien Wilbanks was despised, but that was nothing new. Sheriff Coley might as well retire; he wouldn't get fifty votes. Two opponents were already making noise and the election was half a year away.

One story had eleven voting for the gas chamber and one holding out. 'Probably the nigger,' someone had said, echoing the prevailing sentiment at the Tea Shoppe around seven that morning. A deputy guarding the jury room allegedly whispered to someone somebody knew that it was a six-six split, but this was widely discounted around nine o'clock at the coffee shops. There were two primary theories roaring around the square that morning: first, Miss Callie had screwed things up simply because she was black; second, the Padgitts had dropped some cash on two or three of the jurors, same as they had done on that 'lyin' bitch,' Lydia Vince.

Wiley thought the second had more supporters than the first, though many seemed perfectly willing to believe anything. I was learning that coffee shop gossip was useless.

*

Late Saturday afternoon, I crossed the tracks and drove slowly through Lowtown. The streets were alive with kids on bikes, pickup basketball games, crowded porches, music from the open doors of the honky-tonks, laughter from the men in front of the stores. Everyone was outside, sort of limbering up for the rigors of Saturday night. People waved and stared, more amused at my little car than my pale skin.

There was a crowd on Miss Callie's porch. Al, Max, and Bobby were there along with Reverend Thurston Small and another well-dressed deacon from the church. Esau was in the house tending to his wife. She had been discharged that morning with strict instructions to stay in bed for three days and not lift a finger. Max led me back to her bedroom.

She was sitting in bed, propped up with pillows, reading the Bible. She flashed a smile when she saw me, and said, 'Mr. Traynor, so nice of you to come. Please sit. Esau, fetch Mr. Traynor some tea.' Esau, as always, jumped when she gave orders.

I sat in a stiff wooden chair close to her bed. She did not appear to be the least bit ill to me. 'I'm really concerned about lunch next Thursday,' I began, and we laughed.

'I'm cooking,' she said.

'No you're not. I have a better idea. I'll bring the food.'

'Why does that worry me?'

'I'll buy it somewhere. Something a bit lighter, like a sandwich.'

'A sandwich will be fine,' she said, patting my knee. 'My tomatoes will be ready shortly.'

She stopped patting and smiling and looked away for a moment. 'We didn't do a good job, did we, Mr. Traynor?' Her words were filled with both sadness and frustration.

'It's not a popular verdict,' I said.

'It's not what I wanted,' she said.

And that was as close to the deliberations as she would get for many years. Esau told me later that the other eleven jurors had sworn on a Bible not to talk about their decision. Miss Callie wouldn't swear on the Bible, but she gave them her word that she would guard their secrets.

I left her there to rest and went to the porch, where I spent several hours listening to her sons and their guests talk about life. I sat in a corner, sipping tea, trying to keep myself out of their conversations. At times I would drift away and absorb the sounds of Lowtown on a Saturday night.

The reverend and the deacon left, leaving only Ruffins on the porch. The talk eventually came around to the trial, and the verdict, and how was it playing on the other side of the tracks?

'Did he really threaten the jury?' Max asked me. I told the story, with Esau adding emphasis when needed. They were as shocked as those of us who'd seen it.

'Thank God he's locked up for life,' Bobby

said, and I didn't have the heart to tell them the truth. They were extremely proud of their mother, as they had been forever.

I was tired of the trial. I left around nine, drove slowly and aimlessly back through Lowtown, alone and missing Ginger.

Clanton seethed over the verdict for days. We received eighteen letters to the editor, six of which I ran in the next edition. Half of it was devoted to the trial, and this of course stirred things up even worse.

As the summer dragged on, I was beginning to think the town would never stop talking about Danny Padgitt and Rhoda Kassellaw.

Then suddenly, the two became history. Instantly, in the blink of an eye, literally in less than twenty-four hours, the trial was forgotten.

Clanton, both sides of the tracks, had something much more important to fret over.

Part Two

Part Two

Chapter 21

In a sweeping ruling that left no room for doubt or delay, the Court ordered the immediate termination of the dual school system. No more stalling, no more lawsuits, no more promises. Instant integration, and Clanton was as shocked as every other town in the South.

Harry Rex brought me the Court's opinion and tried to explain its intricacies. It wasn't that complicated. Every school district had to immediately implement a desegregation plan.

'This'll sell some newspapers,' he predicted, unlit cigar crammed in his mouth.

All sorts of meetings were instantly arranged around town, and I covered them all. On a sweltering night in mid-July, a public gathering took place in the gym of the high school. The stands were packed, the floor covered with concerned parents. Mr. Walter Sullivan, the *Times*'s lawyer, also served as the attorney for the school board. He did most of the talking because he wasn't elected in any way. The politicians preferred to hide behind him. He was blunt and said that in six weeks the Ford County school system would open and be fully desegregated.

A smaller meeting was held at the black school on Burley Street. Baggy and I were there, along with Wiley Meek, who took photos. Again Mr. Sullivan explained to the crowd what was about to happen. Twice his remarks were interrupted by applause.

The difference in those two meetings was astounding. The white parents were angry and frightened and I saw several women crying. The fateful day had finally arrived. At the black school there was an air of victory. The parents were concerned, but they were also elated that their children would finally be enrolled in the better schools. Though they had miles to go in housing, employment, and health care, integration into the public schools was an enormous step forward in their battle for civil rights.

Miss Callie and Esau were there. They were treated with great respect by their neighbors. Six years earlier they had walked into the front door of the white school with Sam and fed him to the lions. For three years he was the only black kid in his class, and the family paid a price for it. Now it all seemed worth it, at least to them. Sam wasn't around to interview.

There was also a meeting in the sanctuary of the First Baptist Church. Whites only, and the crowd was slightly upper middle class. Its organizers had been raising money to build a private academy, and now suddenly the fund-raising was more urgent. Several doctors and lawyers were there, and most of the country-club types. Their children were apparently too good to go to school with black children.

They were quickly putting together a plan to open classes in an abandoned factory south of town. The building would be leased for a year or two until their capital campaign was complete. They were scrambling to hire teachers and order books but the most pressing concern, other than running from the blacks, was what to do about a football team. At times there was an air of hysteria, as if a 75 percent white school system would pose grave dangers for their kids.

I wrote long reports and ran bold headlines, and Harry Rex was right. The newspapers were selling. In fact, by late July 1970 our circulation topped five thousand, a stunning turnaround. After Rhoda Kassellaw and desegregation, I was getting a glimpse of what my friend Nick Diener said back at Syracuse. 'A good small town weekly doesn't print newspapers. It prints money.'

I needed news, and in Clanton it was not always available. In a slow week, I would run an overblown story on the latest filing in the Padgitt appeal. It was usually at the bottom of the front page and sounded as if the boy might walk out of Parchman at any minute. I'm not sure my readers cared much anymore. In early August, though, the paper got another boost when Davey Bigmouth Bass explained to me the rituals of high school football.

Wilson Caudle had no interest in sports, which was fine except that everyone else in Clanton lived and died with the Cougars on Friday night. He shoved Bigmouth to the back of the paper and rarely ran photos. I smelled money, and the Cougars became front page news.

My football career ended in the ninth grade, at the hands of a sadistic ex-Marine my soft little prep school had for some reason hired to coach us. Memphis in August is the tropics; football practice should be banned then and there. I was running laps around the practice field, in full gear, helmet and all, in ninety-five-degree heat and humidity, and the coach for some reason refused to give us water. The tennis courts were next to the field, and after I finished vomiting I gazed upon them and saw two girls swatting tennis balls with two guys. With the girls in the scene everything was very pleasant, but what really got my attention were the large bottles of cold water they drank whenever they wanted.

I quit football and took up tennis and girls, and never for an instant regretted it. My school played its games on Saturday afternoons, so I was not baptized in the religion of Friday night football.

I happily became a later convert.

*

254

When the Cougars assembled for their first practice, Bigmouth and Wiley were there to cover it. We ran a large front page photo of four players, two white and two black, and another of the coaching staff, which included a black assistant. Bigmouth wrote columns about the team and its players and prospects, and this was only the first week of practice.

We covered the opening of school, including interviews with students, teachers, and administrators, and our slant was openly positive. In truth, Clanton had little of the racial unrest that was common throughout the Deep South when schools opened that August.

The *Times* did big stories about the cheerleaders, the band, the junior high teams – everything we could possibly think of. And every story had several photos. I don't know how many kids failed to make the pages of our paper, but there weren't many.

The first football game was an annual family brawl against Karaway, a much smaller town that had a much better coach. I sat with Harry Rex and we screamed until we were hoarse. The game was a sell-out and the crowd was mostly white.

But those white folks who had been so adamantly opposed to accepting black students were suddenly transformed that Friday night. In the first quarter of the first game, a star was born when Ricky Patterson, a pint-size black kid who could fly, ran eighty yards the first time he touched the ball. The second time he went forty-five, and from then on whenever they tossed it to him the entire crowd stood and yelled. Six weeks after the desegregation order hit the town, I saw narrow-minded, intolerant rednecks screaming like maniacs and bouncing up and down whenever Ricky got the ball.

Clanton won 34–30 in a cliffhanger, and our coverage of the game was shameless. The entire front page was nothing but football. We immediately initated a Player-of-the-Week, with a $100 scholarship award that went into some vague fund that took us months to figure out. Ricky was our first honoree, and so that required yet another interview with another photo.

When Clanton won its first four games, the *Times* was there to stir up the frenzy. Our circulation reached fifty-five hundred.

One very hot day in early September, I was strolling around the square, going from my office to the bank. I was wearing my usual garb – faded jeans, rumpled cotton button-down shirt with rolled-up sleeves, loafers, no socks. I was then twenty-four years old and because I owned a business I was slowly turning my thoughts away from college and toward a career. Very slowly. I had long hair and still dressed like a student. I generally gave little thought to what I wore or what image I portrayed.

This lack of concern was not shared by all.

Mr. Mitlo grabbed me on the sidewalk and

256

shoved me into his small haberdashery. 'I been waiting for you,' he said with a thick accent, one of the few in Clanton. He was a Hungarian and had some colorful history of escaping from Europe while leaving behind a child or two. He was on my list of human interest stories to pursue as soon as football season was over.

'Look at you!' he sneered as I stood just inside his door, by a rack of belts. But he was smiling and with foreigners it's easy to dismiss their bluntness due to translation problems.

I sort of looked at myself. What exactly was the problem?

Evidently, there were many. 'You are a professional,' he informed me. 'A very important man in this town, and you are dressed like, uh, well . . .' He scratched his bearded chin as he searched for the proper insult.

I tried to help. 'A student.'

'No,' he said, wagging an index finger back and forth as if no student had ever looked that bad. He gave up on the put-down and continued the lecture.

'You are unique – how many people own a newspaper? You are educated, which is rare around here. And from up North! You are young, but you shouldn't look so, so, immature. We must work on your image.'

We went to work, not that I had a choice. He advertised heavily in the *Times*, so I certainly couldn't tell him to take a hike. Plus, he made sense. The student days were gone, the revolution was over. I had escaped Vietnam and the sixties and college, and, though I wasn't ready to settle down to a wife and parenthood, I was beginning to feel my age.

'You must wear suits,' he decided as he went through racks of clothes. Mitlo had been known to walk up to the president of a bank and, in a crowd, comment on a faulty shirt and suit combo, or a drab tie. He and Harry Rex didn't get along at all.

I was not about to start wearing gray suits and wing tips. He pulled out a light blue seersucker suit, found a white shirt, then went straight for the tie rack where he picked out the perfect red-and-gold-striped bow tie. 'Let's try this,' he announced when his selections were finished. 'Over there,' he said, pointing to a dressing room. Thankfully, the store was empty. I had no choice.

I gave up on the bow tie. Mitlo reached up and in a skillful flourish had it fixed in a second. 'Much better,' he said, examining the finished product. I looked at myself in the mirror for a long time. I wasn't sure, but then I was intrigued by the transformation. It gave me character and individuality.

Whether I wanted it or not, the outfit was about to become mine. I had to wear it at least once.

To top it off, he found a white Panama hat that fit nicely on my shaggy head. As he adusted it here and there, he tugged at a patch of hair over my ear and said, 'Too much hair. You are a professional. Cut it.'

He altered the slacks and jacket and pressed the shirt, and the following day I arrived to collect my new outfit. I planned to simply pick it up, take it home, then wait and wait until there was a slow day around town and wear it. I intended to walk straight to Mitlo's so he could see me in his creation.

He, of course, had other plans. He insisted I try it on, and when I did he then insisted that I walk around the entire square to collect my compliments.

'I'm really in a hurry,' I said. Chancery court was in session and downtown was busy.

'I insist,' he said dramatically, wagging the finger as if he would not negotiate for a second.

He adjusted the hat, and the final prop was a long black cigar which he cut, stuffed in my mouth, and lit with a match. 'A powerful image,' he said proudly. 'The town's only publisher. Now off.'

No one recognized me for the first half block. Two farmers in front of the feed store gave me a look, but then I didn't like the way they were dressed either. I felt like Harry Rex with the cigar. Mine was lit, though, and very strong. I sprinted by his office. Mrs. Gladys Wilkins ran her husband's insurance agency. She was about forty, very pretty and always well dressed. When she saw me she stopped dead in her tracks, then said, 'Why Willie Traynor. Don't you look distinguished.'

'Thank you.'

'Sorta reminds me of Mark Twain.'

I walked on, feeling better. Two secretaries did double-takes. 'Love that bow tie,' one of them called to me. Mrs. Clare Ruth Seagraves stopped me and talked on and on about something I'd written months earlier and had forgotten. As she talked she examined my suit and bow tie and hat and didn't even mind the cigar. 'You look quite handsome, Mr. Traynor,' she said finally, and seemed embarrassed by her candor. I walked slower and slower around the square and decided that Mitlo was right. I was a professional, a publisher, an important person in Clanton even if I didn't feel too important, and a new image was in order.

We'd have to find some weaker cigars, though. By the time I completed my tour of the square, I was dizzy and had to sit down.

Mr. Mitlo ordered another blue seersucker and two light gray ones. He decided my wardrobe would not be dark like lawyers' and bankers', but light and cool and a bit unconventional. He dedicated himself to finding me some unique bow ties and proper fabrics for the fall and winter.

Within a month Clanton was accustomed to having a new character around the square. I was getting noticed, especially by the opposite sex. Harry Rex laughed at me, but then his own outfits were comical.

The ladies loved it.

Chapter 22

In late September there were two notable deaths in one week. The first was Mr. Wilson Caudle. He died at home, alone, in the bedroom where he'd secluded himself since the day he walked out of the *Times*. It was odd that I had not spoken to him once in the six months I'd owned the paper, but I'd been too busy to fret over it. I certainly didn't want any advice from Spot. And, sadly, I knew of no one who'd either seen him or talked to him in the past six months.

He died on a Thursday and was buried on a Saturday. On Friday I hustled over to Mr. Mitlo's and we had a wardrobe session regarding the proper funeral attire for someone of my stature. He insisted on a black suit, and he had just the perfect bow tie. It was narrow with black and maroon stripes, very dignified, very respectful, and when it was tied and I was properly turned out, I had to admit that the image was impressive. He pulled out a black felt fedora from his personal collection and proudly loaned it to me for the funeral. He said often that it was a shame American men didn't wear hats anymore.

The final touch was a shiny black wooden cane. When he produced it I just stared. 'I don't need a cane,' I said. It seemed quite foolish.

'It's a walking stick,' he said, thrusting it at me.

'What's the difference?'

He then launched into a baffling history of the crucial role walking sticks had played in the evolution of modern European male fashion. He felt passionately about it, and the more worked up he got, the thicker his accent became, and the less I understood. To shut him up I took the stick.

The following day, when I walked into the Methodist church for Spot's funeral, the ladies stared at me. Some of the men did too, most of them wondering what the hell I was doing with a black hat and a cane. In a whisper just loud enough for me to hear, Stan Atcavage, my banker, said behind me, 'I guess he's gonna sing and dance for us.'

'Been hangin' around Mitlo's again,' someone whispered back.

I accidentally whacked the cane on the pew in front of me, and the noise jolted the mourners. I wasn't sure what one did with a cane while one was seated for a funeral. I squeezed it between my legs and placed the hat in my lap. Portraying the right image took work. I looked around and saw Mitlo. He was beaming at me.

The choir began 'Amazing Grace,' and we fell into a somber mood. Reverend Clinkscale then recited Mr. Caudle's basics – born in 1896, the only child of our beloved Miss Emma Caudle, a widower with no children of his own, a veteran of the First War, and for over fifty years the editor of our county weekly. There he brought to an art form the obituaries, which would forever be Spot's claim to fame.

The reverend rambled on a bit, then a soloist broke the monotony. It was my fourth funeral since landing in Clanton. Except for my mother's, I had never attended one before. They were social events in the small town, and often I heard such gems as, 'Wasn't that a lovely service,' and 'Take care, I'll see you at the funeral,' and, my favorite, 'She would have loved it.'

'She,' of course, was the deceased.

Folks took off work and wore their Sunday best. If you didn't go to funerals, then you were downright peculiar. Since I had enough oddities working against me, I was determined to properly honor the dead.

The second death occurred later that night, and when I heard about it on Monday I went to my apartment and found my pistol.

Malcolm Vince was shot twice in the head as he left a honky-tonk in a very remote part of

Tishomingo County. Tishomingo was dry, the tonk was illegal, and that's why it was hidden so deep in the sticks.

There were no witnesses to the killing. Malcolm had been drinking beer and shooting pool, behaving himself generally and causing no trouble. Two acquaintances told the police that Malcolm left by himself around 11 P.M. after about three hours in the tonk. He was in good spirits and was not drunk. He said good-bye to them, walked outside, and within seconds they heard gunfire. They were almost certain he was not armed.

The joint was at the end of a dirt trail, and a quarter of a mile up the road a sentry guarded a passageway with a shotgun. In theory his job was to alert the owner if the police or other unsavory characters were approaching. Tishomingo was on the state line, and there had historically been feuds with some hoodlums over in Alabama. Tonks were favorite places to settle scores and such. The sentry heard the shots that killed Malcolm, and he was certain no car or truck had fled the scene afterward. Any such vehicle would've had to pass by him.

Whoever killed Malcolm had come from the woods, on foot, and carried out the hit. I talked to the Sheriff of Tishomingo County. He was of the opinion that someone was after Malcolm. It certainly wasn't a garden-variety honky-tonk flare-up.

'Any idea who might be after Mr. Vince?' I

asked, desperately hoping that Malcolm had made some enemies two hours away.

'No idea,' he said. 'The boy hadn't lived here long.'

For two days I carried the pistol in my pocket, then, again, grew weary of that. If the Padgitts wanted to get me or one of the jurors, or Judge Loopus or Ernie Gaddis or anyone they deemed guilty of helping send Danny away, then there was little we could do to stop them.

The paper that week was devoted to Mr. Wilson Caudle. I pulled out some old photos from the archives and plastered them all over the front page. We ran testimonials, stories, and lots of paid announcements of sympathy from his many friends. I then rehashed everything I'd written about him into the longest obituary in the history of the newspaper.

Spot deserved it.

I wasn't sure what to do with the story about Malcolm Vince. He was not a resident of Ford County, thus not entirely eligible for an obituary. Our rules were quite flexible when it came to that issue. A prominent Ford Countian who'd moved away would still qualify for an obituary, but obviously there had to be something to write about. One who'd just passed through the county and either had no family or contributed little could not qualify. Such was the case of Malcolm Vince.

If I exaggerated the story, the Padgitts would

get the satisfaction of further intimidating the county. They would frighten us again. (Of those who'd heard of the killing, no one thought it might be the work of anyone other than the Padgitts.)

If I ignored the story, then I would be running scared and shirking my responsibility as a journalist. Baggy thought it was front page material, but there was no room when I was finished with our farewell to Mr. Caudle. I ran it at the top of page three, with the headline PADGITT WITNESS MURDERED IN TISHOMINGO COUNTY. My first headline had been MALCOLM VINCE MURDERED IN TISHOMINGO COUNTY, but Baggy felt strongly that we should use the Padgitt name with the word 'murdered' in the headline. The story was three hundred words.

I drove to Corinth to snoop around. Harry Rex gave me the name of Malcolm's divorce lawyer, a local act who went by the name of Pud Perryman. His office was on Main Street, between a barbershop and a Chinese seamstress, and when I opened the door I immediately knew that Mr. Perryman was the least successful lawyer I would ever meet. The place reeked of lost cases, dissatisfied clients, and unpaid bills. The carpet was stained and threadbare. The furniture was left over from the fifties. A rancid haze of old and new cigarette smoke hung in layers, dangerously close to my head.

Mr. Perryman himself showed no signs of prosperity. He was around forty-five, potbellied, unkempt, unshaven, red-eyed. The last hangover was wearing off slowly. He informed me he was a divorce and property guy, and I was supposed to be impressed by this. Either he didn't charge enough or he attracted clients with little to sell or fight over.

He hadn't seen Malcolm in a month, he said as he looked for a file among the landfill that covered his desk. The divorce had never been filed. His efforts to work out an agreement with Lydia's lawyer had gone nowhere. 'She flew the coop,' he said.

'Beg your pardon?'

'She's gone. Packed up after the trial over there and hit the road. Took the kid, vanished.'

I really didn't care what happened to Lydia. I was much more concerned with who shot Malcolm. Pud offered a couple of vague theories, but they broke down after a few basic questions. He reminded me of Baggy – a local courthouse gossipmonger who'd make up a rumor if he doesn't hear a new one within an hour.

Lydia had no boyfriends or brothers or anyone else who might want to shoot Malcolm in the heat of a bad divorce. And, of course, there was no divorce. The bad blood hadn't even begun!

Mr. Perryman gave the impression of one who preferred to prattle and tell lies all day, as opposed to tending to his files. I was in his office for almost an hour, and when I finally managed to leave I ran outside for fresh air.

I drove thirty minutes to Iuka, the

Tishomingo County seat, where I found Sheriff Spinner just in time to buy him lunch. Over barbecued chicken in a crowded café, he brought me up to date on the murder. It was a clean hit by someone who knew the area well. They had found nothing – no footprints, no shell casings, nothing. The weapon had been a .44 magnum, and the two shots had practically blown off Malcolm's head. For drama, he unholstered his service revolver and passed it over. 'This is a forty-four,' he said. It was twice as heavy as my meager weapon. I lost what little appetite I had.

They had talked to every acquaintance they could find. Malcolm had lived in the area for about five months. He had no criminal record, no arrests, no reports of fistfights, no dice shooting, disturbances, or drunken brawls. He went to the tonk once a week, where he shot pool and drank beer and never raised his voice. There were no loans or bills past due for more than sixty days. There appeared to be no illicit affairs or jealous husbands.

'I can't find a motive,' the Sheriff said. 'It doesn't make sense.'

I told him about Malcolm's testimony in the Padgitt trial, and about how Danny threatened the jury. He listened intently, and said little afterward. I got the clear impression he preferred to stay in Tishomingo County and wanted no part of the Padgitts.

'That could be your motive,' I said when I finished.

'Revenge?'

'Sure. These are nasty people.'

'Oh, I've heard of them. Guess we're lucky we weren't on that jury, huh?'

Driving back to Clanton, I could not erase the image of the Sheriff's face when he said that. Gone was the swagger of a well-armed man of the law. Spinner was truly grateful he was two counties away, and had nothing to do with the Padgitts.

His investigation was dead. Case closed.

Chapter 23

The only Jew in Clanton was Mr. Harvey Kohn, a dapper little man who'd been selling shoes and handbags to ladies for decades. His store was on the square, next door to the Sullivan law firm, in a row of buildings he'd bought during the Depression. He was a widower and his children had fled Clanton after high school. Once a month Mr. Kohn drove to Tupelo to worship in the nearest synagogue.

Kohn's Shoes aimed at the higher end of the market, which was tricky in a small town like Clanton. The few wealthy ladies in town preferred shopping in Memphis, where they could pay higher prices and talk about it back home. To make his shoes attractive, Mr. Kohn put shockingly high prices on them, then slashed them with deep discounts. The local ladies could then throw out any price they wanted when they showed off their latest purchases.

He ran the store himself, opening early and

staying late, usually with the help of a part-time student. Two years before I arrived in Clanton he hired a sixteen-year-old black kid named Sam Ruffin to unpack inventory, move stock, clean the place, answer the phone. Sam proved to be bright and industrious. He was courteous, mannerly, well dressed, and before long he could be trusted to run the store while Mr. Kohn went home every day at precisely eleven forty-five for a quick lunch and a long nap.

A lady by the name of Iris Durant dropped in around noon one day and found Sam all alone. Iris was forty-one years old, the mother of two teenage boys, one in Sam's class at Clanton High. She was mildly attractive, liked to flirt and wear mini-skirts, and usually selected shoes from Mr. Kohn's more exotic inventory. She tried about two dozen varieties, bought nothing, and took her time about it. Sam knew his products and was very careful with her feet.

She was back the next day, same time, shorter skirt, heavier makeup. Barefoot, she seduced Sam on Mr. Kohn's desk in his small office just behind the cash register. Thus began a torrid affair that would change both their lives.

Several times a week, Iris went shoe shopping. Sam found a more comfortable spot upstairs on an old sofa. He would lock the store for fifteen minutes, turn off the lights, and dash up.

Iris's husband was a sergeant in the Mississippi Highway Patrol. Alarmed at the number of new shoes in her closet, he became suspicious. Suspicion had been a way of life with Iris.

He hired Harry Rex to investigate. A Cub Scout could've caught the lovers. Three straight days she walked into Kohn's at the same time; three straight days Sam quickly locked the front door, eyes darting in all directions; three straight days the lights went off, etc. On the fourth day, Harry Rex and Rafe sneaked in the back of the store. They heard noises upstairs. Rafe barged into the love nest and in five seconds gathered enough evidence to send both of them packing.

Mr. Kohn fired Sam an hour later. Harry Rex filed the divorce that afternoon. Iris was later admitted to the hospital with cuts, abrasions, and a broken nose. Her husband beat her with his fists until she was unconscious. After dark, three uniformed state troopers knocked on the door of Sam's home in Lowtown. They explained to his parents that he was wanted by the police in connection with some vague embezzling charge at Kohn's. If convicted he could be sentenced to twenty years in prison. They also told them, off the record of course, that Sam had been caught having sex with a white lady, another man's wife, and there was a contract on his head. Five thousand bucks.

Iris left town disgraced, divorced, without her children, and afraid to return.

I had heard different versions of Sam's story. It was old gossip by the time I arrived in Clanton, but it was still sensational enough to find its way into many conversations. In the South, it was not unusual for white men to keep black mistresses, but Sam's was the first documented case of a white woman crossing the color line in Clanton.

Baggy had been the one to tell me the story. Harry Rex had confirmed much of it.

Miss Callie refused to talk about it. Sam was her youngest, and he couldn't come home. He had fled, dropped out of high school, and spent the past two years living off his brothers and sisters. Now he was calling me.

I went to the courthouse and dug through drawers of old files. I found no record of an indictment against Sam Ruffin. I asked Sheriff Coley if he had an outstanding warrant. He dodged the question and wanted to know why I was poking around in such an old case. I asked him if Sam would be arrested if he came home. Again, no direct answer. 'Be careful, Mr. Traynor,' he warned, but would not elaborate.

I went to Harry Rex and asked about the now legendary contract on Sam's head. He described his client, Sergeant Durant, as a former Marine, an expert marksman with any number of weapons, a career cop, a hothead who was horribly embarrassed by Iris's indiscretion, and who felt the only honorable way out was to kill her lover. He had thought about killing her, but didn't want to go to prison. He felt safer killing a black kid. A Ford County jury would be more sympathetic.

273

'And he wants to do it himself,' Harry Rex explained. 'That way he can save the five grand.'

He enjoyed delivering such dire news to me, but he did admit that he hadn't seen his client in a year and a half, and he wasn't sure if Mr. Durant hadn't already remarried.

Thursday at noon we settled down at the table on the porch and thanked the Lord for the delicious meal we were about to receive. Esau was at work.

As the garden ripened in late summer, we had enjoyed many vegetarian lunches. Red and yellow tomatoes, cucumbers and onions in vinegar, butter beans, snap beans, peas, okra, squash, boiled potatoes, corn on the cob, and always hot corn bread. Now, as the air was cooler and the leaves were turning, Miss Callie was preparing heartier dishes – duck stew, lamb stew, chili, red beans and rice with pork sausage, and the old standby, pot roast.

The meal that day was chicken and dumplings. I was eating slowly, something she had encouraged me to do. I was half through when I said, 'Sam called me, Miss Callie.'

She paused and swallowed, then said, 'How is he?'

'He's fine. He wants to come home this Christmas, said everybody else was coming back, and he wants to be here.'

'Do you know where he is?' she asked.

'Do you?'

'No.'

'He's in Memphis. We're supposed to meet tomorrow, up there.'

'Why are you meeting with Sam?' She seemed very suspicious of my involvement.

'He wants me to help him. Max and Bobby told him about our friendship. He said he thinks I'm a white person who can be trusted.'

'It could be dangerous,' she said.

'For who?'

'Both of you.'

Her doctor was concerned about her weight. At times she was too, but not always. With particularly heavy dishes, like stews and dumplings, she took small portions and ate slowly. The news of Sam gave her a reason to stop eating altogether. She folded her napkin and began talking.

Sam left Clanton in the middle of the night on a Greyhound bus headed for Memphis. He called Callie and Esau when he arrived there. The next day a friend drove up with some money and clothing. As the story about Iris broke fast around town, Callie and Esau were convinced their youngest son was about to be murdered by the cops. Highway patrol cars eased by their house at all hours of the day and night. There were anonymous phone calls with threats and abusive language.

Mr. Kohn filed some papers in court. A hearing date came and went without Sam's appearance. Miss Callie never saw an official indictment, but then she wasn't sure what one looked like.

Memphis seemed too close, so Sam drifted to Milwaukee where he hid with Bobby for a few months. For two years now, he had drifted from one sibling to the next, always traveling at night, always afraid that he was about to be caught. The older Ruffin children called home often and wrote once a week, but they were afraid to mention Sam. Someone might be listening.

'He was wrong to get involved with a woman like that,' Miss Callie said, sipping tea. I had effectively ruined her lunch, but not mine. 'But he was so young. He didn't chase her.'

The next day I became the unofficial go-between for Sam Ruffin and his parents.

We met in a coffee shop in a shopping mall in south Memphis. From somewhere in the distance, he watched me wait for thirty minutes before he popped in from nowhere and sat across from me. Two years on the run had taught him a few tricks.

His youthful face was showing the strain of life on the lam. Out of habit, he continually looked right and left. He tried mightily to hold eye contact, but he could do it only for a few seconds. Not surprisingly, he was soft-spoken, articulate, very polite. And quite thankful that I had been willing to step forward and explore the possibility of helping him.

He thanked me for the courtesies and friendship I'd shown his mother. Bobby in Milwaukee had shown him the *Times* stories. We talked about his siblings, his movements from UCLA to Duke, then to Toledo, then to Grinnell in Iowa. He couldn't live like that much longer. He was desperate for a resolution to the mess at home so he could get on with a normal life. He finished high school in Milwaukee, and planned eventually to go to law school. But he couldn't do it living like a fugitive.

'There's a fair amount of pressure on me, you know,' he said. 'Seven brothers and sisters, seven PhD's.'

I described my fruitless search for an indictment, my inquiries to Sheriff Coley, and my conversation with Harry Rex about Mr. Durant's current mood. Sam thanked me profusely for this information, and for my willingness to get involved.

'There's no threat of being arrested,' I assured him. 'There is, however, the threat of catching a bullet.'

'I'd rather be arrested,' he said.

'Me too.'

'He's a very scary man,' Sam said of Mr. Durant. A story followed, one in which I did not get all the details. Seems as though Iris was now living in Memphis. Sam kept in touch. She had told him some horrible things about her ex-husband and her two teenaged boys and the threats they'd made against her. She was not welcome anywhere in Ford County. Her life might be in danger too. The boys repeatedly said they hated her and never wanted to see her again.

She was a broken woman who was racked with guilt and suffering a nervous breakdown.

'And it's my fault,' Sam said. 'I was raised better.'

Our meeting lasted an hour, and we promised to get together in a couple of weeks. He handed me two thick letters he'd written to his parents, and we said good-bye. He disappeared in a crowd of shoppers and I couldn't help but ask myself where an eighteen-year-old kid hides? How does he travel, move around? How does he survive day to day? And Sam was not some street kid who'd learned to live by his wits and fists.

I told Harry Rex about our meeting in Memphis. My lofty goal was to somehow convince Mr. Durant to leave Sam alone.

Since I was living under the assumption that my name was on a not-so-favored list somewhere on Padgitt Island, I had no desire to have it added to another list. I swore Harry Rex to secrecy, and had no trouble believing he would protect my role as the intermediary.

Sam would agree to leave Ford County, to finish high school up North, then stay there for college and probably for the rest of his life. The kid simply wanted to be able to see his parents, to have short visits in Clanton, and to be able to live without looking over his shoulder.

Harry Rex didn't care, nor did he want to get involved. He promised to relay the message to Mr. Durant, but he wasn't optimistic it would get a sympathetic ear. 'He's a nasty sumbitch,' he said more than once.

Chapter 24

In early December, I returned to Tishomingo County for a follow-up with Sheriff Spinner. I was not surprised to learn that the investigation of the murder of Malcolm Vince had produced nothing new. More than once, Spinner described it as a 'clean hit,' with nothing left behind but a dead body and two bullets that were virtually untraceable. His men had talked to every possible friend, acquaintance, and coworker, and found no one who knew of any reason why Malcolm would meet such a violent end.

Spinner had also talked to Sheriff Mackey Don Coley, and not surprisingly, our Sheriff had expressed doubt that the murder had anything to do with the Padgitt trial over in Ford County. It appeared as though the two sheriffs had some history, and I was relieved to hear Spinner say, 'Ol' Coley couldn't catch a jaywalker on Main Street.'

I laughed real loud and added, helpfully,

'Yeah, he and the Padgitts go way back.'

'I told him you'd been over, snoopin' around. He said, "That boy's gonna get hurt." Just thought you'd like to know.'

'Thanks,' I said. 'Me and Coley see things differently.'

'Election's a few months away.'

'Yes it is. I hear Coley's got two or three opponents.'

'Just takes one.'

Again, he promised to call if something new developed, but both of us knew that was not going to happen. I left Iuka and drove to Memphis.

Trooper Durant had been quite pleased to learn that his threats were still hanging over the head of Sam Ruffin. Harry Rex had eventually delivered the word that the boy was still on the run but desperately wanted to come home and see his momma.

Durant had not remarried. He was very much alone and extremely bitter and embarrassed about his wife's affair. He ranted at Harry Rex about how his life had been destroyed, and worse, how his two sons were subject to ridicule and abuse because of what their mother did. The white kids at school taunted them daily. The black kids, their new classmates at Clanton High, were smug and made wisecracks about it.

Both boys were expert marksmen and avid hunters, and the three Durants had vowed to put a bullet into Sam Ruffin's head if given the chance. They knew exactly where the Ruffins lived in Lowtown. Durant commented on the annual pilgrimage many blacks from the North made at Christmastime. 'If that boy sneaks home, we'll be waitin',' he promised Harry Rex.

He also had some venom for me, and for my heartwarming stories about Miss Callie and her older children. He guessed correctly that I was the family's contact with Sam.

'You'd better get your nose outta this mess,' Harry Rex warned me after his meeting with Durant. 'This is a nasty character.'

I wasn't anxious to have someone else dreaming of my painful death.

I met Sam at a truck stop near the state line, about a mile into Tennessee. Miss Callie had sent cakes and pies and letters and some cash, an entire cardboard box that filled the other seat in my little Spitfire. It was the first time in two years she had been able to touch him in any way. He tried to read one of her letters, but became emotional and put it back in the envelope. 'I'm so homesick,' he said, wiping huge tears while at the same time trying to hide them from the truckers eating nearby. He was a lost, scared little boy.

With brutal honesty, I recounted the conversation with Harry Rex. Sam had naively thought his offer to stay away from Ford County but visit occasionally would be acceptable to Mr. Durant. He had little grasp of the hatred he had inspired.

He did, however, seem to appreciate the danger.

'He'll kill you, Sam,' I said gravely.

'And he'll get by with it, won't he?'

'What difference will that make to you? You'll be just as dead. Miss Callie would rather have you alive up North than dead in the Clanton cemetery.'

We agreed to meet again in two weeks. He was doing his Christmas shopping, and he would have gifts for his parents and family.

We said good-bye and left the dining area. I was almost to my car when I decided to step back inside and use the men's room. It was in the rear of a tacky gift shop next to the café. I glanced out a window and saw Sam, very suspiciously, jump into a car driven by a white woman. She looked to be older, early forties. Iris, I presumed. Some people never learn.

The Ruffin clan began arriving three days before Christmas. Miss Callie had been cooking for a week. She sent me to the grocery store twice for emergency supplies. I was quickly adopted into the family and given full privileges, the highest of which was to eat whenever and whatever I wanted.

Growing up in that house, the children's lives had been centered around their parents, each other, the Bible, and the kitchen table. And for the holidays there was always a fresh dish of something on the table, and another two or three on the stove or in the oven. The announcement

'Pecan pies are ready!' sent shockwaves through the small house, across the porch, and even into the street. The family gathered at the table where Esau rather quickly thanked the Lord yet again for his family and their health and for the food they were about to 'partake'; then the pies would be cut into thick wedges, laid on saucers, and carried off in all directions.

The same ritual was followed for pumpkin pies, coconut pies, strawberry cakes, the list went on and on. And those were just the light little snacks that carried them from one major meal to the next.

Unlike their mother, the Ruffin children were not the slightest bit heavy. And I soon learned why. They complained that they were unable to eat like this anymore. The food where they lived was bland and much of it was frozen and mass-produced. There were a lot of ethnic foods they simply could not digest. And the people ate in a hurry. The list of complaints grew.

My hunch was that they had been so spoiled by Miss Callie's cooking that nothing would ever measure up.

Carlota, who was single and taught urban studies at UCLA, was especially entertaining when telling stories of the latest wacky food trends sweeping California. Raw foods were the current rage – lunch was a plate of raw carrots and raw celery, all to be choked down with a small cup of hot herbal tea.

Gloria, who taught Italian at Duke, was

considered the luckiest of the seven because she was still in the South. She and Miss Callie compared notes on the different recipes for things such as corn bread, Brunswick stew, and even collard greens. These discussions often turned serious, with the men offering opinions and observations, and more than one argument erupted.

After a three hour lunch, Leon (Leonardo), who taught biology at Purdue, asked me to go for a ride. He was the second oldest, and carried a slight academic air that the others had managed to avoid. He had a beard, smoked a pipe, wore a tweed blazer with worn arm patches, and used a vocabulary that he must've spent hours practicing.

We roamed the streets of Clanton in his car. He wanted to know about Sam, and I told him everything. In my opinion, whatever that was worth, it was too dangerous for him to enter Ford County.

And he wanted to know about the trial of Danny Padgitt. I had sent copies of the *Times* to all of the Ruffins. One of Baggy's reports had emphasized the threat made by Danny to the jurors. The exact quote had been highlighted, 'You convict me, and I'll get every damned one of you.'

'Will he ever be released from prison?' Leon asked.

'Yes,' I said, reluctantly.

'When?'

'No one knows. He got life for murder, life for rape. Ten years is the minimum for each, but I'm told weird things happen in the Mississippi parole system.'

'So it's twenty years minimum?' I'm sure he was thinking about his mother's age. She was fifty-nine.

'No one's sure. There is the possibility of good time, which reduces the minimum.'

He seemed as confused by this as I had been. Truth was, no one connected to either the judicial system or the penal system had been able to answer my questions about Danny's sentence. Parole in Mississippi was a vast dark pit, and I was afraid to get too close.

Leon told me that he had quizzed his mother at length about the verdict. Specifically, did she vote for the life sentence, or did she want death? Her response had been that the jury vowed to keep its deliberations a secret. 'What do you know?' he asked me.

Not much. She had strongly implied to me that she had not agreed with the verdict, but it was nothing definite. In the weeks after the verdict there had been an avalanche of speculation. Most courthouse regulars had settled on the theory that three, maybe four, of the jurors had refused to vote for the death penalty. Miss Callie was generally considered not to be in that group.

'Did the Padgitts get to them?' he asked. We were easing into the long shaded front drive of Clanton High School.

'That's the prevailing theory,' I said. 'But no one really knows. The last death penalty in this county for a white defendant was forty years ago.'

He stopped his car and we looked at the stately oak doors of the school. 'So it's finally integrated,' he said.

'It is.'

'Never thought I'd see it.' He smiled with great satisfaction. 'I used to dream of going to this school. My father worked as a janitor here when I was a little boy, and I would come over on Saturdays and walk those long hallways and see how nice everything was. I understood why I wasn't welcome here, but I never accepted it.'

There was not much I could add to this, so I just listened. He seemed more sad than bitter.

We finally drove away and crossed the tracks. Back in Lowtown, I was amazed at the number of fine automobiles with out-of-state tags that were parked tightly in the streets. Large families sat on porches in the frigid air; children played in the yards and the streets. Other cars arrived, all with brightly wrapped packages in the rear windows.

'Home is where Momma is,' Leon said. 'And everybody comes home for Christmas.'

As we stopped near Miss Callie's, Leon thanked me for befriending his mother. 'She talks about you all the time,' he said.

'It's all about lunch,' I said, and we both laughed. At the front gate, a new aroma wafted

287

from the house. Leon froze, took a long whiff, said, 'Pumpkin pie.' The voice of experience.

At various times, each of the seven professors thanked me for my friendship with Miss Callie. She had shared her life with many, had lots of close friends, but for more than eight months had especially cherished her time with me.

I left them late in the afternoon on Christmas Eve as they were preparing for church. Afterward, there would be gifts and singing. There were more than twenty Ruffins staying in the house; I couldn't imagine where everyone slept, and I was certain no one really cared.

As accepted as I was, I did feel the need to leave them at some point. Later, there would be hugs and tears, and songs and stories, and, though I was certainly welcome to experience all of it, I knew there were times when families needed to be alone.

What did I know about families?

I drove to Memphis, where my childhood home had not seen a Christmas decoration in ten years. My father and I had dinner at a Chinese joint not far from the house. As I choked down bad wonton soup I couldn't help but think of the chaos of Miss Callie's kitchen and all those wonderful dishes being pulled from the oven.

My father worked hard to seem interested in my newspaper. I obligingly sent him a copy each week, but after a few minutes of chitchat I could tell he had never read a word. He was concerned with some ominous connection between the war in Southeast Asia and the bond market.

We ate quickly and went in different directions. Sadly, neither of us had given any thought to exchanging gifts.

Christmas lunch was with BeeBee, who, unlike my father, was delighted to see me. She invited three of her little blue-haired widow friends over for sherry and ham, and the five of us proceeded to get tipsy. I regaled them with stories from Ford County, some accurate, some highly embellished. Hanging around Baggy and Harry Rex, I was learning the art of storytelling.

By 3 P.M., we were all napping. Early the next morning, I raced back to Clanton.

Chapter 25

One frigid day late in January, shots rang out somewhere around the square. I was sitting at my desk, peacefully typing a story about Mr. Lamar Farlowe and his recent reunion in Chicago with his battalion of Army paratroopers, when a bullet shattered a windowpane less than twenty feet from my head. A slow news week thus came to a sudden end.

My bullet was either the second or the third in a fairly rapid sequence. I hit the floor with all sorts of thoughts – Where was my pistol? Were the Padgitts assaulting the town? Were Trooper Durant and his boys after me? On my hands and knees I scrambled to my briefcase as shots continued to crack through the air; they sounded like they were coming from across the street, but in the horror of the moment I really couldn't tell. They sounded much louder after one hit my office.

I emptied the briefcase and then remembered

the pistol was either in my car or my apartment. I was unarmed and felt like such a weakling for not being able to defend myself. Harry Rex and Rafe had trained me better.

I was scared to the point of not being able to move. Then I remembered Bigmouth Bass was in his office downstairs, and like most real men in Clanton he had an arscnal close by. There were handguns in his desk and he kept two hunting rifles on the wall, just in case he got the urge to run out and kill a deer during lunch. Anyone trying to get me would encounter stiff resistance by my staff. I hoped so anyway.

There was a pause in the assault, then shouts of panic and chaos on the streets. It was almost 2 P.M., normally a busy time downtown. I crawled under my desk like I'd been taught in tornado warning drills. From somewhere below I heard Bigmouth yell, 'Stay in your offices!' I could almost see him down there, grabbing a 30.06 and a box of shells, ducking into a doorway in great anticipation. I couldn't imagine a worse place for some nut to start shooting. There were thousands of guns within arm's reach around the Clanton square. Every pickup had two rifles in the window rack and a shotgun under the seat. These people couldn't wait to use their guns!

It wouldn't be long before the locals returned fire. That's when the war would really get ugly.

Then the shots resumed. They weren't getting any closer, I decided as I tried to breathe normally under the desk and analyze things. As the seconds slowly ticked by I realized that the assault was not aimed at me. I just happened to own a nearby window. Sirens approached, then more shots, more shouting. What in the world!

A phone rang downstairs and someone grabbed it quickly.

'Willie! You okay!' Bigmouth yelled from the bottom of the steps.

'Yeah!'

'There's a sniper on top of the courthouse!'

'Great!'

'Stay low!'

'Don't worry!'

I relaxed a little and emerged just enough to grab my phone. I called Wiley Meek at home, but he was already headed our way. Then I crawled across the floor to one of the French doors and opened it. Evidently this caught the attention of our sniper. He shattered a pane four feet above me and the glass fell like heavy rain. I dropped to my stomach and stopped breathing for what seemed like an hour. The gunfire was relentless. Whoever he was he was certainly perturbed about something.

Eight shots, each sounding much louder now that I was outside. A fifteen-second pause as he reloaded, then eight more. I heard glass shatter, bullets ricochet off bricks, bullets split through wooden posts. Somewhere in the midst of the barrage, the voices became silent.

When I could move again, I gently pulled one

of the rocking chairs over on its side, then crawled behind it. The porch had a wrought-iron railing around it, and with that and the chair in front of me, I was concealed and protected. I'm not sure why I felt compelled to move closer to the sniper, but I was twenty-four years old and owned the newspaper and knew that I would write a lengthy story about this dramatic episode. I needed details.

When I finally peeked through the chair and the railing, I saw the sniper. The courthouse had an oddly flattened dome, on top of which was a small cupola with four open windows. He'd made his nest there, and when I first saw him he was peeking just above the sill of one of the windows. He appeared to have a black face with white hair, and this sent more chills through my body. We were dealing with a world-class psycho.

He was reloading, and when he was ready he rose slightly and began shooting completely at random. He appeared to be shirtless, which, given the situation, seemed even stranger since it was around thirty degrees with a chance of light snow later in the afternoon. I was freezing and I was wearing a rather handsome wool suit from Mitlo's.

His chest was white with black stripes, sort of like a zebra. It was a white man who'd painted himself partially black.

All traffic was gone. The city police had blocked the streets and cops were darting about, squatting low and hiding behind their cars. In the store windows an occasional face popped out for a quick scan, then disappeared. The shooting stopped and the sniper ducked low and disappeared for a while. Three county deputies dashed along a sidewalk and into the courthouse. Long minutes passed.

Wiley Meek bounded up the steps of my office and was soon beside me. He was breathing so hard I thought he'd sprinted from his house out in the country. 'He hit us!' he whispered, as if the sniper could hear. He was examining the broken glass.

'Twice,' I said, nodding up at the broken panes.

'Where is he?' he asked as he moved a camera with a long-range lens into position.

'The cupola,' I said, pointing. 'Be careful. He hit that door when I opened it.'

'Have you seen him?'

'Male, white, with black highlights.'

'Oh, one of those.'

'Keep your head down.'

We stayed huddled and crouched for several minutes. More cops scurried about, going nowhere in particular and giving the distinct impression that they were thrilled to be there but had little idea what to do.

'Anybody hurt?' Wiley asked, suddenly anxious that maybe he'd missed some blood.

'How am I supposed to know?'

Then more shots, very quick and startling. We

peeked and saw him from the shoulders up, blazing away. Wiley focused and began taking pictures through the long-range lens.

Baggy and the boys were in the Bar Room on the third floor, not directly under the cupola, but not far from it. In fact, they were probably the closest humans to the sniper when he began his target practice. After the shooting resumed for the ninth or tenth time, they evidently became even more frightened and, convinced they were about to be slaughtered, decided they had to take matters into their own hands. Somehow they managed to pry open the intractable window of their little hideaway. We watched as an electrical cord was thrown out and fell almost to the ground, forty feet below. Baggy's right leg appeared next as he flung it over the brick sill and wiggled his portly body through the opening. Not surprisingly, Baggy had insisted on going first.

'Oh my God,' Wiley said, somewhat gleefully, and raised his camera. 'They're drunk as skunks.'

Clutching the electrical cord with all the grit he could muster, Baggy sprung free from the window and began his descent to safety. His strategy was not apparent. He appeared to give no slack on the cord, his hands frozen to it just above his head. Evidently there was plenty of cord left in the Bar Room, and his cohorts were supposed to ease him down.

As his hands rose higher above his head, his

pants became shorter. Soon they were just below his knees, leaving a long gap of pale white skin before his black socks bunched around his ankles. Baggy wasn't concerned about appearances – before, during, or after the sniper incident.

The shooting stopped, and for a while Baggy just hung there, slowly twisting against the building, about three feet below the window. Major could be seen inside, clinging fiercely to the cord. He had only one leg though, and I worried that it would quickly give out. Behind him I could see two figures, probably Wobble Tackett and Chick Elliot, the usual poker gang.

Wiley began laughing, a low suppressed laugh that shook his entire body.

With each lull in the shooting, the town took a breath, peeked around, and hoped it was over. And each new round scared us more than the last.

Two shots rang out. Baggy lurched as if he'd been hit – though in reality there was no possible way the sniper could even see him, and the suddenness evidently put too much pressure on Major's leg. It collapsed, the cord sprang free, and Baggy screamed as he dropped like a cinder block into a row of thick boxwoods that had been planted by the Daughters of the Confederacy. The boxwoods absorbed the load, and, much like a trampoline, recoiled and sent Baggy to the sidewalk, where he landed like a melon and became the only casualty of the entire episode.

I heard laughter in the distance.

Without a trace of mercy, Wiley recorded the entire spectacle. The photos would be furtively passed around Clanton for years to come.

For a long time Baggy didn't move. 'Leave the sumbitch out there,' I heard a cop yell below us.

'You can't hurt a drunk,' Wiley said as he caught his breath.

Eventually, Baggy rose to all fours. Slowly and painfully, he crawled, like a dog hit by a truck, into the boxwoods that had saved his life, and there he rode out the storm.

A police car had been parked three doors down from the Tea Shoppe. The sniper fired a burst at it, and when the gas tank exploded we forgot about Baggy. The crisis stepped up to the next level as thick smoke poured out from under the car, then we saw flames. The sniper found this sporting, and for a few minutes he hit nothing but cars. I was certain my Spitfire would be irresistible, but perhaps it was too small.

He lost his nerve, though, when fire was eventually returned. Two of Sheriff Coley's men stationed themselves on roofs, and when they unloaded on the cupola the sniper ducked low and was out of business.

'I got him!' one of the deputies shouted down to Sheriff Coley.

We waited for twenty minutes; all was quiet. Baggy's old wing tips and black socks could be seen from under the boxwoods, but the rest was hidden. Occasionally, Major, glass in hand, would look down and yell something at Baggy, who could have been dying for all we knew.

More cops sprinted into the courthouse. We relaxed and sat in the rockers, but we did not take our eyes off the cupola. Bigmouth, Margaret, and Hardy joined us on the balcony. They had watched Baggy's descent from the front window downstairs. Only Margaret was concerned about his injuries.

The police car burned until the fire department eventually showed up and doused it. The doors of the courthouse opened and some of the county employees came out and began smoking furiously. Two deputies managed to retrieve Baggy from the boxwoods. He was barely able to walk, and was obviously in great pain. They placed him in a patrol car and took him away.

Then we saw a deputy in the cupola, and the town was safe again. The five of us hurried over to the courthouse, along with the rest of downtown Clanton.

The third floor was sealed off. Court was not in session, so Sheriff Coley directed us to the courtroom, where he promised a quick briefing. As we were walking into the courtroom, I saw Major, Chick Elliot, and Wobble Tackett being escorted down the hall by a deputy. They were obviously drunk and laughing so hard they had trouble staying on their feet.

Wiley went downstairs to sniff around. A body was about to be removed from the courthouse, and he wanted a shot of the sniper. The white hair, black face, painted stripes – there were a lot of questions.

The deputy sharpshooters had evidently missed. The sniper was identified as Hank Hooten, the local lawyer who had assisted Ernie Gaddis in the prosecution of Danny Padgitt. He was in custody and unharmed.

When Sheriff Coley announced this in the courtroom, we were shocked and bewildered. Our nerves were pretty raw anyway, but this was too much to believe. 'Mr. Hooten was found in the small stairwell that leads up to the cupola,' Coley was saying, but I was too stunned to take notes. 'He did not resist arrest and is now in custody.'

'What was he wearing?' someone asked.

'Nothing.'

'Nothing?'

'Absolutely nothing. He had what appeared to be black shoe polish on his face and chest, but other than that he was as naked as a newborn.'

'What type of weapons?' I asked.

'We found two high-powered rifles, that's all I can say right now.'

'Did he say anything?'

'Not a word.'

Wiley said they wrapped Hank in some sheets and shoved him in the backseat of a patrol car. He shot some photos but was not optimistic. 'There were a dozen cops around him,' he said.

We drove to the hospital to check on Baggy.

His wife worked the night shift in the emergency room. Someone had called her, woke her up, summoned her to the hospital, and when we met her she was in a foul mood. 'Just a broken arm,' she said, obviously disappointed that it was not more serious. 'Some scrapes and bruises. What'd the fool do?'

I looked at Wiley and Wiley looked at me.

'Was he drunk?' she asked. Baggy was always drunk.

'Don't know,' I said. 'He fell out of a window at the courthouse.'

'Oh, brother. He was drunk.'

I gave a quick version of Baggy's escape and tried to make it sound as if he'd done something heroic in the midst of all that gunfire.

'The third floor?' she asked.

'Yes.'

'So he was playing poker, drinking whiskey, and he jumped out of a third-floor window.'

'Basically, yes,' Wiley said, unable to stop himself.

'Not exactly,' I said, but she was already walking away.

Baggy was snoring when we finally got back to his room. The medications had mixed with the whiskey and he appeared comatose. 'He will wish he could sleep forever,' Wiley whispered.

And he was right. The legend of Bouncin' Baggy was told countless times in the years that followed. Wobble Tackett would swear that Chick Elliot let go of the cord first, and Chick would argue that Major's good leg buckled first and caused a chain reaction. The town quickly believed that, whoever let go first, the three idiots Baggy left behind in the Bar Room had intentionally dropped him into the boxwoods.

Two days later, Hank Hooten was sent to the state mental hospital at Whitfield, where he would remain for several years. He was initially indicted for trying to kill half of Clanton, but with time the charges were dropped. He allegedly told Ernie Gaddis that he was not shooting at anyone in particular, didn't want to harm anyone, but was just upset because the town had failed to send Danny Padgitt to his death.

Word eventually drifted back to Clanton that he had been diagnosed as severely schizophrenic. 'Slap-ass crazy,' was the conclusion on the streets.

Never in the history of Ford County had a person lost his mind in such a spectacular fashion.

Chapter 26

One year after I bought the newspaper, I sent BeeBee a check for $55,000 – her loan plus interest at the rate of 10 percent. She had not discussed the matter of interest when she gave me the money, nor had we signed a promissory note. Ten percent was a bit high, and I hoped it would prompt her to send the check back. I sent it, held my breath, watched the mail, and sure enough, about a week later there was a letter from Memphis.

Dear William: I enclose your check, which I was not expecting and have no use for at this time. If, for some unlikely reason, I need the money in the future, then we shall at that time discuss this matter. Your offer of payment makes me extremely proud of you and your integrity. What you have accomplished in one year down there is a source of great pride for me, and I delight in telling my friends about

*your success as a newspaper publisher and
editor.*

*I must confess that I was worried about you
when you came home from Syracuse. You
appeared to lack direction and motivation,
and your hair was too long. You have proven
me wrong, and cut your hair (a little) to boot.
You have also become quite the gentleman in
your dress and manners.*

*You're all I have, William, and I love you
dearly. Please write me more often.*

   Love, BeeBee

*P.S. Did that poor man really take off his
clothes and shoot up the town? What
characters you have down there!*

BeeBee's first husband had died of some
colorful illness in 1924. She then married a
divorced cotton merchant and they had one
child, my poor mother. The second husband, my
grandfather, died in 1938, leaving BeeBee with a
nice bundle. She stopped marrying and had
spent the last thirty-odd years counting her
money, playing bridge, and traveling. As the only
grandchild, I was set to inherit all she had,
though I had no clue as to the extent of her
fortune.

If BeeBee wanted more letters from me, then
she could certainly have them.

I happily tore up the check, walked down to
the bank, and borrowed another $50,000 from

Stan Atcavage. Hardy had found a slightly used offset press in Atlanta, and I bought it for $108,000. We ditched our ancient letterpress and moved into the twentieth century. The *Times* took on a new look – much cleaner print, sharper photos, smarter designs. Our circulation was at six thousand and I could see steady, profitable growth. The elections of 1971 certainly helped.

I was astounded at the number of people who ran for public office in Mississippi. Each county was divided into five districts, and each district had an elected constable, who wore a badge and a gun and whatever uniform he could put together, and if he could afford it, which he always managed, he put lights on his car and had the authority to pull over anyone at any time for any conceivable offense. No training was required. No education. No supervision from the county Sheriff or the city police chief, no one but the voters every four years. In theory he was a summons server, but once elected most constables couldn't resist the powerful urge to strap on a gun and look for folks to arrest.

The more traffic tickets a constable wrote, the more money he earned. It was a part-time job with a nominal salary, but at least one of the five in each county tried to live off the position. This was the guy who caused the most trouble.

Each district had an elected Justice of the Peace, a judicial officer with absolutely no legal training, in 1971 anyway. No education was required for the job. No experience. Just votes. The J.P. judged all the people the constable hauled in, and their relationship was cozy and suspicious. Out-of-state drivers who got nailed by a constable in Ford County were usually in for some abuse at the hands of the J.P.

Each county had five supervisors, five little kings who held the real power. For their supporters they paved roads, fixed culverts, gave away gravel. For their enemies they did little. All county ordinances were enacted by the Board of Supervisors.

Each county also had an elected sheriff, tax collector, tax assessor, chancery court clerk, and coroner. The rural counties shared a state senator and state representative. Other available jobs in 1971 were highway commissioner, public service commissioner, commissioner of agriculture, state treasurer, state auditor, attorney general, lieutenant governor, and governor.

I thought this was a ridiculous and cumbersome system until the candidates for these positions began buying ads in the *Times*. A particularly bad constable over in the Fourth District (also known as 'Beat Four') had eleven opponents by the end of January. Most of these poor boys eased into our offices with an 'announcement' that their wives had handwritten on notebook paper. I would patiently read them, editing, decoding, translating along the way. Then I would take their money and run their little ads, almost all of which began with either 'After months of prayer . . .' or 'Many people have asked me to run . . .'

By late February, the county was consumed with the August election. Sheriff Coley had two opponents with two more threatening. The deadline to file for office was June, and he had yet to do so. This fueled speculation that he might not run.

It took little to fuel speculation about anything when it came to local elections.

Miss Callie clung to the old-fashioned belief that eating in restaurants was a waste of money, and therefore sinful. Her list of potential sins was longer than most folks', especially mine. It took almost six months to convince her to go to Claude's for a Thursday lunch. I argued that if I paid, then we wouldn't be wasting her money. She wouldn't be guilty of any transgression, and if I got hit with another one I really didn't care. Dining out was certainly the most benign in my inventory.

I wasn't worried about being seen in downtown Clanton with a black woman. I didn't care what people said. I wasn't worried about having the only white face in Claude's. What really concerned me, and what almost kept me from suggesting the idea in the first place, was the challenge of getting Miss Callie in and out of my Triumph Spitfire. It wasn't built for hefty folks like her.

She and Esau owned an old Buick that had once held all eight children. Add another hundred pounds and Miss Callie could still slide in and out of the front seat with ease.

She was not getting smaller. Her high blood pressure and high cholesterol were of great concern to her children. She was sixty years old and healthy, but trouble was looming.

We walked to the street and she peered down at my car. It was March and windy with a chance of rain, so the convertible top was up. In its closed state, the two-seater looked even smaller.

'I'm not sure this is going to work,' she announced. It had taken six months to get her that far; we were not turning back. I opened the passenger door and she approached with great caution.

'Any suggestions?' she said.

'Yes, try the rear-end-first method.'

It worked, eventually, and when I started the engine we were shoulder to shoulder. 'White folks sure drive some funny cars,' she said, as frightened as if she were flying in a small plane for the first time. I popped the clutch, spun the tires, and we were off, slinging gravel and laughing.

I parked in front of the office and helped her out. Getting in was far easier. Inside, I introduced her to Margaret Wright and Davey Bigmouth Bass, and I gave her a tour. She was curious about the offset press because the paper now looked so much better. 'Who does the proofreading around here?' she whispered.

'You do,' I said. We were averaging three mistakes per week, according to her. I still got the list every Thursday over lunch.

We took a stroll around the square and eventually made it to Claude's, the black café next to City Cleaners. Claude had been in business for many years and served the best food in town. He didn't need menus because you ate whatever he happened to be cooking that day. Wednesday was catfish and Friday was barbecue, but for the other four days you didn't know what you would eat until Claude told you. He greeted us in a dirty apron and pointed to a table at the front window. The café was half-full and we got some curious stares.

Oddly enough, Miss Callie had never met Claude. I had assumed that every black person in Clanton had at one time bumped into every other one, but Miss Callie explained that was not the case. Claude lived out in the country, and there was an awful rumor over in Lowtown that he did not go to church. She had never been anxious to meet him. They had attended a funeral together years earlier, but had not met.

I introduced them, and when Claude put her name with her face he said, 'The Ruffin family. All them doctors.'

'PhD's,' Miss Callie said, correcting him.

Claude was loud and gruff and charged for his food and did not go to church, so Miss Callie immediately disliked him. He took the hint, didn't really care, and went off to yell at someone in the back. A waitress brought us iced tea and corn bread, and Miss Callie didn't like either. The tea was weak and almost sugarless, according to her, and the corn bread lacked enough salt and was served at room temperature, an unforgivable offense.

'It's a restaurant, Miss Callie,' I said in a low voice. 'Would you relax?'

'I'm trying.'

'No you're not. How can we enjoy a meal if you're frowning at everything?'

'That's a pretty bow tie.'

'Thank you.'

My upgraded wardrobe had pleased no one more than Miss Callie. Negroes liked to dress up and were very fashion conscious, she explained to me. She still referred to herself as a Negro.

In the wake of the civil rights movement and the complicated issues it had spun, it was difficult to know exactly what to call blacks. The older, more dignified ones like Miss Callie preferred to be called 'Negroes.' A notch below them on the social ladder were 'coloreds.'

Though I had never heard Miss Callie use the word, it was not uncommon for upper blacks to refer to the lowest of their kind as 'niggers.'

I could not begin to understand the labels and classes, so I adhered strictly to the safety of 'blacks.' Those on my side of the tracks had an entire dictionary to describe blacks, little of which was endearing.

At that moment, I was the only non-Negro in Claude's, and this bothered no one.

'What y'all eatin'?' Claude yelled from the counter. A blackboard advertised Texas chili, fried chicken, and pork chops. Miss Callie knew the chicken and pork would be sub-par, so we both ordered chili.

I got a gardening report. The winter greens were especially nice. She and Esau were preparing to plant the summer crop. The *Farmer's Almanac* predicted a mild summer with average rain – same prediction every year – and she was excited about warmer weather and lunch back on the porch, where it belonged. I began with Alberto, the oldest, and half an hour later she ended with Sam, the youngest. He was back in Milwaukee, staying with Roberto, working and taking classes at night. All children and grandchildren were doing well.

She wanted to talk about 'poor Mr. Hank Hooten.' She remembered him well from the trial, though he had never spoken to the jury. I passed along the latest news. He was now living in a room with padded walls, where he would remain for some time.

The restaurant filled up quickly. Claude walked by with an armload of plates and said, 'Y'all finished, time to go.' She pretended to be insulted by this, but Claude was famous for telling people to leave as soon as they were finished. On Fridays, when a few whites ventured in for barbeque and the place was packed, he put a clock on his customers and said, loudly, 'You got twenty minutes.'

She pretended to dislike the experience – the idea itself, the restaurant, the cheap tablecloth, the food, Claude, the prices, the crowd, everything. But it was an act. She was secretly delighted to be taken to lunch by a well-dressed young white man. It had not happened to any of her friends.

As I gently pulled her out of the car back in Lowtown, she reached into her purse and took out a small scrap of paper. Only two typos that week; oddly, both were in classifieds, an area that Margaret handled.

I walked her to the house. 'That wasn't so bad now, was it?' I said.

'I enjoyed it. Thank you. Are you coming next Thursday?' She asked the same question each week. The answer was the same too.

Chapter 27

At noon on the Fourth of July the temperature was 101 degrees and the humidity felt even higher. The parade was led by the Mayor, even though he was not yet running for anything. State and local elections were in 1971. The presidential race was in 1972. Judicial elections were in 1973. Municipal elections were in 1974. Mississippians loved voting almost as much as football.

The Mayor sat on the rear seat of a 1962 Corvette and threw candy to the children packed along the sidewalks around the square. Behind him were two high school bands, Clanton's and Karaway's, the Boy Scouts, Shriners on mini-bikes, a new fire truck, a dozen floats, a posse on horseback, veterans from every war that century, a collection of shiny new cars from the Ford dealer, and three restored John Deere tractors. Juror number eight, Mr. Mo Teale, drove one. The rear was protected by a string of city and county police cars, all polished to perfection.

I watched the parade from the third-floor balcony of the Security Bank. Stan Atcavage threw an annual party up there. Since I now owed the bank a sizable sum, I was invited to sip lemonade and watch the festivities.

For a reason no one could remember, the Rotarians were in charge of the speeches. They had parked a long flatbed trailer next to the Confederate sentry and decorated it with bales of hay and red, white, and blue bunting. When the parade was over, the throng moved tightly around the trailer and waited anxiously. An old-fashioned courthouse hanging couldn't have drawn a more expectant audience.

Mr. Mervin Beets, president of the Rotary club, stepped to the microphone and welcomed everyone. Prayer was required for any public event in Clanton, and in the new spirit of desegregation he had invited the Reverand Thurston Small, Miss Callie's minister, to properly get things going. According to Stan, there were noticeably more blacks downtown that year.

With such a crowd, Reverend Small could not be brief. He asked the Lord to bless everyone and everything at least twice. Loudspeakers were hanging from poles all around the courthouse, and his voice echoed throughout downtown.

The first candidate was Timmy Joe Bullock, a terrified young man from Beat Four who wanted to serve as a constable. He walked across the flatbed trailer as if it were a gangplank, and when he stood behind the mike and looked at the crowd he almost fainted. He managed to utter his name, then reached into a pocket where he found his speech. He was not much of a reader, but in ten very long minutes managed to comment on the rise in crime, the recent murder trial, and the sniper. He didn't like murderers and he was especially opposed to snipers. He would work to protect us from both.

Applause was light when he finished. But at least he showed up. There were twenty-two candidates for constable in the five districts, but only seven had the courage to face the crowd. When we finally finished with the constables and the Justices of the Peace, Woody Gates and the Country Boys played a few bluegrass tunes and the crowd appreciated the break.

At various places on the courthouse lawn, food and refreshments were being served. The Lions Club was giving away slices of cold watermelon. The ladies of the garden club were selling homemade ice cream. The Jaycees were barbecuing ribs. The crowd huddled under the ancient oak trees and hid from the sun.

Mackey Don Coley had entered the race for Sheriff in late May. He had three opponents, the most popular of whom was a Clanton city policeman named T. R. Meredith. When Mr. Beets announced that it was time for the Sheriff candidates, the voters left the shade and swarmed around the trailer.

Freck Oswald was running for the fourth time. In the prior three he had finished dead last; he appeared headed for the bottom again but seemed to enjoy the fun of it. He didn't like President Nixon and said harsh things about his foreign policy, especially relations with China. The crowd listened but appeared to be a bit confused.

Tryce McNatt was running for the second time. He began his remarks by saying, 'I really don't give a damn about China.' This was humorous but also stupid. Swearing in public, in the presence of ladies, would cost him many votes. Tryce was upset at the way criminals were being coddled by the system. He was opposed to any effort to build a new jail in Ford County – a waste of taxpayer money! He wanted harsh sentences and more prisons, even chain gangs and forced labor.

I had heard nothing about a new jail.

Because of the Kassellaw murder and the Hank Hooten rampage, violent crime was now out of control in Ford County, according to Tryce. We needed a new Sheriff, one who chased criminals, not befriended them. 'Let's clean up the county!' was his refrain. The crowd was with him.

T. R. Meredith was a thirty-year veteran of law enforcement. He was an awful speaker but he was related to half the county, according to Stan. Stan knew about such things; he was related to the other half. 'Meredith'll win by a thousand votes in the runoff,' he predicted. This caused quite an argument among the other guests.

Mackey Don went last. He had been the Sheriff since 1943, and wanted just one more term. 'He's been saying that for twenty years,' Stan said. Coley rambled on about his experience, his knowledge of the county and its people. When he finished, the applause was polite but certainly not encouraging.

Two gentlemen were running for the office of tax collector, no doubt the least popular position in the county. As they spoke, the crowd drifted away again and headed for the ice cream and watermelons. I walked down to Harry Rex's office, where another party was in progress on the sidewalk.

The speeches continued throughout the afternoon. It was the summer of 1971, and by then at least fifty thousand young Americans had been killed in Vietnam. A similar gathering of people in any other part of the country would have turned into a virulent antiwar rally. The politicians would have been heckled off the stage. Flags and draft cards would've been burned.

But Vietnam was never mentioned that Fourth of July.

I'd had great fun at Syracuse demonstrating on campus and marching in the streets, but such activity was unheard of in the Deep South. It was a war; therefore real patriots were supportive.

We were stopping Communism; the hippies and radicals and peaceniks up North and in California were simply afraid to fight.

I bought a dish of strawberry ice cream from the garden ladies, and as I strolled around the courthouse I heard a commotion. From the third-floor window of the Bar Room, a prankster had dropped down an effigy of Baggy. The stuffed figure was hanging with its hands above its head – just like the real Baggy – and across its chest was a sign that said 'SUGGS.' And to make sure everyone recognized the butt of the joke, an empty bottle of Jack Daniel's protruded from each pants pocket.

I had not seen Baggy that day, nor would I. Later, he claimed to know nothing about the incident. Not surprisingly, Wiley managed to take numerous photos of the effigy.

'Theo's here!' someone yelled, and this excited the crowd. Theo Morton was our long-time state senator. His district covered parts of four counties, and though he lived in Baldwin his wife was from Clanton. He owned two nursing homes and a cemetery, and he had the distinction of having survived three airplane crashes. He was no longer a pilot. Theo was colorful – blunt, sarcastic, hilarious, completely unpredictable on the stump. His opponent was a young man who'd just finished law school and was rumored to be grooming himself for Governor. Warren was his name, and Warren made the mistake of attacking Theo over some suspicious legislation that had been 'sneaked through' the last session and increased the state's support for nursing home patients.

It was a bristling assault. I was standing in the crowd, watching Warren blast away, and just over his left shoulder I could see 'SUGGS' hanging from the window.

Theo began by introducing his wife, Rex Ella, a Mabry from right here in Clanton. He talked about her parents and her grandparents, and her aunts and uncles, and before long Theo had mentioned half the crowd. Clanton was his second home, his district, his people, the constituents he worked so hard to serve down in Jackson.

It was smooth, fluid, off-the-cuff. I was listening to a master on the stump.

He was chairman of the Highways Committee in the state senate, and for a few minutes he bragged about all the new roads he'd built in north Mississippi. His committee handled four hundred separate pieces of legislation each session. Four hundred! Four hundred bills, or laws. As chairman, he was responsible for writing laws. That's what state senators did. They wrote good laws and killed bad laws.

His young opponent had just finished law school, a notable accomplishment. He, Theo, didn't get the chance to go to college because he was off fighting the Japs in World War II. But anyway, his young opponent had evidently neglected his study of the law. Otherwise, he would've passed the bar exam on the first try.

Instead, 'he flunked the bar exam, ladies and gentlemen!'

With perfect timing, someone standing just behind young Warren yelled out, 'That's a damned lie!' The crowd looked at Warren as if he'd lost his mind. Theo turned to the voice and said incredulously, 'A lie?'

He reached into his pocket and whipped out a folded sheet of paper. 'I've got the proof right here!' He pinched a corner of the paper and began waving it about. Without reading a single word of whatever was printed on it, he said, 'How can we trust a man to write our laws when he can't even pass the bar exam? Mr. Warren and I stand on equal footing – neither of us has ever passed the bar exam. Problem is, he had three years of law school to help him flunk it.'

Theo's supporters were yelping with laughter. Young Warren held his ground but wanted to bolt.

Theo hammered away. 'Maybe if he'd gone to law school in Mississippi instead of Tennessee then he'd understand our laws!'

He was famous for such public butcherings. He'd once humiliated an opponent who'd left the pulpit under a cloud. Pulling an 'affidavit' from his pocket, Theo claimed he had proof that the 'ex-reverend' had an affair with a deacon's wife. The affidavit was never read.

The ten-minute limit meant nothing to Theo. He blew through it with a series of promises to cut taxes and waste and do something to make sure murderers got the death penalty more often. When he finally wound down, he thanked the crowd for twenty years of faithful support. He reminded us that in the last two elections the good folks of Ford County had given him, and Rex Ella, almost 80 percent of their votes.

The applause was loud and long, and at some point Warren disappeared. So did I. I was tired of speeches and politics.

Four weeks later, around dusk on the first Tuesday in August, much of the same crowd gathered around the courthouse for the vote counting. It had cooled off considerably; the temperature was only ninety-two with 98 percent humidity.

The final days of the election had been a reporter's dream. There was a fistfight between two Justice of the Peace candidates outside a black church. There were two lawsuits, both of which accused the other side of libel and slander and distributing phony sample ballots. One man was arrested when he was caught in the act of spray painting obscenities on one of Theo's billboards. (As it turned out, after the election, the man had been hired by one of Theo's henchmen to defile the senator's signs. Young Warren still got the blame. 'A common trick,' according to Baggy.) The state's Attorney General was asked to investigate the high number of absentee ballots. 'Typical election,' was Baggy's summary. Things came to a peak on that Tuesday, and the entire county stopped to vote and enjoy the sport of a rural election.

The polls closed at six, and an hour later the square was alive and wired with anticipation. People piled in from the county. They formed little groups around their candidate and even used campaign signs to stake off their territory. Many brought food and drink and most had folding lawn chairs as if they were there to watch a baseball game. Two enormous black chalkboards were placed side by side near the front door of the courthouse, and there the returns were tallied.

'We have the results from North Karaway,' the clerk announced into a microphone so loud it could've been heard five miles away. The festive mood was immediately serious.

'North Karaway's always first,' Baggy said. It was almost eight-thirty, almost dark. We were sitting on the porch outside my office, waiting for the news. We planned to delay press time for twenty-four hours and publish our 'Election Special' on Thursday. It took some time for the clerk to read the vote totals for every candidate for every office. Halfway through she said, 'And in the Sheriff's race.' Several thousand people held their breath.

'Mackey Don Coley, eighty-four. Tryce McNatt, twenty-one. T. R. Meredith, sixty-two, and Freck Oswald, eleven.' A loud cheer went up on the far side of the lawn where Coley's supporters were camped.

'Coley's always tough in Karaway,' Baggy said. 'But he's beat.'

'He's beat?' I asked. The first of twenty-eight precincts were in, and Baggy was already predicting winners.

'Yep. For T.R. to run strong in a place where he has no base shows folks are fed up with Mackey Don. Wait'll you see the Clanton boxes.'

Slowly, the returns dribbled in, from places I'd never heard of: Pleasant Hill, Shady Grove, Klebie, Three Corners, Clover Hill, Green Alley, Possum Ridge, Massey Mill, Calico Ridge. Woody Gates and the Country Boys, who seemed to always be available, filled in the gaps with some bluegrass.

The Padgitts voted at a tiny precinct called Dancing Creek. When the clerk announced the votes from there, and Coley got 31 votes and the other three got 8 combined, there was a refreshing round of boos from the crowd. Clanton East followed, the largest precinct and the one I voted in. Coley got 285 votes, Tryce 47, and when T.R.'s total of 644 was announced, the place went wild.

Baggy grabbed me and we celebrated with the rest of the town. Coley was going down without a runoff.

As the losers slowly learned their fate, they and their supporters packed up and went home. Around eleven, the crowd was noticeably thinner. After midnight, I left the office and strolled around the square, taking in the sounds and images of this wonderful tradition.

I was quite proud of the town. In the aftermath of a brutal murder and its baffling verdict, we had rallied, fought back, and spoken clearly that we would not tolerate corruption. The strong vote against Coley was our way of hitting at the Padgitts. For the second time in a hundred years, they would not own the Sheriff.

T. R. Meredith got 61 percent of the vote, a stunning landslide. Theo got 82 percent, an old-fashioned shellacking. We printed eight thousand copies of our 'Election Edition' and sold every one of them. I became a staunch believer in voting every year. Democracy at its finest.

Chapter 28

A week before Thanksgiving in 1971, Clanton was rocked by the news that one of its sons had been killed in Vietnam. Pete Mooney, a nineteen-year-old staff sergeant, was captured in an ambush near Hue, in central Vietnam. A few hours later his body was found.

I didn't know the Mooneys, but Margaret certainly did. She called me with the news and said she needed a few days off. Her family had lived down the street from the Mooneys for many years. Her son and Pete had been close friends since childhood.

I spent some time in the archives and found the 1966 story of Marvin Lee Walker, a black kid who'd been the county's first death in Vietnam. That had been before Mr. Caudle cared about such things, and the *Times* coverage of the event was shamefully sparse. Nothing on the front page. A hundred-word story on page three with no photo. At the time, Clanton had no idea where Vietnam was.

So a young man who couldn't go to the better schools, probably couldn't vote, and more than likely was too afraid to drink from the public water fountain at the courthouse, had been killed in a country few people in his hometown could find on a map. And his death was the right and proper thing. Communists had to be fought wherever they might be found.

Margaret quietly passed along the details I needed for a story. Pete had graduated from Clanton High School in 1970. He had played varsity football and baseball, lettering in both for three years. He was an honor student who had planned to work for two years, save his money, then go to college. He was unlucky enough to have a high draft number, and in December 1970 he got his notice.

According to Margaret, and this was something I could not print, Pete had been very reluctant to report for basic training. He and his father had fought for weeks over the war. The son wanted to go to Canada and avoid the whole mess. The father was horrified that his son would be labeled a draft dodger. The family name would be ruined, etc. He called the kid a coward. Mr. Mooney had served in Korea and had zero patience for the antiwar movement. Mrs. Mooney tried the role of peacemaker, but in her heart, she too was reluctant to send her son off to such an unpopular war. Pete finally relented, and now he was coming home in a box.

The funeral was at the First Baptist Church, where the Mooneys had been active for many years. Pete had been baptized there at the age of eleven, and this was of great comfort to his family and friends. He was now with the Lord, though still much too young to be called home.

I sat with Margaret and her husband. It was my first and last funeral for a nineteen-year-old soldier. By concentrating on the casket, I could almost avoid the sobbing and, at times, wailing around me. His high school football coach gave a eulogy that drained every eye in the church, mine included.

I could barely see the back of Mr. Mooney, in the front row. What unspeakable grief that poor man was suffering.

After an hour, we escaped and made our way to the Clanton cemetery, where Pete was laid to rest with full military pomp and ceremony. When the lone bugler played 'Taps,' the gut-wrenching cry of Pete's mother made me shudder. She clung to the casket until they began to lower it. His father finally collapsed and was tended to by several deacons.

What a waste, I said over and over as I walked the streets alone, headed generally back to the office. That night, still alone, I cursed myself for being so silent, so cowardly. I was the editor of the newspaper, dammit! Whether I felt entitled to the position or not, I was the only one in town. If I felt strongly about an issue, then I certainly had the power and position to editorialize.

Pete Mooney was preceded in death by more than fifty thousand of his fellow countrymen, although the military did a rotten job of reporting an accurate count.

In 1969, President Nixon and his National Security Adviser, Henry Kissinger, made the decision that the war in Vietnam could not be won, or, rather, that the United States would no longer try and win it. They kept this to themselves. They did not stop the draft. Instead, they pursued the cynical strategy of appearing to be confident of a successful outcome.

From the time this decision was made until the end of the war in 1973, approximately eighteen thousand more men were killed, including Pete Mooney.

I ran my editorial on the front page, bottom half, under a large photo of Pete in his Army uniform. It read:

> *The death of Pete Mooney should make us ask the glaring question – What the hell are we doing in Vietnam? A gifted student, talented athlete, school leader, future community leader, one of our best and brightest, gunned down at the edge of a river we've never heard of in a country we care little about.*
>
> *The official reason, one that goes back twenty years, is that we are there fighting Communism. If we see it spreading, then, in*

the words of ex-President Lyndon Johnson, we are to take '. . . all necessary measures to prevent further aggression.'

Korea, Vietnam. We now have troops in Laos and Cambodia, though President Nixon denies it. Where to next? Are we expected to send our sons anywhere and everywhere in the world to meddle in the civil wars of others?

Vietnam was divided into two countries when the French were defeated there in 1954. North Vietnam is a poor country run by a Communist named Ho Chi Minh. South Vietnam is a poor country that was run by a brutal dictator named Ngo Dinh Diem until he was murdered in a coup in 1963. Since then the country has been run by the military.

Vietnam has been in a state of war since 1946 when the French began their fateful attempt to keep out the Communists. Their failure was spectacular, so we rushed in to show how wars are supposed to be run. Our failure has been even grander than that of the French, and we're not finished yet.

How many more Pete Mooneys will die before our government decides to leave Vietnam to its own course?

And how many other places around the world will we send our troops to fight Communism?

What the hell are we doing in Vietnam? Right now we're burying young soldiers while *the politicians who are running the war contemplate getting out.*

Using bad language would be good for a few slaps on the wrist, but what did I care? Strong language was needed to give light to the blind patriots of Ford County. Before the flood of calls and letters, though, I made a friend.

When I returned from Thursday lunch with Miss Callie (lamb stew indoors by the fire), Bubba Crockett was waiting in my office. He wore jeans, boots, a flannel shirt, long hair, and after he introduced himself he thanked me for the editorial. He had some things he wanted to get off his chest, and since I was as stuffed as a Christmas turkey, I placed my feet on my desk and listened for a long time.

He'd grown up in Clanton, finished school here in 1966. His father owned the nursery two miles south of town; they were landscapers. He got his draft notice in 1967 and gave no thought to doing anything other than racing off to fight Communists. His unit landed in the south, just in time for the Tet Offensive. Two days on the ground, and he had lost three of his closest friends.

The horror of fighting could not accurately be described, though Bubba was descriptive enough for me. Men burning, screaming for help, tripping over body parts, dragging bodies off the battlefield, hours with no sleep, no food, running out of ammo, seeing the enemy crawl toward you

329

at night. His battalion lost a hundred men in the first five days. 'After a week I knew I was going to die,' he said with wet eyes. 'At that point, I became a pretty good soldier. You gotta reach that point to survive.'

He was wounded twice, slight wounds that were treatable in field hospitals. Nothing that would get him home. He talked of the frustration of fighting a war that the government would not allow them to win. 'We were better soldiers,' he said. 'And our equipment was vastly superior. Our commanders were superb, but the fools in Washington wouldn't let them fight a war.'

Bubba knew the Mooney family and had begged Pete not to go. He had watched the burial service from a distance, and he cursed everybody he could see and many he could not.

'These idiots around here still support the war, can you believe that?' he said. 'More than fifty thousand dead and now we're pulling out, and these people will argue with you on the streets of Clanton that it was a great cause.'

'They don't argue with you,' I said.

'They do not. I've punched a couple of them. You play poker?'

I did not, but I'd heard many colorful stories about various poker games around town. Quickly, I thought this might be interesting. 'A little,' I said, figuring I could either find a rule book or get Baggy to teach me.

'We play on Thursday nights, in a shed at the

330

nursery. Several guys who fought over there. You might enjoy it.'

'Tonight?'

'Yeah, around eight. It's a small game, some beer, some pot, some war stories. My buddies want to meet you.'

'I'll be there,' I said, wondering where I could find Baggy.

Four letters were slid under the door that afternoon, all four scathing in their criticism of me and my criticism of the war. Mr. E. L. Green, a veteran of two wars, and a longtime subscriber to the *Times*, though that might soon change, said, among other things:

> *If we don't stop Communism it will spread to every corner of the world. One day it will be at our doorstep, and our children and grandchildren will ask us why we didn't have the courage to stop it before it spread.*

Mr. Herbert Gillenwater's brother was killed in the Korean conflict. He wrote:

> *His death was a tragedy I still struggle with each day. But he was a soldier, a hero, a proud American, and his death helped stop the North Koreans and their allies, the Red Chinese and the Russians. When we are too afraid to fight, then we will ourselves be conquered.*

331

Mr. Felix Toliver from down in Shady Grove suggested that perhaps I'd spent too much time up North where folks were notoriously gun-shy. He said the military had always been dominated by brave young men from the South, and if I didn't believe it then I should do some more research. There were a disproportionate number of Southern casualties in Korea and Vietnam. He concluded, rather eloquently:

> Our freedom was bought at the terrible price of the lives of countless brave soldiers. But what if we had been too afraid to fight? Hitler and the Japanese would still be in power. Much of the civilized world would be in ruins. We would be isolated and eventually destroyed.

I planned to run every single letter to the editor, but I hoped there might be one or two in support of my editorial. The criticism didn't bother me at all. I felt strongly that I was right. And I was developing a rather thick skin, a fine asset for an editor.

After Baggy's quick tutelage, I lost $100 playing poker with Bubba and the boys. They invited me back.

There were five of us around the table, all in our mid-twenties. Three had served in Vietnam – Bubba, Darrell Radke, whose family owned the propane company, and Cedric Young, a black guy with a severe leg injury. The fifth player was

Bubba's older brother David, who had been rejected by the draft because of his eyesight, and who, I think, was there just for the marijuana.

We talked a lot about drugs. None of the three veterans had seen or heard of pot or anything else prior to joining the Army. They laughed at the idea of drugs on the streets of Clanton in the 1960s. In Vietnam, drug use was rampant. Pot was smoked when they were bored and homesick, and it was smoked to calm their nerves in battle. The field hospitals loaded up the injured with the strongest painkillers available, and Cedric got hooked on morphine two weeks after being wounded.

At their urging, I told a few drug stories from college, but I was an amateur among professionals. I don't think they were exaggerating. No wonder we lost the war – everybody was stoned.

They expressed great admiration for my editorial and great bitterness for having been sent over there. Each of the three had been scarred in some way; Cedric's was obvious. Bubba's and Darrel's was more of a smoldering anger, a barely contained rage and desire to lash out, but at whom?

Late in the game, they began swapping stories of gruesome battlefield scenes. I had heard that many soldiers refused to talk about their war experiences. Those three didn't mind at all. It was therapeutic.

They played poker almost every Thursday

night, and I was always welcome. When I left them at midnight, they were still drinking, still smoking pot, still talking about Vietnam. I'd had enough of the war for one day.

Chapter 29

The following week I devoted an entire page to the war controversy I had created. It was covered with letters to the editor, seventeen in all, only two of which were even somewhat supportive of my antiwar feelings. I was called a Communist, a liberal, a traitor, a carpetbagger, and, the worst, a coward because I had not worn the uniform. Every letter was proudly signed, no anonymous mail that week; these folks were fired-up patriots who disliked me and wanted the county to know it.

I didn't care. I had stirred up a hornet's nest and the town was at least debating the war. Most of the debates were one-sided, but I had aroused strong feelings.

The response to those seventeen letters was astounding. A group of high school students came to my rescue with a hand-delivered batch of their own. They were passionately against the war, had no plans to go fight in it, and, furthermore, found it odd that most of the letters the prior week were from folks too old for the armed forces. 'It's our blood, not yours,' was my favorite line.

Many of the the students singled out particular letters I'd printed and went after them with a hatchet. Becky Jenkins was offended by Mr. Robert Earl Huff's statement that '. . . our nation was built by the blood of our soldiers. Wars will always be with us.'

She responded: 'Wars will be with us as long as ignorant and greedy men try to impose their will on others.'

Kirk Wallace took exception to Mrs. Mattie Louise Ferguson's rather exhaustive description of me. In his final paragraph he wrote, 'Sadly, Mrs. Ferguson would not know a Communist, a liberal, a traitor, or a carpetbagger if she met one. Life out in Possum Ridge protects her from such people.'

The following week, I devoted yet another full page to the thirty-one letters from the students. There were also three late arrivals from the warmongering crowd, and I printed them too. The response was another flood of letters, all of which I printed.

Through the pages of the *Times*, we fought the war until Christmas when everyone suddenly called a truce and settled in for the holidays.

Mr. Max Hocutt died on New Year's Day 1972. Gilma knocked on my apartment window early that morning and eventually got me to the door. I'd been asleep for less than five hours, and I needed a full day of hard sleep. Maybe two.

I followed her into the old mansion, my first visit inside in many months, and I was shocked at how badly it was deteriorating. But there were more urgent matters. We walked to the main stairway in the front foyer where Wilma joined us. She pointed a crooked and wrinkled finger upward and said, 'He's up there. First door on the right. We've already been up once this morning.'

Once a day up the stairs was their limit. They now were in their late seventies, and not far behind Mr. Max.

He was lying in a large bed with a dirty white sheet pulled up to his neck. His skin was the color of the sheet. I stood beside him for a moment to make sure he wasn't breathing. I had never been called upon to pronounce someone dead, but this was not a close call – Mr. Max looked as though he'd been dead for a month.

I walked back down the stairs where Wilma and Gilma were waiting right where I'd left them. They looked at me as if I might have a different diagnosis.

'I'm afraid he's dead,' I said.

'We know that,' Gilma said.

'Tell us what to do,' Wilma said.

This was the first corpse I'd been called upon

337

to process, but the next step seemed pretty obvious. 'Well, perhaps we should call Mr. Magargel down at the funeral home.'

'I told you so,' Wilma said to Gilma.

They didn't move, so I went to the phone and called Mr. Magargel. 'It's New Year's Day,' he said. It was apparent my call had awakened him.

'He's still dead,' I said.

'Are you sure?'

'Yes, I'm sure. I just saw him.'

'Where is he?'

'In bed. He went peacefully.'

'Sometimes these old geezers are just sleeping soundly, you know.'

I turned away from the twins so they wouldn't hear me argue about whether their brother was really dead. 'He's not sleeping, Mr. Magargel. He's dead.'

'I'll be there in an hour.'

'Is there anything else we should do?' I asked.

'Like what?'

'I don't know. Notify the police, something like that?'

'Was he murdered?'

'No.'

'Why would you want to call the police?'

'Sorry I asked.'

They invited me into the kitchen for a cup of instant coffee. On the counter was a box of Cream of Wheat, and beside it a large bowl of the cereal, mixed and ready to eat. Evidently,

Wilma or Gilma had prepared breakfast for their brother, and when he didn't come down they went after him.

The coffee was undrinkable until I poured in sugar. They sat across the narrow prep table, watching me curiously. Their eyes were red, but they were not crying.

'We can't live here,' Wilma said, with the finality that came from years of discussion.

'We want you to buy the place,' Gilma added. One barely finished a sentence before the other started another one.

'We sell it to you . . .'

'For a hundred thousand . . .'

'We take the money . . .'

'And move to Florida . . .'

'Florida?' I asked.

'We have a cousin there . . .'

'She lives in a retirement village . . .'

'It's very lovely . . .'

'And they take such good care of you . . .'

'And Melberta is nearby.'

Melberta? I thought she was still around the house somewhere, sneaking through the shadows. They explained that they had placed her in a 'home' a few months back. The 'home' was somewhere north of Tampa. That's where they wanted to go and spend the rest of their days. Their beloved mansion was simply too much for them to maintain. They had bad hips, bad knees, bad eyes. They climbed the stairs once a day – 'twenty-four steps' Gilma informed me – and were terrified of falling down and killing themselves. There wasn't enough money to make it safe, and what money they had they didn't want to waste on housekeepers, grass-cutters, and, now, a driver.

'We want you to buy the Mercedes too . . .'

'We don't drive, you know . . .'

'Max always took us . . .'

Once in a while, just for fun, I would sneak a glance at the odometer of Max's Mercedes. He was averaging less than a thousand miles per year. Unlike the house, the car was in mint condition.

The house had six bedrooms, four floors and a basement, four or five bathrooms, living and dining rooms, library, kitchen, wide sweeping porches that were falling in, and an attic that I felt certain was crammed with family treasures buried there centuries ago. It would take months just to clean it before the remodelers moved in. A hundred thousand dollars was a low price for such a mansion, but there were not enough newspapers sold in the entire state to renovate the place.

And what about all those animals? Cats, birds, rabbits, squirrels, goldfish, the place was a regular zoo.

I had been looking at real estate, but, frankly, I'd been so spoiled by paying them $50 a month that I found it hard to leave. I was twenty-four years old, very single, and I was having a grand time watching the money accumulate in the bank. Why would I risk financial ruin by buying that money pit?

I bought it two days after the funeral.

On a cold, wet Thursday in February, I pulled to a stop in front of the Ruffin residence in Lowtown. Esau was waiting on the porch. 'You trade cars?' he asked, looking at the street.

'No, I still have the little one,' I said. 'That was Mr. Hocutt's.'

'Thought it was black.' There were very few Mercedes in Ford County and it was not difficult keeping track of them.

'It needed painting,' I said. It was now a dark maroon. I had to cover the knives Mr. Hocutt had painted on both front doors, and so while it was in the shop I decided to go with a different color altogether.

Word was out that I had somehow swindled the Hocutts out of their Mercedes. In fact, I had paid blue-book value for it – $9,500. The purchase was approved by Judge Reuben V. Atlee, the longtime chancellor in Ford County. He also approved my purchase of the house for $100,000, an apparently low figure that looked much better after two court-appointed appraisers gave their estimates at $75,000 and $85,000. One reported that any renovation of the Hocutt House would '. . . involve extensive and unforeseen expenditures.'

Harry Rex, my lawyer, made sure I saw this language.

Esau was subdued, and things did not improve inside. The house, as always, simmered in the sauce of some delicious beast she was roasting in the oven. Today it would be rabbit.

I hugged Miss Callie and knew something was terribly wrong. Esau picked up an envelope and said, 'This is a draft notice. For Sam.' He tossed it on the table for me to see, then left the kitchen.

Talk was slow over lunch. They were subdued, preoccupied, and very confused. Esau at times felt the proper thing to do was for Sam to honor whatever commitment his country required. Miss Callie felt like she had already lost Sam once. The thought of losing him again was unbearable.

That night I called Sam and gave him the bad news. He was in Toledo spending a few days with Max. We talked for over an hour, and I was relentless in my conviction that he had no business going to Vietnam. Fortunately, Max felt the same way.

Over the course of the next week, I spent hours on the phone with Sam, Bobby, Al, Leon, Max, and Mario, as we shared our views about what Sam should do. Neither he nor any of his brothers believed the war was just, but Mario and Al felt strongly that it was wrong to break the law. I was by far the biggest dove in the bunch, with Bobby and Leon somewhere in the middle. Sam seemed to twist in the wind and change daily. It was a gut-wrenching decision, but as the days dragged on he appeared to spend more time talking to me. The fact that he had been on the run for two years helped immensely.

After two weeks of soul-searching, Sam slipped into the underground and surfaced in Ontario. He called collect one night and asked me to tell his parents he was okay. Early the next morning, I drove to Lowtown and delivered the news to Esau and Miss Callie that their youngest son had just made the smartest decision of his life.

To them, Canada seemed like a million miles away. Not nearly as far as Vietnam, I told them.

Chapter 30

The second contractor I hired to transform the Hocutt House was Mr. Lester Klump from out in Shady Grove. He had been highly recommended by Baggy, who, of course, knew exactly how to restore a mansion. Stan Atcavage at the bank also recommended Mr. Klump, and since Stan held the mortgage for $100,000 I listened to him.

The first contractor had failed to show, and when I called after waiting for three days his phone had been disconnected. An ominous sign.

Mr. Klump and his son, Lester Junior, spent days going over the house. They were terrified of the project, and knew it would be a regular nightmare if anybody got in a hurry, especially me. They were slow and methodical, even talked slower than most folks in Ford County, and I soon realized that everything they did was in second gear. I probably didn't help matters by explaining that I was already living in very comfortable quarters on the premises; thus I wasn't going to be homeless if they didn't hurry up.

Their reputation was that they were sober and generally finished on time. This put them at the top of the heap in the world of remodeling.

After a few days of scratching our heads and kicking at the gravel, we agreed on a plan whereby they would bill me weekly for their labor and supplies, and I would add 10 percent for their 'overhead,' which I hoped meant profit. It took a week of cursing to get Harry Rex to draft a contract reflecting this. At first he refused and called me all sorts of colorful names.

The Klumps would begin with the cleanup and demolition, then do the roof and porches. When that was over, we'd sit down and plan the next phase. In April 1972 the project began.

At least one of the Klumps appeared every day with a crew. They spent the first month scattering all the varmints and wildlife that had made the property home for decades.

A carload of high school seniors was stopped by a state trooper a few hours after their graduation. The car was full of beer, and the trooper, a rookie fresh from school where they had alerted them to such things, smelled something odd. Drugs had finally made it to Ford County.

There was marijuana in the car. All six students were charged with felony possession and every other crime the cops could possibly throw at them. The town was shocked – how could our innocent little community get infiltrated with drugs? How could we stop it? I low-keyed the story in the paper; no sense beating up on six good kids who'd made a mistake. Sheriff Meredith was quoted as saying that his office would act decisively to 'remove this scourge' from our community. 'This ain't California,' he said.

Typically, everybody in Clanton was suddenly on the lookout for drug dealers, though no one was quite sure what they looked like.

Because the cops were on high alert, and would love nothing more than another drug bust, poker the next Thursday was moved to a different location, one deep in the country. Bubba Crockett and Darrell Radke lived in a dilapidated old cabin with a nonpoker-playing veteran named Ollie Hinds. They called their place the Foxhole. It was hidden in a heavily wooded ravine at the end of a dirt road that you couldn't find in broad daylight.

Ollie Hinds was suffering from every manner of postwar trauma and probably several prewar ones as well. He was from Minnesota and had served with Bubba and survived their horrible nightmares. He had been shot, burned, captured briefly, escaped, and finally sent home when an Army shrink said he was in need of serious help. Apparently he never got it. When I met him he was shirtless, revealing scars and tattoos, and glassy-eyed, which, I would soon learn, was his usual condition.

I was grateful he was not playing poker. A couple of bad hands, and you got the impression he might pull an M-16 and even the score.

The drug bust, and the town's reaction to it, was the source of much humor and ridicule. Folks were acting as though the six teenagers were the very first drug users, and since they'd been caught then the county was on top of the crisis. With some vigilance and tough talk, the plague of illegal drugs could be diverted to another part of the country.

Nixon had mined the harbor at Haiphong and was bombing Hanoi with a fury. I brought this up to get a reaction, but there was little interest in the war that night.

Darrell had heard a rumor that some black kid from Clanton had been drafted and fled to Canada. I said nothing.

'Smart boy,' Bubba said. 'Smart boy.'

The conversation soon returned to drugs. At one point Bubba admired his marijuana cigarette and said, 'Man, this is really smooth. Didn't come from the Padgitts.'

'Came from Memphis,' Darrell said. 'Mexican.'

Since I knew zero about the local drug supply routes, I listened intently for a few seconds then, when it was evident no one would pursue the conversation, said, 'I thought the Padgitts produced pretty good stuff.'

'They should stick to moonshine,' Bubba said.

'It's okay,' Darrell said, 'if you can't get

anything else. They struck it rich a few years back. They started growin' long before anybody else around here. Now they got competition.'

'I hear they're cuttin' back, goin' back to whiskey and stealin' cars,' Bubba said.

'Why?' I asked.

'A lot more narcs now. State, federal, local. They got helicopters and surveillance stuff. Ain't like Mexico where nobody gives a shit what you grow.'

Gunfire erupted outside, not too far away. The others were not fazed by it. 'What might that be?' I asked.

'It's Ollie,' Darrell said. 'After a possum. He puts on night-vision goggles, takes his M-16, goes lookin' for varmints and such. Calls it gook huntin'.'

I luckily lost three hands in a row and found the perfect moment to say good night.

After much delay, the Supreme Court of Mississippi finally affirmed the conviction of Danny Padgitt. Four months earlier it had ruled, by a majority of six to three, that the conviction would stand. Lucien Wilbanks filed a petition for rehearing, which was granted. Harry Rex thought that might signal trouble.

The appeal was reheard, and almost two years after his trial the court finally settled the matter. The vote to affirm the conviction was five to four.

The dissent bought into Lucien's rather

vociferous argument that Ernie Gaddis had been given too much freedom in abusing Danny Padgitt on cross-examination. With his leading questions about the presence of Rhoda's children in the bedroom, watching the rape, Ernie had effectively been allowed to place before the jury highly prejudicial facts that simply were not in evidence.

Harry Rex had read all the briefs and monitored the appeal for me, and he was concerned that Wilbanks had a legitimate argument. If five justices believed it, then the case would be sent back to Clanton for another trial. On the one hand another trial would be good for the newspaper. On the other, I didn't want the Padgitts off their island and running around Clanton causing trouble.

In the end, though, only four justices dissented, and the case was over. I plastered the good news across the front of the *Times* and hoped I would never again hear the name of Danny Padgitt.

Part Three

Chapter 31

Five years and two months after Lester Klump, Sr., and Lester Klump, Jr., first set foot in the Hocutt House, they finished the renovation. The ordeal was over, and the results were splendid.

Once I accepted their languid pace, I settled in for the long haul and worked hard selling ad copy. Twice, during the last year of the project, I had unwisely attempted to live in the house and somehow exist in the midst of the debris. In doing so I had little trouble with the dust, the paint fumes, the blocked hallways, the erratic electricity and hot water, and the absence of heating and air conditioning, but I could never adapt to the early morning hammers and handsaws. They were not early birds, which, as I learned, was unusual for contractors, but they did start in earnest each morning by eight-thirty. I really enjoyed sleeping until ten. The arrangement didn't work, and after each attempt to live in the big house I sneaked back across the gravel drive and returned to the apartment, where things were somewhat quieter.

Only once in five years was I unable to pay the Klumps on time. I refused to borrow money for the project, though Stan Atcavage was always ready to loan it. After work each Friday I would sit down with Lester Senior, usually on a make-shift plywood table in a hallway, and over a cold beer we would tally up the labor and materials for the week, add 10 percent, and I would write him a check. I filed his records away, and for the first two years kept a running total of the cost of the renovation. After two years, though, I stopped adding the weekly to the cumulative. I didn't want to know what it was costing.

I was broke but I didn't care. The money pit had been sealed off; I had teetered on the brink of insolvency, dodged it, and now I could begin stashing it away again.

And I had something magnificent to show for the time, effort, and investment. The house had been built around 1900 by Dr. Miles Hocutt. It had a distinctive Victorian style, with two high gabled roofs in the front, a turret that ran up four levels, and wide covered porches that swept around the house on both sides. Over the years the Hocutts had painted the house blue and yellow, and Mr. Klump, Sr., had even found an area of bright red under three coats of newer paint. I played it safe and stayed with white and beige and light brown trim. The roof was copper.

Outside it was a rather plain Victorian, but I would have years to jazz it up.

Inside, the heart-pine floors on all three levels had been restored to their original beauty. Walls had been removed, rooms and hallways opened up. The Klumps had finally been forced to remove the entire kitchen and build another from the basement up. The fireplace in the living room had actually collapsed under the pressure of relentless jackhammering. I turned the library into a den and knocked out more walls so that upon entering the front foyer you could see through the den to the kitchen in the distance. I added windows everywhere; the house had originally been built like a cave.

Mr. Klump admitted he had never tasted champagne, but he happily chugged it down as we completed our little ceremony on a side porch. I handed him what I hoped would be his last check, we shook hands, posed for a photograph by Wiley Meek, then popped the cork.

Many of the rooms were bare; it would take years to properly decorate the place, and it would require the assistance of someone with far more knowledge and taste than I possessed. Half-empty, though, the house was still spectacular. It needed a party!

I borrowed $2,000 from Stan and ordered wine and champagne from Memphis. I found a suitable caterer from Tupelo. (The only one in Clanton specialized in ribs and catfish and I wanted something a bit classier.)

The official invitation list of three hundred included everybody I knew in town, and a few I did not. The unofficial list was comprised of those who'd heard me say, 'We'll have a huge party when it's finished.' I invited BeeBee and three of her friends from Memphis. I invited my father but he was too worried about inflation and the bond market. I invited Miss Callie and Esau, Reverend Thurston Small, Claude, three clerks from the courthouse, two schoolteachers, an assistant basketball coach, a teller at the bank, and the newest lawyer in town. That made a total of twelve blacks, and I would've invited more if I had known more. I was determined to have the first integrated party in Clanton.

Harry Rex brought moonshine and a large platter of chitlins that almost broke up the festivities. Bubba Crockett and the Foxhole gang arrived stoned and ready to party. Mr. Mitlo wore the only tuxedo. Piston made an appearance, and was seen leaving through the back door with a carry-out bag filled with rather expensive finger food. Woody Gates and the Country Boys played for hours on a side porch. The Klumps were there with all their laborers; it was a fine moment for them and I made sure they got all the credit. Lucien Wilbanks arrived late and was soon in a heated argument about politics with Senator Theo Morton, whose wife, Rex Ella, told me it was the grandest party she'd seen in Clanton in twenty years. Our new Sheriff, Tryce McNatt, dropped by with several of his uniformed deputies. (T. R. Meredith had died of colon cancer the year before.) One of my favorites, Judge Reuben V. Atlee, held court in the den with colorful stories about Dr. Miles Hocutt. Reverend Millard Stark of the First Baptist Church stayed only ten minutes and left quietly when he realized alcohol was being served. Reverend Cargrove of the First Presbyterian Church was seen drinking champagne, and appeared to have a taste for it. Baggy passed out in a second-floor bedroom, where I found him the next afternoon. The Stukes twins, who owned the hardware store, showed up in brand-new, matching overalls. They were seventy years old, lived together, never married, and wore matching overalls every day. There was no dress requirement; the invitation said, 'Open Attire.'

The front lawn was covered with two large white tents, and at times the crowd spilled from under them. The party began at 1 P.M., Saturday afternoon, and would've gone past midnight if the wine and food had lasted. By ten, Woody Gates and his band were exhausted, there was nothing left to drink but a few warm beers, nothing to eat but a few tortilla chips, and nothing left to see. The house had been thoroughly seen and enjoyed.

Late the next morning, I scrambled eggs for BeeBee and her friends. We sat on the front porch and drank coffee and admired the mess made just hours before. It took me a week to clean up.

*

Through the years in Clanton I'd heard plenty of horror stories of imprisonment at the state penitentiary at Parchman. It was in sprawling farmland in the Delta, the richest farming region in the state, two hours west of Clanton. Living conditions were wretched – cramped barracks that were suffocating in the summer and frigid in the winter, ghastly food, scant medical care, a slave system, brutal sex. Forced labor, sadistic guards, the list was endless and pathetic.

When I thought of Danny Padgitt, which I did often, I was always comforted by the belief that he was at Parchman getting what he deserved. He was lucky he hadn't been strapped to a chair in a gas chamber.

My assumption was wrong.

In the late sixties, in an effort to ease the over-crowding at Parchman, the state had built two satellite prisons, or 'camps' as they were known. The plan had been to place a thousand non-violent offenders in more civilized confinement. They would obtain job training, even qualify for work release. One such satellite was near the small town of Broomfield, three hours south of Clanton.

Judge Loopus died in 1972. During the Padgitt trial, his stenographer had been a homely young woman named Darla Clabo. She worked for Loopus for a few years, and after his death left the area. When she walked into my office late one afternoon in the summer of 1977, I knew I had seen her somewhere in the distant past.

Darla introduced herself and I quickly remembered where I'd seen her. For five straight days during the Padgitt trial she had sat below the bench, next to the exhibit table, taking down every word. She was now living in Alabama, and had driven five hours to tell me something. First, she swore me to absolute secrecy.

Her hometown was Broomfield. Two weeks earlier she had been visiting her mother when she saw a familiar face walking down the sidewalk around lunchtime. It was Danny Padgitt, strolling along with a buddy. She was so startled she tripped on the edge of a curb and almost fell into the street.

They walked into a local diner and sat down for lunch. Darla saw them through a window, and decided not to go in. There was a chance Padgitt might recognize her, though she wasn't sure why that frightened her.

The man with him wore the uniform that was common in Broomfield – navy slacks, a short-sleeved white shirt with the words 'Broomfield Correctional Facility' in very small letters over the pocket. He also wore black cowboy boots and no gun whatsoever. She explained that some of the guards who handled the prisoners on work release had the option of carrying a weapon. It was hard to imagine a white man in Mississippi voluntarily declining to carry a gun if given the option, but she suspected that perhaps Danny didn't want his own personal guard to be armed.

Danny was wearing white dungarees and a white shirt, possibly issued by the camp. The two enjoyed a long lunch and appeared to be good friends. From her car, Darla watched them leave the diner. She followed from a distance as they took a leisurely stroll for a few blocks until Danny entered a building that housed the regional office of the Mississippi Highway Department. The guard got into a camp vehicle and drove away.

The following morning, Darla's mother entered the building under the pretext of filing a complaint about a road in need of repair. She was rudely informed that no such procedure existed, and in the ensuing brouhaha managed to catch a glimpse of the young man Darla had carefully described. He was holding a clipboard and appeared to be just another useless pencil pusher.

Darla's mother had a friend whose son worked as a clerk at the Broomfield camp. He confirmed that Danny Padgitt had been moved there in the summer of 1974.

When she finished with the story, she said, 'Are you going to expose him?'

I was reeling, but I could already see the story. 'I will investigate,' I said. 'Depends on what I find.'

'Please do. This ain't right.'

'It's unbelievable.'

'That little punk should be on death row.'

'I agree.'

'I did eight murder trials for Judge Loopus, and that one really sticks with me.'

'Me too.'

She swore me to secrecy again, and left her address. She wanted a copy of the paper if we did the story.

At six the next morning I had no trouble jumping out of bed. Wiley and I drove to Broomfield. Since both the Spitfire and the Mercedes were likely to draw attention in any small town in Mississippi, we took his Ford pickup. We easily found the camp, three miles out of town. We found the highway department office building. At noon we took our positions along Main Street. Since Padgitt would certainly recognize either one of us, we faced the challenge of trying to hide on a busy street in a strange town without acting suspicious. Wiley sat low in his truck, camera loaded and ready. I hid behind a newspaper on a bench.

There was no sign of him the first day. We drove back to Clanton, then early the next morning left again for Broomfield. At eleven-thirty, a prison vehicle stopped in front of the office building. The guard went inside, collected his prisoner, and they walked to lunch.

On July 17, 1977, our front page had four large photos – one of Danny walking along the sidewalk sharing a laugh with the guard, one of them as they entered the City Grill, one of the office building, one of the gate to the Broomfield camp. My headline howled: NO PRISON FOR PADGITT – HE'S OFF AT CAMP.

My report began:

> *Four years after being convicted of the brutal rape and murder of Rhoda Kassellaw, and being sentenced to life in the state penitentiary at Parchman, Danny Padgitt was moved to the state's new satellite camp at Broomfield. After three years there, he enjoys all the perks of a well-connected inmate – an office job with the state highway department, his own personal guard, and long lunches (cheeseburgers and milk shakes) in local cafés where the other patrons have never heard of him or his crimes.*

The story was as venomous and slanted as I could possibly make it. I bullied the waitress at the City Grill into telling me that he had just eaten a cheeseburger with french fries, that he ate there three times a week, and that he always picked up the check. I made a dozen phone calls to the highway department until I found a supervisor who knew something about Padgitt. The supervisor refused to answer questions, and I made him sound like a criminal himself. Penetrating Broomfield camp was just as frustrating. I detailed my efforts and tilted the story so it sounded as though all the bureaucrats were covering up for Padgitt. No one at

Parchman knew a damned thing, or if they did they were unwilling to talk about it. I called the highway commissioner (an elected official), the warden at Parchman (thankfully an appointed position), the Attorney General, the Lieutenant Governor, and finally the Governor himself. They were all too busy, of course, so I chatted with their bootlickers and made them sound like morons.

Senator Theo Morton appeared to be shocked. He promised to get right to the bottom of it and call me back. At press time, I was still waiting.

The reaction in Clanton was mixed. Many of those who called or stopped me on the street were angry and wanted something done. They truly believed that when Padgitt had been sentenced to life and led away in handcuffs, that he would spend the rest of his days in hell at Parchman. A few seemed indifferent and wanted to forget Padgitt altogether. He was old news.

And among some there was the frustrating, almost cynical lack of surprise. They figured the Padgitts had worked their magic once more, found the right pockets, pulled the right strings. Harry Rex was in this camp. 'What's the big fuss, boy? They've bought Governors before.'

The photo of Danny walking down the street, free as a bird, frightened Miss Callie considerably. 'She didn't sleep last night,' Esau mumbled to me when I arrived for lunch that Thursday. 'I wish you hadn't found him.'

Fortunately, the Memphis and Jackson newspapers picked up the story, and it took on a life of its own. They turned up the heat to a point where the politicians had to get involved. The Governor and the Attorney General, along with Senator Morton, were soon jockeying to lead the parade to get the boy sent back to Parchman.

Two weeks after I broke the story, Danny Padgitt was 'reassigned' to the state penitentiary.

The next day, I received two phone calls, one at the office, one at home while I was asleep. Different voices, but with the same message. I was a dead man.

I notified the FBI in Oxford, and two agents visited me in Clanton. I leaked this to a reporter in Memphis, and soon the town knew that I had been threatened, and that the FBI was investigating. For a month, Sheriff McNatt kept a patrol car in front of my office around the clock. Another one sat in my driveway during the night.

After a seven-year hiatus, I was carrying a gun again.

Chapter 32

There was no immediate bloodshed. The threats were not forgotten, but as time passed they became less ominous. I never stopped carrying a gun – it was always within reach – but I lost interest in it. I found it hard to believe that the Padgitts would risk the severe backlash that would come if they knocked off the editor of the local paper. Even if the town was not entirely enamored of me, as opposed to someone as beloved as Mr. Caudle, the uproar would create more pressure than the Padgitts were willing to risk.

They kept to themselves like never before. After the defeat of Mackey Don Coley in 1971, they once again proved quite adept at changing tactics. Danny had given them enough unwanted attention; they were determined to avoid anymore. They retrenched even deeper into Padgitt Island.. They increased security in the wasted belief that the next sheriff, T. R. Meredith, or his successor, Tryce McNatt, might come after them. They grew their crops and smuggled them off the island in planes, boats, pickups, and flatbed trucks ostensibly loaded with timber.

With typical Padgitt shrewdness, and sensing that the marijuana business might become too risky, they began pumping money into legitimate enterprises. They bought a highway contracting company and quickly turned it into a reliable bidder for government projects. They bought an asphalt plant, a Redi-Mix concrete plant, and gravel pits around the northern part of the state. Highway construction was a notably corrupt business in Mississippi, and the Padgitts knew how to play the game.

I watched these activities as closely as possible. This was before the Freedom of Information Act and open-meetings laws. I knew the names of some of the companies the Padgitts had bought, but it was virtually impossible to keep up with them. There was nothing I could print, no story, because on the surface it was all legitimate.

I waited, but for what I wasn't certain. Danny Padgitt would return one day, and when he did he might simply disappear into the island and never be seen again. Or he might do otherwise.

Few people in Clanton did not attend church. Those who did seemed to know exactly which ones did not, and there was a common invitation to 'come worship with us.' The farewell, 'See

366

you on Sunday,' was almost as common as 'Y'all come see us.'

I got hammered with these invitations during my first years in town. Once it was known that the owner and editor of the *Times* did not go to church, I became the most famous derelict in town. I decided to do something about it.

Each week Margaret put together our Religion page, which included a rather extensive menu of churches arranged by denominations. There were also a few ads by the more affluent congregations. And notices for revivals, reunions, potluck suppers, and countless other activities.

Working from this page, and from the phonebook, I made a list of all the churches in Ford County. The total was eighty-eight, but it was a moving target since congregations were always splitting, folding here and popping up over there. My goal was to visit each one of them, something I was sure had never been done, and a feat that would put me in a class by myself among churchgoers.

The denominations were varied and baffling – how could Protestants, all of whom claimed to follow the same basic tenets, get themselves so divided? They agreed basically that (1) Jesus was the only son of God; (2) he was born of a virgin; (3) lived a perfect life; (4) was persecuted by the Jews, arrested and crucified by the Romans; (5) that he arose on the third day and later ascended into heaven; (6) and some believed – though there were many variations – that one must follow Jesus in baptism and faith to make it to heaven.

The doctrine was fairly straightforward, but the devil was in the details.

There were no Catholics, Episcopalians, or Mormons. The county was heavily Baptist, but they were a fractured bunch. The Pentecostals were in second place, and evidently they had fought with themselves as much as the Baptists.

In 1974, I'd begun my epic adventure to visit every church in Ford County. The first had been the Calvary Full Gospel, a rowdy Pentecostal assemblage on a gravel road two miles out of town. As advertised, the service began at ten-thirty, and I found a spot on the back pew, as far away from the action as I could get. I was greeted warmly and word spread that a bona-fide visitor was present. I did not recognize anyone there. Preacher Bob wore a white suit, navy shirt, white tie, and his thick black hair was wound around and plastered tightly at the base of his skull. People started hollering when he was giving the announcements. They waved their hands and shouted during a solo. When the sermon finally began an hour later, I was ready to leave. It lasted for fifty-five minutes, and left me confused and exhausted. At times the building shook with folks stomping the floor. Windows rattled as they were overcome with the spirit and yelled upward. Preacher Bob 'laid hands' on three sick folks suffering vague diseases, and they claimed to be healed. At one point a deacon stood and in an astounding display began uttering something in a tongue I had never heard. He clenched his fists, closed his eyes tightly, and let loose with a steady, fluent flow of words. It was not an act; he wasn't faking. After a few minutes, a young girl in the choir stood and began translating into English. It was a vision God was sending through the deacon. There were those present with unforgiven sins.

'Repent!' Preacher Bob shouted, and heads ducked.

What if the deacon was talking about me? I glanced around and noticed that the door was locked and guarded by two more deacons.

Things finally ran out of gas, and two hours after I sat down I bolted from the building. I needed a drink.

I wrote a pleasant little report about my visit to Calvary Full Gospel and ran it on the Religion page. I commented on the warm atmosphere of the church, the lovely solo by Miss Helen Hatcher, the powerful sermon by Preacher Bob, and so on.

Needless to say, this proved to be very popular.

At least twice a month, I went to church. I sat with Miss Callie and Esau and listened to the Reverend Thurston Small preach for two hours and twelve minutes (I timed every sermon). The briefest was delivered by Pastor Phil Bish at the United Methodist Church of Karaway – seventeen minutes. That church also got the award for being the coldest. The furnace was broken, it was January, and that may have helped shorten the sermon. I sat with Margaret at the First Baptist Church in Clanton and listened to Reverend Millard Stark give his annual sermon on the sins of alcohol. With bad timing, I had a hangover that morning and Stark kept looking at me.

I found the Harvest Tabernacle in the back room of an abandoned service station in Beech Hill, and I sat with six others as a wild-eyed doomsayer named Peter the Prophet yelled at us for almost an hour. My column that week was quite brief.

The Clanton Church of Christ had no musical instruments. The ban was based on Scripture, it was later explained to me. There was a beautiful solo, which I wrote about at length. There was also no emotion whatsoever in the service. For a contrast, I went to the Mount Pisgah Chapel in Lowtown, where the pulpit was surrounded by drums, guitars, horns, and amplifiers. As a warmup for the sermon, a full-blown concert was given with the congregation singing and dancing. Miss Callie referred to Mount Pisgah as a 'lower church.'

On my list, number sixty-four was the Calico Ridge Independent Church, located deep in the hills in the northeastern part of the county. According to the *Times* archives, at this church in 1965 a Mr. Randy Bovee was bitten twice by a rattlesnake during a late Sunday night worship service. Mr. Bovee survived, and for a while the snakes were put away. The legend, however, flourished, and as my Church Notes column gained popularity, I was asked several times if I intended to visit Calico Ridge.

'I plan to visit every church,' was my standard reply.

'They don't like visitors,' Baggy warned me.

I had been greeted so warmly in each church – black or white, large or small, town or country – that I could not imagine Christian folks being rude to a guest.

And they weren't rude at Calico Ridge, but they weren't too happy to see me either. I wanted to see the snakes, but from the safety of the back row. I went on a Sunday night, primarily because legend held that they did not 'take up the serpents' during daylight hours. I searched the Bible in vain for this restriction.

There was no sign of any serpents. There were a few fits and convulsions below the pulpit as the preacher exhorted us to 'come forth and moan and groan in sin!' The choir chanted and hummed to the beat of an electric guitar and a drum, and the meeting took on the spookiness of an ancient tribal dance. I wanted to leave, especially since there were no snakes.

Late in the service, I caught a glimpse of a face I'd seen before. It was a very different face – thin, pale, gaunt, topped with grayish hair. I couldn't place it, but I knew it was familiar. The man was seated in the second row from the front, on the other side of the small sanctuary, and he seemed out of touch with the chaos of the worship service. At times he appeared to be praying, then he would sit while everyone else was standing. Those around him seemed to accept him and ignore him at the same time.

He turned once and looked directly at me. It was Hank Hooten, the ex-lawyer who'd shot up the town in 1971! He'd been taken in a strait-jacket to the state mental hospital, and a few years later there'd been a rumor that he had been released. No one had seen him, though.

For two days after that, I tried to track down Hank Hooten. My calls to the state mental hospital went nowhere. Hank had a brother in Shady Grove, but he refused to talk. I snooped around Calico Ridge, but, typically, no one there would utter a word to a stranger like me.

Chapter 33

Many of those who worshiped diligently on Sunday mornings became less faithful on Sunday nights. During my tour of churches, I heard many preachers chide their followers to return in a few hours to properly complete the observance of the Sabbath. I never counted heads, but as a general rule about half of them did so. I tried a few Sunday night services, usually in an effort to catch some colorful ritual such as snake handling or disease healing or, on one occasion, a 'church conclave' in which a wayward brother was to be put on trial and certainly convicted for fancying another brother's wife. My presence rattled them that night and the wayward brother got a reprieve.

For the most part, I limited my study of comparative religions to the daylight hours.

Others had different Sunday-night rituals. Harry Rex helped a Mexican named Pepe lease a building and open a restaurant one block off the square. Pepe's became moderately successful during the 1970s with decent food that was always on the spicy side. Pepe couldn't resist the peppers, regardless of how they scalded the throats of his gringo customers.

On Sundays all alcohol was banned in Ford County. It could not be sold at retail or in restaurants. Pepe had a back room with a long table and a door that would lock. He allowed Harry Rex and his guests to use the room and eat and drink all we wanted. His margaritas were especially tasty. We enjoyed many colorful meals with spicy dishes, all washed down with strong margaritas. There were usually a dozen of us, all male, all young, about half currently married. Harry Rex threatened our lives if we told anyone about Pepe's back room.

The Clanton city police raided us once, but Pepe suddenly couldn't speak a word of English. The door to the back room was locked, and partially hidden too. Pepe turned off the lights, and for twenty minutes we waited in the dark, still drinking, and listened to the cops try to communicate with Pepe. I don't know why we were worried. The city Judge was a lawyer named Harold Finkley, who was at the end of the table slogging down his fourth or fifth margarita.

Those Sunday nights at Pepe's were often long and rowdy, and afterward we were in no condition to drive. I would walk to my office and sleep on the sofa. I was there snoring off the tequila when the phone rang after midnight. It was a reporter I knew from the big daily in Memphis.

'Are you covering the parole hearing tomorrow?' he asked. Tomorrow? In my toxic fog I had no idea what day it was.

'Tomorrow?' I mumbled.

'Monday, September the eighteenth,' he said slowly.

I was reasonably certain the year was 1978.

'What parole hearing?' I asked, trying desperately to wake myself up and put two thoughts together.

'Danny Padgitt's. You don't know about it?'

'Hell no!'

'It's scheduled for ten A.M. at Parchman.'

'You gotta be kidding!'

'Nope. I just found out. Evidently, they don't advertise these.'

I sat in the darkness for a long time, cursing once again the backwardness of a state that conducted such important matters in such ridiculous ways. How could parole even be considered for Danny Padgitt? Eight years had passed since the murder and his conviction. He had received two life sentences of at least ten years each. We assumed that meant a minimum of twenty years.

I drove home around 3 A.M., slept fitfully for two hours, then woke up Harry Rex, who was in no condition to be dealt with. I picked up sausage biscuits and strong coffee and we met at his office around seven. We were both ill-tempered, and as we plowed through his law books there were sharp words and foul language, not aimed at each other, but at the blurry and toothless parole system passed by the legislature thirty years earlier. Guidelines were only vaguely defined, leaving ample wiggle room for the politicians and their appointees to do as they wished.

Since most law-abiding citizens had no contact with the parole system, it was not a priority with the state legislature. And since most of the state's prisoners were either poor or black, and unable to use the system to their advantage, it was easy to hit them with harsh sentences and keep them locked up. But for an inmate with a few connections and some cash, the parole system was a marvelous labyrinth of contradictory laws that allowed the Parole Board to pass out favors.

Somewhere between the judicial system, the penal system, and the parole system, Danny Padgitt's two 'consecutive' life terms had been changed to two 'concurrent' sentences. They ran side by side, Harry Rex tried to explain.

'What good is that?' I asked.

'It's used in cases where a defendant has multiple charges. Consecutive might give him eighty years in jail, but a fair sentence is ten. So they run 'em side by side.'

I shook my head in disapproval again, and this irritated him.

I finally got Sheriff Tryce McNatt to answer the phone. He sounded as hung over as we were, though he was a strict teetotaler. McNatt knew nothing about the parole hearing. I asked him if he planned to attend, but his day was already filled with important meetings.

I would have called Judge Loopus, but he'd been dead for six years. Ernie Gaddis had retired and was fishing in the Smoky Mountains. His successor, Rufus Buckley, lived in Tyler County and his phone number was unlisted.

At eight o'clock, I jumped in my car with a biscuit and a cup of cold coffee.

An hour west of Ford County the land flattened dramatically and the Delta began. It was a region rich in farming and poor in living conditions, but I was in no mood to take in the sights and offer social commentary. I was too nervous about crashing a clandestine parole hearing.

I was also nervous about setting foot inside Parchman, a legendary hellhole.

After two hours, I saw fences next to fields, then razor wire. Soon there was a sign, and I turned into the main gate. I informed a guard in the booth that I was a reporter, there for a parole hearing. 'Straight ahead, left at the second building,' he said helpfully as he wrote down my name.

There was a cluster of buildings close to the highway, and a row of white-frame houses that would fit on any Maple Street in Mississippi. I

377

chose the Admin A building and sprinted inside, looking for the first secretary. I found her, and she sent me to the next building, second floor. It was just about ten.

There were people at the end of the hallway, loitering outside a room. One was a prison guard, one was a state trooper, one wore a wrinkled suit.

'I'm here for a parole hearing,' I announced.

'In there,' the guard said, pointing. Without knocking, I yanked open the door, as any intrepid reporter would, and stepped inside. Things had just been called to order, and my presence there was certainly not anticipated.

There were five members of the Parole Board, and they were seated behind a slightly elevated table with their name plates in front of them. Along one wall another table held the Padgitt crowd – Danny, his father, his mother, an uncle, and Lucien Wilbanks. Opposite them, behind another table, were various clerks and functionaries of the Board and the prison.

Everyone stared at me as I stormed in. My eyes locked onto Danny Padgitt's, and for a second both of us managed to convey the contempt we felt for the other.

'Can I help you?' a large, badly dressed ole boy growled from the center of the Board. His name was Barrett Ray Jeter, the chairman. Like the other four, he'd been appointed by the Governor as a reward for vote-gathering.

'I'm here for the Padgitt hearing,' I said.

'He's a reporter!' Lucien practically yelled as he was standing. For a second I thought I might get arrested on the spot and be carried deeper into the prison for a life sentence.

'For who?' Jeter demanded.

'*The Ford County Times*,' I said.

'Your name?'

'Willie Traynor.' I was glaring at Lucien and he was scowling at me.

'This is a closed hearing, Mr. Traynor,' Jeter said. The statute wasn't clear as to whether it was open or closed, so it had traditionally been kept quiet.

'Who has the right to attend?' I asked.

'The Parole Board, the parolee, his family, his witnesses, his lawyer, and any witnesses for the other side.' The 'other side' meant the victim's family, which in this setting sounded like the bad guys.

'What about the Sheriff from our county?' I asked.

'He's invited too,' Jeter said.

'Our Sheriff wasn't notified. I talked to him three hours ago. In fact, nobody in Ford County knew of this hearing until after twelve last night.' This caused considerable head-scratching up and down the Parole Board. The Padgitts huddled with Lucien.

By process of elimination, I quickly deduced that I had to become a witness if I wanted to watch the show. I said, as loudly and clearly as possible, 'Well, since there's no one else here from Ford County in opposition, I'm a witness.'

'You can't be a reporter and a witness,' Jeter said.

'Where is that written in the Mississippi Code?' I asked, waving my copies from Harry Rex's law books.

Jeter nodded at a young man in a dark suit. 'I'm the attorney for the Parole Board,' he said politely. 'You can testify in this hearing, Mr. Traynor, but you cannot report it.'

I planned to fully report every detail of the hearing, then hide behind the First Amendment. 'So be it,' I said. 'You guys make the rules.' In less than one minute the lines had been drawn; I was on one side, everybody else was on the other.

'Let's proceed,' Jeter said, and I took a seat with a handful of other spectators.

The attorney for the Parole Board passed out a report. He recited the basics of the Padgitt sentence, and was careful not to use the words 'consecutive' or 'concurrent.' Based on the inmate's 'exemplary' record during his incarceration, he had qualified for 'good time,' a vague concept created by the parole system and not by the state legislature. Subtracting the time the inmate spent in the county jail awaiting trial, he was now eligible for parole.

Danny's caseworker plowed through a lengthy narrative of her relationship with the inmate. She concluded with the gratuitous opinion that he was 'fully remorseful,' 'fully rehabilitated,' 'no threat whatsoever to society,' even ready to become a 'most productive citizen.'

How much did all this cost? I couldn't help but ponder that question. How much? And how long had it taken for the Padgitts to find the right pockets?

Lucien went next. With no one – Gaddis, Sheriff McNatt – not even poor Hank Hooten – to contradict or possibly throttle him, he launched into a fictional recounting of the facts of the crimes, and in particular the testimony of an 'airtight' alibi witness, Lydia Vince. His reconstructed version of the trial had the jury waivering on a verdict of not guilty. I was tempted to throw something at him and start screaming. Maybe that would at least keep him somewhat honest.

I wanted to shout, 'How can he be remorseful if he's so innocent?'

Lucien carped on about the trial and how unfair it had been. He nobly took the blame for not pushing hard for a change of venue, to another part of the state where folks were unbiased and more enlightened. When he finally shut up two of the board members appeared to be asleep.

Mrs. Padgitt testified next and talked about the letters she and her son had exchanged these past eight, very long years. Through his letters, she had seen him mature, seen his faith strengthen, seen him long for his freedom so he could serve his fellow man.

Serve them a stronger blend of pot? Or perhaps a cleaner corn whiskey?

Since tears were expected she gave us some tears. It was part of the show and appeared to have little sway over the Board. In fact, as I watched their faces I got the impression that their decision had been made a long time ago.

Danny went last and did a good job of walking the fine line between denying his crimes and showing remorse for them. 'I have learned from my mistakes,' he said, as if rape and murder were simple indiscretions where no one really got hurt. 'I have grown from them.'

In prison he had been a veritable whirlwind of positive energy – volunteering in the library, singing in the choral group, helping with the Parchman rodeo, organizing teams to go into schools and scare kids away from crime.

Two Board members were listening. One was still asleep. The other two sat in trancelike meditation, apparently brain dead.

Danny shed no tears, but closed with an impassioned plea for his release.

'How many witnesses in opposition?' Jeter announced. I stood, looked around me, saw no one else from Ford County, then said, 'I guess it's just me.'

'Proceed, Mr. Traynor.'

I had no idea what to say, nor did I know what was permissible or objectionable in such a forum. But based on what I had just sat through, I figured I could say anything I damned well pleased. Fat Jeter would no doubt call me down if I ventured into forbidden territory.

I looked up at the Board members, tried my best to ignore the daggers from the Padgitts, and jumped into an extremely graphic description of the rape and the murder. I unloaded everything I could possibly remember, and I put special emphasis on the fact that the two children witnessed some or all of the attack.

I kept waiting for Lucien to object, but there was nothing but silence in their camp. The formerly comatose Board members were suddenly alive, all watching me closely, absorbing the gruesome details of the murder. I described the wounds. I painted the heartbreaking scene of Rhoda dying in the arms of Mr. Deece, and saying, 'It was Danny Padgitt. It was Danny Padgitt.'

I called Lucien a liar and mocked his memory of the trial. It took the jury less than an hour to find the defendant guilty, I explained.

And with a recollection that surprised even me, I recounted Danny's pathetic performance on the witness stand: his lying to cover up his lies; his total lack of truthfulness. 'He should've been indicted for perjury,' I told the Board.

'And when he had finished testifying, instead of returning to his seat, he walked to the jury box, shook his finger in the faces of the jurors, and said, "You convict me, and I'll get every damned one of you."'

A Board member named Mr. Horace Adler

jerked upright in his seat and blurted toward the Padgitts, 'Is that true?'

'It's in the record,' I said quickly before Lucien had the chance to lie again. He was slowly getting to his feet.

'Is that true, Mr. Wilbanks?' Adler insisted.

'He threatened the jury?' asked another board member.

'I have the transcript,' I said. 'I'll be happy to send it to you.'

'Is that true?' Adler asked for the third time.

'There were three hundred people in the courtroom,' I said, staring at Lucien and saying with my eyes, Don't do it. Don't lie about it.

'Shut up, Mr. Traynor,' a Board member said.

'It's in the record,' I said again.

'That's enough!' Jeter shouted.

Lucien was standing and trying to think of a response. Everyone was waiting. Finally, 'I don't remember everything that was said,' he began, and I snorted as loudly as possible. 'Perhaps my client did say something to that effect, but it was an emotional moment, and in the heat of the battle, something like that might have been said. But taken in context –'

'Context my ass!' I yelled at Lucien and took a step toward him as if I might throw a punch. A guard stepped toward me and I stopped. 'It's in black-and-white in the trial transcript!' I said angrily. Then I turned to the Board and said, 'How can you folks sit there and let them lie like this? Don't you want to hear the truth?'

'Anything else, Mr. Traynor?' Jeter asked.

'Yes! I hope this Board will not make a mockery out of our system and let this man go free after eight years. He's lucky to be sitting here instead of on death row, where he belongs. And I hope that the next time you have a hearing on his parole, if there is a next time, you will invite some of the good folks from Ford County. Perhaps the Sheriff, perhaps the prosecutor. And could you notify members of the victim's family? They have the right to be here so you can see their faces when you turn this murderer loose.'

I sat down and fumed. I glared at Lucien Wilbanks and decided that I would work diligently to hate him for the rest of either his life or mine, whichever ended first. Jeter announced a brief recess, and I assumed they needed time to regroup in a back room and count their money. Perhaps Mr. Padgitt could be summoned to provide some extra cash for a Board member or two. To irritate the Board attorney, I scribbled pages of notes for the report he'd prohibited me from writing.

We waited thirty minutes before they filed back in, everyone looking guilty of something. Jeter called for a vote. Two voted in favor of parole, two against, one abstained. 'Parole is denied at this time,' Jeter announced, and Mrs. Padgitt burst into tears. She hugged Danny before they took him away.

Lucien and the Padgitts walked by, very close to me as they left the room. I ignored them and just stared at the floor, exhausted, hungover, shocked at the denial.

'Next we have Charles D. Bowie,' Jeter announced, and there was movement around the tables as the next hopeful was brought in. I caught something about a sex offender, but I was too drained to care. I eventually left the room and walked down the hallway, half-expecting to be confronted by the Padgitts, and that was fine too because I preferred to get it over with.

But they had scattered; there was no sign of them as I left the building and drove through the main gate and back to Clanton.

Chapter 34

The parole hearing was front page news in *The Ford County Times*. I loaded the report with every detail I could remember, and on page five let loose with a blistering editorial about the process. I sent a copy to each member of the Parole Board and to its attorney, and, because I was so worked up, every member of the state legislature, the Attorney General, the Lieutenant Governor, and the Governor received a complimentary copy. Most ignored it, but the attorney for the Parole Board did not.

He wrote me a lengthy letter in which he said he was deeply concerned about my 'willful violation of Parole Board procedures.' He was pondering a session with the Attorney General in which they would 'evaluate the gravity of my actions' and possibly pursue action that would lead to 'far-reaching consequences.'

My lawyer, Harry Rex, had assured me the Parole Board's policy of secret meetings was patently unconstitutional, in clear violation of the First Amendment, and he would happily defend me in federal court. For a reduced hourly rate, of course.

I swapped heated letters with the Board's lawyer for a month before he seemed to lose interest in pursuing me.

Rafe, Harry Rex's chief ambulance chaser, had a sidekick named Buster, a large thick-chested cowboy with a gun in every pocket. I hired Buster for $100 a week to pretend he was my own personal legbreaker. For a few hours a day he would hang around the front of the office, or sit in my driveway or on one of my porches, any place where he might be seen so folks would know that Willie Traynor was important enough to have a bodyguard. If the Padgitts got close enough to take a shot, they would at least get something in return.

After years of steadily gaining weight and ignoring the warnings of her doctors, Miss Callie finally relented. After a particularly bad visit to her clinic, she announced to Esau that she was going on a diet – 1,500 calories a day, except, mercifully, Thursday. A month passed and I couldn't discern any loss of weight. But the day after the *Times* story on the parole hearing, she suddenly looked as though she'd lost fifty pounds.

Instead of frying a chicken, she baked one. Instead of whipping mashed potatoes with butter and thick cream and covering them with gravy, she boiled them. It was still delicious, but my system had become accustomed to its weekly dose of heavy grease.

After the prayer, I handed her two letters from Sam. As always, she read them immediately while I jumped into the lunch. And as always, she smiled and laughed and then finally wiped a tear. 'He's doing fine,' she said, and he was.

With typical Ruffin tenacity, Sam had completed his first college degree, in economics, and was saving his money for law school. He was terribly homesick, and weary of the weather. To boil it all down, he missed his momma. And her cooking.

President Carter had pardoned the draft dodgers, and Sam was wrestling with the decision to stay in Canada, or come home. Many of his expatriate friends up there were vowing to stay and pursue Canadian citizenship, and he was heavily influenced by them. There was also a woman involved, though he had not told his parents.

Sometimes we began with the news, but often it was the obituaries or even the classifieds. Since she read every word, Miss Callie knew who was selling a new litter of beagles and who wanted to buy a good used riding mower. And since she read every word every week, she knew how long a certain small farm or a mobile home had been on the market. She knew prices and values. A car would pass on the street during lunch. She would ask, 'Now, what model is that?'

'A '71 Plymouth Duster,' I would answer.

She would hesitate for a second, then say, 'If it's real clean, it's in the twenty-five-hundred-dollar range.'

Stan Atcavage once needed to sell a twenty-four-foot fishing boat he'd repossessed. I called Miss Callie. She said, 'Yes, a gentleman from Karaway was looking for one three weeks ago.' I checked an old section of the classifieds and found the ad. Stan sold him the boat the next day.

She loved the legal notices, one of the most lucrative sections of the paper. Deeds, foreclosures, divorce filings, probate matters, bankruptcy announcements, annexation hearings, dozens of legal notices were required by law to be published in the county paper. We got them all, and we charged a healthy rate.

'I see where Mr. Everett Wainwright's estate is being probated,' she said.

'I vaguely remember his obituary,' I said with a mouthful. 'When did he die?'

'Five, maybe six months ago. Wasn't much of an obituary.'

'I have to work with whatever the family gives me. Did you know him?'

'He owned a grocery store near the tracks for many years.' I could tell by the inflection in her voice that she did not care for Mr. Everett Wainwright.

'Good guy or bad buy?'

'He had two sets of prices, one for the whites, a higher one for Negroes. His goods were never marked in any way, and he was the only cashier. A white customer would call out, "Say, Mr. Wainwright, how much is this can of condensed milk?" and he'd holler back, "Thirty-eight cents." A minute later I would say, "Pardon me, Mr. Wainwright, but how much is this can of condensed milk?' And he'd snap, "Fifty-four cents." He was very open about it. He didn't care.'

For almost nine years I'd heard stories of the old days. At times I thought I'd heard them all, but Miss Callie's collection was endless.

'Why did you shop there?'

'It was the only store where we could shop. Mr. Monty Griffin ran a nicer store behind the old moviehouse, but we couldn't shop there until twenty years ago.'

'Who stopped you?'

'Mr. Monty Griffin. He didn't care if you had money, he didn't want any Negroes in his store.'

'And Mr. Wainwright didn't care?'

'He cared all right. He didn't want us, but he would take our money.'

She told the story of a Negro boy who loitered around the store until Mr. Wainwright struck him with a broom and sent him away. For revenge, the boy broke into the store once or twice a year for a long time and was never caught. He stole cigarettes and candy, and he also splintered all the broom handles.

'Is it true he left all his money to the Methodist church?' she asked.

'That's the rumor.'

'How much?'

'Around a hundred thousand dollars.'

'Folks say he was trying to buy his way into heaven,' she said. I had long since ceased to be amazed at the gossip Miss Callie heard from the other side of the tracks. Many of her friends worked as housekeepers over there. The maids knew everything.

She had once again nudged the conversation to the topic of the afterlife. Miss Callie was deeply concerned about my soul. She was worried that I had not properly become a Christian; that I had not been 'born again' or 'saved.' My infant baptism, which I could not remember, was thoroughly insufficient in her view. Once a person reaches a certain age, the 'age of accountability,' then, in order to be 'saved' from everlasting damnation in hell, that person must walk down the aisle of a church (the right church was the subject of eternal debate) and make a public profession of faith in Jesus Christ.

Miss Callie carried a heavy burden because I had not done this.

And, after having visited seventy-seven different churches, I had to admit that the vast majority of the people in Ford County shared her beliefs. There were some variations. A powerful sect was the Church of Christ. They clung to the odd notion that they, and only they, were destined for heaven. Every other church was preaching 'sectarian doctrine.' They also believed, as did many congregations, that once a person obtained salvation then it could be lost by bad behavior. The Baptists, the most popular denomination, held firm in 'once saved always saved.'

This was apparently very comforting for several backslidden Baptists I knew in town.

However, there was hope for me. Miss Callie was thrilled that I was attending church and absorbing the gospel. She was convinced, and she prayed about me continually, that one day soon the Lord would reach down and touch my heart. I would decide to follow him, and she and I would spend eternity together.

Miss Callie was truly living for the day when she 'went Home to glory.'

'Reverend Small will preside over the Lord's supper this Sunday,' she said. It was her weekly invitation to sit with her in church. Reverend Small and his long sermons were more than I could bear.

'Thank you, but I'm doing research again this Sunday,' I said.

'God bless you. Where?'

'The Maranatha Primitive Baptist Church.'

'Never heard of it.'

'It's in the phone book.'

'Where is it?'

'Somewhere down in Dumas, I think.'

'Black or white?'

'I'm not sure.'

Number seventy-eight on my list, the Maranatha Primitive Baptist Church, was a little jewel at the foot of a hill, next to a creek, under a cluster of pin oaks that were at least two hundred years old. It was a small white-frame building, narrow and long, with a high-pitched tin roof and a red steeple that was so tall it got lost in the oaks. The front doors were open wide, beckoning any and all to come worship. A cornerstone gave the date as 1813.

I eased into the back pew, my usual place, and sat next to a well-dressed gentleman who'd been around for as long as the church. I counted fifty-six other worshipers that morning. The windows were wide open, and outside a gentle breeze rushed through the trees and soothed the rough edges of a hectic morning. For a century and a half people had gathered there, sat on the same pews, looked through the same windows at the same trees, and worshiped the same God. The choir – all eight – sang a gentle hymn and I drifted back to another century.

The pastor was a jovial man named J. B. Cooper. I'd met him twice over the years while scrambling around trying to put together obituaries. One side benefit to my tour of county churches was the introduction to all the ministers. This really helped spice up my obits.

Pastor Cooper gazed upon his flock and realized I was the only visitor. He called my name, welcomed me, and made some harmless crack about getting favorable coverage in the *Times*. After four years of touring, and seventy-seven rather generous and colorful Church Notes, it was impossible for me to sneak into a service without getting noticed.

I never knew what to expect in these rural churches. More often than not the sermons were loud and long, and many times I wondered how such good people could drag themselves in week after week for a tongue-lashing. Some preachers were almost sadistic in their condemnation of whatever their followers might have done that week. Everything was a sin in rural Mississippi, and not just the basics as set forth in the Ten Commandments. I heard scathing rebukes of television, movies, cardplaying, popular magazines, sports events, cheerleader uniforms, desegregation, mixed-race churches, Disney – because it came on Sunday nights – dancing, social drinking, postmarital sex, everything.

But Pastor Cooper was at peace. His sermon – twenty-eight minutes – was about tolerance and love. Love was Christ's principal message. The one thing Christ wanted us to do was to love one another. For the altar call we sang three verses of 'Just As I Am,' but no one moved. These folks had been down the aisle many times.

As always, I hung around afterward for a few

minutes to speak with Pastor Cooper. I told him how much I enjoyed the service, something I did whether I meant it or not, and I collected the names of the choir members for my column. Church folk were naturally warm and friendly, but at this stage of my tour they wanted to chat forever and pass along little gems that might end up in print. 'My grandfather put the roof on this building in 1902.' 'The tornado of '38 skipped right over us during the summer revival.'

As I was leaving the building, I saw a man in a wheelchair being pushed down the handicap ramp. It was a face I'd seen before, and I walked over to say hello. Lenny Fargarson, the crippled boy, juror number seven or eight, had evidently taken a turn for the worse. During the trial in 1970 he had been able to walk, though it was not a pretty thing to behold. Now he was in a chair. His father introduced himself. His mother was in a cluster of ladies finishing up one last round of goodbyes.

'Got a minute?' Fargarson asked. In Mississippi, that question really meant 'We need to talk and it might take a while.' I sat on a bench under one of the oaks. His father rolled him over, then left us to talk.

'I see your paper every week,' he said. 'You think Padgitt will get out?'

'Sure. It's just a question of when. He can apply for parole once a year, every year.'

'Will he come back here, to Ford County?'

I shrugged because I had no idea. 'Probably. The Padgitts stick close to their land.'

He considered this for some time. He was gaunt and hunched over like an old man. If my memory was correct, he was about twenty-five at the time of the trial. We were roughly about the same age, though he looked twice as old. I had heard the story of his affliction – some injury in a sawmill.

'Does that frighten you?' I asked.

He smiled and said, 'Nothing frightens me, Mr. Traynor. The Lord is my shepherd.'

'Yes he is,' I said, still warm from the sermon. Because of his physical condition and his wheelchair, Lenny was a difficult person to read. He had endured so much. His faith was strong, but I thought for a second that I caught a hint of apprehension.

Mrs. Fargarson was walking toward us.

'Will you be there when he's released?' Lenny asked.

'I'd like to be, but I'm not sure how it's done.'

'Will you call me when you know he's out?'

'Of course.'

Mrs. Fargarson had a pot roast in the oven for Sunday lunch, and she wouldn't take no for an answer. I was suddenly hungry, and there was, as usual, nothing remotely tasty in the Hocutt House. Sunday lunch was typically a cold sandwich and a glass of wine on a side porch, followed by a long siesta.

Lenny lived with his parents on a gravel road

two miles from the church. His father was a rural mail carrier, his mother a schoolteacher. An older sister was in Tupelo. Over roast and potatoes and tea almost as sweet as Miss Callie's, we relived the Kassellaw trial and Padgitt's first parole hearing. Lenny may have been unconcerned about Danny's possible release, but his parents were deeply worried.

Chapter 35

Big news hit Clanton in the spring of 1978. Bargain City was coming! Along with McDonald's and the fast-food joints that followed it around the country, Bargain City was a national chain rapidly marching through the small towns of the South. Most of the town rejoiced. Some of us, though, felt it was the beginning of the end.

The company was taking over the world with its 'big box' discount warehouses that offered everything at very low prices. The stores were spacious and clean and included cafés, pharmacies, banks, even optometrists and travel agents. A small town without a Bargain City store was irrelevant and insignificant.

They optioned fifty acres on Market Street, about a mile from the Clanton square. Some of the neighbors protested, and the city council held a public hearing on whether to allow the store to be built. Bargain City had met opposition before, and it had a well-oiled and highly effective strategy.

The council room was packed with people holding red-and-white Bargain City signs – BARGAIN CITY – A GOOD NEIGHBOR and WE WANT JOBS. Engineers, architects, lawyers, and contractors were there, with their secretaries and wives and children. Their mouthpiece painted a rosy picture of economic growth, sales tax revenues, 150 jobs for the locals, and the best products at the lowest prices.

Mrs. Dorothy Hockett spoke in opposition. Her property was adjacent to the site and she did not want the invasion of noise and lights. The city council seemed sympathetic, but the vote had long since been decided. When no one else would speak against Bargain City, I stood and walked to the podium.

I was driven by a belief that to preserve the downtown area of Clanton we had to protect the stores and shops, cafés and offices around the square. Once we began sprawling, there would be no end to it. The town would spread in a dozen directions, each one siphoning off its own little slice of old Clanton.

Most of the jobs they were promising would be at minimum wage. The increase in sales tax revenues to the city would be at the expense of the merchants Bargain City would quickly drive out of business. The people of Ford County were not going to wake up one day and suddenly start buying more bicycles and refrigerators simply because Bargain City had such dazzling displays.

I mentioned the town of Titus, about an hour south of Clanton. Two years earlier, Bargain City opened there. Since then, fourteen retail stores and one café had closed. Main Street was almost deserted.

I mentioned the town of Marshall, over in the Delta. In the three years since Bargain City opened, the mom-and-pop merchants of Marshall had closed two pharmacies, two small department stores, the feed store, the hardware store, a ladies' boutique, a gift shop, a small bookstore, and two cafés. I'd had lunch in the remaining café and the waitress, who'd worked there for thirty years, told me their business was less than half of what it used to be. The square in Marshall was similar to Clanton's, except that most of the parking spaces were empty. There were very few folks walking the sidewalks.

I mentioned the town of Tackerville, with the same population as Clanton. One year after Bargain City opened there, the town was forced to spend $1.2 million on road improvements to handle the traffic around the development.

I handed the Mayor and councilmen copies of a study by an economics professor at the University of Georgia. He had tracked Bargain City across the South for the previous six years and evaluated the financial and social impact the company had on towns of less than ten thousand. Sales tax revenues remained roughly the same; the sales were simply shifted from the old merchants to Bargain City. Employment was roughly the same; the clerks in the old stores downtown were replaced by the new ones at Bargain City. The company made no substantial investment in the community, other than its land and building. In fact, it would not even allow its money to sit in local banks. At midnight, every night, the day's receipts were wired to the home office in Gainesville, Florida.

The study concluded that expansion was obviously wise for the shareholders of Bargain City, but it was economically devastating for most small towns. And the real damage was cultural. With boarded-up stores and empty sidewalks, the rich town life of main streets and courthouse squares was quickly dying.

A petition in support of Bargain City had 480 names. Our petition in opposition had 12. The council voted unanimously, 5–0, to approve it.

I wrote a harsh editorial and for a month read nasty letters addressed to me. For the first time, I was called a 'tree-hugger.'

Within a month, the bulldozers had completely razed fifty acres. The curbs and gutters were in, and a grand opening was announced for December 1, just in time for Christmas. With money committed, Bargain City wasted no time in building its warehouse. The company had a reputation for shrewd and decisive management.

The store and its parking lot covered about twenty acres. The outparcels were quickly sold to other chains, and before long the city had approved a sixteen-pump self-serve gas station, a convenience store, three fast-food restaurants, a discount shoe store, a discount furniture store, and a large grocery store.

I could not deny advertising to Bargain City. I didn't need their money, but since the *Times* was the only countywide paper, they had to advertise in it. (In response to a zoning flap I stirred up in 1977, a small right-wing rag called the *Clanton Chronicle* was up and running but struggling mightily.)

In mid-November, I met with a representative of the company and we laid out a series of rather expensive ads for the opening. I charged them as much as possible; they never complained.

On December 1, the Mayor, Senator Morton, and other dignitaries cut the ribbon. A rowdy mob burst through the doors and began shopping as if the hungry had found food. Traffic backed up on the highways leading into town.

I refused to give it front page coverage. I buried a rather small story on page seven, and this angered the Mayor and Senator Morton and the other dignitaries. They expected their ribbon cutting to be front and center.

The Christmas season was brutal for the downtown merchants. Three days after Christmas, the first casualty was reported when the old Western Auto store announced it was closing. It had occupied the same building for forty years, selling bicycles and appliances and televisions. Mr. Hollis Barr, the owner, told me that a certain Zenith color TV cost him $438, and he, after several price cuts, was trying to sell it for $510. The identical model was for sale at Bargain City for $399.

The closing of Western Auto was, of course, front page news.

It was followed in January by the closing of Swain's pharmacy next to the Tea Shoppe, and then Maggie's Gifts, next door to Mr. Mitlo's haberdashery. I treated each closing as if it were a death, and my stories had the air of obituaries.

I spent one afternoon with the Stukes twins in their hardware store. It was a wonderful old building, with dusty wooden floors, saggy shelves that held a million items, a wood-burning stove in the back where serious things got debated when business was slow. You couldn't find anything in the store, and you weren't supposed to. The routine was to ask one of the twins about 'the little flat gizmo that screws into the washer at the tip of that rod thing that fits into the gadget that makes the toilet flush.' One of the Stukes would disappear into the slightly organized piles of debris and emerge in a few minutes with whatever it took to make the toilet flush. Such a question could not be asked at Bargain City.

We sat by the stove on a cold winter day and listened to the rantings of one Cecil Clyde Poole, a retired Army major, who, if put in charge of national policy, would nuke everyone but the

Canadians. He would also nuke Bargain City, and in some of the roughest, most colorful language I'd ever heard he ripped and blasted the company with great gusto. We had plenty of time to talk because there were almost no customers. One of the Stukes told me their business was down 70 percent.

The following month they closed the doors to the store their father had opened in 1922. On the front page, I ran a photo of the founder sitting behind a counter in 1938. I also fired off another editorial, sort of a wise-ass 'I-told-you-so' reminder to whoever was out there still reading my little tirades.

'You're preachin' too much,' Harry Rex warned me over and over. 'And nobody's listenin'.'

The front office of the *Times* was seldom attended. There were some tables with copies of the current edition strewn about. There was a counter that Margaret sometimes used to lay out ads. The bell on the front door rang all day long as people came and went. About once a week a stranger would venture upstairs where my office door was usually open. More often than not it was some grieving relative there to discuss an upcoming obituary.

I looked up one afternoon in March 1979 and there was a gentleman in a nice suit standing at my office door. Unlike Harry Rex, whose entrance began on the street and was heard by everyone in the building, this guy had climbed the stairs without making a sound.

His name was Gary McGrew, a consultant from Nashville, whose area of expertise was small-town newspapers. As I fixed a pot of coffee, he explained that a rather well-financed client of his was planning to buy several newspapers in Mississippi during 1979. Because I had seven thousand subscribers, no debt, an offset press, and because we now ran the printing for six smaller weeklies, plus our own shoppers' guides, his client was very interested in buying *The Ford County Times*.

'How interested?' I asked.

'Extremely. If we could look at the books, we could value your company.'

He left and I made a few phone calls to verify his credibility. He checked out fine, and I collected my current financials. Three days later we met again, this time at night. I did not want Wiley or Baggy or anyone else hanging around. News that the *Times* was changing hands would be such hot gossip that they'd open the coffee shops at 3 A.M. instead of 5.

McGrew crunched the numbers like a seasoned analyst. I waited, oddly nervous, as if the verdict might drastically change my life.

'You're clearing a hundred grand after taxes, plus you're taking a salary of fifty grand. Depreciation is another twenty, no interest because you have no debt. That's one-seventy in cash flow, times the standard multiple of six, comes to one million twenty thousand.'

'And the building?' I asked.

He glanced around as if the ceiling might collapse any moment. 'These places typically don't sell for much.'

'A hundred thousand,' I said.

'Okay. And a hundred thousand for the offset press and other equipment. The total value is somewhere in the neighborhood of one-point-two million.'

'Is that an offer?' I asked, even more anxious.

'It might be. I'll have to discuss it with my client.'

I had no intention of selling the *Times*. I had stumbled into the business, gotten a few lucky breaks, worked hard writing stories and obituaries and selling pages of ads, and now, nine years later, my little company was worth over a million dollars.

I was young, still single though I was tired of being lonely and living alone in a mansion with three leftover Hocutt cats that refused to die. I had accepted the reality that I would not find a bride in Ford County. All the good ones were snatched up by their twentieth birthday, and I was too old to compete at that level. I dated all the young divorcées, most of whom were quick to hop in the sack and wake up in my fine home, and dream about spending all the money I was rumored to be making. The only one I really liked, and dated off and on for a year, was saddled with three small children.

But it's funny what a million bucks will do to you. Once it was in play, it was never far from my thoughts. The job became more tedious. I grew to resent the ridiculous obituaries and the endless pressure of the deadlines. I told myself at least once a day that I no longer had to hustle the street selling ads. I could quit the editorials. No more nasty letters to the editor.

A week later, I told Gary McGrew that the *Times* was not for sale. He said his client had decided to buy three papers by the end of the year, so I had time to think about it.

Remarkably, word of our discussions never leaked.

Chapter 36

On a Thursday afternoon in early May, I received a phone call from the attorney for the Parole Board. The next Padgitt hearing would take place the following Monday.

'Convenient timing,' I said.

'Why's that?' he asked.

'We publish every Wednesday, so I don't have time to run a story before the hearing.'

'We don't monitor your paper, Mr. Traynor,' he said.

'I don't believe that,' I snapped.

'What you believe is irrelevant. The Board has decided that you will not be permitted to attend the hearing. You violated our rules last time by reporting on what happened.'

'I'm banned?'

'That's correct.'

'I'll be there anyway.'

I hung up and called Sheriff McNatt. He, too, had been notified of the hearing, but wasn't sure if he could attend. He was hot on the trail of a missing child (from Wisconsin), and it was obvious he had little interest in getting mixed up with the Padgitts.

Our District Attorney, Rufus Buckley, had an armed robbery trial scheduled for Monday in Van Buren County. He promised to send a letter opposing the parole, but the letter never made it. Circuit Judge Omar Noose was presiding over the same trial, so he was off the hook. I began to think that no one would be there to speak in opposition to Padgitt's release.

For fun I asked Baggy to go. He gasped, then quickly let loose with an impressive list of excuses.

I walked over to Harry Rex's with the news. He had an ugly divorce trial starting Monday in Tupelo; otherwise he might have gone with me to Parchman. 'The boy's gonna be released, Willie,' he said.

'We stopped it last year,' I said.

'Once the parole hearings start, it's just a matter of time.'

'But somebody has to fight it.'

'Why bother? He's gettin' out eventually. Why piss off the Padgitts? You won't get any volunteers.'

Volunteers were indeed hard to find as the entire town ducked for cover. I had envisioned an angry mob packing into the parole board hearing and disrupting the meeting.

My angry mob consisted of three people.

Wiley Meek agreed to ride over with me, though he had no interest in speaking. If they were serious about banning me from the room, Wiley would sit through it and give me the details. Sheriff McNatt surprised us with his presence.

Security was tight in the hall outside the hearing room. When the Board attorney saw me he became angry and we exchanged words. Guards in uniforms surrounded me. I was outnumbered and unarmed. I was escorted from the building and placed in my car, then watched by two thick-necked ruffians with low IQs.

According to Wiley, the hearing went like clockwork. Lucien was there with various Padgitts. The Board attorney read a staff report that made Danny sound like an Eagle Scout. His caseworker seconded the nomination. Lucien spoke for ten minutes, the usual lawyerly bullshit. Danny's father spoke last and pleaded emotionally for his son's release. He was desperately needed back home, where the family had interests in timber, gravel, asphalt, trucking, contracting, and freight. He would have so many jobs and work so many hours each week that he couldn't possibly get into more trouble.

Sheriff McNatt gamely stood up for the people of Ford County. He was nervous and not a good speaker, but did a credible job of replaying the crime. Remarkably, he neglected to remind the Board members that a jury drawn

411

from the same pool of people who elected him had been threatened by Danny Padgitt.

By a vote of 4–1, Danny Padgitt was paroled from prison.

Clanton was quietly disappointed. During the trial, the town had a real thirst for blood and was bitter when the jury didn't deliver the death penalty. But nine years had passed, and since the parole hearing it had been accepted that Danny Padgitt would eventually get out. No one expected it so soon, but after the hearing we were over the shock.

His release was influenced by two unusual factors. The first was that Rhoda Kassellaw had no family in the area. There were no grieving parents to arouse sympathy and demand justice. There were no angry siblings to keep the case alive. Her children were gone and forgotten. She had lived a lonely life and left no close friends who were willing to press a grudge against her murderer.

The second was that the Padgitts lived in another world. They were so rarely seen in public, it was not difficult to convince ourselves that Danny would simply go to the island and never be seen again. What difference did it make to the people of Ford County? Prison or Padgitt Island? If we never saw him, we wouldn't be reminded of his crimes. In the nine years since his trial, I had not seen a single Padgitt in Clanton. In my rather harsh editorial about his release, I said 'a cold-blooded killer is once more among us.' But that wasn't really true.

The front page story and the editorial drew not a single letter from the public. Folks talked about the release, but not for long and not very loudly.

Baggy eased into my office late one morning a week after Padgitt's release, and closed the door, always a good sign. He'd picked up some gossip so juicy that it had to be delivered with the door shut.

On a typical day I arrived for work around 11 A.M. And on a typical day he began hitting the sauce around noon, so we usually had about an hour to discuss stories and monitor rumors.

He glanced around as if the walls were bugged, then said, 'It cost the Padgitts a hundred grand to spring the boy.'

The amount did not shock me, nor did the bribe itself, but I was surprised that Baggy had dug up this information.

'No,' I said. This always spurred him to tell more.

'That's what I'm tellin' you,' he said smugly, his usual response when he had the scoop.

'Who got the money?'

'That's the good part. You won't believe it.'

'Who?'

'You'll be shocked.'

'Who?'

Slowly, he went through his extended ritual of lighting a cigarette. In the early years, I would hang in the air as he delayed whatever dramatic news he had picked up, but with experience I had learned that this only slowed down the story. So I resumed my scribbling.

'It shouldn't come as a surprise, I guess,' he said, puffing and pondering. 'Didn't surprise me at all.'

'Are you gonna tell me or not?'

'Theo.'

'Senator Morton?'

'That's what I'm tellin' you.'

I was sufficiently shocked, and I had to give the impression of being so or the story would lose steam. 'Theo?' I asked.

'He's vice chairman of the Corrections Committee in the Senate. Been there forever, knows how to pull the strings. He wanted a hundred grand, the Padgitts wanted to pay it, they cut a deal, the boy walks. Just like that.'

'I thought Theo was above taking bribes,' I said, and I was serious. This drew an exaggerated snort.

'Don't be so naive,' he said. Again, he knew everything.

'Where did you hear it?'

'Can't say.' There was a chance that his poker gang had cooked up the rumor to see how fast it would race around the square before it got back to them. But there was an equally good chance Baggy was on to something. It really didn't matter, though. Cash couldn't be traced.

*

Just when I had stopped dreaming of an early retirement, of cashing in, walking away, jetting off to Europe, and backpacking across Australia, just when I had resettled into my routine of covering stories and writing obits and hawking ads to every merchant in town, Mr. Gary McGrew reentered my life. And he brought his client with him.

Ray Noble was one of three principals in a company that already owned thirty weekly newspapers in the Deep South and wanted to add more. Like my college friend Nick Diener, he had been raised in the family newspaper business and could talk the talk. He swore me to secrecy, then laid out his plan. His company wanted to buy the *Times*, along with the papers in Tyler and Van Buren Counties. They would sell off the equipment in the other two and do all the printing in Clanton because we had a better press. They would consolidate the accounting and much of the ad sales. Their offer of $1.2 million had been at the high end of the appraisal.

Now they were offering $1.3 million. Cash.

'After capital gains, you'll walk away with a cool million,' Noble said.

'I can do the math,' I said, as if I closed such deals on a weekly basis. The words 'cool million' were rumbling through my entire body.

They pressed a little. Offers were on the table for the other two papers, and I got the impression that the deal wasn't exactly coming together as they wished. The key element was the *Times*. We had better equipment and a slightly larger circulation.

I declined again and they left; all three of us knew it was not our last conversation.

Eleven years after he fled Ford County, Sam Ruffin returned in much the same manner as he left – on a bus in the middle of the night. He'd been home for two days before I knew it. I arrived for my Thursday lunch and there sat Sam, rocking on the porch, with a smile as wide as his mother's. Miss Callie looked and acted ten years younger now that he was safely back home. She fried a chicken and cooked every vegetable in her garden. Esau joined us and we feasted for three hours.

Sam now had one college degree under his belt and was planning on law school. He had almost married a Canadian woman but things blew up over her family's heated opposition to the union. Miss Callie was quite relieved to hear of the breakup. Sam had not mentioned the romance in letters to his mother.

He planned to stay in Clanton for a few days, very close to home, venturing out of Lowtown only at night. I promised to talk to Harry Rex, to fish around and see what I could learn about Trooper Durant and his sons. From the legal notices we printed, I knew that Durant had remarried, then divorced for the second time.

He wanted to see the town, so late that afternoon I picked him up in my Spitfire. Hiding under a Detroit Tigers baseball cap, he took in the sights of the small town he still called home. I showed him my office, my house, Bargain City, and the sprawl west of town. We circled the courthouse and I told him the story of the sniper and Baggy's dramatic escape. Much of this he'd heard in letters from Miss Callie.

As I dropped him off in front of the Ruffin home, he said, 'Is Padgitt really out of prison?'

'No one's seen him,' I said. 'But I'm sure he's back home.'

'Do you expect trouble?'

'No, not really.'

'Neither do I. But I can't convince Momma.'

'Nothing will happen, Sam.'

Chapter 37

The single shot that killed Lenny Fargarson was fired from a 30.06 hunting rifle. The killer could have been as far as two hundred yards away from the front porch where Lenny died. Thick woods began just beyond the wide lawn around the house, and there was a good chance whoever pulled the trigger had climbed a tree and had a perfectly concealed view of poor Lenny.

No one heard the shot. Lenny was sitting on the porch, in his wheelchair, reading one of the many books he borrowed each week from the Clanton library. His father was delivering mail. His mother was shopping at Bargain City. In all likelihood, Lenny felt no pain and died instantly. The bullet entered the right side of his head, just over the jaw, and created a massive exit wound above his left ear.

When his mother found him, he'd been dead for some time. She somehow managed to control herself and refrain from touching his body or the scene. Blood was all over the porch, even dripping onto the front steps.

Wiley heard the report on his police scanner. He called me with the chilling announcement, 'It has begun. Fargarson, the crippled boy, is dead.'

Wiley swung by the office, I jumped in his pickup, and we were off to the crime scene. Neither of us said a word, but we were thinking the same thing.

Lenny was still on the porch. The shot had knocked him out of his wheelchair and he lay on his side, with his face toward the house. Sheriff McNatt asked us not to take photos, and we readily complied. The paper would not have used them anyway.

Friends and relatives were flocking over, and they were directed by the deputies to a side door. McNatt used his men to shield the body on the front porch. I backed away and tried to take in that horrible scene – cops hovering over Lenny while those who loved him tried to get a glimpse of him as they hurried inside to console his parents.

When the body was finally loaded onto a gurney and placed in an ambulance, Sheriff McNatt came over and leaned on the pickup next to me.

'Are you thinkin' what I'm thinkin'?' he said.

'Yep.'

'Can you find me a list of the jurors?'

Though we had never printed the names of

the jurors, I had the information in an old file. 'Sure,' I said.

'How long will it take you?' he asked.

'Give me an hour. What's your plan?'

'We gotta notify those folks.'

As we were leaving, the deputies were beginning to comb the thick woods around the Fargarson home.

I took the list to the Sheriff's office, and we looked over it together. In 1977, I had written the obituary for juror number five, Mr. Fred Bilroy, a retired forest ranger who died suddenly of pneumonia. As far as I knew, the other ten were still alive.

McNatt gave the list to three of his deputies. They dispersed to deliver news that no one wanted to hear. I volunteered to tell Callie Ruffin.

She was on the porch watching Esau and Sam wage war over a game of checkers. They were delighted to see me, but the mood quickly changed. 'I have some disturbing news, Miss Callie,' I said somberly. They waited.

'Lenny Fargarson, that crippled boy on the jury with you, was murdered this afternoon.'

She covered her mouth and fell into her rocker. Sam steadied her, then patted her shoulder. I gave a brief description of what happened.

'He was such a good Christian boy,' Miss Callie said. 'We prayed together before we began deliberating.' She wasn't crying, but she was on the verge. Esau went to fetch her a blood pressure pill. He and Sam sat beside her rocker while I sat in the swing. We were all bunched together on the small porch, and for a long time little was said. Miss Callie lapsed into a long, brooding spell.

It was a warm spring night, under a half-moon, and Lowtown was busy with kids on bikes, neighbors talking across fences, a rowdy basketball game under way down the street. A gang of ten-year-olds became infatuated with my Spitfire, and Sam finally ran them off. It was only the second time I had been there after dark. 'Is it like this every night?' I finally asked.

'Yes, when the weather's nice,' Sam said, anxious to talk. 'It was a wonderful place to grow up. Everybody knows everybody. When I was nine years old I broke a car windshield with a baseball. I turned tail and ran, ran straight home, and when I got here Momma was waiting on the front porch. She knew all about it. I had to walk back to the scene of the crime, confess, and promise to make full restitution.'

'And you did,' Esau said.

'Took me six months to work and save a hundred and twenty bucks.'

Miss Callie almost smiled at the memory, but she was too preoccupied with Lenny Fargarson. Though she hadn't seen him in nine years, she had fond memories of him. His death truly saddened her, but it was also terrifying.

Esau fixed sweet tea with lemon, and when he returned from the inside of the house he quietly slid a double-barrel shotgun behind the rocker, within his reach but out of her sight.

As the hours passed, the foot traffic thinned and the neighbors withdrew. I decided that if Miss Callie stayed at home she would be a very difficult target. There were houses next door and across the street. There were no hills or towers or vacant lots within sight.

I didn't mention this, but I'm sure Sam and Esau were having the same thoughts. When she was ready for bed, I said my good nights and drove back to the jail. It was crawling with deputies, and had the carnival-like atmosphere that only a good murder could bring. I couldn't help but flash back nine years to the night Danny Padgitt was arrested and hauled in with blood on his shirt.

Only two of the jurors had not been found. Both had moved, and Sheriff McNatt was trying to track them down. He asked about Miss Callie and I said she was safe. I did not tell him Sam was home.

He closed the door to his office and said he had a favor to ask. 'Tomorrow, can you go talk to Lucien Wilbanks?'

'Why me?'

'Well, I could, but, personally, I can't stand the bastard, and he feels the same way about me.'

'Everybody hates Lucien,' I said.

422

'Except . . .'

'Except . . . Harry Rex?'

'Harry Rex. What if you and Harry Rex go talk to Lucien? See if he will act as go-between to the Padgitts. I mean, at some point I gotta talk to Danny, right?'

'I guess. You're the Sheriff.'

'Just have a chat with Lucien Wilbanks, that's all. Feel him out. If it goes well, then maybe I'll talk to him. It's different if the Sheriff goes bargin' in at first.'

'I'd rather be lashed with a bullwhip,' I said, and I wasn't joking.

'But you'll do it?'

'I'll sleep on it.'

Harry Rex wasn't too thrilled with the idea either. Why should both of us get involved? We kicked it around over an early breakfast at the coffee shop, an unusual meal for us but then we didn't want to miss the first tidal wave of downtown gossip. Not surprisingly, the place was packed with anxious experts who were repeating all sorts of details and theories about the Fargarson murder. We listened more than we talked, and left around eight-thirty.

Two doors down from the coffee shop was the Wilbanks Building. As we walked by, I said, 'Let's do it.'

Pre-Lucien, the Wilbanks family had been a cornerstone of Clanton society, commerce, and law. In the golden years of the last century, they owned land and banks, and all of the men in the family had studied law, some at real Ivy League schools. But they had been in decline for many years. Lucien was the last male Wilbanks of any consequence, and there was an excellent chance he was about to be disbarred.

Ethel Twitty, the longtime secretary, greeted us rudely, almost sneering at Harry Rex, who mumbled to me under his breath, 'Meanest bitch in town.' I think she heard him. It was obvious they had been catfighting for many years. Her boss was in. What did we want?

'We want to see Lucien,' Harry Rex said. 'Why else would we be here?' She rang him up as we waited. 'I don't have all day!' Harry Rex snapped at her at one point.

'Go ahead,' she said, more to get rid of us than anything else. We climbed the steps. Lucien's office was huge, at least thirty feet wide and long with ten-foot ceilings and a row of French doors overlooking the square. It was on the north side, directly across from the *Times*, with the courthouse in between. Thankfully, I couldn't see Lucien's balcony from my porch.

He greeted us indifferently, as if we had interrupted a long serious meditation. Though it was early, his cluttered desk gave the impression of a man who'd worked all night. He had long grayish hair that ran down his neck, and an unfashionable goatee, and the tired red eyes of a serious drinker. 'What's the occasion?' he asked, very slowly. We glared at each other, both conveying as much contempt as possible.

'Had a murder yesterday, Lucien,' Harry Rex said. 'Lenny Fargarson, that crippled boy on the jury.'

'I'm assuming this is off the record,' he said in my direction.

'It is,' I said. 'Completely. Sheriff McNatt asked me to stop by and say hello. I invited Harry Rex.'

'So we're just socializing?'

'Maybe. Just having a little gossip about the murder,' I said.

'I got the details,' he said.

'Have you talked to Danny Padgitt lately?' Harry Rex asked.

'Not since he was paroled.'

'Is he in the county?'

'He's in the state, I'm not sure exactly where. If he crosses the state line without permission he violates the conditions of his parole.'

Why couldn't they parole him to, say, Wyoming? It seemed odd that he would be required to stay close to where he committed his crimes. Get rid of him!

'Sheriff McNatt would like to talk to him,' I said.

'Oh does he? Why should that concern you and me? Tell the Sheriff to go talk to him.'

'It's not that simple, Lucien, and you know it,' Harry Rex said.

'Does the Sheriff have any proof against my client? Any evidence? Ever hear of probable cause, Harry Rex? You can't just round up the usual suspects, you know? Takes a little more than that.'

'There was a direct threat against the jurors,' I said.

'Nine years ago.'

'It was still a threat, and we all remember it. Now, two weeks after he's paroled, one of his jurors is dead.'

'That's not enough, fellas. Show me more and I might consult with my client. Right now there's nothing but naked speculation. Plenty of it, but this town's always good for a flood of gossip.'

'You don't know where he is, do you, Lucien?' Harry Rex said.

'I assume he's on the island, with the rest of them.' He used the word 'them' as if they were a bunch of rats.

'What happens if another juror gets shot?' Harry Rex pressed on.

Lucien dropped a legal pad on his desk and rested there on his elbows. 'What am I supposed to do, Harry Rex? Call the boy up, say "Hey, Danny, I'm sure you're not killin' your jurors, but, if by chance you are, then, hey, be a good boy and stop it." You think he'll listen to me? This wouldn't have happened if the idiot had followed my advice. I insisted that he not take the stand in his own defense. He's an idiot, okay, Harry Rex! You're a lawyer, God knows you've had idiot clients. You can't do a damned thing to control them.'

'What happens if another juror gets shot?' Harry Rex repeated.

'Then I guess another juror will die.'

I jumped to my feet and headed for the door. 'You're a sick bastard,' I said.

'Not a word of this in print,' he snarled behind me.

'Go to hell,' I yelled as I slammed his door.

Late in the afternoon Mr. Magargel called from the funeral home and asked if I could hustle over. Mr. and Mrs. Fargarson were there, picking out a casket and making the final arrangements. As I had done many times, I met them in Parlor C, the smallest viewing room. It was seldom used.

Pastor J. B. Cooper of the Maranatha Primitive Baptist Church was with them, and he was a saint. They leaned on him for every decision.

At least twice a year, I met with a family after the tragic death of a loved one. It was almost always a car wreck or some gruesome farm injury, something unexpected. The surviving members were too shocked to think clearly, too wounded to make decisions. The strong ones simply sleepwalked through the ordeal. The weak ones were often too numb to do anything but cry. Mrs. Fargarson was the stronger of the two, but the horror of finding her son with half his head blown off had reduced her to a shuddering ghost. Mr. Fargarson just stared at the floor.

Pastor Cooper gently extracted the basics, many of which he already knew. Since his spinal injury fifteen years earlier, Lenny had dreamed of going to heaven, of having his body restored, of walking every day hand in hand with his Savior. We worked on some language to this effect, and Mrs. Fargarson was deeply appreciative. She handed me a photo, one of Lenny sitting by a pond with a fishing pole. I promised to put it on the front page.

As always with grieving parents, they thanked me profusely and insisted on hugging me tightly as I tried to leave. Mourners cling to people like that, especially at the funeral home.

I stopped by Pepe's and bought an array of Mexican carryout, then drove to Lowtown, where I found Sam playing basketball, Miss Callie asleep inside, and Esau guarding the house with his shotgun. Eventually, we ate on the porch, though she only nibbled at the foreign food. She wasn't hungry. Esau said she'd eaten little during the day.

I brought my backgammon board and taught Sam the game. Esau preferred checkers. Miss Callie was certain any activity that involved the rolling of dice was patently sinful, but she wasn't up to a lecture. We sat for hours, deep into the night, and watched the rituals of Lowtown. School had just turned out for the summer, the days were longer and hotter.

Buster, my part-time pit bull, drove by every half hour. He would slow in front of the Ruffins,

I'd wave as if things were fine, he'd ease away and return to the driveway of the Hocutt House. A patrol car parked two doors down from the Ruffin house and sat for a long time. Sheriff McNatt had hired three black deputies, and two of them had been assigned to keep an eye on the home.

Others were watching as well. After Miss Callie went to bed, Esau pointed across to the street to the darkened screened porch where the Braxtons lived. 'Tully's over there,' he said. 'Watchin' everythin'.'

'He told me he'd stay up all night,' Sam said. Lowtown would be a dangerous place to start a gunfight.

I left after eleven, crossed the tracks, and drove the empty streets of Clanton. The town pulsed with tension, with anticipation, because whatever had been started was far from over.

Chapter 38

Miss Callie insisted on attending the funeral of Lenny Fargarson. Sam and Esau objected strenuously, but, as always, once she made up her mind, then all conversations were over. I discussed this with Sheriff McNatt, who summed things up by saying, 'She's a grown lady.' He knew of no other jurors who planned to attend, but then it was difficult to monitor such things.

I also called Pastor Cooper to forewarn him. His response was, 'She will be very welcome in our little church. But get here early.'

With rare exceptions blacks and whites did not worship together in Ford County. They fervently believed in the same Lord, but chose very different styles of worshiping him. The majority of whites expected to be outside the church building at five past noon on Sunday, and seated for lunch by twelve-thirty. Blacks really didn't care what time the service broke up, or what time it began for that matter. On my church tour I visited twenty-seven black congregations and never saw a benediction before 1:30 – 3 P.M. was the norm. Several simply went all day, with a short break for lunch in the fellowship hall, then back to the sanctuary for another round.

Such zealotry would have killed a white Christian.

But funerals were very different. When Miss Callie, along with Sam and Esau, walked into the Maranatha Primitive Baptist Church, there were a few quick stares but nothing more. Had they walked in on a Sunday morning for regular worship, there would have been resentment.

We arrived forty-five minutes early, and the lovely little sanctuary was almost filled. I watched through the tall open windows as the cars kept coming. A loudspeaker had been hung from one of the ancient oaks, and a large crowd gathered around it after the building was full. The choir started with 'The Old Rugged Cross,' and the tears began flowing. Pastor Cooper's soothing message was a gentle warning for us not to question why bad things happen to good people. God is always in control, and though we are too small to understand His infinite wisdom and majesty, He will one day reveal Himself to us. Lenny was with Him now, and that was where Lenny longed to be.

They buried him behind the church, in an immaculate little cemetery inside a wrought-iron fence. Miss Callie clutched my hand and prayed fervently when the casket was lowered into the ground. A soloist sang 'Amazing Grace,' then Pastor Cooper thanked us for coming. There was punch and cookies in the fellowship hall behind the sanctuary, and most of the crowd hung around for a few minutes to visit, or to have one last word with Mr. and Mrs. Fargarson.

Sheriff McNatt caught my attention and nodded as if he wanted to talk. We walked to the front of the church where no one could hear us. He was in uniform with his standard toothpick in his mouth. 'Any luck with Wilbanks?' he asked.

'No, just the one meeting,' I said. 'Harry Rex went back yesterday and got nowhere.'

'I guess I'll talk to him,' he said.

'You can, but you won't get anywhere.'

The toothpick shifted from one side of his mouth to the other, in much the same way Harry Rex could slide his cigar over without missing a word. 'We got nothin' else. We've combed the woods around the house, not a track or a trace of anything. You're not printin' this, are you?'

'No.'

'There are a bunch of ol' loggin' trails deep in the woods around the Fargarson place. We've tiptoed everyone of 'em, found absolutely nothin'.'

'So your only evidence is a single bullet.'

'That and a dead body.'

'Has anybody seen Danny Padgitt?'

'Not yet. I keep two cars up on 401, where it turns to go into the island. They can't see everything, but at least the Padgitts know we're there.

There are a hundred ways off and on the island, but only the Padgitts know them all.'

The Ruffins were slowly moving toward us, talking to one of the black deputies.

'She's probably the safest one,' McNatt said.

'Is anybody safe?'

'We'll find out. He'll try again, Willie, you mark my word. I'm convinced of it.'

'Me too.'

Ned Ray Zook owned four thousand acres in the eastern part of the county. He farmed cotton and soybeans, and his operations were large enough to maintain sufficient profits. He was rumored to be one of the few remaining farmers who made good money from the soil. It was on his property, deep in a wooded area, in a converted cattle barn, that Harry Rex had taken me nine years earlier to watch my first and last cockfight.

Sometime during the early hours of June 14, a vandal entered Zook's vast equipment shed and partially drained the oil from the engines of two of his big tractors. The oil was collected in cans and hidden among the supplies, so when the operators arrived around 6 A.M. for the day's work there was no sign of foul play. One operator checked the oil as he was supposed to do, saw the shortage, thought it odd, said nothing, and added four quarts. The other operator had checked his the afternoon before, as was his habit. The second tractor ground to a sudden halt an hour later, as its engine locked up. Its operator hiked half a mile back to the shed and reported the breakdown to the farm manager.

Two hours later, a green-and-yellow service truck bounced along the field road and maneuvered itself close to the disabled tractor. Two servicemen slowly got out, inspected the hot sun and cloudless sky, then walked around the tractor for an initial look. They reluctantly opened up the panels of the service truck and began removing tools and wrenches. The sun baked them and they were soon sweating.

To make their day somewhat more pleasant, they turned on the radio in their truck and cranked up the volume. Merle Haggard could be heard wafting across the soybean field.

The music muffled the crack of a distant rifle shot. It hit Mo Teale directly in the upper back, ripped through his lungs, and tore a hole in his chest as it exited. Teale's partner, Red, said over and over that the only thing he heard was a fierce grunt just a second or two before Mo fell under the front axle. He thought at first that something from the tractor had snapped loose in a violent way and injured Mo. Red dragged him to the truck and raced away, much more concerned about his buddy than what might have injured him. At the equipment shed, the farm manager called an ambulance, but it was too late. Mo Teale died there, on the concrete floor of a small, dusty office. 'Mr. John Deere' we'd called him during the trial. Middle of the front row, bad body language.

At the time of his death he was wearing the same type of bright yellow uniform shirt he'd worn every day of the trial. It made for an easy target.

I saw him at a distance, through the open door. Sheriff McNatt allowed us inside the shed with the now standard prohibition against taking photos. Wiley had left his cameras in his pickup.

Once again Wiley had been monitoring the police scanner when the report came across —' Got a shooting at Ned Ray Zook's farm!' Wiley was always near his scanner, and in those days he wasn't alone. Given the high state of anxiety in the county, every scanner was being listened to and every possible shooting was reason to hop in the pickup and go for a look.

McNatt soon asked us to leave. His men found the cans of oil that had been drained by the vandal, and they found a window that had been pried open for entry into the shed. They would dust for fingerprints and find none. They would look for footprints on the gravel flooring, and find none. They would scour the woods around the soybean field and find no sign of the killer. In the dirt beside the tractor they did find the 30.06 shell, and it was quickly matched with the one that killed Lenny Fargarson.

I hung around the Sheriff's office until well after dark. As expected it was a busy place, with deputies and constables loitering about, comparing stories, creating new details. The phones rang nonstop. And there was a new wrinkle. Random townsfolk, unable to control their curiosity, began stopping by and asking anyone who would listen if there was anything new.

There was not. McNatt barricaded himself in his office with his top boys and tried to decide what to do next. His priority was the protection of the surviving eight jurors. Three were already dead – Mr. Fred Bilroy (of pneumonia), and now Lenny Fargarson and Mo Teale. One juror had moved to Florida two years after the trial. At that moment, each of the eight had a patrol car parked very near their front doors.

I left and went to the office to work on the story about the murder of Mo Teale, but I was sidetracked by the lights at Harry Rex's. He was in his conference room, knee-deep in depositions and files and all sorts of lawyerly debris, the sight of which always gave me an instant headache. We grabbed two beers out of his small office refrigerator and went for a drive.

In a working-class section of town known as Coventry we drove along a narrow street and passed a house with cars parked like fallen dominoes in the front yard. 'That's where Maxine Root lives,' he said. 'She was on the jury.'

I vaguely remembered Mrs. Root. Her small red-brick house had no front porch to speak of, so her neighbors were scattered around the carport in folding lawn chairs. Rifles were visible. Every light in the house was on. A patrol car was parked by the mailbox, two deputies leaning on its hood, smoking cigarettes and watching us very closely as we drove by. Harry Rex stopped and said, 'Evenin', Troy,' to one of the deputies.

'Hey, Harry Rex,' Troy said, taking a step toward us.

'Quite a party they got goin', huh?'

'It'd take a fool to start trouble around here.'

'We're just passin' by,' Harry Rex said.

'Better keep movin',' Troy said. 'They got itchy fingers.'

'Take care.' We eased away and swung around behind the livestock barn north of town where a long shady lane dead-ended near the water tower. Halfway down, the street was lined on both sides with cars. 'Who lives here?' I asked.

'Mr. Earl Youry. He sat on the back row, farthest from the spectators.'

A crowd was huddled on the front porch. Some sat on the steps. Others were in lawn chairs out on the grass. Somewhere in that pack Mr. Earl Youry was hidden and very well protected by his friends and neighbors.

Miss Callie was no less defended. The street in front of her house was packed with cars and barely passable. Groups of men sat on the cars, some smoking, some holding rifles. Next door and across the street the porches and yards were filled with people. Half of Lowtown had gathered there to make sure she felt secure. There was a festival atmosphere, the feeling of a unique event.

With white faces, Harry Rex and I received closer scrutiny. We didn't stop until he could speak with the deputies, and once they approved our presence the pack relaxed. We parked and I walked to the house where Sam met me at the front steps. Harry Rex stayed behind, chatting with the deputies.

She was inside, in her bedroom, reading her Bible with a friend from church. Several deacons were on the porch with Sam and Esau, and they were anxious for details of the Teale murder. I filled them in with as much as I could tell, which wasn't much at all.

Around midnight, the crowd began to slowly break up. Sam and the deputies had organized a rotation of all-night sentries, armed guards on both the front and back porches. There was no shortage of volunteers. Miss Callie never dreamed her pleasant and God-fearing little home would become such an armed fortress, but under the circumstances she could not be disappointed.

We drove the anxious streets to the Hocutt House, where we found Buster asleep in his car in the driveway. We found some bourbon and sat on a front porch, swatting an occasional mosquito and trying to appreciate the situation.

'He's very patient,' Harry Rex said. 'Wait a few days when all these neighbors get tired of porch sittin', when everybody relaxes a little. The jurors can't live long locked inside their homes. He'll wait.'

One chilling little fact that had not been released was a service call received by the tractor dealership a week earlier. At the Anderson farm south of town a tractor had been disabled under similar circumstances. Mo Teale, who was one of four chief mechanics, had not been sent to repair it. Someone else's yellow shirt had been watched through the scope of a hunting rifle.

'He's patient and meticulous,' I agreed. Eleven days had passed between the two murders, and no clues had been left behind. If it was indeed Danny Padgitt, there was a stark contrast between his first murder – Rhoda Kassellaw – and his last two. He'd advanced from a brutal crime of passion to cold-blooded executions. Perhaps that's what nine years in prison had taught him. He'd had plenty of time to remember the faces of the twelve people who'd sent him away, and to plan his revenge.

'He's not finished,' Harry Rex said.

One murder might be considered a random act. Two meant there was a pattern. The third would send a small army of cops and vigilantes onto Padgitt Island for an all-out war.

'He'll wait,' Harry Rex said. 'Probably for a long time.'

'I'm thinking about selling the paper, Harry Rex,' I said.

He took a long drink of bourbon, then said, 'Why would you do that?'

'Money. This company in Georgia is making a serious offer.'

439

'How much?'

'A lot. More than I ever dreamed of. I wouldn't work for a long time. Maybe never.'

The idea of not working hit him hard. His daily routine was ten hours of nonstop chaos with some very emotional and high-strung divorce clients. He often worked nights, when the office was quiet and he could think. He made a comfortable living, but he certainly scraped for every penny. 'How long have you had the paper?' he asked.

'Nine years.'

'Kinda hard to imagine the paper without you.'

'Maybe that's a reason to sell it. I don't want to be another Wilson Caudle.'

'What will you do?'

'Take a break, travel, see the world, find a nice lady, marry her, get her pregnant, have some kids. This is a big house.'

'So you wouldn't move away?'

'To where? This is home.'

Another long sip, then, 'I don't know. Let me sleep on it.' With that, he walked off the porch and drove away.

Chapter 39

With the bodies piling up, it was inevitable the story would attract more attention than the *Times* could give it. The next morning, a reporter I knew from the Memphis paper arrived in my office, and about twenty minutes later one from the Jackson paper joined us. Both covered northern Mississippi, where the hottest news was usually a factory explosion or another indicted county official.

I gave them the background on both murders, the Padgitt parole, and the fear that had gripped the county. We were not competitors – they wrote for large dailies that barely overlapped. Most of my subscribers also took either the Memphis or Jackson papers. The Tupelo daily was also popular.

And, frankly, I was losing interest; not in the current crisis, but in journalism as a vocation. The world was calling me. As I sat there drinking coffee and trading stories with those two veterans, both of whom were older than me, each of whom earned about $40,000 a year, I found it hard to believe that I could walk away right then with a million bucks. It was difficult to stay focused.

They eventually left to pursue their own angles. A few minutes later Sam called with a rather urgent, 'You need to come over.'

A ragtag little unit was still guarding the Ruffin porch. All four were bleary-eyed and in need of sleep. Sam cleared me through the bivouac and we went to the kitchen table where Miss Callie was shelling butter beans, a task she always performed on the rear porch. She gave me a warm smile and the standard bear hug, but she was a troubled woman. 'In here,' she said. Sam nodded and we followed her into her small bedroom. She closed the door behind us as if intruders were lurking, then she disappeared into a narrow closet. We waited awkwardly while she rattled around in there.

She finally emerged with an old spiral note-book, one that had obviously been well hidden. 'Something doesn't make sense,' she said as she sat on the edge of the bed. Sam sat beside her and I backed into an old rocker. She was flipping through the pages of her handwritten notes. 'Here it is,' she said.

'We gave our solemn promises that we would never talk about what happened in the jury room,' she said, 'but this is too important not to tell. When we found Mr. Padgitt guilty, the vote was quick and unanimous. But when we came to the issue of the death penalty, there was some opposition to it. I certainly didn't want to send anyone to die, but I had promised to follow the law. Things got very heated, there were sharp words, even some accusations and threats. Not a pleasant thing to sit through. When the battle lines became clear, there were three people opposed to the death penalty, and they were not about to change their minds.'

She showed me a page in her notebook. In her clear and distinctive handwriting there were two columns – one had nine names, the other had only three – L. Fargarson, Mo Teale, and Maxine Root. I gawked at the names, thinking that maybe I was looking at the killer's list.

'When did you write this?' I asked.

'I kept notes during the trial,' she said.

Why would Danny Padgitt be killing the jurors who refused to give him the death penalty? The ones who had effectively saved his life?

'He's killing the wrong ones, isn't he?' Sam asked. 'I mean, it's all wrong, but if you're out for revenge why go after the folks who tried to save you?'

'As I said, it doesn't make sense,' Miss Callie said.

'You're assuming too much,' I said. 'You're assuming he knows how each juror voted. As far as I know, and I snooped around for a long time, the jurors never told anyone how the vote went. The trial was overshadowed rather quickly by the desegregation order. Padgitt was shipped off to Parchman the same day he was found guilty. There's a good chance he's picking off the easy ones first, and Mr. Fargarson and Mr. Teale just happened to be more accessible.'

'That's very coincidental,' Sam said.

We pondered that for a long time. I wasn't sure if it was plausible; I wasn't sure of anything. Then I had another thought: 'Keep in mind, all twelve jurors voted guilty, and that was just after he made his threat.'

'I suppose,' Miss Callie said, unconvinced. We were trying to make sense of something that was completely incomprehensible.

'Anyway, I need to give this information to the Sheriff,' I said.

'We promised we'd never tell.'

'That was nine years ago, Mother,' Sam said. 'And no one could have predicted what's happening now.'

'It's especially important for Maxine Root,' I said.

'Don't you think some of the other jurors have come forward with this same information?' Sam said.

'Maybe, but it was a long time ago. And I doubt if they kept notes.'

There was a commotion at the front door. Bobby, Leon, and Al had arrived. They had met in St. Louis, then driven all night to Clanton. We had coffee around the kitchen table, and I filled them in on the most recent developments. Miss

Callie suddenly sprang to life and was pondering meals and making a list of vegetables for Esau to pick.

Sheriff McNatt was out making the rounds, visiting each juror. I had to unload on someone, so I barged into Harry Rex's office and waited impatiently while he finished a deposition. When we were alone, I told him about Miss Callie's list and the division of the jurors. He'd been haggling with a room full of lawyers for the past two hours, so he was in a feisty mood.

As usual, he had a different, far more cynical theory.

'Those three were supposed to hang the jury on guilt,' he said after a quick analysis. 'They caved for some reason, probably thought they were doin' the right thing by keepin' him out of the gas chamber, but of course Padgitt ain't thinkin' that way. For nine years he's been pissed because his three stooges didn't hang the jury. He figures he'll get them first, then go after the rest.'

'There's no way Lenny Fargarson was a stooge for Danny Padgitt,' I argued.

'Just because he's crippled?'

'Just because he was a very devout Christian.'

'He was unemployed, Willie. He was once able to work, but he knew his condition would only deteriorate over the years. Maybe he needed money. Hell, everybody needs money. The Padgitts have trucks full of cash.'

'I don't buy it.'

'It makes more sense than any of your screwball theories. What are you sayin' – somebody else is pickin' off the jurors?'

'I didn't say that.'

'Good, because I was about to call you a flamin' dumb-ass.'

'You've called me worse.'

'Not this morning.'

'And under your theory, Mo Teale and Maxine Root also took cash from the Padgitts, then double-crossed Danny on the issue of guilt, then reversed themselves on the issue of death, and will now pay the ultimate price because they didn't hang the jury to begin with? Is that what you're saying, Harry Rex?'

'Damned right!'

'You're a flaming dumb-ass, you know that? Why would an honest, hardworking, crime-hating, churchgoing man like Mo Teale agree to take money from the Padgitts?'

'Maybe they threatened him.'

'Maybe! Maybe they didn't!'

'So what's your best theory?'

'It's Padgitt, and it just so happens that the first two he picked off happened to be two of the three who voted no to the death penalty. He doesn't know how the vote went. He was in Parchman twelve hours after the verdict. He's made his list. Fargarson was first because he was such an easy target. Teale was second because Padgitt could choose the setting.'

'Who's third?'

'I don't know, but these folks won't stay locked in their homes forever. He'll bide his time, let things die down, then secretly start making plans again.'

'He could have some help, you know.'

'Exactly.'

Harry Rex's phone had never stopped ringing. He glared at it during a pause, then said, 'I got work to do.'

'I guess I'll go see the Sheriff. See you later.' I was out of his office when he yelled, 'Say, Willie. One other thing.'

I turned to face him.

'Sell it, take the money, go play for a while. You've earned it.'

'Thanks.'

'But don't leave Clanton, you hear?'

'I won't.'

Mr. Earl Youry ran a road grader for the county. He graded the rural roads that ran into very remote places, out from Possum Ridge and far beyond Shady Grove. Since he worked alone, it was decided that he should hang around the county barn for a few days where he had many friends, all of whom had rifles in their trucks and were on high alert. Sheriff McNatt huddled with Mr. Youry and his supervisor and worked out a plan to keep him safe.

Mr. Youry called the Sheriff and said he had important information. He admitted his recollection was less than thorough, but he was certain that the crippled boy and Mo Teale had been adamant in their refusal to impose the death penalty. He remembered that they had a third vote, maybe it was one of the women, maybe the colored lady. He just couldn't recall exactly, and, after all, it had been nine years. He posed the same question to McNatt – 'Why would Danny Padgitt be killing the jurors who refused to give him the death penalty?'

When I walked into the Sheriff's office, he had just finished his conversation with Mr. Youry, and he was as bewildered as he should have been. I closed the door and relayed my conversation with Miss Callie. 'I saw her notes, Sheriff,' I said. 'The third vote was Maxine Root.'

For an hour we rehashed the same arguments I'd had with Sam and Harry Rex, and again it made no sense. He did not believe that the Padgitts had bought or intimidated either Lenny or Mo Teale; he wasn't so sure about Maxine Root since she came from a rougher family. He more or less agreed with me that the first two killings had been coincidental, and that Padgitt, in all likelihood, did not know how the jurors had voted. Interestingly, he claimed that he found out about a year after the verdict that it had been a 9–3 split on the issue of death, and that Mo Teale had become almost violently opposed to such a sentence.

But, both of us conceded, with Lucien Wilbanks involved it was entirely possible

448

Padgitt knew more about the deliberations than we did. Anything was possible.

And nothing made sense.

While I was sitting in his office, he called Maxine Root. She worked as a bookkeeper at the shoe factory north of town, and had insisted on going to work. McNatt had been in her office that morning, inspecting the place, talking with her boss and coworkers, making sure everyone felt safe. Two of his deputies were outside the building, watching for trouble and waiting to haul Maxine back home at quitting time.

They chatted on the phone like old friends for a few minutes, then McNatt said, 'Say, Maxine, I know that you and Mo Teale and the Fargarson boy were the only three who voted against the death penalty for Danny Padgitt . . .' He paused as she interrupted.

'Well, it's not important how I found out. What's important here is that makes me real nervous about your safety. Extra nervous.'

He listened to her for a few minutes. As she rambled on he interrupted occasionally with such things as: 'Well, Maxine, I can't just charge out there and arrest the boy.'

And, 'You tell your brothers to keep those guns in their trucks.'

And, 'I'm workin' on the case, Maxine, and when I get enough evidence I'll get a warrant for his arrest.'

And, 'It's too late to give him the death

penalty, Maxine. You did what you thought was right at the time.'

She was crying when the conversation ended. 'Poor thing,' McNatt said, 'her nerves are shot to hell.'

'Can't really blame her,' I said. 'I'm ducking under windows myself.'

Chapter 40

The funeral for Mo Teale was held at the Willow Road Methodist Church, number thirty-six on my list and one of my favorites. It was barely in the city limits of Clanton, south of the square. Because I had never met Mr. Teale, I did not go to his funeral. However, there were many in attendance who had never met him.

Had he died of a heart attack at the age of fifty-one, it would have been sudden and tragic and his final service would have drawn an impressive crowd. But being gunned down in a revenge killing by a freshly paroled murderer was simply too much for the curious to resist. The mob included long-forgotten high school acquaintances of Mr. Teale's four adult children, and meddling old widows who seldom missed a good funeral, and out-of-town reporters, and several gentlemen whose only contact with Mo was the fact that they owned John Deere tractors.

I stayed away and worked on his obituary. His

oldest son had been kind enough to stop by the office and give me the details. He was thirty-three – Mo and his wife jump-started their family – and he sold new Fords over in Tupelo. He stayed for almost two hours and desperately wanted me to assure him that Danny Padgitt was about to be hauled in and stoned.

Interment was at the Clanton cemetery. The funeral procession stretched for blocks and, for good measure, swung by the square and proceeded down Jackson Avenue, just outside the *Times*. It did not disrupt traffic at all – everyone was at the funeral.

Using Harry Rex as an intermediary, Lucien Wilbanks arranged a meeting with Sheriff McNatt. I was specifically mentioned by Lucien, and specifically not invited. Didn't matter; Harry Rex took notes and told me everything, with the understanding that nothing would get printed.

Also present in Lucien's office was Rufus Buckley, the District Attorney who had succeeded Ernie Gaddis in 1975. Buckley was a publicity hog who, though reluctant to meddle in Padgitt's parole, was now anxious to lead the mob to lynch him. Harry Rex despised Buckley, and the feelings were mutual. Lucien despised him too, but then Lucien disliked virtually everyone because everyone certainly disliked him. Sheriff McNatt hated Lucien, tolerated Harry Rex, and was forced to work the same side of the street with Buckley, though he loathed him in private.

Given those conflicting sentiments, I was quite pleased not be invited to the meeting.

Lucien began by saying that he had talked with both Danny Padgitt and his father, Gill. They had met somewhere outside of Clanton and away from the island. Danny was doing fine, working each day in the office of the family's highway contracting firm, that office being conveniently located within the safe harbor of Padgitt Island.

Not surprisingly, Danny denied any involvement in the murders of Lenny Fargarson and Mo Teale. He was shocked by what was happening and angry that he was widely considered to be the chief suspect. Lucien emphasized that he grilled Danny at length, even to the point of irritating him, and he never showed the slightest hint of dishonesty.

Lenny Fargarson was shot on the afternoon of May 23. At that time, Danny was in his office, and there were four people who could vouch for his presence there. The Fargarson home was at least a thirty-minute drive from Padgitt Island, and the four witnesses were certain that Danny was either in his office or very close to it throughout the afternoon.

'How many of these witnesses are named Padgitt?' McNatt asked.

'We're not giving names, yet,' Lucien said, stonewalling as any good lawyer should.

Eleven days later, on June 3, Mo Teale was shot at approximately nine-fifteen in the morning. At that precise moment, Danny was standing beside a newly paved highway in Tippah County, getting documents signed by one of the Padgitt construction foremen. The foreman, along with two laborers, was willing to testify as to exactly where Danny was at that moment. The highway job was at least two hours away from Ned Ray Zook's farm in eastern Ford County.

Lucien presented airtight alibis for both murders, though his small audience was very skeptical. Of course the Padgitts would deny everything. And given their capacity to lie, break legs, and bribe with serious cash, they could find witnesses for anything.

Sheriff McNatt voiced his skepticism. He explained to Lucien that his investigation was continuing, and if and when he had probable cause, he would get his arrest warrant and descend upon the island. He had spoken several times with the state police, and if a hundred troopers were necessary to flush out Danny, then so be it.

Lucien said that would not be necessary. If a valid arrest warrant was obtained, he would do his best to bring the boy in himself.

'And if there's another killing,' McNatt said, 'this place will erupt. You'll have a thousand rednecks crossin' the bridge and shootin' every Padgitt they can find.'

Buckley said that he and Judge Omar Noose had spoken twice about the killings, and he was reasonably confident that Noose was 'almost ready' to issue a warrant for Danny's arrest. Lucien attacked him with a barrage of questions about probable cause and sufficient evidence. Buckley argued that the threat by Padgitt during his trial was ample reason to suspect him of the murders.

The meeting deteriorated as the two argued heatedly over nitpicking legalities. The Sheriff finally broke it up by announcing he'd heard enough and walked out of Lucien's office. Buckley followed. Harry Rex hung around and chatted with Lucien in a much more relaxed setting.

'You got liars protectin' liars,' Harry Rex growled as he paced around my office an hour later. 'Lucien tells the truth only when it sounds good, which, for him and his clientele, is not very often. The Padgitts have no concept of what the truth really is.'

'Remember Lydia Vince?' I asked.

'Who?'

'The slut at the trial, the one Wilbanks put on the stand, under oath. She told the jury Danny was in her bed when Rhoda was murdered. The Padgitts found her, bought her testimony, and handed her to Lucien. They're all a bunch of lying thieves.'

'Then her ex got shot, right?'

'Just after the trial. Probably got hit by one of the Padgitt goons. No evidence other than the bullets. No suspects. Nothing. Sounds familiar.'

'McNatt didn't buy anything Lucien said. Neither did Buckley.'

'And you?'

'Naw. I've seen Lucien cry before in front of juries. He can be very persuasive at times, not often, but occasionally. I got the impression he was working way too hard to convince us. It's Danny, and he's got some help.'

'Does McNatt believe that?'

'Yep, but he has no proof. An arrest is a waste of time.'

'It'll keep him off the streets.'

'It's temporary. With no proof you can't keep him in jail forever. He's patient. He's been waiting for nine years.'

Though the pranksters were never identified, and they had enough sense to take their secret to their graves, there was considerable speculation in the months that followed that they were the two teenaged sons of our Mayor. Two youngsters were seen sprinting away from the scene, much too fast to be caught. The Mayor's boys had a long and colorful track record as creative and brazen jokesters.

Under the cover of darkness, they boldly sneaked through a thick hedgerow and came to a stop less than fifty feet from the corner of the front porch of Mr. Earl Youry's house. There they watched and listened to the crowd of friends and neighbors camped out on the front lawn, protecting Mr. Youry. They waited patiently for just the right moment to launch their attack.

A few minutes after eleven, a long strand of eighty-four Black Cat firecrackers was tossed in the general direction of the porch, and when they began popping Clanton almost erupted into an all-out war. Men yelled, ladies screamed, Mr. Youry hit the planks and scurried into his house on all-fours. His sentries out front rolled over in their lawn chairs, clawed around for their guns, and hid low in the grass as the Blacks Cats bounced and popped in a smoky frenzy. It took thirty seconds for all eighty-four to finish exploding, and during that time a dozen heavily armed men were darting behind trees, pointing their guns in every direction, ready to shoot anything that moved.

A part-time deputy named Travis was jolted from his sleep on the hood of his patrol car. He yanked out his .44 Magnum and dashed low and hard in the general direction of the Black Cats. Armed neighbors were scampering everywhere in Mr. Youry's front yard. For some reason, and neither Travis nor his supervisor ever revealed the official explanation, if in fact there was one, he fired a shot into the air. A very loud shot. A shot heard well above the firecrackers. It caused another itchy finger, someone who never admitted to pulling the trigger, to unload a .12-gauge shotgun shell into the trees. No doubt many others would have commenced firing and who knows how many might have been slaughtered had not the other part-time deputy, Jimmy, screamed loudly, 'Hold your fire, you idiots!'

At which point the gunfire ceased immediately, but the Black Cats had a few rounds left. When the last one popped the entire gang of vigilantes walked over to the smoldering patch of grass and inspected things. Word spread that it was just fireworks. Mr. Earl Youry peeked through the front door and eventually eased outside.

Down the street, Mrs. Alice Wood heard the assault and was running to the rear of her house to lock the door when the two youngsters blew by her back entrance, sprinting and laughing furiously. She would report that they were about fifteen and white.

A mile away, in Lowtown, I had just walked down the steps of Miss Callie's front porch when I heard the distant explosions. The late shift – Sam, Leon, and two deacons – jumped to their feet and gazed into the distance. The forty-four sounded like a howitzer. We waited and waited, and when all was still again Leon said, 'Sounds like firecrackers.'

Sam had sneaked inside to check on his mother. He came back and said, 'She's asleep.'

'I'll go check it out,' I said. 'And I'll call if it's anything important.'

Mr. Youry's street was alive with the red and

blue lights of a dozen police cars. Traffic was heavy as the other curious fought to get near the scene. I saw Buster's car parked in a shallow ditch, and when I found him a few minutes later he told me the story. 'Coupla kids,' he said.

I found it funny, but I was in the distinct minority.

Chapter 41

In the nine years since I'd bought the *Times*, I had never left it for more than four days. It went to press every Tuesday, was published every Wednesday, and by every Thursday of my life I was facing a formidable deadline.

One reason for its success was the fact that I wrote so much about so many in a town where so little happened. Each edition had thirty-six pages. Subtracting five for classifieds, three for legals, and about six for advertisements, I was faced each week with the task of filling approximately twenty-two pages with local news.

The obits consumed at least one page, with me in charge of every word. Davey Bigmouth Bass took two pages for sports, though I often had to help with a summary of a junior high football game or an urgent story about a trophy buck shot by some twelve-year-old. Margaret put together one page for Religion and one page for Weddings and another for classifieds. Baggy, whose production nine years earlier had been feeble at best, had succumbed almost completely to booze and was now good for only one story each week, which, of course, he always wanted on the front page. Staff reporters came and went with frustrating regularity. We usually had one on board, sometimes two, and they were often more trouble than they were worth. I had to proofread and edit their work to the point of wishing I had simply done it myself.

And so I wrote. Though I'd studied journalism, I had not noticed a propensity to produce vast amounts of words in short periods of time. But once I suddenly owned the paper, and it was time to sink or swim, I discovered an amazing ability to crank out windy and colorful stories about almost everything, and nothing. A moderately severe car wreck with no fatalities was front page news with breathless quotes from eyewitnesses and ambulance drivers. A small factory expansion sounded like a boon to the nation's Gross National Product. A bake sale at the Baptist Ladies' WMU could run for eight hundred words. A drug arrest sounded as if the Colombians were advancing unchecked upon the innocent children of Clanton. A blood drive by the Civitan Club carried the urgency of a wartime shortage. Three stolen pickups in one week had the feel of organized crime.

I wrote about the people of Ford County. Miss Callie's was my first human interest story, and over the years I tried to run at least one a month. There was a survivor of the Bataan death march, the last local veteran of World War I, a sailor who had been at Pearl Harbor, a retiring minister who'd served one small country congregation for forty-five years, an old missionary who'd lived for thirty-one years in the Congo, a recent graduate who was dancing in a musical on Broadway, a lady who'd lived in twenty-two states, a man who'd been married seven times and was anxious to share his advice with future newlyweds, Mr. Mitlo – our token immigrant, a retiring basketball coach, the short-order cook at the Tea Shoppe who'd been frying eggs forever. And on and on. These stories were immensely popular.

However, after nine years the list of interesting people in Ford County had very few names on it.

I was tired of writing. Twenty pages a week, fifty-two weeks a year.

I woke up each morning thinking of either a new story or a new angle for an old one. Any bit of news or any unusual event was inspiration to puff up a piece and stick it somewhere in the paper. I wrote about dogs, antique trucks, a legendary tornado, a haunted house, a missing pony, Civil War treasure, the legend of a headless slave, a rabid skunk. And all the usual stuff – court proceedings, elections, crime, new businesses, bankrupt businesses, new characters in town. I was tired of writing.

And I was tired of Clanton. With some reluctance the town had come to accept me, especially when it became obvious I wasn't leaving. But it was a very small place, and at times I felt suffocated. I spent so many weekends at home, with little to do but read and write, that I became accustomed to it. And that frustrated me greatly. I tried the poker nights with Bubba Crocket and the Foxhole gang, and the redneck cookouts with Harry Rex and company. But I never felt as though I belonged.

Clanton was changing, and I was not happy with its direction. Like most small towns in the South, it was sprawling in all directions with no plan for its growth. Bargain City was booming, and the area around it was attracting every fast-food franchise imaginable. Downtown was declining, though the courthouse and the county government would always draw people. Strong political leaders were needed, folks with vision, and they were in short supply.

On the other hand, I suspected the town was weary of me. Because of my preachy opposition to the war in Vietnam, I would always be considered a radical liberal. And I did little to diminish this reputation. As the paper grew and the profits increased, and as a direct result my skin got thicker, I editorialized more and more. I railed against closed meetings held by the city council and the county Board of Supervisors. I sued to get access to public records. I spent one year bitching about the almost complete lack of zoning and land-use management in the county, and when Bargain City came to town I said way too much. I ridiculed the state's campaign finance laws, which were designed to allow rich people to elect their favorites. And when Danny Padgitt was set free, I unloaded on the parole system.

Throughout the seventies, I was always on a soapbox. And while this made for interesting reading and sold papers, it also transformed me into something of an oddity. I was viewed as a malcontent, one with a pulpit. I don't think I was ever a bully; I tried hard not to be. But looking back, there were fights I started not only out of conviction but also out of boredom.

As I grew older, I wanted to be a regular citizen. I would always be an outsider, but that didn't bother me anymore. I wanted to come and go, to live in Clanton as I saw fit, then leave for long periods of time when I got bored. Amazing how the prospect of money can change your future.

I became consumed with the dream of walking away, of taking a sabbatical to some place I'd never been, of seeing the world.

The next meeting with Gary McGrew was at a restaurant in Tupelo. He'd been to my office several times. One more visit and the staff would start whispering. Over lunch we again looked at my books, talked about his client's plans, negotiated this point and that one. If I sold, I wanted the owner to honor the new five-year contracts I'd given to Davey Bigmouth Bass, Hardy, and Margaret. Baggy would either retire soon or die of liver poisoning. Wiley had always been a part-timer, and his interest in chasing subjects for photos was waning. He was the only employee I'd told about the negotiations, and he had encouraged me to take the money and run.

McGrew's client wanted me to stay on for at least a year, at a very high salary, and train the new editor. I would not agree to this. If I walked away, then I walked away. I didn't want a boss, and I didn't want the local heat that would come for selling the county's paper to a large firm from outside the state.

Their offer was at $1.3 million. A consultant I'd hired in Knoxville had valued the *Times* at $1.35 million.

'Confidentially, we've bought the papers in Tyler and Van Buren Counties,' McGrew said, late in a very long lunch. 'Things are falling into place.'

He was being almost completely honest. The owner of the paper in Tyler County had agreed in principle, but the documents had not been signed.

'But there's a new wrinkle,' he said. 'The paper in Polk County might be for sale. Frankly, we're taking a look at it if you pass. It's quite a bit cheaper.'

'Ah, more pressure,' I said.

The *Polk County Herald* had four thousand readers and lousy management. I saw it every week.

'I'm not trying to pressure you. I'm just putting everything on the table.'

'I really want a million and a half bucks,' I said.

'That's over the top, Willie.'

'It's high, but you'll earn it back. Might take a little longer, but look ten years down the road.'

'I'm not sure we can go that high.'

'You'll have to if you want the paper.'

A sense of urgency had arisen. McGrew hinted at a deadline, then finally said, 'We've been talking for months now, and my client is anxious to reach a conclusion. He wants to close the deal by the first of next month, or he'll go elsewhere.'

The tactic didn't bother me. I was tired of talking too. Either I sold, or I didn't. It was time to make a decision.

'That's twenty-three days from now,' I said.

'It is.'

'Fair enough.'

The long days of summer arrived, and the insufferable heat and humidity settled in for their annual three-month stay. I made my usual rounds – to the churches on my list, to the softball fields, to the local golf tournament, to the watermelon cuttings. But Clanton was waiting, and the wait was all we talked about.

Inevitably, the noose around the neck of each remaining juror was loosened somewhat. They quite naturally got tired of being prisoners in their homes, of altering their lifelong routines, of having packs of neighbors guard their homes at night. They began to venture out, to try and resume normal lives.

The patience of the killer was unnerving. He had the advantage of time, and he knew his victims would grow weary of all that protection. He knew they would drop their guard, make a mistake. We knew it too.

After missing three consecutive Sundays, for the first time in her life, Miss Callie insisted on going to church. Escorted by Sam, Esau, and Leon, she marched into the sanctuary on Sunday morning and worshiped the Lord as if she'd been gone a year. Her brothers and sisters embraced her, and prayed for her fervently. Reverend Small revised his sermon on the spot and preached on God's protection of his followers. Sam said he went on for almost three hours.

Two days later, Miss Callie slid into the backseat of my Mercedes. With Esau beside her and Sam riding shotgun, we hurried out of Clanton with a deputy behind us. He stopped at the county line, and an hour later we were in Memphis. There was a new shopping mall east of town that was all the rage, and Miss Callie dreamed of seeing it. Over a hundred stores under one roof! For the first time in her life, she ate a pizza; she saw an ice rink, two men holding hands, and a mixed-race family. She approved only of the ice rink.

After a full hour of Sam's atrocious navigating,

we finally found the cemetery in south Memphis. Using a map from the guardhouse, we eventually located the grave of Nicola Rossetti DeJarnette. Miss Callie placed a bouquet of flowers she'd brought from home on the grave, and when it became apparent she planned to spend some time there, we walked away and left her in peace.

In memory of Nicola, Miss Callie wanted Italian food. I had reserved a table at Grisanti's, a Memphis landmark, and we had a long, delightful dinner of lasagna and ravioli stuffed with goat cheese. She managed to overcome her bias against bought food, and, to protect her from sin, I insisted on paying for it.

We didn't want to leave Memphis. For a few hours we had escaped the fear of the unknown and the anxiety of the waiting. Clanton seemed a thousand miles away, and that was too close. Going back late that night, I found myself driving slower and slower.

Though we didn't discuss it, and the conversation grew quieter the closer we got to home, there was a killer loose in Ford County. Miss Callie's name was on his list. If not for the two dead bodies, that would have been impossible to believe.

According to Baggy, and verified by research in the *Times* archives, there had been no unsolved murders that century. Almost every killing had been some impulsive act where the smoking gun had been seen by witnesses. Arrests, trials, and convictions had been prompt.

Now, there was a very smart and very deliberate killer out there, and every one knew his intended victims. For such a law-abiding, God-fearing community, it was inconceivable.

Bobby, Al, Max, and Leon had, at various times, argued strenuously for Miss Callie to go stay with any of them for a month or so. Sam and I, and even Esau, had joined in these rather vigorous requests, but she would not budge. She was in close contact with God, and he would protect her.

In nine years, the only time I lost my temper with Miss Callie, and the only time she rebuked me, was during an argument about spending a month in Milwaukee with Bobby. 'Those big cities are dangerous,' she had said.

'No place is as dangerous as Clanton right now,' I had replied.

Later, when I raised my voice, she told me she did not appreciate my lack of respect, and I quickly shut up.

As we crossed into Ford County late that night, I began watching my rearview mirror. It was silly, but then it wasn't. In Lowtown, the Ruffin home was guarded by a deputy parked in the street, and a friend of Esau's on the porch.

'It's been a quiet night,' the friend said. In other words, no one had been shot or shot at.

Sam and I played checkers for an hour on the porch while she went to sleep.

The waiting continued.

Chapter 42

Nineteen seventy-nine was a year for local elections in Mississippi, my third as a registered voter. It was much quieter than the first two. The Sheriff's race was uncontested, something that was unheard of. There had been a rumor that the Padgitts had bought a new candidate, but after the parole debacle they backed off. Senator Theo Morton drew an opponent who brought me an ad that screamed the question – WHY DID SENATOR MORTON GET DANNY PADGITT PAROLED? CASH! THAT'S WHY! As much as I wanted to run the ad, I had neither the time nor the energy for a libel suit.

There was a constable's race out in Beat Four with thirteen candidates, but other than that the races were fairly lethargic. The county was fixated on the murders of Fargarson and Teale, and, more important, on who might be next. Sheriff McNatt and the investigators from the state police and state crime lab had exhausted every possible clue and lead. All we could do was wait.

As July Fourth approached, there was a noticeable lack of excitement about the annual celebration. Though almost everyone felt safe, there was a dark cloud hanging over the county. Oddly, rumors persisted that something bad would happen when we all gathered around the courthouse on the Fourth. Rumors, though, had never been born with such creativity, nor spread as rapidly, as in the month of June.

On June 25, in a fancy law office in Tupelo, I signed a pile of documents that transferred ownership of the *Times* to a media company owned in part by Mr. Ray Noble of Atlanta. Mr. Noble handed me a check for $1.5 million, and I quickly, and somewhat anxiously, walked it down the street, where my newest friend, Stu Holland, was waiting in his rather spacious office in the Merchants Bank. News of such a deposit in Clanton would leak overnight, so I buried the money with Stu, then drove home.

It was the longest one-hour drive of my life. It was exhilarating because I had cashed in at the market's peak. I had squeezed top dollar out of a well-heeled and honorable buyer who planned to make few changes to my newspaper. Adventure was calling me, and I now had the means to answer.

And it was a sad drive because I was giving up such a large and rewarding part of my life. The paper and I had grown and matured together; me as an adult, it as a prosperous entity. It had become what any small-town paper should be – a lively observer of current events, a recorder of history, an occasional commentator on politics and social issues. As for me, I was a young man who had blindly and doggedly built something from scratch. I suppose I should've felt my age, but all I wanted to do was find a beach. Then a girl.

When I returned to Clanton, I walked into Margaret's office, closed the door, and told her about the sale. She burst into tears, and before long my eyes were moist as well. Her fierce loyalty had always amazed me, and though she, like Miss Callie, worried way too much about my soul, she had grown to love me nonetheless. I explained that the new owners were wonderful people, planned no drastic changes, and had approved her new five-year contract at an increased salary. This made her cry even more.

Hardy did not cry. By then he had been printing the *Times* for almost thirty years. He was moody, cantankerous, drank too much like most pressmen, and if the new owners didn't like him then he'd simply quit and go fishing. He did appreciate the new contract though.

As did Davey Bigmouth Bass. He was shocked at the news, but rallied nicely at the idea of earning more money.

Baggy was on vacation somewhere out West, with his brother, not his wife. Mr. Ray Noble had been reluctant to agree to another five years' of Baggy's sluggish reporting, and I could not, in good conscience, make him a part of the deal. Baggy was on his own.

We had five other employees, and I personally broke the news to each of them. It took all of one afternoon, and when if it was finally over I was drained. I met Harry Rex in the back room at Pepe's and we celebrated with margaritas.

I was anxious to leave town and go somewhere, but it would be impossible until the killings stopped.

For most of June, the Ruffin professors scrambled back and forth to Clanton. They juggled assignments and vacations, trying their best to make sure at least two or three of them were always with Miss Callie. Sam seldom left the house. He stayed in Lowtown to protect his mother, but also to keep his own profile low. Trooper Durant was still around, though he was married again and his two renegade sons had left the area.

Sam spent hours on the porch, reading voraciously, playing checkers with Esau or whoever stopped by to help guard things for a while. He played backgammon with me until he figured out the strategy, then he insisted that we bet a dollar per game. Before long I owed him $50. Such blatant gambling was a deadly secret on Miss Callie's porch.

A hasty reunion was put together for the week

before July Fourth. Because my house had five empty bedrooms and a woeful lack of human activity, I insisted that it be filled with Ruffins. The family had grown considerably since I first met them in 1970. All but Sam were married, and there were twenty-one grandchildren. The total came to thirty-five Ruffins, not counting Sam, Callie, and Esau, and thirty-four made it to Clanton. Leon's wife had a sick father in Chicago.

Of the thirty-four, twenty-three moved into the Hocutt House for a few days. They drifted in from different parts of the country, mostly up North, coming in shifts at all hours of the day, with each new arrival greeted with great ceremony. When Carlota and her husband and two small children arrived at 3 A.M. from Los Angeles, every light in the house came on and Bobby's wife, Bonnie, began cooking pancakes.

Bonnie took over my kitchen, and three times a day I was sent to the grocery store with a list of things she urgently needed. I bought ice cream by the ton and the kids soon learned I would fetch it for them at any hour of the day.

Since my porches were long and wide and seldom used, the Ruffins gravitated toward them. Sam brought Miss Callie and Esau over late in the afternoons for serious visiting. She was desperate to get out of Lowtown. Her warm little house had become a prison.

At various times, I heard her children talk with great concern about their mother. The obvious

474

threat of somehow getting shot was discussed less than her health. Over the years she had managed to lose somewhere around eighty pounds, depending on whose version you heard. Now it was back, and her blood pressure had the doctors concerned. The stress was taking its toll. Esau said she slept fitfully, something she blamed on medications. She was not as spry, didn't smile as much, and had noticeably less energy.

It was all blamed on the 'Padgitt mess.' As soon as he got caught and the killings stopped, then Miss Callie would bounce back.

That was the optimistic view, the one generally shared by most of her children.

On July 2, a Monday, Bonnie and company prepared a light lunch of salads and pizzas. All available Ruffins were there, and we ate on a side porch under slow-moving and practically useless wicker fans. There was a slight breeze, however, and with the temperature in the nineties we were able to enjoy a long lazy meal.

I had yet to find the right moment to tell Miss Callie that I was leaving the paper. I knew she would be shocked, and very disappointed. But I could think of no reason why we couldn't continue our Thursday lunches. It might even be more fun counting the typos and mistakes made by someone else.

In nine years we had missed only seven, all due to illness or dental work.

The lazy postmeal chatter suddenly came to a

halt. There were sirens in the distance, somewhere across town.

The box was twelve inches square, five inches deep, white in color with red and blue stars and stripes. It was gift package from the Bolan Pecan Farm in Hazelhurst, Mississippi, sent to Mrs. Maxine Root by her sister in Concord, California. An Independence Day gift of real American pecans. It came by mail, delivered by the postman around noon, placed in the mailbox of Maxine Root, then hauled inside, past the lone sentry sitting under a tree in the front yard, and into the kitchen where Maxine first saw it.

It had been almost a month since Sheriff McNatt had quizzed her about her vote on the jury. She had reluctantly admitted that she had not been in favor of the death penalty for Danny Padgitt, and she recalled that the two men who stuck with her were Lenny Fargarson and Mo Teale. Since they were now dead, McNatt had delivered the grave news that she might be the next victim.

For years after the trial, Maxine had wrestled with the verdict. The town was bitter over it and she felt the hostility. Thankfully, the jurors kept their vows of silence, and she and Lenny and Mo avoided any additional abuse. With the soothing passage of time, she had been able to distance herself from the aftermath.

Now the world knew how she'd voted. Now a crazy man was stalking her. She was on leave from her job as a bookkeeper. Her nerves were shot; she couldn't sleep; she was sick of hiding in her own home; sick of a yard full of neighbors gathering every night as if it was time for a social event; sick of ducking under every window. She was taking so many different pills that they were all counteracting each other to the point that nothing worked.

She saw the box of pecans and started crying. Someone out there loved her. Her precious sister Jane was thinking about her. Oh how she'd love to be in California with Jane at that very moment.

Maxine started to open the package, then had a thought. She went to the phone and dialed Jane's number. They had not talked in a week.

Jane was at work, thrilled to hear from her. They chatted about this and that, then about the horrible situation in Clanton. 'You're a dear to send the pecans,' Maxine said.

'What pecans?' Jane asked.

A pause. 'The gift box from Bolan Pecans down in Hazelhurst. A big one, three pounds.'

Another pause. 'Not me, sis. Must've been someone else.'

Maxine hung up moments later and examined the box. A sticker on the front said – A Gift from Jane Parham. Of course she knew of no other Jane Parhams.

Very gently, she picked it up. It seemed a bit heavy for a three-pound tin of pecans.

Travis, the part-time deputy, happened by the

house. He was accompanied by one Teddy Ray, a pimple-faced boy with an oversized uniform and a service revolver that he had never fired. Maxine hustled them into the kitchen where the red, white, and blue box sat benignly on the counter. The lone sentry was also tagging along, and for a long minute or so the four of them just stared at the package. Maxine recounted verbatim her conversation with Jane.

With great hesitation, Travis picked up the box and shook it slightly. 'Seems a might heavy for pecans,' he observed. He looked at Teddy Ray, who'd already gone pale, and at the neighbor with a rifle, who seemed ready to duck at anything.

'You think it's a bomb?' the neighbor asked.

'Oh my God,' Maxine mumbled and appeared ready to collapse.

'Could be,' Travis said, then gawked down in horror at what he was holding.

'Get it outside,' Maxine said.

'Shouldn't we call the Sheriff?' Teddy Ray managed to ask.

'I guess so,' Travis said.

'What if it's got a timer or something?' asked the neighbor.

Travis hesitated for a moment, then with the voice of absolutely no experience, said, 'I know what to do.'

They stepped through the kitchen door onto a narrow porch that ran the length of the rear of the house. Travis carefully placed the box at the very edge, three feet or so above the ground. When he removed his .44 Magnum, Maxine said, 'What are you doing?'

'We're gonna see if it's a bomb,' Travis said. Teddy Ray and the neighbor scurried off the porch and took up a safe position in the grass about fifty feet away.

'You're gonna shoot my pecans?' Maxine asked.

'You got a better idea?' Travis snapped back.

'I guess not.'

With most of his body inside the kitchen, Travis leaned out through the screen door with his thick right arm, and his rather large head, and took aim. Maxine was right behind him, crouching low and peeking around his waist.

The first shot missed the porch entirely, though it took the breath out of Maxine. Teddy Ray shouted, 'Nice shot,' and he and the neighbor had a quick laugh.

Travis aimed and fired again.

The explosion ripped the porch completely from the house, tore a gaping hole in the back wall behind the kitchen, and sprayed shrapnel for a hundred yards. It shattered windows, peeled up planks, and it wounded the four observers. Teddy Ray and the neighbor both took bits of metal in their chests and legs. Travis's right arm and his firing hand were mangled. Maxine was hit twice in the head – one piece of glass ripped off the lobe of her right ear, and a small nail penetrated her right jaw.

479

For a moment, they were all unconscious, knocked silly by three pounds of plastic explosives packed with nails, glass, and ball bearings.

As the sirens continued to wail across town, I went to the phone and called Wiley Meek. He was just about to call me. 'They tried to blow up Maxine Root,' he said.

I told the Ruffins there'd been an accident and left them on the porch. When I got near the subdivision where the Roots lived, the main roads were blocked and traffic was being turned away. I hustled over to the hospital and found a young doctor I knew. He said that there were four injured, none of whom appeared to be in grave danger.

Judge Omar Noose was holding court in Clanton that afternoon. In fact, he later said that he heard the explosion. Rufus Buckley and Sheriff McNatt met with him for over an hour in chambers, and what they discussed was never revealed. As we waited in the courtroom, Harry Rex and most of the other lawyers loitering there were certain that they were debating how to handle an arrest warrant for Danny Padgitt when there was so little proof that he'd done anything wrong.

But something had to be done. Someone had to be arrested. The Sheriff had a population to protect; he had to take action, even if it wasn't entirely proper.

We got a report that Travis and Teddy Ray had been transported to one of the hospitals in Memphis for surgery. Maxine and her neighbor were under the knife at that very moment. Again, it was the opinion of the doctors that no life was in jeopardy. Travis might lose his right arm, though.

How many people in Ford County knew how to make package bombs? Who had access to explosives? Who had motive? As we argued these questions in the courtroom, they were evidently being argued back in chambers as well. Noose, Buckley, and McNatt were all elected officials. The good people of Ford County needed their protection. Since Danny Padgitt was the only conceivable suspect, Judge Noose finally issued a warrant for his arrest.

Lucien was notified, and he took the news without objection. At that moment, not even Padgitt's lawyer could argue with the strategy of bringing him in for processing. He could always be released later.

A few minutes after 5 P.M., a convoy of police cars blew out of Clanton and headed for Padgitt Island. Harry Rex now owned a police scanner (there were quite a few new ones in town) and we sat in his office, sipping beer, listening to it squawk with unchecked fury. It had to be the most exciting arrest in the history of our county, and many of us wanted to be there. Would the Padgitts block the road and thwart the arrest? Would there be gunfire? A small war?

From the chatter, we were able to follow most of what was happening. At Highway 42, McNatt and his men were met by ten 'units' of the state highway patrol. We assumed a 'unit' meant nothing more than a car, but it sounded far more serious. They proceeded to Highway 401, turned onto the county road that led to the island, and at the bridge where everyone expected some dramatic showdown, there sat Danny Padgitt in the car with his lawyer.

The voices on the scanner were quick and anxious:

'He's with his lawyer!'

'Wilbanks?'

'Yep.'

'Let's shoot both of them.'

'They're gettin' out of the car.'

'Wilbanks is holdin' up his hands. Smart-ass!'

'It's Danny Padgitt, all right. Hands held high.'

'I'd like to knock that smile off his face.'

'They got the cuffs on him.'

'Dammit!' Harry Rex yelled across his desk. 'I wanted some gunfire. Just like in the old days.'

We were at the jail an hour later when the parade of red and blue lights came swarming in. Sheriff McNatt had wisely placed Padgitt in the patrol car of a state trooper; otherwise his deputies might have roughed him up during the ride. Two of their colleagues were in surgery in Memphis, and feelings were pretty raw.

A mob had gathered outside the jail. Padgitt was jeered and cursed as he was rushed inside, then the Sheriff angrily told the hotheads to go home.

Seeing him in handcuffs brought a great sense of relief. And the news that he was in custody was like a balm for the entire county. The heavy cloud had been lifted. Clanton came to life that night.

When I returned to the Hocutt House after dark, the Ruffin clan was in a festive mood. Miss Callie was as relaxed as I'd seen her in a long time. We sat on the porch for a long time, telling stories, laughing, listening to Aretha Franklin and the Temptations, even listening to an occasional burst of fireworks.

Chapter 43

Unknown to anyone, Lucien Wilbanks and Judge Noose struck a deal in the hectic hours before the arrest. The Judge was worried about what might happen if Danny Padgitt chose to retreat into the safety of the island, or, worse, resist the arrest with force. The county was a powder keg waiting for a match. The cops were ready for blood because of Teddy Ray and Travis, whose gunslinging stupidity was being temporarily ignored while they recovered from their wounds. And Maxine Root came from a notoriously rough family of loggers, a large fierce clan known to hunt year round, live off their land, and leave no grudge unchallenged.

Lucien appreciated the situation. He agreed to deliver his client on one condition – he wanted an immediate bail hearing. He had at least a dozen witnesses who were willing to provide 'airtight' alibis for Danny, and Lucien wanted the folks in Clanton to hear their testimony. He truly believed that someone else was behind the killings, and it was important to convince the town.

Lucien was also one month away from being disbarred in an unrelated mess. He knew the end was coming, and the bail hearing would be his last performance.

Noose agreed to a hearing and set it for 10 A.M. the next day, July 3. In a scene eerily reminiscent of one nine years earlier, Danny Padgitt once again packed the Ford County Courthouse. It was a hostile crowd, anxious to get a look at him, hopeful that he might be strung up on the spot. Maxine Root's family arrived early and sat near the front. They were angry, thick-chested, bearded men in overalls. They frightened me, and we were ostensibly on the same side. Maxine was reported to be resting well and expected home in a few days.

The Ruffins had little to do that morning, so the excitement at the courthouse could not be missed. Miss Callie herself insisted on arriving early and getting a good seat. She was happy to be downtown again. She wore a Sunday dress and delighted in sitting in such a public gathering surrounded by her family.

The reports from the hospital in Memphis were mixed. Teddy Ray had been sewn together and was recuperating. Travis had had a rough night, and there was much concern about saving his arm. Their comrades were in the courtroom in full force, waiting for another chance to scowl at the bomb maker.

I saw Mr. and Mrs. Fargarson sitting in the rear, two rows from the back, and I couldn't begin to comprehend what they were thinking.

There were no Padgitts present; they had enough sense to stay clear of the courtroom. The sight of one of them would've touched off a riot. Harry Rex whispered that they were huddled together upstairs in the jury room, with the door locked. We never saw them.

Rufus Buckley arrived with his entourage to represent the State of Mississippi. One advantage in selling the *Times* was that I would never be forced to spend time with him. He was arrogant and pompous, and everything he did was designed to get him to the Governor's office.

As I waited and watched the courtroom fill up, I realized it was the last time I would cover such a proceeding for the *Times*. I found no sadness in that. I had mentally checked out, mentally spent some of the money. And now that Danny was in custody, I was even more anxious to escape Clanton and go see the world.

There would be a trial in a few months. Another Danny Padgitt circus, but I doubted seriously if it would be held in Ford County. I didn't care. It would be a story for someone else.

At 10 A.M., all seats were filled and a thick row of spectators lined the walls. Fifteen minutes later, there was a shuffle behind the bench, a door opened, and Lucien Wilbanks emerged. It had the feel of a sporting event; he was a player; we all wanted to boo. Two bailiffs quickly followed him, and one announced, 'All rise for the Court!'

Judge Noose ambled forth in his black robe and sat on his throne. 'Please be seated,' he said into the microphone. He surveyed the crowd and seemed astonished at the number of us out there.

He nodded, a side door opened, and Danny Padgitt, handcuffed, shackled at the ankles, and sporting the orange jail jumpsuit he'd worn before, was led in by three deputies. It took a few minutes to unlock him from his various restraints, and when he was finally free he leaned over and whispered something to Lucien.

'This is a bail hearing,' Noose announced, and the courtroom was still and quiet. 'There's no reason why it cannot be handled judiciously and briefly.'

It would be much briefer than anyone anticipated.

A cannon exploded somewhere above us, and for a split second I thought we'd all been shot. Something cracked sharply through the heavy air of the courtroom, and for a town so jittery to begin with we all froze in one horrible snapshot of disbelief. Then Danny Padgitt grunted in a delayed reaction, and all hell broke loose. Women screamed. Men screamed. Someone yelled, 'Get down!' as half the spectators ducked low, some hitting the floor. Someone shouted, 'He's been shot!'

I lowered my head a few inches, but I didn't

want to miss anything. Every deputy yanked out a service revolver and looked in a different direction for someone to shoot. They pointed up and down, front and back, here and there.

Though we argued about it for years, the second shot was no more than three seconds behind the first. It hit Danny in the ribs, but it had not been necessary. The first had gone through his head. The second shot drew the attention of a deputy in the front of the courtroom. I was ducking even lower, but I saw him pointing to the balcony.

The double doors to the courtroom flew open, and the stampede was on. In the hysteria that followed, I stayed in my seat and tried to take in everything. I remember seeing Lucien Wilbanks hovering over his client. And Rufus Buckley on his hands and knees, scurrying in front of the jury box in an effort to escape. And I'll never forget Judge Noose, sitting calmly at the bench, reading glasses perched on the tip of his nose, watching the chaos as if he saw it every week.

Each second seemed to last a minute.

The shots that hit Danny were fired from the ceiling above the balcony. And, though the balcony was filled with people, no one saw the rifle drop down a few inches ten feet above their heads. Like the rest of us, they were preoccupied with getting a first glance at Danny Padgitt.

The county had patched and renovated the courtroom at various times over the decades, whenever a few spare bucks could be squeezed from the coffers. Back in the late sixties, in an effort to improve the lighting, a dropped ceiling had been installed. The sniper found the perfect spot on a heating duct just above a panel in the ceiling. There, in the dark crawl space, he waited patiently, watching the courtroom below through a five-inch slit he'd created by lifting one of the water-stained panels.

When I thought the shooting was over, I crept closer to the bar. The cops were yelling for everybody to get out of the courtroom. They were shoving people and barking all sorts of contradictory instructions. Danny was under the table, attended to by Lucien and several deputies. I could see his feet, and they were not moving. A minute or two passed, and the confusion was subsiding. Suddenly, there was more gunfire; thankfully, now it was outside. I looked out a courtroom window and saw people scampering into the stores around the square. I saw an old man point upward, sort of above my head, to something on the top of the courthouse.

Sheriff McNatt had just found the crawl space when he heard shots above him. He and two deputies climbed the stairs to the third floor, then slowly took the cramped circular stairway through the dome. The door to the cupola was jammed shut, but just above it they could hear the anxious footsteps of the sniper. And they could hear shell casings hit the floor.

His only target was the law offices of Lucien Wilbanks, specifically the upstairs windows.

With great deliberation he was blowing them out, one by one. Downstairs, Ethel Twitty was under her desk, bawling and screaming at the same time.

I finally left the courtroom and hustled downstairs to the main floor, where the crowd was waiting, uncertain what to do. The police chief was telling everyone to stay inside. Between bursts of gunfire, the chatter was fast and nervous. When the shooting started, we gawked at one another. Each one of us was thinking, 'How long will this go on?'

I huddled with the Ruffin family. Miss Callie had fainted when the first shot jolted the courtroom. Max and Bobby were clutching her, anxious to get her home.

After holding the town hostage for an hour, the sniper ran out of ammunition. He saved the last bullet for himself, and when he pulled the trigger he fell hard on the small passage door in the floor of the cupola. Sheriff McNatt waited a few minutes, then managed to shove the door up and open. The body of Hank Hooten was naked again. And as dead as fresh roadkill.

A deputy ran down the stairs and yelled, 'It's over! He's dead! It's Hank Hooten!'

The bewildered expressions were almost amusing. Hank Hooten? Everyone said the name but no words came out. Hank Hooten?

'That lawyer who went crazy.'

'I thought he got sent away.'

'Isn't he in Whitfield?'

'Thought he was dead.'

'Who's Hank Hooten?' Carlota asked me, but I was too confused to give an answer. We spilled outside under the shade trees and lingered for a while, not certain whether we should stay in case there was another incredible event, or go home and try to comprehend the one we'd just lived through. The Ruffin clan left quickly; Miss Callie was not feeling well.

Eventually, an ambulance carrying Danny Padgitt pulled away from the courthouse and left in no hurry whatsoever. The removal of Hank Hooten was a bit more demanding, but with time they wrestled down his corpse, then rolled it out of the courthouse on a gurney, covered from head to toe with a white sheet.

I walked to my office, where Margaret and Wiley were sipping fresh coffee and waiting for me. We were too stunned to engage in intelligent conversation. The entire town was muted.

I eventually made some phone calls, found who I wanted, and around noon left the office. As I drove around the square, I saw Mr. Dex Pratt, who owned the local glass company and ran an ad in the *Times* every week, on the balcony at Lucien's, already removing the French doors and replacing panes. I was sure Lucien was home by then, already hitting the sauce on his porch, from where he could see the dome and the cupola of the courthouse.

Whitfield was three hours to the south. I

wasn't sure if I would make it that far, because at any moment I was likely to turn right, head west, cross the river at Greenville or Vicksburg, and be somewhere deep in Texas by dusk. Or take a left, head east, and find a very late dinner somewhere close to Atlanta.

What madness. How did such a pleasant little town end up in such a nightmare? I just wanted out.

I was near Jackson before I came out of my trance.

The state mental hospital was twenty miles east of Jackson on an interstate highway. I bluffed my way through the guardhouse, using the name of a doctor I'd located fishing around with the phone.

Dr. Vero was very busy, and I read magazines for an hour outside his office. When I informed the girl at the desk that I was not leaving, and that I would follow him home if necessary, he somehow found the time to squeeze me in.

Vero had long hair and a grayish beard. His accent was clearly upper midwest. Two diplomas on his wall tracked him through Northwestern and Johns Hopkins, though in the dingy light of his debris-strewn office I couldn't read the details.

I told him what had happened that morning in Clanton. After my narrative he said, 'I can't talk about Mr. Hooten. As I explained on the phone, we have a doctor-patient privilege.'

492

'Had. Not have.'

'It survives, Mr. Traynor. It's still alive, and I'm afraid I can't discuss this patient.'

I'd been around Harry Rex long enough to know that you never took no for an answer. I launched into a long and detailed account of the Padgitt case, from the trial to the parole to the last month and the tension in Clanton. I told the story of seeing Hank Hooten late one Sunday night in the Calico Ridge Independent Church, and how no one seemed to know anything about him during the last years of his life.

My angle was that the town needed to know what made him snap. How sick was he? Why was he released? There were many questions, and before 'we' could put the tragic episode behind 'us,' then 'we' needed the truth. I caught myself pleading for information.

'How much will you print?' he asked, breaking the ice.

'I'll print what you tell me to print. And if something's off-limits, just say so.'

'Let's take a walk.'

On a concrete bench, in a small shaded courtyard, we sipped coffee from paper cups. 'This is what you can print,' Vero began. 'Mr. Hooten was admitted here in January 1971. He was diagnosed as schizophrenic, confined here, treated here, and released in October 1976.'

'Who diagnosed him?' I asked.

'We now go off the record. Agreed?'

'Agreed.'

493

'This must be confidential, Mr. Traynor. I must have your word on this.'

I put away my pen and notepad and said, 'I swear on the Bible that this will not be printed.'

He hesitated for a long time, took several sips of his coffee, and for a moment I thought he might clam up and ask me to leave. Then he relaxed a little, and said, 'I treated Mr. Hooten initially. His family had a history of schizophrenia. His mother and possibly his grandmother suffered from it. Quite often genetics play a role in the disease. He was institutionalized while he was in college, and remarkably, managed to finish law school. After his second divorce, he moved to Clanton in the mid-sixties, looking for a place to start over. Another divorce followed. He adored women, but could not survive in a relationship. He was quite enamored with Rhoda Kassellaw and claimed he asked her to marry him repeatedly. I'm sure the young lady was somewhat wary of him. Her murder was very traumatic. And when the jury refused to send her killer to death, he, shall I say, slipped over the edge.'

'Thank you for using layman's terms,' I said. I remembered the diagnosis around town – 'slap-ass crazy.'

'He heard voices, the principal one being that of Miss Kassellaw. Her two small children also talked to him. They begged him to protect her, to save her. They described the horror of watching their mother get raped and murdered in her own bed, and they blamed Mr. Hooten for not saving her. Her killer, Mr. Padgitt, also tormented him with taunts from prison. On many occasions I watched by closed circuit as Mr. Hooten screamed at Danny Padgitt from his room here.'

'Did he mention the jurors?'

'Oh yes, all the time. He knew that three of them – Mr. Fargarson, Mr. Teale, and Mrs. Root – had refused to bring back a death penalty. He would scream their names in the middle of the night.'

'That's amazing. The jurors vowed to never discuss their deliberations. We didn't know how they voted until a month ago.'

'Well, he was the assistant prosecutor.'

'Yes, he was.' I vividly remembered Hank Hooten sitting beside Ernie Gaddis at the trial, never saying a word, looking bored and detached from the proceedings. 'Did he express a desire to seek revenge?'

A sip of coffee, another pause as he debated whether to answer. 'Yes. He hated them. He wanted them dead, along with Mr. Padgitt.'

'Then why was he released?'

'I can't talk about his release, Mr. Traynor. I wasn't here at the time, and there might be some liability on the part of this institution.'

'You weren't here?'

'I left for two years to teach in Chicago. When I returned eighteen months ago, Mr. Hooten was gone.'

'But you've reviewed his file.'

'Yes, and his condition improved dramatically while I was away. The doctors found the right mix of antipsychotic drugs and his symptoms diminished substantially. He was released to a community treatment program in Tupelo, and from there he sort of fell off our radar. Needless to say, Mr. Traynor, the treatment of the mentally ill is not a priority in this state, nor in many others. We are grossly understaffed and underfunded.'

'Would you have released him?'

'I cannot answer that. At this point, Mr. Traynor, I think I've said enough.'

I thanked him for his time, for his candor, and once again promised to protect his confidence. He asked for a copy of whatever I printed.

I stopped at a fast-food place in Jackson for a cheeseburger. At a pay phone I called the office, half-wondering if I'd missed more shootings. Margaret was relieved to hear my voice.

'You must come home, Willie, and quickly,' she said.

'Why?'

'Callie Ruffin has had a stroke. She's in the hospital.'

'Is it serious?'

'I'm afraid so.'

Chapter 44

A county bond issue in 1977 had paid for a handsome renovation to our hospital. At one end of the main floor there was a modern, though quite dark, chapel where I'd once sat with Margaret and her family as her mother passed away. It was there that I found the Ruffins, all eight children, all twenty-one grandchildren, and every spouse but Leon's wife. Reverend Thurston Small was there, along with a sizable contingent from the church. Esau was upstairs in the intensive care unit, waiting outside Miss Callie's room.

Sam told me that she had awakened from a nap with a sharp pain in her left arm, then numbness in her leg, and before long she was mumbling incoherently. An ambulance rushed her to the hospital. The doctor was certain it was initially a stroke, one that precipitated a mild heart attack. She was being heavily medicated and monitored. The last report from the doctor had been around 8 P.M.; her condition was described as 'serious but stable.'

Visitors were not allowed, so there was little to do but wait and pray and greet friends as they came and went. After an hour in the chapel, I was ready for bed. Max, third in the birth order but the undeniable leader, organized a schedule for the night. At least two of Miss Callie's children would be somewhere in the hospital at all times.

We checked with the doctor again around eleven, and he sounded reasonably optimistic that she was still stable. She was 'asleep' as he put it, but upon further questioning admitted that they had her knocked out to prevent another stroke. 'Go home and rest,' he said. 'Tomorrow could be a long day.' We left Mario and Gloria in the chapel, and moved en masse to the Hocutt House where we ate ice cream on a side porch. Sam had taken Esau home to Lowtown. I was delighted that the rest of the family preferred staying at my place.

Of the thirteen adults there, only Leon and Carlota's husband, Sterling, would touch alcohol. I opened a bottle of wine, and the three of us passed on the ice cream.

Everyone was exhausted, especially the children. The day had begun with an adventure to the courthouse for a peek at the man who'd been terrorizing our community. That seemed like a week ago. Around midnight, Al gathered the family together in my den for one last word of prayer. A 'chain prayer' as he called it, in which every adult and child gave thanks for something and asked for God's protection of Miss Callie. Sitting there on my sofa, fervently holding hands with Bonnie and with Mario's wife, I felt the presence of the Lord. I knew my beloved friend, their mother and grandmother, would be fine.

Two hours later I was lying in bed, wide awake, still hearing the sharp crack of the rifle in the courtroom, the thud of the bullet as it hit Danny, the panic that followed. I rewound and replayed every word of Dr. Vero's, and wondered in what manner of hell poor Hank Hooten had been living for the past few years. Why had he been set loose on society again?

And I worried about Miss Callie, though her condition seemed to be under control and she was in good hands.

I eventually slept for two hours, then eased downstairs where I found Mario and Leon drinking coffee at the kitchen table. Mario had left the hospital an hour earlier; there'd been no change. They were already plotting the stringent weight reduction plan the family would impose on Miss Callie when she was back home. And she would begin an exercise program that would include long walks each day around Lowtown. Regular checkups, vitamins, lean foods.

They were serious about this new health regimen, though everyone knew that Miss Callie would do exactly as she wished.

*

A few hours later, I began the chore of boxing up the things and junk I'd collected in nine years, and cleaning out my office. The new editor was a pleasant lady from Meridian, Mississippi, and she wanted to get started by the weekend. Margaret offered to help, but I wanted to go slowly and reminisce as I emptied drawers and files. It was a personal moment, and I preferred to be alone.

Mr. Caudle's books were finally removed from the dusty shelves where they had been placed long before I arrived. I planned to store them somewhere at home, in case an ancestor of his showed up and asked questions.

My emotions were mixed. Everything I touched brought back a story, a deadline, a trip deep into the county to chase a lead, interview a witness, or meet someone I hoped would be interesting enough for a profile. And the sooner I finished the packing, the closer I would be to walking out of the building and catching an airplane.

Bobby Ruffin called at nine-thirty. Miss Callie was awake, sitting up, sipping some tea, and they were allowing visitors for a few minutes. I hurried to the hospital. Sam met me in the hall and led me through the maze of rooms and cubicles in ICU. 'Don't talk about anything that happened yesterday, okay?' he said as we walked.

'Sure.'

'Nothing exciting. They won't even allow the

grandkids in; afraid that would make her heart rate go crazy. Everything is real quiet.'

She was awake, but barely. I had expected to see the bright eyes and brilliant smile, but Miss Callie was barely conscious. She recognized me, we hugged, I patted her right hand. The left one had an IV. Sam, Esau, and Gloria were in the room.

I wanted a few minutes alone so I could finally tell her I was selling the paper, but she was in no condition for such news. She'd been awake for almost two hours, and she obviously needed more sleep. Perhaps in a day or so we could have a lively chat about it.

After fifteen minutes, the doctor showed up and asked us to leave. We left, we came back, and the vigil continued throughout the Fourth of July, though we were not allowed inside the ICU again.

The Mayor decided there would be no fireworks for the Fourth. We'd heard enough explosions, suffered enough from gunpowder. Given the town's lingering jumpiness, there was no organized objection. The bands marched, the parade went on, the political speeches were the same as before, though with fewer candidates. Senator Theo Morton was a conspicuous no-show. There was ice cream, lemonade, barbecue, cotton candy – the usual food and snacks on the courthouse lawn.

But the town was subdued. Or maybe it was

just me. Maybe I was just so tired of the place that nothing seemed right about it. I certainly had the remedy.

After the speeches, I left the square and drove back to the hospital, a little detour that was becoming monotonous. I spoke to Fuzzy, who swept the hospital parking lot, and to Ralph, who washed the windows of the lobby. I stopped by the canteen and bought another lemonade from Hazel, then spoke to Mrs. Esther Ellen Trussel, who was manning the front information desk on behalf of the Pink Ladies, the hospital's auxiliary. In the waiting room on the second floor I found Bobby with Al's wife; they were watching television like two zombies. I had just opened a magazine when Sam came running in.

'She's had another heart attack!' he said.

The three of us jumped to our feet as if we had somewhere to go.

'It just happened! They got the red team in there!'

'I'll call the house,' I said, and stepped to the pay phone in the hall. Max answered the phone, and fifteen minutes later the Ruffins were streaming into the chapel.

The doctors took forever before giving us an update. It was almost eight P.M. before her treating physician entered the chapel. Doctors are notoriously hard to read, but his heavy eyes and wrinkled brow conveyed an unmistakable message. As he described a 'significant cardiac arrest' the eight children of Miss Callie deflated as a group. She was on a respirator, no longer able to breathe by herself.

Within an hour, the chapel was full of her friends. Reverend Thurston Small led a nonstop prayer group near the altar, and people joined it and left it as they wished. Poor Esau sat on the back row, slumped over, thoroughly drained. His grandchildren surrounded him, all very quiet and respectful.

For hours, we waited. And though we tried to smile and be optimistic, there was a feeling of doom. It was as if the funeral had already begun.

Margaret stopped by and we chatted in the hallway. Later, Mr. and Mrs. Fargarson found me and asked to speak to Esau. I led them into the chapel, where they were welcomed warmly by the Ruffins, all of whom expressed great sympathy for the loss of their son.

By midnight we were numb and rapidly losing track of time. Minutes dragged by, then I would look at the clock on the wall and wonder where the past hour went. I wanted to leave, if only to walk outside and breathe fresh air. The doctor, however, had warned us to stay close.

The horror of the ordeal hit when he gathered us around and gravely said it was time for a 'final moment with the family.' There were gasps, then tears. I'll never forget hearing Sam say out loud, 'A final moment?'

'This is it?' Gloria asked in absolute terror.

Frightened and bewildered, we followed the doctor out of the chapel, down the hall, up a flight of stairs, all of us moving with the heavy feet of someone marching to his own execution. The nurses helped herd us through the maze in ICU, their faces telling us what we dreaded the most.

As the family filed into the cramped little room, the doctor touched my arm and said, 'This should be just for the family.'

'Right,' I said, stopping.

'It's okay,' Sam said. 'He's with us.'

We packed around Miss Callie and her machines, most of which had been disconnected. The two smallest grandchildren were placed at the foot of her bed. Esau stood closest to her, gently patting her face. Her eyes were closed; she did not appear to be breathing.

She was very much at peace. Her husband and children touched some part of her, and the crying was heartbreaking. I was in a corner, wedged behind Gloria's husband and Al's wife, and I simply could not believe where I was or what I was doing.

When Max got his emotions under control, he touched Miss Callie's arm and said, 'Let us pray.' We bowed our heads and most of the crying stopped, for a moment anyway. 'Dear Lord, not our will but yours. Into thine hands we commend the spirit of this faithful child of God. Prepare a place for her now in your heavenly kingdom. Amen.'

At sunrise, I was sitting on the porch outside my

office. I wanted to be alone, to have a good cry in private. The crying around my house was more than I could bear.

As I had dreamed of traveling the world, I had the recurring vision of returning to Clanton with gifts for Miss Callie. I'd bring her a silver vase from England, linens from the Italy she would never see, perfumes from Paris, chocolates from Belgium, an urn from Egypt, a small diamond from the mines of South Africa. I would present these to her on her porch, before we had lunch, then we would talk about the places they came from. I would send her postcards at every stop. We would review my photographs in great detail. Through me, she would vicariously see the world. She would always be there, waiting eagerly for my return, anxious to see what I'd brought her. She would fill her home with little pieces of the world, and own things that no one, black or white, had ever owned in Clanton.

I ached with the loss of my dear friend. Its suddenness was cruel, as it always is. Its depth was so immense that I could not, at that time, imagine a recovery.

As the town slowly came to life below me, I walked to my desk, shoved some boxes out of the way, and sat down. I took my pen, and for a long time stared at a blank notepad. Eventually, slowly, with great agony, I began the last obituary.

The Broker

Chapter 1

In the waning hours of a presidency that was destined to arouse less interest from historians than any since perhaps that of William Henry Harrison (thirty-one days from inauguration to death), Arthur Morgan huddled in the Oval Office with his last remaining friend and pondered his final decisions. At that moment he felt as though he'd botched every decision in the previous four years, and he was not overly confident that he could, somehow, so late in the game, get things right. His friend wasn't so sure either, though, as always, he said little and whatever he did say was what the President wanted to hear.

They were about pardons – desperate pleas from thieves and embezzlers and liars, some still in jail and some who'd never served time but who nonetheless wanted their good names cleared and their beloved rights restored. All claimed to be friends, or friends of friends, or die-hard supporters, though only a few had ever gotten the chance to proclaim their support before that eleventh hour. How sad that after four tumultuous years of leading the free world it would all fizzle into one miserable pile of requests from a bunch of crooks. Which thieves should be allowed to steal again? That was the momentous question facing the President as the hours crept by.

The last friend was Critz, an old fraternity pal from their days at Cornell when Morgan ran the student government while Critz stuffed the ballot boxes. In the past four years, Critz had served as press secretary, chief of staff, national security advisor, and even secretary of state, though that appointment lasted for only three months and was hastily rescinded when Critz's unique style of diplomacy nearly ignited World War III. Critz's last appointment had taken place the previous October, in the final frantic weeks of the reelection onslaught. With the polls showing President Morgan trailing badly in at least forty states, Critz seized control of the campaign and managed to alienate the rest of the country, except, arguably, Alaska.

It had been a historic election; never before had an incumbent president received so few electoral votes. Three to be exact, all from Alaska, the only state Morgan had not visited, at Critz's advice. Five hundred and thirty-five for the challenger, three for President Morgan. The word 'landslide' did not even begin to capture the enormity of the shellacking.

Once the votes were counted, the challenger, following bad advice, decided to contest the results in Alaska. Why not go for all 538 electoral votes? he reasoned. Never again would a candidate for the presidency have the opportunity to completely whitewash his opponent, to throw the mother of all shutouts. For six weeks the President suffered even more while lawsuits raged in Alaska. When the supreme court there eventually awarded him the state's three electoral votes, he and Critz had a very quiet bottle of champagne.

President Morgan had become enamored of Alaska, even though the certified results gave him a scant seventeen-vote margin.

He should have avoided more states.

He even lost Delaware, his home, where the once-enlightened electorate had allowed him to serve eight wonderful years as governor. Just as he had never found the time to visit Alaska, his opponent had totally ignored Delaware – no organization to speak of, no television ads, not a single campaign stop. And his opponent still took 52 percent of the vote!

Critz sat in a thick leather chair and held a notepad with a list of a hundred things that needed to be done immediately. He watched his President move slowly from one window to the next, peering into the darkness, dreaming of what might have been. The man was depressed and humiliated. At fifty-eight his life was over, his career a wreck, his marriage crumbling. Mrs. Morgan had already moved back to Wilmington and was openly laughing at the idea of living in a cabin in Alaska. Critz had secret doubts about his friend's ability to hunt and fish for the rest of his life, but the prospect of living two thousand miles from Mrs. Morgan was very appealing. They might have carried Nebraska if the rather blue-blooded First Lady had not referred to the football team as the 'Sooners'.

The Nebraska Sooners!

Overnight, Morgan fell so far in the polls in both Nebraska and Oklahoma that he never recovered.

And in Texas she took a bite of prizewinning chili and began vomiting. As she was rushed to the hospital a microphone captured her still-famous words: 'How can you backward people eat such a putrid mess?'

Nebraska has five electoral votes. Texas has thirty-four. Insulting the local football team was a mistake they could have survived. But no candidate could overcome such a belittling description of Texas chili.

What a campaign! Critz was tempted to write a book. Someone needed to record the disaster.

Their partnership of almost forty years was ending. Critz had lined up a job with a defense contractor for $200,000 a year, and he would hit the lecture circuit at $50,000 a speech if anybody was desperate enough to pay it. After dedicating

4

his life to public service, he was broke and aging quickly and anxious to make a buck.

The President had sold his handsome home in Georgetown for a huge profit. He'd bought a small ranch in Alaska, where the people evidently admired him. He planned to spend the rest of his days there, hunting, fishing, perhaps writing his memoirs. Whatever he did in Alaska, it would have nothing to do with politics and Washington. He would not be the senior states-man, the grand old man of anybody's party, the sage voice of experience. No farewell tours, convention speeches, endowed chairs of political science. No presidential library. The people had spoken with a clear and thunderous voice. If they didn't want him, then he could certainly live without them.

'We need to make a decision about Cuccinello,' Critz said. The President was still standing at a window, looking at nothing in the darkness, still pondering Delaware. 'Who?'

'Figgy Cuccinello, that movie director who was indicted for having sex with a young starlet.'

'How young?'

'Fifteen, I think.'

'That's pretty young.'

'Yes, it is. He fled to Argentina, where he's been for ten years. Now he's homesick, wants to come back and start making dreadful movies again. He says his art is calling him home.'

'Perhaps the young girls are calling him home.'

'That too.'

'Seventeen wouldn't bother me. Fifteen's too young.'

'His offer is up to five million.'

The President turned and looked at Critz. 'He's offering five million for a pardon?'

'Yes, and he needs to move quickly. The money has to be wired out of Switzerland. It's three in the morning over there.'

'Where would it go?'

'We have accounts offshore. It's easy.'

'What would the press do?'

'It would be ugly.'

'It's always ugly.'

'This would be especially ugly.'

'I really don't care about the press,' Morgan said.

Then why did you ask? Critz wanted to say.

'Can the money be traced?' the President asked and turned back to the window.

'No.'

With his right hand, the President began scratching the back of his neck, something he always did when wrestling with a difficult decision. Ten minutes before he almost nuked North Korea, he'd scratched until the skin broke and blood oozed onto the collar of his white shirt. 'The answer is no,' he said. 'Fifteen is too young.'

Without a knock, the door opened and Artie Morgan, the President's son, barged in holding a Heineken in one hand and some papers in the other. 'Just talked to the CIA,' he said casually. He wore faded jeans and no socks. 'Maynard's on the way over.' He dumped the papers on the desk and left the room, slamming the door behind him.

Artie would take the $5 million without hesitation, Critz thought to himself, regardless of the girl's age. Fifteen was certainly not too young for Artie. They might have carried Kansas if Artie hadn't been caught in a Topeka motel room with three cheerleaders, the oldest of whom was seventeen. A grandstanding prosecutor had finally dropped the charges – two days after the election – when all three girls signed affidavits claiming they had not had sex with Artie. They were about to, in fact had been just seconds away from all manner of frolicking, when one of their mothers knocked on the motel room door and prevented an orgy.

The President sat in his leather rocker and pretended to flip through some useless papers. 'What's the latest on Backman?' he asked.

In his eighteen years as director of the CIA, Teddy Maynard had been to the White House less than ten times. And never for dinner (he always declined for health reasons), and never to say howdy to a foreign hotshot (he couldn't have cared less). Back when he could walk, he had occasionally stopped by to confer with whoever happened to be president, and perhaps one or two of his policy makers. Now, since he was in a wheelchair, his conversations with the White House were by phone. Twice, a vice president had actually been driven out to Langley to meet with Mr. Maynard.

The only advantage of being in a wheelchair was that it provided a wonderful excuse to go or stay or do whatever he damn well pleased. No one wanted to push around an old crippled man.

A spy for almost fifty years, he now preferred the luxury of looking directly behind himself when he moved about. He traveled in an unmarked white van – bulletproof glass, lead walls, two heavily armed boys perched behind the heavily armed driver – with his wheelchair clamped to the floor in the rear and facing back, so that Teddy could see the traffic that could not see him. Two other vans followed at a distance, and any misguided attempt to get near the director would be instantly terminated. None was expected. Most of the world thought Teddy Maynard was either dead or idling away his final days in some secret nursing home where old spies were sent to die.

Teddy wanted it that way.

He was wrapped in a heavy gray quilt, and tended to by Hoby, his faithful aide. As the van moved along the Beltway at a constant sixty miles an hour, Teddy sipped green tea poured from a thermos by Hoby, and watched the cars behind them. Hoby sat next to the wheelchair on a leather stool made especially for him.

A sip of tea and Teddy said, 'Where's Backman right now?'

'In his cell,' Hoby answered.

'And our people are with the warden?'

'They're sitting in his office, waiting.'

Another sip from a paper cup, one carefully guarded with both hands. The hands were frail, veiny, the color of skim milk, as if they had already died and were patiently waiting for the rest of the body. 'How long will it take to get him out of the country?'

'About four hours.'

'And the plan is in place?'

'Everything is ready. We're waiting on the green light.'

'I hope this moron can see it my way.'

Critz and the moron were staring at the walls of the Oval Office, their heavy silence broken occasionally by a comment about Joel Backman. They had to talk about something, because neither would mention what was really on his mind.

Can this be happening?

Is this finally the end?

Forty years. From Cornell to the Oval Office. The end was so abrupt that they had not had enough time to properly prepare for it. They had been counting on four more years. Four years of glory as they carefully crafted a legacy, then rode gallantly into the sunset.

Though it was late, it seemed to grow even

darker outside. The windows that overlooked the Rose Garden were black. A clock above the fireplace could almost be heard as it ticked nonstop in its final countdown.

'What will the press do if I pardon Backman?' the President asked, not for the first time.

'Go berserk.'

'That might be fun.'

'You won't be around.'

'No, I won't.' After the transfer of power at noon the next day, his escape from Washington would begin with a private jet (owned by an oil company) to an old friend's villa on the island of Barbados. At Morgan's instructions, the televisions had been removed from the villa, no newspapers or magazines would be delivered, and all phones had been unplugged. He would have no contact with anyone, not even Critz, and especially not Mrs. Morgan, for at least a month. He wouldn't care if Washington burned. In fact, he secretly hoped that it would.

After Barbados, he would sneak up to his cabin in Alaska, and there he would continue to ignore the world as the winter passed and he waited on spring.

'Should we pardon him?' the President asked.

'Probably,' Critz said.

The President had shifted to the 'we' mode now, something he invariably did when a potentially unpopular decision was at hand. For the easy ones, it was always 'I'. When he needed a crutch, and especially when he would need someone to blame, he opened up the decision-making process and included Critz.

Critz had been taking the blame for forty years, and though he was certainly used to it, he was nonetheless tired of it. He said, 'There's a very good chance we wouldn't be here had it not been for Joel Backman.'

'You may be right about that,' the President said. He had always maintained that he had been elected because of his brilliant campaigning, charismatic personality, uncanny grasp of the issues, and clear vision for America. To finally admit that he owed anything to Joel Backman was almost shocking.

But Critz was too calloused, and too tired, to be shocked.

Six years ago, the Backman scandal had engulfed much of Washington and eventually tainted the White House. A cloud appeared over a popular president, paving the way for Arthur Morgan to stumble his way into the White House.

Now that he was stumbling out, he relished the idea of one last arbitrary slap in the face to the Washington establishment that had shunned him for four years. A reprieve for Joel Backman would rattle the walls of every office building in D.C. and shock the press into a blathering frenzy. Morgan liked the idea. While he sunned away on Barbados, the city would gridlock once again as congressmen demanded hearings and prosecutors performed for the cameras and the

11

insufferable talking heads prattled nonstop on cable news.

The President smiled into the darkness.

On the Arlington Memorial Bridge, over the Potomac River, Hoby refilled the director's paper cup with green tea. 'Thank you,' Teddy said softly. 'What's our boy doing tomorrow when he leaves office?' he asked.

'Fleeing the country.'

'He should've left sooner.'

'He plans to spend a month in the Caribbean, licking his wounds, ignoring the world, pouting, waiting for someone to show some interest.'

'And Mrs. Morgan?'

'She's already back in Delaware playing bridge.'

'Are they splitting?'

'If he's smart. Who knows?'

Teddy took a careful sip of tea. 'So what's our leverage if Morgan balks?'

'I don't think he'll balk. The preliminary talks have gone well. Critz seems to be on board. He has a much better feel of things now than Morgan. Critz knows that they would've never seen the Oval Office had it not been for the Backman scandal.'

'As I said, what's our leverage if he balks?'

'None, really. He's an idiot, but he's a clean one.'

They turned off Constitution Avenue onto 18th Street and were soon entering the east gate of the White House. Men with machine guns materialized from the darkness, then Secret Service agents in black trench coats stopped the van. Code words were used, radios squawked, and within minutes Teddy was being lowered from the van. Inside, a cursory search of his wheelchair revealed nothing but a crippled and bundled-up old man.

Artie, minus the Heineken, and again without knocking, poked his head through the door and announced: 'Maynard's here.'

'So he's alive,' the President said.

'Barely.'

'Then roll him in.'

Hoby and a deputy named Priddy followed the wheelchair into the Oval Office. The President and Critz welcomed their guests and directed them to the sitting area in front of the fireplace. Though Maynard avoided the White House, Priddy practically lived there, briefing the President every morning on intelligence matters.

As they settled in, Teddy glanced around the room, as if looking for bugs and listening devices. He was almost certain there were none; that practice had ended with Watergate. Nixon laid enough wire in the White House to juice a small city, but, of course, he paid for it. Teddy, however, was wired. Carefully hidden above the axle of his wheelchair, just inches below his seat, was a powerful recorder that would capture every sound made during the next thirty minutes.

He tried to smile at President Morgan, but he wanted to say something like: You are without a doubt the most limited politician I have ever encountered. Only in America could a moron like you make it to the top.

President Morgan smiled at Teddy Maynard, but he wanted to say something like: I should have fired you four years ago. Your agency has been a constant embarrassment to this country.

Teddy: I was shocked when you carried a single state, albeit by seventeen votes.

Morgan: You couldn't find a terrorist if he advertised on a billboard.

Teddy: Happy fishing. You'll get even fewer trout than votes.

Morgan: Why didn't you just die, like everyone promised me you would?

Teddy: Presidents come and go, but I never leave.

Morgan: It was Critz who wanted to keep you. Thank him for your job. I wanted to sack your ass two weeks after my inauguration.

Critz said loudly, 'Coffee anyone?'

Teddy said, 'No,' and as soon as that was established, Hoby and Priddy likewise declined. And because the CIA wanted no coffee, President Morgan said, 'Yes, black with two sugars.' Critz nodded at a secretary who was waiting in a half-opened side door.

He turned back to the gathering and said, 'We don't have a lot of time.'

14

Teddy said quickly, 'I'm here to discuss Joel Backman.'

'Yes, that's why you're here,' the President said.

'As you know,' Teddy continued, almost ignoring the President, 'Mr. Backman went to prison without saying a word. He still carries some secrets that, frankly, could compromise national security.'

'You can't kill him,' Critz blurted.

'We cannot target American citizens, Mr. Critz. It's against the law. We prefer that someone else do it.'

'I don't follow,' the President said.

'Here's the plan. If you pardon Mr. Backman, and if he accepts the pardon, then we will have him out of the country in a matter of hours. He must agree to spend the rest of his life in hiding. This should not be a problem because there are several people who would like to see him dead, and he knows it. We'll relocate him to a foreign country, probably in Europe where he'll be easier to watch. He'll have a new identity. He'll be a free man, and with time people will forget about Joel Backman.'

'That's not the end of the story,' Critz said.

'No. We'll wait, perhaps a year or so, then we'll leak the word in the right places. They'll find Mr. Backman, and they'll kill him, and when they do so, many of our questions will be answered.'

A long pause as Teddy looked at Critz, then

the President. When he was convinced they were thoroughly confused, he continued. 'It's a very simple plan, gentlemen. It's a question of who kills him.'

'So you'll be watching?' Critz asked.

'Very closely.'

'Who's after him?' the President asked.

Teddy refolded his veiny hands and recoiled a bit, then he looked down his long nose like a schoolteacher addressing his little third graders. 'Perhaps the Russians, the Chinese, maybe the Israelis. There could be others.'

Of course there were others, but no one expected Teddy to reveal everything he knew. He never had; never would, regardless of who was president and regardless of how much time he had left in the Oval Office. They came and went, some for four years, others for eight. Some loved the espionage, others were only concerned with the latest polls. Morgan had been particularly inept at foreign policy, and with a few hours remaining in his administration, Teddy certainly was not going to divulge any more than was necessary to get the pardon.

'Why would Backman take such a deal?' Critz asked.

'He may not,' Teddy answered. 'But he's been in solitary confinement for six years. That's twenty-three hours a day in a tiny cell. One hour of sunshine. Three showers a week. Bad food – they say he's lost sixty pounds. I hear he's not doing too well.'

Two months ago, after the landslide, when Teddy Maynard conceived this pardon scheme, he had pulled a few of his many strings and Backman's confinement had grown much worse. The temperature in his cell was lowered ten degrees, and for the past month he'd had a terrible cough. His food, bland at best, had been run through the processor again and was being served cold. His toilet flushed about half the time. The guards woke him up at all hours of the night. His phone privileges were curtailed. The law library that he used twice a week was suddenly off-limits. Backman, a lawyer, knew his rights, and he was threatening all manner of litigation against the prison and the government, though he had yet to file suit. The fight was taking its toll. He was demanding sleeping pills and Prozac.

'You want me to pardon Joel Backman so you can arrange for him to be murdered?' the President asked.

'Yes,' Teddy said bluntly. 'But we won't actually arrange it.'

'But it'll happen.'

'Yes.'

'And his death will be in the best interests of our national security?'

'I firmly believe that.'

Chapter 2

The isolation wing at Rudley Federal Correctional Facility had forty identical cells, each a twelve-foot square with no windows, no bars, green-painted concrete floors and cinder-block walls, and a door that was solid metal with a narrow slot at the bottom for food trays and a small open peephole for the guards to have a look occasionally. The wing was filled with government informants, drug snitches, Mafia misfits, a couple of spies – men who needed to be locked away because there were plenty of folks back home who would gladly slice their throats. Most of the forty inmates in protective custody at Rudley had requested the I-wing.

Joel Backman was trying to sleep when two guards clanged open his door and switched on his light. 'The warden wants you,' one said, and there was no elaboration. They rode in silence in a prison van across the frigid Oklahoma prairie, past other buildings holding less-secure criminals, until they arrived at the administration building. Backman, handcuffed for no apparent reason, was hurried inside, up two flights of stairs, then down a long hall to the big office where lights were on and something important was going down. He saw a clock on a wall; it was almost 11:00 p.m.

He'd never met the warden, which was not at all unusual. For many good reasons the warden didn't circulate. He wasn't running for office, nor was he concerned with motivating the troops. With him were three other suits, all earnest-looking men who'd been chatting for some time. Though smoking was strictly prohibited in offices owned by the U.S. government, an ashtray was full and a thick fog hung close to the ceiling.

With absolutely no introduction, the warden said, 'Sit over there, Mr. Backman.'

'A pleasure to meet you,' Backman said as he looked at the other men in the room. 'Why, exactly, am I here?'

'We'll discuss that.'

'Could you please remove these handcuffs? I promise not to kill anyone.'

The warden snapped at the nearest guard, who quickly found a key and freed Backman. The guard then scrambled out of the room, slamming the door behind him, much to the displeasure of the warden, a very nervous man.

He pointed and said, 'This is Special Agent Adair of the FBI. This is Mr. Knabe from the

Justice Department. And this is Mr. Sizemore, also from Washington.'

None of the three moved in the direction of Mr. Backman, who was still standing and looking quite perplexed. He nodded at them, in a halfhearted effort to be polite. His efforts were not returned.

'Please sit,' the warden said, and Backman finally took a chair. 'Thank you. As you know, Mr. Backman, a new president is about to be sworn in. President Morgan is on the way out. Right now he is in the Oval Office wrestling with the decision of whether to grant you a full pardon'.

Backman was suddenly seized with a violent cough, one brought on in part by the near arctic temperature in his cell and in part by the shock of the word 'pardon.'

Mr. Knabe from Justice handed him a bottle of water, which he gulped and splashed down his chin and finally managed to stifle the cough. 'A pardon?' he mumbled.

'A full pardon, with some strings attached.'

'But why?'

'I don't know why, Mr. Backman, nor is it my business to understand what's happening. I'm just the messenger.'

Mr. Sizemore, introduced simply as 'from Washington', but without the baggage of title or affiliation, said, 'It's a deal, Mr. Backman. In return for a full pardon, you must agree to leave the country, never return, and live with a new

20

identity in a place where no one can find you.'

No problem there, thought Backman. He didn't want to be found.

'But why?' he mumbled again. The bottle of water in his left hand could actually be seen shaking.

As Mr. Sizemore from Washington watched it shake, he studied Joel Backman, from his closely cropped gray hair to his battered dime-store running shoes, with his black prison-issue socks, and couldn't help but recall the image of the man in his prior life. A magazine cover came to mind. A fancy photo of Joel Backman in a black Italian suit, impeccably tailored and detailed and groomed and looking at the camera with as much smugness as humanly possible. The hair was longer and darker, the handsome face was fleshy and wrinkle free, the waistline was thick and spoke of many power lunches and four-hour dinners. He loved wine and women and sports cars. He had a jet, a yacht, a place in Vail, all of which he'd been quite eager to talk about. The bold caption above his head read: THE BROKER – IS THIS THE SECOND MOST POWERFUL MAN IN WASHINGTON?

The magazine was in Mr. Sizemore's brief-case, along with a thick file on Joel Backman. He'd scoured it on the flight from Washington to Tulsa.

According to the magazine article, the broker's income at the time was reported to be in excess of $10 million a year, though he'd been coy with the reporter. The law firm he founded had two hundred lawyers, small by Washington standards, but without a doubt the most powerful in political circles. It was a lobbying machine, not a place where real lawyers practiced their craft. More like a bordello for rich companies and foreign governments.

Oh, how the mighty have fallen, Mr. Sizemore thought to himself as he watched the bottle shake.

'I don't understand,' Backman managed to whisper.

'And we don't have time to explain,' Mr. Sizemore said. 'It's a quick deal, Mr. Backman. Unfortunately, you don't have time to contemplate things. A snap decision is required. Yes or no. You want to stay here, or you want to live with another name on the other side of the world?'

'Where?'

'We don't know where, but we'll figure it out.'

'Will I be safe?'

'Only you can answer that question, Mr. Backman.'

As Mr. Backman pondered his own question, he shook even more.

'When will I leave?' he asked slowly. His voice was regaining strength for the moment, but another violent cough was always waiting.

'Immediately,' said Mr. Sizemore, who had seized control of the meeting and relegated the warden, the FBI, and the Justice Department to being spectators.

'You mean, like, right now?'

'You will not return to your cell.'

'Oh darn,' Backman said, and the others couldn't help but smile.

'There's a guard waiting by your cell,' the warden said. 'He'll bring whatever you want.'

'There's always a guard waiting by my cell,' Backman snapped at the warden. 'If it's that sadistic little bastard Sloan, tell him to take my razor blades and slash his own wrists.'

Everyone swallowed hard and waited for the words to escape through the heating vents. Instead, they cut through the polluted air and rattled around the room for a moment.

Mr. Sizemore cleared his throat, reshuffled his weight from the left buttock to the right, and said, 'There are some gentlemen waiting in the Oval Office, Mr. Backman. Are you going to accept the deal?'

'The President is waiting on me?'

'You could say that.'

'He owes me. I put him there.'

'This really is not the time to debate such matters, Mr. Backman,' Mr. Sizemore said calmly.

'Is he returning the favor?'

'I'm not privy to the President's thoughts.'

'You're assuming he has the ability to think.'

'I'll just call and tell them the answer is no.'

'Wait.'

Backman drained the bottle of water and asked for another. He wiped his mouth with a sleeve, then said, 'Is it like a witness protection program, something like that?'

'It's not an official program, Mr. Backman. But, from time to time, we find it necessary to hide people.'

'How often do you lose one?'

'Not too often.'

'Not too often? So there's no guarantee I'll be safe.'

'Nothing is guaranteed. But your odds are good.'

Backman looked at the warden and said, 'How many years do I have left here, Lester?'

Lester was jolted back into the conversation. No one called him Lester, a name he hated and avoided. The nameplate on his desk declared him to be L. Howard Cass. 'Fourteen years, and you can address me as Warden Cass.'

'Cass my ass. Odds are I'll be dead in three. A combination of malnutrition, hypothermia, and negligent health care should do it. Lester here runs a really tight ship, boys.'

'Can we move along?' Mr. Sizemore said.

'Of course I'll take the deal,' Backman said. 'What fool wouldn't?'

Mr. Knabe from Justice finally moved. He opened a briefcase and said, 'Here's the paperwork.'

'Who do you work for?' Backman asked Mr. Sizemore.

'The President of the United States.'

'Well, tell him I didn't vote for him because I

24

was locked away. But I certainly would have, if given the chance. And tell him I said thanks, okay?'

'Sure.'

Hoby poured another cup of green tea, decaffeinated now because it was almost midnight, and handed it to Teddy, who was wrapped in a blanket and staring at the traffic behind them. They were on Constitution Avenue, leaving downtown, almost to the Roosevelt Bridge. The old man took a sip and said, 'Morgan is too stupid to be selling pardons. Critz, however, worries me.'

'There's a new account on the island of Nevis,' Hoby said. 'It popped up two weeks ago, opened by an obscure company owned by Floyd Dunlap.'

'And who's he?'

'One of Morgan's fund-raisers.'

'Why Nevis?'

'It's the current hot spot for offshore activity.'

'And we're covering it?'

'We're all over it. Any transfers should take place in the next forty-eight hours.'

Teddy nodded slightly and glanced to his left for a partial look at the Kennedy Center. 'Where's Backman?'

'He's leaving prison.'

Teddy smiled and sipped his tea. They crossed the bridge in silence, and when the Potomac was behind them, he finally said, 'Who'll get him?'

'Does it really matter?'

'No, it doesn't. But it will be quite enjoyable watching the contest.'

Wearing a well-worn but starched and pressed khaki military uniform, with all the patches and badges removed, and shiny black combat boots and a heavy navy parka with a hood that he pulled snugly around his head, Joel Backman strutted out of the Rudley Federal Correctional Facility at five minutes after midnight, fourteen years ahead of schedule. He had been there, in solitary confinement, for six years, and upon leaving he carried with him a small canvas bag with a few books and some photos. He did not look back.

He was fifty-two years old, divorced, broke, thoroughly estranged from two of his three children and thoroughly forgotten by every friend he'd ever made. Not a single one had bothered to maintain a correspondence beyond the first year of his confinement. An old girlfriend, one of the countless secretaries he'd chased around his plush offices, had written for ten months, until it was reported in *The Washington Post* that the FBI had decided it was unlikely that Joel Backman had looted his firm and his clients of the millions that had first been rumored. Who wants to be pen pals with a broke lawyer in prison? A wealthy one, maybe.

His mother wrote him occasionally, but she was ninety-one years old and living in a low-rent nursing home near Oakland, and with each letter he got the impression it would be her last. He wrote her once a week, but doubted if she was able to read anything, and he was almost certain that no one on staff had the time or interest to read to her. She always said, 'Thanks for the letter,' but never mentioned anything he'd said. He sent her cards on special occasions. In one of her letters she had confessed that no one else remembered her birthday.

The boots were very heavy. As he plodded along the sidewalk he realized that he'd spent most of the past six years in his socks, no shoes. Funny the things you think about when you get sprung with no warning. When was the last time he'd worn boots? And how soon could he shuck the damn things?

He stopped for a second and looked toward the sky. For one hour each day, he'd been allowed to roam a small patch of grass outside his prison wing. Always alone, always watched by a guard, as if he, Joel Backman, a former lawyer who'd never fired a gun in anger, might suddenly become dangerous and maim someone. The 'garden' was lined with ten feet of chain-link topped with razor wire. Beyond it was an empty drainage canal, and beyond that was an endless, treeless prairie that stretched to Texas, he presumed.

Mr. Sizemore and Agent Adair were his escorts. They led him to a dark green sport-utility vehicle that, though unmarked, practically screamed 'government issue' to anyone looking. Joel crawled into the backseat, alone, and began praying. He closed his eyes tightly, gritted his teeth, and asked God to please allow the engine to start, the wheels to move, the gates to open, the paperwork to be sufficient; please, God, no cruel jokes. This is not a dream, God, please!

Twenty minutes later, Sizemore spoke first. 'Say, Mr. Backman, are you hungry?'

Mr. Backman had ceased praying and had begun crying. The vehicle had been moving steadily, though he had not opened his eyes. He was lying on the rear seat, fighting his emotions and losing badly.

'Sure,' he managed to say. He sat up and looked outside. They were on an interstate highway, a green sign flew by – Perry Exit. They stopped in the parking lot of a pancake house, less than a quarter of a mile from the interstate. Big trucks were in the distance, their diesel engines grinding along. Joel watched them for a second, and listened. He glanced upward again and saw a half-moon.

'Are we in a hurry?' he asked Sizemore as they entered the restaurant.

'We're on schedule,' came the reply.

They sat at a table near the front window, with Joel looking out. He ordered french toast and fruit, nothing heavy because he was afraid his system was too accustomed to the gruel he'd been living on. Conversation was stiff; the two government boys were programmed to say little and were thoroughly incapable of small talk. Not that Joel wanted to hear anything they had to say.

He tried not to smile. Sizemore would report later that Backman glanced occasionally at the door and seemed to keep a close eye on the other customers. He did not appear to be frightened; quite the contrary. As the minutes dragged on and the shock wore off, he seemed to adjust quickly and became somewhat animated. He devoured two orders of french toast and had four cups of black coffee.

A few minutes after 4:00 a.m. they entered the gates of Fort Summit, near Brinkley, Texas. Backman was taken to the base hospital and examined by two physicians. Except for a head cold and the cough, and general gauntness, he wasn't in bad shape. He was then taken to a hangar where he met a Colonel Gantner, who instantly became his best friend. At Gantner's instructions, and under his close supervision, Joel changed into a green army jumpsuit with the name HERZOG stenciled above the right pocket. 'Is that me?' Joel asked, looking at the name.

'It is for the next forty-eight hours,' Gantner said.

'And my rank?'

'Major.'

'Not bad.'

At some point during this quick briefing, Mr. Sizemore from Washington and Agent Adair slipped away, never to be seen again by Joel

Backman. With the first hint of sunlight, Joel stepped through the rear hatch of a C-130 cargo plane and followed Gantner to the upper level, to a small bunk room where six other soldiers were preparing for a long flight.

'Take that bunk,' Gantner said, pointing to one close to the floor.

'Can I ask where we're going?' Joel whispered.

'You can ask, but I can't answer.'

'Just curious.'

'I'll brief you before we land.'

'And when might that be?'

'In about fourteen hours.'

With no windows to distract him, Joel situated himself on his bunk, pulled a blanket over his head, and was snoring by takeoff.

Chapter 3

Critz slept a few hours, then left home long before the inauguration mess began. Just after dawn, he and his wife were whisked off to London on one of his new employer's many private jets. He was to spend two weeks there, then return to the grind of the Beltway as a new lobbyist playing a very old game. He hated the idea. For years he'd watched the losers cross the street and start new careers twisting the arms of their former colleagues, selling their souls to anyone with enough money to buy whatever influence they advertised. It was such a rotten business. He was sick of the political life, but, sadly, he knew nothing else.

He'd make some speeches, maybe write a book, hang on for a few years hoping someone remembered him. But Critz knew how quickly the once powerful are forgotten in Washington.

President Morgan and Director Maynard had agreed to sit on the Backman story for twenty-four hours, until well after the inauguration. Morgan didn't care; he'd be in Barbados. Critz, however, did not feel bound by any agreement, especially one made with the likes of Teddy Maynard. After a long dinner with lots of wine, sometime around 2:00 a.m. in London, he called a White House correspondent for CBS and whispered the basics of the Backman pardon. As he predicted, CBS broke the story during its early-morning gossip hour, and before 8:00 a.m. the news was roaring around D.C.

Joel Backman had been given a full and unconditional pardon at the eleventh hour!

There were no details of his release. When last heard from, he'd been tucked away in a maximum-security facility in Oklahoma.

In a very nervous city, the day began with the pardon storming onto center stage and competing with a new President and his first full day in office.

The bankrupt law firm of Pratt & Bolling now found itself on Massachusetts Avenue, four blocks north of Dupont Circle; not a bad location, but not nearly as classy as the old place on New York Avenue. A few years earlier, when Joel Backman was in charge – it was Backman, Pratt & Bolling then – he had insisted on paying the highest rent in town so he could stand at the vast windows of his vast office on the eighth floor and look down at the White House.

Now the White House was nowhere in sight;

there were no power offices with grand vistas; the building had three floors, not eight. And the firm had shrunk from two hundred highly paid lawyers to about thirty struggling ones. The first bankruptcy – commonly referred to within the offices as Backman I – had decimated the firm, but it had also miraculously kept its partners out of prison. Backman II had been caused by three years of vicious infighting and suing among the survivors. The firm's competitors were fond of saying that Pratt & Bolling spent more time suing itself than those it was hired to sue.

Early that morning, though, the competitors were quiet. Joel Backman was a free man. The broker was loose. Would he make a comeback? Was he returning to Washington? Was it all true? Surely not.

Kim Bolling was currently locked away in alcohol rehab, and from there he would be sent straight to a private mental facility for many years. The unbearable strain of the last six years had driven him over the edge, to a point of no return. The task of dealing with the latest nightmare from Joel Backman fell into the rather large lap of Carl Pratt.

It had been Pratt who had uttered the fateful 'I do' twenty-two years earlier when Backman had proposed a marriage of their two small firms. It had been Pratt who had labored strenuously for sixteen years to clean up behind Backman as the firm expanded and the fees poured in and all ethical boundaries were blurred beyond recognition. It had been Pratt who'd fought weekly with his partner, but who, over time, had come to enjoy the fruits of their enormous success.

And it had been Carl Pratt who'd come so close to a federal prosecution himself, just before Joel Backman heroically took the fall for everyone. Backman's plea agreement, and the agreement that exculpated the firm's other partners, required a fine of $10 million, thus leading directly to the first bankruptcy – Backman I.

But bankruptcy was better than jail, Pratt reminded himself almost daily. He lumbered around his sparse office early that morning, mumbling to himself and trying desperately to believe that the news was simply not true. He stood at his small window and gazed at the gray brick building next door, and asked himself how it could happen. How could a broke, disbarred, disgraced former lawyer/lobbyist convince a lame-duck president to grant a last-minute pardon?

By the time Joel Backman went to prison, he was probably the most famous white-collar criminal in America. Everybody wanted to see him hang from the gallows.

But, Pratt conceded to himself, if anyone in the world could pull off such a miracle, it was Joel Backman.

Pratt worked the phones for a few minutes, tapping into his extensive network of Washington gossipmongers and know-it-alls. An old friend who'd somehow managed to survive in the Executive Department under four presidents – two from each party – finally confirmed the truth.

'Where is he?' Pratt asked urgently, as if Backman might resurrect himself in D.C. at any moment.

'No one knows,' came the reply.

Pratt locked his door and fought the urge to open the office bottle of vodka. He had been forty-nine years old when his partner was sent to prison for twenty years with no parole, and he often wondered what he would do when he was sixty-nine and Backman got out.

At that moment, Pratt felt as though he'd been cheated out of fourteen years.

The courtroom had been so crowded that the judge postponed the hearing for two hours until the demand for seating could be organized and somewhat prioritized. Every prominent news organization in the country was screaming for a place to sit or stand. Big shots from Justice, the FBI, the Pentagon, the CIA, the NSA, the White House, and Capitol Hill were pressing for seats, all claiming that their best interests would be served if they could be present to watch the lynching of Joel Backman. When the defendant finally appeared in the tense courtroom, the crowd suddenly froze and the only sound was that of the court reporter prepping his steno machine.

Backman was led to the defense table, where his small army of lawyers packed tightly around him as if bullets were expected from the mob in the gallery. Gunfire would not have been a surprise, though the security rivaled that of a presidential visit. In the first row directly behind the defense table sat Carl Pratt and a dozen or so other partners, or soon-to-be-former partners, of Mr. Backman. They had been searched most aggressively, and for good reason. Though they seethed with hatred for the man, they were also pulling for him. If his plea agreement fell through because of a last-second hitch or disagreement, then they would be fair game again, with nasty trials just around the corner.

At least they were sitting on the front row, out with the spectators, and not at the defense table where the crooks were kept. At least they were alive. Eight days earlier, Jacy Hubbard, one of their trophy partners, had been found dead in Arlington National Cemetery, in a contrived suicide that few people believed. Hubbard had been a former senator from Texas who had given up his seat after twenty-four years for the sole, though unannounced, purpose of offering his significant influence to the highest bidder. Of course Joel Backman would never allow such a big fish to escape his net, so he and the rest of Backman, Pratt & Bolling had hired Hubbard for a million bucks a year because good ol' Jacy could get himself into the Oval Office anytime he wanted.

Hubbard's death had worked wonders in helping Joel Backman to see the government's point of view. The logjam that had delayed the plea negotiations was suddenly broken. Not only would Backman accept twenty years, he wanted to do it quickly. He was anxious for protective custody!

The government's lawyer that day was a high-ranking career prosecutor from Justice, and with such a big and prestigious crowd he could not help but grandstand. He simply couldn't use one word when three would suffice; there were too many people out there. He was onstage, a rare moment in a long dull career, when the nation happened to be watching. With a savage blandness he launched into a reading of the indictment, and it was quickly apparent that he possessed almost no talent at theatrics, virtually no flair for drama, though he tried mightily. After eight minutes of stultifying monologue, the judge, peering sleepily over reading glasses, said, 'Would you speed it up, sir, and lower your voice at the same time.'

There were eighteen counts, alleging crimes ranging from espionage to treason. When they were all read, Joel Backman was so thoroughly vilified that he belonged in the same league with Hitler. His lawyer immediately reminded the court, and everyone else present, that nothing in the indictment had been proven, that it was in fact just a recitation of one side of the case, the government's heavily slanted view of things. He explained that his client would be pleading guilty to only four of the eighteen counts – unauthorized possession of military documents. The judge then read the lengthy plea agreement, and for twenty minutes nothing was said. The artists on the front row sketched the scene with a fury, their images bearing almost no likeness to reality.

Hiding on the back row, seated with strangers, was Neal Backman, Joel's oldest son. He was, at that moment, still an associate with Backman, Pratt & Bolling, but that was about to change. He watched the proceedings in a state of shock, unable to believe that his once powerful father was pleading guilty and about to be buried in the federal penal system.

The defendant was eventually herded to the bench, where he looked up as proudly as possible and faced the judge. With lawyers whispering in both ears, he pled guilty to his four counts, then was led back to his seat. He managed to avoid eye contact with everyone.

A sentencing date was set for the following month. As Backman was handcuffed and taken away, it became obvious to those present that he would not be forced to divulge his secrets, that he would indeed be incarcerated for a very long time while his conspiracies faded away. The crowd slowly broke up. The reporters got half the story they wanted. The big men from the agencies left without speaking – some were pleased that secrets had been protected, others were furious that crimes were being hidden. Carl

Pratt and the other beleaguered partners headed for the nearest bar.

The first reporter called the office just before 9:00 a.m. Pratt had already alerted his secretary that such calls were expected. She was to tell everyone that he was to be busy in court on some lengthy matter and might not be back in the office for months. Soon the phone lines were gridlocked and a seemingly productive day was shot to hell. Every lawyer and other employee dropped everything and whispered of nothing but the Backman news. Several watched the front door, half expecting the ghost to come looking for them.

Behind a locked door and alone, Pratt sipped a Bloody Mary and watched the nonstop news on cable. Thankfully, a busload of Danish tourists had been kidnapped in the Philippines, otherwise Joel Backman would have been the top story. But he was running a close second, as all kinds of experts were brought in, powdered up, and placed in the studio under the lights where they prattled on about the man's legendary sins.

A former Pentagon chief called the pardon 'a potential blow to our national security.' A retired federal judge, looking every day of his ninety-plus years, called it, predictably, 'a miscarriage of justice.' A rookie senator from Vermont admitted he knew little about the Backman scandal but he was nonetheless enthusiastic about being on live cable and said he planned to call for all sorts of investigations. An unnamed White House official said the new President was 'quite disturbed' by the pardon and planned to review it, whatever that meant.

And on and on. Pratt mixed a second Bloody Mary.

Going for the gore, a 'correspondent' – not simply a 'reporter' – dug up a piece on Senator Jacy Hubbard, and Pratt reached for the remote. He turned up the volume when a large photo of Hubbard's face was flashed on the screen. The former senator had been found dead with a bullet in the head the week before Backman pled guilty. What appeared at first to be a suicide was later called suspicious, though no suspect had ever been identified. The pistol was unmarked and probably stolen. Hubbard had been an active hunter but had never used handguns. The powder residue on his right hand was suspicious. An autopsy revealed a stout concentration of alcohol and barbiturates in his system. The alcohol could certainly be predicted but Hubbard had never been known to use drugs. He'd been seen a few hours earlier with an attractive young lady at a Georgetown bar, which was fairly typical.

The prevailing theory was that the lady slipped him enough drugs to knock him out, then handed him over to the professional killers. He was hauled to a remote section of the Arlington National Cemetery and shot once in the head. His body came to rest on the grave of his brother, a decorated Vietnam hero. A nice touch, but those who knew him well claimed he seldom talked about his family and many knew nothing of the dead brother.

The unspoken theory was that Hubbard was killed by the same people who wanted a shot at Joel Backman. And for years afterward Carl Pratt and Kim Bolling paid serious money for professional bodyguards just in case their names were on the same list. Evidently, they were not. The details of the fateful deal that nailed Backman and killed Hubbard had been handled by those two, and with time Pratt had loosened the security around himself, though he still carried a Ruger with him everywhere.

But Backman was far away, with the distance growing every minute. Oddly enough, he, too, was thinking of Jacy Hubbard and the people who might have killed him. He had plenty of time to think – fourteen hours in a fold-down bunk on a rattling cargo plane did much to deaden the senses, for a normal person anyway. But for a freshly released former convict who'd just walked out of six years in solitary lockdown, the flight was quite stimulating.

Whoever killed Jacy Hubbard would want very much to kill Joel Backman, and as he bumped along at 24,000 feet he pondered some serious questions. Who had lobbied for his pardon? Where did they plan to hide him? Who, exactly, were 'they'?

Pleasant questions, really. Less than twenty-four hours earlier his questions had been: Are they trying to starve me to death? Freeze me? Am I slowly losing my mind in this twelve-by-twelve cell? Or losing it rapidly? Will I ever see my grandchildren? Do I want to?

He liked the new questions better, troubling as they were. At least he would be able to walk down a street somewhere and breathe the air and feel the sun and perhaps stop at a café and sip a strong coffee.

He'd had a client once, a wealthy cocaine importer who'd been snared in a DEA sting. The client had been such a valuable catch that the feds offered him a new life with a new name and a new face if he would squeal on the Colombians. Squeal he did, and after surgery he was reborn on the north side of Chicago, where he ran a small bookshop. Joel had dropped in one day years later and found the client sporting a goatee, smoking a pipe, looking rather cerebral and earthy. He had a new wife and three stepchildren, and the Colombians never had a clue.

It's a big world out there. Hiding is not that difficult.

Joel closed his eyes, grew still, listened to the steady hum of the four engines, and tried to tell himself that wherever he was headed he would not live like a man on the run. He would adapt, he would survive, he would not live in fear.

There was a muted conversation under way

42

two bunks down, two soldiers swapping stories about all the girls they'd had. He thought of Mo the mob snitch who, for the last four years, had occupied the cell next to Joel's, and who, for about twenty-two hours a day, was the only human he could chat with. He couldn't see him, but they could hear each other through a vent. Mo didn't miss his family, his friends, his neighborhood, or food or drink or sunshine. All Mo talked about was sex. He told long, elaborate stories about his escapades. He told jokes, some of the dirtiest Joel had ever heard. He even wrote poems about old lovers and orgies and fantasies.

He wouldn't miss Mo and his imagination.

Unwillingly, he dozed off again.

Colonel Gantner was shaking him, whispering loudly, 'Major Herzog, Major Herzog. We need to talk.' Backman squeezed out of his bunk, and followed the colonel along the dark cramped aisle between the bunks and into a small room, somewhere closer to the cockpit. 'Take a seat,' Gantner said. They huddled over a small metal table.

Gantner was holding a file. 'Here's the deal,' he began. 'We land in about an hour. The plan is for you to be sick, so sick that an ambulance from the base hospital will meet the plane at the landing field. The Italian authorities will do their usual quick inspection of the paperwork, and they might actually take a look at you. Probably not. We'll be at a U.S. military base, and soldiers come and go all the time. I have a passport for

43

you. I'll do the talking with the Italians, then you'll be taken by ambulance to the hospital.'

'Italians?'

'Yes. Ever hear of the Aviano Air Base?'

'No.'

'Didn't think so. It's been around in U.S. hands since we ran the Germans off in 1945. It's in the northeast part of Italy, near the Alps.'

'Sounds lovely.'

'It's okay, but it's a base.'

'How long will I be there?'

'That's not my decision. My job is to get you from this airplane to the base hospital. There, someone else takes over. Take a look at this bio for Major Herzog, just in case.'

Joel spent a few minutes reading the fictional history of Major Herzog and memorizing the details on the fake passport.

'Remember, you're very ill and sedated,' Gantner said. 'Just pretend you're in a coma.'

'I've been in one for six years.'

'Would you like some coffee?'

'What time is it where we're going?'

Gantner looked at his watch and did a quick calculation. 'We should land around one a.m.'

'I'd love some coffee.'

Gantner gave him a paper cup and a thermos, and disappeared.

After two cups, Joel felt the engines reduce power. He returned to his bunk and tried to close his eyes.

★

As the C-130 rolled to a stop, an air force ambulance backed itself close to the rear hatch. The troops ambled off, most still half asleep. A stretcher carrying Major Herzog rolled down the gateway and was carefully lifted into the ambulance. The nearest Italian official was sitting inside a U.S. military jeep, watching things halfheartedly and trying to stay warm. The ambulance pulled away, in no particular hurry, and five minutes later Major Herzog was rolled into the small base hospital and tucked away in a tiny room on the second floor where two military policemen guarded his door.

Chapter 4

Fortunately for Backman, though he had no way of knowing and no reason to care, at the eleventh hour President Morgan also pardoned an aging billionaire who'd escaped prison by fleeing the country. The billionaire, an immigrant from some Slavic state who'd had the option of redoing his name upon his arrival decades earlier, had chosen in his youth the title of Duke Mongo. The Duke had given trainloads of money to Morgan's presidential campaign. When it was revealed that he'd spent his career evading taxes it was also revealed he'd spent several nights in the Lincoln Bedroom, where, over a friendly nightcap, he and the President discussed pending indictments. According to the third person present for the nightcap, a young tart who was currently serving as the Duke's fifth wife, the President promised to throw his weight around over at the IRS and call off the dogs. Didn't happen. The indictment was thirty-eight pages long, and before it rolled off the printer the billionaire, minus wife number five, took up residence in Uruguay where he thumbed his nose north while living in a palace with soon-to-be wife number six.

Now he wanted to come home so he could die with dignity, die as a real patriot, and be buried on his Thoroughbred farm just outside Lexington, Kentucky. Critz cut the deal, and minutes after signing the pardon for Joel Backman, President Morgan granted complete clemency to Duke Mongo.

It took a day for the news to leak – the pardons, for good reason, were not publicized by the White House – and the press went insane. Here was a man who cheated the federal government out of $600 million over a twenty-year period, a crook who deserved to be locked away forever, and he was about to fly home in his mammoth jet and spend his final days in obscene luxury. The Backman story, sensational as it was, now had serious competition from not only the kidnapped Danish tourists but also the country's largest tax cheater.

But it was still a hot item. Most of the major morning papers along the East Coast ran a picture of 'The Broker' somewhere on the front page. Most ran long stories about his scandal, his guilty plea, and now his pardon.

Carl Pratt read them all online, in a huge messy office he kept above his garage in northwest Washington. He used the place to hide, to stay away from the wars that raged within his firm, to avoid the partners he couldn't stand. He could drink there and no one would care. He could throw things, and curse at the walls, and do whatever he damn well pleased because it was his sanctuary.

The Backman file was in a large cardboard storage box, one he kept hidden in a closet. Now it was on a worktable, and Pratt was going through it for the first time in many years. He'd saved everything – news articles, photos, inter-office memos, sensitive notes he'd taken, copies of the indictments, Jacy Hubbard's autopsy report.

What a miserable history.

In January of 1996, three young Pakistani computer scientists made an astounding discovery. Working in a hot, cramped flat on the top floor of an apartment building on the outskirts of Karachi, the three linked together a series of Hewlett-Packard computers they'd purchased online with a government grant. Their new 'supercomputer' was then wired to a sophisticated military satellite telephone, one also provided by the government. The entire operation was secret and funded off the books by the military. Their objective was simple: to locate, and then try to access, a new Indian spy satellite hovering three hundred miles above Pakistan. If they successfully tapped into the satellite, then they hoped to monitor its surveillance. A secondary dream was to try to manipulate it.

The stolen intelligence was at first exciting, then proved to be virtually useless. The new Indian 'eyes' were doing much the same thing the old ones had been doing for ten years – taking thousands of photographs of the same military installations. Pakistani satellites had been sending back photos of Indian army bases and troop movements for the same ten years. The two countries could swap pictures and learn nothing.

But another satellite was accidentally discovered, then another and another. They were neither Pakistani nor Indian, and they were not supposed to be where they were found – each about three hundred miles above the earth, moving north-northeast at a constant speed of 120 miles per hour, and each maintaining a distance of four hundred miles from the other. Over ten days, the terribly excited hackers monitored the movements of at least six different satellites, all apparently part of the same system, as they slowly approached from the Arabian Peninsula, swept through the skies over Afghanistan and Pakistan, then headed off for western China.

They told no one, but instead managed to procure a more powerful satellite telephone from the military, claiming it was needed to follow up some unfinished work with the Indian surveillance. After a month of methodical, twenty-four-hour monitoring, they had pieced together a global web of nine identical satellites, all linked to each other, and all carefully designed to be invisible to everyone except the men who launched them.

They code-named their discovery Neptune.

The three young wizards had been educated in the United States. The leader was Safi Mirza, a former Stanford graduate assistant who'd worked briefly at Breedin Corp, a renegade U.S. defense contractor that specialized in satellite systems. Fazal Sharif had an advanced degree in computer science from Georgia Tech.

The third and youngest member of the Neptune gang was Farooq Khan, and it was Farooq who finally wrote the software that penetrated the first Neptune satellite. Once inside its computer system, Farooq began downloading intelligence so sensitive that he and Fazal and Safi knew they were entering no-man's-land. There were clear color pictures of terrorist training camps in Afghanistan, and government limousines in Beijing. Neptune could listen as Chinese pilots bantered back and forth at twenty thousand feet, and it could watch a suspicious fishing boat as it docked in Yemen. Neptune followed an armored truck, presumably Castro's, through the streets of Havana. And in a live video feed that shocked the three, Arafat himself was clearly seen stepping into an alley in his compound in Gaza, lighting a cigarette, then urinating.

For two sleepless days, the three peeked inside the satellites as they crossed Pakistan. The software was in English, and with Neptune's preoccupation with the Middle East, Asia, and China, it was easy to assume Neptune belonged to the United States, with Britain and Israel a distant second and third. Perhaps it was a joint U.S.-Israeli secret.

After two days of eavesdropping, they fled the apartment and reorganized their little cell in a friend's farmhouse ten miles outside of Karachi. The discovery was exciting enough, but they, and Safi in particular, wanted to go one step further. He was quite confident he could manipulate the system.

His first success was watching Fazal Sharif read a newspaper. To protect the identity of their location, Fazal took a bus into downtown Karachi, and wearing a green cap and sunglasses, he bought a newspaper and sat on a park bench near a certain intersection. With Farooq feeding commands through a ramped-up satphone, a Neptune satellite found Fazal, zoomed down close enough to pick off the headlines of his newspaper, and relayed it all back to the farmhouse where it was watched in muted disbelief.

The electro-optical imaging relays to Earth were of the highest resolution known to technology at that time, down to about four feet – equal to the sharpest images produced by U.S. military reconnaissance satellites and about twice as sharp as the best European and American commercial satellites.

For weeks and months, the three worked nonstop writing home-brewed software for their discovery. They discarded much of what they wrote, but as they fine-tuned the successful programs they became even more amazed at Neptune's possibilities.

Eighteen months after they first discovered Neptune, the three had, on four Jaz 2-gigabyte disks, a software program that not only increased the speed at which Neptune communicated with its numerous contacts on Earth but also allowed Neptune to jam many of the navigation, communications, and reconnaissance satellites already in orbit. For lack of a better code name, they called their program JAM.

Though the system they called Neptune belonged to someone else, the three conspirators were able to control it, to thoroughly manipulate it, and even to render it useless. A bitter fight erupted. Safi and Fazal got greedy and wanted to sell JAM to the highest bidder. Farooq saw nothing but trouble with their creation. He wanted to give it to the Pakistani military and wash his hands of the entire matter.

In September of 1998, Safi and Fazal traveled to Washington and spent a frustrating month trying to penetrate military intelligence through Pakistani contacts. Then a friend told them about Joel Backman, the man who could open any door in Washington.

But getting in his door was a challenge. The broker was a very important man with important clients and lots of significant people demanding small segments of his time. His flat fee for a one-hour consultation with a new client was $5,000 and that was for those lucky enough to be looked upon with favor by the great man. Safi borrowed $2,000 from an uncle in Chicago and promised to pay Mr. Backman the rest in ninety days. Documents in court later revealed that their first meeting took place on October 24, 1998, in the offices of Backman, Pratt & Bolling. The meeting would eventually destroy the lives of everyone present.

Backman at first had seemed skeptical of JAM and its incredible capabilities. Or perhaps he'd grasped its potential immediately and chosen to play it sly with his new clients. Safi and Fazal dreamed of selling JAM to the Pentagon for a fortune, whatever Mr. Backman thought their product might fetch. And if anyone in Washington could get a fortune for JAM, it was Joel Backman.

Early on, he had called in Jacy Hubbard, his million-dollar mouthpiece who still played golf once a week with the President and went barhopping with big shots on Capitol Hill. He was colorful, flamboyant, combative, thrice-divorced, and quite fond of expensive whiskeys – especially when purchased by lobbyists. He had survived politically only because he was known as the dirtiest campaigner in the history of the U.S.

Senate, no small feat. He was known to be anti-Semitic, and during the course of his career he developed close ties with the Saudis. Very close. One of many ethics investigations revealed a $1 million campaign contribution from a prince, the same one Hubbard went skiing with in Austria.

Initially, Hubbard and Backman argued over the best way to market JAM. Hubbard wanted to peddle it to the Saudis, who, he was convinced, would pay $1 billion for it. Backman had taken the rather provincial view that such a dangerous product should be kept at home. Hubbard was convinced he could cut a deal with the Saudis in which they would promise that JAM would never be used against the United States, their ostensible ally. Backman was afraid of the Israelis – their powerful friends in the United States, their military, and, most important, their secret spy services.

At that time Backman, Pratt & Bolling represented many foreign companies and governments. In fact, the firm was 'the' address for anyone looking for instant clout in Washington. Pay their frightening fees, and you had yourself access. Its endless list of clients included the Japanese steel industry, the South Korean government, the Saudis, most of the Caribbean banking conspiracy, the current regime in Panama, a Bolivian farming cooperative that grew nothing but cocaine, and on and on. There were many legitimate clients, and many that were not so clean.

The rumor about JAM slowly leaked around their offices. It could potentially be the largest fee the firm had yet seen, and there had been some startling ones. As weeks passed, other partners in the firm presented varying scenarios for the marketing of JAM. The notion of patriotism was slowly forgotten – there was simply too much money out there! The firm represented a Dutch company that built avionics for the Chinese air force, and with that entrée a lucrative deal could be struck with the Beijing government. The South Koreans would rest easier if they knew exactly what was happening to the north. The Syrians would hand over their national treasury for the ability to neutralize Israeli military communications. A certain drug cartel would pay billions for the ability to track DEA interdiction efforts.

Each day Joel Backman and his band of greedy lawyers grew richer. In the firm's largest offices, they talked of little else.

The doctor was rather brusque and appeared to have little time for his new patient. It was, after all, a military hospital. With scarcely a word he checked the pulse, heart, lungs, blood pressure, reflexes, and so on, then from out of the blue announced, 'I think you're dehydrated.'

'How's that?' Backman asked.

'Happens a lot with long flights. We'll start a drip. You'll be okay in twenty-four hours.'

'You mean, like an IV?'

'That's it.'

'I don't do IVs.'

'Beg your pardon.'

'I didn't stutter. I don't do needles.'

'We took a sample of your blood.'

'Yeah, that was blood going out, not something coming in. Forget it, Doc, I'm not doing an IV.'

'But you're dehydrated.'

'I don't feel dehydrated.'

'I'm the doctor, and I say you're dehydrated.'

'Then give me a glass of water.'

Half an hour later, a nurse entered with a big smile and a handful of medications. Joel said no to the sleeping pills, and when she sort of waved a hypodermic he said, 'What's that?'

'Ryax.'

'What the hell is Ryax?'

'It's a muscle relaxer.'

'Well, it just so happens that my muscles are very relaxed right now. I haven't complained of unrelaxed muscles. I haven't been diagnosed with unrelaxed muscles. No one has asked me if my muscles are relaxed. So you can take that Ryax and stick it up your own ass and we'll both be relaxed and happier.'

She almost dropped the needle. After a long painful pause in which she was completely speechless, she managed to utter, 'I'll check with the doctor.'

'You do that. On second thought, why don't you poke him in his rather fat ass. He's the one who needs to relax.' But she was already out of the room.

On the other side of the base, a Sergeant McAuliffe pecked on his keyboard and sent a message to the Pentagon. From there it was sent almost immediately to Langley where it was read by Julia Javier, a veteran who'd been selected by Director Maynard himself to handle the Backman matter. Less than ten minutes after the Ryax incident, Ms. Javier stared at her monitor, mumbled the word 'Dammit,' then walked upstairs.

As usual, Teddy Maynard was sitting at the end of a long table, wrapped in a quilt, reading one of the countless summaries that got piled on his desk every hour.

Ms. Javier said, 'Just heard from Aviano. Our boy is refusing all medications. Won't take an IV. Won't take a pill.'

'Can't they put something in his food?' Teddy said at low volume.

'He's not eating.'

'What's he saying?'

'That his stomach is upset.'

'Is that possible?'

'He's not spending time on the toilet. Hard to say.'

'Is he taking liquids?'

'They took him a glass of water, which he refused. Insisted on bottled water only. When he got one, he inspected the cap to make sure the seal had not been broken.'

Teddy shoved the current report away and rubbed his eyes with his knuckles. The first plan had been to sedate Backman in the hospital, with either an IV or a regular injection, knock him out cold, keep him drugged for two days, then slowly bring him back with some delightful blends of their most up-to-date narcotics. After a few days in a haze, they would start the sodium pentothal treatment, the truth serum, which, when used with their veteran interrogators, always produced whatever they were after.

The first plan was easy and foolproof. The second one would take months and success was far from guaranteed.

'He's got big secrets, doesn't he?' Teddy said.

'No doubt.'

'But we knew that, didn't we?'

'Yes, we did.'

Chapter 5

Two of Joel Backman's three children had already abandoned him when the scandal broke. Neal, the oldest, had written his father at least twice a month, though in the early days of the sentence the letters had been quite difficult to write.

Neal had been a twenty-five-year-old rookie associate at the Backman firm when his father went to prison. Though he knew little about JAM and Neptune, he was nonetheless harassed by the FBI and eventually indicted by federal prosecutors.

Joel's abrupt decision to plead guilty was aided mightily by what happened to Jacy Hubbard, but it was also pushed along by the mistreatment of his son by the authorities. All charges against Neal were dropped in the deal. When his father left for twenty years, Neal was immediately terminated by Carl Pratt and escorted from the firm's offices by armed security. The Backman name was a curse, and employment was impossible around Washington. A pal from law school had an uncle who was a retired judge, and after calls here and there Neal landed in the small town of Culpeper, Virginia, working in a five-man firm and thankful for the opportunity.

He craved the anonymity. He thought about changing his name. He refused to discuss his father. He did title work, wrote wills and deeds, and settled nicely into the routine of small-town living. He eventually met and married a local girl and they quickly produced a daughter, Joel's second grandchild, and the only one he had a photo of.

Neal read about his father's release in the *Post*. He discussed it at length with his wife, and briefly with the partners of his firm. The story might be causing earthquakes in D.C., but the tremors had not reached Culpeper. No one seemed to know or care. He wasn't the broker's son; he was simply Neal Backman, one of many lawyers in a small Southern town.

A judge pulled him aside after a hearing and said, 'Where are they hiding your old man?'

To which Neal replied respectfully, 'Not one of my favorite subjects, Your Honor.' And that was the end of the conversation.

On the surface, nothing changed in Culpeper. Neal went about his business as if the pardon had been granted to a man he didn't know. He waited on a phone call; somewhere down the road his father would eventually check in.

After repeated demands, the supervising nurse passed the hat and collected almost three bucks in change. This was delivered to the patient they still called Major Herzog, an increasingly cranky sort whose condition was no doubt worsening because of hunger. Major Herzog took the money and proceeded directly to the vending machines he'd found on the second floor, and there he bought three small bags of Fritos corn chips and two Dr Peppers. All were consumed within minutes, and an hour later he was on the toilet with raging diarrhea.

But at least he wasn't quite as hungry, nor was he drugged and saying things he shouldn't say.

Though technically a free man, fully pardoned and all that, he was still confined to a facility owned by the U.S. government, and still living in a room not much larger than his cell at Rudley. The food there had been dreadful, but at least he could eat it without fear of being sedated. Now he was living on corn chips and sodas. The nurses were only slightly friendlier than the guards who tormented him. The doctors just wanted to dope him, following orders from above, he was certain. Somewhere close by was a little torture chamber where they were waiting to pounce on him after the drugs had worked their miracles.

He longed for the outside, for fresh air and

sunshine, for plenty of food, for a little human contact with someone not wearing a uniform. And after two very long days he got it.

A stone-faced young man named Stennett appeared in his room on the third day and began pleasantly by saying, 'Okay, Backman, here's the deal. My name's Stennett.'

He tossed a file on the blankets, on Joel's legs, next to some old magazines that were being read for the third time. Joel opened the file. 'Marco Lazzeri?'

'That's you, pal, a full-blown Italian now. That's your birth certificate and national ID card. Memorize all the info as soon as possible.'

'Memorize it? I can't even read it.'

'Then learn. We're leaving in about three hours. You'll be taken to a nearby city where you'll meet your new best friend who'll hold your hand for a few days.'

'A few days?'

'Maybe a month, depends on how well you make the transition.'

Joel laid down the file and stared at Stennett. 'Who do you work for?'

'If I told you, then I'd have to kill you.'

'Very funny. The CIA?'

'The USA, that's all I can say, and that's all you need to know.'

Joel looked at the metal-framed window, complete with a lock, and said, 'I didn't notice a passport in the file.'

'Yes, well, that's because you're not going

anywhere, Marco. You're about to live a very quiet life. Your neighbors will think you were born in Milan but raised in Canada, thus the bad Italian you're about to learn. If you get the urge to travel, then things could get very dangerous for you.'

'Dangerous?'

'Come on, Marco. Don't play games with me. There are some really nasty people in this world who'd love to find you. Do what we tell you, and they won't.'

'I don't know a word of Italian.'

'Sure you do – pizza, spaghetti, caffè latte, bravo, opera, mamma mia. You'll catch on. The quicker you learn and the better you learn, the safer you'll be. You'll have a tutor.'

'I don't have a dime.'

'That's what they say. None that they could find, anyway.' He pulled some bills out of his pocket and laid them on the file. 'While you were tucked away, Italy abandoned the lira and adopted the euro. There's a hundred of them. One euro is about a dollar. I'll be back in an hour with some clothes. In the file is a small dictionary, two hundred of your first words in Italian. I suggest you get busy.'

An hour later Stennett was back with a shirt, slacks, jacket, shoes, and socks, all of the Italian variety. 'Buon giorno,' he said.

'Hello to you,' Backman said.

'What's the word for car?'

'Macchina.'

'Good, Marco. It's time to get in the macchina.'

Another silent gentleman was behind the wheel of the compact, nondescript Fiat. Joel folded himself into the backseat with a canvas bag that held his net worth. Stennett sat in the front. The air was cold and damp and a thin layer of snow barely covered the ground. When they passed through the gates of the Aviano Air Base, Joel Backman had the first twinge of freedom, though the slight wave of excitement was heavily layered with apprehension.

He watched the road signs carefully; not a word from the front seat. They were on Route 251, a two-lane highway, headed south, he thought. The traffic soon grew heavy as they approached the city of Pordenone.

'What's the population of Pordenone?' Joel asked, breaking the thick silence.

'Fifty thousand,' Stennett said.

'This is northern Italy, right?'

'Northeast.'

'How far away are the Alps?'

Stennett nodded in the general direction of his right and said, 'About forty miles that way. On a clear day, you can see them.'

'Can we stop for a coffee somewhere?' Joel asked.

'No, we, uh, are not authorized to stop.'

So far the driver appeared to be completely deaf.

They skirted around the northern edge of

Pordenone and were soon on A28, a four-lane where everyone but the truckers appeared to be very late for work. Small cars whizzed by them while they puttered along at a mere one hundred kilometers per hour. Stennett unfolded an Italian newspaper, *La Repubblica*, and blocked half the windshield with it.

Joel was very content to ride in silence and gaze at the countryside flying by. The rolling plain appeared to be very fertile, though it was late January and the fields were empty. Occasionally, above a terraced hillside, an ancient villa could be seen.

He'd actually rented one once. A dozen or so years earlier, wife number two had threatened to walk out if he didn't take her somewhere for a long vacation. Joel was working eighty hours a week with time to spare for even more work. He preferred to live at the office, and judging by the way things were going at home, life would've certainly been more peaceful there. A divorce, however, would've cost too much money, so Joel announced to everyone that he and his dear wife would spend a month in Tuscany. He acted as though it had all been his idea – 'a monthlong wine and culinary adventure through the heart of Chianti!'

They found a fourteenth-century monastery near the medieval village of San Gimignano, complete with housekeepers and cooks, even a chauffeur. But on the fourth day of the adventure, Joel received the alarming news that the Senate Appropriations Committee was considering deleting a provision that would wipe out $2 billion for one of his defense-contractor clients. He flew home on a chartered jet and went to work whipping the Senate back into shape. Wife number two stayed behind, where, as he would later learn, she began sleeping with the young chauffeur. For the next week he called daily and promised to return to the villa to finish their vacation, but after the second week she stopped taking his calls.

The appropriations bill was put back together in fine fashion.

A month later she filed for divorce, a raucous contest that would eventually cost him over three million bucks.

And she was his favorite of the three. They were all gone now, all scattered forever. The first, the mother of two of his children, had remarried twice since Joel, and her current husband had gotten rich selling liquid fertilizer in third world countries. She had actually written him in prison, a cruel little note in which she praised the judicial system for finally dealing with one of its biggest crooks.

He couldn't blame her. She packed up after catching him with a secretary, the bimbo that became wife number two.

Wife number three had jumped ship soon after his indictment.

What a sloppy life. Fifty-two years, and what's to show for a career of bilking clients, chasing secretaries around the office, putting the squeeze on slimy little politicians, working seven days a week, ignoring three surprisingly stable children, crafting the public image, building the boundless ego, pursuing money money money? What are the rewards for the reckless pursuit of the great American dream?

Six years in prison. And now a fake name because the old one is so dangerous. And about a hundred dollars in his pocket.

Marco? How could he look himself in the mirror every morning and say, 'Buon giorno, Marco'?

Sure beat the hell out of 'Good morning, Mr. Felon.'

Stennett didn't as much read the newspaper as he wrestled with it. Under his perusal, it jerked and popped and wrinkled, and at times the driver glanced over in frustration.

A sign said Venice was sixty kilometers to the south, and Joel decided to break the monotony. 'I'd like to live in Venice, if that's all right with the White House.'

The driver flinched and Stennett's newspaper dropped six inches. The air in the small car was tense for a moment until Stennett managed a grunt and a shrug. 'Sorry,' he said.

'I really need to pee,' Joel said. 'Can you get authorization to stop for a potty break?'

They stopped north of the town of Conegliano, at a modern roadside servizio. Stennett bought a round of corporate espressos.

67

Joel took his to the front window where he watched the traffic speed by while he listened to a young couple snipe at each other in Italian. He heard none of the two hundred words he'd tried to memorize. It seemed an impossible task.

Stennett appeared by his side and watched the traffic. 'Have you spent much time in Italy?' he asked.

'A month once, in Tuscany.'

'Really? A whole month? Must've been nice.'

'Four days actually, but my wife stayed for a month. She met some friends. How about you? Is this one of your hangouts?'

'I move around.' His face was as vague as his answer. He sipped from the tiny cup and said, 'Conegliano, known for its Prosecco.'

'The Italian answer to champagne,' Joel said.

'Yes. You're a drinking man?'

'Haven't touched a drop in six years.'

'They didn't serve it in prison?'

'Nope.'

'And now?'

'I'll ease back into it. It was a bad habit once.'

'We'd better go.'

'How much longer?'

'Not far.'

Stennett headed for the door, but Joel stopped him. 'Hey, look, I'm really hungry. Could I get a sandwich for the road?'

Stennett looked at a rack of ready-made panini. 'Sure.'

'How about two?'

'No problem.'

A27 led south to Treviso, and when it became apparent they would not bypass the city, Joel began to assume the ride was about to end. The driver slowed, made two exits, and they were soon bouncing through the narrow streets of the city.

'What's the population of Treviso?' Joel asked.

'Eighty-five thousand,' Stennett answered.

'What do you know about the city?'

'It's a prosperous little city that hasn't changed much in five hundred years. It was once a staunch ally of Venice back when these towns all fought with each other. We bombed the hell out of it in World War Two. A nice place, not too many tourists.'

A good place to hide, Joel thought. 'Is this my stop?'

'Could be.'

A tall clock tower beckoned all the traffic into the center of the city where it inched along around the Piazza dei Signori. Scooters and mopeds zipped between cars, their drivers seemingly fearless. Joel soaked in the quaint little shops – the tabaccheria with racks of newspapers blocking the door, the farmacia with its neon green cross, the butcher with all manner of hams hanging in the window, and of course the tiny sidewalk cafés where all tables were taken with people who appeared content to sit and read and gossip and sip espresso for hours. It was almost 11:00 a.m. What could those people possibly do for a living if they broke for coffee an hour before lunch?

It would be his challenge to find out, he decided.

The nameless driver wheeled into a temporary parking place. Stennett pecked numbers on a cell phone, waited, then spoke quickly in Italian. When he was finished, he pointed through the windshield and said, 'You see that café over there, under the red-and-white awning? Caffè Donati?'

Joel strained from the backseat and said, 'Yeah, I got it.'

'Walk in the front door, past the bar on your right, on to the back where there are eight tables. Have a seat, order a coffee, and wait.'

'Wait for what?'

'A man will approach you after about ten minutes. You will do what he says.'

'And if I don't?'

'Don't play games, Mr. Backman. We'll be watching.'

'Who is this man?'

'Your new best friend. Follow him, and you'll probably survive. Try something stupid, and you won't last a month.' Stennett said this with a certain smugness, as if he might enjoy being the one who rubbed out poor Marco.

'So it's adios for us, huh?' Joel said, gathering his bag.

'Arrivederci, Marco, not adios. You have your paperwork?'

'Yes.'

70

'Then arrivederci.'

Joel slowly got out of the car and began walking away. He fought the urge to glance over his shoulder to make sure Stennett, his protector, was paying attention and still back there, shielding him from the unknown. But he did not turn around. Instead, he tried to look as normal as possible as he strolled down the street carrying a canvas bag, the only canvas bag he saw at that moment in the center of Treviso.

Stennett was watching, of course. And who else? Certainly his new best friend was over there somewhere, partially hiding behind a newspaper, giving signals to Stennett and the rest of the static. Joel stopped for a second in front of the tabaccheria and scanned the headlines of the Italian newspapers, though he understood not a single word. He stopped because he could stop, because he was a free man with the power and the right to stop wherever he wanted, and to start moving whenever he chose to.

He entered Caffè Donati and was greeted with a soft 'Buon giorno' from the young man wiping off the bar.

'Buon giorno,' Joel managed in reply, his first real words to a real Italian. To prevent further conversation, he kept walking, past the bar, past a circular stairway where a sign pointed to a café upstairs, past a large counter filled with beautiful pastries. The back room was dark and cramped and choking under a fog of cigarette smoke. He sat down at one of two empty tables and ignored

71

the glances of the other patrons. He was terrified of the waiter, terrified of trying to order, terrified of being unmasked so early in his flight, and so he just sat with his head down and read his new identity papers.

'Buon giorno,' the young lady said at his left shoulder.

'Buon giorno,' Joel managed to reply. And before she could rattle off anything on the menu, he said, 'Espresso.' She smiled, said something thoroughly incomprehensible, to which he replied, 'No.'

It worked, she left, and for Joel it was a major victory. No one stared at him as if he was some ignorant foreigner. When she brought the espresso he said, 'Grazie,' very softly, and she actually smiled at him. He sipped it slowly, not knowing how long it would have to last, not wanting to finish it so he might be forced to order something else.

Italian whirled around him, the soft incessant chatter of friends gossiping at a rapid-fire pace. Did English sound this fast? Probably so. The idea of learning the language well enough to be able to understand what was being said around him seemed thoroughly impossible. He looked at his paltry little list of two hundred words, then for a few minutes tried desperately to hear a single one of them spoken.

The waitress happened by and asked a question. He gave his standard reply of 'No,' and again it worked.

So Joel Backman was having an espresso in a small bar on Via Verde, at the Piazza dei Signori, in the center of Treviso, in the Veneto, in northeast Italy, while back at Rudley Federal Correctional Facility his old pals were still locked down in protective isolation with lousy food and watery coffee and sadistic guards and silly rules and years to go before they could even dream of life on the outside.

Contrary to previous plans, Joel Backman would not die behind bars at Rudley. He would not wither away in mind and body and spirit. He had cheated his tormentors out of fourteen years, and now he sat unshackled in a quaint café an hour from Venice.

Why was he thinking of prison? Because you can't just walk away from six years of anything without the aftershocks. You carry some of the past with you, regardless of how unpleasant it was. The horror of prison made his sudden release so sweet. It would take time, and he promised himself to focus on the present. Don't even think about the future.

Listen to the sounds, the rapid chatter of friends, the laughter, the guy over there whispering into a cell phone, the pretty waitress calling into the kitchen. Take in the smells – the cigarette smoke, the rich coffee, the fresh pastries, the warmth of an ancient little room where locals had been meeting for centuries.

And he asked himself for the hundredth time, Why, exactly, was he here? Why had he been whisked away from prison, then out of the country? A pardon is one thing, but why a full-blown international getaway? Why not hand him his walking papers, let him say so long to dear ol' Rudley and live his life, same as all the other freshly pardoned criminals?

He had a hunch. He could venture a fairly accurate guess.

And it terrified him.

Luigi appeared from nowhere.

Chapter 6

Luigi was in his early thirties, with dark sad eyes and dark hair half covering his ears, and at least four days' worth of stubble on his face. He was bundled in some type of heavy barn jacket that, along with the unshaven face, gave him a handsome peasant look. He ordered an espresso and smiled a lot. Joel immediately noticed that his hands and nails were clean, his teeth were straight. The barn jacket and whiskers were part of the act. Luigi had probably gone to Harvard.

His perfect English was accented just enough to convince anyone that he was really an Italian. He said he was from Milan. His Italian father was a diplomat who took his American wife and their two children around the world in service to his country. Joel was assuming Luigi knew plenty about him, so he prodded to learn what he could about his new handler.

He didn't learn much. Marriage – none.

College – Bologna. Studies in the United States – yes, somewhere in the Midwest. Job – government. Which government – couldn't say. He had an easy smile that he used to deflect questions he didn't want to answer. Joel was dealing with a professional, and he knew it.

'I take it you know a thing or two about me,' Joel said.

The smile, the perfect teeth. The sad eyes almost closed when he smiled. The ladies were all over this guy. 'I've seen the file.'

'The file? The file on me wouldn't fit in this room.'

'I've seen the file.'

'Okay, how long did Jacy Hubbard serve in the U.S. Senate?'

'Too long, I'd say. Look, Marco, we're not going to relive the past. We have too much to do now.'

'Can I have another name? I'm not crazy about Marco.'

'It wasn't my choice.'

'Well, who picked Marco?'

'I don't know. It wasn't me. You ask a lot of useless questions.'

'I was a lawyer for twenty-five years. It's an old habit.'

Luigi drained what was left of his espresso and placed some euros on the table. 'Let's go for a walk,' he said, standing. Joel lifted his canvas bag and followed his handler out of the café, onto the sidewalk, and down a side street with less traffic.

They had walked only a few steps when Luigi stopped in front of the Albergo Campeol. 'This is your first stop,' he said.

'What is it?' Joel asked. It was a four-story stucco building wedged between two others. Colorful flags hung above the portico.

'A nice little hotel. "Albergo" means hotel. You can also use the word "hotel" if you want, but in the smaller cities they like to say albergo.'

'So it's an easy language.' Joel was looking up and down the cramped street – evidently his new neighborhood.

'Easier than English.'

'We'll see. How many do you speak?'

'Five or six.'

They entered and walked through the small foyer. Luigi nodded knowingly at the clerk behind the front desk. Joel managed a passable 'Buon giorno' but kept walking, hoping to avoid a more involved reply. They climbed three flights of stairs and walked to the end of a narrow hallway. Luigi had the key to room 30, a simple but nicely appointed suite with windows on three sides and a view of a canal below.

'This is the nicest one,' Luigi said. 'Nothing fancy, but adequate.'

'You should've seen my last room.' Joel tossed his bag on the bed and began opening curtains.

Luigi opened the door to the very small closet. 'Look here. You have four shirts, four slacks, two jackets, two pairs of shoes, all in your size. Plus a heavy wool overcoat – it gets quite cold here in

Treviso.' Joel stared at his new wardrobe. The clothes were hanging perfectly, all pressed and ready to wear. The colors were subdued, tasteful, and every shirt could be worn with every jacket and pair of slacks. He finally shrugged and said, 'Thanks.'

'In the drawer over there you'll find a belt, socks, underwear, everything you'll need. In the bathroom you'll find all the necessary toiletries.'

'What can I say?'

'And here on the desk are two sets of glasses.' Luigi picked up a pair of glasses and held them to the light. The small rectangular lenses were secured by thin black metal, very European frames. 'Armani,' Luigi said, with a trace of pride.

'Reading glasses?'

'Yes, and no. I suggest you wear them every moment you're outside this room. Part of the disguise, Marco. Part of the new you.'

'You should've met the old one.'

'No thanks. Appearance is very important to Italians, especially those of us from here in the north. Your attire, your glasses, your haircut, everything must be put together properly or you will get noticed.'

Joel was suddenly self-conscious, but, then, what the hell. He'd been wearing prison garb for longer than he cared to remember. Back in the glory days he routinely dropped $3,000 for a finely tailored suit.

Luigi was still lecturing. 'No shorts, no black

socks and white sneakers, no polyester slacks, no golf shirts, and please don't start getting fat.'

'How do you say "Kiss my ass" in Italian?'

'We'll get to that later. Habits and customs are important. They're easy to learn and quite enjoyable. For example, never order cappuccino after ten-thirty in the morning. But an espresso can be ordered at any hour of the day. Did you know that?'

'I did not.'

'Only tourists order cappuccino after lunch or dinner. A disgrace. All that milk on a full stomach.' For a moment Luigi frowned as if he might just vomit for good measure.

Joel raised his right hand and said, 'I swear I'll never do it.'

'Have a seat,' Luigi said, waving at the small desk and its two chairs. They sat down and tried to get comfortable. He continued: 'First, the room. It's in my name, but the staff thinks that a Canadian businessman will be staying here for a couple of weeks.'

'A couple of weeks?'

'Yes, then you'll move to another location.' Luigi said this as ominously as possible, as if squads of assassins were already in Treviso, looking for Joel Backman. 'From this moment on, you will be leaving a trail. Keep that in mind: everything you do, everyone you meet – they're all part of your trail. The secret of survival is to leave behind as few tracks as possible. Speak to very few people, including the clerk at the front desk and the housekeeper. Hotel personnel watch their guests, and they have good memories. Six months from now someone might come to this very hotel and start asking questions about you. He might have a photograph. He might offer bribes. And the clerk might suddenly remember you, and the fact that you spoke almost no Italian.'

'I have a question.'

'I have very few answers.'

'Why here? Why a country where I cannot speak the language? Why not England or Australia, someplace where I could blend in easier?'

'That decision was made by someone else, Marco. Not me.'

'That's what I figured.'

'Then why did you ask?'

'I don't know. Can I apply for a transfer?'

'Another useless question.'

'A bad joke, not a bad question.'

'Can we continue?'

'Yes.'

'For the first few days I will take you to lunch and dinner. We'll move around, always going to different places. Treviso is a nice city with lots of cafés and we'll try them all. You must start thinking of the day when I will not be here. Be careful who you meet.'

'I have another question.'

'Yes, Marco.'

'It's about money. I really don't like being

broke. Are you guys planning to give me an allowance or something? I'll wash your car and do other chores.'

'What is allowance?'

'Cash, okay? Money in my pocket.'

'Don't worry about money. For now, I take care of the bills. You will not be hungry.'

'All right.'

Luigi reached deep in the barn jacket and pulled out a cell phone. 'This is for you.'

'And who, exactly, am I going to call?'

'Me, if you need something. My number is on the back.'

Joel took the phone and laid it on the desk. 'I'm hungry. I've been dreaming of a long lunch with pasta and wine and dessert, and of course espresso, certainly not cappuccino at this hour, then perhaps the required siesta. I've been in Italy for four days now, and I've had nothing but corn chips and sandwiches. What do you say?'

Luigi glanced at his watch. 'I know just the place, but first some more business. You speak no Italian, right?'

Joel rolled his eyes and exhaled mightily in frustration. Then he tried to smile and said, 'No, I've never had the occasion to learn Italian, or French, or German, or anything else. I'm an American, okay, Luigi? My country is larger than all of Europe combined. All you need is English over there.'

'You're Canadian, remember?'

'Okay, whatever, but we're isolated. Just us and the Americans.'

'My job is to keep you safe.'

'Thank you.'

'And to help us do that, you need to learn a lot of Italian as quickly as possible.'

'I understand.'

'You will have a tutor, a young student by the name of Ermanno. You will study with him in the morning and again in the afternoon. The work will be difficult.'

'For how long?'

'As long as it takes. That depends on you. If you work hard, then in three or four months you should be on your own.'

'How long did it take you to learn English?'

'My mother is American. We spoke English at home, Italian everywhere else.'

'That's cheating. What else do you speak?'

'Spanish, French, a few more. Ermanno is an excellent teacher. The classroom is just down the street.'

'Not here, in the hotel?'

'No, no, Marco. You must think about your trail. What would the bellboy or the housekeeper say if a young man spent four hours a day in this room with you?'

'God forbid.'

'The housekeeper would listen at the door and hear your lessons. She would whisper to her supervisor. Within a day or two the entire staff would know that the Canadian businessman is studying intensely. Four hours a day!'

'Gotcha. Now about lunch.'

Leaving the hotel, Joel managed to smile at the clerk, a janitor, and the bell captain without uttering a word. They walked one block to the center of Treviso, the Piazza dei Signori, the main square lined with arcades and cafés. It was noon and the foot traffic was heavier as the locals hurried about for lunch. The air was getting colder, though Joel was quite comfortable tucked inside his new wool overcoat. He tried his best to look Italian.

'Inside or outside?' Luigi asked.

'Inside,' Joel said, and they ducked into the Caffè Beltrame, overlooking the piazza. A brick oven near the front was heating the place, and the aroma of the daily feast was steaming from the rear. Luigi and the headwaiter both spoke at the same time, then they laughed, then a table was found by a front window.

'We're in luck,' Luigi said as they took off their coats and sat down. 'The special today is faraona con polenta.'

'And what might that be?'

'Guinea fowl with polenta.'

'What else?'

Luigi was studying one of the blackboards hanging from a rough-hewn crossbeam. 'Panzerotti di funghi al burro – fried mushroom pastries. Conchiglie con cavalfiori – pasta shells with cauliflower. Spiedino di carne misto alla griglia – grilled shish kabob of mixed meats.'

'I'll have it all.'

'Their house wine is pretty good.'

'I prefer red.'

Within minutes the café was crowded with locals, all of whom seemed to know each other. A jolly little man with a dirty white apron sped by the table, slowed just long enough to make eye contact with Joel, and wrote down nothing as Luigi spat out a long list of what they wanted to eat. A jug of house wine arrived with a bowl of warm olive oil and a platter of sliced focaccia, and Joel began eating. Luigi was busy explaining the complexities of lunch and breakfast, the customs and traditions and mistakes made by tourists trying to pass themselves off as authentic Italians.

With Luigi, everything would be a learning experience.

Though Joel sipped and savored the first glass of wine, the alcohol went straight to his brain. A wonderful warmth and numbness embraced his body. He was free, many years ahead of schedule, and sitting in a rustic little café in an Italian town he'd never heard of, drinking a nice local wine, and inhaling the smells of a delicious feast. He smiled at Luigi as the explanations continued, but at some point Joel drifted into another world.

Ermanno claimed to be twenty-three years old but looked no more than sixteen. He was tall and painfully thin, and with sandy hair and hazel eyes he looked more German than Italian. He was also very shy and quite nervous, and Joel did not like the first impression.

They met Ermanno at his tiny apartment, on the third floor of an ill-kept building six blocks or so from Joel's hotel. There were three small rooms – kitchen, bedroom, living area – all sparsely furnished, but then Ermanno was a student so such surroundings were not unexpected. But the place looked as though he had just moved in and might be moving out at any minute.

They sat around a small desk in the center of the living room. There was no television. The room was cold and dimly lit, and Joel couldn't help but feel as if he had been placed in some underground highway where fugitives are kept alive and moved about in secret. The warmth of a two-hour lunch was fading quickly.

His tutor's nervousness didn't help matters.

When Ermanno was unable to take control of the meeting, Luigi quickly stepped in and kicked things off. He suggested that they study each morning from 9:00 a.m. to 11:00 a.m., break for two hours, then resume around 1:30 and study until they were tired. This seemed to suit Ermanno and Joel, who thought about asking the obvious: If my new guy here is a student, how does he have the time to teach me all day long? But he let it pass. He'd pursue it later.

Oh, the questions he was accumulating.

Ermanno eventually relaxed and described the

language course. When he spoke slowly, his accent was not intrusive. But when he rushed things, as he was prone to do, his English might as well have been Italian. Once Luigi interrupted and said, 'Ermanno, it's important to speak very slowly, at least in the first few days.'

'Thank you,' Joel said, like a true smartass.

Ermanno's cheeks actually reddened and he offered a very timid 'Sorry.'

He handed over the first batch of study aids – course book number one, along with a small tape player and two cassettes. 'The tapes follow the book,' he said, very slowly. 'Tonight, you should study chapter one and listen to each tape several times. Tomorrow we'll begin there.'

'It will be very intense,' Luigi added, applying more pressure, as if more was needed.

'Where did you learn English?' Joel asked.

'At the university,' Ermanno said. 'In Bologna.'

'So you haven't studied in the United States?'

'Yes, I have,' he said, shooting a quick nervous glance at Luigi, as if whatever happened in the States was something he preferred not to talk about. Unlike Luigi, Ermanno was an easy read, obviously not a professional.

'Where?' Joel asked, probing, seeing how much he could get.

'Furman,' Ermanno said. 'A small school in South Carolina.'

'When were you there?'

Luigi came to the rescue, clearing his throat.

'You will have plenty of time for this small talk later. It is important for you to forget English, Marco. From this day forward, you will live in a world of Italian. Everything you touch has an Italian name for it. Every thought must be translated. In one week you'll be ordering in restaurants. In two weeks you'll be dreaming in Italian. It's total, absolute immersion in the language and culture, and there's no turning back.'

'Can we start at eight in the morning?' Joel asked.

Ermanno glanced and fidgeted, finally said, 'Perhaps eight-thirty.'

'Good, I'll be here at eight-thirty.'

They left the apartment and strolled back to the Piazza dei Signori. It was mid-afternoon, traffic was noticeably quieter, the sidewalks almost deserted. Luigi stopped in front of the Trattoria del Monte. He nodded at the door, said, 'I'll meet you here at eight for dinner, okay?'

'Yes, okay.'

'You know where your hotel is?'

'Yes, the albergo.'

'And you have a map of the city?'

'Yes.'

'Good. You're on your own, Marco.' And with that Luigi ducked into an alley and disappeared. Joel watched him for a second, then continued his walk to the main square.

He felt very much alone. Four days after

leaving Rudley, he was finally free and unaccompanied, perhaps unobserved, though he doubted it. He decided immediately that he would move around the city, go about his business, as if no one was watching him. And he further decided, as he pretended to examine the items in the window of a small leather shop, that he would not live the rest of his life glancing over his shoulder.

They wouldn't find him.

He drifted until he found himself at Piazza San Vito, a small square where two churches had been sitting for seven hundred years. The Santa Lucia and San Vito were both closed, but, according to the ancient brass plate, they would reopen from 4:00 p.m. to 6:00 p.m. What kind of place closes from noon to four?

The bars weren't closed, just empty. He finally mustered the courage to sneak into one. He pulled up a stool, held his breath, and said the word 'Birra' when the bartender got close.

The bartender shot something back, waited for a response, and for a split second Joel was tempted to bolt. But he saw the tap, pointed at it as if it was perfectly clear what he wanted, and the bartender reached for an empty mug.

The first beer in six years. It was cool, heavy, tasty, and he savored every drop. A soap opera rattled from a television somewhere at the end of the bar. He listened to it from time to time, understood not a single word, and worked hard to convince himself that he could master the language. As he was making the decision to leave and drift back to his hotel, he looked through the front window.

Stennett walked by.

Joel ordered another beer.

Chapter 7

The Backman affair had been closely chronicled by Dan Sandberg, a veteran of *The Washington Post*. In 1998, he'd broken the story about certain highly classified papers leaving the Pentagon without authorization. The FBI investigation that soon followed kept him busy for half a year, during which he filed eighteen stories, most of them on the front page. He had reliable contacts at the CIA and the FBI. He knew the partners at Backman, Pratt & Bolling and had spent time in their offices. He hounded the Justice Department for information. He'd been in the courtroom the day Backman hurriedly pled guilty and disappeared.

A year later he'd written one of two books about the scandal. His sold a respectable 24,000 copies in hardback, the other about half of that.

Along the way, Sandberg built some key relationships. One in particular grew into a valuable, if quite unexpected, source. A month before Jacy Hubbard's death, Carl Pratt, then very much under indictment, as were most of the senior partners of the firm, had contacted Sandberg and arranged a meeting. They eventually met more than a dozen times while the scandal ran its course, and in the ensuing years had become drinking buddies. They sneaked away at least twice year to exchange gossip.

Three days after the pardon story first broke, Sandberg called Pratt and arranged a meeting at their favorite place, a college bar near Georgetown University.

Pratt looked awful, as if he'd been drinking for days. He ordered vodka; Sandberg stuck with beer.

'So where's your boy?' Sandberg asked with a grin.

'He's not in prison anymore, that's for sure.' Pratt took a near lethal slug of the vodka and smacked his lips.

'No word from him?'

'None. Not me, not anyone at the firm.'

'Would you be surprised if he called or stopped by?'

'Yes and no. Nothing surprises me with Backman.' More vodka. 'If he never set foot in D.C. again, I wouldn't be surprised. If he showed up tomorrow and announced the opening of a new law firm, I wouldn't be surprised.'

'The pardon surprised you.'

'Yes, but that wasn't Backman's deal, was it?'

'I doubt it.' A coed walked by and Sandberg gave her a look. Twice-divorced, he was always on the prowl. He sipped his beer and said, 'He can't practice law, can he? I thought they yanked his license.'

'That wouldn't stop Backman. He'd call it "government relations" or "consulting" or something else. It's lobbying, that's his speciality, and you don't need a license for that. Hell, half the lawyers in this city couldn't find the nearest courthouse. But they can damned sure find Capitol Hill.'

'What about clients?'

'It's not gonna happen. Backman ain't coming back to D.C. Unless you've heard something different?'

'I've heard nothing. He vanished. Nobody at the prison is talking. I can't get a word from the penal folks.'

'What's your theory?' Pratt asked, then drained his glass and seemed poised for more.

'I found out today that Teddy Maynard went to the White House late on the nineteenth. Only someone like Teddy could squeeze it out of Morgan. Backman walked away, probably with an escort, and vanished.'

'Witness protection?'

'Something like that. The CIA has hidden people before. They have to. There's nothing official on the books, but they have the resources.'

'So why hide Backman?'

'Revenge. Remember Aldrich Ames, the biggest mole in CIA history?'

'Sure.'

'Now locked away securely in a federal pen. Don't you know the CIA would love to have a crack at him? They can't do it because it's against the law – they cannot target a U.S. citizen, either here or abroad.'

'Backman wasn't a CIA mole. Hell, he hated Teddy Maynard, and the feeling was very mutual.'

'Maynard won't kill him. He'll just set things up so someone else will have the pleasure.'

Pratt was getting to his feet. 'You want another one of those?' he asked, pointing at the beer.

'Later, maybe.' Sandberg picked up his pint for the second time and took a drink.

When Pratt returned with a double vodka, he sat down and said, 'So you think Backman's days are numbered?'

'You asked my theory. Let me hear yours.'

A reasonable pull on the vodka, then, 'Same result, but from a slightly different angle.' Pratt stuck his finger in the drink, stirred it, then licked his finger, thinking for a few seconds. 'Off the record, okay?'

'Of course.' They had talked so much over the years that everything was off the record.

'There was an eight-day period between Hubbard's death and Backman's plea. It was a very scary time. Both Kim Bolling and I were under FBI protection, around the clock, around the block, everywhere. Quite odd, really. The FBI was doing its best to send us to prison forever and at the same time felt compelled to protect us.' A sip, as he glanced around to see if any of the college students were eavesdropping. They were not. 'There were some threats, some serious movements by the same people who killed Jacy Hubbard. The FBI debriefed us later, months after Backman was gone and things settled down. We felt a bit safer, but Bolling and I paid armed security for two years afterward. I still glance in the rearview mirror. Poor Kim has lost his mind.'

'Who made the threats?'

'The same people who'd love to find Joel Backman.'

'Who?'

'Backman and Hubbard had made a deal to sell their little product to the Saudis for a trainload of money. Very pricey, but far less than the cost of building a brand-new satellite system. The deal fell through. Hubbard gets himself killed. Backman hurries off to jail, and the Saudis are not happy at all. Neither are the Israelis, because they wanted to make a deal too. Plus, they were furious that Hubbard and Backman would deal with the Saudis.' He paused and took a drink, as if he needed the fortitude to finish the story. 'Then you have the folks who built the system in the first place.'

'The Russians?'

'Probably not. Jacy Hubbard loved Asian girls. He was last seen leaving a bar with a gorgeous young leggy thing, long black hair, round face, from somewhere on the other side of the world. Red China uses thousands of people here to gather information. All their U.S. students, businessmen, diplomats, this place is crawling with Chinese who are snooping around. Plus, their intelligence service has some very effective agents. For a matter like this, they wouldn't hesitate to go after Hubbard and Backman.'

'You're sure it's Red China?'

'No one's sure, okay? Maybe Backman knows, but he never told anyone. Keep in mind, the CIA didn't even know about the system. They got caught with their pants down, and ol' Teddy's still trying to catch up.'

'Fun and games for Teddy, huh?'

'Absolutely. He fed Morgan a line about national security. Morgan, no surprise, falls for it. Backman walks. Teddy sneaks him out of the country, then watches to see who shows up with a gun. It's a no-lose game for Teddy.'

'It's brilliant.'

'It's beyond brilliant, Dan. Think about it. When Joel Backman meets his maker, no one will ever know about it. No one knows where he is now. No one will know who he is when his body is found.'

'If it's found.'

'Exactly.'

'And Backman knows this?'

Pratt drained the second drink and wiped his mouth with a sleeve. He was frowning. 'Backman's not stupid by any measure. But a lot of what we know came to light after he went away. He survived six years in prison, he probably figures he can survive anything.'

Critz ducked into a pub not far from the Connaught Hotel in London. A light rain grew steadier and he needed a place to stay dry. Mrs. Critz was back at the small apartment that was on loan from their new employer, so Critz had the luxury of sitting in a crowded pub where no one knew him and knocking back a couple of pints. A week in London now with a week to go before he pushed himself back across the Atlantic, back to D.C. where he would take a miserable job lobbying for a company that made, among other hardware, defective missiles that the Pentagon hated but nonetheless would be forced to buy because the company had all the right lobbyists.

He found an empty booth, one partially visible through a fog of tobacco smoke, and wedged himself into it and settled in behind his pint. How nice it was to drink alone without the worry of being spotted by someone who would rush over and say, 'Hey, Critz, what were you idiots thinking with that Berman veto?' Yakety-yakety-yak.

He absorbed the cheery British voices of neighbors coming and going. He didn't even mind the smoke. He was alone and unknown and he quietly reveled in his privacy.

His anonymity was not complete, however. From behind him a small man wearing a battered sailor's cap appeared and fell into the booth across the table, startling Critz.

'Mind if I join you, Mr. Critz?' the sailor said with a smile that revealed large yellow teeth. Critz would remember the dingy teeth.

'Have a seat,' Critz said warily. 'You got a name?'

'Ben.' He wasn't British, and English was not his native tongue. Ben was about thirty, with dark hair, dark brown eyes, and a long pointed nose that made him rather Greek-looking.

'No last name, huh?' Critz took a sip from his glass and said, 'How, exactly, do you know my name?'

'I know everything about you.'

'Didn't realize I was that famous.'

'I wouldn't call it fame, Mr. Critz. I'll be brief. I work for some people who desperately want to find Joel Backman. They'll pay serious money, cash. Cash in a box, or cash in a Swiss bank, doesn't matter. It can be done quickly, within hours. You tell us where he is, you get a million bucks, no one will ever know.'

'How did you find me?'

'It was simple, Mr. Critz. We're, let's say, professionals.'

'Spies?'

'It's not important. We are who we are, and we're going to find Mr. Backman. The question is, do you want the million bucks?'

'I don't know where he is.'

'But you can find out.'

'Maybe.'

'Do you want to do business?'

'Not for a million bucks.'

'Then how much?'

'I'll have to think about it.'

'Then think quickly.'

'And if I can't get the information?'

'Then we'll never see you again. This meeting never took place. It's very simple.'

Critz took a long pull on his pint and contemplated things. 'Okay, let's say I'm able to get this information – I'm not too optimistic – but what if I get lucky? Then what?'

'Take a Lufthansa flight from Dulles to Amsterdam, first class. Check into the Amstel Hotel on Biddenham Street. We'll find you, just like we found you here.'

Critz paused and committed the details to memory. 'When?' he asked.

'As soon as possible, Mr. Critz. There are others looking for him.'

Ben vanished as quickly as he had materialized, leaving Critz to peer through the smoke and wonder if he'd just witnessed a dream. He left the pub an hour later, with his face hidden under an umbrella, certain that he was being watched.

Would they watch him in Washington too? He had the unsettling feeling that they would.

Chapter 8

The siesta didn't work. The wine at lunch and the two afternoon beers didn't help. There was simply too much to think about.

Besides, he was too rested; there was too much sleep in his system. Six years in solitary confinement reduces the human body to such a passive state that sleep becomes a principal activity. After the first few months at Rudley, Joel was getting eight hours a night and a hard nap after lunch, which was understandable since he'd slept so little during the previous twenty years when he was holding the republic together during the day and chasing skirts till dawn. After a year he could count on nine, sometimes ten hours of sleep. There was little else to do but read and watch television. Out of boredom, he once conducted a survey, one of his many clandestine polls, by passing a sheet of paper from cell to cell while the guards were themselves napping, and of the thirty-seven respondents on his block the average was eleven hours of sleep a day. Mo, the Mafia snitch, claimed sixteen hours and could often be heard snoring at noon. Mad Cow Miller registered the lowest at just three hours, but the poor guy had lost his mind years earlier and so Joel was forced to discount his responses to the survey.

There were bouts of insomnia, long periods of staring into the darkness and thinking about the mistakes and the children and grandchildren, about the humiliation of the past and the fear of the future. And there were weeks when sleeping pills were delivered to his cell, one at a time, but they never worked. Joel always suspected they were nothing more than placebos.

But in six years there had been too much sleep. Now his body was well rested. His mind was working overtime.

He slowly got up from the bed where he'd been lying for an hour, unable to close his eyes, and walked to the small table where he picked up the cell phone Luigi had given him. He took it to the window, punched the numbers taped to its back, and after four rings he heard a familiar voice.

'Ciao, Marco. Come stai?'

'Just checking to see if this thing works,' Joel said.

'You think I'd give you a defective phone?' Luigi asked.

'No, of course not.'

'How was your nap?'

101

'Uh, nice, very nice. I'll see you at dinner.'

'Ciao.'

Where was Luigi? Lurking nearby with a phone in his pocket, just waiting for Joel to call? Watching the hotel? If Stennett and the driver were still in Treviso, along with Luigi and Ermanno, that would add up to four 'friends' of some variety assigned to keep tabs on Joel Backman.

He gripped the phone and wondered who else out there knew about the call. Who else was listening? He glanced at the street below and wondered who was down there. Only Luigi?

He dismissed those thoughts and sat at the table. He wanted some coffee, maybe a double espresso to get the nerves buzzing, certainly not a cappuccino because of the late hour, but he wasn't ready to pick up the phone and place an order. He could handle the 'Hello' and the 'Coffee', but there would be a flood of other words he did not yet know.

How can a man survive without strong coffee? His favorite secretary had once brought forth his first cup of some jolting Turkish brew at exactly six-thirty every morning, six days a week. He'd almost married her. By ten each morning, the broker was so wired he was throwing things and yelling at subordinates and juggling three calls at once while senators were on hold.

The flashback did not please him. They seldom did. There were plenty of them, and for six years in solitary he'd waged a ferocious mental war to purge his past.

Back to the coffee, which he was afraid to order because he was afraid of the language. Joel Backman had never feared a damn thing, and if he could keep track of three hundred pieces of legislation moving through the maze of Congress, and if he could make one hundred phone calls a day while rarely looking at a Rolodex or a directory, then he could certainly learn enough Italian to order coffee. He arranged Ermanno's study materials neatly on the table and looked at the synopsis. He checked the batteries in the small tape player and fiddled with the tapes. The first page of lesson one was a rather crude color drawing of a family living room with Mom and Pop and the kids watching television. The objects were labeled in both English and Italian – door and porta, sofa and sofà, window and finestra, painting and quadro, and so on. The boy was ragazzo, the mother was madre, the old man teetering on a cane in the corner was the grandfather, or il nonno.

A few pages later was the kitchen, then the bedroom, then the bath. After an hour, still without coffee, Joel was walking softly around his room pointing and whispering the name of everything he saw: bed, letto; lamp, lampada; clock, orologio; soap, sapone. There were a few verbs thrown in for caution: to speak, parlare; to eat, mangiare; to drink, bere; to think, pensare. He stood before the small mirror (specchio) in his bathroom (bagno) and tried to convince himself that he was really Marco. Marco

Lazzeri. 'Sono Marco, sono Marco,' he repeated. I am Marco. I am Marco. Silly at first, but that must be put aside. The stakes were too high to cling to an old name that could get him killed. If being Marco would save his neck, then Marco he was.

Marco. Marco. Marco.

He began looking for words that were not in the drawings. In his new dictionary he found carta igienica for toilet paper, guanciale for pillow, soffitto for ceiling. Everything had a new name, every object in his room, in his own little world, everything he could see at that moment became something new. Over and over, as his eyes bounced from one article to another, he uttered the Italian word.

And what about himself? He had a brain, cervello. He touched a hand, mano; an arm, braccio; a leg, gamba. He had to breathe, respirare; see, vedere; touch, toccare; hear, sentire; sleep, dormire; dream, sognare. He was digressing now, and he caught himself. Tomorrow Ermanno would begin with lesson one, the first blast of vocabulary with emphasis on the basics: greetings and salutations, polite talk, numbers one through a hundred, the days of the week, the months of the year, even the alphabet. The verbs to be (essere) and to have (avere) were both conjugated in the present, simple past, and future.

When it was time for dinner, Marco had memorized all of the first lesson and had listened to the tape of it a dozen times. He stepped into the very cool night and walked happily in the general direction of Trattoria del Monte, where he knew Luigi would be waiting with a choice table and some excellent suggestions from the menu. On the street, and still reeling from several hours of rote memorization, he noticed a scooter, a bike, a dog, a set of twin girls, and he was hit hard with the reality that he knew none of those words in his new language.

All of it had been left in his hotel room.

With food waiting, though, he plowed ahead, undaunted and still confident that he, Marco, could become a somewhat respectable Italian. At a table in the corner, he greeted Luigi with a flourish. 'Buona sera, signore, come sta?'

'Sto bene, grazie, e tu?' Luigi said with an approving smile. Fine, thanks, and you?

'Molto bene, grazie,' Marco said. Very well, thank you.

'So you've been studying?' Luigi said.

'Yes, there's nothing else to do.'

Before Marco could unwrap his napkin, a waiter stopped by with a straw-covered flask of the house red. He quickly poured two glasses and then disappeared. 'Ermanno is a very good teacher,' Luigi was saying.

'You've used him before?' Marco asked casually.

'Yes.'

'So how often do you bring in someone like me and turn him into an Italian?'

Luigi gave a smile and said, 'From time to time.'

'That's hard to believe.'

'Believe what you want, Marco. It's all fiction.'

'You talk like a spy.'

A shrug, no real response.

'Who do you work for, Luigi?'

'Who do you think?'

'You're part of the alphabet – CIA, FBI, NSA. Maybe some obscure branch of military intelligence.'

'Do you enjoy meeting me in these nice little restaurants?' Luigi asked.

'Do I have a choice?'

'Yes. If you keep asking these questions, then we'll stop meeting. And when we stop meeting, your life, shaky as it is, will become even more fragile.'

'I thought your job was to keep me alive.'

'It is. So stop asking questions about me. I assure you there are no answers.'

As if he were on the payroll, the waiter appeared with perfect timing and dropped two large menus between them, effectively changing whatever course the conversation was taking. Marco frowned at the list of dishes and was once again reminded of how far his Italian had to go. At the bottom he recognized the words caffè, vino, and birra.

'What looks good?' he asked.

'The chef is from Siena, so he likes Tuscan dishes. The risotto with porcini mushrooms is great for a first course. I've had the steak florentine, outstanding.'

Marco closed his menu and savored the aroma from the kitchen. 'I'll take both.'

Luigi closed his too and waved at the waiter. After he ordered, they sipped the wine for a few minutes in silence. 'A few years ago,' Luigi began, 'I woke up one morning in a small hotel room in Istanbul. Alone, with about five hundred dollars in my pocket. And a fake passport. I didn't speak a single word of Turkish. My handler was in the city, but if I contacted him then I would be forced to find a new career. In exactly ten months I was supposed to return to the same hotel to meet a friend who would take me out of the country.'

'Sounds like basic CIA training.'

'Wrong part of the alphabet,' he said, then paused, took a sip, and continued. 'Since I enjoy eating, I learned to survive. I absorbed the language, the culture, everything around me. I managed quite nicely, blended in with the surroundings, and ten months later when I met my friend I had more than a thousand dollars.'

'Italian, English, French, Spanish, Turkish – what else?'

'Russian. They dropped me in Stalingrad for a year.'

Marco almost asked who 'they' might be, but he let it pass. There would be no answer; besides, he thought he knew.

'So I've been dropped here?' Marco asked.

The waiter plunked down a basket of mixed breads and a small bowl of olive oil. Luigi began dipping and eating, and the question was either forgotten or ignored. More food followed, a small tray of ham and salami with olives, and the conversation lagged. Luigi was a spy, or a counterspy, or an operative, or an agent of some strain, or simply a handler or a contact, or maybe a stringer, but he was first and foremost an Italian. All the training possible could not divert his attention from the challenge at hand when the table was covered.

As he ate, he changed subjects. He explained the rigors of a proper Italian dinner. First, the anitpasti – usually a plate of mixed meats, such as they had before them. Then the first course, primi, which is usually a reasonably sized serving of pasta, rice, soup, or polenta, the purpose of which is to sort of limber up the stomach in preparation for the main course, the secondi – a hearty dish of meat, fish, pork, chicken, or lamb. Be careful with desserts, he warned ominously, glancing around to make sure the waiter wasn't listening. He shook his head sadly as he explained that many good restaurants now buy them off premises, and they're loaded with so much sugar or cheap liqueur that they practically rot your teeth out.

Marco managed to appear sufficiently shocked at this national scandal.

'Learn the word "gelato," ' he said, his eyes glowing again.

'Ice cream,' Marco said.

'Bravo. The best in the world. There's a gelateria down the street. We'll go there after dinner.'

Room service terminated at midnight. At 11:55, Marco slowly picked up the phone and punched number four twice. He swallowed deeply, then held his breath. He'd been practicing the dialogue for thirty minutes.

After a few lazy rings, during which time he almost hung up twice, a sleepy voice answered and said, 'Buona sera.'

Marco closed his eyes and plunged ahead. 'Buona sera. Vorrei un caffè, per favore. Un espresso doppio.'

'Sì, latte e zucchero?' Milk and sugar?

'No, senza latte e zucchero.'

'Sì, cinque minuti.'

'Grazie.' Marco quickly hung up before risking further dialogue, though given the enthusiasm on the other end he doubted it seriously. He jumped to his feet, pumped a fist in the air, and patted himself on the back for completing his first conversation in Italian. No hitches whatsoever. Both parties understood all of what the other said.

At 1:00 a.m., he was still sipping his double espresso, savoring it even though it was no longer warm. He was in the middle of lesson three, and with sleep not even a distant thought, he was thinking of maybe devouring the entire textbook for his first session with Ermanno.

He knocked on the apartment door ten minutes early. It was a control thing. Though he tried to resist it, he found himself impulsively reverting to his old ways. He preferred to be the one who decided when the lesson would begin. Ten minutes early or twenty minutes late, the time was not important. As he waited in the dingy hallway he flashed back to a high-level meeting he'd once hosted in his enormous conference room. It was packed with corporate executives and honchos from several federal agencies, all summoned there by the broker. Though the conference room was fifty steps down the hall from his own office, he made his entrance twenty minutes late, apologizing and explaining that he'd been on the phone with the office of the prime minister of some minor country.

Petty, petty, petty. The games he played.

Ermanno was seemingly unimpressed. He made his student wait at least five minutes before he opened the door with a timid smile and a friendly 'Buon giorno, Signor Lazzeri.'

'Buon giorno, Ermanno. Come stai?'

'Molto bene, grazie, e tu?'

'Molto bene, grazie.'

Ermanno opened the door wider, and with the sweep of a hand said, 'Prego.' Please come in.

Marco stepped inside and was once again struck by how sparse and temporary everything looked. He placed his books on the small table in the center of the front room and decided to keep his coat on. The temperature was about forty outside and not much warmer in this tiny apartment.

'Vorrebbe un caffè?' Ermanno asked. Would you like a coffee?

'Sì, grazie.' He'd slept about two hours, from four to six, then he'd showered, dressed, and ventured into the streets of Treviso, where he'd found an early bar where the old gentlemen gathered and had their espressos and all talked at once. He wanted more coffee, but what he really needed was a bite to eat. A croissant or a muffin or something of that variety, something he had not yet learned the name of. He decided he could hold off hunger until noon, when he would once again meet Luigi for another foray into Italian cuisine.

'You are a student, right?' he asked when Ermanno returned from the kitchen with two small cups.

'Non inglese, Marco, non inglese.'

And that was the end of English. An abrupt end; a harsh, final farewell to the mother tongue. Ermanno sat on one side of the table, Marco on the other, and at exactly eight-thirty they, together, turned to page one of lesson one. Marco read the first dialogue in Italian, Ermanno gently made corrections, though he was quite impressed with his student's preparation. The vocabulary was thoroughly memorized, but the

111

accent needed work. An hour later, Ermanno began pointing at various objects around the room – rug, book, magazine, chair, quilt, curtains, radio, floor, wall, backpack – and Marco responded with ease. With an improving accent, he rattled off the entire list of polite expressions – good day, how are you, fine thanks, please, see you later, goodbye, good night – and thirty others. He rattled off the days of the week and the months of the year. Lesson one was completed after only two hours and Ermanno asked if they needed a break. 'No.' They turned to lesson two, with another page of vocabulary that Marco had already mastered and more dialogue that he delivered quite impressively.

'You've been studying,' Ermanno mumbled in English.

'Non inglese, Ermanno, non inglese,' Marco corrected him. The game was on – who could show more intensity. By noon, the teacher was exhausted and ready for a break, and they were both relieved to hear the knock on the door and the voice of Luigi outside in the hallway. He entered and saw the two of them squared off across the small, littered table, as if they'd been arm wrestling for several hours.

'Come va?' Luigi asked. How's it going?

Ermanno gave him a weary look and said, 'Molto intenso.' Very intense.

'Vorrei pranzare,' Marco announced, slowly rising to his feet. I'd like some lunch.

Marco was hoping for a nice lunch with some

English thrown in to make things easier and perhaps relieve the mental strain of trying to translate every word he heard. However, after Ermanno's glowing summary of the morning session, Luigi was inspired to continue the immersion through the meal, or at least the first part of it. The menu contained not a word of English, and after Luigi explained each dish in incomprehensible Italian, Marco threw up his hands and said, 'That's it. I'm not speaking or listening to Italian for the next hour.'

'What about your lunch?'

'I'll eat yours.' He gulped the red wine and tried to relax.

'Okay then. I suppose we can do English for one hour.'

'Grazie,' Marco said before he caught himself.

Chapter 9

Midway through the morning session the following day, Marco abruptly changed direction. In the middle of a particularly tedious piece of dialogue he ditched the Italian and said, 'You're not a student.'

Ermanno looked up from the study guide, paused for a moment, then said, 'Non inglese, Marco. Soltanto Italiano.' Only Italian.

'I'm tired of Italian right now, okay? You're not a student.'

Deceit was difficult for Ermanno, and he paused a bit too long. 'I am,' he said, without much conviction.

'No, I don't think so. You're obviously not taking classes, otherwise you wouldn't be able to spend all day teaching me.'

'Maybe I have classes at night. Why does it matter?'

'You're not taking classes anywhere. There are no books here, no student newspaper, none of the usual crap that students leave lying around everywhere.'

'Perhaps it's in the other room.'

'Let me see.'

'Why? Why is it important?'

'Because I think you work for the same people Luigi works for.'

'And what if I do?'

'I want to know who they are.'

'Suppose I don't know? Why should you be concerned? Your task is to learn the language.'

'How long have you lived here, in this apartment?'

'I don't have to answer your questions.'

'See, I think you got here last week; that this is a safe house of some sort; that you're not really who you say you are.'

'Then that would make two of us.' Ermanno suddenly stood and walked through the tiny kitchen to the rear of the apartment. He returned with some papers, which he slid in front of Marco. It was a registration packet from the University of Bologna, with a mailing label listing the name of Ermanno Rosconi, at the address where they were now sitting.

'I resume classes soon,' Ermanno said. 'Would you like some more coffee?'

Marco was scanning the forms, comprehending just enough to get the message. 'Yes, please,' he said. It was just paperwork – easily faked. But if it was a forgery, it was a very good one. Ermanno disappeared into the kitchen and began running water.

Marco shoved his chair back and said, 'I'm going for a walk around the block. I need to clear my head.'

The routine changed at dinner. Luigi met him in front of a tobacco shop facing the Piazza dei Signori, and they strolled along a busy alley as shopkeepers were closing up. It was already dark and very cold, and smartly bundled businessmen hurried home, their heads covered with hats and scarves.

Luigi had his gloved hands buried deep in the wool pockets of his knee-length rough fabric duster, one that could've been handed down by his grandfather or purchased last week in Milan at some hideously expensive designer shop. Regardless, he wore it stylishly, and once again Marco was envious of the casual elegance of his handler.

Luigi was in no hurry and seemed to enjoy the cold. He offered a few comments in Italian, but Marco refused to play along. 'English, Luigi,' he said twice. 'I need English.'

'All right. How was your second day of class?'

'Good. Ermanno's okay. No sense of humor, but an adequate teacher.'

'You're making progress?'

'How could I not make progress?'

'Ermanno tells me you have an ear for the language.'

116

'Ermanno is a bad con man and you know it. I'm working hard because a lot depends on it. I'm drilled by him six hours a day, then I spend three hours at night cramming. Progress is inevitable.'

'You work very hard,' Luigi repeated. He suddenly stopped and looked at what appeared to be a small deli. 'This, Marco, is dinner.'

Marco stared with disapproval. The storefront was no more than fifteen feet across. Three tables were crammed in the window and the place appeared to be packed. 'Are you sure?' Marco asked.

'Yes, it's very good. Lighter food, sandwiches and stuff. You're eating by yourself. I'm not going in.'

Marco looked at him and started to protest, then he caught himself and smiled as if he gladly accepted the challenge.

'The menu is on a chalkboard above the cashier, no English. Order first, pay, then pick up your food at the far end of the counter, which is not a bad to place to sit if you can get a stool. Tip is included.'

Marco asked, 'What's the specialty of the house?'

'The ham and artichoke pizza is delicious. So are the panini. I'll meet you over there, by the fountain, in one hour.'

Marco gritted his teeth and entered the café, very alone. As he waited behind two young ladies he desperately searched the chalkboard for

117

something he could pronounce. Forget taste. What was important was the ordering and paying. Fortunately, the cashier was a middle-aged lady who enjoyed smiling. Marco gave her a friendly 'Buona sera,' and before she could shoot something back he ordered a 'panino prosciutto e formaggio' – ham and cheese sandwich – and a Coca-Cola.

Good ol' Coca-Cola. The same in any language.

The register rattled and she offered a blur of words that he did not understand. But he kept smiling and said, 'Sì,' then handed over a twenty-euro bill, certainly enough to cover things and bring back some change. It worked. With the change was a ticket. 'Numero sessantasette,' she said. Number sixty-seven.

He held the ticket and moved slowly along the counter toward the kitchen. No one gawked at him, no one seemed to notice. Was he actually passing himself off as an Italian, a real local? Or was it so obvious that he was an alien that the locals didn't bother to look? He had quickly developed the habit of evaluating how other men were dressed, and he judged himself to be in the game. As Luigi had told him, the men of northern Italy were much more concerned with style and appearance than Americans. There were more jackets and tailored slacks, more sweaters and ties. Much less denim, and virtually no sweatshirts or other signs of indifference to appearance.

Luigi, or whoever had put together his wardrobe, one no doubt paid for by the American taxpayers, had done a fine job. For a man who'd worn the same prison garb for six years, Marco was quickly adjusting to things Italian.

He watched the plates of food as they popped up along the counter near the grill. After about ten minutes, a thick sandwich appeared. A server grabbed it, snatched off a ticket, and yelled, 'Numero sessantasette.' Marco stepped forward without a word and produced his ticket. The soft drink came next. He found a seat at a small corner table and thoroughly enjoyed the solitude of his dinner. The deli was loud and crowded, a neighborhood place where many of the customers knew each other. Their greetings involved hugs and kisses and long hellos, even longer goodbyes. Waiting in line to order caused no problems, though the Italians seemed to struggle with the basic concept of one standing behind the other. Back home there would've been sharp words from the customers and perhaps swearing from the cashier.

In a country where a three-hundred-year-old house is considered new, time has a different meaning. Food is to be enjoyed, even in a small deli with few tables. Those seated close to Joel seemed poised to take hours to digest their pizza and sandwiches. There was simply too much talking to do!

The brain-dead pace of prison life had

flattened all his edges. He'd kept his sanity by reading eight books a week, but even that exercise had been for escape and not necessarily for learning. Two days of intensive memorizing, conjugating, pronouncing, and listening like he'd never listened before left him mentally exhausted.

So he absorbed the roar of Italian without trying to understand any of it. He enjoyed its rhythm and cadence and laughter. He caught a word every now and then, especially in the greetings and farewells, and considered this to be progress of some sort. Watching the families and friends made him lonely, though he refused to dwell on it. Loneliness was twenty-three hours a day in a small cell with little mail and nothing but a cheap paperback to keep him company. He'd seen loneliness; this was a day at the beach.

He tried hard to linger over his ham and cheese, but he could only stretch it so far. He reminded himself to order fries the next time because fries can be toyed with until long after they're cold, thus extending the meal far beyond what would be considered normal back home. Reluctantly, he surrendered his table. Almost an hour after he entered the café, he left the warmth of it and walked to the fountain where the water had been turned off so it wouldn't freeze. Luigi strolled up a few minutes later, as if he'd been loitering in the shadows, waiting. He had the nerve to suggest a gelato, an ice cream, but Marco was already shivering. They walked to the hotel and said good night.

*

Luigi's field supervisor had diplomatic cover at the U.S. consulate in Milan. His name was Whitaker, and Backman was the least of his priorities. Backman was not involved in intelligence, or counterintelligence, and Whitaker had a full load in those arenas without having to worry about an ex–Washington power broker who'd been stashed away in Italy. But he dutifully prepared his daily summaries and sent them to Langley. There they were received and reviewed by Julia Javier, the veteran with access to Mr. Maynard himself. It was because of Ms. Javier's watchful eye that Whitaker was so diligent in Milan. Otherwise, the daily summaries may not have been so prompt.

Teddy wanted a briefing.

Ms. Javier was summoned to his office on the seventh floor, to the 'Teddy Wing', as it was known throughout Langley. She entered his 'station', as he preferred it to be called, and once again found him parked at the end of a long wide conference table, sitting high in his jacked-up wheelchair, bundled in blankets from the chest down, wearing his standard black suit, peering over stacks of summaries, with Hoby hovering nearby ready to fetch another cup of the wretched green tea that Teddy was convinced was keeping him alive.

He was barely alive, but then Julia Javier had been thinking that for years now.

Since she didn't drink coffee and wouldn't

touch the tea, nothing was offered. She took her customary seat to his right, sort of the witness chair that all visitors were expected to take – his right ear caught much more than his left – and he managed a very tired 'Hello, Julia.'

Hoby, as always, sat across from her and prepared to take notes. Every sound in the 'station' was being captured by some of the most sophisticated recording devices modern technology had created, but Hoby nonetheless went through the charade of writing it all down.

'Brief me on Backman,' Teddy said. A verbal report such as this was expected to be concise, to the point, with not a single unnecessary word thrown in.

Julia looked at her notes, cleared her throat, and began speaking for the hidden recorders. 'He's in place in Treviso, a nice little town in northern Italy. Been there for three full days, seems to be making the adjustment quite well. Our agent is in complete contact, and the language tutor is a local who's doing a nice job. Backman has no money and no passport, and so far has been quite willing to stick close to the agent. He has not used the phone in his hotel room, nor has he tried to use his cell phone for anything other than to call our agent. He has shown no desire to explore or to wander about. Evidently, the habits learned in prison are hard to break. He's staying close to his hotel. When he's not being tutored or eating, he stays in his room and studies Italian.'

'How is his language?'

'Not bad. He's fifty-two years old, so it won't be quick.'

'I learned Arabic when I was sixty,' Teddy said proudly, as if sixty was a century ago.

'Yes, I know,' she said. Everyone at Langley knew it. 'He is studying extremely hard and making progress, but it's only been three days. The tutor is impressed.'

'What does he talk about?'

'Not the past, not old friends and old enemies. Nothing that would interest us. He's closed that off, for now anyway. Idle conversation tends to be about his new home, the culture and language.'

'His mood?'

'He just walked out of prison fourteen years early and he's having long meals and good wine. He's quite happy. Doesn't appear to be home-sick, but of course he doesn't really have a home. Never talks about his family.'

'His health?'

'Seems fine. The cough is gone. Appears to be sleeping. No complaints.'

'How much does he drink?'

'He's careful. Enjoys wine at lunch and dinner and a beer in a nearby bar, but nothing excessive.'

'Let's try and crank up the booze, okay? See if he'll talk more.'

'That's our plan.'

'How secure is he?'

'Everything's bugged – phones, room, language lessons, lunches, dinners. Even his shoes have mikes. Both pairs. His overcoat has a Peak 30 sewn into the lining. We can track him virtually anywhere.'

'So you can't lose him?'

'He's a lawyer, not a spy. As of now, he seems very content to enjoy his freedom and do what he's told.'

'He's not stupid, though. Remember that, Julia. Backman knows there are some very nasty people who would love to find him.'

'True, but right now he's like a toddler clinging to his mother.'

'So he feels safe?'

'Under the circumstances, yes.'

'Then let's give him a scare.'

'Now?'

'Yes.' Teddy rubbed his eyes and took a sip of tea. 'What about his son?'

'Level-three surveillance, not much happening in Culpeper, Virginia. If Backman tries to contact anyone, it will be Neal Backman. But we'll know it in Italy before we know it in Culpeper.'

'His son is the only person he trusts,' Teddy said, stating what Julia had said many times.

'Very true.'

After a long pause he said, 'Anything else, Julia?'

'He's writing a letter to his mother in Oakland.'

Teddy gave a quick smile. 'How nice. Do we have it?'

'Yes, our agent took a picture of it yesterday, we just got it. Backman hides it in between the pages of a local tourism magazine in his hotel room.'

'How long is it?'

'Two good paragraphs. Evidently a work in progress.'

'Read it to me,' Teddy said as he leaned his head back against his wheelchair and closed his eyes.

Julia shuffled papers and pushed up her reading glasses. 'No date, handwritten, which is a chore because Backman's penmanship is lousy. "Dear Mother: I'm not sure when or if you will ever receive this letter. I'm not sure if I will ever mail it, which could affect whether or not you get it. At any rate, I'm out of prison and doing better. In my last letter I said things were going well in the flat country of Oklahoma. I had no idea at that time that I would be pardoned by the President. It happened so quickly that I still find it hard to believe." Second paragraph. "I'm living on the other side of the world, I can't say where because this would upset some people. I would prefer to be in the United States, but that is not possible. I had no say in the matter. It's not a great life but it's certainly better than the one I had a week ago. I was dying in prison, in spite of what I said in my letters. Didn't want to worry you. Here, I'm free, and that's the most important thing in the world. I can walk down the street, eat in a café, come and go as I please, do pretty much whatever I want. Freedom, Mother, something I dreamed of for years and thought was impossible."'

She laid it down and said, 'That's as far as he's gotten.'

Teddy opened his eyes and said, 'You think he's stupid enough to mail a letter to his mother?'

'No. But he's been writing her once a week for a long time. It's a habit, and it's probably therapeutic. He has to talk to somebody.'

'Are we still watching her mail?'

'Yes, what little she receives.'

'Very well. Scare the hell out of him, then report back.'

'Yes sir.' Julia gathered her papers and left the office. Teddy picked up a summary and adjusted his reading glasses. Hoby went to a small kitchen nearby.

Backman's mother's phone had been tapped in the nursing home in Oakland, and so far it had revealed nothing. The day the pardon was announced two very old friends had called with lots of questions and some subdued congratulations, but Mrs. Backman had been so bewildered she was eventually sedated and napped for hours. None of her grandchildren – the three produced by Joel and his various wives – had called her in the past six months.

Lydia Backman had survived two strokes and

was confined to a wheelchair. When her son was at his pinnacle she lived in relative luxury in a spacious condo with a full-time nurse. His conviction had forced her to give up the good life and live in a nursing home with a hundred others.

Surely Backman would not try to contact her.

Chapter 10

After a few days of dreaming about the money, Critz began spending it, at least mentally. With all that cash, he wouldn't be forced to work for the sleazy defense contractor, nor would he be forced to hustle audiences on the lecture circuit. (He wasn't convinced the audiences were out there to begin with, in spite of what his lecture agent had promised him.)

Critz was thinking about retirement! Somewhere far away from Washington and all the enemies he'd made there, somewhere on a beach with a sailboat nearby. Or maybe he'd move to Switzerland and stay close to his new fortune buried in his new bank, all wonderfully tax free and growing by the day.

He made a phone call and got the flat in London for a few more days. He encouraged Mrs. Critz to shop more aggressively. She, too, was tired of Washington and deserved an easier life.

Partly because of his greedy enthusiasm, and partly because of his natural ineptitude, and also because of his lack of sophistication in intelligence matters, Critz blundered badly from the start. For such an old hand at the Washington game, his mistakes were inexcusable.

First, he used the phone in his borrowed flat, thus making it easy for someone to nail down his exact location. He called Jeb Priddy, the CIA liaison who had been stationed in the White House during the last four years. Priddy was still at his post but expected to be called back to Langley soon. The new President was settling in, things were chaotic, and so on, according to Priddy, who seemed slightly irritated by the call. He and Critz had never been close, and Priddy knew immediately that the guy was fishing. Critz eventually said he was trying to find an old pal, a senior CIA analyst he'd once played a lot of golf with. Name was Daly, Addison Daly, and he'd left Washington for a stint in Asia. Did Priddy perhaps know where he was now?

Addison Daly was tucked away at Langley and Priddy knew him well. 'I know the name,' Priddy said. 'Maybe I can find him. Where can I reach you?'

Critz gave him the number at the flat. Priddy called Addison Daly and passed along his suspicions. Daly turned on his recorder and called London on a secure line. Critz answered the phone and went overboard with his delight at hearing from an old friend. He rambled on about how wonderful life was after the White House, after all those years playing the political game, how nice it was being a private citizen. He was anxious to renew old friendships and get serious about his golf game.

Daly played along well. He offered that he, too, was contemplating retirement – almost thirty years in the service – and that he caught himself looking forward to an easier life.

How's Teddy these days? Critz wanted to know. And how's the new president? What's the mood in Washington with the new administration?

Nothing changes much, Daly mused, just another bunch of fools. By the way, how's former president Morgan?

Critz didn't know, hadn't talked to him, in fact might not talk to him for many weeks. As the conversation was winding down, Critz said with a clumsy laugh, 'Don't guess anybody's seen Joel Backman?'

Daly managed to laugh too – it was all a big joke. 'No,' he said, 'I think the boy's well hidden.'

'He should be.'

Critz promised to call as soon as he returned to D.C. They'd play eighteen holes at one of the good clubs, then have a drink, just like in the old days!

What old days? Daly asked himself after he hung up.

An hour later, the phone conversation was played for Teddy Maynard.

Since the first two calls had been somewhat encouraging, Critz pressed on. He'd always been one to work the phones like a maniac. He subscribed to the shotgun theory – fill the air with calls and something will happen. A rough plan was coming together. Another old pal had once been a senior staffer to the chairman of the Senate Intelligence Committee, and though he was now a well-connected lobbyist, he had, allegedly, maintained close ties to the CIA.

They talked politics and golf and eventually, much to Critz's delight, the pal asked what, exactly, was President Morgan thinking when he pardoned Duke Mongo, the biggest tax evader in the history of America? Critz claimed to have been opposed to the pardon but managed to steer the conversation along to the other controversial reprieve. 'What's the gossip on Backman?' he asked.

'You were there,' answered his pal.

'Yes, but where did Maynard stash him? That's the big question.'

'So it was a CIA job?' his friend asked.

'Of course,' Critz said with the voice of authority. Who else could sneak him out of the country in the middle of the night?

'That's interesting,' said his pal, who then became very quiet. Critz insisted on a lunch the following week, and that's where they left the conversation.

As Critz feverishly worked the phone, he

marveled once again at his endless list of contacts. Power did have its rewards.

Joel, or Marco, said goodbye to Ermanno at five-thirty in the afternoon, completing a three-hour session that had gone virtually nonstop. Both were exhausted.

The chilly air helped clear his head as he walked the narrow streets of Treviso. For the second day, he dropped by a small corner bar and ordered a beer. He sat in the window and watched the locals hurry about, some rushing home from work, others shopping quickly for dinner. The bar was warm and smoky, and Marco once again drifted back to prison. He couldn't help himself – the change had been too drastic, the freedom too sudden. There was still the lingering fear that he would wake up and find himself locked in the cell with some unseen prankster laughing hysterically in the distance.

After the beer he had an espresso, and after that he stepped into the darkness and shoved both hands deep into his pockets. When he turned the corner and saw his hotel, he also saw Luigi pacing nervously along the sidewalk, smoking a cigarette. As Marco crossed the street, Luigi came after him. 'We are leaving, immediately,' he said.

'Why?' Marco asked, glancing around, looking for bad guys.

'I'll explain later. There's a travel bag on your

bed. Pack your things as quickly as possible. I'll wait here.'

'What if I don't want to leave?' Marco asked.

Luigi clutched his left wrist, thought for a quick second, then gave a very tight smile. 'Then you might not last twenty-four hours,' he said as ominously as possible. 'Please trust me.'

Marco raced up the stairs and down the hall, and was almost to his room before he realized that the sharp pain in his stomach was not from heavy breathing but from fear.

What had happened? What had Luigi seen or heard, or been told? Who, exactly, was Luigi in the first place and who was he taking orders from? As Marco yanked his clothes out of the tiny closet and flung them toward the bed he asked all these questions, and many more. When everything was packed, he sat for a moment and tried to collect his thoughts. He took deep breaths, exhaled slowly, told himself that whatever was happening was just part of the game.

Would he be running forever? Always packing in a hurry, fleeing one room in search of another? It still beat the hell out of prison, but it would take its toll.

And how could anyone possibly have found him this soon? He'd been in Treviso only four days.

When his composure was somewhat restored, he walked slowly down the hall, down the stairs, through the lobby where he nodded at the gawking clerk but said nothing, and out the front door. Luigi snatched his bag and tossed it into the trunk of a compact Fiat. They were on the outskirts of Treviso before a word was spoken.

'Okay, Luigi, what's up?' Marco asked.

'A change of scenery.'

'Got that. Why?'

'Some very good reasons.'

'Oh, well, that explains everything.'

Luigi drove with his left hand, shifted gears frantically with his right, and kept the accelerator as close to the floor as possible while ignoring the brakes. Marco was already perplexed as to how a race of people could spend two and a half leisurely hours over lunch, then hop in a car for a ten-minute drive across town at breakneck speed.

They drove an hour, generally in a southward direction, avoiding the highways by clinging to the back roads. 'Is someone behind us?' Marco asked more than once as they sped around tight curves on two wheels.

Luigi just shook his head. His eyes were narrow, his eyebrows pinched together, his jaw clenched tightly when the cigarette wasn't near. He somehow managed to drive like a maniac while smoking calmly and never glancing behind them. He was determined not to speak, and that reinforced Marco's determination to have a conversation.

'You're just trying to scare me, aren't you, Luigi? We're playing the spy game – you're the

134

master, I'm the poor schmuck with the secrets. Scare the hell out of me and keep me dependent and loyal. I know what you're doing.'

'Who killed Jacy Hubbard?' Luigi asked, barely moving his lips.

Backman suddenly wanted to go quiet. The mere mention of Hubbard made him freeze for a second. The name always brought the same flashback: a police photo of Jacy slumped against his brother's grave, the left side of his head blown away, blood everywhere – on the tombstone, on his white shirt. Everywhere.

'You have the file,' Backman said. 'It was a suicide.'

'Oh yes. And if you believed that, then why did you decide to plead guilty and beg for protective custody in prison?'

'I was scared. Suicides can be contagious.'

'Very true.'

'So you're saying that the boys who did the Hubbard suicide are after me?'

Luigi confirmed it with a shrug.

'And somehow they found out I was hiding in Treviso?'

'It's best not to take chances.'

He would not get the details, if, in fact, there were any. He tried not to, but he instinctively glanced over his shoulder and saw the dark road behind them. Luigi looked into his rearview mirror, and managed a satisfactory smile, as if to say: They're back there, somewhere.

Joel sank a few inches in his seat and closed his

eyes. Two of his clients had died first. Safi Mirza had been knifed outside a Georgetown nightclub three months after he hired Backman and handed over the only copy of JAM. The knife wounds were severe enough, but a poison had been injected, probably with the thrust of the blade. No witnesses. No clues. A very unsolved murder, but one of many in D.C. A month later Fazal Sharif had disappeared in Karachi, and was presumed dead.

JAM was indeed worth a billion dollars, but no one would ever enjoy the money.

In 1998, Backman, Pratt & Bolling had hired Jacy Hubbard for $1 million a year. The marketing of JAM was his first big challenge. To prove his worth, Hubbard bullied and bribed his way into the Pentagon in a clumsy and ill-fated effort to confirm the existence of the Neptune satellite system. Some documents – doctored but still classified – were smuggled out by a Hubbard mole who was reporting everything to his superiors. The highly sensitive papers purported to show the existence of Gamma Net, a fictitious Star Wars–like surveillance system with unheard-of capabilities. Once Hubbard 'confirmed' that the three young Pakistanis were indeed correct – their Neptune was a U.S. project – he proudly reported his findings to Joel Backman and they were in business.

Since Gamma Net was supposedly the creation of the U.S. military, JAM was worth even more. The truth was that neither the Pentagon nor the CIA knew about Neptune.

The Pentagon then leaked its own fiction – a fabricated breach of security by a mole working for ex-senator Jacy Hubbard and his powerful new boss, the broker himself. The scandal erupted. The FBI raided the offices of Backman, Pratt & Bolling in the middle of the night, found the Pentagon documents that everyone presumed to be authentic, and within forty-eight hours a highly motivated team of federal prosecutors had issued indictments against every partner in the firm.

The killings soon followed, with no clues as to who was behind them. The Pentagon brilliantly neutralized Hubbard and Backman without tipping its hand as to whether it actually owned and created the satellite system. Gamma Net or Neptune, or whatever, was effectively shielded under the impenetrable web of 'military secrets'.

Backman the lawyer wanted a trial, especially if the Pentagon documents were questionable, but Backman the defendant wanted to avoid a fate similar to Hubbard's.

If Luigi's mad dash out of Treviso was designed to frighten him, then the plan suddenly began working. For the first time since his pardon, Joel missed the safety of his little cell in maximum security.

The city of Padua was ahead, its lights and traffic growing by the mile. 'What's the population of Padua?' Marco asked, his first words in half an hour.

'Two hundred thousand. Why do Americans always want to know the population of every village and city?'

'Didn't realize it was a problem.'

'Are you hungry?'

The dull throbbing in his stomach was from fear, not hunger, but he said 'Sure' anyway. They ate a pizza at a neighborhood bar just beyond the outer ring of Padua, and were quickly back in the car and headed south.

They slept that night in a tiny country inn – eight closet-sized rooms – that had been in the same family since Roman times. There was no sign advertising the place; it was one of Luigi's stopovers. The nearest road was narrow, neglected, and virtually free of any vehicle built after 1970. Bologna was not far away.

Luigi was next door, through a thick stone wall that went back for centuries. When Joel Backman/Marco Lazzeri crawled under the blankets and finally got warm, he couldn't see a flicker of light anywhere. Total blackness. And total quiet. It was so quiet he couldn't close his eyes for a long time.

Chapter 11

After the fifth report that Critz had called with questions about Joel Backman, Teddy Maynard threw a rare tantrum. The fool was in London, working the phones furiously, for some reason trying to find someone, anyone, who might lead him to information about Backman.

'Someone's offered Critz money,' Teddy barked at Wigline, an assistant deputy director.

'But there's no way Critz can find out where Backman is,' Wigline said.

'He shouldn't be trying. He'll only complicate matters. He must be neutralized.'

Wigline glanced at Hoby, who had suddenly stopped his note-taking. 'What are you saying, Teddy?'

'Neutralize him.'

'He's a U.S. citizen.'

'I know that! He's also compromising an operation. There is precedent. We've done it before.' He didn't bother to tell them what the precedent was, but they assumed that since Teddy often created his own precedents, then it would do no good to argue the matter.

Hoby nodded as if to say: Yes, we've done it before.

Wigline clenched his jaw and said, 'I assume you want it done now.'

'As soon as possible,' Teddy said. 'Show me a plan in two hours.'

They watched Critz as he left his borrowed apartment and began his long, late-afternoon walk, one that usually ended with a few pints. After half an hour at a languid pace he neared Leicester Square and entered the Dog and Duck, the same pub as the day before.

He was on his second pint at the far end of the main bar, first floor, before the stool next to him cleared and an agent named Greenlaw wedged in and yelled for a beer.

'Mind if I smoke?' Greenlaw asked Critz, who shrugged and said, 'This ain't America.'

'A Yank, huh?' Greenlaw said.

'Yep.'

'Live here?'

'No, just visiting.' Critz was concentrating on the bottles on the wall beyond the bar, avoiding eye contact, wanting no part of the conversation. He had quickly come to adore the solitude of a crowded pub. He loved to sit and drink and listen to the rapid banter of the Brits and know that not a soul had a clue as to who he was. He was, though, still wondering about the little guy named Ben. If they were watching him, they were doing a great job of staying in the shadows.

Greenlaw gulped his beer in an effort to catch up with Critz. It was crucial to order the next two at the same time. He puffed a cigarette, then added his smoke to the cloud above them. 'I've been here for a year,' he said.

Critz nodded without looking. Get lost.

'I don't mind driving on the wrong side, or the lousy weather, but what really bugs me here are the sports. You ever watch a cricket match? Lasts for four days.'

Critz managed to grunt and offer a lame 'Such a stupid sport.'

'It's either soccer or cricket, and these people go nuts over both. I just survived the winter here without the NFL. It was pure misery.'

Critz was a loyal Redskins season-ticket holder and few things in life excited him as much as his beloved team. Greenlaw was a casual fan but had spent the day memorizing statistics in a CIA safe house north of London. If football didn't work, then politics would be next. If that didn't work, there was a fine-looking lady waiting outside, though Critz did not have a reputation as a philanderer.

Critz was suddenly homesick. Sitting in a pub, far from home, far from the frenzy of the Super Bowl – two days away and virtually ignored by the British press – he could hear the crowd and feel the excitement. If the Redskins had survived the playoffs, he would not be drinking pints in

London. He would be at the Super Bowl, fifty-yard-line seats, furnished by one of the many corporations he could lean on.

He looked at Greenlaw and said, 'Patriots or Packers?'

'My team didn't make it, but I always pull for the NFC.'

'Me too. Who's your team?'

And that was perhaps the most fatal question Robert Critz would ever ask. When Greenlaw answered, 'Redskins,' Critz actually smiled and wanted to talk. They spent a few minutes establishing pedigree – how long each had been a Redskins fan, the great games they'd seen, the great players, the Super Bowl championships. Greenlaw ordered another round and both seemed ready to replay old games for hours. Critz had talked to so few Yanks in London, and this guy was certainly an easy one to get on with.

Greenlaw excused himself and went to find the restroom. It was upstairs, the size of a broom closet, a one-holer like so many johns in London. He latched the door for a few seconds of privacy and quickly whipped out a cell phone to report his progress. The plan was in place. The team was just down the street, waiting. Three men and the fine-looking lady.

Halfway through his fourth pint, and with a polite disagreement under way over Sonny Jurgensen's touchdown-to-interception ratio, Critz finally needed to pee. He asked directions and disappeared. Greenlaw deftly dropped into Critz's glass one small white tablet of Rohypnol – a strong, tasteless, odorless sedative. When Mr. Redskins returned he was refreshed and ready to drink. They talked about John Riggins and Joe Gibbs and thoroughly enjoyed themselves as poor Critz's chin began to drop.

'Wow,' he said, his tongue already thick. 'I'd better be going. Old lady is waiting.'

'Yeah, me too,' Greenlaw said, raising his glass. 'Drink up.'

They drained their pints and stood to leave; Critz in front, Greenlaw waiting to catch him. They made it through the crowd packed around the front door and onto the sidewalk where a cold wind revived Critz, but only for a second. He forgot about his new pal, and in less than twenty steps was wobbling on rubbery legs and grasping for a lamp pole. Greenlaw grabbed him as he was falling, and for the benefit of a young couple passing by said loudly, 'Dammit, Fred, you're drunk again.'

Fred was far beyond drunk. A car appeared from nowhere and slowed by the sidewalk. A back door swung open, and Greenlaw shoveled a half-dead Critz into the rear seat. The first stop was a warehouse eight blocks away. There Critz, thoroughly unconscious now, was transferred to a small unmarked panel truck with a double rear door. While Critz lay on the floor of the van, an agent used a hypodermic needle and injected him with a massive dose of very pure heroin. The presence of heroin always squelched the autopsy results, at the family's insistence of course.

With Critz barely breathing, the van left the warehouse and drove to Whitcomb Street, not far from his apartment. The killing required three vehicles – the van, followed by a large and heavy Mercedes, and a trail car driven by a real Brit who would hang around and chat with the police. The trail car's primary purpose was to keep the traffic as far behind the Mercedes as possible.

On the third pass, with all three drivers talking to each other, and with two agents, including the fine-looking lady, hiding on the sidewalk and also listening, the rear doors of the van were shoved open, Critz fell onto the street, the Mercedes aimed for his head and got it with a sickening thump, then everyone disappeared but the Brit in the trail car. He slammed on his brakes, jumped out and ran to the poor drunk who'd just stumbled into the street and been run over, and looked around quickly for other witnesses.

There were none, but a taxi was approaching in the other lane. He flagged it down, and soon other traffic stopped. Before long, a crowd was gathering and the police arrived. The Brit in the trail car may have been the first on the scene, but he saw very little. He saw the man stumble between those two parked cars over there, into the street, and get hit by a large black car. Or maybe it was dark green. Not sure of the make or model. Never thought about looking at the license plates. No clue as to the description of the hit-and-run driver. He was too shocked by the sight of the drunk suddenly appearing at the edge of the street.

By the time the body of Bob Critz was loaded into an ambulance for the trip to the morgue, Greenlaw, the fine-looking lady, and two other members of the team were on a train leaving London and headed for Paris. They would scatter for a few weeks, then return to England, their home base.

Marco wanted breakfast primarily because he could smell it – ham and sausages on the grill somewhere deep in the main house – but Luigi was anxious to move on. 'There are other guests and everyone eats at the same table,' he explained as they hurriedly threw their bags in his car. 'Remember, you're leaving a trail, and the signora forgets nothing.'

They sped down the country lane in search of wider roads.

'Where are we going?' Marco asked.

'We'll see.'

'Stop playing games with me!' he growled and Luigi actually flinched. 'I'm a perfectly free man who could get out of this car anytime I want!'

'Yes, but –'

'Stop threatening me! Every time I ask a question you give me these vague threats about how I won't last twenty-four hours on my own. I want to know what's going on. Where are we headed? How long will we be there? How long will you be around? Give me some answers, Luigi, or I'll disappear.'

Luigi turned onto a four-lane and a sign said that Bologna was thirty kilometers ahead. He waited for the tension to ease a bit, then said, 'We're going to Bologna for a few days. Ermanno will meet us there. You will continue your lessons. You'll be placed in a safe house for several months. Then I'll disappear and you'll be on your own.'

'Thank you. Why was that so difficult?'

'The plan changes.'

'I knew Ermanno wasn't a student.'

'He is a student. He's also part of the plan.'

'Do you realize how ridiculous the plan is? Think about it, Luigi. Someone is spending all this time and money trying to teach me another language and another culture. Why not just put me back on the cargo plane and stash me in some place like New Zealand?'

'That's a great idea, Marco, but I'm not making those decisions.'

'Marco my ass. Every time I look in the mirror and say Marco I want to laugh.'

'This is not funny. Do you know Robert Critz?'

Marco paused for a moment. 'I met him a few times over the years. Never had much use for him. Just another political hack, like me, I guess.'

'Close friend of President Morgan, chief of staff, campaign director.'

'So?'

'He was killed last night in London. That makes five people who've died because of you – Jacy Hubbard, the three Pakistanis, now Critz. The killing hasn't stopped, Marco, nor will it. Please be patient with me. I'm only trying to protect you.'

Marco slammed his head into the headrest and closed his eyes. He could not begin to put the pieces together.

They made a quick exit and stopped for gas. Luigi returned to the car with two small cups of strong coffee. 'Coffee to go,' Marco said pleasantly. 'I figured such evils would be banned in Italy.'

'Fast food is creeping in. It's very sad.'

'Just blame the Americans. Everybody else does.'

Before long they were inching through the rush hour traffic on the outskirts of Bologna. Luigi was saying, 'Our best cars are made around here, you know. Ferraris, Lamborghinis, Maseratis, all the great sports cars.'

'Can I have one?'

'It's not in the budget, sorry.'

'What, exactly, is in the budget?'

'A very quiet, simple life.'

'That's what I thought.'

'Much better than your last one.'

Marco sipped his coffee and watched the traffic. 'Didn't you study here?'

'Yes. The university is a thousand years old.

One of the finest in the world. I'll show it to you later.'

They exited the main thoroughfare and wound through a gritty suburb. The streets became shorter and narrower and Luigi seemed to know the place well. They followed the signs pointing them toward the center of the city, and the university. Luigi suddenly swerved, jumped a curb, and wedged the Fiat into a slot barely wide enough for a motorcycle. 'Let's eat something,' he said, and, once they managed to squeeze themselves out of the car, they were on the sidewalk, walking quickly through the cool air.

Marco's next hiding place was a dingy hotel a few blocks from the outer edge of the old city. 'Budget cuts already,' he mumbled as he followed Luigi through the cramped lobby to the stairs.

'It's just for a few days,' Luigi said.

'Then what?' Marco was struggling with his bags up the narrow stairway. Luigi was carrying nothing. Thankfully the room was on the second floor, a rather small space with a tiny bed and curtains that hadn't been opened in days.

'I like Treviso better,' Marco said, staring at the walls.

Luigi yanked open the curtains. The sunlight helped only slightly. 'Not bad,' he said, without conviction.

'My prison cell was nicer.'

'You complain a lot.'

'With good reason.'

'Unpack. I'll meet you downstairs in ten minutes. Ermanno is waiting.'

Ermanno appeared as rattled as Marco by the sudden change in location. He was harried and unsettled, as if he'd chased them all night from Treviso. They walked with him a few blocks to a run-down apartment building. No elevators were evident, so they climbed four flights of stairs and entered a tiny, two-room flat that had even less furniture than the apartment in Treviso. Ermanno had obviously packed in a hurry and unpacked even faster.

'Your dump's worse than mine,' Marco said, taking it in.

Spread on a narrow table and waiting for action were the study materials they'd used the day before.

'I'll be back for lunch,' Luigi said, and quickly disappeared.

'Andiamo a studiare,' Ermanno announced. Let's study.

'I've already forgotten everything.'

'But we had a good session yesterday.'

'Can't we just go to a bar and drink? I'm really not in the mood for this.' But Ermanno had assumed his position across the table and was turning pages in his manual. Marco reluctantly settled into the seat across from him.

Lunch and dinner were forgettable. Both were quick snacks in fake trattorias, the Italian version of fast food. Luigi was in a foul mood and insisted, quite harshly at times, that they speak only Italian. Luigi spoke slowly, clearly, and repeated everything four times until Marco figured it out, then he moved along to the next phrase. It was impossible to enjoy food under such pressure.

At midnight, Marco was in his bed, in his cold room, wrapped tightly with the thin blanket, sipping orange juice he had ordered himself, and memorizing list after list of verbs and adjectives.

What could Robert Critz have possibly done to get himself killed by people who might also be looking for Joel Backman? The question itself was too bizarre to ask. He couldn't begin to contemplate an answer. He assumed Critz was present when the pardon was granted; ex-president Morgan was incapable of making such a decision by himself. Beyond that, though, it was impossible to see Critz involved at a higher level. He had proven for decades that he was nothing more than a good hatchet man. Very few people trusted him.

But if people were still dying, then it was urgent that he learn the verbs and adjectives scattered on his bed. Language meant survival, and movement. Luigi and Ermanno would soon disappear, and Marco Lazzeri would be left to fend for himself.

Chapter 12

Marco escaped his claustrophobic room, or 'apartment' as it was called, and went for a long walk at daybreak. The sidewalks were almost as damp as the frigid air. With a pocket map Luigi had given him, all in Italian of course, he made his way into the old city, and once past the ruins of the ancient walls at Porta San Donato, he headed west on Via Irnerio along the north edge of the university section of Bologna. The sidewalks were centuries old and covered with what appeared to be miles of arching porticoes.

Evidently street life began late in the university section. An occasional car passed, then a bike or two, but the foot traffic was still asleep. Luigi had explained that Bologna had a history of left-wing, communist leanings. It was a rich history, one that Luigi promised to explore with him.

Ahead Marco saw a small green neon sign that was indifferently advertising the Bar Fontana, and as he walked toward it he soon picked up the scent of strong coffee. The bar was wedged tightly into the corner of an ancient building – but then they were all ancient. The door opened reluctantly, and once inside Marco almost smiled at the aromas – coffee, cigarettes, pastries, breakfast on a grill in the rear. Then the fear hit, the usual apprehension of trying to order in an unknown language.

Bar Fontana was not for students, or for women. The crowd was his age, fifty and up, somewhat oddly dressed, with enough pipes and beards to identify it as a hangout for faculty. One or two glanced his way, but in the center of a university with 100,000 students it was difficult for anyone to draw attention.

Marco got the last small table near the back, and when he finally nestled into his spot with his back to the wall he was practically shoulder to shoulder with his new neighbors, both of whom were lost in their morning papers and neither of whom appeared to notice him. In one of Luigi's lectures on Italian culture he had explained the concept of space in Europe and how it differed significantly from that in the States. Space is shared in Europe, not protected. Tables are shared, the air evidently is shared because smoking bothers no one. Cars, houses, buses, apartments, cafés – so many important aspects of life are smaller, thus more cramped, thus more willingly shared. It's not offensive to go nose to nose with an acquaintance during routine conversation because no space is being violated.

Talk with your hands, hug, embrace, even kiss at times.

Even for a friendly people, such familiarity was difficult for Americans to understand.

And Marco was not yet prepared to yield too much space. He picked up the wrinkled menu on the table and quickly settled on the first thing he recognized. Just as the waiter stopped and glanced down at him he said, with all the ease he could possibly exude, 'Espresso, e un panino al formaggio.' A small cheese sandwich.

The waiter nodded his approval. Not a single person glanced over to check out his accented Italian. No newspapers dipped to see who he might be. No one cared. They heard accents all the time. As he placed the menu back on the table, Marco Lazzeri decided that he probably liked Bologna, even if it turned out to be a nest for Communists. With so many students and faculty coming and going, and from all over the world, foreigners were accepted as part of the culture. Perhaps it was rather cool to have an accent and dress differently. Perhaps it was okay to openly study the language.

One sign of a foreigner was that he noticed everything, his eyes darting around as if he knew he was trespassing into a new culture and didn't want to get caught. Marco would not be caught taking in the sights in the Bar Fontana. He removed a booklet of vocabulary sheets and tried mightily to ignore the people and scenes he wanted to watch. Verbs, verbs, verbs. Ermanno kept saying that to master Italian, or any Romance language for that matter, you had to know the verbs. The booklet had one thousand of the basic verbs, and Ermanno claimed that it was a good starting point.

As tedious as rote memorization was, Marco was finding an odd pleasure in it. He found it quite satisfying to zip through four pages – one hundred verbs, or nouns, or anything for that matter – and not miss a one. When he got one wrong, or missed a pronunciation, he went back to the beginning and punished himself by starting over. He had conquered three hundred verbs when his coffee and sandwich arrived. He took a sip, went back to work as if the food was much less important than the vocab, and was somewhere over four hundred when Rudolph arrived.

The chair on the other side of Marco's small round table was vacant, and this caught the attention of a short fat man, dressed entirely in faded black, with wild bunches of gray frizzy hair protruding from all parts of his head, some of it barely suppressed by a black beret that somehow managed to stay aboard. 'Buon giorno. È libera?' he asked politely, gesturing toward the chair. Marco wasn't sure what he said but it was obvious what he wanted. Then he caught the word 'libera' and assumed it meant 'free' or 'vacant'.

'Sì,' Marco managed with no accent, and the man removed a long black cape, draped it over the chair, then maneuvered himself into position. When he came to rest they were less than three feet apart. Space is different here, Marco kept telling himself. The man placed a copy of *L'Unità* on the table, making it rock back and forth. For an instant Marco was worried about his espresso. To avoid conversation, he buried himself even deeper into Ermanno's verbs.

'American?' his new friend said, in English with no foreign accent.

Marco lowered the booklet and looked into the glowing eyes not far away. 'Close. Canadian. How'd you know?'

He nodded at the booklet and said, 'English to Italian vocabulary. You don't look British, so I figure you're American.' Judging by his accent, he was probably not from the upper Midwest. Not from New York or New Jersey; not from Texas or the South, or Appalachia, or New Orleans. As vast sections of the country were eliminated, Marco was beginning to think of California. And he was beginning to get very nervous. The lying would soon start, and he hadn't practiced enough.

'And where are you from?' he asked.

'Last stop was Austin, Texas. That was thirty years ago. Name's Rudolph.'

'Good morning, Rudolph, a pleasure. I'm Marco.' They were in kindergarten where only first names were needed. 'You don't sound Texan.'

'Thank God for that,' he said with a pleasant

laugh, one that barely revealed his mouth. 'Originally from San Francisco.'

The waiter leaned in and Rudolph ordered black coffee, then something else in rapid Italian. The waiter had a follow-up, as did Rudolph, and Marco understood none of it.

'What brings you to Bologna?' Rudolph asked. He seemed anxious to chat; probably rare that he cornered a fellow North American in his favorite café.

Marco lowered his booklet and said, 'Just traveling around Italy for a year, seeing the sights, trying to pick up some of the language.'

Half of Rudolph's face was covered with an unkempt gray beard that began fairly high up the cheekbones and sprang in all directions. Most of his nose was visible, as was part of his mouth. For some odd reason, one that no one would ever understand because no one would ever dare ask such a ridiculous question, he had developed the habit of shaving a small round spot under his lower lip and comprising most of his upper chin. Other than that sacred ground, the wild frizzy whiskers were allowed to run free and apparently go unwashed. The top of his head was pretty much the same – acres of untouched bright gray brush sprouting from all around the beret.

Because so many of his features were masked, his eyes got all the attention. They were dark green and projected rays that, from under a set of thick sagging eyebrows, took in everything.

'How long in Bologna?' Rudolph asked.

'Got here yesterday. I have no schedule. And you, what brings you here?' Marco was anxious to keep the conversation away from himself.

The eyes danced and never blinked. 'I've been here for thirty years. I'm a professor at the university.'

Marco finally took a bite of his cheese sandwich, partly out of hunger, but more importantly to keep Rudolph talking.

'Where's your home?' he asked.

Following the script, Marco said, 'Toronto. Grandparents immigrated there from Milan. I have Italian blood but never learned the language.'

'The language is not hard,' Rudolph said, and his coffee arrived. He grabbed the small cup and thrust it deep into the beard. Evidently it found his mouth. He smacked his lips and leaned forward a bit as though he wanted to talk. 'You don't sound Canadian,' he said, and those eyes appeared to be laughing at him.

Marco was struggling under the labor of looking, acting, and sounding Italian. He'd had no time to even think about putting on Canadian airs. How, exactly, does one sound Canadian? He took another bite, a huge one, and through his food said, 'Can't help that. How did you get here from Austin?'

'A long story.'

Marco shrugged as if he had plenty of time.

'I was once a young professor at the University of Texas law school. When they found out I was

157

a Communist they began pressuring me to leave. I fought them. They fought back. I got louder, especially in the classroom. Communists didn't fare too well in Texas in the early seventies, doubt if much has changed. They denied me tenure, ran me out of town, so I came here to Bologna, the heart of Italian communism.'

'What do you teach here?'

'Jurisprudence. Law. Radical left-wing legal theories.'

A powdered brioche of some sort arrived and Rudolph ate half of it with the first bite. A few crumbs dropped from the depths of his beard.

'Still a Communist?' Marco asked.

'Of course. Always. Why would I change?'

'Seems to have run its course, don't you think? Not such a great idea after all. I mean, look at what a mess Russia is in because of Stalin and his legacy. And North Korea, they're starving there while the dictator builds nuclear warheads. Cuba is fifty years behind the rest of the world. The Sandinistas were voted out in Nicaragua. China is turning to free market capitalism because the old system broke down. It really doesn't work, does it?'

The brioche had lost its appeal; the green eyes were narrow. Marco could see a tirade coming, probably one laced with obscenities in both English and Italian. He glanced around quickly and realized that there was a very good chance the Communists had him outnumbered in the Bar Fontana.

158

And what had capitalism done for him?

Much to his credit, Rudolph smiled and shrugged and said with an air of nostalgia, 'Maybe so, but it sure was fun being a Communist thirty years ago, especially in Texas. Those were the days.'

Marco nodded at the newspaper and said, 'Ever read papers from home?'

'Home is here, my friend. I became an Italian citizen and haven't been back to the States in twenty years.'

Backman was relieved. He had not seen American newspapers since his release, but he assumed there had been coverage. Probably old photos as well. His past seemed safe from Rudolph.

Marco wondered if that was his future – Italian citizenship. If any at all. Fast-forward twenty years, and would he still be drifting through Italy, not exactly glancing over his shoulder but always thinking about it?

'You said "home,"' Rudolph interrupted. 'Is that the U.S. or Canada?'

Marco smiled and nodded to a far-off place. 'Over there, I guess.' A small mistake, but one that should not have been made. To quickly shift to another subject, he said, 'This is my first visit to Bologna. Didn't know it was the center of Italian communism.'

Rudolph lowered his cup and made a smacking sound with his partially concealed lips. Then with both hands he gently pawed his beard backward, much like an old cat slicking down his whiskers. 'Bologna is a lot of things, my friend,' he said, as if a lengthy lecture was starting. 'It's always been the center of free thought and intellectual activity in Italy, thus its first nickname, la dotta, which means the learned. Then it became the home of the political left and received its second nickname, la rossa, the red. And the Bolognesi have always been very serious about their food. They believe, and they're probably right, that this is the stomach of Italy. Thus, the third nickname of la grassa, the fat, an affectionate term because you won't see many overweight people here. Me, I was fat when I arrived.' He patted his stomach proudly with one hand while finishing off the brioche with the other.

A frightening question suddenly hit Marco: Was it possible that Rudolph was part of the static? Was he a teammate of Luigi and Ermanno and Stennett and whoever else was out there in the shadows working so hard to keep Joel Backman alive? Surely not. Surely he was what he said he was – a professor. An oddball, a misfit, an aging Communist who'd found a better life somewhere else.

The thought passed, but it was not forgotten. Marco finished his little sandwich and decided they'd talked enough. He suddenly had a train to catch for another day of sightseeing. He managed to extricate himself from the table and got a fond farewell from Rudolph. 'I'm here every morning,' he said. 'Come back when you can stay longer.'

'Grazie,' Marco said. 'Arrivederci.'

Outside the café, Via Irnerio was stirring to life as small delivery vans began their routes. Two of the drivers yelled at each other, probably friendly obscenities Marco would never understand. He hustled away from the café just in case old Rudolph thought of something else to ask him and came charging out. He turned down a side street, Via Capo di Lucca – he was learning that they were well marked and easy to find on his map – and zigzagged his way toward the center. He passed another cozy little café, then backtracked and ducked inside for a cappuccino.

No Communists bothered him there, no one seemed to even notice him. Marco and Joel Backman savored the moment – the delicious strong drink, the warm thick air, the quiet laughter of those doing the talking. Right now not a single person in the world knew exactly where he was, and it was indeed an exhilarating feeling.

At Marco's insistence, the morning sessions were beginning at eight, not thirty minutes later. Ermanno, the student, still needed long hours of hard sleep but he couldn't argue with his pupil's intensity. Marco arrived for each lesson with his vocabulary lists thoroughly memorized, his situational dialogues perfected, and his urgent desire to absorb the language barely under control. At one point he suggested they begin at seven.

The morning he met Rudolph, Marco studied intensely for two uninterrupted hours, then abruptly said, 'Vorrei vedere l'università.' I'd like to see the university.

'Quando?' Ermanno asked. When?

'Adesso. Andiamo a fare una passeggiata.' Now. Let's go for a walk.

'Penso che dobbiamo studiare.' I think we should study.

'Sì. Possiamo studiare a camminando.' We can study while we're walking.

Marco was already on his feet, grabbing his coat. They left the depressing building and headed in the general direction of the university.

'Questa via, come si chiama?' Ermanno asked. What's the name of this street?

'È Via Donati,' Marco answered without looking for a street sign.

They stopped in front of a small crowded shop and Ermanno asked, 'Che tipo di negozio è questo?' What kind of store is this?

'Una tabaccheria.' A tobacco store.

'Che cosa puoi comprare in questo negozio?' What can you buy here?

'Posso comprare molte cose. Giornali, riviste, francobolli, sigarette.' I can buy many things. Newspapers, magazines, stamps, cigarettes.

The session became a roving game of name that thing. Ermanno would point and say, 'Cosa è quello?' What's that? A bike, a policeman, a blue car, a city bus, a bench, a garbage can, a student, a telephone booth, a small dog, a café, a pastry shop. Except for a lamppost, Marco was quick with the Italian word for each. And the all-important verbs – walking, talking, seeing, studying, buying, thinking, chatting, breathing, eating, drinking, hurrying, driving – the list was endless and Marco had the proper translations at his disposal.

A few minutes after ten, and the university was finally coming to life. Ermanno explained that there was no central campus, no American-style quadrangle lined with trees and such. The Università degli Studi was found in dozens of handsome old buildings, some five hundred years old, most of them packed end to end along Via Zamboni, though over the centuries the school had grown and now covered an entire section of Bologna.

The Italian lesson was forgotten for a block or two as they were swept along in wave of students hustling to and from their classes. Marco caught himself looking for an old man with bright gray hair – his favorite Communist, his first real acquaintance since walking out of prison. He had already made up his mind to see Rudolph again.

At 22 Via Zamboni, Marco stopped and gazed at a sign between the door and a window: FACOLTÀ DI GIURISPRUDENZA.

'Is this the law school?' he asked.

'Sì.'

163

Rudolph was somewhere inside, no doubt spreading left-wing dissent among his impressionable students.

They ambled on, in no hurry as they continued to play name that thing and enjoy the energy of the street.

Chapter 13

The lezione-a-piedi – lesson on foot – continued the next day when Marco revolted after an hour of tedious grammar straight from the textbook and demanded to go for a walk.

'Ma, deve imparare la grammatica,' Ermanno insisted. You must learn grammar.

Marco was already putting on his coat. 'That's where you're wrong, Ermanno. I need real conversation, not sentence structure.'

'Sono io l'insegnante.' I am the teacher.

'Let's go. Andiamo. Bologna is waiting. The streets are filled with happy young people, the air is alive with the sounds of your language, all just waiting for me to absorb.' When Ermanno hesitated, Marco smiled at him and said, 'Please, my friend. I've been locked in a small cell about the size of this apartment for six years. You can't expect me to stay here. There's a vibrant city out there. Let's go explore it.'

Outside the air was clear and brisk, not a

cloud anywhere, a gorgeous winter day that drew every warm-blooded Bolognese into the streets for errands and long-winded chats with old friends. Pockets of intense conversation materialized as sleepy-eyed students greeted each other and housewives gathered to trade the gossip. Elderly gentlemen dressed in coats and ties shook hands and then all talked at once. Street merchants called out with their latest bargains.

But for Ermanno it was not a walk in the park. If his student wanted conversation, then he would certainly earn it. He pointed to a policeman and said to Marco, in Italian of course, 'Go to that policeman and ask directions for the Piazza Maggiore. Get them right, then repeat them to me.'

Marco walked very slowly, whispering some words, trying to recall others. Always start with a smile and the proper greeting. 'Buon giorno,' he said, almost holding his breath.

'Buon giorno,' answered the policeman.

'Mi può aiutare?' Can you help me?

'Certamente.' Certainly.

'Sono Canadese. Non parlo molto bene.' I'm Canadian. I don't speak Italian very well.

'Allora.' Okay. The policeman was still smiling, now quite anxious to help.

'Dov'è la Piazza Maggiore?'

The policeman turned and gazed into the distance, toward the central part of Bologna. He cleared his throat and Marco braced for the torrent of directions. Just a few feet away and listening to every sound was Ermanno.

With a beautifully slow cadence, he said in Italian, and pointing of course the way they all do, 'It's not too far away. Take this street, turn at the next right, that's Via Zamboni, follow it until you see the two towers. Turn on Via Rizzoli, and go for three blocks.'

Marco listened as hard as possible, then tried to repeat each phrase. The policeman patiently went through the exercise again. Marco thanked him, repeated as much as he could to himself, then unloaded it on Ermanno.

'Non c'è male,' he said. Not bad. The fun was just starting. As Marco was enjoying his little triumph, Ermanno was searching for the next unsuspecting tutor. He found him in an old man shuffling by on a cane and with a thick newspaper under his arm. 'Ask him where he bought the newspaper,' he instructed his student.

Marco took his time, followed the gentleman for a few steps, and when he thought he had the words together he said, 'Buon giorno, scusi.' The old man stopped and stared, and for a moment looked as though he might lift his cane and whack it across Marco's head. He did not offer the customary 'Buon giorno.'

'Dov'è ha comprato questo giornale?' Where did you buy this newspaper?

The old man looked at the newspaper as if it were contraband, then looked at Marco as if he'd cursed him. He jerked his head to the left and

167

said something like, 'Over there.' And his part of the conversation was over. As he shuffled away, Ermanno eased beside Marco and said in English, 'Not much for conversation, huh?'

'I guess not.'

They stepped inside a small café, where Marco ordered a simple espresso for himself. Ermanno could not be content with simple things; instead he wanted regular coffee with sugar but without cream, and a small cherry pastry, and he made Marco order everything and get it perfect. At their table, Ermanno laid out several euro notes of various denominations, along with the coins for fifty cents and one euro, and they practiced numbers and counting. He then decided he wanted another regular coffee, this time with no sugar but just a little cream. Marco took two euros and came back with the coffee. He counted the change.

After the brief break, they were back on the street, drifting along Via San Vitale, one of the main avenues of the university, with porticoes covering the sidewalks on both sides and thousands of students jostling to early classes. The street was crammed with bicycles, the preferred mode of getting around. Ermanno had been studying for three years in Bologna, so he said, though Marco believed little of what he heard from either his tutor or his handler.

'This is Piazza Verdi,' Ermanno said, nodding to a small plaza where a protest of some sort was stuttering to a start. A long-haired relic from the seventies was adjusting a microphone, no doubt prepping for a screeching denunciation of American misdeeds somewhere. His cohorts were trying to unravel a large, badly painted homemade banner with a slogan not even Ermanno could understand. But they were too early. The students were half asleep and more concerned with being late for class.

'What's their problem?' Marco asked as they walked by.

'I'm not sure. Something to do with the World Bank. There's always a demonstration here.'

They walked on, flowing with the young crowd, picking their way through the foot traffic, and headed generally to il centro.

Luigi met them for lunch at a restaurant called Testerino, near the university. With American taxpayers footing the bill, he ordered often and with no regard for price. Ermanno, the broke student, seemed ill at ease with such extravagance, but, being an Italian, he eventually warmed to the idea of a long lunch. It lasted for two hours and not a single word of English was spoken. The Italian was slow, methodical, and often repeated, but it never yielded to English. Marco found it difficult to enjoy a fine meal when his brain was working overtime to hear, grasp, digest, understand, and plot a response to the last phrase thrown at him. Often the last phrase had passed over his head with only a word or two being somewhat recognizable when the whole thing was suddenly chased by another.

And his two friends were not just chatting for the fun of it. If they caught the slightest hint that Marco was not following, that he was simply nodding so they would keep talking so he could eat a bite, then they stopped abruptly and said, 'Che cosa ho detto?' What did I say?

Marco would chew for a few seconds, buying time to think of something – in Italian dammit! – that might get him off the hook. He was learning to listen, though, to catch the key words. Both of his friends had repeatedly said that he would always understand much more than he could say.

The food saved him. Of particular importance was the distinction between tortellini (small pasta stuffed with pork) and tortelloni (larger pasta stuffed with ricotta cheese). The chef, upon realizing that Marco was a Canadian very curious about Bolognese cuisine, insisted on serving both dishes. As always, Luigi explained that both were exclusively the creations of the great chefs of Bologna.

Marco simply ate, trying his best to devour the delicious servings while avoiding the Italian language.

After two hours, Marco insisted on a break. He finished his second espresso and said goodbye. He left them in front of the restaurant and walked away, alone, his ears ringing and his head spinning from the workout.

He made a two-block loop off Via Rizzoli. Then he did it again to make sure no one was following. The long porticoed walkways were ideal for ducking and hiding. When they were thick with students again he crossed Piazza Verdi, where the World Bank protest had yielded to a fiery speech that, for a moment, made Marco quite happy he could not understand Italian. He stopped at 22 Via Zamboni and once again looked at the massive wooden door that led to the law school. He walked through it and tried his best to appear as if this was his turf. No directory was in sight, but a student bulletin board advertised apartments, books, companion-ship, almost everything, it seemed, including a summer studies program at Wake Forest Law School.

Through the hallway, the building yielded to an open courtyard where students were milling around, chatting on cell phones, smoking, waiting for classes.

A stairway to his left caught his attention. He climbed to the third floor, where he finally located a directory of sorts. He understood the word 'uffici', and followed a corridor past two classrooms until he found the faculty offices. Most had names, a few did not. The last belonged to Rudolph Viscovitch, so far the only non-Italian name in the building. Marco knocked and no one answered. He twisted the knob but the door was locked. He quickly removed from his coat pocket a sheet of paper he'd taken from the Albergo Campeol in Treviso and scribbled a note:

Dear Rudolph: I was wandering around the campus, stumbled upon your office and wanted to say hello. Maybe I'll catch you again at the Bar Fontana. Enjoyed our chat yesterday. Nice to hear English occasionally. Your Canadian friend, Marco Lazzeri

He slid it under the door and walked down the stairs behind a group of students. Back on Via Zamboni, he drifted along with no particular destination in mind. He stopped for a gelato, then slowly made his way back to his hotel. His dark little room was too cold for a nap. He promised himself again that he would complain to his handler. Lunch had cost more than three nights' worth of his room. Surely Luigi and those above him could spring for a nicer place.

He dragged himself back to Ermanno's cupboard-sized apartment for the afternoon session.

Luigi waited patiently at Bologna Centrale for the nonstop Eurostar from Milano. The train station was relatively quiet, the lull before the five o'clock rush hour. At 3:35, precisely on schedule, the sleek bullet blew in for a quick stop and Whitaker bounced off.

Since Whitaker never smiled, they barely said hello. After a cursory handshake was complete, they walked to Luigi's Fiat. 'How's our boy?' Whitaker asked as soon as he slammed the door.

'Doing fine,' Luigi said as he started the engine and drove away. 'He's studying hard. There's not much else for him to do.'

'And he's staying close?'

'Yes. He likes to walk around the city, but he's afraid to venture too far. Plus, he has no money.'

'Keep him broke. How's his Italian?'

'He's learning rapidly.' They were on the Via dell' Indipendenza, a wide avenue that was taking them directly south, into the center of the city. 'Very motivated.'

'Is he scared?'

'I think so.'

'He's smart, and he's a manipulator, Luigi, don't forget that. And because he's smart, he's also very frightened. He knows the danger.'

'I told him about Critz.'

'And?'

'He was bewildered.'

'Did it scare him?'

'Yes, I think so. Who got Critz?'

'I'm assuming we did, but you never know. Is the safe house ready?'

'Yes.'

'Good. Let's see Marco's apartment.'

Via Fondazza was a quiet residential street in the southeast section of the old city, a few blocks south of the university section. As in the rest of Bologna, the walkways on both sides of the street were covered with porticoes. Doors to the homes and apartments opened directly onto the sidewalks. Most had building directories on brass

173

plaques next to intercoms, but the one at 112 Via Fondazza did not. It was unmarked and had been for the three years it had been leased to a mysterious businessman in Milan who paid the rent but seldom used it. Whitaker had not seen it in more than a year; not that it was much of an attraction. It was a simple apartment of about six hundred square feet; four rooms with basic furnishings that cost 1,200 euros a month. It was a safe house, nothing more or less; one of three currently under his control in northern Italy.

There were two bedrooms, a tiny kitchen, and a living area with a sofa, a desk, two leather chairs, no television. Luigi pointed to the phone and they discussed, in near coded language, the bugging device that had been installed and could never be detected. There were two hidden mikes in each room, powerful little collectors that missed no human sound. There were also two microscopic cameras – one hidden in a crack of an old tile high above the den, and from there it offered a view of the front door. The other was hidden in a cheap light fixture hanging from a kitchen wall, with a clear view of the rear door.

They would not be watching his bedroom, and Luigi said he was relieved by that. If Marco managed to find a woman willing to visit him, they could catch her coming and going with the camera in the den, and that was certainly enough for Luigi. If he got really bored, he could hit a switch and listen for fun.

The safe house was bordered to the south by another apartment, with a thick stone wall separating the two. Luigi was staying there, hiding next door in a five-room flat slightly larger than Marco's. His rear door opened into a small garden that could not be seen from the safe house, thus concealing his movements. His kitchen had been converted into a high-tech snooping room where he could switch on a camera anytime he wanted and take a look at what was happening next door.

'Will they study here?' Whitaker asked.

'Yes. I think it's secure enough. Plus I can monitor things.'

Whitaker walked through each room again. When he'd seen enough he said, 'Everything's set up next door?'

'Everything. I've spent the last two nights there. We're ready.'

'How soon can you move him?'

'This afternoon.'

'Very well. Let's go see the boy.'

They walked north along Via Fondazza until it came to an end, then northwest along a wider avenue, Strada Maggiore. The rendezvous point was a small café called Lestre's. Luigi found a newspaper and sat alone at a table. Whitaker found another newspaper and sat nearby, each man ignoring the other. At precisely four-thirty, Ermanno and his student stopped by for a quick espresso with Luigi.

When the greetings were exchanged and the

coats removed, Luigi asked, 'Are you tired of Italian, Marco?'

'I'm sick of it,' Marco replied with a smile.

'Good. Let's talk English.'

'God bless you,' Marco said.

Whitaker sat five feet away, partially hidden behind a newspaper, smoking a cigarette as if he had no interest in anyone around him. He of course knew of Ermanno, but had never actually seen him. Marco was another story.

Whitaker had been in Washington for a stint at Langley a dozen or so years earlier, back when everyone knew the broker. He remembered Joel Backman as a political force who spent almost as much time cultivating his oversized image as he did representing his important clients. He'd been the epitome of money and power, the perfect fat cat who could bully and cajole and throw around enough money to get whatever he wanted.

Amazing what six years in prison could do. He was very thin now, and looking quite European behind the Armani eyewear. He had the beginnings of a salt-and-pepper goatee. Whitaker was certain that virtually no one from back home could walk into Lestre's at that moment and identify Joel Backman.

Marco caught the man five feet away glancing over one time too often but thought nothing of it. They were chatting in English, and perhaps few people did so, at Lestre's anyway. Nearer the university, one could hear several languages in every coffee shop.

Ermanno excused himself after one espresso. A few minutes later Whitaker left too. He walked a few blocks and found an Internet café, one he'd used before. He plugged in his laptop, got online, and typed a message to Julia Javier at Langley:

Fondazza flat is ready to go, should move in tonight. Laid eyes on our man, having a coffee with our friends. Would not have known him otherwise. Adjusting nicely to a new life. All is in order here; no problems whatsoever.

After dark, the Fiat stopped in the middle of Via Fondazza, and its contents were quickly unloaded. Marco packed light because he owned practically nothing. Two bags of clothes and some Italian study books, and he was completely mobile. When he stepped into his new apartment, the first thing he noticed was that it was sufficiently heated. 'This is more like it,' he said to Luigi.

'I'll move the car. Have a look around.'

He looked around, counted four rooms with nice furnishings, nothing extravagant but a huge step up from the last place. Life was improving – ten days ago he'd been in prison.

Luigi returned in a rush. 'What do you think?'

'I'll keep it. Thank you.'

'Don't mention it.'

'And thank the folks in Washington too.'

'Did you see the kitchen?' Luigi asked, flipping on a light switch.

'Yes, it's perfect. How long do I stay here, Luigi?'

'I don't make those decisions. You know that.'

'I know.'

They were back in the den. 'A couple of things,' Luigi said. 'First, Ermanno will come here each day to study. Eight until eleven, then two until five or whenever you wish to stop.'

'Wonderful. Please get the boy a new flat, would you? His dump is an embarrassment to the American taxpayers.'

'Second, this is a very quiet street, mainly apartments. Come and go quickly, don't chat with your neighbors, don't make any friends. Remember, Marco, you are leaving a trail. Make it wide enough and someone will find you.'

'I heard you the first ten times.'

'Then hear me again.'

'Relax, Luigi. My neighbors will never see me, I promise. I like it here. It's much nicer than my prison cell.'

Chapter 14

The memorial service for Robert Critz was held in a country club–like mausoleum in a ritzy suburb of Philadelphia, the city of his birth but a place he'd avoided for at least the past thirty years. He died without a will and without a thought as to his final arrangements, leaving poor Mrs. Critz with the burden of not only getting him home from London but then deciding how to properly dispose of him. A son pressed the idea of cremation and a rather neat interment in a marble vault, one shielded from the weather. By that point Mrs. Critz would have agreed to almost any plan. Flying seven hours across the Atlantic (in coach) with her husband's remains somewhere below her, in a rather stark air-transport box made especially for dead humans, had nearly pushed her over the edge. And then there had been the chaos at the airport when no one was there to greet her and take charge. What a mess!

The service was by invitation only, a condition laid down by former president Arthur Morgan, who, after only two weeks on Barbados, was quite unwilling to return and be seen by anyone. If he was truly saddened by the death of his lifelong friend, he didn't show it. He'd haggled over the details of the service with the Critz family until he was almost asked to stay away. The date had been moved because of Morgan. The order of service didn't suit him. He reluctantly agreed to deliver a eulogy, but only if it could be very brief. Truth was, he'd never liked Mrs. Critz and she'd never liked him.

To the small circle of friends and family, it seemed implausible that Robert Critz would get so drunk in a London pub that he would stagger into a busy street and fall in front of a car. When the autopsy revealed a significant level of heroin, Mrs. Critz had become so distraught that she insisted that the report be sealed and buried. She had refused to tell even her children about the narcotic. She was absolutely certain her husband had never touched an illicit drug – he drank too much but few people knew it – but she nonetheless was determined to protect his good name.

The London police had readily agreed to lock away the autopsy findings and close the case. They had their questions all right, but they had many other cases to keep them busy, and they also had a widow who couldn't wait to get home and put it all behind her.

The service began at two on a Thursday afternoon – the time also dictated by Morgan so that the private jet could fly nonstop from Barbados to Philly International – and lasted for an hour. Eighty-two people had been invited, and fifty-one showed up, a fair majority of them more curious to see President Morgan than to say goodbye to ol' Critz. A semi-Protestant minister of some variety presided. Critz had not seen the inside of a church in forty years, except for weddings and funerals. The minister was faced with the difficult task of bringing to life the memory of a man he'd never met, and though he tried gamely he failed completely. He read from the book of Psalms. He offered a generic prayer that would've fit a deacon or a serial killer. He offered soothing words to the family, but, again, they were total strangers to him.

Rather than a heart-warming send-off, the service was as cold as the gray marble walls of the faux chapel. Morgan, with a bronze tan too ridiculous for February, attempted to humor the small crowd with some anecdotes about his old pal, but he came off as a man going through the motions and wanting desperately to get back on the jet.

Hours in the Caribbean sun had convinced Morgan that the blame for his disastrous reelection campaign could be placed squarely at the feet of Robert Critz. He'd told no one of this conclusion; there really was no one to confide in since the beach mansion was deserted except for him and the staff of natives. But he'd already begun to carry a grudge, to question the friendship.

He didn't linger when the service finally ran out of gas and came to an end. He offered obligatory hugs to Mrs. Critz and her children, spoke briefly with some old friends, promised to see them in a few weeks, then rushed away with his mandatory Secret Service escort. News cameras had been stationed along a fence outside the grounds, but they caught no glimpse of the former president. He was ducking in the rear of one of two black vans. Five hours later he was by the pool watching another Caribbean sunset.

Though the memorial drew a small crowd, it nonetheless was being keenly observed by others. While it was actually in progress, Teddy Maynard had a list of all fifty-one people in attendance. There was no one suspicious. No name raised an eyebrow.

The killing was clean. The autopsy was buried, thanks in part to Mrs. Critz, and thanks also in part to strings pulled at levels much higher than the London police. The body was now ashes and the world would quickly forget about Robert Critz. His idiotic foray into the Backman disappearance had ended with no damage to the plan.

The FBI had tried, and failed, to mount a hidden camera inside the chapel. The owner had balked, then refused to bend despite enormous pressure. He did allow hidden cameras outside, and these provided close shots of all the mourners as they entered and left. The live feeds were edited, the list of fifty-one quickly compiled, and an hour after the service ended the director was given a briefing.

The day before the death of Robert Critz, the FBI received some startling information. It was completely unexpected, unsolicited, and delivered by a desperate corporate crook staring at forty years in a federal prison. He'd been the manager of a large mutual fund who had been caught skimming fees; just another Wall Street scandal involving only a few billion bucks. But his mutual fund was owned by an international banking cabal, and over the years the crook had worked his way into the inner core of the organization. The fund was so profitable, thanks in no small measure to his talent for skimming, that the profits could not be ignored. He was voted onto the board of directors and given a luxury condo in Bermuda, the corporate head-quarters for his very secretive company.

In his desperation to avoid spending the rest of his life in prison, he became willing to share secrets. Banking secrets. Offshore dirt. He claimed he could prove that former president Morgan, during his last day in office, had sold at least one pardon for $3 million. The money had been wired from a bank on Grand Cayman to a bank in Singapore, both banks being secretly controlled by the cabal he'd just left. The money was still hiding in Singapore, in an account opened by a shell corporation that was really owned by an old crony of Morgan's. The money, according to the snitch, was intended for Morgan's use.

When the wire transfers and the accounts were confirmed by the FBI, a deal was suddenly put on the table. The crook was now facing only two years of light house arrest. Cash for a presidential pardon was such a sensational crime that it became a high priority at the Hoover Building.

The informant was unable to identify whose money had left Grand Cayman, but it seemed quite obvious to the FBI that only two of the people pardoned by Morgan had the potential of paying such a bribe. The first and likeliest was Duke Mongo, the geriatric billionaire who held the record for the most dollars illegally hidden from the IRS, at least by an individual. The corporate category was still open for debate. However, the informant felt strongly that Mongo was not involved because he had a long, ugly history with the banks in question. He preferred the Swiss, and this was verified by the FBI.

The second suspect was, of course, Joel Backman. Such a bribe would not be unexpected from an operator like Backman. And while the FBI had believed for many years that he had not hidden a fortune, there had always been doubt. When he was the broker he had relationships with banks in both Switzerland and the Caribbean. He had a web of shadowy friends, contacts in important places. Bribes, payoffs, campaign contributions, lobbying fees – it was all familiar turf for the broker.

The director of the FBI was an embattled soul named Anthony Price. Three years earlier he had been appointed by President Morgan, who then tried to fire him six months later. Price begged for more time and got it, but the two fought constantly. For some reason he could never quite remember, Price had also decided to prove his manhood by crossing swords with Teddy Maynard. Teddy hadn't lost many battles in the CIA's secret war with the FBI, and he certainly wasn't frightened by Anthony Price, the latest in a long line of lame ducks.

But Teddy didn't know about the cash-for-pardon conspiracy that now consumed the director of the FBI. The new President had vowed to get rid of Anthony Price and revamp his agency. He'd also promised to finally put Maynard out to pasture, but such threats had been heard many times in Washington.

Price suddenly had a beautiful opportunity to secure his job, and possibly eliminate Maynard at the same time. He went to the White House and briefed the national security advisor, who'd been confirmed the day before, on the suspicious account in Singapore. He strongly implicated former president Morgan in the scheme. He argued that Joel Backman should be located and hauled back to the United States for questioning and possible indictment. If proven to be true, it would be an earthshaking scandal, unique and truly historic.

The national security advisor listened intently. After the briefing, he walked directly to the office of the vice president, cleared out the staffers, locked the door, and unloaded everything he'd just heard. Together, they told the President.

As usual, there was no love lost between the new man in the Oval Office and his predecessor. Their campaign had been loaded with the same mean-spiritedness and dirty tricks that have become standard behavior in American politics. Even after a landslide of historic proportions and the thrill of reaching the White House, the new President was unwilling to rise above the mud. He adored the idea of once again humiliating Arthur Morgan. He could see himself, after a sensational trial and conviction, stepping in at the last minute with a pardon of his own to salvage the image of the presidency.

What a moment!

At six the following morning, the vice president was driven in his usual armed caravan to the CIA headquarters at Langley. Director Maynard had been summoned to the White House, but, suspecting some ploy, had begged off, claiming he was suffering from vertigo and confined to his office by his doctors. He often slept and ate there, especially when his vertigo was in high gear and kept him dizzy. Vertigo was one of his many handy ailments.

The meeting was brief. Teddy was sitting at

the end of his long conference table, in his wheelchair, wrapped tightly in blankets, with Hoby at his side. The vice president entered with only one aide, and after some awkward chitchat about the new administration and such, he said, 'Mr. Maynard, I'm here on behalf of the President.'

'Of course you are,' Teddy said with a very tight smile. He was expecting to be fired; finally, after eighteen years and numerous threats, this was it. Finally, a president with the stones to replace Teddy Maynard. He had prepped Hoby for the moment. As they waited for the vice president, Teddy had laid out his fears.

Hoby was scribbling on his customary legal pad, waiting to write the words he'd been dreading for many years: Mr. Maynard, the President requests your resignation.

Instead, the vice president said something completely unexpected. 'Mr. Maynard, the President wants to know about Joel Backman.'

Nothing made Teddy Maynard flinch. 'What about him?' he said without hesitation.

'He wants to know where he is and how long it will take to bring him home.'

'Why?'

'I can't say.'

'Then neither can I.'

'It's very important to the President.'

'I appreciate that. But Mr. Backman is very important to our operations right now.'

The vice president blinked first. He glanced at

his aide, who was consumed with his own note-taking and completely useless. They would not under any circumstances tell the CIA about the wire transfers and the bribes for pardons. Teddy would figure out a way to use that information to his advantage. He would steal their little nugget and survive yet another day. No sir, Teddy would either play ball with them or finally get himself fired.

The vice president inched forward on his elbows and said, 'The President is not going to compromise on this, Mr. Maynard. He will have this information, and he'll have it very soon. Otherwise, he will ask for your resignation.'

'He won't get it.'

'Need I remind you that you serve at his pleasure?'

'You need not.'

'Very well. The lines are clear. You come to the White House with the Backman file and discuss it with us at length, or the CIA will soon have a new director.'

'Such bluntness is rare among your breed, sir, with all due respect.'

'I'll take that as a compliment.'

The meeting was over.

Leaking like an old dike, the Hoover Building practically sprayed gossip onto the streets of Washington. And there to collect it was, among many others, Dan Sandberg of *The Washington Post*. His sources, though, were far better than those of the average investigative journalist, and it wasn't long before he picked up the scent of the pardon scandal. He worked an old mole in the new White House and got a partial confirmation. The outline of the story began to take shape, but Sandberg knew the hard details would be virtually impossible to confirm. He stood no chance of seeing the wire-transfer records.

But if it happened to be true – a sitting president selling pardons for some serious retirement cash – Sandberg could not imagine a bigger story. A former president indicted, put on trial, maybe convicted and sent to jail. It was unthinkable.

He was at his landfill of a desk when the call came from London. It was an old friend, another hard-charging reporter who wrote for *The Guardian*. They talked a few minutes about the new administration, which was the official topic in Washington. It was, after all, early February with heavy snow on the ground and Congress mired in its annual committee work. Life was relatively slow and there was little else to talk about.

'Anything on the death of Bob Critz?' his friend asked.

'No, just a funeral yesterday,' Sandberg replied. 'Why?'

'A few questions about how the poor chap went down, you know. That, and we can't get near the autopsy.'

'What kind of questions? I thought it was open-and-shut.'

'Maybe, but it got shut really fast. Nothing concrete, mind you, just fishing to see if there's anything amiss over there.'

'I'll make some calls,' Sandberg said, already very suspicious.

'Do that. Let's talk in a day or so.'

Sandberg hung up and stared at his blank computer monitor. Critz would certainly have been present when the last-minute pardons were granted by Morgan. Given their paranoia, there was a good chance that only Critz was in the Oval Office with Morgan when the decisions were made and the paperwork signed.

Perhaps Critz knew too much.

Three hours later, Sandberg left Dulles for London.

Chapter 15

Long before dawn, Marco once again awoke in a strange bed in a strange place, and for a long time worked hard gathering his thoughts – recalling his movements, analyzing his bizarre situation, planning the day ahead, trying to forget his past while trying to predict what might happen in the next twelve hours. Sleep was fitful at best. He had dozed for a few hours; it felt like four or five but he couldn't be sure because his rather warm little room was completely dark. He removed the earphones; as usual, he'd fallen asleep sometime after midnight with happy Italian dialogue ringing in his ears.

He was thankful for the heat. They'd frozen him at Rudley and his last hotel stop had been just as cold. The new apartment had thick walls and windows and a heating system that worked overtime. When he decided the day was properly organized, he slowly placed his feet on the very warm tile floor and again thanked Luigi for the change of residence.

How long he might stay here was uncertain, like most of the future they'd planned for him. He switched on the light and checked his watch – almost five. In the bathroom he switched on another light and studied himself in the mirror. The growth under his nose and along the sides of his mouth and covering his chin was coming in quite a bit grayer than he had hoped. In fact, after a week of cultivation, it was now obvious that his goatee would be at least 90 percent gray, with just a few lonely specks of dark brown thrown in. What the hell. He was fifty-two years old. It was part of the disguise and looked quite distinctive. With the thin face, hollow cheeks, short haircut, and little funky rectangular designer eyeglass frames, he could easily pass for Marco Lazzeri on any street in Bologna. Or Milan or Florence or all the other places he wanted to visit.

An hour later he stepped outside, under the cold, silent porticoes built by laborers who'd been dead for three hundred years. The wind was sharp and biting, and once again he reminded himself to complain to his handler about the lack of proper winter clothing. Marco didn't read papers and didn't watch television and thus had no idea about weather forecasts. But it was certainly getting colder.

He hustled along under the low porticoes of Via Fondazza, headed toward the university, the only person moving about. He refused to use the map tucked away in his pocket. If he got lost he might pull it out and concede a momentary defeat, but he was determined to learn the city by walking and observing. Thirty minutes later, with the sun finally showing some life, he emerged onto Via Irnerio on the northern edge of the university section. Two blocks east and he saw the pale green sign for Bar Fontana. Through the front window he saw a shock of gray hair. Rudolph was already there.

Out of habit, Marco waited for a moment. He glanced down Via Irnerio, from the direction he'd just come, waiting for someone to sneak out of the shadows like a silent bloodhound. When no one appeared, he went inside.

'My friend Marco,' Rudolph said with a smile as they exchanged greetings. 'Please sit.'

The café was half full, with the same academic types buried in their morning papers, lost in their own worlds. Marco ordered a cappuccino while Rudolph refilled his meerschaum pipe. A pleasant aroma engulfed their little corner of the place.

'Got your note the other day,' Rudolph was saying as he shot a cloud of pipe smoke across the table. 'Sorry I missed you. So where have you been?'

Marco had been nowhere, but as the laid-back Canadian tourist with Italian roots he had put together a mock itinerary. 'A few days in Florence,' he said.

'Ah, what a beautiful city.'

They talked about Florence for a while, with Marco rambling on about the sites and art and history of a place he knew only from a cheap guidebook Ermanno had loaned him. It was in Italian, of course, which meant he'd labored hours with a dictionary translating it into something he could kick back and forth with Rudolph as if he'd spent weeks there.

The tables grew crowded and the latecomers packed around the bar. Luigi had explained to him early on that in Europe when you get a table, it's yours for the day. No one is rushed out the door so someone can be seated. A cup of coffee, a newspaper, something to smoke, and it doesn't matter how long you hold a table while others come and go.

They ordered another round and Rudolph repacked his pipe. For the first time Marco noticed tobacco stains on the wild whiskers closest to his mouth. On the table were three morning newspapers, all Italian.

'Is there a good English newspaper here in Bologna?' Marco asked.

'Why do you ask?'

'Oh, I don't know. Sometimes I'd like to know what's happening across the ocean.'

'I'll pick up the *Herald Tribune* occasionally. It makes me so happy that I live here, away from all the crime and traffic and pollution and politicians and scandals. U.S. society is so rotten. And the government is the height of hypocrisy – the world's brightest democracy. Hah! Congress is bought and paid for by the rich.'

When he looked as though he wanted to spit, Rudolph suddenly sucked on his pipe and began grinding away on the stem. Marco held his breath, waiting for another venomous assault on the United States. A moment passed; they both sipped coffee.

'I hate the U.S. government,' Rudolph grumbled bitterly.

Attaboy, thought Marco. 'What about the Canadian?' he asked.

'I give you higher marks. Slightly higher.'

Marco pretended to be relieved and decided to change the subject. He said he was thinking of going to Venice next. Of course, Rudolph had been there many times and had lots of advice. Marco actually took notes, as if he couldn't wait to hop a train. And then there was Milano, though Rudolph wasn't too keen on it because of all the 'right-wing fascists' lurking there. 'It was Mussolini's center of power, you know,' he said, leaning in low as if the other Communists in Bar Fontana might erupt in violence at the very mention of the little dictator's name.

When it became apparent that Rudolph was willing to sit and talk through most of the morning, Marco began his exit. They agreed to meet at the same place, same time, the following Monday.

A light snow had begun, enough to leave tracks

for the delivery vans on Via Irnerio. As Marco left the warm café behind, he once again marveled at the foresight of Bologna's ancient city planners who designed some twenty miles of covered sidewalks in the old town. He went a few blocks farther east and turned south on Via dell' Indipendenza, a wide elegant avenue built in the 1870s so the higher classes who lived in the center would have an easy walk to the train station north of town. When he crossed Via Marsala he stepped in a pile of shoveled snow and flinched as the frozen mush soaked his right foot.

He cursed Luigi for his inadequate wardrobe – if it was going to snow then common sense would dictate that a person needed some boots. This led to a lengthy internal tirade about the lack of funding Marco felt he was receiving from whoever in hell was in charge of his current cover. They'd dumped him in Bologna, Italy, and they were obviously spending a fair amount on language lessons and safe houses and personnel and certainly food to keep him alive. In his opinion, they were wasting valuable time and money. The better plan would be to sneak him into London or Sydney where there were lots of Americans and everyone spoke English. He could blend in much easier.

The man himself strode alongside him. 'Buon giorno,' Luigi said.

Marco stopped, smiled, offered a handshake and said, 'Well, buon giorno, Luigi. Are you following me again?'

'No. I was out for a walk, saw you pass on the other side of the street. I love the snow, Marco. How about you?'

They were walking again, at a leisurely pace. Marco wanted to believe his friend, but he doubted if their meeting was an accident. 'It's okay. It's much prettier here in Bologna than in Washington, D.C., during rush hour traffic. What, exactly, do you do all day long, Luigi? Mind if I ask?'

'Not at all. You can ask all you want.'

'That's what I figured. Look, I have two complaints. Actually three.'

'No surprise. Have you had coffee?'

'Yes, but I'll take some more.'

Luigi nodded to a small corner café just ahead. They stepped inside and found all the tables taken, so they stood along the crowded bar and sipped espresso. 'What's the first complaint?' Luigi said in a low voice.

Marco moved closer, they were practically nose to nose. 'The first two complaints are closely related. First, it's the money. I don't want a lot, but I would like to have some sort of stipend. No one likes to be broke, Luigi. I'd feel better if I had a little cash in my pocket and knew I didn't have to hoard it.'

'How much?'

'Oh, I don't know. I haven't negotiated an allowance in a long time. What about a hundred euros a week for starters. That way I can buy newspapers, books, magazines, food – you know, just the basics. Uncle Sam's paying my rent and I'm very grateful. Come to think of it, he's been paying my rent for the past six years.'

'You could still be in prison, you know.'

'Oh, thank you, Luigi. I hadn't thought of that.'

'I'm sorry, that was unkind on my –'

'Listen, Luigi, I'm lucky to be here, okay. But, at the same time, I am now a fully pardoned citizen of some country, not sure which one, but I have the right to be treated with a little dignity. I don't like being broke, and I don't like begging for money. I want the promise of a hundred euros a week.'

'I'll see what I can do.'

'Thank you.'

'The second complaint?'

'I would like some money so I can buy some clothes. Right now my feet are freezing because it's snowing outside and I don't have proper footwear. I'd also like a heavier coat, perhaps a couple of sweaters.'

'I'll get them.'

'No, I want to buy them, Luigi. Get me the cash and I'll do my own shopping. It's not asking too much.'

'I'll try.'

They backed away a few inches and each took a sip. 'The third complaint?' Luigi said.

'It's Ermanno. He's losing interest very fast. We spend six hours a day together and he's getting bored with the whole thing.'

Luigi rolled his eyes in frustration. 'I can't just snap my fingers and find another language teacher, Marco.'

'You teach me. I like you, Luigi, we have good times together. You know Ermanno is dull. He's young and wants to be in school. But you would be a great teacher.'

'I am not a teacher.'

'Then please find someone else. Ermanno doesn't want to do it. I'm afraid I'm not making much progress.'

Luigi looked away and watched two elderly gentlemen enter and shuffle by. 'I think he's leaving anyway,' he said. 'Like you said, he really wants to go back to school.'

'How long will my lessons last?'

Luigi shook his head as if he had no idea. 'That's not my decision.'

'I have a fourth complaint.'

'Five, six, seven. Let's hear them all, then maybe we could go a week with no complaints.'

'You've heard it before, Luigi. It's sort of my standing objection.'

'Is that a lawyer thing?'

'You've watched too much American television. I really want to be transferred to London. There are ten million people there, they all speak English. I won't waste ten hours a day trying to learn a language. Don't get me wrong, Luigi, I love Italian. The more I study, the more beautiful it becomes. But, come on, if you're going to hide me, then stash me someplace where I can survive.'

'I've already passed this along, Marco. I'm not making these decisions.'

'I know, I know. Just keep the pressure on, please.'

'Let's go.'

The snow was heavier as they left the café and resumed their walk under the covered sidewalk. Smartly dressed businessmen hustled by them on the way to work. The early shoppers were out – mainly housewives headed for the market. The street itself was busy as small cars and scooters dodged the city buses and tried to avoid the accumulating slush.

'How often does it snow here?' Marco asked.

'A few times each winter. Not much, and we have these lovely porticoes to keep us dry.'

'Good call.'

'Some date back a thousand years. We have more than any other city in the world, did you know that?'

'No. I have very little to read, Luigi. If I had some money then I could buy books, then I could read and learn such things.'

'I'll have the money at lunch.'

'And where is lunch?'

'Ristorante Cesarina, Via San Stefano, one o'clock?'

'How can I refuse?'

Luigi was sitting with a woman at a table near the front of the restaurant when Marco entered, five minutes early. A serious conversation had just been interrupted. The woman stood, reluctantly, and offered a limp hand and a somber face as Luigi introduced her as Signora Francesca Ferro. She was attractive, in her mid-forties, perhaps a bit too old for Luigi, who tended to gawk at the university girls. She radiated an air of sophisticated irritation. Marco wanted to say: Excuse me, but I was invited here for lunch.

As they settled into their seats Marco noticed what was left of two fully smoked cigarettes in the ashtray. Luigi's water glass was almost completely empty. The two had been sitting there for at least twenty minutes. In very deliberate Italian, Luigi said to Marco, 'Signora Ferro is a language teacher and a local guide.' Pause, to which Marco offered a weak 'Sì.'

He glanced at the signora and smiled, to which she responded with a forced smile of her own. She appeared to be bored with him already.

Luigi continued in Italian. 'She is your new Italian teacher. Ermanno will teach you in the mornings, and Signora Ferro in the afternoons.' Marco understood all of it. He managed a fake smile in her direction and said, 'Va bene.' That's good.

'Ermanno wants to resume his studies at the university next week,' Luigi said.

'I thought so,' Marco said in English.

Francesca fired up another cigarette and crunched her full red lips around it. She exhaled a huge cloud of smoke and said, 'So, how is your

Italian?' It was a rich, almost husky voice, one no doubt enriched by years of smoking. Her English was slow, very refined, and without an accent.

'Terrible,' Marco said.

'He's doing fine,' Luigi said. The waiter delivered a bottle of mineral water and handed over three menus. La signora disappeared behind hers. Marco followed her lead. A long silent spell followed as they contemplated food and ignored each other.

When the menus finally came down she said to Marco, 'I'd like to hear you order in Italian.'

'No problem,' he said. He'd found some things he could pronounce without drawing laughter. The waiter appeared with his pen and Marco said, 'Sì, allora, vorrei un'insalata di pomodori, e una mezza porzione di lasagna.' Yes, okay, I'd like a salad with tomatoes and a half portion of lasagna. Once again he was very thankful for transatlantic goodies such as spaghetti, lasagna, ravioli, and pizza.

'Non c'è male,' she said. Not bad.

She and Luigi stopped smoking when the salads arrived. Eating gave them a break in the awkward conversation. No wine was ordered, though much was needed.

His past, her present, and Luigi's shadowy occupation were all off-limits, so they bobbed and weaved through the meal with light talk about the weather, almost all of it mercifully in English.

When the espressos were finished Luigi

grabbed the check and they hurried from the restaurant. In the process, and while Francesca wasn't looking, he slid an envelope to Marco and whispered, 'Here are some euros.'

'Grazie.'

The snow was gone, the sun was up and bright. Luigi left them at the Piazza Maggiore and vanished, as only he could do. They walked in silence for a while, until she said, 'Che cosa vorrebbe vedere?' What would you like to see?

Marco had yet to step inside the main cathedral, the Basilica di San Petronio. They walked to its sweeping front steps and stopped. 'It's both beautiful and sad,' she said in English, with the first hint of a British accent. 'It was conceived by the city council as a civic temple, not a cathedral, in direct opposition to the pope in Rome. The original design was for it to be even larger than Saint Peter's Cathedral, but along the way the plans fell short. Rome opposed it, and diverted money elsewhere, some of which went to the founding of the university.'

'When was it built?' Marco asked.

'Say that in Italian,' she instructed.

'I can't.'

'Then listen: 'Quando è stata costruita?' Repeat that for me.'

Marco repeated it four times before she was satisfied.

'I don't believe in books or tapes or such things,' she said as they continued to gaze upward at the vast cathedral. 'I believe in conversation, and more conversation. To learn to speak the language, then you have to speak it, over and over and over, just like when you were a child.'

'Where did you learn English?' he asked.

'I can't answer that. I've been instructed to say nothing about my past. And yours too.'

For a split second, Marco came very close to turning around and walking away. He was sick of people who couldn't talk to him, who dodged his questions, who acted as if the whole world was filled with spies. He was sick of the games.

He was a free man, he kept telling himself, completely able to come and go and make whatever decision he felt like. If he got sick of Luigi and Ermanno and now Signora Ferro, then he could tell the whole bunch, in Italian, to choke on a panino.

'It was begun in 1390, and things went smoothly for the first hundred years or so,' she said. The bottom third of the façade was a handsome pink marble; the upper two-thirds was an ugly brown brick that hadn't been layered with the marble. 'Then it fell on hard times. Obviously, the outside was never completed.'

'It's not particularly pretty.'

'No, but it's quite intriguing. Would you like to see the inside?'

What else was he supposed to do for the next three hours? 'Certamente,' he said.

They climbed the steps and stopped at the front door. She looked at a sign and said, 'Mi dica.' Tell me. 'What time does the church close?'

Marco frowned hard, rehearsed some words, and said, 'La chiesa chiude alle sei.' The church closes at six.

'Ripeta.'

He repeated it three times before she allowed him to stop, and they stepped inside. 'It's named in honor of Petronio, the patron saint of Bologna,' she said softly. The central floor of the cathedral was big enough for a hockey match with large crowds on both sides. 'It's huge,' Marco said, in awe.

'Yes, and this is about one-fourth of the original design. Again, the pope got worried and applied some pressure. It cost a tremendous amount of public money, and eventually the people got tired of building.'

'It's still very impressive.' Marco was aware that they were chatting in English, which suited him fine.

'Would you like the long tour or the short one?' she asked. Though the inside was almost as cold as the outside, Signora Ferro seemed to be thawing just a bit.

'You're the teacher,' he said.

They drifted to the left and waited for a small group of Japanese tourists to finish studying a large marble crypt. Other than the Japanese, the cathedral was empty. It was a Friday in February, not exactly peak tourist season. Later in the afternoon he would learn that Francesca's very seasonal tourist work was quite slow in the winter months. That confession was the only bit of personal data she divulged.

Because business was so slow, she felt no urge to race through the Basilica di San Petronio. They saw all twenty-two side chapels and looked at most of the paintings, sculptures, glasswork, and frescoes. The chapels were built over the centuries by wealthy Bolognese families who paid handsomely for commemorative art. Their construction was a history of the city, and Francesca knew every detail. She showed him the well-preserved skull of Saint Petronio himself sitting proudly on an altar, and an astrological clock created in 1655 by two scientists who relied directly on Galileo's studies at the university.

Though sometimes bored with the intricacies of paintings and sculptures, and inundated with names and dates, Marco gamely held on as the tour inched around the massive structure. Her voice captivated him, her rich slow delivery, her perfectly refined English.

Long after the Japanese had abandoned the cathedral, they made it back to the front door and she said, 'Had enough?'

'Yes.'

They stepped outside and she immediately lit a cigarette.

'How about some coffee?' he said.

'I know just the place.'

He followed her across the street to Via Clavature; a few steps down and they ducked into Rosa Rose. 'It's the best cappuccino around the square,' she assured him as she ordered two at the bar. He started to ask her about the Italian prohibition of drinking cappuccino after ten-thirty in the morning, but let it pass. As they waited she carefully removed her leather gloves, scarf, overcoat. Perhaps this coffee would last for a while.

They took a table near the front window. She stirred in two sugars until things were just perfect. She hadn't smiled in the past three hours, and Marco was not expecting one now.

'I have a copy of the materials you're using with the other tutor,' she said, reaching for the cigarettes.

'Ermanno.'

'Whoever, I don't know him. I suggest that each afternoon we do conversation based on what you have covered that morning.'

He was in no position to argue with whatever she was suggesting. 'Fine,' he said with a shrug.

She lit a cigarette, then sipped the coffee.

'What did Luigi tell you about me?' Marco asked.

'Not much. You're a Canadian. You're taking a long vacation through Italy and you want to study the language. Is that true?'

'Are you asking personal questions?'

'No, I simply asked if that was true.'

'It's true.'

'It's not my business to worry about such matters.'

'I didn't ask you to worry.'

He saw her as the stoic witness on the stand, sitting arrogantly in front of the jury, thoroughly convinced that she would not bend or break regardless of the barrage of cross-examination. She had mastered the distracted pouty look so popular among European women. She held the cigarette close to her face, her eyes studying everything on the sidewalk and seeing nothing.

Idle chitchat was not one of her specialties.

'Are you married?' he asked, the first hint of cross-examination.

A grunt, a fake smile. 'I have my orders, Mr. Lazzeri.'

'Please call me Marco. And what should I call you?'

'Signora Ferro will do for now.'

'But you're ten years younger than me.'

'Things are more formal here, Mr. Lazzeri.'

'Evidently.'

She snubbed out the cigarette, took another sip, and got down to business. 'Today is your free day, Mr. Lazzeri. We've done English for the last time. Next lesson, we do nothing but Italian.'

'Fine, but I'd like for you to keep one thing in mind. You're not doing me any favors, okay? You're getting paid. This is your profession. I'm a Canadian tourist with plenty of time, and if we don't get along, then I'll find someone else to study with.'

'Have I offended you?'

'You could smile more.'

She nodded slightly and her eyes were instantly moist. She looked away, through the window, and said, 'I have so little to smile about.'

Chapter 16

The shops along Via Rizzoli opened at 10:00 a.m. on Saturday and Marco was waiting, studying the merchandise in the windows. With the five hundred fresh euros in his pocket, he swallowed hard, told himself he had no choice but to go in and survive his first real shopping experience in Italian. He'd memorized words and phrases until he fell asleep, but as the door closed behind him he prayed for a nice young clerk who spoke perfect English.

Not a word. It was an older gentleman with a warm smile. In less than fifteen minutes, Marco had pointed and stuttered and, at times, done quite nicely when asking sizes and prices. He left with a pair of modestly priced and youthful-looking hiking boots, the style he'd seen occasionally around the university when the weather was bad, and a black waterproof parka with a hood that rolled up in the collar. And he left with almost three hundred euros in his pocket. Hoarding cash was his newest priority.

He hustled back to his apartment, changed into the boots and the parka, then left again. The thirty-minute walk to Bologna Centrale took almost an hour with the snaking and circuitous route he used. He never looked behind him, but instead would duck into a café and study the foot traffic, or suddenly stop at a pastry shop and admire the delicacies while watching the reflections in the glass. If they were following, he didn't want them to know he was suspicious. And the practice was important. Luigi had told him more than once that soon he would be gone, and Marco Lazzeri would be left alone in the world.

The question was, how much could he trust Luigi? Neither Marco Lazzeri nor Joel Backman trusted anyone.

There was a moment of anxiety at the train station when he walked inside, saw the crowd, studied the overhead schedules of arrivals and departures, and looked about desperately for the ticket window. By habit, he also searched for anything in English. But he was learning to shove the anxiety aside and push on. He waited in line and when a window was open he stepped up quickly, smiled at the little lady on the other side of the glass, offered a pleasant 'Buon giorno,' and said, 'Vado a Milano.' I'm going to Milan.

She was already nodding.

'Alle tredici e venti,' he said. At 1:20.

'Sì, cinquanta euro,' she said. Fifty euros.

211

He gave her a one-hundred-euro bill because he wanted the change, then walked away clutching his ticket and patting himself on the back. With an hour to kill, he left the station and wandered down Via Boldrini two blocks until he found a café. He had a panino and a beer and enjoyed both while watching the sidewalk, expecting to see no one of any interest.

The Eurostar arrived precisely on schedule, and Marco followed the crowd as it hurried on board. It was his first train ride in Europe and he wasn't exactly sure of the protocol. He'd studied his ticket over lunch and saw nothing to indicate a seat assignment. Selection appeared to be random and haphazard and he grabbed the first available window seat. His car was less than half full when the train began moving, at exactly 1:20.

They were soon out of Bologna and the countryside was flying by. The rail track followed M4, the main auto route from Milano to Parma, Bologna, Ancona, and the entire eastern coast of Italy. After half an hour, Marco was disappointed in the scenery. It was hard to appreciate when zipping along at one hundred miles an hour; things were rather blurry and a handsome landscape was gone in a flash. And there were too many factories bunched along the line, near the transportation routes.

He soon realized why he was the only person in his car who was remotely interested in things outside. Those above the age of thirty were lost in newspapers and magazines and looked completely at ease, even bored. The younger ones were sound asleep. After a while Marco nodded off too.

The conductor woke him, saying something completely incomprehensible in Italian. He caught the word 'biglietto' on the second or third try and quickly handed over his ticket. The conductor scowled at it as if he might toss poor Marco off at the next bridge, then abruptly marked it with a punch and gave it back with a wide toothy grin.

An hour later a rush of gibberish over the loudspeaker announced something to do with Milano, and the scenery began to change dramatically. The sprawling city soon engulfed them as the train slowed, then stopped, then moved again. It passed block after block of postwar apartment buildings packed tightly together, with wide avenues separating them. Ermanno's guidebook gave the population of Milano at four million; an important city, the unofficial capital of northern Italy, the country's center for finance, fashion, publishing, and industry. A hard-working industrial city with, of course, a beautiful center and a cathedral worth the visit.

The tracks multiplied and fanned out as they entered the sprawling rail yards of Milano Centrale. They came to a stop under the vast dome of the station, and when Marco stepped onto the platform he was startled at the sheer size of the place. As he walked along the platform he counted at least a dozen other tracks lined in perfect rows, most with trains waiting patiently for their passengers. He stopped at the end, in the frenzy of thousands of people coming and going, and studied the departures: Stuttgart, Rome, Florence, Madrid, Paris, Berlin, Geneva.

All of Europe was within his reach, just a few hours away.

He followed the signs down to the front entrance and found the taxi stand, where he waited in line briefly before he hopped in the backseat of a small white Renault. 'Aeroporto Malpensa,' he said to the driver. They crawled through heavy Milano traffic until they reached the perimeter. Twenty minutes later they left the autostrada for the airport. 'Quale compagnia aerea?' the driver said over his shoulder. Which airline?

'Lufthansa,' Marco said. At Terminal 2 the cab found a spot at the curb, and Marco turned loose another forty euros. The automatic doors opened to a mass of people, and he was thankful he had no plane to catch. He checked the departures and found what he wanted – a direct flight to Dulles. He circled around the terminal until he found the Lufthansa check-in desk. A long line was waiting, but with typical German efficiency things were moving quickly.

The first prospect was an attractive redhead of about twenty-five who appeared to be traveling alone, which was something he preferred.

Anyone with a partner might be tempted to talk about the strange man back at the airport with his rather odd request. She was second in line at the business-class desk. As he watched her he also spotted prospect number two: a denim-clad student with long scruffy hair, unshaven face, well-worn backpack, and a University of Toledo sweatshirt – the perfect fit. He was well back in the line, listening to music on bright yellow headphones.

Marco followed the redhead as she left the counter with her boarding card and carry-on bags. The flight was still two hours away, so she drifted through the crowd to the duty-free shop, where she stopped to inspect the latest in Swiss watches. Seeing nothing to buy, she wandered around the corner to a newsstand and bought two fashion magazines. As she was headed to the gate, and the first security checkpoint, Marco sucked in his gut and made his move. 'Excuse me, miss, excuse me.' She couldn't help but turn and look at him, but she was too suspicious to say anything.

'Are you by chance going to Dulles?' he asked with a huge smile and the pretense of being out of breath, as if he'd just sprinted to catch her.

'Yes,' she snapped. No smile. American.

'So was I, but my passport has just been stolen. Don't know when I'll get home.' He was pulling an envelope out of his pocket. 'This is a birthday card for my father. Could you please drop it in the box when you get to Dulles? His birthday is next Tuesday, and I'm afraid I won't make it. Please.'

She looked at both him and the envelope suspiciously. It was just a birthday card, not a bomb or a gun.

He was yanking something else out of his pocket. 'Sorry, there's no stamp. Here's a euro. Please, if you don't mind.'

The face finally cracked, and she almost smiled. 'Sure,' she said, taking both the envelope and the euro and placing them in her purse.

'Thank you so much,' Marco said, ready to burst into tears. 'It's his ninetieth birthday. Thank you.'

'Sure, no problem,' she said.

The kid with the yellow headphones was more complicated. He, too, was an American, and he also fell for the lost passport story. But when Marco tried to hand over the envelope, he looked around warily as if they might be breaking the law.

'I don't know, man,' he said, taking a step back. 'I don't think so.'

Marco knew better than to push. He backed away and said as sarcastically as possible, 'Have a nice flight.'

Mrs. Ruby Ausberry of York, Pennsylvania, was one of the last passengers at check-in. She had taught world history in high school for forty years and was now having a delightful time spending her retirement funds traveling to places she'd only seen in textbooks. This was the last

216

leg of a three-week adventure through most of Turkey. She was in Milano only for a connecting flight from Istanbul to Washington. The nice gentleman approached her with a desperate smile and explained that his passport had just been stolen. He would miss his father's ninetieth birthday. She gladly took the card and placed it in her bag. She cleared security and walked a quarter of a mile to the gate, where she found a scat and made herself a nest.

Behind her, less than fifteen feet away, the redhead reached a decision. It could be one of those letter bombs after all. It certainly didn't seem thick enough to carry explosives, but what did she know about such things? There was a waste can near the window – a sleek chrome can with a chrome top (they were, after all, in Milano) – and she casually walked over and dropped the letter into the garbage.

What if it explodes there? she wondered as she sat back down. It was too late. She wasn't about to go over and fish it out. And if she did, then what? Track down someone in a uniform and try to explain in English that there was a chance she was holding a letter bomb? Come on, she told herself. She grabbed her carry-on and moved to the other side of the gate, as far away as possible from the waste can. And she couldn't keep her eyes off it.

The conspiracy grew. She was the first one on the 747 when they began boarding. Only with a glass of champagne did she finally relax. She'd watch CNN as soon as she got home to Baltimore. She was convinced there would be carnage at Milano's Malpensa airport.

Marco's taxi ride back to Milano Centrale cost forty-five euros, but he didn't question the driver. Why bother? The return ticket to Bologna was the same – fifty euros. After a day of shopping and traveling he was down to around one hundred euros. His little stash of cash was dwindling rapidly.

It was almost dark when the train slowed at the station in Bologna. Marco was just another weary traveler when he stepped onto the platform, but he was silently bursting with pride at the day's accomplishments. He'd purchased clothing, bought rail tickets, survived the madness of both the train station and the airport in Milano, hired two cabs, and delivered his mail, a rather full day without a hint of anyone knowing who or where he was.

And he'd never been asked to show a passport or any type of identification.

Luigi had taken a different train, the 11:45 express to Milano. But he stepped off at Parma and got lost in the crowd. He found a cab and took a short ride to the meeting place, a favorite café. He waited almost an hour for Whitaker, who had missed one train in Milano and caught the next one. As usual, Whitaker was in a foul mood, which was made even worse by having to meet on a Saturday. They ordered quickly and as soon as the waiter was gone, Whitaker said, 'I don't like this woman.'

'Francesca?'

'Yes, the travel guide. We've never used her before, right?'

'Right. Relax, she's fine. She doesn't have a clue.'

'What does she look like?'

'Reasonably attractive.'

'Reasonably attractive can mean anything, Luigi. How old is she?'

'I never ask that question. Forty-five is a good guess.'

'Is she married?'

'Yes, no children. She married an older man who's in very bad health. He's dying.'

As always, Whitaker was scribbling notes, thinking about the next question. 'Dying? Why is he dying?'

'I think it's cancer. I didn't ask a lot of questions.'

'Perhaps you should ask more questions.'

'Perhaps she doesn't want to talk about certain things – her age and her dying husband.'

'Where'd you find her?'

'It wasn't easy. Language tutors are not exactly lined up like taxi drivers. A friend recommended her. I asked around. She has a good reputation in the city. And she's available. It's almost impossible to find a tutor willing to spend three hours every day with a student.'

'Every day?'

'Most weekdays. She agreed to work every afternoon for the next month or so. It's the slow season for guides. She might have a job once or twice a week, but she'll try to be on call. Relax, she's good.'

'What's her fee?'

'Two hundred euros a week, until spring when tourism picks up.'

Whitaker rolled his eyes as if the money would come directly from his salary. 'Marco's costing too much,' he said, almost to himself.

'Marco has a great idea. He wants to go to Australia or New Zealand or someplace where the language won't be a problem.'

'He wants a transfer?'

'Yes, and I think it's a great idea. Let's dump him on someone else.'

'That's not our decision, is it, Luigi?'

'I guess not.'

The salads arrived and they were quiet for a moment. Then Whitaker said, 'I still don't like this woman. Keep looking for someone else.'

'There is no one else. What are you afraid of?'

'Marco has a history with women, okay? There's always the potential for romance. She could complicate things.'

'I've warned her. And she needs the money.'

'She's broke?'

'I get the impression things are very tight. It's the slow season, and her husband is not working.'

Whitaker almost smiled, as if this was good

news. He stuffed a large wedge of tomato in his mouth and chomped on it while peering around the trattoria to see if anyone was eavesdropping on their hushed conversation in English. When he was finally able to swallow, he said, 'Let's talk about e-mail. Marco was never much of a hacker. Back in his glory days he lived on the phone – had four or five of them in his office, two in his car, one in his pocket – always juggling three conversations at once. He bragged about charging five thousand bucks just to take a phone call from a new client, that sort of crap. Never used the computer. Those who worked for him have said that he occasionally read e-mails. He rarely sent them, and when he did it was always through a secretary. His office was high-tech, but he hired people to do the grunt work. He was too much of a big shot.'

'What about prison?'

'No evidence of e-mail. He had a laptop which he used only for letters, never e-mail. It looks as though everyone abandoned him when he took the fall. He wrote occasionally to his mother and his son, but always used regular mail.'

'Sounds completely illiterate.'

'Sounds like it, but Langley's concerned that he might try and contact someone on the outside. He can't do it by phone, at least not now. He has no address he can use, so mail is probably out of the question.'

'He'd be stupid to mail a letter,' Luigi said. 'It might divulge his whereabouts.'

'Exactly. Same for the phone, fax, everything but e-mail.'

'We can track e-mail.'

'Most of it, but there are ways around it.'

'He has no computer and no money to buy one.'

'I know, but, hypothetically, he could sneak into an Internet café, use a coded account, send the e-mail, then clean his trail, pay a small fee for the rental, and walk away.'

'Sure, but who's gonna teach him how to do that?'

'He can learn. He can find a book. It's unlikely, but there's always a chance.'

'I'm sweeping his apartment every day,' Luigi said. 'Every inch of it. If he buys a book or lays down a receipt, I'll know it.'

'Scope out the Internet cafés in the neighborhood. There are several of them in Bologna now.'

'I know them.'

'Where's Marco right now?'

'I don't know. It's Saturday, a day off. He's probably roaming the streets of Bologna, enjoying his freedom.'

'And he's still scared?'

'He's terrified.'

Mrs. Ruby Ausberry took a mild sedative and slept for six of the eight hours it took to fly from Milano to Dulles International. The lukewarm coffee they served before landing did little to clear the cobwebs, and as the 747 taxied to the gate she dozed off again. She forgot about the birthday card as they were herded onto the cattle cars on the tarmac and driven to the main terminal. She forgot about it as she waited with the mob to claim her baggage and plod through customs. And she forgot about it when she saw her beloved granddaughter waiting for her at the arrival exit.

She forgot about it until she was safely at home in York, Pennsylvania, and shuffling through her shoulder bag for a souvenir. 'Oh my,' she said as the card fell onto the kitchen table. 'I was supposed to drop this off at the airport.' Then she told her granddaughter the story of the poor guy in the Milan airport who'd just lost his passport and would miss his father's ninetieth birthday.

Her granddaughter looked at the envelope. 'Doesn't look like a birthday card,' she said. She studied the address: R. N. Backman, Attorney at Law, 412 Main Street, Culpeper, Virginia, 22701.

'There's no return address,' the granddaughter said.

'I'll mail it first thing in the morning,' Mrs. Ausberry said. 'I hope it arrives before the birthday.'

Chapter 17

At ten Monday morning in Singapore, the mysterious $3 million sitting in the account of Old Stone Group, Ltd, made an electronic exit and began a quiet journey to the other side of the world. Nine hours later, when the doors of the Galleon Bank and Trust opened on the Caribbean island of Saint Christopher, the money arrived promptly and was deposited in a numbered account with no name. Normally it would have been a completely anonymous transaction, one of several thousand that Monday morning, but Old Stone now had the full attention of the FBI. The bank in Singapore was cooperating fully. The bank on Saint Christopher was not, though it would soon get the opportunity to participate.

When Director Anthony Price arrived in his office at the Hoover Building before dawn on Monday, the hot memo was waiting. He canceled everything planned for that morning.

He huddled with his team and waited for the money to land on Saint Christopher.

Then he called the vice president.

It took four hours of undiplomatic arm-breaking to shake the information loose on Saint Christopher. At first the bankers refused to budge, but what small quasi-nation can withstand the full might and fury of the world's only superpower? When the vice president threatened the prime minister with economic and banking sanctions that would destroy what little economy the island was clinging to, he finally knuckled under and turned on his bankers.

The numbered account could be directly traced to Artie Morgan, the thirty-one-year-old son of the former president. He'd been in and out of the Oval Office during the final hours of his father's administration, sipping Heinekens and occasionally dispensing advice to both Critz and the President.

The scandal was ripening by the hour.

From Grand Cayman to Singapore and now to Saint Christopher, the wiring bore the telltale signs of an amateur trying to cover his tracks. A professional would've split the money eight ways and parked it in several different banks in different countries, and the wires would've been months apart. But even a rookie like Artie should've been able to hide the cash. The offshore banks he selected were secretive enough to protect him. The break for the feds had been the mutual-fund crook desperate to avoid prison.

However, there was still no evidence as to the source of the money. In his last three days in office, President Morgan granted twenty-two pardons. All went unnoticed except two: Joel Backman and Duke Mongo. The FBI was hard at work digging for financial dirt on the other twenty. Who had $3 million? Who had the resources to get it? Every friend, family member, and business associate was being scrutinized by the feds.

A preliminary analysis repeated what was already known. Mongo had billions and was certainly corrupt enough to bribe anyone. Backman, too, could pull it off. A third possibility was a former New Jersey state legislator whose family made a bundle in government road contracts. Twelve years earlier he'd gone to 'federal camp' for a few months and now wanted his rights restored.

The President was off in Europe, in the middle of his get-acquainted tour, his first victory lap around the world. He wouldn't be back for three days, and the vice president decided to wait. They would watch the money, double- and triple-check the facts and details, and when he returned they would brief him with an airtight case. A cash-for-pardon scandal would electrify the country. It would humiliate the opposition party and weaken its resolve in Congress. It would ensure that Anthony Price would head the FBI for a few more years. It would finally send old Teddy Maynard off to the retirement home. There was simply no downside to the launching of a full federal blitz against an unsuspecting ex-president.

His tutor was waiting in the back pew of the Basilica di San Francesco. She was still bundled, with her gloved hands stuck partially in the pockets of her heavy overcoat. It was snowing again outside, and in the vast, cold, empty sanctuary the temperature was not much warmer. He sat beside her and offered a soft 'Buon giorno.'

She acknowledged him with just enough of a smile to be considered polite, and said, 'Buon giorno.' He kept his hands in his pockets too, and for a long time they sat like two frozen hikers hiding from the weather. As usual, her face was sad and her thoughts were on something other than this bumbling Canadian businessman who wanted to speak her language. She was aloof and distracted and Marco was fed up with her attitude. Ermanno was losing interest by the day. Francesca was barely tolerable. Luigi was always back there, lurking and watching, but he, too, seemed to be losing interest in the game.

Marco was beginning to think that the break was about to happen. Cut the lifeline and set him adrift to sink or swim on his own. So be it. He'd been free for almost a month. He'd learned enough Italian to survive. He could certainly learn more by himself.

'So how old is this one?' he said after it

became apparent that he was expected to speak first.

She shifted slightly, cleared her throat, took her hands out of her pockets, as if he'd awakened her from a deep sleep. 'It was begun in 1236 by some Franciscan monks. Thirty years later the main sanctuary here was complete.'

'A rush job.'

'Yes, quite fast. Over the centuries the chapels sort of sprang up along both sides. The sacristy was built, then the bell tower. The French, under Napoleon, deconsecrated it in 1798 and turned it into a customs house. In 1886 it was converted back to a church, then restored in 1928. When Bologna was bombed by the Allies its façade was extensively damaged. It's had a rough history.'

'It's not very pretty on the outside.'

'Bombing will do that.'

'I guess you picked the wrong side.'

'Bologna did not.'

No sense refighting the war. They paused as their voices seemed to float up and echo slightly around the dome. Backman's mother had taken him to church a few times each year as a child, but that halfhearted effort at pursuing a faith had been abandoned quickly in high school and totally forgotten over the past forty years. Not even prison could convert him, unlike some of the other inmates. But it was still difficult for a man with no convictions to understand how any style of meaningful worship could be conducted in a such a cold, heartless museum.

'It seems so empty. Does anyone ever worship in this place?'

'There's a daily mass and services on Sunday. I was married here.'

'You're not supposed to talk about yourself. Luigi will get mad.'

'Italian, Marco, no more English.' In Italian, she asked him, 'What did you study this morning with Ermanno?'

'La famiglia.'

'La sua famiglia. Mi dica.' Tell me about your family.

'It's a real mess,' he said in English.

'Sua moglie?' Your wife?

'Which one? I have three.'

'Italian.'

'Quale? Ne ho tre.'

'L'ultima.' The last one.

Then he caught himself. He was not Joel Backman, with three ex-wives and a screwed-up family. He was Marco Lazzeri from Toronto, with a wife, four children, and five grand-children. 'I was kidding,' he said in English. 'I have one wife.'

'Mi dica, in Italiano, di sua moglie?' Tell me about your wife.

In very slow Italian, Marco described his fictional wife. Her name is Laura. She is fifty-two years old. She lives in Toronto. She works for a small company. She does not like to travel. And so on.

Every sentence was repeated at least three times. Every mispronunciation was met with a grimace and a quick 'Ripeta.' Over and over, Marco went on and on about a Laura who did not exist. And when he finished with her, he was led to his oldest child, another creation, this one named Alex. Thirty years old, a lawyer in Vancouver, divorced with two kids, etc., etc.

Fortunately, Luigi had given him a little biography on Marco Lazzeri, complete with all the data he was now reaching for in the back of a frigid church. She prodded him on, urging perfection, cautioning against speaking too fast, the natural tendency.

'Deve parlare lentamente,' she kept saying. You must speak slowly.

She was strict and no fun, but also very motivational. If he could learn to speak Italian half as well as she spoke English, then he would be ahead of the pack. If she believed in constant repetition, then so did he.

As they were discussing his mother, an elderly gentleman entered the church and sat in the pew directly in front of them. He was soon lost in meditation and prayer. They decided to make a quiet exit. A light snow was still falling and they stopped at the first café for espresso and a smoke.

'Adesso, possiamo parlare della sua famiglia?' he asked. Can we talk about your family now?

She smiled, showed teeth, a rarity, and said, 'Benissimo, Marco.' Very good. 'Ma, non possiamo. Mi dispiace.' But, I'm sorry. We cannot.

'Perchè non?' Why not?

'Abbiamo delle regole.' We have rules.

'Dov'è suo marito?' Where is your husband?

'Qui, a Bologna.' Here, in Bologna.

'Dov'è lavora?' Where does he work?

'Non lavora.'

After her second cigarette they ventured back onto the covered sidewalks and began a thorough lesson about snow. She delivered a short sentence in English, and he was supposed to translate it. It is snowing. It never snows in Florida. Maybe it will snow tomorrow. It snowed twice last week. I love the snow. I don't like snow.

They skirted the edge of the main plaza and stayed under the porticoes. On Via Rizzoli they passed the store where Marco bought his boots and his parka and he thought she might like to hear his version of that event. He could handle most of the Italian. He let it pass, though, since she was so engrossed in the weather. At an intersection they stopped and looked at Le Due Torri, the two surviving towers that the Bolognesi were so proud of.

There were once more than two hundred towers, she said. Then she asked him to repeat the sentence. He tried, butchered the past tense and the number, and was then asked to repeat the damn sentence until he got it right.

In medieval times, for reasons present-day Italians cannot explain, their ancestors seized

231

upon the unusual architectural compulsion of building tall slender towers in which to live. Since tribal wars and local hostilities were epidemic, the towers were meant principally for protection. They were effective lookout posts and valuable during attacks, though they proved to be less than practical as living quarters. To protect the food, the kitchens were often on the top floor, three hundred or so steps above the street, which made it difficult to find dependable domestic help. When fights broke out, the warring families were known to simply launch arrows and fling spears at each other from one offending tower to the other. No sense fighting in the streets like common folk.

They also became quite the status symbol. No self-respecting noble could allow his neighbor and/or rival to have a taller tower, so in the twelfth and thirteenth centuries a curious game of one-upmanship raged over the skyline of Bologna as the nobles tried to keep up with the Joneses. The city was nicknamed la turrita, the towered one. An English traveler described it as a 'bed of asparagus'.

By the fourteenth century organized government was gaining a foothold in Bologna, and those with vision knew that the warring nobles had to be reined in. The city, whenever it had enough muscle to get away with it, tore down many of the towers. Age and gravity took care of others; poor foundations crumbled after a few centuries.

In the late 1800s, a noisy campaign to tear them all down was narrowly approved. Only two survived – Asinelli and Garisenda. Both stand near each other at the Piazza di Porto Ravegnana. Neither stands exactly straight, with Garisenda drifting off to the north at an angle that rivals the more famous, and far prettier, one in Pisa. The two old survivors have evoked many colorful descriptions over the decades. A French poet likened them to two drunk sailors staggering home, trying to lean on one another for support. Ermanno's guidebook referred to them as the 'Laurel and Hardy' of medieval architecture.

La Torre degli Asinelli was built in the early twelfth century, and, at 97.2 meters, is twice as tall as its partner. Garisenda began leaning as it was almost completed in the thirteenth century, and was chopped in half in an effort to stop the tilt. The Garisenda clan lost interest and abandoned the city in disgrace.

Marco had learned the history from Ermanno's book. Francesca didn't know this, and she, like all good guides, took fifteen cold minutes to talk about the famous towers. She formulated a simple sentence, delivered it perfectly, helped Marco stumble through it, then grudgingly went to the next one.

'Asinelli has four hundred and ninety-eight steps to the top,' she said.

'Andiamo,' Marco said quickly. Let's go. They entered the thick foundation through a narrow door, followed a tight circular staircase up fifty feet or so to where the ticket booth had been stuck in a corner. He bought two tickets at three euros each, and they started the climb. The tower was hollow, with the stairs fixed to the outside walls.

Francesca said she hadn't climbed it in at least ten years, and seemed excited about their little adventure. She took off, up the narrow, sturdy oak steps, with Marco keeping his distance behind. An occasional small open window allowed light and cold air to filter in. 'Pace yourself,' she called over her shoulder, in English, as she slowly pulled away from Marco. On that snowy February afternoon there were no others climbing to the top of the city.

He paced himself and she was soon out of sight. About halfway up, he stopped at a large window so the wind could cool his face. He caught his breath, then took off again, even slower now. A few minutes later, he stopped again, his heart pounding away, his lungs working overtime, his mind wondering if he could make it. After 498 steps he finally emerged from the boxlike attic and stepped onto the top of the tower. Francesca was smoking a cigarette, gazing upon her beautiful city, no sign of sweat anywhere on her face.

The view from the top was panoramic. The red tile roofs of the city were covered with two inches of snow. The pale green dome of San Bartolomeo was directly under them, refusing any accumulation. 'On a clear day, you can see the Adriatic Sea to the east, and the Alps to the north,' she said, still in English. 'It's just beautiful, even in the snow.'

'Just beautiful,' he said, almost panting. The wind whipped through the metal bars between the brick posts, and it was much colder above Bologna than on its streets.

'The tower is the fifth-tallest structure in old Italy,' she said proudly. He was certain she could name the other four.

'Why was this tower saved?' he asked.

'Two reasons, I think. It was well designed and well built. The Asinelli family was strong and powerful. And it was used as a prison briefly in the fourteenth century, when many of the other towers were demolished. Truthfully, no one really knows why this one was spared.' Three hundred feet up, and she was a different person. Her eyes were alive, her voice radiant.

'This always reminds me of why I love my city,' she said with a rare smile. Not at him, not at anything he said, but at the rooftops and skyline of Bologna. They stepped to the other side and looked in the distance to the southwest. On a hill above the city they could see the outline of Santuario di San Luca, the guardian angel of the city.

'Have you been there?' she asked.

'No.'

'We'll do it one day when the weather is nice, okay?'

'Sure.'

'We have so much to see.'

Maybe he wouldn't fire her after all. He was so starved for companionship, especially from the opposite sex, that he could tolerate her aloofness and sadness and mood swings. He would study even harder to gain her approval.

If the climb to the top of the Asinelli Tower had buoyed her spirits, the trip down brought back the same old dour demeanor. They had a quick espresso near the towers and said goodbye. As she walked away, no superficial hug, no cheek-pecking, not even a cursory handshake, he decided he would give her one more week.

He put her on secret probation. She had seven days to become nice, or he'd simply stop the lessons. Life was too short.

She was very pretty, though.

The envelope had been opened by his secretary, just like all the other mail from yesterday and the day before. But inside the first envelope was another, this one addressed simply to Neal Backman. In bold print on the front and back were the dire warnings: PERSONAL, CONFIDENTIAL, TO BE OPENED ONLY BY NEAL BACKMAN.

'You might want to look at the one on top,' the secretary said as she hauled in his daily stack of mail at 9:00 a.m. 'The envelope was postmarked two days ago in York, Pennsylvania.' When she closed the door behind her, Neal examined the envelope. It was light brown in

236

color, with no markings other than what had been hand-printed by the sender. The printing look vaguely familiar.

With a letter opener, he slowly cut along the top of the envelope, then pulled out a single sheet of folded white paper. It was from his father. It was a shock, but then it was not.

Dear Neal: *Feb. 21*

I'm safe for now but I doubt it will last. I need your help. I have no address, no phone, no fax, and I'm not sure I would use them if I could. I need access to e-mail, something that cannot be traced. I have no idea how to do this, but I know you can figure it out. I have no computer and no money. There is a good chance you are being watched, so whatever you do, you must not leave a trail. Cover your tracks. Cover mine. Trust no one. Watch everything. Hide this letter, then destroy it. Send me as much money as possible. You know I'll pay it back. Never use your real name on anything. Use the following address:

Sr. Rudolph Viscovitch, Università degli Studi, University of Bologna, Via Zamboni 22, 44041, Bologna, Italy. Use two envelopes – the first for Viscovitch, the second for me. In your note to him ask him to hold the package for Marco Lazzeri.

     Hurry!   *Love, Marco*

Neal placed the letter on his desk and walked

over to lock his door. He sat on a small leather sofa and tried to arrange his thoughts. He had already decided his father was out of the country, otherwise he would've made contact weeks earlier. Why was he in Italy? Why was the letter mailed from York, Pennsylvania?

Neal's wife had never met her father-in-law. He'd been in prison for two years when they met and married. They had sent photos of the wedding, and later a photo of their child, Joel's second granddaughter.

Joel was not a topic Neal liked to talk about it. Or think about. He had been a lousy father, absent for most of his childhood, and his astounding plunge from power had embarrassed everyone close to him. Neal had grudgingly sent letters and cards during the incarceration, but he could truthfully say, at least to himself and his wife, that he did not miss his father. He'd rarely been around the man.

Now he was back, asking for money that Neal did not have, assuming with no hesitation that Neal would do exactly as he was instructed, perfectly willing to endanger someone else.

Neal walked to his desk and read the letter again, then again. It was the same scarcely readable chicken scratch he'd seen throughout his life. And it was his same method of operation, whether at home or at the office. Do this, this, and this, and everything will work. Do it my way, and do it now! Hurry! Risk everything because I need you.

And what if everything worked smoothly and the broker came back? He certainly wouldn't have time for Neal and the granddaughter. If given the chance, Joel Backman, fifty-two, would once again rise to glory in the power circles of Washington. He'd make the right friends, hustle the right clients, marry the right woman, find the right partners, and within a year he'd once again work from a vast office where he would charge outrageous fees and bully congressmen.

Life had been much simpler with his father in prison.

What would he tell Lisa, his wife? Honey, that $2,000 we have buried in our savings account has just been spoken for. Plus a few hundred bucks for an encrypted e-mail system. And you and the baby keep the doors locked at all times because life just became much more dangerous.

With the day shot to hell, Neal buzzed his secretary and asked her to hold his calls. He stretched out on the sofa, kicked off his loafers, closed his eyes, and began massaging his temples.

Chapter 18

In the nasty little war between the CIA and the FBI, both sides often used certain journalists for tactical reasons. Preemptive strikes could be launched, counterattacks blunted, hasty retreats glossed over, even damage control could be implemented by manipulating the press. Dan Sandberg had cultivated sources on both sides for almost twenty years and was perfectly willing to be used when the information was correct, and exclusive. He was also willing to assume the role of courier, cautiously moving between the armies with sensitive gossip to see how much the other side knew. In his effort to confirm the story that the FBI was investigating a cash-for-pardon scandal, he contacted his most reliable source at the CIA. He was met with the usual stonewall, one that lasted less than forty-eight hours.

His contact at Langley was Rusty Lowell, a frazzled career man with shifting titles. Whatever

240

he was paid to do, his real job was watching the press and advising Teddy Maynard on how to use and abuse it. He was not a snitch, not one to pass along anything that wasn't true. After years of working at the relationship, Sandberg was reasonably confident that most of what he got from Lowell was doled out by Teddy himself.

They met at Tyson's Corner Mall, over in Virginia, just off the Beltway, in the back of a cheap pizzeria on the upper-level food court. They each bought one slice of pepperoni and cheese and a soft drink, then found a booth where no one could see them. The usual rules applied: (1) everything was off the record and deep background; (2) Lowell would give the green light before Sandberg could run any story; and (3) if anything Lowell said was contradicted by another source, he, Lowell, would have the chance to review it and offer the last word.

As an investigative journalist, Sandberg hated the rules. However, Lowell had never been wrong, and he was not talking to anyone else. If Sandberg wanted to mine this rich source, he had to play by the rules.

'They've found some money,' Sandberg began. 'And they think it's linked to a pardon.'

Lowell's eyes always betrayed him because he was never deceitful. They narrowed immediately and it was obvious that this was something new.

'Does the CIA know this?' Sandberg asked.

'No,' Lowell said bluntly. He had never been afraid of the truth. 'We've been watching some

241

accounts offshore, but nothing's happened. How much money?'

'A lot. I don't know how much. And I don't know how they found it.'

'Where did it come from?'

'They don't know for sure, but they're desperate to link it to Joel Backman. They're talking to the White House.'

'And not us.'

'Evidently not. It reeks of politics. They'd love to pin a scandal on President Morgan, and Backman would be the perfect conspirator.'

'Duke Mongo would be a nice target too.'

'Yes, but he's practically dead. He's had a long, colorful career as a tax cheat, but now he's out to pasture. Backman has secrets. They want to haul him back, run him through the grinder over at Justice, blow the top off Washington for a few months. It will humiliate Morgan.'

'The economy's sliding like hell. What a wonderful diversion.'

'Like I said, it's all about politics.'

Lowell finally took a bite of pizza and chewed it quickly as he thought. 'Can't be Backman. They're way off target.'

'You're sure.'

'I'm positive. Backman had no idea a pardon was in the works. We literally yanked him out of his cell in the middle of the night, made him sign some papers, then shipped him out of the country before sunrise.'

'And where did he go?'

'Hell, I don't know. And if I did I wouldn't tell you. The point is that Backman had no time to arrange a bribe. He was buried so deep in prison he couldn't even dream of a pardon. It was Teddy's idea, not his. Backman's not their man.'

'They intend to find him.'

'Why? He's a free man, fully pardoned, not some convict on the run. He can't be extradited, unless of course they squeeze an indictment.'

'Which they can do.'

Lowell frowned at the table for a second or two. 'I can't see an indictment. They have no proof. They have some suspicious money sitting in a bank, as you say, but they don't know where it came from. I assure you it's not Backman's money.'

'Can they find him?'

'They're gonna put the pressure on Teddy, and that's why I wanted to talk.' He shoved the half-eaten pizza aside and leaned in closer. 'There will soon be a meeting in the Oval Office. Teddy will be there, and he'll be asked by the President to see the sensitive stuff on Backman. He will refuse. Then it's showdown time. Will the Prez have the guts to fire the old man?'

'Will he?'

'Probably. At least Teddy is expecting it. This is his fourth president, which, as you know, is a record, and the first three have all wanted to fire him. Now, though, he's old and ready to go.'

'He's been old and ready to go forever.'

'True, but he's run a tight ship. This time it's different.'

'Why doesn't he just resign?'

'Because he's a cranky, contrary, stubborn old son of a bitch, you know that.'

'That's well established.'

'And if he gets fired, he's not going peacefully. He'd like balanced coverage.'

'Balanced coverage' was their long-standing buzzword for 'slant it our way'.

Sandberg slid his pizza away too and cracked his knuckles. 'Here's the story as I see it,' he said, part of the ritual. 'After eighteen years of solid leadership at the CIA, Teddy Maynard gets sacked by a brand-new president. The reason is that Maynard refused to divulge details of sensitive ongoing operations. He stood his ground to protect national security, and stared down the President, who, along with the FBI, wants classified information so that it, the FBI, can pursue an investigation relating to pardons granted by former president Morgan.'

'You cannot mention Backman.'

'I'm not ready to use names. I don't have confirmation.'

'I assure you the money did not come from Backman. And if you use his name at this point, there's a chance he'll see it and do something stupid.'

'Like what?'

'Like, run for his life.'

'Why is that stupid?'

'Because we don't want him running for his life.'

'You want him dead?'

'Of course. That's the plan. We want to see who kills him.'

Sandberg settled back against the hard plastic bench and looked away. Lowell picked slices of pepperoni off his cold rubbery pizza, and for a long time they thought in silence. Sandberg drained his Diet Coke, and finally said, 'Teddy somehow convinced Morgan to pardon Backman, who's stashed away somewhere as bait for the kill.'

Lowell was looking away but nodding.

'And the killing will answer some questions over at Langley?'

'Perhaps. That's the plan.'

'Does Backman know why he was pardoned?'

'We certainly haven't told him, but he's fairly bright.'

'Who's after him?'

'Some very dangerous people who carry grudges.'

'Do you know who?'

A nod, a shrug, a nonanswer. 'There are several with potential. We'll watch closely and maybe learn something. Maybe not.'

'And why are they carrying grudges?'

Lowell laughed at the ridiculous question. 'Nice try, Dan. You've been asking that for six years now. Look, I gotta go. Work on the balanced piece and let me see it.'

'When is the meeting with the President?'

'Not sure. As soon as he gets back.'

'And if Teddy's terminated?'

'You'll be the first person I call.'

As a small-town lawyer in Culpeper, Virginia, Neal Backman was earning far less than what he had dreamed about in law school. Back then, his father's firm was such a force in D.C. that he could easily see himself making the big bucks after only a few years of practice. The greenest associates at Backman, Pratt & Bolling started at $100,000 a year, and a rising junior partner thirty years of age would earn three times as much. During his second year of law school, a local magazine put the broker on the cover and talked about his expensive toys. His income was estimated at $10 million a year. This had caused quite a stir around law school, something Neal was not uncomfortable with. He could remember thinking how wonderful the future would be with all that earning potential.

However, less than a year after signing on as a green associate, he was sacked by the firm after his father pled guilty, and was literally thrown out of the building.

But Neal had soon stopped dreaming of the big money and the glitzy lifestyle. He was perfectly content to practice law with a nice little firm on Main Street and hopefully take home $50,000 a year. Lisa stopped working when their daughter was born. She managed the finances and kept their lives on budget.

After a sleepless night, he awoke with a rough idea of how to proceed. The most painful issue had been whether or not to tell his wife. Once he decided not to, the plan began to take shape. He went to the office at eight, as usual, and puttered online for an hour and a half, until he was sure the bank was open. As he walked down Main Street he found it impossible to believe that there might be people lurking nearby watching his movements. Still, he would take no chances.

Richard Koley ran the nearest branch of Piedmont National Bank. They went to church together, hunted grouse, played softball for the Rotary Club. Neal's law firm had banked there forever. The lobby was empty at such an early hour, and Richard was already at his desk with a tall cup of coffee, *The Wall Street Journal,* and evidently very little to do. He was pleasantly surprised to see Neal, and for twenty minutes they talked about college basketball. When they eventually got around to business, Richard said, 'So what can I do for you?'

'Just curious,' Neal said casually, delivering lines he'd been rehearsing all morning. 'How much might I borrow with just my signature?'

'Bit of a jam, huh?' Richard was grabbing the mouse and already glancing at the monitor, where all answers were stored.

'No, nothing like that. Rates are so low and I've got my eye on a hot stock.'

'Not a bad strategy, really, though I certainly

247

can't advertise it. With the Dow at ten thousand again you wonder why more folks don't load up with credit and buy stocks. It would certainly be good for the old bank.' He managed an awkward banker's chuckle at his own quick humor. 'Income range?' he asked, tapping keys, somber-faced now.

'It varies,' Neal said. 'Sixty to eighty.'

Richard frowned even more, and Neal couldn't tell if it was because he was sad to learn his friend made so little, or because his friend earned so much more than he. He'd never know. Small-town banks were not known for over-paying their people.

'Total debts, outside the mortgage?' he asked, tapping again.

'Hmmm, let's see.' Neal closed his eyes and ran through the math again. His mortgage was almost $200,000 and Piedmont held that. Lisa was so opposed to debt that their own little balance sheet was remarkably clean. 'Car loan of about twenty grand,' he said. 'Maybe a thousand or so on the credit cards. Not much, really.'

Richard nodded his approval and never took his eyes off the monitor. When his fingers left the keyboard, he shrugged and turned into the generous banker. 'We could do three thousand on a signature. Six percent interest, for twelve months.'

Since he'd never borrowed with no collateral, Neal wasn't sure what to expect. He had no idea what his signature would command, but somehow $3,000 sounded about right. 'Can you go four thousand?' he asked.

Another frown, another hard study of the monitor, then it revealed the answer. 'Sure, why not? I know where to find you, don't I?'

'Good. I'll keep you posted on the stock.'

'Is this a hot tip, something on the inside?'

'Give me a month. If the price goes up, I'll come back and brag a little.'

'Fair enough.'

Richard was opening a drawer, looking for forms. Neal said, 'Look, Richard, this is just between us boys, okay? Know what I mean? Lisa won't be signing the papers.'

'No problem,' the banker said, the epitome of discretion. 'My wife doesn't know half of what I do on the financial end. Women just don't understand.'

'You got it. And along those lines, would it be possible to get the funds in cash?'

A pause, a puzzled look, but then anything was possible at Piedmont National. 'Sure, give me an hour or so.'

'I need to run to the office and sue a guy, okay? I'll be back around noon to sign everything and get the money.'

Neal hustled to his office, two blocks away, with a nervous pain in his stomach. Lisa would kill him if she found out, and in a small town secrets were hard to bury. In four years of a very happy marriage they had made all decisions

249

together. Explaining the loan would be painful, though she would probably come around if he told the truth.

Repaying the money would pose a challenge. His father had always been one to make easy promises. Sometimes he came through, sometimes he didn't, and he was never too concerned one way or the other. But that was the old Joel Backman. The new one was a desperate man with no friends, no one to trust.

What the hell. It was only $4,000. Richard would keep it quiet. Neal would worry about the loan later. He was, after all, a lawyer. He could squeeze in some extra fees here and there, put in a few more hours.

His primary concern at that moment was the package to be shipped to Rudolph Viscovitch.

With the cash bulging in his pocket, Neal fled Culpeper during the lunch hour and hurried up to Alexandria, ninety minutes away. He found the store, Chatter, in a small strip mall on Russell Road, a mile or so from the Potomac River. It advertised itself online as the place to go for the latest in telecom gadgetry, and one of the few places in the United States where one could purchase unlocked cell phones that would work in Europe. As he browsed for a few moments, he was astounded at the selection of phones, pagers, computers, satellite phones – everything one could possibly need to keep in touch. He couldn't browse for long – there was a four o'clock deposition in his office. Lisa would be making one of her many daily check-ins to see what, if anything, was happening downtown.

He asked a clerk to show him the Ankyo 850 PC Pocket Smartphone, the greatest technological marvel to hit the market in the past ninety days. The clerk removed it from a display case and, with great enthusiasm, switched languages and described it as 'Full QWERTY keyboard, tri-band operation on five continents, eighty megabyte built-in memory, high-speed data connectivity with EGPRS, wireless LAN access, Bluetooth wireless technology, IPv4 and IPv6 dual stack support, infrared, Pop-Port interface, Symbian operating system version 7.0S, Series 80 platform.'

'Automatic switching between bands?'

'Yes.'

'Covered by European networks?'

'Of course.'

The smartphone was slightly larger than the typical business phone, but it was comfortable in the hand. It had a smooth metallic surface with a rough plastic back cover that prevented sliding when in use.

'It's larger,' the clerk was saying. 'But it's packed with goodies – e-mail, multimedia messaging, camera, video player, complete word processing, Internet browsing – and complete wireless access almost anywhere in the world. Where are you going with it?'

'Italy.'

'It's ready to go. You'll just need to open an account with a service provider.'

Opening an account meant paperwork. Paperwork meant leaving a trail, something Neal was determined not to do. 'What about a prepaid SIM card?' he asked.

'We got 'em. For Italy it's called a TIM – Telecom Italia Mobile. It's the largest provider in Italy, covers about ninety-five percent of the country.'

'I'll take it.'

Neal slid down the lower part of the cover to reveal a full keypad. The clerk explained, 'It's best to hold it with both hands and type with the thumbs. You can't fit all ten fingers on the keypad.' He took it from Neal and demonstrated the preferred method of thumb-typing.

'Got it,' Neal said. 'I'll take it.'

The price was $925 plus tax, plus another $89 for the TIM card. Neal paid in cash as he simultaneously declined the extended warranty, rebate registration, owner's program, anything that would create paperwork and leave a trail. The clerk asked for his name and address and Neal declined. At one point he said, with great irritation, 'Is it possible to simply pay for this and leave?'

'Well, sure, I guess,' the clerk said.

'Then let's do it. I'm in a hurry.'

He left and drove half a mile to a large office supply store. He quickly found a Hewlett-Packard Tablet PC with integrated wireless capability. Another $440 got invested in his father's security, though Neal would keep the laptop and hide it in his office. Using a map he'd downloaded, he found the PackagePost in another strip mall nearby. Inside, at a shipping desk, he hurriedly wrote two pages of instructions for his father, then folded them into an envelope containing a letter and more instructions he'd prepared earlier that morning. When he was certain no one was watching, he wedged twenty $100 bills in the small black carrying case that came with the Ankyo marvel. Then he placed the letter and the instructions, the smartphone, and the case inside a mailing carton from the store. He sealed it tightly, and on the outside he wrote with a black marker PLEASE HOLD FOR MARCO LAZZERI. The carton was then placed inside another, slightly larger one that was addressed to Rudolph Viscovitch at Via Zamboni 22, Bologna. The return address was PackagePost, 8851 Braddock Road, Alexandria, Virginia 22302. Because he had no choice, he left his name, address, and phone number on the registry, in case the package got returned. The clerk weighed the package and asked about insurance. Neal declined, and prevented more paperwork. The clerk added the international stamps, and finally said, 'Total is eighteen dollars and twenty cents.'

Neal paid him and was assured again that it would be mailed that afternoon.

Chapter 19

In the semidarkness of his small apartment, Marco went through his early-morning routine with his usual efficiency. Except for prison, when he had little choice and no motivation to hit the ground running, he'd never been one to linger after waking. There was too much to do, too much to see. He'd often arrived at his office before 6:00 a.m. breathing fire and looking for the day's first brawl, and often after only three or four hours of sleep.

Those habits were returning now. He wasn't attacking each day, wasn't looking for a fight, but there were other challenges.

He showered in less than three minutes, another old habit that was aided mightily on Via Fondazza by a severe shortage of warm water. Over the lavatory he shaved and worked carefully around the quite handsome growth he was cultivating on his face. The mustache was almost complete; the chin was solid gray. He looked nothing like Joel Backman, nor did he sound like him. He was training himself to speak much slower and in a softer voice. And of course he was doing so in another language.

His quick morning routine included a little espionage. Beside his bed was a chest of drawers where he kept his things. Four drawers, all the same size, with the last one six inches above the floor. He took a very thin strand of white thread he'd unraveled from a bed sheet; the same thread he used every day. He licked both ends, leaving as much saliva as possible, then stuck one end under the bottom of the last drawer. The other end was stuck to the side brace of the chest, so that when the drawer was opened the invisible thread was pulled out of position.

Someone, Luigi he presumed, entered his room every day while he was studying with either Ermanno or Francesca and went through the drawers.

His desk was in the small living room, under the only window. On it he kept an assortment of papers, notepads, books; Ermanno's guide to Bologna, a few copies of the *Herald Tribune*, a sad collection of free shopping guides he'd gathered from Gypsies who passed them out on the streets, his well-used Italian-English dictionary, and the growing pile of study aids Ermanno was burdening him with. The desk was only moderately well organized, a condition that irritated him. His old lawyer's desk, one that wouldn't fit in his current living room, had been famous for its meticulous order. A secretary fussed over it late every afternoon.

But amid the rubble was an invisible scheme. The desk's surface was some type of hardwood that had been nicked and marked over the decades. One defect was a small stain of some sort – Marco had decided it was probably ink. It was about the size of a small button and was located almost in the dead center of the desk. Every morning, as he was leaving, he placed the corner of a sheet of scratch paper directly in the center of the ink stain. Not even the most diligent of spies would have noticed.

And they didn't. Whoever sneaked in for the daily sweep had never, not once, been careful enough to place the papers and books back in their precise location.

Every day, seven days a week, even on the weekends when he was not studying, Luigi and his gang entered and did their dirty work. Marco was considering a plan whereby he would wake up one Sunday morning with a massive headache, telephone Luigi, still the only person he talked to on the cell phone, and ask him to fetch some aspirin or whatever they used in Italy. He would go through the ruse of nursing himself, staying in bed, keeping the apartment dark, until late in the afternoon when he would call Luigi again and announce he felt much better and needed something to eat. They would walk around the corner, have a quick bite, then Marco would suddenly feel like returning to his apartment. They would be gone for less than an hour.

Would someone else handle the sweep?

The plan was taking shape. Marco wanted to know who else was watching him. How large was the net? If their concern was simply to keep him alive, then why would they sift through his apartment every day? What were they afraid of?

They were afraid he would disappear. And why should that frighten them so? He was a free man, perfectly free to move about. His disguise was good. His language skills were rudimentary but passable and improving daily. Why should they care if he simply drifted away? Caught a train and toured the country? Never came back? Wouldn't that make their lives easier?

And why keep him on such a short leash, with no passport and very little cash?

They were afraid he would disappear.

He turned off the lights and opened the door. It was still dark outside under the arcaded sidewalks of Via Fondazza. He locked the door behind him and hurried away, off in search of another early-morning café.

Through the thick wall, Luigi was awakened by a buzzer somewhere in the distance; the same buzzer that awakened him most mornings at such dreadful hours.

'What's that?' she said.

'Nothing,' he said as he flung the covers in her direction and stumbled, naked, out of the room. He hurried across the den to the kitchen, where

257

he unlocked the door, stepped inside, closed and locked it, and looked at the monitors on a folding table. Marco was leaving through his front door, as usual. And at ten minutes after six, again, nothing unusual about that. It was a very frustrating habit. Damn Americans.

He pushed a button and the monitor went silent. Procedures required him to get dressed immediately, hit the streets, find Marco, and watch him until Ermanno made contact. But Luigi was growing tired of procedures. And he had Simona waiting.

She was barely twenty, a student from Naples, an absolute doll he'd met a week earlier at a club he'd discovered. Last night had been their first together, and it would not be their last. She was already sleeping again when he returned and buried himself under the blankets.

It was cold outside. He had Simona. Whitaker was in Milan, probably still asleep and probably in bed with an Italian woman. There was absolutely no one monitoring what he, Luigi, would do for the entire day. Marco was doing nothing but drinking coffee.

He pulled Simona close and fell asleep.

It was a clear, sunny day in early March. Marco finished a two-hour session with Ermanno. As always, when the weather cooperated, they walked the streets of central Bologna and spoke nothing but Italian. The verb of the day had been 'fare', translated as 'to do' or 'to make', and as far as Marco could tell it was one of the most versatile and overused verbs in the entire language. The act of shopping was 'fare la spesa', translated as 'to make the expenses, or to do the acquisitions'. Asking a question was 'fare la domanda', 'to make a question'. Having breakfast was 'fare la colazione', 'to do breakfast'.

Ermanno signed off a little early, again claiming he had studies of his own to pursue. More often than not, when a strolling lesson came to an end, Luigi made his appearance, taking the handoff from Ermanno, who vanished with remarkable speed. Marco suspected that such coordination was meant to give him the impression that he was always being watched.

They shook hands and said goodbye in front of Feltrinelli's, one of the many bookstores in the university section. Luigi appeared from around a corner and offered the usual hearty 'Buon giorno. Pranziamo?' Are we having lunch?

'Certamente.'

The lunches were becoming less frequent, with Marco getting more chances to dine by himself and handle the menu and the service.

'Ho trovato un nuovo ristorante.' I have found a new restaurant.

'Andiamo.' Let's go.

It wasn't clear what Luigi did with his time during the course of a day, but there was no doubt he spent hours scouring the city for different cafés, trattorias, and restaurants. They had never eaten at the same place twice.

They walked through some narrow streets and came to Via dell' Indipendenza. Luigi did most of the talking, always in very slow, deliberate, precise Italian. He'd forgotten English as far as Marco was concerned.

'Francesca can't study this afternoon,' he said.

'Why not?'

'She has a tour. A group of Australians called her yesterday. Her business is very slow this time of the year. Do you like her?'

'Am I supposed to like her?'

'Well, that would be nice.'

'She's not exactly warm and fuzzy.'

'Is she a good teacher?'

'Excellent. Her perfect English inspires me to study more.'

'She says you study very hard, and that you are a nice man.'

'She likes me?'

'Yes, as a student. Do you think she's pretty?'

'Most Italian women are pretty, including Francesca.'

They turned onto a small street, Via Goito, and Luigi pointed just ahead. 'Here,' Luigi said, and they stopped at the door to Franco Rossi's. 'I've never been here, but I hear it's very good.'

Franco himself greeted them with a smile and open arms. He wore a stylish dark suit that contrasted nicely with his thick gray hair. He took their coats and chatted with Luigi as if they were old friends. Luigi was dropping names and Franco was approving of them. A table near the front window was selected. 'Our best one,' Franco said with a gush. Marco looked around and didn't see a bad table.

'The antipasti here are superb,' Franco said modestly, as if he hated to brag about his food. 'My favorite of the day, however, would be the sliced mushroom salad. Lino adds some truffles, some Parmesan, a few sliced apples . . .' At that point Franco's words faded as he kissed the tips of his fingers. 'Really good,' he managed to say with his eyes closed, dreaming.

They agreed on the salad and Franco was off to welcome the next guests. 'Who's Lino?' asked Marco.

'His brother, the chef.' Luigi dipped some Tuscan bread in a bowl of olive oil. A waiter stopped by and asked about wine. 'Certainly,' Luigi said. 'I'd like something red, from the region.'

There was no question about it. The waiter stabbed his pen at the wine list and said, 'This one here, a Liano from Imola. It is fantastic.' He took a whiff of air just to emphasize the point. Luigi had no choice. 'We'll try it.'

'We were talking about Francesca,' Marco said. 'She seems so distracted. Is something wrong with her?'

Luigi dipped some bread in the olive oil and chewed on a large bite while debating how much to tell Marco. 'Her husband is not well,' he said.

'Does she have children?'

'I don't think so.'

'What's wrong with her husband?'

'He's very sick. I think he's older. I've never met him.'

Il Signore Rossi was back to guide them through the menus, which wasn't really needed. He explained that the tortellini just happened to be the best in Bologna, and particularly superb that day. Lino would be happy to come out of the kitchen and verify this. After the tortellini, an excellent choice would be the veal filet with truffles.

For more than two hours they followed Franco's advice, and when they left they pushed their stomachs back down Via dell' Indipendenza and discussed their siestas.

He found her by accident at the Piazza Maggiore. He was having an espresso at an outdoor table, braving the chill in the bright sunshine, after a vigorous thirty-minute walk, when he saw a small group of fair-haired seniors coming out of the Palazzo Comunale, the city's town hall. A familiar figure was leading, a thin, slightly built woman who held her shoulders high and straight, her dark hair falling out from under a burgundy beret. He left one euro on the table and headed toward them. At the fountain of Neptune, he eased in behind the group – ten in all – and listened to Francesca at work. She was explaining that the gigantic bronze image of the Roman god of the sea was sculpted by a Frenchman over a three-year period, from 1563 to 1566. It was commissioned by a bishop under an urban beautification program aimed at pleasing the pope. Legend has it that before he began the actual work, the Frenchman was concerned about the ample nudity of the project – Neptune is stark naked – so he sent the design to the pope in Rome for approval. The pope wrote back, 'For Bologna, it's okay.'

Francesca was a bit livelier with the real tourists than she was with Marco. Her voice had more energy, her smile came quicker. She was wearing a pair of very stylish eyeglasses that made her look ten years younger. Hiding behind the Australians, he watched and listened for a long time without being noticed.

She explained that the Fontana del Nettuno is now one of the most famous symbols of the city, and perhaps the most popular backdrop for photos. Cameras were pulled from every pocket, and the tourists took their time posing in front of Neptune. At one point, Marco managed to move close enough to make eye contact with Francesca. When she saw him she instinctively smiled, then said a soft 'Buon giorno.'

'Buon giorno. Mind if I tag along?' he asked in English.

'No. Sorry I had to cancel.'

'No problem. How about dinner?'

She glanced around as if she'd done something wrong.

'To study, of course. Nothing more,' he said.

'No, I'm sorry,' she said. She looked beyond

him, across the piazza to the Basilica di San Petronio. 'That little café over there,' she said, 'beside the church, at the corner. Meet me there at five and we'll study for an hour.'

'Va bene.'

The tour continued a few steps to the west wall of the Palazzo Comunale, where she stopped them in front of three large framed collections of black-and-white photos. The history lesson was that during World War II the heart of the Italian Resistance was in and around Bologna. The Bolognesi hated Mussolini and his fascists and the German occupiers, and worked diligently in the underground. The Nazis retaliated with a vengeance – their well-publicized rule was that they would murder ten Italians for every one German soldier killed by the Resistance. In a series of fifty-five massacres in and around Bologna they murdered thousands of young Italian fighters. Their names and faces were on the wall, forever memorialized.

It was a somber moment, and the elderly Australians inched closer to look at the heroes. Marco moved closer too. He was struck by their youthfulness, by their promise that was forever lost – slaughtered for their bravery.

As Francesca moved on with her group, he stayed behind, staring at the faces that covered much of the long wall. There were hundreds, maybe thousands of them. A pretty female face here and there. Brothers. Fathers and sons. An entire family.

Peasants willing to die for their country and their beliefs. Loyal patriots with nothing to give but their lives. But not Marco. No sir. When forced to choose between loyalty and money, Marco had done what he always did. He'd gone for the money. He'd turned his back on his country.

All for the glory of cash.

She was standing inside the door of the café, waiting, not drinking anything but, of course, having a smoke. Marco had decided that her willingness to meet so late for a lesson was further evidence of her need for the work.

'Do you feel like walking?' she said before she said hello.

'Of course.' He'd walked several miles with Ermanno before lunch, then for hours after lunch waiting on her. He'd walked enough for one day, but then what else was there to do? After a month of doing several miles a day he was in shape. 'Where?'

'It's a long one,' she said.

They wound through narrow streets, heading to the southwest, chatting slowly in Italian, discussing the morning's lesson with Ermanno. She talked about the Australians, always an easy and amiable group. Near the edge of the old city they approached the Porta Saragozza and Marco realized where he was, and where he was going.

'Up to San Luca,' he said.

'Yes. The weather is very clear, the night will be beautiful. Are you okay?'

His feet were killing him but he would never think of declining. 'Andiamo,' he said. Let's go.

Sitting almost one thousand feet above the city on the Colle della Guardia, one of the first foothills of the Apennines, the Santuario di San Luca has, for eight centuries, looked over Bologna as its protector and guardian. To get up to it, without getting wet or sunburned, the Bolognesi decided to do what they'd always done best – build a covered sidewalk. Beginning in 1674, and continuing without interruption for sixty-five years, they built arches; 666 arches over a walkway that eventually runs for 3.6 kilometers, the longest porticoed sidewalk in the world.

Though Marco had studied the history, the details were much more interesting when they came from Francesca. The hike up was a steady climb, and they paced themselves accordingly. After a hundred arches, his calves were screaming for relief. She, on the other hand, glided along as if she could climb mountains. He kept waiting for all that cigarette smoking to slow her down.

To finance such a grandiose and extravagant project, Bologna used its considerable wealth. In a rare display of unity among the feuding factions, each arch of the portico was funded by a different group of merchants, artisans, students, churches, and noble families. To record their achievement, and to secure their immortality, they were allowed to hang plaques opposite their arches. Most had disappeared over time.

Francesca stopped for a brief rest at the 170th arch, where one of the few remaining plaques still hung. It was known as 'la Madonna grassa,' the fat Madonna. There were fifteen chapels en route. They stopped again between the eighth and ninth chapels, where a bridge had been built to straddle a road. Long shadows were falling through the porticoes as they trudged up the steepest part of the incline. 'It's well lighted at night,' she assured him. 'For the trip down.'

Marco wasn't thinking about the trip down. He was still looking up, still gazing at the church, which at times seemed closer and at other times seemed to be sneaking away from them. His thighs were aching now, his steps growing heavier.

When they reached the crest and stepped from under the 666th portico, the magnificent basilica spread before them. Its lights were coming on as darkness surrounded the hills above Bologna, and its dome glowed in shades of gold. 'It's closed now,' she said. 'We'll have to see it another day.'

During the hike up, he'd caught a glimpse of a bus easing down the hill. If he ever decided to visit San Luca again for the sole purpose of wandering through another cathedral, he'd be sure to take the bus.

'This way,' she said softly, beckoning him over. 'I know a secret path.'

He followed her along a gravel trail behind the church to a ledge where they stopped and took in the city below them. 'This is my favorite spot,' she said, breathing deeply, as if trying to inhale the beauty of Bologna.

'How often do you come here?'

'Several times a year, usually with groups. They always take the bus. Sometimes on a Sunday afternoon I'll enjoy the walk up.'

'By yourself?'

'Yes, by myself.'

'Could we sit somewhere?'

'Yes, there is a small bench hidden over there. No one knows about it.' He followed her down a few steps, then along a rocky path to another ledge with views just as spectacular.

'Are your legs tired?' she asked.

'Of course not,' he lied.

She lit a cigarette and enjoyed it as few people could possibly enjoy one. They sat in silence for a long time, both resting, both thinking and gazing at the shimmering lights of Bologna.

Marco finally spoke. 'Luigi tells me your husband is very ill. I'm sorry.'

She glanced at him with a look of surprise, then turned away. 'Luigi told me the personal stuff is off-limits.'

'Luigi changes the rules. What has he told you about me?'

'I haven't asked. You're from Canada,

traveling around, trying to learn Italian.'

'Do you believe that?'

'Not really.'

'Why not?'

'Because you claim to have a wife and a family, yet you leave them for a long trip to Italy. And if you're just a businessman off on a pleasure trip, then where does Luigi fit in? And Ermanno? Why do you need those people?'

'Good questions. I have no wife.'

'So it's all a lie.'

'Yes.'

'What's the truth?'

'I can't tell you.'

'Good. I don't want to know.'

'You have enough problems, don't you, Francesca?'

'My problems are my business.'

She lit another cigarette. 'Can I have one of those?' he asked.

'You smoke?'

'Many years ago.' He picked one from the pack and lit it. The lights from the city grew brighter as the night engulfed them.

'Do you tell Luigi everything we do?' he asked.

'I tell him very little.'

'Good.'

Chapter 20

Teddy's last visit to the White House was scheduled for 10:00 a.m. He planned to be late. Beginning at seven that morning, he met with his unofficial transition team – all four deputy directors and his senior people. In quiet little conferences he informed those he'd trusted for many years that he was on the way out, that it had been inevitable for a long time, that the agency was in good shape and life would go on.

Those who knew him well sensed an air of relief. He was, after all, pushing eighty and his legendary bad health was actually getting worse.

At precisely 8:45, while meeting with William Lucat, his deputy director for operations, he summoned Julia Javier for their Backman meeting. The Backman case was important, but in the scheme of global intelligence it was mid-list.

How odd that an operation dealing with a

disgraced former lobbyist would be Teddy's downfall.

Julia Javier sat next to the ever vigilant Hoby, who was still taking notes that no one would ever see, and began matter-of-factly. 'He's in place, still in Bologna, so if we had to activate now we could do so.'

'I thought the plan was to move him to a village in the countryside, someplace where we could watch him more closely,' Teddy said.

'That's a few months down the road.'

'We don't have a few months.' Teddy turned to Lucat and said, 'What happens if we push the button now?'

'It'll work. They'll get him somewhere in Bologna. It's a nice city with almost no crime. Murders are unheard of, so his death will get some attention if his body is found there. The Italians will quickly realize that he's not – what's his name, Julia?'

'Marco,' Teddy said without looking at notes. 'Marco Lazzeri.'

'Right, they'll scratch their heads and wonder who the hell he is.'

Julia said, 'There's no clue as to his real identity. They'll have a body, a fake ID, but no family, no friends, no address, no job, nothing. They'll bury him like a pauper and keep the file open for a year. Then they'll close it.'

'That's not our problem,' Teddy said. 'We're not doing the killing.'

'Right,' said Lucat. 'It'll be a bit messier in the

city, but the boy likes to wander the streets. They'll get him. Maybe a car will hit him. The Italians drive like hell, you know.'

'It won't be that difficult, will it?'

'I wouldn't think so.'

'And what are our chances of knowing when it happens?' Teddy asked.

Lucat scratched his beard and looked across the table at Julia, who was biting a nail and looking over at Hoby, who was stirring green tea with a plastic stick. Lucat finally said, 'I'd say fifty-fifty, at the scene anyway. We'll be watching twenty-four/seven, but the people who'll take him out will be the best of the best. There may be no witnesses.'

Julia added, 'Our best chance will be later, a few weeks after they bury the pauper. We have good people in place. We'll listen closely. I think we'll hear it later.'

Lucat said, 'As always, when we're not pulling the trigger, there's a chance we won't know for sure.'

'We cannot screw this up, understand? It'll be nice to know that Backman is dead – God knows he deserves it – but the goal of the operation is to see who kills him,' Teddy said as his white wrinkled hands slowly lifted a paper cup of green tea to his mouth. He slurped it loudly, crudely.

Maybe it was time for the old man to fade away in a retirement home.

'I'm reasonably confident,' Lucat said. Hoby wrote that down.

'If we leak it now, how long before he's dead?' Teddy asked.

Lucat shrugged and looked away as he pondered the question. Julia was chewing another nail. 'It depends,' she said cautiously. 'If the Israelis move, it could happen in a week. The Chinese are usually slower. The Saudis will probably hire a freelance agent; it could take a month to get one on the ground.'

'The Russians could do it in a week,' Lucat added.

'I won't be here when it happens,' Teddy said sadly. 'And no one on this side of the Atlantic will ever know. Promise me you'll give me a call.'

'This is the green light?' Lucat asked.

'Yes. Careful how you leak it, though. All hunters must be given an equal chance at the prey.'

They gave Teddy their final farewells and left his office. At nine-thirty, Hoby pushed him into the hall and to the elevator. They rode down eight levels to the basement where the bulletproof white vans were waiting for his last trip to the White House.

The meeting was brief. Dan Sandberg was sitting at his desk at the *Post* when it began in the Oval Office a few minutes after ten. And he hadn't moved twenty minutes later when the call came from Rusty Lowell. 'It's over,' he said.

'What happened?' Sandberg asked, already pecking at his keyboard.

'As scripted. The President wanted to know about Backman. Teddy wouldn't budge. The President said he was entitled to know everything. Teddy agreed but said the information was going to be abused for political purposes and it would compromise a sensitive operation. They argued briefly. Teddy got himself fired. Just like I told you.'

'Wow.'

'The White House is making an announcement in five minutes. You might want to watch.'

As always, the spin began immediately. The somber-faced press secretary announced that the President had decided to 'pursue a fresher course with our intelligence operations.' He praised Director Maynard for his legendary leadership and seemed downright saddened by the prospect of having to find his successor. The first question, shot from the front row, was whether Maynard resigned or had been fired.

'The President and Director Maynard reached a mutual understanding.'

'What does that mean?'

'Just what I said.'

And so it went for thirty minutes.

Sandberg's front-page story the following morning dropped two bombs. It began with the definite confirmation that Maynard had been fired after he refused to divulge sensitive information for what he deemed to be raw political purposes. There was no resignation, no 'reaching of a mutual understanding.' It was an old-fashioned sacking. The second blast announced to the world that the President's insistence on obtaining intelligence data was directly tied to a new FBI investigation into the selling of pardons. The cash-for-pardon scandal had been a distant rumbling until Sandberg opened the door. His scoop practically stopped traffic on the Arlington Memorial Bridge.

While Sandberg was hanging around the press room, reveling in his coup, his cell phone rang. It was Rusty Lowell, who abruptly said, 'Call me on a land line, and do it quickly.' Sandberg went to a small office for privacy and dialed Lowell's number at Langley.

'Lucat just got fired,' Lowell said. 'At eight o'clock this morning he met with the President in the Oval Office. He was asked to step in as the interim director. He said yes. They met for an hour. The President pushed on Backman. Lucat wouldn't budge. Got himself fired, just like Teddy.'

'Damn, he's been there a hundred years.'

'Thirty-eight to be exact. One of the best men here. A great administrator.'

'Who's next?'

'That's a very good question. We're all afraid of the knock on the door.'

'Somebody's got to run the agency.'

'Ever meet Susan Penn?'

'No. I know who she is, but I never met her.'

'Deputy director for science and technology. Very loyal to Teddy, hell we all are, but she's also a survivor. She's in the Oval Office right now. If she's offered the interim, she'll take it. And she'll give up Backman to get it.'

'He is the President, Rusty. He's entitled to know everything.'

'Of course. And it's a matter of principle. Can't really blame the guy. He's new on the job, wants to flex his muscle. Looks like he'll fire us all until he gets what he wants. I told Susan Penn to take the job to stop the bleeding.'

'So the FBI should know about Backman real soon?'

'Today, I would guess. Not sure what they'll do when they find out where he is. They're weeks away from an indictment. They'll probably just screw up our operation.'

'Where is he?'

'Don't know.'

'Come on, Rusty, things are different now.'

'The answer is no. End of story. I'll keep you posted on the bloodletting.'

An hour later, the White House press secretary met with the press and announced the appointment of Susan Penn as interim director of the CIA. He made much of the fact that she was the first female to hold the position, thus proving once again how determined this President was to labor diligently for the cause of equal rights.

Luigi was sitting on the edge of his bed, fully dressed and all alone, waiting for the signal from next door. It came at fourteen minutes after 6:00 a.m. – Marco was becoming such a creature of habit. Luigi walked to his control room and pushed a button to silence the buzzer that indicated that his friend had exited through the front door. A computer recorded the exact time and within seconds someone at Langley would know that Marco Lazzeri had just left their safe house on Via Fondazza at precisely 6:14.

He hadn't trailed him in a few days. Simona had been sleeping over. He waited a few seconds, slipped out his rear door, cut through a narrow alley, then peeked through the shadows of the arcades along Via Fondazza. Marco was to his left, headed south and walking at his usual brisk pace, which was getting faster the longer he stayed in Bologna. He was at least twenty years older than Luigi, but with his penchant for walking miles every day he was in better shape. Plus he didn't smoke, didn't drink much, didn't seem to be interested in ladies and the nightlife, and he'd spent the last six years in a cage. Little wonder he could roam the streets for hours, doing nothing.

He wore the new hiking boots every day. Luigi had not been able to get his hands on them. They remained bug-free, leaving no signal behind. Whitaker worried about this in Milan, but then he worried about everything. Luigi was convinced that Marco might walk for a hundred miles within the city, but he wasn't leaving town.

He'd disappear for a while, go exploring or sightseeing, but he could always be found.

He turned onto Via Santo Stefano, a main avenue that ran from the southeast corner of old Bologna into the thick of things around Piazza Maggiore. Luigi crossed over and followed from the other side. As he practically jogged along, he quickly radioed Zellman, a new guy in town, sent by Whitaker to tighten the web. Zellman was waiting on Strada Maggiore, another busy avenue between the safe house and the university.

Zellman's arrival was an indication of the plan moving forward. Luigi knew most of the details now, and was somewhat saddened by the fact that Marco's days were numbered. He wasn't sure who would take him out, and he got the impression that Whitaker didn't know either.

Luigi was praying that he would not be called upon to do the deed. He'd killed two other men, and preferred to avoid such messes. Plus, he liked Marco.

Before Zellman picked up the trail, Marco vanished. Luigi stopped and listened. He ducked into the darkness of a doorway, just in case Marco had stopped too.

He heard him back there, walking a little too heavily, breathing a little too hard. A quick left on a narrow street, Via Castellata, a sprint for fifty yards, then another left onto Via de' Chiari, and a complete change of direction, from due north to due west, a hard pace for a long time until he came to an opening, a small square called Piazza Cavour. He knew the old city so well now, the avenues, alleys, dead ends, intersections, the endless maze of crooked little streets, the names of every square and many of the shops and stores. He knew which tobacco stores opened at six and which waited until seven. He could find five coffee shops that were filled by sunrise, though most waited until daylight. He knew where to sit in the front window, behind a newspaper, with a view of the sidewalk and wait for Luigi to stroll by.

He could lose Luigi anytime he wanted, though most days he played along and kept his trails wide and easy to follow. But it was the fact that he was being watched so closely that spoke volumes.

They don't want me to disappear, he kept saying to himself. And why? Because I'm here for a reason.

He swung wide to the west of the city, far away from where he might be expected to be. After almost an hour of zigzagging through and looping around dozens of short streets and alleys, he stepped onto Via Irnerio and watched the foot traffic. Bar Fontana was directly across the street. There was no one watching it.

Rudolph was tucked away in the rear, head buried low in the morning paper, pipe smoke rising in a lazy blue spiral. They hadn't seen each other in ten days, and after the usual warm greetings his first question was 'Did you make it to Venice?'

Yes, a delightful visit. Marco dropped the names of all the places he'd memorized from the guidebook. He raved about the beauty of the canals, the amazing variety of bridges, the smothering hordes of tourists. A fabulous place. Couldn't wait to go back. Rudolph added some of his own memories. Marco described the church of San Marco as if he'd spent a week there.

Where to next? Rudolph inquired. Probably south, toward warmer weather. Maybe Sicily, the Amalfi coast. Rudolph, of course, adored Sicily and described his visits there. After half an hour of travel talk, Marco finally got around to business. 'I'm traveling so much, I really have no address. A friend from the States is sending me a package. I gave him your address at the law school. Hope you don't mind.'

Rudolph was relighting his pipe. 'It's already here. Came yesterday,' he said, with heavy smoke pouring out with the words.

Marco's heart skipped a beat. 'Was there a return address?'

'Some place in Virginia.'

'Good.' His mouth was instantly dry. He took a sip of water and tried to conceal his excitement. 'Hope it wasn't a problem.'

'Not at all.'

'I'll swing by later and pick it up.'

'I'm in the office from eleven to twelve-thirty.'

'Good, thanks.' Another sip. 'Just curious, how big is the package?'

Rudolph chewed on the stem of his pipe and said, 'A small cigar box maybe.'

A cold rain started at mid-morning. Marco and Ermanno were walking through the university area and found shelter in a quiet little bar. They finished the lesson early, primarily because the student pushed so hard. Ermanno was always ready to quit early.

Since Luigi had not booked lunch, Marco was free to roam, presumably without being followed. But he was careful just the same. He did his loops and backtracking maneuvers, and felt silly as always. Silly or not, they were now standard procedure. Back on Via Zamboni he drifted behind a group of students strolling aimlessly along. At the door to the law school he ducked inside, bounded up the stairs, and within seconds was knocking on Rudolph's half-opened door.

Rudolph was at his ancient typewriter, hammering away at what appeared to be a personal letter. 'Over there,' he said, pointing to a pile of rubble covering a table that hadn't been cleared in decades. 'That brown thing on top.'

Marco picked up the package with as little interest as possible. 'Thanks again, Rudolph,' he said, but Rudolph was typing again and in no mood for a visit. He'd clearly been interrupted.

'Don't mention it,' he said over his shoulder, releasing another cloud of pipe smoke.

'Is there a restroom nearby?' Marco asked.

'Down the hall, on your left.'

'Thanks. See you around.'

There was a prehistoric urinal and three wooden stalls. Marco went into the far one, locked the door, lowered the lid, and took a seat. He carefully opened his package and unfolded the sheets of paper. The first one was plain, white, no letterhead of any kind. When he saw the words 'Dear Marco', he felt like crying.

> *Dear Marco:*
>
> *Needless to say, I was thrilled to hear from you. I thanked God when you were released and I pray for your safety now. As you know, I will do anything to help.*
>
> *Here is a smartphone, state of the art and all that. The Europeans are ahead of us with cell phone and wireless Internet technology, so this should work fine over there. I've written some instructions on another sheet of paper. I know this will sound like Greek, but it's really not that complicated.*
>
> *Don't try and call – it's too easy to track. Plus, you would have to use a name and set up an account. E-mail is the way. By using KwyteMail with encryption, it's impossible to track our messages. I suggest that you e-mail only me. I can then handle the relays.*
>
> *On this end I have a new laptop that I keep near me at all times.*

This will work, Marco. Trust me. As soon as you're online, e-mail and we can chat.

Good Luck, Grinch   *(March 5)*

Grinch? A code or something. He had not used their real names.

Marco studied the sleek device, thoroughly bewildered by it but also determined to get the damn thing going. He probed its small case, found the cash, and counted it slowly as if it were gold. The door opened and closed; someone was using the urinal. Marco could hardly breathe. Relax, he kept telling himself.

The restroom door opened and closed again, and he was alone. The page of instructions was handwritten, obviously when Neal didn't have a lot of time. It read:

Ankyo 850 PC Pocket Smartphone – fully charged battery – 6 hours talk time before recharging, recharger included.

Step 1) Find Internet café with wireless access – list enclosed

Step 2) Either enter café or get within 200 feet of it

Step 3) Turn on, switch is in upper right-hand corner

Step 4) Watch screen for 'Access Area' then the question 'Access Now?' Press 'Yes' under screen; wait.

Step 5) Then push keypad switch, bottom right, and unfold keypad

Step 6) Press Wi-Fi access on screen

Step 7) Press 'Start' for Internet browser

Step 8) At cursor, type 'www.kwytemail.com'

Step 9) Type user name 'Grinch456'

Step 10) Type pass phrase 'post hoc ergo propter hoc'

Step 11) Press 'Compose' to bring up New Message Form

Step 12) Select my e-mail address: 123Grinch@kwytemail.com

Step 13) Type your message to me

Step 14) Click on 'Encrypt Message'

Step 15) Click 'Send'

Step 16) Bingo – I'll have the message

More notes followed on the other side, but Marco needed to pause. The smartphone was growing heavier by the minute as it inspired more questions than answers. For a man who'd never been in an Internet café, he could not begin to understand how one could be used from across the street. Or within two hundred feet.

Secretaries had always handled the e-mail flood. He'd been much too busy to sit in front of a monitor.

There was an instruction booklet that he opened at random. He read a few lines and didn't understand a single phrase. Trust Neal, he told himself.

You have no choice here, Marco. You have to master this damn thing.

From a Web site called www.AxEss.com Neal

had printed a list of free wireless Internet places in Bologna – three cafés, two hotels, one library, and one bookstore.

Marco folded his cash, stuck it in his pocket, then slowly put his package back together. He stood, flushed the toilet for some reason, and left the restroom. The phone, the papers, the case, and the small recharger were easily buried in the deep pockets of his parka.

The rain had turned to snow when he left the law school, but the covered sidewalks protected him and the crowd of students hurrying to lunch. As he drifted away from the university area, he pondered ways to hide the wonderful little assets Neal had sent him. The phone would never leave his person. Nor would the cash. But the paperwork – the letter, the instructions, the manual – where could he stash them? Nothing was protected in his apartment. He saw in a store window an attractive shoulder bag of some sort. He went and inquired. It was a Silvio brand laptop case, navy blue, waterproof, made of a synthetic fabric that the saleslady could not translate. It cost sixty euros, and Marco reluctantly placed them on the counter. As she finished the sale, he carefully placed the smartphone and its related items into the bag. Outside, he flung it over his shoulder and tucked it snugly under his right arm.

The bag meant freedom for Marco Lazzeri. He would guard it with his life.

He found the bookstore on Via Ugo Bassi.

The magazines were on the second level. He stood by the rack for five minutes, holding a soccer weekly while watching the front door for anyone suspicious. Silly. But it was a habit now. The Internet hookups were on the third floor, in a small coffee shop. He bought a pastry and a Coke and found a narrow booth where he could sit and watch everyone going and coming.

No one could find him there.

He pulled out his Ankyo 850 with as much confidence as he could muster and glanced through its manual. He reread Neal's instructions. He followed them nervously, typing on the tiny keypad with both thumbs, the way it was illustrated in the owner's manual. After each step he looked up to check the movements around the café.

The steps worked perfectly. He was online in short order, much to his amazement, and when the codes worked he was looking at a screen that was giving him the okay to write a message. Slowy, he moved his thumbs around and typed his first wireless Internet e-mail:

Grinch: Got the package. You'll never know how much it means to me. Thank you for your help. Are you sure our messages are completely secure? If so, I will tell you more about my situation. I fear I am not safe. It's about 8:30 a.m. your time. I'll send this message now, and check back in a few hours. Love, Marco

286

He sent the message, turned the machine off, then stayed for an hour poring over the manual. Before he left to meet Francesca, he turned it on again and followed the route to get online. On the screen he tapped 'Google Search', then typed in 'Washington Post'. Sandberg's story caught his attention, and he scrolled through it.

He'd never met Teddy Maynard, but they had spoken several times by phone. Very tense conversations. The man had been practically dead ten years ago. In his other life Joel had butted heads a few times with the CIA, usually over shenanigans his defense-contractor clients were trying to pull.

Outside the bookstore, Marco sized up the street, saw nothing of interest, and began another long walk.

Cash for pardons? What a sensational story, but it was asking too much to believe that an outgoing president would take bribes like that. During his spectacular fall from power, Joel had read many things about himself, about half of them true. He'd learned the hard way to believe little of what got printed.

Chapter 21

At an unnamed, unnumbered, nondescript building on Pinsker Street in downtown Tel Aviv, an agent named Efraim entered from the sidewalk and walked past the elevator to a dead-end corridor with one locked door. There was no knob, no handle. He pulled a device that resembled a small television remote from his pocket and aimed it at the door. Thick tumblers fell somewhere inside, a sharp click, and the door opened into one of the many safe houses maintained by the Mossad, the Israeli secret police. It had four rooms – two with bunk beds where Efraim and his three colleagues slept, a small kitchen where they cooked their simple meals, and a large cluttered workroom where they spent hours every day planning an operation that had been practically dormant for six years but was suddenly one of the Mossad's highest priorities.

The four were members of *kidon*, a small, tight

unit of highly skilled field agents whose primary function was assassination. Quick, efficient, silent killing. Their targets were enemies of Israel who could not be brought to trial because its courts could not get jurisdiction. Most targets were in Arab and Islamic countries, but *kidon* were often used in the former Soviet bloc, Europe, Asia, even North Korea and the United States. They had no boundaries, no restraints, nothing to stop them from taking out those who wanted to destroy Israel. The men and women of *kidon* were fully licensed to kill for their country. Once a target was approved, in writing, by the current prime minister, an operation plan was put into place, a unit was organized, and the enemy of Israel was as good as dead. Obtaining such approval at the top had rarely been difficult.

Efraim tossed a bag of pastries onto one of the folding tables where Rafi and Shaul were plowing through research. Amos was in a corner at the computer, studying maps of Bologna, Italy.

Most of their research was stale; it included pages of mainly useless background on Joel Backman, information that had been collected years ago. They knew everything about his chaotic personal life – the three ex-wives, the three children, the former partners, the girlfriends, the clients, the old lost friends from the power circles in D.C. When his killing had been approved six years earlier, another *kidon* had worked urgently putting together the background on Backman. A preliminary plan to kill him in a car accident in D.C. had been jettisoned when he suddenly pled guilty and fled to prison. Not even a *kidon* could reach him in protective custody at Rudley.

The background was important now only because of his son. Since his surprise pardon and disappearance seven weeks earlier, the Mossad had kept two agents close to Neal Backman. They rotated every three or four days so no one in Culpeper, Virginia, would get suspicious; small towns with their nosy neighbors and bored cops presented enormous challenges. One agent, a pretty lady with a German accent, had actually chatted with Neal on Main Street. She claimed to be a tourist and needed directions to Montpelier, the nearby home of President James Madison. She flirted, or tried her best to, and was perfectly willing go further. He didn't take the bait. They'd bugged his home and office, and they listened to cell phone conversations. From a lab in Tel Aviv, they read every one of his office e-mails and those from home as well. They monitored his bank account and his credit card spending. They knew he'd made a quick trip to Alexandria six days earlier, but they did not know why.

They were watching Backman's mother too, in Oakland, but the poor lady was fading fast. For years they had debated the idea of slipping her one of the poison pills from their amazing arsenal. They would then ambush her son at her funeral. However, the *kidon* manual on assassination prohibited the killing of family members unless said members were also involved in threats to Israeli security.

But the idea was still debated, with Amos being its most vocal proponent.

They wanted Backman dead, but they also wanted him to live a few hours before passing on. They needed to chat with him, to ask some questions, and if the answers weren't forthcoming they knew how to make him talk. Everyone talked when the Mossad really wanted answers.

'We have found six agents who speak Italian,' Efraim said. 'Two will be here this afternoon at three, for a meeting.' None of the four spoke Italian, but all spoke perfect English, as well as Arabic. Among them there were eight other languages.

Each of the four had combat experience, extensive computer training, and were skilled at crossing borders (with and without paperwork), interrogation, disguises, and forgery. And they had the ability to kill in cold blood with no regrets. The average age was thirty-four, and each had been involved with at least five successful *kidon* assassinations.

When fully operational, their *kidon* would have twelve members. Four would carry out the actual killing, and the other eight would provide cover, surveillance, and tactical support, and would clean up after the hit.

'Do we have an address?' Amos asked from the computer.

'No, not yet,' said Efraim. 'And I'm not sure we'll get one. This is coming through counterintelligence.'

'There are half a million people in Bologna,' Amos said almost to himself.

'Four hundred thousand,' said Shaul. 'And a hundred thousand of those are students.'

'We're supposed to get a picture of him,' Efraim said, and the other three stopped what they were doing and looked up. 'There's a photo of Backman somewhere, one taken recently, after prison. Getting a copy is a possibility.'

'That would certainly be helpful,' Rafi said.

They had a hundred old photos of Joel Backman. They had studied every square centimeter of his face, every wrinkle, every vein in his eyes, every strand of hair on his head. They had counted his teeth, and they had copies of his dental records. Their specialists across town at the headquarters of Israel's Central Institute for Intelligence and Special Duties, better known as Mossad, had prepared excellent computer images of what Backman would look like now, six years after the world last saw him. There was a series of digital projections of Backman's face at a hefty 240 pounds, his weight when he pled guilty. And another series of Backman at 180, his rumored weight now. They had worked with his hair, leaving it natural, and predicting its color for a fifty-two-year-old man. They colored it black and red and brown. They cut it and left it longer. They put a dozen different pairs of glasses on his face, then added a beard, first a dark one, then a gray one.

It all came back to the eyes. Study the eyes.

Though Efraim was the leader of the unit, Amos had seniority. He had been assigned to Backman in 1998 when the Mossad first heard rumors of the JAM software that was being shopped around by a powerful Washington lobbyist. Working through their ambassador in Washington, the Israelis pursued the purchase of JAM, thought they had a deal, but were stiff-armed when Backman and Jacy Hubbard took their goods elsewhere.

The selling price was never made known. The deal was never consummated. Some money changed hands, but Backman, for some reason, did not deliver the product.

Where was it now? Had it ever existed in the first place?

Only Backman knew.

The six-year hiatus in the hunt for Joel Backman had given Amos ample time to fill in some gaps. He believed, as did his superiors, that the so-called Neptune satellite system was a Red Chinese creation; that the Chinese had spent a hefty chunk of their national treasury in building it; that they had stolen valuable technology from the Americans to do so; that they had brilliantly disguised the launching of the system and fooled U.S., Russian, and Israeli satellites; and that they had been unable to reprogram the system to override the software JAM had uploaded. Neptune was useless without JAM, and the Chinese would give up their Great Wall to get their hands on it and Backman.

Amos, and Mossad, also believed that Farooq Khan, the last surviving member of the trio and the principal author of the software, had been tracked down by the Chinese and murdered eight months ago. Mossad was on his trail when he disappeared.

They also believed the Americans were still not sure who built Neptune, and this intelligence failure was an ongoing, almost permanent embarrassment. American satellites had dominated the skies for forty years and were so effective they could see through clouds, spot a machine gun under a tent, intercept a wire transfer from a drug dealer, eavesdrop on a conversation in a building, and find oil under the desert with infrared imagery. They were vastly superior to anything the Russians had put up. For another system of equal or better technology to be designed, built, launched, and to become operational without the knowledge of the CIA and the Pentagon had been unthinkable.

Israeli satellites were very good, but not as good as the Americans'. Now it appeared to the intelligence world that Neptune was more advanced than anything the United States had ever launched.

These were only assumptions; little had been

confirmed. The only copy of JAM had been hidden. Its creators were dead.

Amos had lived the case for almost seven years, and he was thrilled to have a new *kidon* in place and was urgently making plans. Time was very short. The Chinese would blow up half of Italy if they thought Backman would end up in the rubble. The Americans might try and get him too. On their soil he was protected by their Constitution, with its layers of safeguards. The laws required that he be treated fairly then tucked away in prison and protected around the clock. But on the other side of the world he was fair game.

Kidon had been used to neutralize a few wayward Israelis, but never at home. The Americans would do the same.

Neal Backman kept his new, very thin laptop in the same old battered briefcase he hauled home every night. Lisa had not noticed it because he never took it out. He kept it close, always within a step or two.

He changed his morning routine slightly. He'd bought a card from Jerry's Java, a fledgling coffee and doughnut chain that was trying to lure customers with fancy coffee and free newspapers, magazines, and wireless Internet access. The franchise had converted an abandoned drive-through taco hut at the edge of town, jazzed it up with funky decor, and in its first two months was doing a booming business.

There were three cars in front of him at the drive-through window. His laptop was on his knees, just under the steering wheel. At the curb, he ordered a double mocha, no whipped cream, and waited for the cars in front to inch forward. He pecked away with both hands as he waited. Once online, he quickly went to KwyteMail. He typed in his user name – Grinch123 – then his pass phrase – post hoc ergo propter hoc. Seconds later there it was – the first message from his father.

Neal held his breath as he read, then exhaled mightily and eased forward in line. It worked! The old man had figured it out!

Quickly, he typed:

Marco: Our messages cannot be traced. You can say anything you want, but it's always best to say as little as possible. Delighted you're there and out of Rudley. I'll go online each day at this time – at precisely 7:50 a.m. EST. Gotta run. Grinch

He placed the laptop in the passenger seat, lowered his window, and paid almost four bucks for a cup of coffee. As he pulled away, he kept glancing at the computer to see how long the access signal would last. He turned onto the street, drove no more than two hundred feet, and the signal was gone.

Last November, after Arthur Morgan's

astounding defeat, Teddy Maynard began devising his Backman pardon strategy. With his customary meticulous planning, he prepared for the day when moles would leak the word of Backman's whereabouts. To tip the Chinese, and do so in a manner that would not arouse suspicion, Teddy began looking for the perfect snitch.

Her name was Helen Wang, a fifth-generation Chinese American who'd worked for eight years at Langley as an analyst on Asian issues. She was very smart, very attractive, and spoke passable Mandarin Chinese. Teddy got her a temporary assignment at the State Department, and there she began cultivating contacts with diplomats from Red China, some of whom were spies themselves and most of whom were constantly on the prowl for new agents.

The Chinese were notorious for their aggressive tactics in recruiting spies. Each year 25,000 of their students were enrolled in American universities, and the secret police tracked them all. Chinese businessmen were expected to cooperate with central intelligence when they returned home. The thousands of American companies doing business on the mainland were constantly monitored. Their executives were researched and watched. The good prospects were sometimes approached.

When Helen Wang 'accidentally' let it slip that her background included a few years at the CIA, and that she hoped to return soon, she quickly had the attention of intelligence chiefs in Beijing. She accepted an invitation from a new friend to have lunch at a swanky D.C. restaurant, then dinner. She played her role beautifully, always reticent about their overtures but always reluctantly saying yes. Her detailed memos were hand delivered to Teddy after every encounter.

When Backman was suddenly freed from prison, and it became apparent he'd been stashed away and would not surface, the Chinese put tremendous pressure on Helen Wang. They offered her $100,000 for information about his location. She appeared to be frightened by the offer, and for a few days broke off contact. With perfect timing, Teddy got her assignment at State canceled and called her back to Langley. For two weeks she had nothing to do with her old friends undercover at the Chinese embassy.

Then she called them and the payoff soon climbed to $500,000. Helen turned nasty and demanded $1 million, claiming that she was risking her career and her freedom and it was certainly worth more money than that. The Chinese agreed.

The day after Teddy was fired, she called her handler and requested a secret meeting. She gave him a sheet of paper with wiring instructions to a bank account in Panama, one that was secretly owned by the CIA. When the money was received, she said, they would meet again and she would have the location of Joel Backman.

She would also give them a recent photo of Joel Backman.

The drop was a 'brush by', an actual physical meeting between mole and handler, done in such a way that no one would notice anything unusual. After work, Helen Wang stopped at a Kroger store in Bethesda. She walked to the end of aisle twelve, where the magazines and paperbacks were displayed. Her handler was loitering at the rack with a copy of *Lacrosse Magazine*. Helen picked up another copy of the same magazine and quickly slid an envelope into it. She flipped pages with passable boredom, then put the magazine back on the rack. Her handler was shuffling through the sports weeklies. Helen wandered away, but only after she saw him take her copy of *Lacrosse Magazine*.

For a change, the cloak-and-dagger routine wasn't needed. Helen's friends at the CIA weren't watching because they had arranged the drop. They'd known her handler for many years.

The envelope contained one sheet of paper – an eight-by-ten color xerox photo of Joel Backman as he was apparently walking down the street. He was much thinner, had the beginnings of a grayish goatee, European-style eyeglasses, and was dressed like a local. Handwritten at the bottom of the page was: Joel Backman, Via Fondazza, Bologna, Italy. The handler gawked at it as he sat in his car, then he sped away to the embassy of the People's Republic of China on Wisconsin Avenue NW in Washington.

*

At first the Russians seemed to have no interest in the whereabouts of Joel Backman. Their signals were read a variety of ways at Langley. No early conclusions were made, none were possible. For years the Russians had secretly maintained that the so-called Neptune system was one of their own, and this had contributed mightily to the confusion at the CIA.

Much to the surprise of the intelligence world, Russia was managing to keep aloft about 160 reconnaissance satellites a year, roughly the same number as the former Soviet Union. Its robust presence in space had not diminished, contrary to what the Pentagon and the CIA had predicted.

In 1999, a defector from the GRU, the Russian military's intelligence arm and successor to the KGB, informed the CIA that Neptune was not the property of the Russians. They had been caught off guard as badly as the Americans. Suspicion was focused on the Red Chinese, who were far behind in the satellite game.

Or were they?

The Russians wanted to know about Neptune, but they were not willing to pay for information about Backman. When the overtures from Langley were largely ignored, the same color photo sold to the Chinese was anonymously e-mailed to four Russian intelligence chiefs operating under diplomatic cover in Europe.

The leak to the Saudis was handled through an executive of an American oil company stationed in Riyadh. His name was Taggett and he'd lived there for more than twenty years. He was fluent in Arabic and moved in the social circles as easily as any foreigner. He was especially close to a mid-level bureaucrat in the Saudi Foreign Ministry office, and over late-afternoon tea he told him that his company had once been represented by Joel Backman. Further, and much more important, Taggett claimed to know where Backman was hiding.

Five hours later, Taggett was awakened by a buzzing doorbell. Three young gentlemen in business suits pushed their way into his apartment and demanded a few moments of his time. They apologized, explained that they were with some branch of the Saudi police, and really needed to talk. When pressed, Taggett reluctantly passed on the information he had been coached to disclose.

Joel Backman was hiding in Bologna, Italy, under a different name. That was all he knew.

Could he find out more? they asked.

Perhaps.

They asked him if he would leave the next morning, return to his company's headquarters in New York, and dig for more information about Backman. It was very important to the Saudi government and the royal family.

Taggett agreed to do so. Anything for the king.

Chapter 22

Every year in May, just before Ascension Day,
the people of Bologna march up the Colle della
Guardia from the Saragozza gate, along the
longest continuous arcade in the world, through
all 666 arches and past all fifteen chapels, to the
summit, to the Santuario di San Luca. In the
sanctuary they remove their Madonna and
proceed back down to the city, where they parade
her through the crowded streets and finally place
her in the Cathedral of San Pietro, where she
stays for eight days until another parade takes her
home. It's a festival unique to Bologna, and has
gone on uninterrupted since 1476.

As Francesca and Joel sat in the Santuario di
San Luca, Francesca was describing the ritual
and how much it meant to the people of
Bologna. Pretty, but just another empty church
as far as Marco was concerned.

They had taken the bus this time, thus
avoiding the 666 arches and the 3.6-kilometer

hike up the hill. His calves still hurt from the last visit to San Luca, three days ago.

She was so distracted by weightier matters that she was lapsing into English and didn't seem to realize it. He did not complain. When she finished with the festival, she began pointing to the interesting elements in the cathedral – the architecture and construction of the dome, the painting of the frescoes. Marco was fighting desperately to pay attention. The domes and faded frescoes and marble crypts and dead saints were all running together now in Bologna, and he caught himself thinking of warmer weather. Then they could stay outdoors and talk. They could visit the city's lovely parks and if she so much as mentioned a cathedral he would revolt.

She wasn't thinking of warmer weather. Her thoughts were elsewhere.

'You've already done that one,' he interrupted when she pointed at a painting above the baptistery.

'I'm sorry. Am I boring you?'

He started to blurt out the truth, but instead said, 'No, but I've seen enough.'

They left the sanctuary and sneaked around behind the church, to her secret pathway that led down a few steps to the best view of the city. The last snow was melting quickly on the red tiled roofs. It was the eighteenth of March.

She lit a cigarette and seemed content to loiter in silence and admire Bologna. 'Do you like my city?' she asked, finally.

'Yes, very much.'

'What do you like about it?'

After six years in prison, any city would do. He thought for a moment, then said, 'It's a real city, with people living where they work. It's safe and clean, timeless. Things haven't changed much over the centuries. The people enjoy their history and they're proud of their accomplishments.'

She nodded slightly, approving of his analysis. 'I'm baffled by Americans,' she said. 'When I guide them through Bologna they're always in a hurry, always anxious to see one sight so they can cross it off the list and move on to the next. They're always asking about tomorrow, and the next day. Why is this?'

'I'm the wrong person to ask.'

'Why?'

'I'm Canadian, remember?'

'You're not Canadian.'

'No, I'm not. I'm from Washington.'

'I've been there. I've never seen so many people racing around, going nowhere. I don't understand the desire for such a hectic life. Everything has to be so fast – work, food, sex.'

'I haven't had sex in six years.'

She gave him a look that conveyed many questions. 'I really don't want to talk about that.'

'You brought it up.'

She puffed on the cigarette as the air cleared. 'Why haven't you had sex in six years?'

'Because I was in prison, in solitary confinement.'

She flinched slightly and her spine seemed to straighten. 'Did you kill someone?'

'No, nothing like that. I'm pretty harmless.'

Another pause, another puff. 'Why are you here?'

'I really don't know.'

'How long will you stay?'

'Maybe Luigi can answer that.'

'Luigi,' she said as if she wanted to spit. She turned and began walking. He followed along because he was supposed to. 'What are you hiding from?' she asked.

'It's a very, very long story, and you really don't want to know.'

'Are you in danger?'

'I think so. I'm not sure how much, but let's just say that I'm afraid to use my real name and I'm afraid to go home.'

'Sounds like danger to me. Where does Luigi fit in?'

'He's protecting me, I think.'

'For how long?'

'I really don't know.'

'Why don't you simply disappear?'

'That's what I'm doing now. I'm in the middle of my disappearance. And from here, where would I go? I have no money, no passport, no identification. I don't officially exist.'

'This is very confusing.'

'Yes. Why don't we drop it.'

305

He glanced away for a second and did not see her fall. She was wearing black leather boots with low heels, and the left one twisted violently on a rock in the narrow pathway. She gasped and fell hard onto the walkway, bracing herself at the last second with both hands. Her purse flew forward. She shrieked something in Italian. Marco quickly knelt down to grab her.

'It's my ankle,' she said, grimacing. Her eyes were already moist, her pretty face twisted in pain.

He gently lifted her from the wet pathway and carried her to a nearby bench, then retrieved her purse. 'I must've tripped,' she kept saying. 'I'm sorry.' She fought the tears but soon gave up.

'It's okay, it's okay,' Marco said, kneeling in front of her. 'Can I touch it?'

She slowly lifted her left leg, but the pain was too great.

'Let's leave the boot on,' Marco said, touching it with great care.

'I think it's broken,' she said. She pulled a tissue from her purse and wiped her eyes. She was breathing heavy and gritting her teeth. 'I'm sorry.'

'It's okay.' Marco looked around; they were very much alone. The bus up to San Luca had been virtually empty, and they had seen no one in the past ten minutes. 'I'll, uh, go inside and find help.'

'Yes, please.'

'Don't move. I'll be right back.' He patted her

knee and she managed a smile. Then he hustled away, almost falling himself. He ran to the rear of the church and saw no one. Where, exactly, does one find an office in a cathedral? Where is the curator, administrator, head priest? Who's in charge of this place? Outside, he circled San Luca twice before he saw a custodian emerge from a partially hidden door by the gardens.

'Mi può aiutare?' he called out. Can you help me?

The custodian stared and said nothing. Marco was certain he had spoken clearly. He walked closer and said, 'La mia amica si é fatta male.' My lady friend is hurt.

'Dov'è?' the man grunted. Where?

Marco pointed and said, 'Lì, dietro alla chiesa.' Over there, behind the church.

'Aspetti.' Wait. He turned and walked back to the door and opened it.

'Si sbrighi, per favora.' Please hurry.

A minute or two dragged by, with Marco waiting nervously, wanting to dash back and check on Francesca. If she'd broken a bone, then shock might set in quickly. A larger door below the baptistery opened, and a gentleman in a suit came rushing out with the custodian behind him.

'La mia amica è caduta,' Marco said. My friend fell.

'Where is she?' asked the gentleman in excellent English. They were cutting across a small brick patio, dodging unmelted snow.

'Around back, by the lower ledge. It's her

ankle; she thinks she broke it. We might need an ambulance.'

Over his shoulder the gentleman snapped something at the custodian, who disappeared.

Francesca was sitting on the edge of the bench with as much dignity as possible. She held the tissue at her mouth; the crying had stopped. The gentleman didn't know her name, but he had obviously seen her before at San Luca. They chatted in Italian, and Marco missed most of it.

Her left boot was still on, and it was agreed that it should remain so, to prevent swelling. The gentleman, Mr. Coletta, seemed to know his first aid. He examined her knees and hands. They were scratched and sore, but there was no bleeding. 'It's just a bad sprain,' she said. 'I really don't think it's broken.'

'An ambulance will take forever,' the gentleman said. 'I'll drive you to the hospital.'

A horn honked nearby. The custodian had fetched a car and pulled up as close as possible.

'I think I can walk,' Francesca said gamely, trying to stand.

'No, we'll help you,' Marco said. Each grabbed an elbow and slowly raised her to her feet. She grimaced when she put pressure on the foot, but said, 'It's not broken. Just a sprain.' She insisted on walking. They half carried her toward the car.

Mr. Coletta took charge and arranged them in the backseat so that her feet were in Marco's lap, elevated, and her back was resting against the left rear door. When his passengers were properly in place, he jumped behind the wheel and shifted gears. They crawled in reverse along a shrub-lined alley, then onto a narrow paved road. Soon, they were moving down the hill, headed for Bologna.

Francesca put on her sunglasses to cover her eyes. Marco noticed a trickle of blood on her left knee. He took the tissue from her hand and began to dab it. 'Thank you,' she whispered. 'I'm sorry I've ruined your day.'

'Please stop that,' he said with a smile.

It was actually the best day with Francesca. The fall was humbling her and making her seem human. It was evoking, however unwilling, honest emotions. It was allowing sincere physical contact, one person genuinely trying to help another. It was shoving him into her life. Whatever happened next, whether at the hospital or at her home, he would at least be there for a moment. In the emergency, she was needing him, though she certainly didn't want that.

As he held her feet and stared blankly out the window, Marco realized how desperately he craved a relationship of any kind, with any person.

Any friend would do.

At the foot of the hill, she said to Mr. Coletta, 'I would like to go to my apartment.'

He looked in the rearview mirror and said, 'But I think you should see a doctor.'

'Maybe later. I'll rest for a bit and see how it

feels.' The decision was made; arguing would've been useless.

Marco had some advice too, but he held it. He wanted to see where she lived.

'Very well,' said Mr. Coletta.

'It's Via Minzoni, near the train station.'

Marco smiled to himself, quite proud that he knew the street. He could picture it on a map, at the northern edge of the old city, a nice section but not the high-rent district. He had walked it at least once. In fact, he'd found an early-hours coffee bar at a spot where the street ended at the Piazza dei Martiri. As they zipped along the perimeter, in the mid-afternoon traffic, Marco glanced at every street sign, took in every intersection, and knew exactly where he was at all times.

Not another word was spoken. He held her feet, her stylish but well-used black boots slightly soiling his wool slacks. At that moment, he couldn't have cared less. When they turned onto Via Minzoni, she said, 'Down about two blocks, on the right.' A moment later she said, 'Just ahead. There's a spot behind that green BMW.'

They gently extracted her from the rear seat and got her to the sidewalk, where she shook free for a second and tried to walk. The ankle gave way; they caught her. 'I'm on the second floor,' she said, gritting her teeth. There were eight apartments. Marco watched carefully as she pushed the button next to the name of Giovanni Ferro. A female voice answered.

310

'Francesca,' she said, and the door clicked. They stepped into a foyer that was dark and shabby. To the right was an elevator with its door open, waiting. The three of them filled it tightly. 'I'm really fine now,' she said, obviously trying to lose both Marco and Mr. Coletta.

'We need to get some ice on it,' Marco said as they began a very slow ride up.

The elevator made a noisy stop, its door finally opened, and they shuffled out, both men still holding Francesca by the elbows. Her apartment was only a few steps away, and when they arrived at the door Mr. Coletta had gone far enough.

'I'm very sorry about this,' he said. 'If there are medical bills, would you please call me?'

'No, you're very kind. Thank you so much.'

'Thank you,' Marco said, still attached to her. He pushed the doorbell and waited as Mr. Coletta ducked back in the elevator and left them. She pulled away and said, 'This is fine, Marco. I can manage from here. My mother is house-sitting today.'

He was hoping for an invitation inside, but he was in no position to push on. The episode had run its course as far as he was concerned, and he had learned much more than he could have expected. He smiled, released her arm, and was about to say goodbye when a lock clicked loudly from inside. She turned toward the door, and in doing so put pressure on her wounded ankle. It

311

buckled again, causing her to gasp and reach for him.

The door opened just as Francesca fainted.

Her mother was Signora Altonelli, a seventyish lady who spoke no English and for the first few hectic minutes thought Marco had somehow harmed her daughter. His bumbling Italian proved inadequate, especially under the pressure of the moment. He carried Francesca to the sofa, raised her feet, and conveyed the concept of 'Ghiaccio, ghiaccio.' Ice, get some ice. She reluctantly backed away, then disappeared into the kitchen.

Francesca was stirring by the time her mother returned with a wet washcloth and a small plastic bag of ice.

'You fainted,' Marco said, hovering over her. She clutched his hand and looked about wildly.

'Chi è?' her mother said suspiciously. Who's he?

'Un amico.' A friend. He patted her face with the washcloth and she rallied quickly. In some of the fastest Italian he had yet to experience, she explained to her mother what had happened. The machine-gun bursts back and forth made him dizzy as he tried to pick off an occasional word, then he simply gave up. Suddenly, Signora Altonelli smiled and patted him on the shoulder with great approval. Good boy.

When she disappeared, Francesca said, 'She's gone to make coffee.'

'Great.' He had pulled a stool next to the sofa, and he sat close by, waiting. 'We need to get some ice on this thing,' he said.

'Yes, we should.'

They both looked at her boots. 'Will you take them off?' she asked.

'Sure.' He unzipped the right boot and removed it as though that foot had been injured too. He went even slower with the left one. Every little movement caused pain, and at one point he said, 'Would you prefer to do it?'

'No, please, go ahead.' The zipper stopped almost exactly at the ankle. The swelling made it difficult to ease the boot off. After a few long minutes of delicate wiggling, while the patient suffered with clenched teeth, the boot was off.

She was wearing black stockings. Marco studied them, then announced, 'These have to come off.'

'Yes, they do.' Her mother returned and fired off something in Italian. 'Why don't you wait in the kitchen?' Francesca said to Marco.

The kitchen was small but impeccably put together, very modern with chrome and glass and not a square inch of wasted space. A high-tech coffeepot gurgled on a counter. The walls above a small breakfast nook were covered in bright abstract art. He waited and listened to both of them chatter at once.

They got the stockings off without further injury. When Marco returned to the living room,

Signora Altonelli was arranging the ice around the left ankle.

'She says it's not broken,' Francesca said to him. 'She worked in a hospital for many years.'

'Does she live in Bologna?'

'Imola, a few miles away.'

He knew exactly where it was, on the map anyway. 'I guess I should be going now,' he said, not really wanting to go but suddenly feeling like a trespasser.

'I think you need some coffee,' Francesca said. Her mother darted away, back into the kitchen.

'I feel like I'm intruding,' he said.

'No, please, after all you've done today, it's the least I can do.'

Her mother was back, with a glass of water and two pills. Francesca gulped it all down and propped her head up on some pillows. She exchanged short sentences with her mother, then looked at him and said, 'She has a chocolate torta in the refrigerator. Would you like some?'

'Yes, thank you.'

And her mother was off again, humming now and quite pleased that she had someone to care for and someone to feed. Marco resumed his place on the stool. 'Does it hurt?'

'Yes, it does,' she said, smiling. 'I cannot lie. It hurts.'

He could think of no appropriate response, so he ventured back to common ground. 'It all happened so fast,' he said. They spent a few

314

minutes rehashing the fall. Then they were silent. She closed her eyes and appeared to be napping. Marco crossed his arms over his chest and stared at a huge, very odd painting that covered almost an entire wall.

The building was ancient, but from the inside Francesca and her husband had fought back as determined modernists. The furniture was low, sleek black leather with bright steel frames, very minimalist. The walls were covered with baffling contemporary art.

'We can't tell Luigi about this,' she whispered.

'Why not?'

She hesitated, then let it go. 'He is paying me two hundred euros a week to tutor you, Marco, and he's complaining about the price. We've argued. He has threatened to find someone else. Frankly, I need the money. I'm getting one or two jobs a week now; it's still the slow season. Things will pick up in a month when the tourists come south, but right now I'm not earning much.'

The stoic façade was long gone. He couldn't believe that she was allowing herself to be so vulnerable. The lady was frightened, and he would break his neck to help her.

She continued: 'I'm sure he will terminate my services if I skip a few days.'

'Well, you're about to skip a few days.' He glanced at the ice wrapped around her ankle.

'Can we keep it quiet? I should be able to move around soon, don't you think?'

'We can try to keep it quiet, but Luigi has a way of knowing things. He follows me closely. I'll call in sick tomorrow, then we'll figure out something the next day. Maybe we could study here.'

'No. My husband is here.'

Marco couldn't help but glance over his shoulder. 'Here?'

'He's in the bedroom, very ill.'

'What's –'

'Cancer. The last stages. My mother sits with him when I'm working. A hospice nurse comes in each afternoon to medicate him.'

'I'm sorry.'

'So am I.'

'Don't worry about Luigi. I'll tell him I'm thrilled with your teaching style, and that I will refuse to work with anyone else.'

'That would be a lie, wouldn't it?'

'Sort of.'

Signora Altonelli was back with a tray of torta and espresso. She placed it on a bright red coffee table in the middle of the room and began slicing. Francesca took the coffee but didn't feel like eating. Marco ate as slowly as humanly possible and sipped from his small cup as if it might be his last. When Signora Altonelli insisted on another slice, and a refill, he grudgingly accepted.

Marco stayed about an hour. Riding down in the elevator, he realized that Giovanni Ferro had not made a sound.

Chapter 23

Red China's principal intelligence agency, the Ministry of State Security, or MSS, used small, highly trained units to carry out assassinations around the world, in much the same manner as the Russians, Israelis, British, and Americans.

One notable difference, though, was that the Chinese had come to rely upon one unit in particular. Instead of spreading the dirty work around like other countries, the MSS turned first to a young man the CIA and Mossad had been watching with great admiration for several years. His name was Sammy Tin, the product of two Red Chinese diplomats who were rumored to have been selected by the MSS to marry and reproduce. If ever an agent were perfectly cloned, it was Sammy Tin. Born in New York City and raised in the suburbs around D.C., he'd been educated by private tutors who bombarded him with foreign languages from the time he left diapers. He entered the University of Maryland at the age of sixteen, left it with two degrees at the age of twenty-one, then studied engineering in Hamburg, Germany. Somewhere along the way he picked up bomb-making as a hobby. Explosives became his passion, with an emphasis on controlled explosions from odd packages – envelopes, paper cups, ballpoint pens, cigarette packages. He was an expert marksman, but guns were simple and bored him. The Tin Man loved his bombs.

He then studied chemistry under an assumed name in Tokyo, and there he mastered the art and science of killing with poisons. By the time he was twenty-four he had a dozen different names, about that many languages, and crossed borders with a vast array of passports and disguises. He could convince any customs agent anywhere that he was Japanese, Korean, or Taiwanese.

To round out his education, he spent a grueling year in training with an elite Chinese army unit. He learned to camp, cook over a fire, cross raging rivers, survive in the ocean, and live in the wilderness for days. When he was twenty-six, the MSS decided the boy had studied enough. It was time to start killing.

As far as Langley could tell, he began notching his astounding body count with the murders of three Red Chinese scientists who'd gotten too cozy with the Russians. He got them over dinner at a restaurant in Moscow. While their body-guards waited outside, one got his throat slit in the men's room while he finished up at the urinal. It took an hour to find his body, crammed in a rather small garbage can. The second made the mistake of worrying about the first. He went to the men's room, where the Tin Man was waiting, dressed as a janitor. They found him with his head stuffed down the toilet, which had been clogged and was backing up. The third died seconds later at the table, where he was sitting alone and becoming very worried about his two missing colleagues. A man in a waiter's jacket hurried by, and without slowing thrust a poison dart into the back of his neck.

As killings go, it was all quite sloppy. Too much blood, too many witnesses. Escape was dicey, but the Tin Man got a break and managed to dash through the busy kitchen unnoticed. He was on the loose and sprinting through a back alley by the time the bodyguards were summoned. He ducked into the dark city, caught a cab, and twenty minutes later entered the Chinese embassy. The next day he was in Beijing, quietly celebrating his first success.

The audacity of the attack shocked the intelligence world. Rival agencies scrambled to find out who did it. It ran so contrary to how the Chinese normally eliminated their enemies. They were famous for their patience, the discipline to wait and wait until the timing was perfect. They would chase until their prey simply gave up. Or they would ditch one plan and go to the next, carefully waiting for their opportunity.

When it happened again a few months later in Berlin, the Tin Man's legend was born. A French executive had handed over some bogus high-tech secrets dealing with mobile radar. He got flung from the balcony of a fourteenth-floor hotel room, and when he landed beside the pool it upset quite a few sunbathers. Again, the killing was much too visible.

In London, the Tin Man blew a man's head off with a cell phone. A defector in New York's Chinatown lost most of his face when a cigarette exploded. Sammy Tin was soon getting credit for most of the more dramatic intelligence killings in that underworld. The legend grew rapidly. Though he kept four or five trusted members in his unit, he often worked alone. He lost a man in Singapore when their target suddenly emerged with some friends, all with guns. It was a rare failure, and the lesson from it was to stay lean, strike fast, and don't keep too many people on the payroll.

As he matured, the hits became less dramatic, less violent, and much easier to conceal. He was now thirty-three, and without a doubt the most feared agent in the world. The CIA spent a fortune trying to track his movements. They knew he was in Beijing, hanging around his luxurious apartment. When he left, they tracked him to Hong Kong. Interpol was alerted when he boarded a nonstop flight to London, where he changed passports and at the last moment boarded an Alitalia flight to Milan.

Interpol could only watch. Sammy Tin often traveled with diplomatic cover. He was no criminal; he was an agent, a diplomat, a businessman, a professor, anything he needed to be.

A car was waiting for him at Milan's Malpensa airport, and he vanished into the city. As far as the CIA could tell, it had been four and a half years since the Tin Man had set foot in Italy.

Mr. Elya certainly looked the part of a wealthy Saudi businessman, though his heavy wool suit was almost black, a little too dark for Bologna, and its pinstripes were much too thick for anything designed in Italy. And his shirt was pink, with a glistening white collar, not a bad combo, but, well, it was still pink. Through the collar was a gold bar, also too thick, that pushed the knot of the tie up tightly for the choking look, and at each end of the bar was a diamond. Mr. Elya was into diamonds – a large one on each hand, dozens of smaller ones clustered in his Rolex, a couple more in the gold cuffs of his shirt. The shoes appeared to Stefano to be Italian, brand new, brown, but much too light to go with the suit.

As a whole, the package simply wasn't working. It was trying mightily, though. Stefano had time to analyze his client while they rode in virtual silence from the airport, where Mr. Elya and his assistant had arrived by private jet, to the center of Bologna. They were in the rear of a black Mercedes, one of Mr. Elya's conditions, with a driver who was silent in the front seat along with the assistant, who evidently spoke only Arabic. Mr. Elya's English was passable, quick bursts of it, usually followed with something in Arabic to the assistant, who felt compelled to write down everything his master said.

After ten minutes in the car with them, Stefano was already hoping they would finish well before lunch.

The first apartment he showed them was near the university, where Mr. Elya's son would soon arrive to study medicine. Four rooms on the second floor, no elevator, solid old building, nicely furnished, certainly luxurious for any student – 1,800 euros a month, one year's lease, utilities extra. Mr. Elya did nothing but frown, as if his spoiled son would require something much nicer. The assistant frowned too. They frowned all the way down the stairs, into the car, and said nothing as the driver hurried to the second stop.

It was on Via Remorsella, one block west of Via Fondazza. The flat was slightly larger than the first, had a kitchen the size of a broom closet, was badly furnished, had no view whatsoever, was twenty minutes away from the university, cost 2,600 euros a month, and even had a strange odor to it. The frowning stopped, they liked the place. 'This will be fine,' Mr. Elya said, and Stefano breathed a sigh of relief. With a bit of luck, he wouldn't have to entertain them over lunch. And he'd just earned a nice commission.

They hurried over to the office of Stefano's company, where paperwork was produced at a record pace. Mr. Elya was a busy man with an urgent meeting in Rome, and if the rental couldn't be completed right then, on the spot, then forget everything!

The black Mercedes sped them back to the airport, where a rattled and exhausted Stefano said thanks and farewell and hurried away as quickly as possible. Mr. Elya and his assistant walked across the tarmac to his jet and disappeared inside. The door closed.

The jet didn't move. Inside, Mr. Elya and his assistant had ditched their business garb and were dressed casually. They huddled with three other members of their team. After waiting for about an hour, they finally left the jet, hauled their substantial baggage to the private terminal, then into waiting vans.

Luigi had become suspicious of the navy blue Silvio bag. Marco never left it in his apartment. It was never out of his sight. He carried it everywhere, strapped over his shoulder and tucked tightly under his right arm as if it contained gold.

What could he possibly possess now that required such protection? He rarely carried his study materials anywhere. If he and Ermanno studied inside, they did so in Marco's apartment. If they studied outside, it was all conversation and no books were used.

Whitaker in Milano was suspicious too, especially since Marco had been spotted in an Internet café near the university. He sent an agent named Krater to Bologna to help Zellman and Luigi keep a closer eye on Marco and his troublesome bag. With the noose tightening and fireworks expected, Whitaker was asking Langley for even more muscle on the streets.

But Langley was in chaos. Teddy's departure, though certainly not unexpected, had turned the place upside down. The shock waves from Lucat's sacking were still being felt. The President was threatening a major overhaul, and the deputy directors and high-level administrators were spending more time protecting their butts than watching their operations.

It was Krater who got the radio message from Luigi that Marco was drifting toward Piazza Maggiore, probably in search of his late-afternoon coffee. Krater spotted him as he strode across the square, dark blue bag under his right arm, looking very much like a local. After studying a rather thick file on Joel Backman, it was nice to finally lay eyes on him. If the poor guy only knew.

But Marco wasn't thirsty, not yet anyway. He passed the cafés and shops, then suddenly, after a furtive glance, stepped into Albergo Nettuno, a fifty-room boutique hotel just off the piazza. Krater radioed Zellman and Luigi, who was particularly puzzled because Marco had no reason whatsoever to be entering a hotel. Krater waited five minutes, then walked into the small lobby, absorbing everything he saw. To his right was a lobby area with some chairs and a few travel magazines strewn over a wide coffee table. To his left was a small empty phone room with its door open, then another room that was not empty. Marco sat there, alone, hunched over the small table under the wall-mounted phone, his blue bag open. He was too busy to see Krater walk by.

'May I help you, sir?' the clerk said from the front desk.

'Yes, thanks, I wanted to inquire about a room,' Krater said in Italian.

'For when?'

'Tonight.'

'I'm sorry, but we have no vacancies.'

Krater picked up a brochure at the desk. 'You're always full,' he said with a smile. 'It's a popular place.'

'Yes, it is. Perhaps another time.'

'Do you by chance have Internet access?'

'Of course.'

'Wireless?'

'Yes, the first hotel in the city.'

He backed away and said, 'Thanks. I'll try again another time.'

'Yes, please.'

He passed the phone room on the way out. Marco had not looked up.

With both thumbs he was typing his text and hoping he would not be asked to leave by the clerk at the front desk. The wireless access was something the Nettuno advertised, but only for its guests. The coffee shops, libraries, and one of the bookstores offered it free to anyone who ventured in, but not the hotels.

His e-mail read:

Grinch: I once dealt with a banker in Zurich, name of Mikel Van Thiessen, at Rhineland Bank, on Bahnhofstrasse, downtown Zurich. See if you can determine if he's still there. If not, who took his place? Do not leave a trail!
   Marco

He pushed Send, and once again prayed that he'd done things right. He quickly turned off the Ankyo 850 and tucked it away in his bag. As he left, he nodded at the clerk, who was on the phone.

Two minutes after Krater came out of the hotel, Marco made his exit. They watched him from three different points, then followed him as he mixed easily with the late-afternoon rush of people leaving work. Zellman circled back, entered the Nettuno, went to the second phone room on the left, and sat in the seat where Marco had been less than twenty minutes earlier. The clerk, puzzled now, pretended to be busy behind his desk.

An hour later, they met in a bar and retraced his movements. The conclusion was obvious, but still hard to swallow – since Marco had not used the phone, he was freeloading on the hotel's wireless Internet access. There was no other reason to randomly enter the hotel lobby, sit in a phone room for less than ten minutes, then abruptly leave. But how could he do it? He had no laptop, no cell phone other than the one Luigi had loaned him, an outdated device that would only work in the city and could in no way be upgraded to go online. Had he obtained some high-tech gadget? He had no money.

Theft was a possibility.

They kicked around various scenarios. Zellman left to e-mail the disturbing news to Whitaker. Krater was dispatched to begin window shopping for an identical blue Silvio bag.

Luigi was left to contemplate dinner.

His thoughts were interrupted by a call from Marco himself. He was in his apartment, not feeling too well, his stomach had been jumpy all afternoon. He'd canceled his lesson with Francesca, and now he was begging off dinner.

Chapter 24

If Dan Sandberg's phone rang before 6:00 a.m., the news was never good. He was a night owl, a nocturnal creature who often slept until it was time to have breakfast and lunch together. Everyone who knew him also knew that it was pointless to phone early.

It was a colleague at the *Post*. 'You got scooped, buddy,' he announced gravely.

'What?' Sandberg snapped.

'The *Times* just wiped your nose for you.'

'Who?'

'Backman.'

'What?'

'Go see for yourself.'

Sandberg ran to the den of his messy apartment and attacked his desk computer. He found the story, written by Heath Frick, a hated rival at *The New York Times*. The front-page headline read FBI PARDON PROBE SEARCHES FOR JOEL BACKMAN.

Citing a host of unnamed sources, Frick reported that the FBI's cash-for-pardon investigation had intensified and was expanding to include specific individuals who were granted reprieves by former president Arthur Morgan. Duke Mongo was named as a 'person of interest,' a euphemism often tossed about when the authorities wanted to taint a person they were unable to formally indict. Mongo, though, was hospitalized and rumored to be gasping for his last breath.

The probe was now focusing its attention on Joel Backman, whose eleventh-hour pardon had shocked and outraged many, according to Frick's gratuitous analysis. Backman's mysterious disappearance had only fueled the speculation that he'd bought himself a pardon and fled to avoid the obvious questions. Old rumors were still out there, Frick reminded everyone, and various unnamed and supposedly trustworthy sources hinted that the theory about Backman burying a fortune had not been officially laid to rest.

'What garbage!' Sandberg snarled as he scrolled down the screen. He knew the facts better than anyone. This crap could not be substantiated. Backman had not paid for a pardon.

No one even remotely connected with the former president would say a word. For now, the probe was just a probe, with no formal investigation under way, but the heavy federal artillery was not far away. An eager U.S. attorney was clamoring to get started. He didn't have his grand jury yet, but his office was sitting on go, waiting on word from the Justice Department.

Frick wrapped it all up with two paragraphs about Backman, historical rehash that the paper had run before.

'Just filler!' Sandberg fumed.

The President read it too but had a different reaction. He made some notes and saved them until seven-thirty, when Susan Penn, his interim director of the CIA, arrived for the morning briefing. The PDB – president's daily briefing – had historically been handled by the director himself, always in the Oval Office and normally the first item of the day's business. But Teddy Maynard and his rotten health had changed the routine, and for the past ten years the briefings had been done by someone else. Now traditions were being honored again.

An eight- to ten-page summary of intelligence matters was placed on the President's desk precisely at 7:00 a.m. After almost two months in office, he had developed the habit of reading every word of it. He found it fascinating. His predecessor had once boasted that he read hardly anything – books, newspapers, magazines. Certainly not legislation, policies, treaties, or daily briefings. He'd often had trouble reading his own speeches. Things were much different now.

330

Susan Penn was driven in an armored car from her Georgetown home to the White House, where she arrived each morning at 7:15. Along the way she read the daily summary, which was prepared by the CIA. On page four that morning was an item about Joel Backman. He was attracting the attention of some very dangerous people, perhaps even Sammy Tin.

The President greeted her warmly and had coffee waiting by the sofa. They were alone, as always, and they went right to work.

'You've seen *The New York Times* this morning?' he asked.

'Yes.'

'What are the chances that Backman paid for a pardon?'

'Very slim. As I've explained before, he had no idea one was in the works. He didn't have time to arrange things. Plus, we're quite confident he didn't have the money.'

'Then why was Backman pardoned?'

Susan Penn's loyalty to Teddy Maynard was fast becoming history. Teddy was gone, and would soon be dead, but she, at the age of forty-four, had a career left. Perhaps a long one. She and the President were working well together. He seemed in no hurry to appoint his new director.

'Frankly, Teddy wanted him dead.'

'Why? What is your recollection of why Mr. Maynard wanted him dead?'

'It's a long story –'

'No, it's not.'

'We don't know everything.'

'You know enough. Tell me what you know.'

She tossed her copy of the summary on the sofa and took a deep breath. 'Backman and Jacy Hubbard got in way over their heads. They had this software, JAM, that their clients had stupidly brought to the United States, to their office, looking for a fortune.'

'These clients were the young Pakistanis, right?'

'Yes, and they're all dead.'

'Do you know who killed them?'

'No.'

'Do you know who killed Jacy Hubbard?'

'No.'

The President stood with his coffee and walked to his desk. He sat on the edge and glared across the room at her. 'I find it hard to believe that we don't know these things.'

'Frankly, so do I. And it's not because we haven't tried. It's one reason Teddy worked so hard to get Backman pardoned. Sure, he wanted him dead, just on general principle – the two have a history and Teddy has always considered Backman to be a traitor. But he also felt strongly that Backman's murder might tell us something.'

'What?'

'Depends on who kills him. If the Russians do it, then we can believe the satellite system belonged to the Russians. Same for the Chinese. If the Israelis kill him, then there's a good chance

Backman and Hubbard tried to sell their product to the Saudis. If the Saudis get to him, then we can believe that Backman double-crossed them. We're almost certain that the Saudis thought they had a deal.'

'But Backman screwed them?'

'Maybe not. We think Hubbard's death changed everything. Backman packed his bags and ran away to prison. All deals were off.'

The President walked back to the coffee table and refilled his cup. He sat across from her and shook his head. 'You expect me to believe that three young Pakistani hackers tapped into a satellite system so sophisticated that we didn't even know about it?'

'Yes. They were brilliant, but they also got lucky. Then they not only hacked their way in, but they wrote some amazing programs that manipulated it.'

'And that's JAM?'

'That's what they called it.'

'Has anybody ever seen the software?'

'The Saudis. That's how we know that it not only exists but probably works as well as advertised.'

'Where is the software now?'

'No one knows, except, maybe, Backman himself.'

A long pause as the President sipped his lukewarm coffee. Then he rested his elbows on his knees and said, 'What's best for us, Susan? What's in our best interests?'

She didn't hesitate. 'To follow Teddy's plan. Backman will be eliminated. The software hasn't been seen in six years, so it's probably gone too. The satellite system is up there, but whoever owns it can't play with it.'

Another sip, another pause. The President shook his head and said, 'So be it.'

Neal Backman didn't read *The New York Times*, but he did a quick search each morning for his father's name. When he ran across Frick's story, he attached it to an e-mail and sent it with the morning message from Jerry's Java.

At his desk, he read the story again, and relived the old rumors of how much money the broker had buried while the firm was collapsing. He'd never asked his father the question point-blank, because he knew he would not get a straight answer. Over the years, though, he had come to accept the common belief that Joel Backman was as broke as most convicted felons.

Then why did he have the nagging feeling that the cash-for-pardon scheme could be true? Because if anyone buried so deep in a federal prison could pull off such a miracle, it was his father. But how did he get to Bologna, Italy? And why? Who was after him?

The questions were piling up, the answers more elusive than ever.

As he sipped his double mocha and stared at his locked office door, he once again asked himself the great question: How does one go about locating a certain Swiss banker without the use of phones, faxes, regular mail, or e-mail?

He'd figure it out. He just needed time.

The *Times* story was read by Efraim as he rode the train from Florence to Bologna. A call from Tel Aviv had alerted him, and he found it online. Amos was four seats behind him, also reading it on his laptop.

Rafi and Shaul would arrive early the next morning, Rafi on a flight from Milan, Shaul on a train from Rome. The four Italian-speaking members of the *kidon* were already in Bologna, hurriedly putting together the two safe houses they would need for the project.

The preliminary plan was to grab Backman under the darkened porticoes along Via Fondazza or another suitable side street, preferably early in the morning or after dark. They would sedate him, shove him in a van, take him to a safe house, and wait for the drugs to wear off. They would interrogate him, eventually kill him with poison, and drive his body two hours north to Lake Garda where he'd be fed to the fish.

The plan was rough and fraught with pitfalls, but the green light had been given. There was no turning back. Now that Backman was getting so much attention, they had to strike quickly.

The race was also fueled by the fact that the Mossad had good reason to believe that Sammy Tin was either in Bologna, or somewhere close.

The nearest restaurant to her apartment was a
lovely old trattoria called Nino's. She knew the
place well and had known the two sons of old
Nino for many years. She explained her pre-
dicament, and when she arrived both of them
were waiting and practically carried her inside.
They took her cane, her bag, her coat, and
walked her slowly to their favorite table, which
they'd moved closer to the fireplace. They
brought her coffee and water, and offered
anything else she could possibly want. It was
mid-afternoon, the lunch crowd was gone.
Francesca and her student had Nino's to
themselves.

When Marco arrived a few minutes later, the
two brothers greeted him like family. 'La
professoressa la sta aspettando,' one of them
said. The teacher is waiting.

The fall on the gravel at San Luca and the
sprained ankle had transformed her. Gone was
the frosty indifference. Gone was the sadness, at
least for now. She smiled when she saw him,
even reached up, grabbed his hand, and pulled
him close so they could blow air kisses at both
cheeks, a custom Marco had been observing for
two months but had yet to engage in. This was,
after all, his first female acquaintance in Italy.
She waved him to the chair directly across from
her. The brothers swarmed around, taking his
coat, asking him about coffee, anxious to see
what an Italian lesson would look and sound like.

'How's your foot?' Marco asked, and made the mistake of doing so in English. She put her finger to her lips, shook her head, and said, 'Non inglese, Marco. Solamente Italiano.'

He frowned and said, 'I was afraid of that.'

Her foot was very sore. She had kept it on ice while she was reading or watching television, and the swelling had gone down. The walk to the restaurant had been slow, but it was important to move about. At her mother's insistence, she was using a cane. She found it both useful and embarrassing.

More coffee and water arrived, and when the brothers were convinced that things were perfect with their dear friend Francesca and her Canadian student, they reluctantly retreated to the front of the restaurant.

'How is your mother?' he asked in Italian.

Very well, very tired. She has been sitting with Giovanni for a month now, and it's taking a toll.

So, thought Marco, Giovanni is now available for discussion. How is he?

Inoperable brain cancer, she said, and it took a few tries to get the translation right. He has been suffering for almost a year, and the end is quite close. He is unconscious. It's a pity.

What was his profession, what did he do?

He taught medieval history at the university for many years. They met there – she was a student, he was her professor. At the time he was married to a woman he disliked immensely. They had two sons. She and her professor fell in love and began an affair which lasted almost ten years before he divorced his wife and married Francesca.

Children? No, she said with sadness. Giovanni had two, he didn't want any more. She had regrets, many regrets.

The feeling was clear that the marriage had not been a happy one. Wait till we get around to mine, thought Marco.

It didn't take long. 'Tell me all about you,' she said. 'Speak slowly. I want the accents to be as good as possible.'

'I'm just a Canadian businessman,' Marco began in Italian.

'No, really. What's your real name?'

'No.'

'What is it?'

'For now it's Marco. I have a long history, Francesca, and I can't talk about it.'

'Very well, do you have children?'

Ah, yes. For a long time he talked about his three children – their names, ages, occupations, residences, spouses, children. He added some fiction to move along his narrative, and he pulled off a small miracle by making the family sound remotely normal. Francesca listened intently, waiting to pounce on any wayward pronunciation or improperly conjugated verb. One of Nino's boys brought some chocolates and lingered long enough to say, with a huge smile, 'Parla molto bene, signore.' You speak very well, sir.

She began to fidget after an hour and Marco could tell she was uncomfortable. He finally convinced her to leave, and with great pleasure he walked her back down Via Minzoni, her right hand tightly fixed to his left elbow while her left hand worked the cane. They walked as slowly as possible. She dreaded the return to her apartment, to the deathwatch, the vigil. He wanted to walk for miles, to cling to her touch, to feel the hand of someone who needed him.

At her apartment they traded farewell kisses and made arrangements to meet at Nino's tomorrow, same time, same table.

Jacy Hubbard spent almost twenty-five years in Washington; a quarter of a century of major-league hell-raising with an astounding string of disposable women. The last had been Mae Szun, a beauty almost six feet tall with perfect features, deadly black eyes, and a husky voice that had no trouble at all getting Jacy out of a bar and into a car. After an hour of rough sex, she had delivered him to Sammy Tin, who finished him off and left him at his brother's grave.

When sex was needed to set up a kill, Sammy preferred Mae Szun. She was a fine MSS agent in her own right, but the legs and face added a dimension that had proved deadly on at least three occasions. He summoned her to Bologna, not to seduce but to hold hands with another agent and pretend to be happily married tourists. Seduction, though, was always a possibility.

Especially with Backman. Poor guy had just spent six years locked up, away from women.

Mae spotted Marco as he moved in a crowd down Strada Maggiore, headed in the general direction of Via Fondazza. With amazing agility, she picked up her pace, pulled out a cell phone, and managed to gain ground on him while still looking like a bored window shopper.

Then he was gone. He suddenly took a left, turned down a narrow alley, Via Begatto, and headed north, away from Via Fondazza. By the time she made the turn, he was out of sight.

Chapter 25

Spring was finally arriving in Bologna. The last flurries of snow had fallen. The temperature had approached fifty degrees the day before, and when Marco stepped outside before dawn he thought about swapping his parka for one of the other jackets. He took a few steps under the dark portico, let the temperature sink in, then decided it was still chilly enough to keep the parka. He'd return in a couple of hours and he could switch then if he wanted. He crammed his hands in his pockets and took off on the morning hike.

He could think of nothing but the *Times* story. To see his name plastered across the front page brought back painful memories, and that was unsettling enough. But to be accused of bribing the President was actionable at law, and in another life he would have started the day by shotgunning lawsuits at everyone involved. He would have owned *The New York Times*.

But what kept him awake were the questions.

What would the attention mean for him now? Would Luigi snatch him again and run away?

And the most important: Was he in more danger today than yesterday?

He was surviving nicely, tucked away in a lovely city where no one knew his real name. No one recognized his face. No one cared. The Bolognesi went about their lives without disturbing others.

Not even he recognized himself. Each morning when he finished shaving and put on his glasses and his brown corduroy driver's cap, he stood at the mirror and said hello to Marco. Long gone were the fleshy jowls and puffy dark eyes, the thicker, longer hair. Long gone was the smirk and the arrogance. Now he was just another quiet man on the street.

Marco was living one day at a time, and the days were piling up. No one who read the *Times* story knew where Marco was or what he was doing.

He passed a man in a dark suit and instantly knew he was in trouble. The suit was out of place. It was a foreign variety, something bought off the rack in a low-end store, one he'd seen every day in another life. The white shirt was the same monotonous button-down he'd seen for thirty years in D.C. He'd once considered floating an office memo banning blue-and-white cotton button-downs, but Carl Pratt had talked him out of it.

He couldn't tell the color of the tie.

It was not the type of suit you'd ever see under the porticoes along Via Fondazza before dawn, or at any other time for that matter. He took a few steps, glanced over his shoulder, and saw that the suit was now following him. White guy, thirty years old, thick, athletic, the clear winner in a footrace or a fistfight. So Marco used another strategy. He suddenly stopped, turned around, and said, 'You want something?'

To which someone else said, 'Over here, Backman.'

Hearing his name stopped him cold. For a second his knees were rubbery, his shoulders sagged, and he told himself that no, he was not dreaming. In a flash he thought of all the horrors the word 'Backman' brought with it. How sad to be so terrified of your own name.

There were two of them. The one with the voice arrived on the scene from the other side of Via Fondazza. He had basically the same suit, but with a bold white shirt with no buttons on the collar. He was older, shorter, and much thinner. Mutt and Jeff. Thick 'n' Thin.

'What do you want?' Marco said.

They were slowly reaching for their pockets. 'We're with the FBI,' the thick one said. American English, probably Midwest.

'Sure you are,' Marco said.

They went through the required ritual of flashing their badges, but under the darkness of the portico Marco could read nothing. The dim light over an apartment door helped a little. 'I can't read those,' he said.

'Let's take a walk,' said the thin one. Boston, Irish. 'Walk' came out 'wok'.

'You guys lost?' Marco said without moving. He didn't want to move, and his feet were quite heavy anyway.

'We know exactly where we are.'

'I doubt that. You got a warrant?'

'We don't need one.'

The thick one made the mistake of touching Marco's left elbow, as if he would help him move along to where they wanted to go. Marco jerked away. 'Don't touch me! You boys get lost. You can't make an arrest here. All you can do is talk.'

'Fine, let's go have a chat,' said the thin one.

'I don't have to talk.'

'There's a coffee shop a couple of blocks away,' said the thick one.

'Great, have some coffee. And a pastry. But leave me alone.'

Thick 'n' Thin looked at each other, then glanced around, not sure what to do next, not sure what plan B entailed.

Marco wasn't moving; not that he felt very safe where he was, but he could almost see a dark car waiting around the corner.

Where the hell is Luigi right now? he asked himself. Is this part of his conspiracy?

He'd been discovered, found, unmasked, called by his real name on Via Fondazza. This

344

would certainly mean another move, another safe house.

The thin one decided to take control of the encounter. 'Sure, we can meet right here. There are a lot of folks back home who'd like to talk to you.'

'Maybe that's why I'm over here.'

'We're investigating the pardon you bought.'

'Then you're wasting a helluva lot of time and money, which would surprise no one.'

'We have some questions about the transaction.'

'What a stupid investigation,' Marco said, spitting the words down at the thin one. For the first time in many years he felt like the broker again, berating some haughty bureaucrat or dimwitted congressman. 'The FBI spends good money sending two clowns like you all the way to Bologna, Italy, to tackle me on a sidewalk so you can ask me questions that no fool in his right mind would answer. You're a couple of dumbasses, you know that? Go back home and tell your boss that he's a dumbass too. And while you're talking to him, tell him he's wasting a lot of time and money if he thinks I paid for a pardon.'

'So you deny –'

'I deny nothing. I admit nothing. I say nothing, except that this is the FBI at its absolute worst. You boys are in deep water and you can't swim.'

Back home they'd slap him around a little,

push him, curse him, swap insults. But on foreign soil they weren't sure how to behave. Their orders were to find him, to see if he did in fact live where the CIA said he was living. And if found, they were supposed to jolt him, scare him, hit him with some questions about wire transfers and offshore accounts.

They had it all mapped out and had rehearsed it many times. But under the porticoes of Via Fondazza, Mr. Lazzeri was annihilating their plans.

'We're not leaving Bologna until we talk,' said the thick one.

'Congratulations, you're in for a long vacation.'

'We have our orders, Mr. Backman.'

'And I've got mine.'

'Just a few questions, please,' said the thin one.

'Go see my lawyer,' Marco said, and began to walk away, in the direction of his apartment.

'Who's your lawyer?'

'Carl Pratt.'

They weren't moving, weren't following, and Marco picked up his pace. He crossed the street, glanced quickly at his safe house, but didn't slow down. If they wanted to follow, they waited too long. By the time he darted onto Via del Piombo, he knew they could never find him. These were his streets now, his alleys, his darkened doorways to shops that wouldn't open for three more hours.

They found him on Via Fondazza only because they knew his address.

At the southwestern edge of old Bologna, near the Porto San Stefano, he caught a city bus and rode it for half an hour, until he stopped near the train station at the northern perimeter. There he caught another bus and rode into the center of the city. The buses were filling; the early risers were getting to work. A third bus took him across the city again to the Porta Saragozza, where he began the 3.6-kilometer hike up to San Luca. At the four-hundredth arch he stopped to catch his breath, and between the columns he looked down and waited for someone to come sneaking up behind him. There was no one back there, as he expected.

He slowed his pace and finished the climb in fifty-five minutes. Behind the Santuario di San Luca he followed the narrow pathway where Francesca had fallen, and finally parked himself on the bench where she had waited. From there, his early-morning view of Bologna was magnificent. He removed his parka to cool off. The sun was up, the air was as light and clear as any he'd ever breathed, and for a long time Marco sat very much alone and watched the city come to life.

He treasured the solitude, and the safety of the moment. Why couldn't he make the climb every morning, and sit high above Bologna with nothing to do but think, and maybe read the newspapers? Perhaps call a friend on the phone and catch up on the gossip?

He'd have to find the friends first.

It was a dream that would not come true.

With Luigi's very limited cell phone he called Ermanno and canceled their morning session. Then he called Luigi and explained that he didn't feel like studying.

'Is something wrong?'

'No. I just need a break.'

'That's fine, Marco, but we're paying Ermanno to teach you, okay? You need to study every day.'

'Drop it, Luigi. I'm not studying today.'

'I don't like this.'

'And I don't care. Suspend me. Kick me out of school.'

'Are you upset?'

'No, Luigi, I'm fine. It's a beautiful day, springtime in Bologna, and I'm going for a long walk.'

'Where?'

'No thanks, Luigi. I don't want company.'

'What about lunch?'

Hunger pains shot through Marco's stomach. Lunch with Luigi was always delicious and he always grabbed the check. 'Sure.'

'Let me think. I'll call you back.'

'Sure, Luigi. Ciao.'

They met at twelve-thirty at Caffè Atene, an ancient dive in an alley, down a few steps from street level. It was a tiny place, with small square tables practically touching each other. The waiters jostled around with trays of food held high overhead. Chefs yelled from the kitchen. The cramped dining room was smoky, loud, and packed with hungry people who enjoyed talking at full volume as they ate. Luigi explained that the restaurant had been around for centuries, tables were impossible to get, and the food was, of course, superb. He suggested they share a plate of calamari to get things started.

After a morning of arguing with himself up at San Luca, Marco had decided not to tell Luigi about his encounter with the FBI. At least not then, not that morning. He might do it the next day, or the next, but for the moment he was still sorting things out. His principal reason for holding back was that he did not want to pack up and run again, not on Luigi's terms.

If he ran, he would be alone.

He couldn't begin to imagine why the FBI would be in Bologna, evidently without the knowledge of Luigi and whoever he was working for. He was assuming Luigi knew nothing of their presence. He certainly seemed to be much more concerned with the menu and the wine list. Life was good. Everything was normal.

The lights went out. Suddenly, Caffè Atene was completely dark, and in the next instant a waiter with a tray of someone's lunch came crashing across their table, yelling and cursing and spilling himself onto both Luigi and Marco. The legs of the antique table buckled and its edge crashed hard onto Marco's lap. At about the same time, a foot or something hit him hard on the left shoulder. Everyone was yelling. Glass was breaking. Bodies were getting shoved, then from the kitchen someone screamed, 'Fire!'

The scramble outside and onto the street was completed without serious injury. The last person out was Marco, who ducked low to avoid the stampede while searching for his navy blue Silvio bag. As always, he had hung its strap over the back of his chair, with the bag resting so close to his body he could usually feel it. It had disappeared in the melee.

The Italians stood in the street and stared in disbelief at the café. Their lunch was in there, half eaten and now being ruined. Finally, a thin light puff of smoke emerged and made its way through the door and into the air. A waiter could be seen running by the front tables with a fire extinguisher. Then some more smoke, but not much.

'I lost my bag,' Marco said to Luigi as they watched and waited.

'The blue one?'

How many bags do I carry around, Luigi? 'Yes, the blue one.' He already had suspicions that the bag had been snatched.

A small fire truck with an enormous siren arrived, slid to a stop, and kept wailing as the firemen raced inside. Minutes passed, and the Italians began to drift away. The decisive ones left to find lunch elsewhere while there was still

350

time. The others just kept gawking at this horrible injustice.

The siren was finally neutralized. Evidently the fire was too, and without the need for water being sprayed all over the restaurant. After an hour of discussion and debate and very little firefighting, the situation was under control. 'Something in the restroom,' a waiter yelled to one of his friends, one of the few remaining weakened and unfed patrons. The lights were back on.

They allowed them back inside to get their coats. Some who'd left in search of other meals were returning to get their things. Luigi became very helpful in the hunt for Marco's bag. He discussed the situation with the headwaiter, and before long half the staff was scouring the restaurant. Among the excited chatter, Marco heard a waiter say something about a 'smoke bomb.'

The bag was gone, and Marco knew it.

They had a panino and a beer at a sidewalk café, under the sun where they could watch pretty girls stroll by. Marco was preoccupied with the theft, but he worked hard to appear unconcerned.

'Sorry about the bag,' Luigi said at one point.

'No big deal.'

'I'll get you another cell phone.'

'Thanks.'

'What else did you lose?'

'Nothing. Just some maps of the city, some aspirin, a few euros.'

In a hotel room a few blocks away, Zellman and Krater had the bag on the bed, its contents neatly arranged. Other than the Ankyo smartphone, there were two maps of Bologna, both well marked and well used but revealing little, four $100 bills, the cell phone Luigi had loaned him, a bottle of aspirin, and the owner's manual for the Ankyo.

Zellman, the more agile computer whiz of the two, plugged the smartphone into an Internet access jack and was soon fiddling with the menu. 'This is good stuff,' he was saying, quite impressed with Marco's gadget. 'The absolute latest toy on the market.'

Not surprisingly, he was stopped by the password. They would have to dissect it at Langley. With his laptop, he e-mailed a message to Julia Javier, passing along the serial number and other information.

Within two hours of the theft, a CIA agent was sitting in the parking lot outside Chatter in suburban Alexandria, waiting for the store to open.

Chapter 26

From a distance he watched her shuffle along gamely, bravely, with her cane down the sidewalk beside Via Minzoni. He followed and was soon fifty feet away. Today she wore brown suede boots, no doubt for the support. The boots had low heels. Flat shoes would've been more comfortable, but then she was Italian and fashion always took priority. The light brown skirt stopped at her knees. She was wearing a tight wool sweater, bright red in color, and it was the first time he'd seen her when she wasn't bundled up for cold weather. No overcoat to hide her really nice figure.

She was walking cautiously and limping slightly, but with a determination that gave him heart. It was just coffee at Nino's, for an hour or two of Italian. And it was all for him!

And the money.

For a moment he thought about her money. Whatever the dire situation with her poor husband, and her seasonal work as a tour guide, she managed to dress stylishly and live in a beautifully decorated apartment. Giovanni had been a professor. Perhaps he'd saved carefully over the years, and now his illness was straining their budget.

Whatever. Marco had his own problems. He'd just lost $400 in cash and his only lifeline to the outside world. People who weren't supposed to know his whereabouts now knew his exact address. Nine hours earlier he'd heard his real name used on Via Fondazza.

He slowed and allowed her to enter Nino's, where she was again greeted like a beloved member of the family by Nino's boys. Then he circled the block to give them time to get her situated, to fuss over her, bring her coffee, chat for a moment and catch up on the neighborhood gossip. Ten minutes after she arrived, he walked through the door and got bear-hugged by Nino's youngest son. A friend of Francesca's was a friend for life.

Her moods changed so much that Marco did not know what to expect. He was still touched by the warmth of yesterday, but he knew that the indifference could return today. When she smiled and grabbed his hand and started all the cheek pecking he knew instantly the lesson would be the highlight of a rotten day.

When they were finally alone he asked about her husband. Things had not changed. 'It's only a matter of days,' she said with stiff lip, as if she'd already accepted death and was ready for the grieving.

He asked about her mother, Signora Altonelli, and got a full report. She was baking a pear torta, one of Giovanni's favorites, just in case he got a whiff of it from the kitchen.

'And how was your day?' she asked.

It would be impossible to fictionalize a worse set of occurrences. From the shock of hearing his real name barked through the darkness, to being the victim of a carefully staged theft, he couldn't imagine a worse day.

'A little excitement during lunch,' he said.

'Tell me about it.'

He described his hike up to San Luca, to the spot where she fell, her bench, the views, the canceled session with Ermanno, lunch with Luigi, the fire but not the loss of his bag. She had not noticed the absence of it until he told the story.

'There's so little crime in Bologna,' she said, half apologetic. 'I know Caffè Atene. It's not a place for thieves.'

These were probably not Italians, he wanted to say, but managed to nod gravely as if to say: Yes, yes, what's the world coming to?

When the small talk was over, she switched gears like a stern professor and said she was in the mood to tackle some verbs. He said he was not, but his moods were unimportant. She drilled him on the future tense of abitare (to live) and vedere (to see). Then she made him weave both verbs in all tenses into a hundred random sentences. Far from being distracted, she pounced on any wayward accent. A grammatical mistake prompted a quick reprimand, as if he'd just insulted the entire country.

She had spent the day penned up in her apartment, with a dying husband and a busy mother. The lesson was her only chance to release some energy. Marco, however, was exhausted. The stress of the day was taking its toll, but Francesca's high-octane demands took his mind off his fatigue and confusion. One hour passed quickly. They recharged with more coffee, and she launched into the murky and difficult world of the subjunctive – present, imperfect, and past perfect. Finally, he began to founder. She tried to prop him up with reassurances that the subjunctive sinks a lot of students. But he was tired and ready to sink.

He surrendered after two hours, thoroughly drained and in need of another long walk. It took fifteen minutes to say goodbye to Nino's boys. He happily escorted her back to her apartment. They hugged and pecked cheeks and promised to study tomorrow.

If he walked as directly as possible, his apartment was twenty-five minutes away. But he had not walked directly to any place in more than a month.

He began to wander.

*

At 4:00 p.m., eight of the *kidon* were on Via Fondazza, at various points – one drinking coffee at a sidewalk café, three strolling aimlessly a block apart, one cruising back and forth on a scooter, and one looking out a window from the third floor.

Half a mile away, outside the central city, on the second floor above a flower shop owned by an elderly Jew, the four other members of the *kidon* were playing cards and waiting nervously. One, Ari, was one of the top English interrogators within the Mossad.

They played with little conversation. The night ahead would be long and unpleasant.

Throughout the day, Marco had struggled with the question of whether to return to Via Fondazza. The FBI boys could still be there, ready for another ugly confrontation. He felt sure they would not be stiff-armed so easily. They wouldn't simply call it quits and catch a plane. They had superiors back home who demanded results.

Though far from certain, he had a strong hunch that Luigi was behind the theft of his Silvio bag. The fire had not really been a fire; it was more of a diversion, a reason for the lights to go off and a cover for someone to grab the bag.

He didn't trust Luigi because he trusted no one.

They had his cute little smartphone. Neal's

codes were in there somewhere. Could they be broken? Could the trail lead to his son? Marco had not the slightest idea how those things worked, what was possible, what was impossible.

The urge to leave Bologna was overwhelming. Where to go and how to get there were questions he had not sorted out. He was rambling now, and he felt vulnerable, almost helpless. Every face glancing at him was someone else who knew his real name. At a crowded bus stop he cut the line and climbed on, not sure where he was going. The bus was packed with weary commuters, shoulder to shoulder as they bounced along. Through the windows he watched the foot traffic under the marvelous crowded porticoes of the city center.

At the last second he jumped off, then walked three blocks along Via San Vitale until he saw another bus. He rode in circles for almost an hour, then finally stepped off near the train station. He drifted with another crowd, then darted across Via dell' Indipendenza to the bus station. Inside he found the departures, saw that one was leaving in ten minutes for Piacenza, an hour and a half away with five stops in between. He bought a ticket for thirty euros and hid in the restroom until the last minute. The bus was almost full. The seats were wide with high headrests, and as the bus moved slowly through heavy traffic, Marco almost nodded off. Then he caught himself. Sleeping was not permissible.

This was it – the escape he'd been contemplating since the first day in Bologna. He'd become convinced that to survive he would be forced to disappear, to leave Luigi behind and make it on his own. He had often wondered exactly how and when the flight would begin. What would trigger it? A face? A threat? Would he take a bus or train, cab or plane? Where would he go? Where would he hide? Would his rudimentary Italian get him through it? How much money would he have at the time?

This was it. It was happening. There was no turning back now.

The first stop was the small village of Bazzano, fifteen kilometers west of Bologna. Marco got off the bus and did not get back on. Again, he hid in the restroom of the station until the bus was gone, then crossed the street to a bar where he ordered a beer and asked the bartender about the nearest hotel.

Over his second beer he asked about the train station, and learned that Bazzano did not have one. Only buses, said the bartender.

Albergo Cantino was near the center of the village, five or six blocks away. It was dark when he arrived at the front desk, with no bags, something that did not go unnoticed by the signora who handled things.

'I'd like a room,' he said in Italian.

'For how many nights?'

'Only one.'

'The rate is fifty-five euros.'

'Fine.'

'Your passport, please.'

'Sorry, but I lost it.'

Her plucked and painted eyebrows arched in great suspicion, then she began shaking her head. 'Sorry.'

Marco laid two hundred-euro bills on the counter in front of her. The bribe was obvious – just take the cash, no paperwork, and give me a key.

More shaking, more frowning.

'You must have a passport,' she said. Then she folded her arms across her chest, jerked her chin upward, braced for the next exchange. There was no way she was going to lose.

Outside, Marco walked the streets of the strange town. He found a bar and ordered coffee; no more alcohol, he had to keep his wits.

'Where can I find a taxi?' he asked the bartender.

'At the bus station.'

By 9:00 p.m. Luigi was walking the floors of his apartment, waiting for Marco to return next door. He called Francesca and she reported that they had studied that afternoon; in fact they'd had a delightful lesson. Great, he thought.

His disappearance was part of the plan, but Whitaker and Langley thought it would take a few more days. Had they lost him already? That quickly? There were now five agents very close by – Luigi, Zellman, Krater, and two others sent from Milano.

Luigi had always questioned the plan. In a city the size of Bologna it was impossible to maintain physical surveillance of a person twenty-four hours a day. Luigi had argued almost violently that the only way for the plan to work was to stash Backman away in a small village where his movements were limited, his options few, and his visitors much more visible. That had been the original plan, but the details had been abruptly changed in Washington.

At 9:12, a buzzer quietly went off in the kitchen. He hurried to the monitors in the kitchen. Marco was home. His front door was opening. Luigi stared at the digital image from the hidden camera in the ceiling of the living room next door.

Two strangers – not Marco. Two men in their thirties, dressed like regular guys. They closed the door quickly, quietly, professionally, then began looking around. One carried a small black bag of some sort.

They were good, very good. To pick the lock of the safe house they had to be very good.

Luigi smiled with excitement. With a little luck, his cameras were about to record Marco getting nabbed. Maybe they would kill him right there in the living room, captured on film. Perhaps the plan would work after all.

He flipped the audio switches and increased the volume. Language was crucial here. Where were they from? What was their tongue? There were no sounds, though, as they moved about silently. They whispered once or twice, but he could barely hear it.

Chapter 27

The taxi made an abrupt stop on Via Gramsci, near the bus and train stations. From the backseat, Marco handed over enough cash, then ducked between two parked cars and was soon lost in the darkness. His escape from Bologna had been very brief indeed, but then it wasn't exactly over. He zigzagged out of habit, looping back, watching his own trail.

On Via Minzoni he moved quickly under the porticoes and stopped at her apartment building. He didn't have the luxury of second thoughts, of hesitating or guessing. He rang twice, desperately hoping that Francesca, and not Signora Altonelli, would answer.

'Who is it?' came that lovely voice.

'Francesca, it's me, Marco. I need some help.'

A very slight pause, then, 'Yes, of course.'

She met him at her door on the second floor and invited him in. Much to his dismay, Signora Altonelli was still there, standing in the kitchen door with a hand towel, watching his entrance very closely.

'Are you all right?' Francesca asked in Italian.

'English, please,' he said, looking and smiling at her mother.

'Yes, of course.'

'I need a place to stay tonight. I can't get a room because I have no passport. I can't even bribe my way into a small hotel.'

'That's the law in Europe, you know.'

'Yes, I'm learning.'

She waved at the sofa, then turned to her mother and asked her to make some coffee. They sat down. He noticed she was barefoot and moving about without the cane, though she still needed it. She wore tight jeans and a baggy sweater and looked as cute as a coed.

'Why don't you tell me what's going on?' she said.

'It's a complicated story and I can't tell you most of it. Let's just say that I don't feel very safe right now, that I really need to leave Bologna, as soon as possible.'

'Where are you going?'

'I'm not sure. Somewhere out of Italy, out of Europe, to a place where I'll hide again.'

'How long will you hide?'

'A long time. I'm not sure.'

She stared at him coldly, without blinking. He stared back because even when cold, the eyes were beautiful. 'Who are you?' she asked.

'Well, I'm certainly not Marco Lazzeri.'

'What are you running from?'

'My past, and it's rapidly catching up with me. I'm not a criminal, Francesca. I was once a lawyer. I got in some trouble. I served my time. I've been fully pardoned. I'm not a bad guy.'

'Why is someone after you?'

'It was a business deal six years ago. Some very nasty people are not happy with how the deal was finished. They blame me. They would like to find me.'

'To kill you?'

'Yes. That's what they'd like to do.'

'This is very confusing. Why did you come here? Why did Luigi help you? Why did he hire me and Ermanno? I don't understand.'

'And I can't answer those questions. Two months ago I was in prison, and I thought I would be there for another fourteen years. Suddenly, I'm free. I was given a new identity, brought here, hidden first in Treviso, now Bologna. I think they want to kill me here.'

'Here! In Bologna!'

He nodded and looked toward the kitchen as Signora Altonelli appeared with a tray of coffee, and also a pear torta that had not yet been sliced. As she placed it delicately on a small plate for Marco, he realized that he had not eaten since lunch.

Lunch with Luigi. Lunch with the fake fire and the stolen smartphone. He thought of Neal again and worried about his safety.

'It's delicious,' he said to her mother in

Italian. Francesca was not eating. She watched every move he made, every bite, every sip of coffee. When her mother went back to the kitchen, she said, 'Who does Luigi work for?'

'I'm not sure. Probably the CIA. You know the CIA?'

'Yes. I read spy novels. The CIA put you here?'

'I think the CIA got me out of prison, out of the country, and here to Bologna where they've hidden me in a safe house while they try and figure out what to do with me.'

'Will they kill you?'

'Maybe.'

'Luigi?'

'Possibly.'

She placed her cup on the table and fiddled with her hair for a while. 'Would you like some water?' she asked as she got to her feet.

'No thanks.'

'I need to move a little,' she said as she carefully placed weight on her left foot. She walked slowly into the kitchen, where things were quiet for a moment before an argument broke out. She and her mother were disagreeing rather heatedly, but they were forced to do so in loud, tense whispers.

It dragged on for a few minutes, died down, then flared up as neither side seemed ready to yield. Finally, Francesca came limping back with a small bottle of San Pellegrino and took her place on the sofa.

'What was that all about?' he asked.

'I told her you wanted to sleep here tonight. She misunderstood.'

'Come on. I'll sleep in the closet. I don't care.'

'She's very old-fashioned.'

'Is she staying here tonight?'

'She is now.'

'Just give me a pillow. I'll sleep on the kitchen table.'

Signora Altonelli was a different person when she returned to remove the coffee tray. She glared at Marco as if he'd already molested her daughter. She glared at Francesca as if she wanted to slap her. She huffed around the kitchen for a few minutes, then retired somewhere back in the apartment.

'Are you sleepy?' Francesca asked.

'No. You?'

'No. Let's talk.'

'Okay.'

'Tell me everything.'

He slept a few hours on the sofa, and was awakened by Francesca tapping on his shoulder. 'I have an idea,' she said. 'Follow me.'

He followed her to the kitchen, where a clock read 4:15. On the counter by the sink was a disposable razor, a can of shaving cream, a pair of eyeglasses, and a bottle of hair something or other – he couldn't translate it. She handed him a small burgundy leather case and said, 'This is a passport. Giovanni's.'

He almost dropped it. 'No, I can't –'

'Yes, you can. He won't be needing it. I insist.'

Marco slowly opened it and looked at the distinguished face of a man he'd never meet. The expiration date was seven months away, so the photo was almost five years old. He found the birthday – Giovanni was now sixty-eight years old, a good twenty years older than his wife.

During the cab ride back from Bazzano, he'd thought of nothing but a passport. He'd thought about stealing one from an unsuspecting tourist. He'd thought about buying one somewhere on the black market but had no idea where to go. And he'd pondered Giovanni's, one that, sadly, was about to be useless. Null and void.

But he'd dismissed the thought for fear of endangering Francesca. What if he got caught? What if an immigration guard at an airport got suspicious and called his supervisor over? But his biggest fear was getting caught by the people who were chasing him. The passport could implicate her, and he would never do that.

'Are you sure?' he asked. Now that he was holding the passport he really wanted to keep it.

'Please, Marco, I want to help. Giovanni would insist.'

'I don't know what to say.'

'We have work to do. There's a bus for Parma that leaves in two hours. It would be a safe way out of town.'

'I want to get to Milano,' he said.

'Good idea.'

She took the passport and opened it. They studied the photo of her husband. 'Let's start with that thing around your mouth,' she said.

Ten minutes later the mustache and goatee were gone, his face completely shaven. She held a mirror for him as he hovered over the kitchen sink. Giovanni at sixty-three had less gray hair than Marco at fifty-two, but then he'd not had the experience of a federal indictment and six years in prison.

He assumed the hair coloring was something she used, but he was not about to ask. It promised results in an hour. He sat in a chair facing the table with a towel draped over his shoulders while she gently worked the solution through his hair. Very little was said. Her mother was asleep. Her husband was still and quiet and heavily medicated.

Not long ago Giovanni the professor had worn round tortoiseshell eyeglasses, light brown, quite the academic look, and when Marco put them on and studied his new look he was startled at the change. His hair was much darker, his eyes much different. He hardly recognized himself.

'Not bad' was her assessment of her own work. 'It will do for now.'

She brought in a navy corduroy sports coat, with well-worn patches on the elbows. 'He's about two inches shorter than you,' she said. The sleeves needed another inch, and the jacket would've been tight through the chest, but

Marco was so thin these days that anything would swallow him.

'What's your real name?' she said as she tugged on the sleeves and adjusted the collar.

'Joel.'

'I think you should travel with a briefcase. It will look normal.'

He couldn't argue. Her generosity was overwhelming, and he needed every damned bit of it. She left, then came back with a beautiful old briefcase, tan leather with a silver buckle.

'I don't know what to say,' Marco mumbled.

'It's Giovanni's favorite, a gift from me twenty years ago. Italian leather.'

'Of course.'

'If you get caught somehow with the passport, what will you say?' she asked.

'I stole it. You're my tutor. I was in your home as a guest. I managed to find the drawer with your documents, and I stole your husband's passport.'

'You're a good liar.'

'At one time, I was one of the best. If I get caught, Francesca, I will protect you. I promise. I will tell lies that will baffle everyone.'

'You won't get caught. But use the passport as little as possible.'

'Don't worry. I'll destroy it as soon as I can.'

'Do you need money?'

'No.'

'Are you sure? I have a thousand euros here.'

'No, Francesca, but thanks.'

'You'd better hurry.'

He followed her to the front door where they stopped and looked at each other. 'Do you spend much time online?' he asked.

'A little each day.'

'Check out Joel Backman, start with *The Washington Post*. There's a lot of stuff there, but don't believe everything you read. I'm not the monster they've created.'

'You're not a monster at all, Joel.'

'I don't know how to thank you.'

She took his right hand and squeezed it with both of hers. 'Will you ever return to Bologna?' she asked. It was more of an invitation than a question.

'I don't know. I really don't have any idea what's about to happen. But, maybe. Can I knock on your door if I make it back?'

'Please do. Be careful out there.'

He stood in the shadows of Via Minzoni for a few minutes, not wanting to leave her, not ready to begin the long journey.

Then there was a cough from under the darkened porticoes across the street, and Giovanni Ferro was on the run.

Chapter 28

As the hours passed with excruciating slowness, Luigi gradually moved from worry to panic. One of two things had happened: either the hit had already occurred, or Marco had gotten wind of something and was trying to flee. Luigi worried about the stolen bag. Was it too strong a move? Had it scared Marco to the point of disappearing?

The expensive smartphone had shaken everyone. Their boy had been doing much more than studying Italian, walking the streets, and sampling every café and bar in town. He'd been planning, and communicating.

The smartphone was in a lab in the basement of the American embassy in Milan, where, according to the latest from Whitaker, and they were talking every fifteen minutes, the technicians had been unable to crack its codes.

A few minutes after midnight, the two

intruders next door evidently got tired of waiting. As they were making their exit, they spoke a few words loud enough to be recorded. It was English with a trace of an accent. Luigi had immediately called Whitaker and reported that they were probably Israeli.

He was correct. The two agents were instructed by Efraim to leave the apartment and take up other positions.

When they left, Luigi decided to send Krater to the bus station and Zellman to the train station. With no passport, Marco could not buy a plane ticket. Luigi decided to ignore the airport. But, as he told Whitaker, if their boy can somehow buy a state-of-the-art cell phone PC that cost about a thousand bucks, maybe he could also find himself a passport.

By 3:00 a.m. Whitaker was yelling in Milano and Luigi, who couldn't yell for security reasons, could only curse, which he was doing in English and Italian and holding his own in both languages.

'You've lost him, dammit!' Whitaker screeched.

'Not yet!'

'He's already dead!'

Luigi hung up again, for the third time that morning.

The *kidon* pulled back around 3:30 a.m. They would all rest for a few hours, then plan the day ahead.

*

He sat with a wino on a bench in a small park, not far down Via dell' Indipendenza from the bus station. The wino had been nursing a jug of pink fluid for most of the night, and every five minutes or so he managed to lift his head and utter something at Marco, five feet away. Marco mumbled back, and whatever he said seemed to please the wino. Two of his colleagues were completely comatose and were huddled nearby like dead soldiers in a trench. Marco didn't feel exactly safe, but then he had more serious problems.

A few people loitered in front of the bus station. Around five-thirty activity increased when a large group of what appeared to be Gypsies came bustling out, all speaking loudly at once, obviously delighted to be off the bus after a long ride from somewhere. More departing passengers were arriving, and Marco decided it was time to leave the wino. He entered the station behind a young couple and their child and followed them to the ticket counter where he listened as they bought tickets to Parma. He did the same, then hurried to the restroom and again hid in a stall.

Krater was sitting in the station's all-night diner, drinking bad coffee behind a newspaper while he watched the passengers come and go. He watched Marco walk by. He noted his height, build, age. The walk was familiar, though much slower. The Marco Lazzeri he'd been following for weeks could walk as fast as most men could jog. This fellow's pace was much slower, but then there was nowhere to go. Why hurry? On the streets Lazzeri was always trying to lose them, and at times he was successful.

But the face was very different. The hair was much darker. The brown corduroy cap was gone, but then it was an accessory and easy to lose. The tortoiseshell eyeglasses caught Krater's attention. Glasses were wonderful diversions but so often they were overplayed. Marco's stylish Armani frames had fit him perfectly, slightly altering his appearance without calling attention to his face. The round glasses on this guy begged for attention.

The facial hair was gone; a five-minute job, something anyone would do. The shirt was not one Krater had seen before, and he'd been in Marco's apartment with Luigi during sweeps when they looked at every item of clothing. The faded jeans were very generic, and Marco had purchased a similar pair. The blue sports coat with worn elbow patches, along with the handsome attaché, kept Krater in his chair. The jacket had many miles on it, something Marco could not have acquired. The sleeves were a bit short, but that was not uncommon. The briefcase was made of fine leather. Marco might somehow find and spend some cash on a smartphone, but why waste it on such an expensive briefcase? His last bag, the navy blue Silvio he'd owned until about sixteen hours ago when Krater grabbed it during the melee at Caffè Atene, had cost sixty euros.

Krater watched him until he rounded a corner and was out of sight. A possibility, nothing more. He sipped his coffee and for a few minutes contemplated the gentleman he'd just seen.

Marco stood in the stall with his jeans bunched around his ankles, feeling quite silly but much more concerned with a good cover at this point. The door opened. The wall to the left of the door had four urinals; across were six lavatories, and next to them were the four stalls. The other three were empty. There was very little traffic at the moment. Marco listened carefully, waiting to hear the sounds of human relief – the zipper, the jangle of a belt buckle, the deep sigh men often make, the spray of urine.

Nothing. There was no noise from the lavatories, no one washing their hands. The doors to the other three stalls did not open. Maybe it was the custodian making his rounds, and doing so very quietly.

In front of the lavatories, Krater bent low and saw the jeans around the ankles in the last stall. Next to the jeans was the fine briefcase. The gentleman was taking care of his business and in no hurry about it.

The next bus left at 6:00 a.m. for Parma; after that there was a 6:20 departure for Florence. Krater hurried to the booth and bought tickets for both. The clerk looked at him oddly, but Krater couldn't have cared less. He went back to the restroom. The gentleman in the last stall was still there.

Krater stepped outside and called Luigi. He gave a description of the man, and explained that he appeared to be in no hurry to leave the men's room.

'The best place to hide,' Luigi said.

'I've done it many times.'

'Do you think it's Marco?'

'I don't know. If it is, it's a very good disguise.'

Rattled by the smartphone, the $400 in American cash, and the disappearance, Luigi was not taking chances. 'Follow him,' he said.

At 5:55, Marco pulled up his jeans, flushed, grabbed his briefcase, and took off for the bus. Waiting on the platform was Krater, nonchalantly eating an apple with one hand and holding a newspaper with the other. When Marco headed for the bus to Parma, so did Krater.

A third of the seats were empty. Marco took one on the left side, halfway back, by a window. Krater was looking away when he passed by, then found a seat four rows behind him.

The first stop was Modena, thirty minutes into the trip. As they entered the city, Marco decided to take stock of the faces behind him. He stood and made his way to the rear, to the restroom, and along the way gave a casual glance to each male.

When he locked himself in the restroom, he closed his eyes and said to himself, 'Yes, I've seen that face before.'

377

Less than twenty-four hours earlier, in Caffè Atene, just a few minutes before the lights went out. The face had been in a long mirror that lined the wall with an old coatrack, above the tables. The face had been seated nearby, behind him, with another man.

It was a familiar face. Maybe he'd even seen it before somewhere in Bologna.

Marco returned to his seat as the bus slowed and approached the station. Think quickly, man, he kept telling himself, but keep your cool. Don't panic. They've followed you out of Bologna; you can't let them follow you out of the country.

As the bus stopped, the driver announced their arrival in Modena. A brief stop; a departure in fifteen minutes. Four passengers waddled down the aisle and got off. The others kept their seats; most were dozing anyway. Marco closed his eyes and allowed his head to drift to his left, against the window, fast asleep now. A minute passed and two peasants climbed aboard, wild-eyed and clutching heavy cloth bags.

When the driver returned and was situating himself behind the wheel, Marco suddenly eased from his seat, slid quickly along the aisle, and hopped off the bus just as the door was closing. He walked quickly into the station, then turned around and watched the bus back away. His pursuer was still on board.

Krater's first move was to sprint off the bus, perhaps arguing with the driver in the process, but then no driver will fight to keep someone on board. He caught himself, though, because Marco obviously knew he was being followed. His last-second exit only confirmed what Krater had suspected. It was Marco all right, running like a wounded animal.

Problem was, he was loose in Modena and Krater was not. The bus turned onto another street, then stopped for a traffic light. Krater rushed to the driver, holding his stomach, begging to get off before he vomited all over the place. The door flew open, Krater jumped off and ran back toward the station.

Marco wasted no time. When the bus was out of sight, he hurried to the front of the station where three taxis were lined up. He jumped into the backseat of the first one and said, 'Can you take me to Milano?' His Italian was very good.

'Milano?'

'Sì, Milano.'

'È molto caro!' It's very expensive.

'Quanto?'

'Duecento euro.' Two hundred euros.

'Andiamo.'

After an hour of scouring the Modena bus station and the two streets next to it, Krater called Luigi with the news that was not all good, and not all bad. He'd lost his man, but the mad dash for freedom confirmed that it was indeed Marco.

Luigi's reaction was mixed. He was frustrated that Krater had been outfoxed by an amateur.

He was impressed that Marco could effectively change his appearance and elude a small army of assassins. And he was angry at Whitaker and the fools in Washington who kept changing the plans and had now created an impending disaster for which he, Luigi, would no doubt get the blame.

He called Whitaker, yelled and cursed some more, then headed for the train station with Zellman and the two others. They'd meet up with Krater in Milano, where Whitaker was promising a full-court press with all the muscle he could pull in.

Leaving Bologna on the direct Eurostar, Luigi had a wonderful idea, one he could never mention. Why not just simply call the Israelis and the Chinese and tell them that Backman was last seen in Modena, headed west to Parma and probably Milano? They wanted him much more than Langley did. And they could certainly do a better job of finding him.

But orders were orders, even though they kept changing.

All roads led to Milano.

Chapter 29

The cab stopped a block away from the Milano central train station. Marco paid the driver, thanked him more than once, wished him well back home in Modena, then walked past a dozen more taxis that were waiting for arriving passengers. Inside the mammoth station, he drifted with the crowd, up the escalators, into the controlled frenzy of the platform area where a dozen tracks brought the trains. He found the departure board and studied his options. A train left for Stuttgart four times a day, and its seventh stop was Zurich. He picked up a schedule, bought a cheap city guide with a map, then found a table at a café among a row of shops. Time could not be wasted, but he needed to figure out where he was. He had two espressos and a pastry while his eyes watched the crowd. He loved the mob, the throng of people coming and going. There was safety in those numbers.

His first plan was to take a walk, about thirty

minutes, to the center of the city. Somewhere along the way he would find an inexpensive clothing store and change everything – jacket, shirt, pants, shoes. They had spotted him in Bologna. He couldn't risk it again.

Surely, somewhere in the center of the city, near the Piazza del Duomo, there was an Internet café where he could rent a computer for fifteen minutes. He had little confidence in his ability to sit in front of a strange machine, turn the damn thing on, and not only survive the jungle of the Internet but get a message to Neal. It was 10:15 a.m. in Milan, 4:15 a.m. in Culpeper, Virginia. Neal would be checking in live at 7:50.

Somehow he'd make the e-mail work. He had no choice.

The second plan, the one that was looking better and better as he watched a thousand people casually hop on trains that would have them scattered throughout Europe in a matter of hours, was to run. Buy a ticket right now and get out of Milano and Italy as soon as possible. His new hair color and Giovanni's eyeglasses and old professor's jacket had not fooled them in Bologna. If they were that good, they would surely find him anywhere.

He compromised with a walk around the block. The fresh air always helped, and after four blocks his blood was pumping again. As in Bologna, the streets of Milano fanned out in all directions like a spiderweb. The traffic was heavy and at times hardly moved. He loved the traffic, and he especially loved the crowded sidewalks that gave him cover.

The shop was called Roberto's, a small haberdashery wedged between a jewelry store and a bakery. The two front windows were packed with clothing that would hold up for about a week, which fit Marco's time frame perfectly. A clerk from the Middle East spoke worse Italian than Marco, but he was fluent in pointing and grunting and he was determined to transform his customer. The blue jacket was replaced with a dark brown one. The new shirt was a white pullover with short sleeves. The slacks were low-grade wool, very dark navy. Alterations would take a week, so Marco asked the clerk for a pair of scissors. In the mildewy dressing room, he measured as best he could, then cut the pants off himself. When he walked out in his new ensemble, the clerk looked at the ragged edges where the cuffs should have been and almost cried.

The shoes Marco tried on would have crippled him before he made it back to the train station, so he stayed with his hiking boots for the moment. The best purchase was a tan straw hat that Marco bought because he'd seen one just before entering the store.

What did he care about fashion at this point?

The new getup cost him almost four hundred euros, money he hated to part with, but he had no choice. He tried to swap Giovanni's briefcase, which was certainly worth more than everything he was wearing, but the clerk was too depressed over the butchered slacks. He was barely able to offer a weak thanks and goodbye. Marco left with the blue jacket, faded jeans, and the old shirt folded up in a red shopping bag; again, something different to carry around.

He walked a few minutes and saw a shoe store. He bought a pair of what appeared to be slightly modified bowling shoes, without a doubt the ugliest items in what turned out to be a very nice store. They were black with some manner of burgundy striping, hopefully built for comfort and not attractiveness. He paid 150 euros for them, only because they were already broken in. It took two blocks before he could muster the courage to look down at them.

Luigi got himself followed out of Bologna. The kid on the scooter saw him leave the apartment next to Backman's, and it was the manner in which he left that caught his attention. He was jogging, and gaining speed with each step. No one runs under the porticoes on Via Fondazza. The scooter hung back until Luigi stopped and quickly crawled into a red Fiat. He drove a few blocks, then slowed long enough for another man to jump into the car. They took off at breakneck speed, but in city traffic the scooter had no trouble keeping up. When they wheeled into the train station and parked illegally, the kid on the scooter saw it all and radioed Efraim again.

Within fifteen minutes, two Mossad agents dressed as traffic policemen entered Luigi's apartment, setting off alarms – some silent, some barely audible. While three agents waited on the street, providing cover, the three inside kicked open the kitchen door and found the astounding collection of electronic surveillance equipment.

When Luigi, Zellman, and a third agent stepped onto the Eurostar to Milano, the kid on the scooter had a ticket too. His name was Paul, the youngest member of the *kidon* and the most fluent speaker of Italian. Behind the bangs and baby face was a twenty-six-year-old veteran of half a dozen killings. When he radioed that he was on the train and it was moving, two more agents entered Luigi's apartment to help dissect the equipment. One alarm, though, could not be silenced. Its steady ring penetrated the walls just enough to attract attention from a few neighbors along the street.

After ten minutes, Efraim called a halt to the break-in. The agents scattered, then regrouped in one of their safe houses. They had not been able to determine who Luigi was or who he worked for, but it was obvious he'd been spying on Backman around the clock.

As the hours passed with no sign of Backman, they began to believe that he had fled. Could Luigi lead them to him?

In central Milano, at the Piazza del Duomo, Marco gawked at the mammoth Gothic cathedral that took only three hundred years to complete. He strolled along the Galleria Vittorio Emanuele, the magnificent glass-domed gallery that Milano is famous for. Lined with cafés and bookshops, the gallery is the center of the city's life, its most popular meeting place. With the temperature approaching sixty degrees, Marco had a sandwich and a cola outdoors where the pigeons swarmed every wayward crumb. He watched elderly Milanesi stroll through the gallery, women arm in arm, men stopping to chat as if time was irrelevant. To be so lucky, he thought.

Should he leave immediately, or should he lay low for a day or two? That was the new urgent question. In a crowded city of four million people, he could vanish for as long as he wanted. He'd get a map, learn the streets, spend hours hiding in his room and hours walking the alleys.

But the bloodhounds behind him would have time to regroup.

Shouldn't he leave now, while they were back there scrambling and scratching their heads?

Yes he should, he decided. He paid the waiter and glanced down at his bowling shoes. They were indeed comfortable but he couldn't wait to burn them. On a city bus he saw an ad for an Internet café on Via Verri. Ten minutes later he entered the place. A sign on the wall gave the rates – ten euros per hour, minimum of thirty minutes. He ordered an orange juice and paid for half an hour. The clerk nodded in the general direction of a table where a bunch of computers were waiting. Three of the eight were being used by people who obviously knew what they were doing. Marco was already lost.

But he faked it well. He sat down, grabbed a keyboard, stared at the monitor and wanted to pray, but plowed ahead as if he'd been hacking for years. It was surprisingly easy; he went to the KwyteMail site, typed his user name, 'Grinch456', then his pass phrase, 'post hoc ergo propter hoc', waited ten seconds, and there was the message from Neal:

Marco: Mikel Van Thiessen is still with Rhineland Bank, now the vice president of client services. Anything else? Grinch.

At exactly 7:50 EST, Marco typed a message:

Grinch: Marco here – live and in person. Are you there?

He sipped his juice and stared at the screen. Come on, baby, make this thing work. Another sip. A lady across the table was talking to her monitor. Then the message:

I'm here, loud and clear. What's up?

Marco typed: *They stole my Ankyo 850. There's a good chance the bad guys have it and they're picking it to pieces. Any chance they can discover you?*

387

Neal: *Only if they have the user name and pass phrase. Do they?*

Marco: *No, I destroyed them. There's no way they can get around a password?*

Neal: *Not with KwyteMail. It's totally secure and encrypted. If they have the PC and nothing more, then they're out of luck.*

Marco: *And we're completely safe now?*

Neal: *Yes, absolutely. But what are you using now?*

Marco: *I'm in an Internet café, renting a computer, like a real hacker.*

Neal: *Do you want another Ankyo smartphone?*

Marco: *No, not now, maybe later. Here's the deal. Go see Carl Pratt. I know you don't like him, but at this point I need him. Pratt was very close to former senator Ira Clayburn from North Carolina. Clayburn ruled the Senate Intelligence Committee for many years. I need Clayburn now. Go through Pratt.*

Neal: *Where's Clayburn now?*

Marco: *I don't know – I just hope he's still alive. He came from the Outer Banks of NC, some pretty remote place. He retired the year after I went to federal camp. Pratt can find him.*

Neal: *Sure, I'll do it as soon as I can sneak away.*

Marco: *Please be careful. Watch your back.*

Neal: *Are you okay?*

Marco: *I'm on the run. I left Bologna early this morning. I'll try to check in the same time tomorrow. Okay?*

Neal: *Keep your head down. I'll be here tomorrow.*

Marco signed off with a smug look. Mission accomplished. Nothing to it. Welcome to the age of high-tech wizardry and gadgetry. He made sure his exit was clean from KwyteMail, then finished his orange juice and left the café. He headed in the direction of the train station, stopping first at a leather shop where he managed an even swap of Giovanni's fine briefcase for a black one of patently inferior quality; then at a cheap jewelry store where he paid eighteen euros for a large round-faced watch with a bright red plastic band, something else to distract anyone looking for Marco Lazzeri, formerly of Bologna; then at a used-book shop where he spent two euros on a well-worn hardback containing the poetry of Czeslaw Milosz, all in Polish of course, anything to confuse the bloodhounds; and, finally, at a secondhand accessory store where he bought a pair of sunglasses and a wooden cane, which he began using immediately on the sidewalk.

The cane reminded him of Francesca. It also slowed him down, changed his gait. With time to spare he shuffled into Milano Centrale and bought a ticket for Stuttgart.

Whitaker got the urgent message from Langley that Luigi's safe house had been broken into, but there was absolutely nothing he could do about it. All the agents from Bologna were now in Milano, scrambling frantically. Two were at the train station, looking for the needle in the haystack. Two were at Malpensa airport, twenty-seven miles from downtown. Two were at Linate airport, which was much closer and handled primarily European flights. Luigi was at the central bus station, still arguing by cell phone that perhaps Marco wasn't even in Milano. Just because he took the bus from Bologna to Modena, and headed in the general direction of northwest, didn't necessarily mean he was going to Milano. But Luigi's credibility at the moment was somewhat diminished, at least in Whitaker's substantial opinion, so he was banished to the bus station where he watched ten thousand people come and go.

Krater got closest to the needle.

For sixty euros, Marco purchased a first-class ticket in hopes that he could avoid the exposure of traveling by coach. For the ride north, the first-class car was the last one, and Marco climbed aboard at five-thirty, forty-five minutes before departure. He settled into his seat, hid his face as much as possible behind the sunglasses and the tan straw hat, opened the book of Polish poetry, and gazed out at the platform where passengers walked by his train. Some were barely five feet away, all in a hurry.

Except one. The guy on the bus was back; the face from Caffè Atene; probably the sticky-fingered thug who'd grabbed his blue Silvio bag; the same bloodhound who'd been a step too slow off the bus in Modena about eleven hours ago. He was walking but not going anywhere.

His eyes were squinted, his forehead wrinkled in a deep frown. For a professional, he was much too obvious, thought Giovanni Ferro, who, unfortunately, now knew much more than he wanted to know about ducking and hiding and covering tracks.

Krater had been told that Marco would probably head either south to Rome, where he had more options, or north to Switzerland, Germany, France – virtually the entire continent to choose from. For five hours Krater had been strolling along the twelve platforms, watching as the trains came and went, mixing with the crowds, not concerned at all with who was getting off but paying desperate attention to who was getting on. Every blue jacket of any shade or style got his attention, but he had yet to see one with the worn elbow patches.

It was in the cheap black briefcase wedged between Marco's feet, in seat number seventy of the first-class car to Stuttgart. Marco watched Krater amble along the platform, paying very close attention to the train whose final destination was Stuttgart. He was holding what appeared to be a ticket, and as he walked out of sight Marco could swear that he got on the train.

Marco fought the urge to get off. The door to his cabin opened, and Madame entered.

Chapter 30

Once it was determined that Backman had disappeared, and was not finally dead at the hands of someone else, a frenetic five hours passed before Julia Javier found the information that should've been close by. It was found in a file that had been locked away in the director's office, and once guarded by Teddy Maynard himself. If Julia had ever seen the information, she could not remember. And, in the chaos, she was certainly not going to admit anything.

The information had come, reluctantly, from the FBI years earlier when Backman was being investigated. His financial dealings were under great scrutiny because the rumors were wild that he'd bilked a client and buried a fortune. So where was the money? In search of it, the FBI had been piecing together his travel history when he abruptly pled guilty and was sent away. The guilty plea didn't close the Backman file, but it certainly removed the pressure. With time, the travel research was completed, and eventually sent over to Langley.

In the month before Backman was indicted, arrested, and released on a very restricted bail arrangement, he had made two quick trips to Europe. For the first one, he'd flown Air France business class with his favorite secretary to Paris, where they frolicked for a few days and saw the sights. She later told investigators that Backman had spent one long day dashing off to Berlin for some quick business, but made it back in time for dinner at Alain Ducasse. She did not accompany him.

There were no records of Backman traveling by a commercial airliner to Berlin, or anywhere else within Europe, during that week. A passport would've been required, and the FBI was positive he had not used his. A passport would not have been required for a train ride. Geneva, Bern, Lausanne, and Zurich are all within four hours of Paris by train.

The second trip was a seventy-two-hour sprint from Dulles, first class on Lufthansa to Frankfurt, again for business, though no business contacts had been discovered there. Backman had paid for two nights in a luxury hotel in Frankfurt, and there was no evidence that he had slept elsewhere. Like Paris, the banking centers of Switzerland are within a few hours' train ride from Frankfurt.

When Julia Javier finally found the file and

read the report, she immediately called Whitaker and said, 'He's headed for Switzerland.'

Madame had enough luggage for an affluent family of five. A harried porter helped her haul the heavy suitcases on board and into the first-class car, which she consumed with herself, her belongings, and her perfume. The cabin had six seats, at least four of which she laid claim to. She sat in one across from Marco and wiggled her ample rear as if to make it expand. She glanced at him, cowering against the window, and gushed over a sultry 'Bonsoir.' French, he thought, and since it didn't seem right to respond in Italian, he relied on old faithful. 'Hello.'

'Ah, American.'

With languages, identities, names, cultures, backgrounds, lies, lies, and more lies all swirling around, he managed to say with no conviction whatsoever, 'No, Canadian.'

'Ah, yes,' she said, still arranging bags and settling in. Evidently American would've been more welcome than Canadian. Madame was a robust woman of sixty, with a tight red dress, thick calves, and stout black pumps that had traveled a million miles. Her heavily decorated eyes were puffy, and the reason was soon evident. Long before the train moved, she pulled out a large flask, unscrewed its top which became a cup, and knocked back a shot of something strong. She swallowed hard, then smiled at Marco and said, 'Would you like a drink?'

'No thanks.'

'It's a very good brandy.'

'No thanks.'

'Very well.' She poured another one, drained it, then put away the flask.

A long train ride just got longer.

'Where are you going?' she asked in very good English.

'Stuttgart. And you?'

'Stuttgart, then on to Strasbourg. Can't stay too long in Stuttgart, you know.' Her nose wrinkled as if the entire city was swimming in raw sewage.

'I love Stuttgart,' Marco said, just to watch it unwrinkle.

'Oh, well.' Her shoes caught her attention. She kicked them off with little regard as to where they might land. Marco braced for a jolt of foot odor but then realized it had little chance of competing with the cheap perfume.

In self-defense, he pretended to nod off. She ignored him for a few minutes, then said loudly, 'You speak Polish?' She was looking at his book of poetry.

He jerked his head as if he'd just been awakened. 'No, not exactly. I'm trying to learn it, though. My family is Polish.' He held his breath as he finished, half expecting her to unleash a torrent of proper Polish and bury him with it.

'I see,' she said, not really approving.

At exactly 6:15, an unseen conductor blew a

whistle and the train started to move. Fortunately, there were no other passengers assigned to Madame's car. Several had walked down the aisle and stopped, glanced in, seen the congestion, then moved on to another cabin where there was more room.

Marco watched the platform intensely as they began moving. The man from the bus was nowhere to be seen.

Madame worked the brandy until she began snoring. She was awakened by the conductor who punched their tickets. A porter came through with a pushcart loaded with drinks. Marco bought a beer and offered one to his cabinmate. His offer was greeted with another mammoth wrinkle of the nose, as if she'd rather drink urine.

Their first stop was Como/San Giovanni, a two-minute break during which no one got on. Five minutes later they stopped at Chiasso. It was almost dark now, and Marco was pondering a quick exit. He studied the itinerary; there were four more stops before Zurich, one in Italy and three in Switzerland. Which country would work best?

He couldn't risk being followed now. If they were on the train, then they had stuck to him from Bologna, through Modena and Milano, through various disguises. They were professionals, and he was no match for them. Sipping his beer, Marco felt like a miserable amateur.

Madame was staring at the butchered hems of his slacks. Then he caught her glancing down at the modified bowling shoes, and for that he didn't blame her at all. Then the bright red watchband caught her attention. Her face conveyed the obvious – she did not approve of his low sense of fashion. Typical American, or Canadian, or whatever he was.

He caught a glimpse of lights shimmering off Lake Lugano. They were snaking through the lake region, gaining altitude. Switzerland was not far away.

An occasional drifter moved down the darkened aisle outside their cabin. They would look in, through the glass door, then move along toward the rear, where there was a restroom. Madame had plopped her large feet in the seat opposite her, not too far from Marco. An hour into the trip, and she had managed to spread her boxes and magazines and clothing throughout the entire cabin. Marco was afraid to leave his scat.

Fatigue finally set in, and Marco fell asleep. He was awakened by the racket at the Bellinzona station, the first stop in Switzerland. A passenger entered the first-class car and couldn't find the right seat. He opened the door to Madame's cabin, looked around, didn't like what he saw, then went off to yell at the conductor. They found him a spot elsewhere. Madame hardly looked up from her fashion magazines.

The next stretch was an hour and forty

minutes, and when Madame went back to her flask Marco said, 'I'll try some of that.' She smiled for the first time in hours. Though she certainly didn't mind drinking alone, it was always more pleasant with a friend. A couple of shots, though, and Marco was nodding off again.

The train jerked as it slowed for the stop at Arth-Goldau. Marco's head jerked too, and his hat fell off. Madame was watching him closely. When he opened his eyes for good, she said, 'A strange man has been looking at you.'

'Where?'

'Where? Here, of course, on this train. He's been by at least three times. He stops at the door, looks closely at you, then sneaks away.'

Maybe it's my shoes, thought Marco. Or my slacks. Watchband? He rubbed his eyes and tried to act as though it happened all the time.

'What does he look like?'

'Blond hair, about thirty-five, cute, brown jacket. Do you know him?'

'No, I have no idea.' The man on the bus at Modena had neither blond hair nor a brown jacket, but those minor points were irrelevant now. Marco was frightened enough to switch plans.

Zug was twenty-five minutes away, the last stop before Zurich. He could not run the risk of leading them to Zurich. Ten minutes out, he announced he needed to use the restroom. Between his seat and the door was Madame's obstacle course. As he began stepping through it, he placed his briefcase and cane in his seat.

He walked past four cabins, each with at least three passengers, none of whom looked suspicious. He went to the restroom, locked the door, and waited until the train began to slow. Then it stopped. Zug was a two-minute layover, and the train so far had been ridiculously on time. He waited one minute, then walked quickly back to his cabin, opened the door, said nothing to Madame, grabbed his briefcase and his cane, which he was perfectly prepared to use as a weapon, and raced to the rear of the train where he jumped onto the platform.

It was a small station, elevated with a street below. Marco flew down the steps to the sidewalk where a lone taxi sat with a driver unconscious behind the wheel. 'Hotel, please,' he said, startling the driver, who instinctively grabbed the ignition key. He asked something in German and Marco tried Italian. 'I need a small hotel. I don't have a reservation.'

'No problem,' the driver said. As they pulled away, Marco looked up and saw the train moving. He looked behind him, and saw no one giving chase.

The ride took all of four blocks, and when they stopped in front of an A-frame building on a quiet side street the driver said in Italian, 'This hotel is very good.'

'Looks fine. Thanks. How far away is Zurich by car?'

'Two hours, more or less. Depends on the traffic.'

'Tomorrow morning, I need to be in downtown Zurich at nine o'clock. Can you drive me there?'

The driver hesitated for a second, his mind thinking of cold cash. 'Perhaps,' he said.

'How much will it cost?'

The driver rubbed his chin, then shrugged and said, 'Two hundred euros.'

'Good. Let's leave here at six.'

'Six, yes, I'll be here.'

Marco thanked him again and watched as he drove away. A bell rang when he entered the front door of the hotel. The small counter was deserted, but a television was chattering away somewhere close by. A sleepy-eyed teenager finally appeared and offered a smile. 'Guten abend,' he said.

'Parla inglese?' Marco asked.

He shook his head, no.

'Italiano?'

'A little.'

'I speak a little too,' Marco said in Italian. 'I'd like a room for one night.'

The clerk pushed over a registration form, and from memory Marco filled in the name on his passport, and its number. He scribbled in a fictional address in Bologna, and a bogus phone number as well. The passport was in his coat pocket, close to his heart, and he was prepared to reluctantly pull it out.

But it was late and the clerk was missing his television show. With atypical Swiss inefficiency, he said, also in Italian, 'Forty-two euros,' and didn't mention the passport.

Giovanni laid the cash on the counter, and the clerk gave him a key to room number 26. In surprisingly good Italian, he arranged a wake-up call for 5:00 a.m. Almost as an afterthought, he said, 'I lost my toothbrush. Would you have an extra?'

The clerk reached into a drawer and pulled out a box full of assorted necessities – toothbrushes, toothpaste, disposable razors, shaving cream, aspirin, tampons, hand cream, combs, even condoms. Giovanni selected a few items and handed over ten euros.

A luxury suite at the Ritz could not have been more welcome than room 26. Small, clean, warm, with a firm mattress, and a door that bolted twice to keep away the faces that had been haunting him since early morning. He took a long, hot shower, then shaved and brushed his teeth forever.

Much to his relief, he found a minibar in a cabinet under the television. He ate a packet of cookies, washed them down with two small bottles of whiskey, and when he crawled under the covers he was mentally drained and physically exhausted. The cane was on the bed, nearby. Silly, but he couldn't help it.

Chapter 31

In the depths of prison he'd dreamed of Zurich, with its blue rivers and clean shaded streets and modern shops and handsome people, all proud to be Swiss, all going about their business with a pleasant seriousness. In another life he'd ridden the quiet electric streetcars with them as they headed into the financial district. Back then he'd been too busy to travel much, too important to leave the fragile workings of Washington, but Zurich was one of the few places he'd seen. It was his kind of city: unburdened by tourists and traffic, unwilling to spend its time gawking at cathedrals and museums and worshiping the last two thousand years. Not at all. Zurich was about money, the refined management of it as opposed to the naked cash grab Backman had once perfected.

He was on a streetcar again, one he'd caught near the train station, and was now moving steadily along Bahnhofstrasse, the main avenue of downtown Zurich, if in fact it had one. It was almost 9:00 a.m. He was among the last wave of the sharply dressed young bankers headed for UBS and Credit Suisse and a thousand lesser-known but equally rich institutions. Dark suits, shirts of various colors but not many white ones, expensive ties with thicker knots and fewer designs, dark brown shoes with laces, never tassels. The styles had changed slightly in the past six years. Always conservative, but with some dash. Not quite as stylish as the young professionals in his native Bologna, but quite attractive.

Everyone was reading something as they moved along. Streetcars passed from the other direction. Marco pretended to be engrossed in a copy of *Newsweek*, but he was really watching everyone else.

No one was watching him. No one seemed offended by his bowling shoes. In fact, he'd seen another pair on a casually dressed young man near the train station. His straw hat was getting no attention. The hems of his slacks had been repaired slightly after he'd purchased a cheap sewing kit from the hotel desk, then spent half an hour trying to tailor his pants without drawing blood. His outfit cost a fraction of those around him, but what did he care? He'd made it to Zurich without Luigi and all those others, and with a little more luck he'd make it out.

At Paradeplatz the streetcars wheeled in from east and west and stopped. They emptied quickly as the young bankers scattered in droves and headed for the buildings. Marco moved with the crowd, his hat now left behind under the seat in the streetcar.

Nothing had changed in seven years. The Paradeplatz was still the same – an open plaza lined with small shops and cafés. The banks around it had been there for a hundred years; some announced their names from neon signs, others were hidden so well they couldn't be found. From behind his sunglasses he soaked in as much of the surroundings as he could while sticking close to three young men with gym bags slung over their shoulders. They appeared to be headed for Rhineland Bank, on the east side. He followed them inside, into the lobby, where the fun began.

The information desk hadn't moved in seven years; in fact, the well-groomed lady sitting behind it looked vaguely familiar. 'I'd like to see Mr. Mikel Van Thiessen,' he said as softly as possible.

'And your name?'

'Marco Lazzeri.' He would use 'Joel Backman' later, upstairs, but he was hesitant to use it here. Hopefully, Neal's e-mails to Van Thiessen had alerted him to the alias. The banker had been asked to remain in town, if at all possible, for the next week or so.

She was on the phone and also pecking at a keyboard. 'It will be just a moment, Mr. Lazzeri,' she said. 'Would you mind waiting?'

'No,' he said. Waiting? He'd been dreaming of this for years. He took a chair, crossed his legs, saw the shoes, then put his feet under the chair. He was certain that he was being watched from a dozen different camera angles now, and that was fine. Maybe they would recognize Backman sitting in the lobby, maybe they wouldn't. He could almost see them up there, gawking at the monitors, scratching their heads, saying, 'Don't know, he's much thinner, gaunt, even.'

'And the hair. It's obviously a bad coloring job.'

To help them Joel removed Giovanni's tortoiseshell glasses.

Five minutes later, a stern-faced security type in a much lesser suit approached him from nowhere and said, 'Mr. Lazzeri, would you follow me?'

They rode a private elevator up to the third floor where Marco was led into a small room with thick walls. All the walls seemed to be thick at Rhineland Bank. Two other security agents were waiting. One actually smiled, the other did not. They asked him to place both hands on a biometric fingerprint scanner. It would compare his fingerprints to the ones he left behind almost seven years ago, at this same place, and when the perfect match was made there would be more smiles, then a nicer room, a nicer lobby, the offer of coffee or juice. Anything, Mr. Backman.

He asked for orange juice because he'd had no breakfast. The security agents were back in their cave. Mr. Backman was now being serviced by Elke, one of Mr. Van Thiessen's shapely assistants. 'He'll be out in just a minute,' she explained. 'He wasn't expecting you this morning.'

Kinda hard to make appointments when you're hiding in toilet stalls. Joel smiled at her. Ol' Marco was history now. Finally laid to rest after a good two-month run. Marco had served him well, kept him alive, taught him the basics of Italian, walked him around Treviso and Bologna, and introduced him to Francesca, a woman he would not soon forget.

But Marco would also get him killed, so he ditched him there on the third floor of the Rhineland Bank, while looking at Elke's black stiletto heels and waiting on her boss. Marco was gone, never to return.

Mikel Van Thiessen's office was designed to smack his visitors with a powerful right hook. Power in the massive Persian rug. Power in the leather sofa and chairs. Power in the ancient mahogany desk that wouldn't have fit in the cell at Rudley. Power in the array of electronic gadgets at his disposal. He met Joel at the powerful oak door and they shook hands properly, but not like old friends. They had met exactly once before.

If Joel had lost sixty pounds since their last visit, Van Thiessen had found most of it. He was much grayer too, not nearly as crisp and sharp as the younger bankers Joel had seen on the

406

streetcar. Van Thiessen directed his client to the leather chairs while Elke and another assistant scurried around to fetch coffee and pastries.

When they were alone, with the door shut, Van Thiessen said, 'I've been reading about you.'

'Oh really. And what have you read?'

'Bribing a president for a pardon, come on, Mr. Backman. Is it really that easy over there?'

Joel couldn't tell if he was joking or not. Joel was in an upbeat mood, but he didn't exactly feel like swapping one-liners.

'I didn't bribe anyone, if that's what you're suggesting.'

'Yes, well, the newspapers are certainly filled with speculation.' His tone was more accusatory than jovial, and Joel decided not to waste time. 'Do you believe everything you read in the newspapers?'

'Of course not, Mr. Backman.'

'I'm here for three reasons. I want access to my security box. I want to review my account. I want to withdraw ten thousand dollars in cash. After that, I may have another favor or two.'

Van Thiessen shoved a small cookie in his mouth and chewed rapidly. 'Yes, of course. I don't think we'll have a problem with any of that.'

'Why should you have a problem?'

'Not a problem, sir. I'll just need a few minutes.'

'For what?'

'I'll need to consult with a colleague.'

'Can you do so quickly?'

Van Thiessen practically bolted from the room and slammed the door behind him. The pain in Joel's stomach was not from hunger. If the wheels came off now, he had no plan B. He'd walk out of the bank with nothing, hopefully make it across the Paradeplatz to a streetcar, and once on board he would have no place to go. The escape would be over. Marco would be back, and Marco would eventually get him killed.

As time came to an abrupt halt, he kept thinking about the pardon. With it, his slate was wiped clean. The U.S. government was in no position to pressure the Swiss to freeze his account. The Swiss didn't freeze accounts! The Swiss were immune from pressure! That's why their banks were filled with loot from around the world.

They were the Swiss!

Elke retrieved him and asked if he would follow her downstairs. In other days, he would've followed Elke anywhere, but now it was only downstairs.

He'd been to the vault during his prior visit. It was in the basement, several levels below ground, though the clients never knew how deep into Swiss soil they were descending. Every door was a foot thick, every wall appeared to be made of lead, every ceiling had surveillance cameras. Elke handed him off to Van Thiessen again.

Both thumbs were scanned for matching prints. An optical scanner took his photo. 'Number seven,' Van Thiessen said, pointing. 'I'll meet you there,' he said, and left through a door.

Joel walked down a short hallway, passing six windowless steel doors until he came to the seventh. He pushed a button, all sorts of things tumbled and clicked inside, and the door finally opened. He stepped inside, where Van Thiessen was waiting.

The room was a twelve-foot square, with three walls lined with individual vaults, most about the size of a large shoe box.

'Your vault number?' he asked.

'L2270.'

'Correct.'

Van Thiessen stepped to his right, bent slightly to face L2270. On the vault's small keypad he punched some numbers, then straightened himself and said, 'If you wish.'

Under Van Thiessen's watchful eyes, Joel stepped to his vault and entered the code. As he did so, he softly whispered the numbers, forever seared in his memory: 'Eighty-one, fifty-five, ninety-four, ninety-three, twenty-three.' A small green light began blinking on the keypad. Van Thiessen smiled and said, 'I'll be waiting at the front. Just ring when you're finished.'

When he was alone, Joel removed the steel box from his vault and pulled open the top. He picked up the padded mailing envelope and opened it. There were the four two-gigabyte Jaz disks that had once been worth $1 billion.

He allowed himself a moment, but no more than sixty seconds. He was, after all, very safe at that time, and if he wanted to reflect, what was the harm?

He thought of Safi Mirza, Fazal Sharif, and Farooq Khan, the brilliant boys who'd discovered Neptune, then wrote reams of software to manipulate the system. They were all dead now, killed by their naïve greed and their choice of lawyer. He thought of Jacy Hubbard, the brash, gregarious, infinitely charismatic crook who had snowed the voters for an entire career and finally gotten much too greedy. He thought of Carl Pratt and Kim Bolling and dozens of other partners he'd brought into their prosperous firm, and the lives that had been wrecked by what he was now holding in his hand. He thought of Neal and the humiliation he'd caused his son when the scandal engulfed Washington and prison became not only a certainty but a sanctuary.

And he thought of himself, not in selfish terms, not in pity, not passing the blame to anyone else. What a miserable mess of a life he'd lived, so far anyway. As much as he'd like to go back and do it differently, he had no time to waste on such thoughts. You've only got a few years left, Joel, or Marco, or Giovanni, or whatever the hell your name is. For the first time in your rotten life, why don't you do what's right, as opposed to what's profitable?

He put the disks in the envelope, the envelope in his briefcase, then replaced the steel box in the vault. He rang for Van Thiessen.

Back in the power office, Van Thiessen handed him a file with one sheet of paper in it. 'This is a summary of your account,' he was saying. 'It's very straightforward. As you know, there's been no activity.'

'You guys are paying one percent interest,' Joel said.

'You were aware of our rates when you opened the account, Mr. Backman.'

'Yes, I was.'

'We protect your money in other ways.'

'Of course.' Joel closed the file and handed it back. 'I don't want to keep this. Do you have the cash?'

'Yes, it's on the way up.'

'Good. I need a few things.'

Van Thiessen pulled over his writing pad and stood ready with his fountain pen. 'Yes,' he said.

'I want to wire a hundred thousand to a bank in Washington, D.C. Can you recommend one?'

'Certainly. We work closely with Maryland Trust.'

'Good, wire the money there, and with the wire open a generic savings account. I will not be writing checks, just making withdrawals.'

'In what name?'

'Joel Backman and Neal Backman.' He was

getting used to his name again, not ducking when he said it. Not cowering in fear, waiting for gunfire. He liked it.

'Very well,' Van Thiessen said. Anything was possible.

'I need some help in getting back to the U.S. Could your girl check the Lufthansa flights to Philadelphia and New York?'

'Of course. When, and from where?'

'Today, as soon as possible. I'd like to avoid the airport here. How far away is Munich by car?'

'By car, three to four hours.'

'Can you provide a car?'

'I'm sure we can arrange that.'

'I prefer to leave from the basement here, in a car driven by someone not dressed like a chauffeur. Not a black car either, something that will not attract attention.'

Van Thiessen stopped writing and shot a puzzled look. 'Are you in danger, Mr. Backman?'

'Perhaps. I'm not sure, and I'm not taking chances.'

Van Thiessen pondered this for a few seconds, then said, 'Would you like for us to make the airline reservations?'

'Yes.'

'Then I need to see your passport.'

Joel pulled out Giovanni's borrowed passport. Van Thiessen studied it for a long time, his stoic banker's face betraying him. He was confused and worried. He finally managed, 'Mr.

412

Backman, you will be traveling with someone else's passport.'

'That's correct.'

'And this is a valid passport?'

'It is.'

'I assume you do not have one of your own.'

'They took it a long time ago.'

'This bank cannot take part in the commission of a crime. If this is stolen, then –'

'I assure you it's not stolen.'

'Then how did –'

'Let's just say it's borrowed, okay?'

'But using someone else's passport is a violation of the law.'

'Let's not get hung up on U.S. immigration policy, Mr. Van Thiessen. Just get the schedules. I'll pick the flights. Your girl makes the reservations using the bank's account. Deduct it from my balance. Get me a car and a driver. Deduct that from my balance, if you wish. It's all very simple.'

It was just a passport. Hell, other clients had three or four of them. Van Thiessen handed it back to Joel and said, 'Very well. Anything else?'

'Yes, I need to go online. I'm sure your computers are secure.'

'Absolutely.'

His e-mail to Neal read:

Grinch – With a bit of luck, I should arrive in U.S. tonight. Get a new cell phone today.

Don't let it out of your sight. Tomorrow morning call the Hilton, Marriott, and Sheraton, in downtown Washington. Ask for Giovanni Ferro. That's me. Call Carl Pratt first thing this morning, on the new phone. Push hard to get Senator Clayburn in D.C. We will cover his expenses. Tell him it's urgent. A favor to an old friend. Don't take no for an answer. No more e-mails until I get home. Marco

After a quick sandwich and a cola in Van Thiessen's office, Joel Backman left the bank building riding shotgun in a shiny green BMW four-door sedan. For good measure, he kept a Swiss newspaper in front of his face until they were on the autobahn. The driver was Franz. Franz fancied himself a Formula One hopeful, and when Joel let it be known that he was in somewhat of a hurry, Franz slipped into the left lane and hit 150 kilometers per hour.

Chapter 32

At 1:55 p.m., Joel Backman was sitting in a lavishly large seat in the first-class section of a Lufthansa 747 as it began its push back from the gate at the Munich airport. Only when it started to move did he dare pick up the glass of champagne he'd been staring at for ten minutes. The glass was empty by the time the plane stopped at the end of the runway for its final check. When the wheels lifted off the pavement, Joel closed his eyes and allowed himself the luxury of a few hours of relief.

His son, on the other hand, and at exactly the same moment, 7:55 Eastern Standard time, was stressed to the point of throwing things. How the hell was he supposed to go buy a new cell phone immediately, then call Carl Pratt again and solicit old favors that did not exist, and somehow cajole a retired and cantankerous old senator from Ocracoke, North Carolina, to drop what he was doing and return immediately to a city he evidently disliked immensely? Not to mention the obvious: he, Neal Backman, had a rather full day at the office. Nothing as pressing as rescuing his wayward father, but still a pretty full docket with clients and other important matters.

He left Jerry's Java, but instead of going to the office he went home. Lisa was bathing their daughter and was surprised to see him. 'What's wrong?' she said.

'We have to talk. Now.'

He began with the mysterious letter post-marked from York, Pennsylvania, and went through the $4,000 loan, as painful as it was, then the smartphone, the encrypted e-mails, pretty much the entire story. She took it calmly, much to his relief.

'You should've told me,' she said more than once.

'Yes, and I'm sorry.'

There was no fight, no arguing. Loyalty was one of her strongest traits, and when she said, 'We have to help him,' Neal hugged her.

'He'll pay back the money,' he assured her.

'We'll worry about the money later. Is he in danger?'

'I think so.'

'Okay, what's the first step?'

'Call the office and tell them I'm in bed with the flu.'

Their entire conversation was captured live and

in perfect detail by a tiny mike planted by the Mossad in the light fixture above where they were sitting. It was wired to a transmitter hidden in their attic, and from there it was relayed to a high-frequency receiver a quarter of a mile away in a seldom-used retail office space recently leased for six months by a gentleman from D.C. There, a technician listened to it twice, then quickly e-mailed his field agent in the Israeli embassy in Washington.

Since Backman's disappearance in Bologna more than twenty-four hours ago, the bugs planted around his son had been monitored even more closely.

The e-mail to Washington concluded with 'JB's coming home.'

Fortunately, Neal did not mention the name 'Giovanni Ferro' during the conversation with Lisa. Unfortunately, he did mention two of the three hotels – the Marriott and the Sheraton.

Backman's return was given the highest priority possible. Eleven Mossad agents were located on the East Coast; all were ordered to D.C. immediately.

Lisa dropped their daughter off at her mother's, then she and Neal sped south to Charlottesville, thirty minutes away. In a shopping center north of town they found the office for U.S. Cellular. They opened an account, bought a phone, and within thirty minutes were back on the road. Lisa drove while Neal tried to find Carl Pratt.

Aided by generous helpings of champagne and wine, Joel managed to sleep for several hours over the Atlantic. When the plane landed at JFK at 4:30 p.m., the relaxation was gone, replaced by uncertainties and a compulsion to look over his shoulder.

At immigration, he at first stepped into line with the returning Americans, a much shorter line. The mob waiting across the way for non-U.S. was embarrassing. Then he caught himself, glanced around, began cursing under his breath, and hustled over to the foreigners.

How stupid can you be?

A thick-necked uniformed kid from the Bronx was yelling at people to follow this line, not that one, and hurry up while you're at it. Welcome to America. Some things he had not missed.

The passport officer frowned at Giovanni's passport, but then he'd frowned at all the others too. Joel had been watching him carefully from behind a pair of cheap sunglasses.

'Could you remove your sunglasses, please?' the officer said.

'Certamente,' Joel said loudly, anxious to prove his Italianness. He took off the sunglasses, squinted as if blinded, then rubbed his eyes while the officer tried to study his face. Reluctantly, he stamped the passport and handed it over without a word. With nothing to declare, the customs officials barely looked at him. Joel hustled through the terminal and found the line at the taxi stand. 'Penn Station,' he said. The driver resembled Farooq Khan, the youngest of the three, just a boy, and as Joel studied him from the backseat he pulled his briefcase closer.

Moving against the rush hour traffic, he was at Penn Station in forty-five minutes. He bought an Amtrak ticket to D.C., and at 7:00 left New York for Washington.

The taxi parked on Brandywine Street in northwest Washington. It was almost eleven, and most of the fine homes were dark. Backman spoke to the driver, who was already reclining and ready for a nap.

Mrs. Pratt was in bed and struggling with sleep when she heard the doorbell. She grabbed her robe and hurried down the stairs. Her husband slept in the basement most nights, mainly because he snored but also because he was drinking too much and suffering from insomnia. She presumed he was there now.

'Who is it?' she asked through the intercom.

'Joel Backman,' came the answer, and she thought it was a prank.

'Who?'

'Donna, it's me, Joel. I swear. Open the door.'

She peeped through the hole in the door and did not recognize the stranger. 'Just a minute,' she said, then ran to the basement where Carl was watching the news. A minute later he was at the door, wearing a Duke sweat suit and holding a pistol.

'Who is it?' he demanded through the intercom.

'Carl, it's me, Joel. Put the gun down and open the door.'

The voice was unmistakable. He opened the door and Joel Backman walked into his life, an old nightmare back for more. There were no hugs, no handshakes, hardly a smile. The Pratts quietly examined him because he looked so different – much thinner, hair darker and shorter, strange clothing. He got a 'What are you doing here?' from Donna.

'That's a good question,' he said coolly. He had the advantage of planning. They were caught completely off guard. 'Will you put that gun down?'

Pratt put the gun on a side table.

'Have you talked to Neal?' Backman asked.

'All day long.'

'What's going on, Carl?' Donna asked.

'I don't really know.'

'Can we talk? That's why I'm here. I don't trust phones anymore.'

'Talk about what?' she demanded.

'Could you make us some coffee, Donna?' Joel asked pleasantly.

'Hell no.'

'Scratch the coffee.'

Carl had been rubbing his chin, assessing things. 'Donna, we need to talk in private. Old law firm stuff. I'll give you the rundown later.'

She shot them both a look that clearly said,

Go straight to hell, then stomped back up the stairs. They stepped into the den. Carl said, 'Would you like something to drink?'

'Yes, something strong.'

He went to a small wet bar in a corner and poured single malts – doubles. He handed Joel a drink and without the slightest effort at a smile said, 'Cheers.'

'Cheers. It's good to see you, Carl.'

'I bet it is. You weren't supposed to see anyone for another fourteen years.'

'Counting the days, huh?'

'We're still cleaning up after you, Joel. A bunch of good folks got hurt. I'm sorry if Donna and I aren't exactly thrilled to see you. I can't think of too many people in this town who'd like to give you a hug.'

'Most would like to shoot me.'

Carl gave a wary look over at the pistol.

'I can't worry about that,' Backman continued. 'Sure, I'd like to go back and change some things, but I don't have that luxury. I'm running for my life now, Carl, and I need some help.'

'Maybe I don't want to get involved.'

'I can't blame you. But I need a favor, a big one. Help me now, and I promise I'll never show up on your doorstep again.'

'I'll shoot the next time.'

'Where's Senator Clayburn? Tell me he's still alive.'

'Yes, very much so. And you caught some luck.'

'What?'

'He's here, in D.C.'

'Why?'

'Hollis Maples is retiring, after a hundred years in the Senate. They had a bash for him tonight. All the old boys are in town.'

'Maples? He was drooling in his soup ten years ago.'

'Well, now he can't see his soup. He and Clayburn were as tight as ticks.'

'Have you talked to Clayburn?'

'Yes.'

'And?'

'It might be a tough one, Joel. He didn't like the sound of your name. Something about being shot for treason.'

'Whatever. Tell him he can broker a deal that will make him feel like a real patriot.'

'What's the deal?'

'I have the software, Carl. The whole package. Picked it up this morning from a vault in a bank in Zurich where it's been sitting for more than six years. You and Clayburn come to my room in the morning, and I'll show it to you.'

'I really don't want to see it.'

'Yes you do.'

Pratt sucked down two ounces of scotch. He walked back to the bar and refilled his glass, took another toxic dose, then said, 'When and where?'

'The Marriott on Twenty-second Street. Room five-twenty. Nine in the morning.'

'Why Joel? Why should I get involved?'

'A favor to an old friend.'

'I don't owe you any favors. And the old friend left a long time ago.'

'Please, Carl. Bring in Clayburn, and you'll be out of the picture by noon tomorrow. I promise you'll never see me again.'

'That is very tempting.'

He asked the driver to take his time. They cruised through Georgetown, along K Street, with its late-night restaurants and bars and college hangouts all packed with people living the good life. It was March 22 and spring was coming. The temperature was around sixty-five and the students were anxious to be outside, even at midnight.

The cab slowed at the intersection of I Street and 14th and Joel could see his old office building in the distance on New York Avenue. Somewhere in there, on the top floor, he'd once ruled his own little kingdom, with his minions running behind him, jumping at every command. It was not a nostalgic moment. Instead he was filled with regret for a worthless life spent chasing money and buying friends and women and all the toys a serious big shot could want. They drove on, past the countless office buildings, government on one side, lobbyists on the other.

He asked the driver to change streets, to move on to more pleasant sights. They turned onto Constitution and drove along the Mall, past the

Washington Monument. His youngest child, Anna Lee, had begged him for years to take her for a springtime walk along the Mall, like the other kids in her class. She wanted to see Mr. Lincoln and spend a day at the Smithsonian. He'd promised and promised until she was gone. Anna Lee was in Denver now, he thought, with a child he'd never seen.

As the dome of the Capitol drew nearer, Joel suddenly had enough. This little trip down memory lane was depressing. The memories in his life were too unpleasant.

'Take me to the hotel,' he said.

Chapter 33

Neal made the first pot of coffee, then stepped outside onto the cool bricks of the patio and admired the beauty of an early-spring daybreak.

If his father had indeed arrived back in D.C., he would not be asleep at six-thirty in the morning. The night before, Neal had coded his new phone with the numbers of the Washington hotels, and as the sun came up he started with the Sheraton. No Giovanni Ferro. Then the Marriott.

'One moment, please,' the operator said, then the phone to the room began ringing. 'Hello,' came a familiar voice.

'Marco, please,' Neal said.

'Marco here. Is this the Grinch?'

'It is.'

'Where are you right now?'

'Standing on my patio, waiting for the sun.'

'And what type of phone are you using?'

'It's a brand-new Motorola that I've kept in my pocket since I bought it yesterday.'

'You're sure it's secure.'

'Yes.'

A pause as Joel breathed deeply. 'It's good to hear your voice, son.'

'And yours as well. How was your trip?'

'Very eventful. Can you come to Washington?'

'When?'

'Today, this morning.'

'Sure, everybody thinks I have the flu. I'm covered at the office. When and where?'

'Come to the Marriott on Twenty-second Street. Walk in the lobby at eight forty-five, take the elevator to the sixth floor, then the stairs down to the fifth. Room five-twenty.'

'Is all this necessary?'

'Trust me. Can you use another car?'

'I don't know. I'm not sure who –'

'Lisa's mother. Borrow her car, make sure no one is following you. When you get to the city, park it at the garage on Sixteenth then walk to the Marriott. Watch your rear at all times. If you see anything suspicious, then call me and we'll abort.'

Neal glanced around his backyard, half expecting to see agents dressed in black moving in on him. Where did his father pick up the cloak-and-dagger stuff? Six years in solitary maybe? A thousand spy novels?

'Are you with me?' Joel snapped.

'Yeah, sure. I'm on my way.'

★

Ira Clayburn looked like a man who'd spent his life on a fishing boat, as opposed to one who'd served thirty-four years in the U.S. Senate. His ancestors had fished the Outer Banks of North Carolina, around their home at Ocracoke, for a hundred years. Ira would've done the same, except for a sixth-grade math teacher who discovered his exceptional IQ. A scholarship to Chapel Hill pulled him away from home. Another one to Yale got him a master's. A third, to Stanford, placed the title of 'Doctor' before his name. He was happily teaching economics at Davidson when a compromise appointment sent him to the Senate to fill an unexpired term. He reluctantly ran for a full term, and for the next three decades tried his best to leave Washington. At the age of seventy-one he finally walked away. When he left the Senate, he took with him a mastery of U.S. intelligence that no politician could equal.

He agreed to go to the Marriott with Carl Pratt, an old friend from a tennis club, only out of curiosity. The Neptune mystery had never been solved, as far as he knew. But then he'd been out of the loop for the last five years, during which time he'd been fishing almost every day, happily taking his boat out and trolling the waters from Hattcras to Cape Lookout.

During the twilight of his Senate career, he had watched Joel Backman become the latest in a long line of hotshot lobbyists who perfected the art of twisting arms for huge fees. He was leaving Washington when Jacy Hubbard, another cobra who got what he deserved, was found dead.

He had no use for their ilk.

When the door to room 520 opened, he stepped inside behind Carl Pratt and came face-to-face with the devil himself.

But the devil was quite pleasant, remarkably gracious, a different man. Prison.

Joel introduced himself and his son Neal to Senator Clayburn. All hands were properly shaken, all thanks duly given. The table in the small suite was covered with pastries, coffee, and juice. Four chairs had been pulled around in a loose circle, and they sat down.

'This shouldn't take long,' Joel said. 'Senator, I need your help. I don't know how much you know about the rather messy affair that sent me away for a few years . . .'

'I know the basics, but there have always been questions.'

'I'm pretty sure I know the answers.'

'Whose satellite system is it?'

Joel couldn't sit. He walked to the window, looked out at nothing, then took a deep breath. 'It was built by Red China, at an astronomical cost. As you know, the Chinese are far behind us in conventional weapons, so they're spending heavily on the high-tech stuff. They stole some of our technology, and they successfully launched the system – nicknamed Neptune – without the knowledge of the CIA.'

'How did they do that?'

'Something as low-tech as forest fires. They torched twenty thousand acres one night in a northern province. It created an enormous cloud and in the middle of it they launched three rockets, each with three satellites.'

'The Russians did that once,' Clayburn said.

'And the Russians got fooled by their own trick. They missed Neptune too – everybody did. No one in the world knew it existed until my clients stumbled across it.'

'Those Pakistani students.'

'Yes, and all three are dead.'

'Who killed them?'

'I suspect agents of Red China.'

'Who killed Jacy Hubbard?'

'Same.'

'And how close are these people to you?'

'Closer than I would like.'

Clayburn reached for a doughnut and Pratt drained a glass of orange juice. Joel continued, 'I have the software – JAM as they called it. There was only one copy.'

'The one you tried to sell?' Clayburn said.

'Yes. And I really want to get rid of it. It's proving to be quite deadly, and I'm desperate to hand it over. I'm just not sure who should get it.'

'What about the CIA?' Pratt said, because he had yet to say anything.

Clayburn was already shaking his head no.

'I can't trust them,' Joel said. 'Teddy

Maynard got me pardoned so he could sit back and watch someone else kill me. Now there's an interim director.'

'And a new President,' Clayburn said. 'The CIA is a mess right now. I wouldn't go near it.' And with that Senator Clayburn stepped over the line, becoming an advisor, not just a curious spectator.

'Who do I talk to?' Joel asked. 'Who can I trust?'

'DIA, the Defense Intelligence Agency,' Clayburn said without hesitation. 'The head guy there is Major Wes Roland, an old friend.'

'How long has he been there?'

Clayburn thought for a second, then said, 'Ten, maybe twelve years. He has a ton of experience, smart as hell. And an honorable man.'

'And you can talk to him?'

'Yes. We've kept in touch.'

'Doesn't he report to the director of the CIA?' Pratt asked.

'Yes, everyone does. There are now at least fifteen different intelligence agencies – something I fought against for twenty years – and by law they all report to the CIA.'

'So Wes Roland will take whatever I give him and tell the CIA?' Joel asked.

'He has no choice. But there are different ways to go about it. Roland is a sensible man, and he knows how to play the politics. That's how he's survived this long.'

'Can you arrange a meeting?'

'Yes, but what will happen at the meeting?'

'I'll throw JAM at him and run out of the building.'

'And in return?'

'It's an easy deal, Senator. I don't want money. Just a little help.'

'What?'

'I prefer to discuss it with him. With you in the room, of course.'

There was a gap in the conversation as Clayburn stared at the floor and weighed the issues. Neal walked to the table and selected a croissant. Joel poured more coffee. Pratt, obviously hungover, worked another tall glass of orange juice.

Finally, Clayburn sat back in his chair and said, 'I assume this is urgent.'

'Worse than urgent. If Major Roland is available, I would meet with him right now. Anywhere.'

'I'm sure he'll drop whatever he's doing.'

'The phone's over there.'

Clayburn stood and stepped toward the desk. Pratt cleared his throat and said, 'Look, fellas, at this point in the game, I'd like to check out. I don't want to hear any more. Don't want to be a witness, or a defendant, or another casualty. So if you'll just excuse me, I'll be heading back to the office.'

He didn't wait for a response. He was gone in an instant, with the door closing hard behind him. They watched it for a few seconds, somewhat taken aback by the abrupt exit.

'Poor Carl,' Clayburn said. 'Always afraid of his shadow.' He picked up the phone and went to work.

In the middle of the fourth call, and the second straight to the Pentagon, Clayburn placed his hand over the receiver and said to Joel, 'They prefer to meet at the Pentagon.'

Joel was already shaking his head. 'No. I'm not going in there with the software until there's a deal. I'll leave it behind and give it to them later, but I'm not walking in there with it.'

Clayburn relayed this, then listened for a long time. When he covered the receiver again he asked, 'The software, what's it on?'

'Four disks,' Joel said.

'They have to verify it, you understand?'

'Okay, I'll take two disks with me into the Pentagon. That's about half of it. They can take a quick look.'

Clayburn huddled over the receiver and repeated Joel's conditions. Again, he listened for a long time, then he asked Joel, 'Will you show me the disks?'

'Yes.'

He placed the call on hold while Joel picked up his briefcase. He removed the envelope, then the four disks, and placed them on the bed for Neal and Clayburn to gawk at. Clayburn went back to the phone and said, 'I'm looking at four disks. Mr. Backman assures me it is what it is.'

He listened for a few minutes, then punched the hold button again.

'They want us at the Pentagon right now,' he said.

'Let's go.'

Clayburn hung up and said, 'Things are hopping over there. I think the boys are excited. Shall we go?'

'I'll meet you in the lobby in five minutes,' Joel said.

When the door closed behind Clayburn, Joel quickly gathered the disks and stuck two of them into his coat pocket. The other two – numbers three and four – were placed back in the briefcase, which he handed to Neal as he said, 'After we leave, go to the front desk and get another room. Insist on checking in now. Call this room, leave me a message and tell me where you are. Stay there until you hear from me.'

'Sure, Dad. I hope you know what you're doing.'

'Just cutting a deal, son. Like in the old days.'

The taxi dropped them at the south lot of the Pentagon, near the Metro stop. Two uniformed members of Major Roland's staff were waiting with credentials and instructions. They walked them through the security clearances and got their photos made for their temporary ID cards. The entire time Clayburn was griping about how easy it was back in the old days.

Old days or not, he had made a quick

transition from the skeptical critic to a major player, and he was thoroughly engaged in Backman's plot. As they hiked along the wide corridors of the second floor, he reminisced about how simple life had been when there were two superpowers. We always had the Soviets. The bad guys were easy to identify.

They took the stairs to the third floor, C wing, and were led by the staffers through a set of doors and into a suite of offices where they were obviously expected. Major Roland himself was standing by, waiting. He was about sixty, still looking trim and fit in his khaki uniform. Introductions were made, and he invited them into his conference room. At one end of the long, wide center table, three technicians were busy checking out a large computer that had evidently just been rolled in.

Major Roland asked Joel's permission to have two assistants present. Certainly. Joel had no objection.

'Would you mind if we video the meeting?' Roland asked.

'For what purpose?' Joel asked.

'Just to have it on film in case someone higher up wants to see it.'

'Such as?'

'Perhaps the President.'

Joel looked at Clayburn, his only friend in the room, and a tenuous one at best.

'What about the CIA?' Joel asked.

'Maybe.'

'Let's forget the video, at least initially. Maybe at some point during the meeting, we'll agree to switch on the camera.'

'Fair enough. Coffee or soft drinks?'

No one was thirsty. Major Roland asked the computer technicians if their equipment was ready. It was, and he asked them to step outside the room.

Joel and Clayburn sat on one side of the conference table. Major Roland was flanked by his two deputies on the opposite side. All three had pens and notepads ready to go. Joel and Clayburn had nothing.

'Let's start and finish a conversation about the CIA,' Backman began, determined to be in charge of the proceedings. 'As I understand the law, or at least the way things once worked around here, the director of the CIA is in charge of all intelligence activities.'

'That's correct,' Roland said.

'What will you do with the information I am about to give you?'

The major glanced to his right, and the look that passed between him and the deputy there conveyed a lot of uncertainty. 'As you said, sir, the director is entitled to know and have everything.'

Backman smiled and cleared his throat. 'Major, the CIA tried to get me killed, okay? And, as far as I know, they're still after me. I don't have much use for the guys over at Langley.'

'Mr. Maynard's gone, Mr. Backman.'

'And someone took his place. I don't want money, Major. I want protection. First, I want my own government to leave me alone.'

'That can be arranged,' Roland said with authority.

'And I'll need some help with a few others.'

'Why don't you tell us everything, Mr. Backman? The more we know, the more we can help you.'

With the exception of Neal, Joel Backman didn't trust another person on the face of the earth. But the time had come to lay it all on the table and hope for the best. The chase was over; there was no place else to run.

He began with Neptune itself, and described how it was built by Red China, how the technology was stolen from two different U.S. defense contractors, how it was launched under cover and fooled not only the U.S. but also the Russians, the British, and the Israelis. He narrated the lengthy story of the three Pakistanis – their ill-fated discovery, their fear of what they found, their curiosity at being able to communicate with Neptune, and their brilliance in writing software that could manipulate and neutralize the system. He spoke harshly of his own giddy greed in shopping JAM to various governments, hoping to make more money than anyone could dream of. He pulled no punches when recalling the recklessness of Jacy Hubbard, and the foolishness of their schemes to peddle their product. Without hesitation, he admitted his mistakes and took full responsibility for the havoc he'd caused. Then he pressed on.

No, the Russians had no interest in what he was selling. They had their own satellites and couldn't afford to negotiate for more.

No, the Israelis never had a deal. They were on the fringes, close enough to know that a deal with the Saudis was looming. The Saudis were desperate to purchase JAM. They had a few satellites of their own, but nothing to match Neptune.

Nothing could match Neptune, not even the latest generation of American satellites.

The Saudis had actually seen the four disks. In a tightly controlled experiment, two agents from their secret police were given a demonstration of the software by the three Pakistanis. It took place in a computer lab on the campus of the University of Maryland, and it had been a dazzling, very convincing display. Backman had watched it, as had Hubbard.

The Saudis offered $100 million for JAM. Hubbard, who fancied himself a close friend of the Saudis, was the point man during the negotiations. A 'transaction fee' of $1 million was paid, the money wired to an account in Zurich. Hubbard and Backman countered with half a billion.

Then all hell broke loose. The feds attacked with warrants, indictments, investigations, and the Saudis got spooked. Hubbard got murdered.

Joel fled to the safety of prison, leaving a wide path of destruction behind and some angry people with serious grudges.

The forty-five-minute summary ended without a single interruption. When Joel finished, none of the three on the other side of the table was taking notes. They were too busy listening.

'I'm sure we can talk to the Israelis,' Major Roland said. 'If they're convinced the Saudis will never get their hands on JAM, then they'll rest much easier. We've had discussions with them over the years. JAM has been a favorite topic. I'm quite sure they can be placated.'

'What about the Saudis?'

'They've asked about it too, at the highest levels. We have a lot of common interests these days. I'm confident they'll relax if they know that we have it and no one else will get it. I know the Saudis well, and I think they'll write it off as a bad deal. There is the small matter of the transaction fee.'

'A million bucks is chump change to them. It's not negotiable.'

'Very well. I guess that leaves the Chinese.'

'Any suggestions?'

Clayburn had yet to speak. He leaned forward on his elbows and said, 'In my opinion, they'll never forget it. Your clients basically hijacked a zillion-dollar system and rendered it useless without their homemade software. The Chinese have nine of the best satellites ever built floating around up there and they can't use them. They are not going to forgive and forget, and you really can't blame them. Unfortunately, we have little leverage with Beijing on delicate intelligence matters.'

Major Roland was nodding. 'I'm afraid I must agree with the senator. We can let them know that we have the software, but this is something they'll never forget.'

'I don't blame them. I'm just trying to survive, that's all.'

'We'll do what we can with the Chinese, but it may not be much.'

'Here's the deal, gentlemen. You give me your word that you'll get the CIA out of my life, and that you'll act quickly to appease the Israelis and the Saudis. Do whatever is possible with the Chinese, which I understand may be very little. And you give me two passports – one Australian and one Canadian. As soon as they're ready, and this afternoon would not be too soon, you bring them to me and I'll hand over the other two disks.'

'It's a deal,' Roland said. 'But, of course, we need to have a look at the software.'

Joel reached into his pocket and removed disks one and two. Roland called the computer technicians back in, and the entire group huddled around the large monitor.

A Mossad agent with the code name of Albert thought he saw Neal Backman enter the lobby of the Marriott on 22nd Street. He called his supervisor, and within thirty minutes two other agents were inside the hotel. Albert again saw Neal Backman an hour later, as he left an elevator carrying a briefcase that he had not carried into the hotel, went to the front desk, and appeared to fill out a registration form. Then he pulled out his wallet and handed over a credit card.

He returned to the elevator, where Albert missed him by a matter of seconds.

The knowledge that Joel Backman was probably staying at the Marriott on 22nd Street was extremely important, but it also posed enormous problems. First, the killing of an American on American soil was an operation so delicate that the prime minister would have to be consulted. Second, the actual assassination itself was a logistical nightmare. The hotel had six hundred rooms, hundreds of guests, hundreds of employees, hundreds of visitors, no less than five conventions in progress. Thousands of potential witnesses.

However, a plan came together quickly.

Chapter 34

They had lunch with the senator in the rear of a Vietnamese deli near Dupont Circle, a place they judged to be safe from lobbyists and old-timers who might see them together and start one of the hot rumors that kept the city alive and gridlocked. For an hour, as they struggled with spicy noodles almost too hot to eat, Joel and Neal listened as the fisherman from Ocracoke regaled them with endless stories of his glory days in Washington. He said more than once that he did not miss politics, yet his memories of those days were filled with intrigue, humor, and many friendships.

Clayburn had started the day thinking that a bullet in the head would've been too good for Joel Backman, but when they said goodbye on the sidewalk outside the café he was begging him to please come see his boat, and bring Neal too. Joel had not been fishing since childhood, and he knew he would never make it to the Outer

Banks, but out of gratitude he promised to try.

Joel came closer to a bullet in the head than he would ever know. As he and Neal strolled along Connecticut Avenue after lunch, they were closely watched by the Mossad. A sharpshooter was ready in the rear of a rented panel truck. Final approval, though, was still hung up in Tel Aviv. And the sidewalk was very crowded.

Using the yellow pages in his hotel room, Neal had found a men's shop that advertised over-night alterations. He was anxious to help – his father desperately needed some new clothes. Joel bought a navy three-piece suit, a white dress shirt, two ties, some chinos and casual clothes, and, thankfully, two pairs of black dress shoes. The total was $3,100, and he paid in cash. The bowling shoes were left in a wastebasket, though the salesman had been somewhat complimentary of them.

At exactly 4:00 p.m., while sitting in a Starbucks coffee shop on Massachusetts Avenue, Neal took his cell phone and dialed the number given by Major Roland. He handed the phone to his father.

Roland himself answered. 'We're on our way,' he said.

'Room five-twenty,' Joel said, eyes watching the other coffee drinkers. 'How many are coming?'

'It's a nice group,' Roland said.

'I don't care how many you bring, just leave everybody else in the lobby.'

'I can do that.'

They forgot the coffee and walked ten blocks back to the Marriott, with every step watched closely by well-armed Mossad agents. Still no action in Tel Aviv.

The Backmans were in the room for a few minutes when there was a knock on the door.

Joel shot a nervous glance at his son, who froze and looked as anxious as his father. This could be it, Joel said to himself. The epic journey that began on the streets of Bologna, on foot, then a cab, then a bus to Modena, a taxi all the way to Milan, more little hikes, more cabs, then the train destined for Stuttgart, but with an unexpected detour in Zug, where another driver took the cash and hauled him into Zurich, two streetcars, then Franz and the green BMW doing 150 kilometers all the way to Munich, where the warm and welcome arms of Lufthansa brought him home. This could be the end of the road.

'Who is it?' Joel asked as he stepped to the door.

'Wes Roland.'

Joel looked through the peephole, saw no one. He took a deep breath and opened the door. The major was now wearing a sports coat and tie, and he was all alone and empty-handed. At least he appeared to be alone. Joel glanced down the hall and saw people trying to hide. He quickly closed the door and introduced Roland to Neal.

'Here are the passports,' Roland said,

reaching into his coat pocket and pulling out two broken-in passports. The first had a dark blue cover with AUSTRALIA in gold letters. Joel opened it and looked at the photo first. The technicians had taken the Pentagon security photo, lightened the hair considerably, removed the eyeglasses and a few of the wrinkles, and produced a pretty good image. His name was Simon Wilson McAvoy. 'Not bad,' Joel said.

The second was bound in navy blue, with CANADA in gold letters on the outside. Same photo, and the Canadian name of Ian Rex Hatteboro. Joel nodded his approval and handed both to Neal for his inspection.

'There is some concern about the grand jury investigation into the pardon scandal,' Roland said. 'We didn't discuss it earlier.'

'Major, you and I both know I'm not involved in that affair. I expect the CIA to convince the boys over at Hoover that I'm clean. I had no idea a pardon was in the works. It's not my scandal.'

'You may be called to appear before a grand jury.'

'Fine. I'll volunteer. It'll be a very short appearance.'

Roland seemed satisfied. He was just the messenger. He began to look around for his end of the bargain. 'Now, about that software,' he said.

'It's not here,' Joel said, with unnecessary drama. He nodded at Neal, who left the room. 'Just a minute,' he said to Roland, whose eyebrows were arching up while his eyes grew narrow.

'Is there a problem?' he said.

'Not at all. The package is in another room. Sorry, but I've been acting like a spy for too long.'

'Not a bad practice for a man in your position.'

'I guess it's now a way of life.'

'Our technicians are still playing with the first two disks. It's really an impressive piece of work.'

'My clients were smart boys, and good boys. Just got greedy, I guess. Like a few others.'

There was a knock on the door, and Neal was back. He handed the envelope to Joel, who removed the two disks, then gave them to Roland. 'Thanks,' he said. 'It took guts.'

'Some people have more guts than brains, I guess.'

The exchange was over. There was nothing left to say. Roland made his way to the door. He grabbed the doorknob, then thought of something else. 'Just so you know,' he said gravely, 'the CIA is reasonably certain that Sammy Tin landed in New York this afternoon. The flight came from Milan.'

'Thanks, I guess,' Joel said.

When Roland left the hotel room with the envelope, Joel stretched out on the bed and closed his eyes. Neal found two beers in the minibar and fell into a nearby chair. He waited a few minutes, sipped his beer, then finally said, 'Dad, who is Sammy Tin?'

'You don't want to know.'

'Oh, yeah. I want to know everything. And you're going to tell me.'

At 6:00 p.m., Lisa's mother's car stopped outside a hair salon on Wisconsin Avenue in Georgetown. Joel got out and said goodbye. And thanks. Neal sped away, anxious to get home.

Neal had made the appointment by phone a few hours earlier, bribing the receptionist with the promise of $500 in cash. A stout lady named Maureen was waiting, not too happy to be working late but nonetheless anxious to see who would drop that kind of money on a quick coloring job.

Joel paid first, thanked both the receptionist and Maureen for their flexibility, then sat in front of a mirror.

'You want it washed?' Maureen said.

'No. Let's hurry.'

She put her fingers in his hair and said, 'Who did this?'

'A lady in Italy.'

'What color do you have in mind?'

'Gray, solid gray.'

'Natural?'

'No, beyond natural. Let's get it almost white.'

She rolled her eyes at the receptionist. We get all kinds in here.

446

Maureen went to work. The receptionist went home, locking the door behind her. A few minutes into the project, Joel asked, 'Are you working tomorrow?'

'Nope, it's my day off. Why?'

'Because I need to come in around noon for another session. I'll be in the mood for something darker tomorrow, something to hide the gray you're doing now.'

Her hands stopped. 'What's with you?'

'Meet me here at noon, and I'll pay a thousand bucks in cash.'

'Sure. What about the next day?'

'I'll be fine when some of the gray is gone.'

Dan Sandberg had been loafing at his desk at the *Post* late in the afternoon when the call came. The gentleman on the other end identified himself as Joel Backman, said he wanted to talk. Sandberg's caller ID showed an unknown number.

'The real Joel Backman?' Sandberg said, scrambling for his laptop.

'The only one I know.'

'A real pleasure. Last time I saw you, you were in court, pleading guilty to all sorts of bad stuff.'

'All of which was wiped clean with a presidential pardon.'

'I thought you were tucked away on the other side of the world.'

'Yeah, I got tired of Europe. Kinda missed my

447

old stomping grounds. I'm back now, ready to do business again.'

'What kind of business?'

'My specialty, of course. That's what I wanted to talk about.'

'I'd be delighted. But I'll have to ask questions about the pardon. Lots of wild rumors out there.'

'That's the first thing we'll cover, Mr. Sandberg. How about tomorrow morning at nine?'

'I wouldn't miss it. Where do we meet?'

'I'll have the presidential suite at the Hay-Adams. Bring a photographer if you like. The broker is back in town.'

Sandberg hung up and called Rusty Lowell, his best source at the CIA. Lowell was out, and as usual no one had any idea where he was. He tried another source at Langley, but found nothing.

Whitaker sat in the first-class section of the Alitalia flight from Milano to Dulles. Up front, the booze was free and free-flowing, and Whitaker tried his best to get hammered. The call from Julia Javier had been a shock. She had begun pleasantly enough with the question 'Anyone seen Marco over there, Whitaker?'

'No, but we're looking.'

'Do you think you'll find him?'

'Yes, I'm quite sure he'll turn up.'

'The director is very anxious right now,

Whitaker. She wants to know if you're going to find Marco.'

'Tell her yes, we'll find him!'

'And where are you looking, Whitaker?'

'Between here, in Milano, and Zurich.'

'Well, you're wasting your time, Whitaker, because ol' Marco has popped up here in Washington. Met with the Pentagon this afternoon. Slipped right through your fingers, Whitaker, made us look stupid.'

'What!'

'Come home, Whitaker, and get here quickly.'

Twenty-five rows back, Luigi was crouching low in coach, rubbing knees with a twelve-year-old girl who was listening to some of the raunchiest rap he'd ever heard. He was on his fourth drink himself. It wasn't free and he didn't care what it cost.

He knew Whitaker was up there making notes on exactly how to pin all the blame on Luigi. He should be doing the same, but for the moment he just wanted to drink. The next week in Washington would be quite unpleasant.

At 6:02 p.m., eastern standard time, the call came from Tel Aviv to halt the Backman killing. Stand down. Abort. Pack up and withdraw, there would be no dead body this time.

For the agents it was welcome news. They were trained to move in with great stealth, do their deed, disappear with no clues, no evidence, no trail. Bologna was a far better place than the crowded streets of Washington, D.C.

An hour later, Joel checked out of the Marriott and enjoyed a long walk through the cool air. He stayed on the busy streets, though, and didn't waste any time. This wasn't Bologna. This city was far different after hours. Once the commuters were gone and the traffic died down, things got dangerous.

The clerk at the Hay-Adams preferred credit, something plastic, something that would not upset the bookkeeping. Rarely did a client insist on paying in cash, but this client wouldn't take no for an answer. The reservation had been confirmed, and with a proper smile he handed over a key and welcomed Mr. Ferro to their hotel.

'Any bags, sir?'

'None.'

And that was the end of their little conversation.

Mr. Ferro headed for the elevators carrying only a cheap black-leather briefcase.

Chapter 35

The presidential suite at the Hay-Adams was on the eighth floor, with three large windows overlooking H Street, then Lafayette Park, then the White House. It had a king-size bedroom, a bathroom well appointed with brass and marble, and a sitting room with period antiques, a slightly out-of-date television and phones, and a fax machine that was seldom used. It went for $3,000 a night, but then what did the broker care about such things?

When Sandberg knocked on the door at nine, he waited only a second before it was yanked open and a hearty 'Morning, Dan!' greeted him. Backman lunged for his right hand and as he pumped it furiously he dragged Sandberg into his domain.

'Glad you could make it,' he said. 'Would you like some coffee?'

'Yeah, sure, black.'

Sandberg dropped his satchel onto a chair and

watched Backman pour from a silver coffeepot. Much thinner, with hair that was shorter and almost white, gaunt through the face. There was a slight resemblance to defendant Backman, but not much.

'Make yourself at home,' Backman was saying. 'I've ordered some breakfast. Should be up in a minute.'

He carefully set two cups with saucers on the coffee table in front of the sofa, and said, 'Let's work here. You plan to use a recorder?'

'If that's all right.'

'I prefer it that way. Eliminates misunderstandings.' They took their positions. Sandberg placed a small recorder on the table, then got his pad and pen ready. Backman was all smiles as he sat low in his chair, legs casually crossed, the confident air of a man who wasn't afraid of any question. Sandberg noticed the shoes, hard rubber soles that had barely been used. Not a scuff or speck of dirt anywhere on the black leather. Typically, the lawyer was put together – navy suit, bright white shirt with cuffs, gold links, a collar bar, a red-and-gold tie that begged for attention.

'Well, the first question is, where have you been?'

'Europe, knocking about, seeing the Continent.'

'For two months?'

'Yep, that's enough.'

'Anyplace in particular?'

'Not really. I spent a lot of time on the trains over there, a marvelous way to travel. You can see so much.'

'Why have you returned?'

'This is home. Where else would I go? What else would I do? Bumming around Europe sounds like great fun, and it was, but you can't make a career out of it. I've got work to do.'

'What kind of work?'

'The usual. Government relations, consulting.'

'That means lobbying, right?'

'My firm will have a lobbying arm, yes. That will be a very important part of our business, but by no means the centerpiece.'

'And what firm is that?'

'The new one.'

'Help me out here, Mr. Backman.'

'I'm opening a new firm, the Backman Group, offices here, New York, and San Francisco. We'll have six partners initially, should be up to twenty in a year or so.'

'Who are these people?'

'Oh, I can't name them now. We're hammering out the details, negotiating the fine points, pretty sensitive stuff. We plan to cut the ribbon on the first of May, should be a big splash.'

'No doubt. This will not be a law firm?'

'No, but we plan to add a legal section later.'

'I thought you lost your license when . . .'

'I did, yes. But with the pardon, I'm now eligible to sit for the bar exam again. If I get a hankering to start suing people, then I'll brush up on the books and get a license. Not in the near future, though, there's just too much work to do.'

'What kind of work?'

'Getting this thing off the ground, raising capital, and, most important, meeting with potential clients.'

'Could you give me the names of some clients?'

'Of course not, but just hang on for a few weeks and that information will be available.'

The phone on the desk rang, and Backman frowned at it. 'Just a second. It's a call I've been waiting on.' He walked over and picked it up. Sandberg heard, 'Backman, yes, hello, Bob. Yes, I'll be in New York tomorrow. Look, I'll call you back in an hour, okay? I'm in the middle of something.' He hung up and said, 'Sorry about that.'

It was Neal, calling as planned, at exactly 9:15, and he would call every ten minutes for the next hour.

'No problem,' said Sandberg. 'Let's talk about your pardon. Have you seen the stories about the alleged buying of presidential pardons?'

'Have I seen the stories? I have a defense team in place, Dan. My guys are all over this. If and when the feds manage to put together a grand jury, if they ever get that far, I've informed them that I want to be the first witness. I have absolutely nothing to hide, and the suggestion that I paid for a pardon is actionable at law.'

'You plan to sue?'

'Absolutely. My lawyers are preparing a massive libel action now against *The New York Times* and that hatchet man, Heath Frick. It'll be ugly. It'll be a nasty trial, and they're gonna pay me a bunch of money.'

'You're sure you want me to print that?'

'Hell yes! And while we're at it, I commend you and your newspaper for the restraint you've shown so far. It's rather unusual, but admirable nonetheless.'

Sandberg's story of this visit to the presidential suite was big enough to begin with. Now, however, it had just been thrust onto the front page, tomorrow morning.

'Just for the record, you deny paying for the pardon?'

'Categorically, vehemently denied. And I'll sue anybody who says I did.'

'So why were you pardoned?'

Backman reshifted his weight and was about to launch into a long one when the door buzzer erupted. 'Ah, breakfast,' he said, jumping to his feet. He opened the door and a white-jacketed waiter pushed in a cart holding caviar and all the trimmings, scrambled eggs with truffles, and a bottle of Krug champagne in a bucket of ice. While Backman signed the check the waiter opened the bottle.

'One glass or two?' the waiter asked.

'A glass of champagne, Dan?'

Sandberg couldn't help but glance at his watch. Seemed a bit early to start with the booze, but then why not? How often would he be sitting in the presidential suite looking over at the White House sipping on bubbly that cost $300 a bottle? 'Sure, but just a little.'

The waiter filled two glasses, put the Krug back in the ice, and left the room just as the phone rang again. This time it was Randall from Boston, and he'd have to sit by the phone for another hour while Backman finished his business.

He slammed down the receiver and said, 'Eat a bite, Dan, I ordered enough for the both us.'

'No, thanks, I had a bagel earlier.' He took the champagne and had a drink.

Backman dipped a wafer into a $500 pile of caviar and stuck it in his mouth, like a teenager with a corn chip and salsa. He chomped on it as he paced, glass in hand.

'My pardon?' he said. 'I asked President Morgan to review my case. Frankly, I didn't think he had any interest, but he's a very astute person.'

'Arthur Morgan?'

'Yes, very underrated as a president, Dan. He didn't deserve the shellacking he got. He will be missed. Anyway, the more Morgan studied the case, the more concerned he became. He saw through the government's smoke screen. He caught their lies. As an old defense lawyer himself, he understood the power of the feds

456

when they want to nail an innocent person.'

'Are you saying you were innocent?'

'Absolutely. I did nothing wrong.'

'But you pled guilty.'

'I had no choice. First, they indicted me and Jacy Hubbard on bogus charges. We didn't budge. 'Bring on the trial,' we said. 'Give us a jury.' We scared the feds so bad that they did what they always do. They went after our friends and families. Those gestapo idiots indicted my son, Dan, a kid fresh out of law school who knew nothing about my files. Why didn't you write about that?'

'I did.'

'Anyway, I had no choice but to take the fall. It became a badge of honor for me. I pled guilty so all charges would be dropped against my son and my partners. President Morgan figured this out. That's why I was pardoned. I deserved it.'

Another wafer, another mouthful of gold, another slurp of Krug to wash it all down. He was pacing back and forth, jacket off now, a man with many burdens to unload. Then he suddenly stopped and said, 'Enough about the past, Dan. Let's talk about tomorrow. Look at that White House over there. Have you ever been there for a state dinner, black tie, marine color guard, slinky ladies in beautiful gowns?'

'No.'

Backman was standing in the window, gazing at the White House. 'Twice I've done that,' he said with a trace of sadness. 'And I'll be back.

Give me two, maybe three years, and one day they'll hand deliver a thick invitation, heavy paper, gold embossed lettering: The President and First Lady request the honor of your presence . . .'

He turned and looked smugly at Sandberg. 'That's power, Dan. That's what I live for.'

Good copy, but not exactly what Sandberg was after. He jolted the broker back to reality with a sharp 'Who killed Jacy Hubbard?'

Backman's shoulders dropped and he walked to the ice bucket for another round. 'It was a suicide, Dan, plain and simple. Jacy was humiliated beyond belief. The feds destroyed him. He just couldn't handle it.'

'Well, you're the only person in town who believes it was a suicide.'

'And I'm the only person who knows the truth. Print that, would you.'

'I will.'

'Let's talk about something else.'

'Frankly, Mr. Backman, your past is much more interesting than your future. I have a pretty good source that tells me that you were pardoned because the CIA wanted you released, that Morgan caved under pressure from Teddy Maynard, and that they hid you somewhere so they could watch and see who nailed you first.'

'You need new sources.'

'So you deny –'

'I'm here!' Backman spread his arms so Sandberg could see everything. 'I'm alive! If the

458

CIA wanted me dead, then I'd be dead.' He swallowed some champagne, and said, 'Find a better source. You want some eggs? They're getting cold.'

'No thanks.'

Backman scooped a large serving of scrambled eggs onto a small plate and ate them as he moved around the room, from window to window, never too far away from his view of the White House. 'They're pretty good, got truffles.'

'No thanks. How often do you have this for breakfast?'

'Not often enough.'

'Did you know Bob Critz?'

'Sure, everybody knew Critz. He'd been around as long as I had.'

'Where were you when he died?'

'San Francisco, staying with a friend, saw it on the news. Really sad. What's Critz got to do with me?'

'Just curious.'

'Does this mean you're out of questions?'

Sandberg was flipping back through his notes when the phone rang again. It was Ollie this time, and Backman would have to call him back.

'I have a photographer downstairs,' Sandberg said. 'My editor would like some photos.'

'Of course.'

Joel put on his jacket, checked his tie, hair, and teeth in a mirror, then had another scoop of caviar while the photographer arrived and unloaded some gear. He fiddled with the lighting while Sandberg kept the recorder on and tossed up a few questions.

The best shot, according to the photographer, but also one that Sandberg thought was quite nice, was a wide one of Joel on the burgundy leather sofa, with a portrait on the wall behind him. He posed for a few by the window, trying to get the White House in the distance.

The phone kept ringing, and Joel finally ignored it. Neal was supposed to call back every five minutes in the event a call went unanswered, ten if Joel picked up. After twenty minutes of shooting, the phone was driving them crazy.

The broker was a busy man.

The photographer finished, collected his gear, and left. Sandberg hung around for a few minutes, then finally headed for the door. As he was leaving he said, 'Look, Mr. Backman, this will be a big story tomorrow, no doubt about that. But just so you know, I don't buy half the crap you've told me today.'

'Which half?'

'You were guilty as hell. So was Hubbard. He didn't kill himself, and you ran to prison to save your ass. Maynard got you pardoned. Arthur Morgan didn't have a clue.'

'Good. That half is not important.'

'What is?'

'The broker is back. Make sure that's on the front page.'

Maureen was in a much better mood. Her day

off had never been worth a thousand bucks. She escorted Mr. Backman to a private parlor in the rear, away from the gaggle of ladies getting worked on in the front of the salon. Together, they studied colors and shades, and finally selected one that would be easy to maintain. To her, 'maintain' meant the hope of $1,000 every five weeks.

Joel really didn't care. He'd never see her again.

She turned the white into gray and added enough brown to take five years off his face. Vanity was not at stake here.

Youth didn't matter. He just wanted to hide.

Chapter 36

His last guests in the suite made him cry. Neal, the son he hardly knew, and Lisa, the daughter-in-law he'd never met, handed him Carrie, the two-year-old granddaughter he'd only dreamed about. She cried too, at first, but then settled down as her grandfather walked her around and showed her the White House just over there. He walked her from window to window, from room to room, bouncing her and chatting away as if he'd had experience with a dozen grandkids. Neal took more photos, but these were of a different man. Gone was the flashy suit; he was wearing chinos and a plaid button-down. Gone were the bluster and arrogance; he was a simple grandfather clinging to a beautiful little girl.

Room service delivered a late lunch of soups and salads. They enjoyed a quiet family meal, Joel's first in many, many years. He ate with only one hand because the other balanced Carrie on his knee, which never stopped its steady bounce.

He warned them of tomorrow's story in the *Post*, and explained the motives behind it. It was important for him to be seen in Washington, and in the most visible way possible. It would buy him some time, confuse everyone who might still be looking for him. It would create a splash, and be talked about for days, long after he was gone.

Lisa wanted answers as to how much danger he was in, and Joel confessed that he wasn't sure. He would drop out for a while, move around, always being careful. He'd learned a lot in the past two months.

'I'll be back in a few weeks,' he said. 'And I'll drop in from time to time. Hopefully, after a few years things will be safer.'

'Where are you going now?' Neal asked.

'I'm taking the train to Philly, then I'll catch a flight to Oakland. I would like to visit my mother. It would be nice if you'd drop her a card. I'll take my time, eventually end up somewhere in Europe.'

'Which passport will you use?'

'Not the ones I got yesterday.'

'What?'

'I'm not about to allow the CIA to monitor my movements. Barring an emergency, I'll never use them.'

'So how do you travel?'

'I have another passport. A friend loaned it to me.'

Neal gave him a look of suspicion, as if he knew what 'friend' meant. Lisa missed it,

463

though, and little Carrie picked that moment to relieve herself. Joel was quick to hand her to her mother.

While Lisa was in the bathroom changing the diaper, Joel lowered his voice and said, 'Three things. First, get a security firm to sweep your home, office, and cars. You might be surprised. It'll cost about ten grand, and it must be done. Second, I'd like for you to locate an assisted-living place somewhere close to here. My mother, your grandmother, is stuck out there in Oakland with no one to check on her. A good place will cost three to four thousand a month.'

'I take it you have the money.'

'Third, yes, I have the money. It's in an account here at Maryland Trust. You're listed as one of the owners. Withdraw twenty-five thousand to cover the expenses you've incurred so far, and keep the rest close by.'

'I don't need that much.'

'Well, spend some, okay? Loosen up a little. Take the girl to Disney World.'

'How will we correspond?'

'For now, e-mail, the Grinch routine. I'm quite the hacker, you know.'

'How safe are you, Dad?'

'The worst is over.'

Lisa was back with Carrie, who wanted to return to the bouncing knee. Joel held her for as long as he could.

Father and son entered Union Station together

while Lisa and Carrie waited in the car. The bustle of activity made Joel anxious again; old habits would be hard to break. He pulled a small carry-on bag, loaded with all of his possessions.

He bought a ticket to Philadelphia, and as they slowly made their way to the platform area Neal said, 'I really want to know where you're going.'

Joel stopped and looked at him. 'I'm going back to Bologna.'

'There's a friend there, right?'

'Yes.'

'Of the female variety?'

'Oh yes.'

'Why am I not surprised?'

'Can't help it, son. It was always my weakness.'

'She's Italian?'

'Very much so. She's really special.'

'They were all special.'

'This one saved my life.'

'Does she know you're coming back?'

'I think so.'

'Please be careful, Dad.'

'I'll see you in a month or so.'

They hugged and said goodbye.

Author's Note

My background is law, certainly not satellites or espionage. I'm more terrified of high-tech electronic gadgets today than a year ago. (These books are still written on a thirteen-year-old word processor. When it stutters, as it seems to do more and more, I literally hold my breath. When it finally quits, I'm probably done too.)

It's all fiction, folks. I know very little about spies, electronic surveillance, satellite phones, smartphones, bugs, wires, mikes, and the people who use them. If something in this novel approaches accuracy, it's probably a mistake.

Bologna, however, is very real. I had the great luxury of tossing a dart at a map of the world to find a place to hide Mr. Backman. Almost anywhere would work. But I adore Italy and all things Italian, and I have to confess that I was not blindfolded when I threw the dart.

My research (too severe a word) led me to Bologna, a delightful old city that I immediately came to adore. My friend Luca Patuelli showed me around. He knows all the chefs in Bologna, no small feat, and in the course of our tedious work I put on about ten pounds.

Thanks to Luca, to his friends, and to their warm and magical city. Thanks also to Gene McDade, Mike Moody, and Bert Colley.

The Last Juror

John Grisham

In 1970, one of Mississippi's more colourful weekly newspapers, *The Ford County Times*, went bankrupt. To the surprise and dismay of many, ownership was assumed by a 23 year-old college drop-out, named Willie Traynor. The future of the paper looked grim until a young mother was brutally raped and murdered by a member of the notorious Padgitt family. Willie Traynor reported all the gruesome details, and his newspaper began to prosper.

The murderer, Danny Padgitt, was tried before a packed courtroom in Clanton, Mississippi. The trial came to a startling and dramatic end when the defendant threatened revenge against the jurors if they convicted him. Nevertheless, they found him guilty, and he was sentenced to life in prison.

But in Mississippi in 1970, 'life' didn't necessarily mean 'life', and nine years later Danny Padgitt managed to get himself paroled. He returned to Ford County, and the retribution began.

'*The Last Juror* sees Grisham at the absolute peak of his form . . . page-turning urgency'
Mail on Sunday

'Masterful… when Grisham gets in the courtroom he lets rip, drawing scenes so real they're not just alive, they're pulsating… quality thriller writing'
Daily Mirror

'*The Last Juror* does not need to coast on its author's megapopularity. It's a reminder of how the Grisham juggernaut began.'
New York Times

'Wholly engrossing…. Grisham's story-telling knack has not deserted him; and the hint that something more serious is at stake than the solution of a crime gives the narrative an extra depth'
Evening Standard

arrow books

ALSO AVAILABLE IN ARROW

The King of Torts

John Grisham

The Office of the Public Defender is not known as a training ground for bright young litigators. Clay Carter has been there too long, and, like most of his colleagues, dreams of a better job in a real firm. When he reluctantly takes the case of a young man charged with a random street killing, he assumes it is just another of the many senseless murders that hit D.C. every week.

As he digs into the background of his client, Clay stumbles upon a conspiracy too horrible to believe. He suddenly finds himself in the middle of a complex case against one of the largest pharmaceutical companies in the world, looking at the kind of enormous settlement that would totally change his life – that would make him, almost overnight, the legal profession's newest king of torts.

'Grisham reigns supreme . . . *The King of Torts* is another tremendous tour de force'
Sunday Express

'A rollercoaster ride'
The Times

'This novel has incident to burn, a clean, pacy style and a conclusion that will blindside the reader' *Daily Telegraph*

'Grisham at his best, combining a gripping plot and an illuminating insight into the seamier side of legal business' Mariella Frostrup.
Open Book

arrow books

ALSO AVAILABLE IN ARROW

The Summons

John Grisham

Ray Atlee is a professor of law at the University of Virginia. He's forty-three, newly single, and still enduring the after-shocks of a surprise divorce. He has a younger brother, Forrest, who redefines the notion of a family's black sheep.

And he has a father, a very sick old man who lives alone in the ancestral home in Clanton, Mississippi. He is known to all as Judge Atlee, a beloved and powerful official who has towered over local law and politics for forty years. No longer on the bench, the Judge has withdrawn to the Atlee mansion and become a recluse.

With the end in sight, Judge Atlee issues a summons for both sons to return home to Clanton, to discuss the details of his estate. It is typed by the Judge himself, on his handsome old stationery, and gives the date and time for Ray and Forrest to appear in his study.

Ray reluctantly heads south, to his hometown, to the place where he grew up, which he prefers now to avoid. But the family meeting does not take place. The Judge dies too soon, and in doing so leaves behind a shocking secret known only to Ray.

And perhaps someone else.

'No one does it better than Grisham'
Sunday Telegraph

arrow books

ALSO AVAILABLE IN ARROW

The Brethren

John Grisham

The perfect scam: the wrong victim.

Trumble is a minimum security federal prison, home to drug dealers, bank robbers, swindlers, embezzlers, tax evaders, and three former judges who call themselves The Brethren. They meet each day in the law library where they spend hours writing letters. They are fine-tuning a mail scam, and it's starting to really work. The money is pouring in.

Then their little scam goes awry. It ensnares the wrong victim, a powerful man on the outside, a man with dangerous friends, and The Brethren's days of quietly marking time are over.

'Grisham spins out a compelling, beautifully written thriller . . . it's all absolutely brilliant'
Independent on Sunday

'An engaging and fast-paced story of powerful men in high places and blackmail gone awry, it will hook you from the first page and won't let you go'
New York Post

'Completely gripping'
Mirror

'A lively and fast-paced story'
Times Literary Supplement

arrow books

ALSO AVAILABLE IN ARROW

The Runaway Jury

John Grisham

Every jury has a leader and the verdict belongs to him.

In Biloxi, Mississippi, a landmark trial with hundreds of millions of dollars at stake begins routinely, then swerves mysteriously off course. The jury is behaving strangely, and at least one juror is convinced he's being watched. Soon they have to be sequestered. Then a tip from an anonymous young woman suggests she is able to predict the juror's increasingly odd behaviour.

Is the jury somehow being manipulated, or even controlled? And, more importantly, why?

'A marvellous read'
Sunday Telegraph

'This book is a joy. One of those books you regret having to finish'
Daily Express

'Grisham creates a terrific level of suspense. I could not put it down'
Mail on Sunday

'Riveting... Grisham is a superb, instinctive storyteller'
The Times

arrow books

ALSO AVAILABLE IN ARROW

The Firm

John Grisham

The job of his dreams is about to become his worst nightmare.

Mitchell McDeere had qualified third in his class at Harvard, and offers poured in from every law firm in America.

The firm was small, but well-respected. They were prepared to match, and then exceed Mitch's wildest dreams, eighty thousand a year, a BMW and a low-interest mortgage.

Soon the house, the car and the job were his. Then the nightmares began: the secret files, the bugs in the new bedroom, the mysterious deaths of colleagues, and the millions of dollars of mob money pouring through the office into the Cayman Islands, dollars that the FBI would do anything to trace.

Now Mitch was in the place where dreams end and nightmares begin...

'Slickly plotted . . . unputdownable'
Mail on Sunday

'A furiously paced thriller'
Sunday Times

'Enthralling characters and mesmeric plot'
Time Out

arrow books

ALSO AVAILABLE IN ARROW

A Time To Kill

John Grisham

When Carl Lee Hailey guns down the hoodlums who have
raped his ten-year-old child, the people of Clanton see it as a
crime of blood and call for his acquittal.

But when extremists outside Clanton hear that a black man
has killed two white men, they invade the town, determined
to destroy anything and anyone that opposes their sense of
justice.

Jake Brigance has been hired to defend Hailey. It's the kind
of case that can make or break a young lawyer. But in the
maelstrom of Clanton, it is also the kind of case that could get
a young lawyer killed.

'The best thriller writer alive'
Ken Follett, *Evening Standard*

'Grisham is a natural storyteller'
Daily Telegraph

'A giant of the thriller genre'
Time Out

'Leaves one eager for more'
Spectator

arrow books